Women & Men
Men & Women

Women & Men
Men & Women

AN
ANTHOLOGY
OF SHORT STORIES

EDITED BY
WILLIAM SMART

**ST. MARTIN'S PRESS
NEW YORK**

Library of Congress Catalog Card Number: 74-23280
Copyright © 1975 by St. Martin's Press, Inc.
All Rights Reserved.
Manufactured in the United States of America.
For information, write: St. Martin's Press, Inc.,
175 Fifth Avenue, New York, N.Y. 10010

Since this page cannot accommodate all of the copyright notices, the page that follows constitutes an extension of the copyright page.

ACKNOWLEDGMENTS

CYRILLY ABELS, LITERARY AGENT: "Brooklyn," from *Soul Clap Hands and Sing* by Paule Marshall. Copyright © 1961 by Paule Marshall. Reprinted by permission of Cyrilly Abels, Literary Agent.

JONATHAN CAPE LTD.: "Songs My Father Sang Me," from *The Demon Lover* by Elizabeth Bowen. Reprinted by permission of Jonathan Cape Ltd.

CURTIS BROWN LTD.: "A Good Investment," from *Spring Song and Other Stories* by Joyce Cary. Copyright 1954 by Arthur Lucius Michael Cary and David Alexander Ogilvie (Executors of the Estate of Joyce Cary). Reprinted by permission of Curtis Brown Ltd.

JOHN CUSHMAN ASSOCIATES: The following stories by Doris Lessing are reprinted by permission of the author and John Cushman Associates. "A Man and Two Women" and "One off the Short List," from *A Man and Two Women*. Copyright © 1958, 1962, and 1963 by Doris Lessing. "Winter in July," from *African Stories*. Copyright © 1951, 1953, 1954, 1957, 1958, 1962, 1963, 1964, 1965 by Doris Lessing.

FARRAR, STRAUS & GIROUX, INC.: The following stories are reprinted by permission of Farrar, Straus & Giroux, Inc. "The Magic Barrel," from *The Magic Barrel* by Bernard Malamud. Copyright © 1954, 1958 by Bernard Malamud. "A Country Love Story," from *Children Are Bored on Sunday* by Jean Stafford. Copyright 1950 by Jean Stafford. This story originally appeared in *The New Yorker*. "Reservations: A Love Story," from *The Collected Stories of Peter Taylor* by Peter Taylor. Copyright © 1960 by Peter Taylor. This story originally appeared in *The New Yorker*.

HARCOURT BRACE JOVANOVICH, INC.: "Rope," from *Flowering Judas and Other Stories* by Katherine Anne Porter. Copyright 1930, 1958 by Katherine Anne Porter. Reprinted by permission of Harcourt Brace Jovanovich, Inc.

HARPER & ROW, PUBLISHERS, INC.: The following are reprinted by permission of Harper & Row, Publishers, Inc. "A Good Investment," from *Spring Song and Other Stories* by Joyce Cary. Copyright 1954 by Arthur Lucius Michael Cary and David Alexander Ogilvie (Executors of the Estate of Joyce Cary). "The Five-forty-eight," from *The Housebreaker of Shady Hill and Other Stories* by John Cheever. Copyright 1954 by John Cheever.

ALFRED A. KNOPF, INC.: The following are reprinted by permission of Alfred A. Knopf, Inc. "Songs My Father Sang Me," from *Ivy Gripped the Stairs and Other Stories* by Elizabeth Bowen. Copyright 1946 and renewed 1974 by Elizabeth Bowen. "A Dill Pickle," from *The Short Stories of Katherine Mansfield*. Copyright 1920 by Alfred A. Knopf, Inc. and renewed 1948 by J. Middleton Murry.

BILL MC CARTNEY: Cover photograph, "Night Faces, 1970," by Bill McCartney. Black and white. Used by permission of photographer.

HAROLD MATSON COMPANY, INC.: "Debut," by Kristin Hunter. Copyright 1973 by Kristin Hunter. Reprinted by permission of Harold Matson Company, Inc.

WILLIAM MORRIS AGENCY, INC.: "The Dentist's Wife," by William Melvin Kelley. Copyright © 1968 by William Melvin Kelley. Reprinted by permission of William Morris Agency, Inc. This story originally appeared in the October 1968 issue of *Playboy Magazine*.

RANDOM HOUSE, INC.: "The Old Chevalier," from *Seven Gothic Tales* by Isak Dinesen. Copyright 1934 and renewed 1962 by Isak Dinesen. Reprinted by permission of Random House, Inc.

RUSSELL & VOLKENING, INC.: "The Nightingales Sing," from *An Afternoon* by Elizabeth Parsons, published by The Viking Press in 1946. Copyright © 1946 by Elizabeth Parsons Warner. Reprinted by permission of Russell & Volkening, Inc. as agents for the author.

CHARLES SCRIBNER'S SONS: "The Short Happy Life of Francis Macomber," from *The Short Stories of Ernest Hemingway*. Copyright 1936 by Ernest Hemingway. Reprinted by permission of Charles Scribner's Sons.

SIMON & SCHUSTER, INC.: The following stories by Doris Lessing are reprinted by permission of Simon & Schuster, Inc. "A Man and Two Women" and "One off the Short List," from *A Man and Two Women* by Doris Lessing. Copyright © 1958, 1962, 1963 by Doris Lessing. "Winter in July," from *African Stories* by Doris Lessing. Copyright © 1951, 1953, 1954, 1957, 1958, 1962, 1964, 1965 by Doris Lessing.

UNIVERSITY OF IOWA PRESS: "The Beach Umbrella," from *The Beach Umbrella* by Cyrus Colter. Copyright © 1970 by Cyrus Colter. Reprinted by permission of the author and the University of Iowa Press.

VANGUARD PRESS, INC.: "Accomplished Desires," from *The Wheel of Love* by Joyce Carol Oates. Copyright © 1970, 1969, 1968, 1967, 1966, 1965 by Joyce Carol Oates. Reprinted by permission of Vanguard Press, Inc.

THE VIKING PRESS, INC.: The following stories are reprinted by permission of The Viking Press, Inc. "Araby," from *Dubliners* by James Joyce. Copyright © 1967 by the Estate of James Joyce. All rights reserved. "The Odour of Chrysanthemums," "Samson and Delilah," and "The White Stocking," from *The Complete Short Stories of D. H. Lawrence*. Copyright 1922 by Thomas B. Seltzer, Inc. Copyright renewed 1950 by Frieda Lawrence. All rights reserved "An Interest in Life," from *The Little Disturbances of Man* by Grace Paley. Copyright © 1959 by Grace Paley.

HOPE MC KAY VIRTUE: "Truant," from *Gingertown* by Claude McKay. Copyright 1960 by Hope McKay Virtue. Reprinted by permission of Hope McKay Virtue.

A. WATKINS, INC.: "Astronomer's Wife," from *The White Horses of Vienna* by Kay Boyle. Copyright 1936 by Kay Boyle, renewed © 1964. Reprinted by permission of A. Watkins, Inc.

ZIEGLER-ROSS AGENCY: "Oh, the Wonder" by Jeremy Larner. Copyright © 1965 by Jeremy Larner. This story originally appeared in *Paris Review,* 1965. Reprinted by permission of the Ziegler-Ross Agency.

Preface

As the title implies, all of the stories in this anthology are about relationships between the sexes. The book is not a collection of romantic love stories or titillating sexual fantasies but of serious works of fiction that explore frustrations, conflicts, pleasures, discoveries, and disappointments. Too often students think of literature as little more than entertainment, or fancy embroidery, or extremely complicated puzzles that only English teachers can solve. Thus, they turn to disciplines such as sociology and psychology to find out about the world and human behavior. Yet good fiction, in its exact delineations of character and action, provides insights into the subtleties and complexities of human behavior that certainly are no less valuable than the information gathered and processed by the seemingly more objective methods of science. And the best way to demonstrate this, I believe, is by beginning with interesting subject matter and then showing that writers do not simply blurt out stories but are in fact as careful and precise as scientists in employing the techniques and devices of their craft. In other words, paying attention to subject matter does not mean that classes must turn into rap sessions about "Life"—free-for-alls of opinion and personal experience —but that students progress from interest in *what* the story says to analysis of *how* it says it.

Thus, *Women & Men/Men & Women* attempts to be simultaneously both an anthology of outstanding short stories and virtually a casebook on relationships between the sexes—a great subject that has called forth great writing. The stories are arranged in five sections corresponding to what appear to be different kinds of relationships. Part 1, "Awakenings," contains stories about initial experiences, falling in love, and courtship; the stories in Part 2 are about marriages. Part 3, "Exploitations," contains stories that show how men and women use each other for selfish ends; and the stories in Part 4, "Reassessments," portray women and men revising previous expectations or relationships in the light of subsequent experience. Finally, Part 5, "Impasses," contains stories about people trapped in situations that seem unresolvable, because they either cannot have a relationship they desire or cannot get out of one they are in.

Perhaps few will agree that this particular ordering is the best one possible. All I can say is that the categories were not decided at the outset but rather were discovered in the course of reading an enormous number of stories. Within each section the stories have been arranged to reveal an increasing complexity, and stories that embody conflicting points of view are frequently juxtaposed. Two writers, D. H. Lawrence and Doris Lessing, are represented by three stories each, partly because they have written so well on relationships between women and men and partly to give the reader the opportunity to study at least two writers more thoroughly than is usually possible.

Finally, although Virginia Woolf in *A Room of One's Own* claimed that the best writers have androgynous minds, it seemed proper in a book of this sort, which tries to give a balanced perspective on sexual relationships, that the writers should be divided evenly between women and men. What I hope the book will show, however, is that the highest literary art—regardless of the author's gender—is not sexist, or sexually chauvinistic, because it is the ability of the best writers to embody the multiple ironies and complex ambiguities of real life that gives their works a permanent claim on our attention. Simple villains and simple heroes or heroines are neither interesting nor lifelike, and neither sex has a patent on virtue or meanness. Writers tell us so better than anyone else.

Probably few editors have felt as many debts of gratitude as I do on the completion of this book. Though compiling an anthology is hardly a great achievement, it is always a lot of work, and in the case of *Women & Men/Men & Women* I must say that I could not possibly have done it without the collaboration of seven students who joined me in an experimental course at Sweet Briar College. For over half a year the eight of us read and talked. Collectively, we read all the stories of virtually every major short story writer of the nineteenth and twentieth centuries, more than five thousand stories in all. We read, we discussed, we re-read, we re-discussed, and even after my collaborators went home for the summer vacation we continued our discussions in letters flying back and forth across the country. I hardly know how to thank them, other than by saying that the experience was one of the most rewarding of my life and that I wish I could always have students as intelligent, energetic, and enthusiastic as Kathy Abromitis, Wendy Congdon, Elliott Graham, Ebet Little, Denise Montgomery, Johna Pierce, and Charlene Thomas. It seems superfluous to dedicate to them a book that is so much their own.

William Smart

Contents

Part 1 AWAKENINGS

James Joyce *Araby*	3
Kristin Hunter *Debut*	8
Elizabeth Parsons *The Nightingales Sing*	15
Jeremy Larner *Oh, the Wonder!*	27
Isak Dinesen *The Old Chevalier*	43
Bernard Malamud *The Magic Barrel*	61

Part 2 MARRIAGES

Peter Taylor *Reservations: A Love Story*	77
D. H. Lawrence *The White Stocking*	98
Katherine Anne Porter *Rope*	117
Doris Lessing *A Man and Two Women*	123
Cyrus Colter *The Beach Umbrella*	138
Grace Paley *An Interest in Life*	156

xii   Contents

Part 3   EXPLOITATIONS

Doris Lessing	*One off the Short List*	171
John Cheever	*The Five-forty-eight*	191
Joyce Carol Oates	*Accomplished Desires*	202
Ernest Hemingway	*The Short Happy Life of Francis Macomber*	217
William Melvin Kelley	*The Dentist's Wife*	242

Part 4   REASSESSMENTS

Joyce Cary	*A Good Investment*	257
Katherine Mansfield	*A Dill Pickle*	271
Kay Boyle	*Astronomer's Wife*	277
Elizabeth Bowen	*Songs My Father Sang Me*	282
Claude McKay	*Truant*	293
D. H. Lawrence	*Samson and Delilah*	304

Part 5   IMPASSES

Anton Chekhov	*The Lady with the Dog*	319
Doris Lessing	*Winter in July*	333
Jean Stafford	*A Country Love Story*	363
Paule Marshall	*Brooklyn*	374
D. H. Lawrence	*Odour of Chrysanthemums*	389

Women & Men
Men & Women

1
awakenings

James Joyce
Araby

Though Joyce left Dublin in 1902, it is both the setting and the center of everything he wrote for the rest of his life. During nearly forty years of "exile" in Trieste, Zurich, and Paris, Joyce labored steadily to re-create his native city and its inhabitants as representative of the world in microcosm. In doing so, his major works became increasingly complex in their use of language, symbol, and myth, from Dubliners *(1914), a collection of short stories, and* A Portrait of the Artist as a Young Man *(1916) to* Ulysses *(1922) and* Finnegan's Wake *(1939), perhaps the most arcane novel ever published.*

North Richmond Street, being blind, was a quiet street except at the hour when the Christian Brothers' School set the boys free. An uninhabited house of two stories stood at the blind end, detached from its neighbors in a square ground. The other houses of the street, conscious of decent lives within them, gazed at one another with brown imperturbable faces.

The former tenant of our house, a priest, had died in the back drawing-room. Air, musty from having been long enclosed, hung in all the rooms, and the waste room behind the kitchen was littered with old useless papers. Among these I found a few paper-covered books, the pages of which were curled and damp: *The Abbot,* by Walter Scott, *The Devout Communicant* and *The Memoirs of Vidocq.* I liked the last best because its leaves were yellow. The wild garden behind the house contained a central apple-tree and a few straggling bushes under one of which I found the late tenant's rusty bicycle-pump. He had been a very charitable priest; in his will he had left all his money to institutions and the furniture of his house to his sister.

When the short days of winter came dusk fell before we had well eaten our dinners. When we met in the street the houses had grown sombre. The space of sky above us was the color of ever-changing violet and towards it the lamps of the street lifted their feeble lanterns. The cold air stung us and we played till our bodies glowed. Our shouts echoed in the silent street. The career of our play brought us through the dark muddy lanes behind the houses where we ran the gauntlet of the rough tribes from the cottages, to the back doors of the dark dripping gardens where odors arose from the ashpits, to the dark odorous stables where a coachman smoothed and combed the horse or shook music from the buckled harness. When we returned to the street light from the kitchen windows had filled the areas. If my uncle was seen turning the corner we hid in the shadow until we had seen him safely housed. Or if Mangan's sister came out on the doorstep to call her brother in to his tea we watched her from our shadow peer up and down the street. We waited to see whether she would remain or go in and, if she remained, we left our shadow and walked up to Mangan's steps resignedly. She was waiting for us, her figure defined by the light from the half-opened door. Her brother always teased her before he obeyed and I stood by the railings looking at her. Her dress swung as she moved her body and the soft rope of her hair tossed from side to side.

Every morning I lay on the floor in the front parlor watching her door. The blind was pulled down to within an inch of the sash so that I could not be seen. When she came out on the doorstep my heart leaped. I ran to the hall, seized my books and followed her. I kept her brown figure always in my eye and, when we came near the point at which our ways diverged, I quickened my pace and passed her. This happened morning after morning. I had never spoken to her, except for a few casual words, and yet her name was like a summons to all my foolish blood.

Her image accompanied me even in places the most hostile to romance. On Saturday evenings when my aunt went marketing I had to go to carry some of the parcels. We walked through the flaring streets, jostled by drunken men and bargaining women, amid the curses of laborers, the shrill litanies of shop-boys who stood on guard by the barrels of pigs' cheeks, the nasal chanting of street-singers, who sang a *come-all-you* about O'Donovan Rossa, or a ballad about the troubles in our native land. These noises converged in a single sensation of life for me: I imagined that I bore my chalice safely through a throng of foes. Her name sprang to my lips at moments in strange prayers and praises which I myself did not understand. My eyes were often full of tears (I could not tell why) and at times a flood from my heart seemed to pour itself out into my bosom. I thought little of the future. I did not know whether I would ever speak to her or not or, if I spoke to her, how I could tell her of my confused adoration. But my body was like a harp and her words and gestures were like fingers running upon the wires.

One evening I went into the back drawing-room in which the priest had died. It was a dark rainy evening and there was no sound in the house. Through one of the broken panes I heard the rain impinge upon the earth, the fine incessant needles of water playing in the sodden beds. Some distant lamp or lighted window gleamed below me. I was thankful that I could see so little. All my senses seemed to desire to veil themselves and, feeling that I was about to slip from them, I pressed the palms of my hands together until they trembled, murmuring: *"O love! O love!"* many times.

At last she spoke to me. When she addressed the first words to me I was so confused that I did not know what to answer. She asked me was I going to *Araby*. I forgot whether I answered yes or no. It would be a splendid bazaar, she said she would love to go.

"And why can't you?" I asked.

While she spoke she turned a silver bracelet round and round her wrist. She could not go, she said, because there would be a retreat that week in her convent. Her brother and two other boys were fighting for their caps and I was alone at the railings. She held one of the spikes, bowing her head towards me. The light from the lamp opposite our door caught the white curve of her neck, lit up her hair that rested there and, falling, lit up the hand upon the railing. It fell over one side of her dress and caught the white border of a petticoat, just visible as she stood at ease.

"It's well for you," she said.

"If I go," I said, "I will bring you something."

What innumerable follies laid waste my waking and sleeping thoughts after that evening! I wished to annihilate the tedious intervening days. I chafed against the work of school. At night in my bedroom and by day in the classroom her image came between me and the page I strove to read. The syllables of the word *Araby* were called to me through the silence in which my soul luxuriated and cast an Eastern enchantment over me. I asked for leave to go to the bazaar on Saturday night. My aunt was surprised and hoped it was not some Freemason affair. I answered few questions in class. I watched my master's face pass from amiability to sternness; he hoped I was not beginning to idle. I could not call my wandering thoughts together. I had hardly any patience with the serious work of life which, now that it stood between me and my desire, seemed to me child's play, ugly monotonous child's play.

On Saturday morning I reminded my uncle that I wished to go to the bazaar in the evening. He was fussing at the hallstand, looking for the hat-brush, and answered me curtly:

"Yes, boy, I know."

As he was in the hall I could not go into the front parlor and lie at the window. I left the house in bad humor and walked slowly towards the school. The air was pitilessly raw and already my heart misgave me.

When I came home to dinner my uncle had not yet been home. Still it was early. I sat staring at the clock for some time and, when its ticking began to irritate me, I left the room. I mounted the staircase and gained the upper part of the house. The high cold empty gloomy rooms liberated me and I went from room to room singing. From the front window I saw my companions playing below in the street. Their cries reached me weakened and indistinct and, leaning my forehead against the cool glass, I looked over at the dark house where she lived. I may have stood there for an hour, seeing nothing but the brown-clad figure cast by my imagination, touched discreetly by the lamplight at the curved neck, and the hand upon the railings and at the border below the dress.

When I came downstairs again I found Mrs. Mercer sitting at the fire. She was an old garrulous woman, a pawnbroker's widow, who collected used stamps for some pious purpose. I had to endure the gossip of the tea-table. The meal was prolonged beyond an hour and still my uncle did not come. Mrs. Mercer stood up to go: she was sorry she couldn't wait any longer, but it was after eight o'clock and she did not like to be out late, as the night air was bad for her. When she had gone I began to walk up and down the room, clenching my fists. My aunt said:

"I'm afraid you may put off your bazaar for this night of Our Lord."

At nine o'clock I heard my uncle's latchkey in the halldoor. I heard him talking to himself and heard the hallstand rocking when it had received the weight of his overcoat. I could interpret these signs. When he was midway through his dinner I asked him to give me the money to go to the bazaar. He had forgotten.

"The people are in bed and after their first sleep now," he said.

I did not smile. My aunt said to him energetically:

"Can't you give him the money and let him go? You've kept him late enough as it is."

My uncle said he was very sorry he had forgotten. He said he believed in the old saying: "All work and no play makes Jack a dull boy." He asked me where I was going and, when I had told him a second time he asked me did I know *The Arab's Farewell to his Steed*. When I left the kitchen he was about to recite the opening lines of the piece to my aunt.

I held a florin tightly in my hand as I strode down Buckingham Street towards the station. The sight of the streets thronged with buyers and glaring with gas recalled to me the purpose of my journey. I took my seat in a third-class carriage of a deserted train. After an intolerable delay the train moved out of the station slowly. It crept onward among ruinous houses and over the twinkling river. At Westland Row Station a crowd of people pressed to the carriage doors; but the porters moved them back, saying that it was a special train for the bazaar. I remained alone in the bare carriage. In a few minutes the train drew up beside an improvised wooden platform. I passed out on to the road and saw by the lighted dial of a clock that it was ten minutes to ten. In front of me was a large building which displayed the magical name.

I could not find any sixpenny entrance and, fearing that the bazaar would be closed, I passed in quickly through a turnstile, handing a shilling to a weary-looking man. I found myself in the big hall girdled at half its height by a gallery. Nearly all the stalls were closed and the greater part of the hall was in darkness. I recognized a silence like that which pervades a church after a service. I walked into the center of the bazaar timidly. A few people were gathered about the stalls which were still open. Before a curtain, over which the words *Café Chantant* were written in colored lamps, two men were counting money on a salver. I listened to the fall of the coins.

Remembering with difficulty why I had come I went over to one of the stalls and examined porcelain vases and flowered tea-sets. At the door of the stall a young lady was talking and laughing with two young gentlemen. I remarked their English accents and listened vaguely to their conversation.

"O, I never said such a thing!"

"O, but you did!"

"O, but I didn't!"

"Didn't she say that?"

"Yes. I heard her."

"O, there's a . . . fib!"

Observing me the young lady came over and asked me did I wish to buy anything. The tone of her voice was not encouraging; she seemed to have spoken to me out of a sense of duty. I looked humbly at the great jars that stood like eastern guards at either side of the dark entrance to the stall and murmured:

"No, thank you."

The young lady changed the position of one of the vases and went back to the two young men. They began to talk of the same subject. Once or twice the young lady glanced at me over her shoulder.

I lingered before her stall, though I knew my stay was useless, to make my interest in her wares seem the more real. Then I turned away slowly and walked down the middle of the bazaar. I allowed the two pennies to fall against the sixpence in my pocket. I heard a voice call from one end of the gallery that the light was out. The upper part of the hall was now completely dark.

Gazing up into the darkness I saw myself as a creature driven and derided by vanity; and my eyes burned with anguish and anger.

Kristin Hunter

Debut

A graduate of the University of Pennsylvania at the age of twenty, Kristin Hunter has worked as an advertising copywriter, Information Officer for the City of Philadelphia, and director of comprehensive health services at Temple University. She has been a John Hay Whitney fellow, and in 1968 she was recipient of the National Council on Interracial Books for Children award. Since 1964 she has published five novels: God Bless the Child; The Landlord; The Soul Brothers and Sister Lou; Boss Cat; *and* Guests in the Promised Land.

"Hold *still,* Judy," Mrs. Simmons said around the spray of pins that protruded dangerously from her mouth. She gave the thirtieth tug to the tight sash at the waist of the dress. "Now walk over there and turn around slowly."

The dress, Judy's first long one, was white organdy over taffeta, with spaghetti straps that bared her round brown shoulders and a floating skirt and a wide sash that cascaded in a butterfly effect behind. It was a dream, but Judy was sick and tired of the endless fittings she had endured so that she might wear it at the Debutantes' Ball. Her thoughts leaped ahead to the Ball itself . . .

"*Slowly,* I said!" Mrs. Simmons' dark, angular face was always grim, but now it was screwed into an expression resembling a prune. Judy, starting nervously, began to revolve by moving her feet an inch at a time.

Her mother watched her critically. "No, it's still not right. I'll just have to rip out that waistline seam again."

"Oh, Mother!" Judy's impatience slipped out at last. "Nobody's going to notice all those little details."

"They will too. They'll be watching you every minute, hoping to see something wrong. You've got to be the *best.* Can't you get that through your head?" Mrs. Simmons gave a sigh of despair. "You better start noticin' 'all those little details' yourself. I can't do it for you all your life. Now turn around and stand up straight."

"Oh, Mother," Judy said, close to tears from being made to turn and pose while her feet itched to be dancing, "I can't stand it any more!"

"You can't stand it, huh? How do you think *I* feel?" Mrs. Simmons said in her harshest tone.

Judy was immediately ashamed, remembering the weeks her mother had spent at the sewing machine, pricking her already tattered fingers with needles and pins, and the great weight of sacrifice that had been borne on Mrs. Simmons' shoulders for the past two years so that Judy might bare hers at the Ball.

"All right, take it off," her mother said. "I'm going to take it up the street to Mrs. Luby and let her help me. It's got to be right or I won't let you leave the house."

"Can't we just leave it the way it is, Mother?" Judy pleaded without hope of success. "I think it's perfect."

"You would," Mrs. Simmons said tartly as she folded the dress and prepared to bear it out of the room. "Sometimes I think I'll never get it through your head. You got to look just right and act just right. That Rose Griffin and those other girls can afford to be careless, maybe, but you can't. You're gonna be the darkest, poorest one there."

Judy shivered in her new lace strapless bra and her old, childish knit snuggies. "You make it sound like a battle I'm going to instead of just a dance."

"It is a battle," her mother said firmly. "It starts tonight and it goes on for the rest of your life. The battle to hold your head up and get someplace and be somebody. We've done all we can for you, your father and I. Now you've got to start fighting some on your own." She gave Judy a slight smile; her voice softened a little. "You'll do all right, don't worry. Try and get some rest this afternoon. Just don't mess up your hair."

"All right, Mother," Judy said listlessly.

She did not really think her father had much to do with anything that happened to her. It was her mother who had ingratiated her way into the Gay

Charmers two years ago, taking all sorts of humiliation from the better-dressed, better-off, lighter-skinned women, humbly making and mending their dresses, fixing food for their meetings, addressing more mail and selling more tickets than anyone else. The club had put it off as long as they could, but finally they had to admit Mrs. Simmons to membership because she worked so hard. And that meant, of course, that Judy would be on the list for this year's Ball.

Her father, a quiet carpenter who had given up any other ambitions years ago, did not think much of Negro society or his wife's fierce determination to launch Judy into it. "Just keep clean and be decent," he would say. "That's all anybody has to do."

Her mother always answered, "If that's all *I* did we'd still be on relief," and he would shut up with shame over the years when he had been laid off repeatedly and her days' work and sewing had kept them going. Now he had steady work but she refused to quit, as if she expected it to end at any moment. The intense energy that burned in Mrs. Simmons' large dark eyes had scorched her features into permanent irony. She worked day and night and spent her spare time scheming and planning. Whatever her personal ambitions had been, Judy knew she blamed Mr. Simmons for their failure; now all her schemes revolved around their only child.

Judy went to her mother's window and watched her stride down the street with the dress until she was hidden by the high brick wall that went around two sides of their house. Then she returned to her own room. She did not get dressed because she was afraid of pulling a sweater over her hair—her mother would notice the difference even if it looked all right to Judy—and because she was afraid that doing anything, even getting dressed, might precipitate her into the battle. She drew a stool up to her window and looked out. She had no real view, but she liked her room. The wall hid the crowded tenement houses beyond the alley, and from its cracks and bumps and depressions she could construct any imaginary landscape she chose. It was how she had spent most of the free hours of her dreamy adolescence.

"Hey, can I go?"

It was the voice of an invisible boy in the alley. As another boy chuckled, Judy recognized the familiar ritual; if you said yes, they said, "Can I go with you?" It had been tried on her dozens of times. She always walked past, head in the air, as if she had not heard. Her mother said that was the only thing to do; if they knew she was a lady, they wouldn't dare bother her. But this time a girl's voice, cool and assured, answered.

"If you think you're big enough," it said.

It was Lucy Mae Watkins; Judy could picture her standing there in a tight dress with bright, brazen eyes.

"I'm big enough to give you a baby," the boy answered.

Judy would die if a boy ever spoke to her like that, but she knew Lucy Mae could handle it. Lucy Mae could handle all the boys, even if they ganged up on her, because she had been born knowing something other girls had to learn.

"Aw, you ain't big enough to give me a shoe-shine," she told him.

"Come here and I'll show you how big I am," the boy said.

"Yeah, Lucy Mae, what's happenin'?" another boy said. "Come here and tell us."

Lucy Mae laughed. "What I'm puttin' down is too strong for little boys like you."

"Come here a minute, baby," the first boy said. "I got a cigarette for you."

"Aw, I ain't studyin' your cigarettes," Lucy Mae answered. But her voice was closer, directly below Judy. There were the sounds of a scuffle and Lucy Mae's muffled laughter. When she spoke her voice sounded raw and cross. "Come on now, boy. Cut it out and give me the damn cigarette." There was more scuffling, and the sharp crack of a slap, and then Lucy Mae said, "Cut it out, I said. Just for that I'm gonna take 'em all." The clack of high heels rang down the sidewalk with a boy's clumsy shoes in pursuit.

Judy realized that there were three of them down there. "Let her go, Buster," one said. "You can't catch her now."

"Aw, hell, man, she took the whole damn pack," the one called Buster complained.

"That'll learn you!" Lucy Mae's voice mocked from down the street. "Don't mess with nothin' you can't handle."

"Hey, Lucy Mae. Hey, I heard Rudy Grant already gave you a baby," a second boy called out.

"Yeah. Is that true, Lucy Mae?" the youngest one yelled.

There was no answer. She must be a block away by now.

For a moment the hidden boys were silent; then one of them guffawed directly below Judy, and the other two joined in the secret male laughter that was oddly high-pitched and feminine.

"Aw man, I don't know what you all laughin' about," Buster finally grumbled. "That girl took all my cigarettes. You got some, Leroy?"

"Naw," the second boy said.

"Me neither," the third one said.

"What we gonna do? I ain't got but fifteen cent. Hell, man, I want more than a feel for a pack of cigarettes." There was an unpleasant whine in Buster's voice. "Hell, for a pack of cigarettes I want a bitch to come across."

"She will next time, man," the boy called Leroy said.

"She better," Buster said. "You know she better. If she pass by here again, we gonna jump her, you hear?"

"Sure, man," Leroy said. "The three of us can grab her easy."

"Then we can all three of us have some fun. Oh, *yeah*, man," the youngest boy said. He sounded as if he might be about fourteen.

Leroy said, "We oughta get Roland and J.T. too. For a whole pack of cigarettes she oughta treat all five of us."

"Aw, man, why tell Roland and J.T.?" the youngest voice whined "They ain't in it. Them was *our* cigarettes."

"They was *my* cigarettes, you mean," Buster said with authority. "You guys better quit it before I decide to cut you out."

"Oh, man, don't do that. We with you. You know that."

"Sure Buster, we your aces, man."

"All right, that's better." There was a minute of silence.

Then, "What we gonna do with the girl, Buster?" the youngest one wanted to know.

"When she come back we gonna jump the bitch, man. We gonna jump her and grab her. Then we gonna turn her every way but loose." He went on, spinning a crude fantasy that got wilder each time he retold it, until it became so secretive that their voices dropped to a low indistinct murmur punctuated by guffaws. Now and then Judy could distinguish the word "girl" or the other word they used for it; these words always produced the loudest guffaws of all. She shook off her fear with the thought that Lucy Mae was too smart to pass there again today. She had heard them at their dirty talk in the alley before and had always been successful in ignoring it; it had nothing to do with her, the wall protected her from their kind. All the ugliness was on their side of it, and this side was hers to fill with beauty.

She turned on her radio to shut them out completely and began to weave her tapestry to its music. More for practice than anything else, she started by picturing the maps of the places to which she intended to travel, then went on to the faces of her friends. Rose Griffin's sharp, Indian profile appeared on the wall. Her coloring was like an Indian's too and her hair was straight and black and glossy. Judy's hair, naturally none of these things, had been "done" four days ago so that tonight it would be "old" enough to have a gloss as natural-looking as Rose's. But Rose, despite her handsome looks, was silly; her voice broke constantly into high-pitched giggles and she became even sillier and more nervous around boys.

Judy was not sure that she knew how to act around boys either. The sisters kept boys and girls apart at the Catholic high school where her parents sent her to keep her away from low-class kids. But she felt that she knew a secret: tonight, in that dress, with her hair in a sophisticated upsweep, she would be transformed into a poised princess. Tonight all the college boys her mother described so eagerly would rush to dance with her, and then from somewhere *the boy* would appear. She did not know his name; she neither knew nor cared whether he went to college, but she imagined that he would be as dark as she was, and that there would be awe and diffidence in his manner as he bent to kiss her hand . . .

A waltz swelled from the radio; the wall, turning blue in deepening twilight, came alive with whirling figures. Judy rose and began to go through the steps she had rehearsed for so many weeks. She swirled with a practiced smile on her face, holding an imaginary skirt at her side; turned, dipped, and flicked on her bedside lamp without missing a fraction of the beat. Faster and faster she danced with her imaginary partner, to an inner music that was better than the sounds on the radio. She was "coming out," and tonight the world would discover what it had been waiting for all these years.

"Aw git it, baby." She ignored it as she would ignore the crowds that lined the streets to watch her pass on her way to the Ball.

"Aw, do your number." She waltzed on, safe and secure on her side of the wall.

"Can I come up there and do it with you?"

At this she stopped, paralyzed. Somehow they had come over the wall or around it and into her room.

"Man, I sure like the view from here," the youngest boy said. "How come we never tried this view before?"

She came to life, ran quickly to the lamp and turned if off, but not before Buster said, "Yeah, and the back view is fine, too."

"Aw, she turned off the light," a voice complained.

"Put it on again, baby, we don't mean no harm."

"Let us see you dance some more. I bet you can really do it."

"Yeah, I bet she can shimmy on down."

"You know it, man."

"Come on down here, baby," Buster's voice urged softly, dangerously. "I got a cigarette for you."

"Yeah, and he got something else for you, too."

Judy, flattened against her closet door, gradually lost her urge to scream. She realized that she was shivering in her underwear. Taking a deep breath, she opened the closet door and found her robe. She thought of going to the window and yelling down, "You don't have anything I want. Do you understand?" But she had more important things to do.

Wrapping her hair in a protective plastic, she ran a full steaming tub and dumped in half a bottle of her mother's favorite cologne. At first she scrubbed herself furiously, irritating her skin. But finally she stopped, knowing she would never be able to get cleaner than this again. She could not wash away the thing they considered dirty, the thing that made them pronounce "girl" in the same way as the other four-letter words they wrote on the wall in the alley; it was part of her, just as it was part of her mother and Rose Griffin and Lucy Mae. She relaxed then because it was true that the boys in the alley did not have a thing she wanted. She had what they wanted, and the knowledge replaced her shame with a strange, calm feeling of power.

After her bath she splashed on more cologne and spent forty minutes on her makeup, erasing and retracing her eyebrows six times until she was satisfied. She went to her mother's room then and found the dress, finished and freshly pressed, on its hanger.

When Mrs. Simmons came upstairs to help her daughter she found her sitting on the bench before the vanity mirror as if it were a throne. She looked young and arrogant and beautiful and perfect and cold.

"Why, you're dressed already," Mrs. Simmons said in surprise. While she stared, Judy rose with perfect, icy grace and glided to the center of the room. She stood there motionless as a mannequin.

"I want you to fix the hem, Mother," she directed. "It's still uneven in back."

Her mother went down obediently on her knees muttering, "It looks all right to me." She put in a couple of pins. "That better?"

"Yes," Judy said with a brief glance at the mirror. "You'll have to sew it on me, Mother. I can't take it off now. I'd ruin my hair."

Mrs. Simmons went to fetch her sewing things, returned and surveyed her daughter. "You sure did a good job on yourself, I must say," she admitted grudgingly. "Can't find a thing to complain about. You'll look as good as anybody there."

"Of course, Mother," Judy said as Mrs. Simmons knelt and sewed. "I don't know what you were so worried about." Her secret feeling of confidence had returned, stronger than ever, but the evening ahead was no longer a vague girlish fantasy she had pictured on the wall; it had hard, clear outlines leading up to a definite goal. She would be the belle of the Ball because she knew more than Rose Griffin and her silly friends; more than her mother, more, even then Lucy Mae, because she knew better than to settle for a mere pack of cigarettes.

"There," her mother said, breaking the thread. She got up. "I never expected to get you ready this early. Ernest Lee won't be here for another hour."

"That silly Ernest Lee," Judy said, with a new contempt in her young voice. Until tonight she had been pleased by the thought of going to the dance with Ernest Lee; he was nice, she felt comfortable with him, and he might even be the awe-struck boy of her dream. He was a dark, serious neighborhood boy who could not afford to go to college; Mrs. Simmons had reluctantly selected him to take Judy to the dance because all the Gay Charmers' sons were spoken for. Now, with an undertone of excitement, Judy said, "I'm going to ditch him after the first dance, Mother. You'll see. I'm going to come home with one of the college boys."

"It's very nice, Ernest Lee," she told him an hour later when he handed her the white orchid, "but it's rather small. I'm going to wear it on my wrist, if you don't mind." And then, dazzzling him with a smile of sweetest cruelty, she stepped back and waited while he fumbled with the door.

"You know, Edward, I'm not worried about her any more," Mrs. Simmons said to her husband after the children were gone. Her voice became harsh and grating. "Put down that paper and listen to me! Aren't you interested in your child?—That's better," she said as he complied meekly. "I was saying, I do believe she's learned what I've been trying to teach her, after all."

Elizabeth Parsons

The Nightingales Sing

Born in Hartford, Connecticut, Elizabeth Parsons was published regularly by The New Yorker *during the 1940's and early fifties. Her only book, a collection of short stories entitled* An Afternoon, *was published in 1946. A writer of great sensitivity to the ambience of delicate situations, Elizabeth Parsons has written very little since the mid-fifties. For many years she has spent her summers on the island of Vinalhaven off the coast of Maine; the rest of the time she and her husband live in New York City.*

Through the fog the car went up the hill, whining in second gear, up the sandy road that ran between the highest and broadest stone walls that Joanna had ever seen. There were no trees at all, only the bright-green, cattle-cropped pastures sometimes visible above the walls, and sweetfern and juniper bushes, all dim in the opaque air and the wan light of an early summer evening. Phil, driving the creaking station wagon with dexterous recklessness, said to her, "I hope it's the right road. Nothing looks familiar in this fog and I've only been here once before."

"It was nice of him to ask us—me especially," said Joanna, who was young and shy and grateful for favors.

"Oh, he loves company," Phil said. "I wish we could have gotten away sooner to be here to help him unload the horses, though. Still, Chris will be there."

"Is Chris the girl who got thrown today?" Joanna asked, remembering the slight figure in the black coat going down in a spectacular fall with a big bay horse. Phil nodded, and brought the car so smartly around a bend that the two tack boxes in the back of it skidded across the floor. Then he stopped, at last on the level, at a five-barred gate that suddenly appeared out of the mist.

"I'll do the gate," said Joanna, and jumped out. It opened easily and she swung it back against the fence and held it while Phil drove through; then the engine stalled, and in the silence she stood for a moment, her head raised, sniffing the damp, clean air. There was no sound—not the sound of a bird, or a lamb, or the running of water over stones, or of wind in leaves; there was only a great stillness and a sense of height and strangeness and the smell of grass and dried dung. This was the top of the world, this lost hillside, green and bare, ruled across by enormous old walls—the work, so it seemed, of giants. In the air there was a faint movement as of a great wind far away, breathing through the fog. Joanna pulled the gate shut and got in again with Phil and they drove on along the smooth crest of the hill, the windshield wipers swinging slowly to and fro and Phil's sharp, red-headed profile drawn clearly against the gray background. She was grateful to him for taking her to the horse show that afternoon, but she was timid about the invitation to supper that it had led to. Still, there was no getting out of it now. Phil was the elder brother of a school friend of hers, Carol Watson—he was so old he might as well have been of another generation and there was about him, still incredibly unmarried at the age of thirty one, the mysterious aura that bachelor elder brothers always possess. Carol was supposed to have come with them but she had developed chickenpox the day before. However, Phil had kindly offered to take Joanna just the same, since he had had to ride, and he had kept a fatherly eye on her whenever he could. Then a friend of his named Sandy Sheldon, a breeder of polo ponies, had asked him to stop at his farm for supper on the way home. Phil had asked Joanna if she wanted to go and she had said yes, knowing that he wanted to.

Being a good child, she had telephoned her family to tell them she would not be home until late.

"*Whose* place?" her mother's faraway voice had asked, doubtfully. "Well, don't be late, will you, dear? And call me up when you're leaving, won't you? It's a miserable night to be driving."

"I can't call you," Joanna had said. "There's no telephone."

"Couldn't you call up from somewhere after you've left?" the faint voice had said. "You know how Father worries, and Phil's such a fast driver."

"I'll try to." Exasperation had made Joanna's voice stiff. What earthly good was *telephoning?* She hung up the receiver with a bang, showing a temper she would not have dared display in the presence of her parents.

Now, suddenly, out of the fog great buildings loomed close, and they drove through an open gate into a farmyard with gray wooden barns on two sides of it and stone walls on the other two sides. A few white hens rushed away across the dusty ground, and a gray cat sitting on the pole of a blue dump cart stared coldly at the car as Phil stopped it beside a battered horse van. The instant he stopped, a springer ran barking out of one of the barn doors, and a man appeared behind him and came quickly out to them, up to Joanna's side of the car, where he put both hands on the door and bent his head a little to look in at them.

"Sandy, this is Joanna Gibbs," said Phil.

Sandy looked at her without smiling, but not at all with unfriendliness, only with calm consideration. "Hello, Joanna," he said, and opened the door for her.

"Hello," she said, and then forgot to be shy, for, instead of uttering the kind of asinine, polite remarks she was accustomed to hearing from strangers, he did not treat her as a stranger at all, but said immediately, "You're just in time to help put the horses away. Chris keeled over the minute we got here and I had to send her to bed, and Jake's gone after one of the cows that's strayed off." He spoke in a light, slow, Western voice. He was a small man about Phil's age, with a flat freckled face, light-brown, intelligent eyes, and faded brown hair cut short all over his round head. He looked very sturdy and stocky, walking toward the van beside Phil's thin New England elegance, and he had a self-confidence that sprang simply from his own good nature.

"Quite a fog you greet us with," said Phil, taking off his coat and hanging it on the latch of the open door of the van. Inside in the gloom four long, shining heads were turned toward them, and one of the horses gave a gentle, anxious whinny.

"Yes, we get them once in a while," said Sandy. "I like 'em."

"So do I," said Joanna.

He turned to her and said, "Look, there's really no need in your staying out here. Run in the house, where it's warm, and see if the invalid's all right. You go through that gate." He pointed to a small sagging gate at a gap in the wall.

"All right, I will," she answered, and she started off across the yard toward the end gable of a house she could see rising dimly above some apple trees, the spaniel going with her.

"Joanna!" Sandy called after her, just as she reached the gate.

"Yes?" She turned back. The two men were standing by the runway of the van. They both looked at her, seeing a tall young girl in a blue dress and sweater, with her hair drawn straight back over her head and tied at the back of her neck in a chignon with a black bow, and made more beautiful and airy than she actually was by the watery air.

"Put some wood on the kitchen fire as you go in, will you?" Sandy shouted to her. "The woodbox is right by the stove."

"All right," she answered again, and she and the spaniel went through the little gate in the wall.

A path led from the gate, under the apple trees where the grass was cut short and neat, to a door in the ell of the house. The house itself was big and old and plain, almost square, with a great chimney settled firmly across the ridgepole, and presumably it faced down the hill toward the sea. It was conventional and unimposing, with white painted trim and covered with gray old shingles. There was a lilac bush by the front door and a bed of unbudded red lilies around one of the apple trees, but except for these there was neither shrubbery nor flowers. It looked austere and pleasing to Joanna, and she went in through the door in the ell and saw the woodbox beside the black stove. As she poked some pieces of birch wood down into the snapping fire, a girl's voice called from upstairs, "Sandy?"

Joanna put the lid on the stove and went through a tiny hallway into a living room. An enclosed staircase went up out of one corner and she went to it and called up it, "Sandy's in the barn. Are you all right?"

"Oh, I'm fine," the voice answered, hard and clear. "Just a little shaky when I move around. Come on up."

Joanna climbed up. Immediately at the top of the stairs was a big square bedroom, papered in a beautiful faded paper with scrolls and wheat sheaves. On a four-posted bed lay a girl not many years older than Joanna, covered to the chin with a dark patchwork quilt. Her short black hair stood out against the pillow, and her face was colorless and expressionless and at the same time likeable and amusing. She did not sit up when Joanna came in; she clasped her hands behind her head and looked at her with blue eyes under lowered black lashes.

"You came with Phil, didn't you?" she asked.

"Yes," said Joanna, moving hesitantly up to the bed and leaning against one of the footposts. "They're putting the horses away and they thought I'd better come in and see how you were."

"Oh, I'm fine," said Chris again. "I'll be O.K. in a few minutes. I lit on my head, I guess, by the way it feels, but I don't remember a thing."

Joanna remembered. It had not seemed possible that that black figure could emerge, apparently from directly underneath the bay horse and, after sitting a minute on the grass with hanging head, could get up and walk grimly away, ignoring the animal who had made such a clumsy error and was being led out by an attendant in a long tan coat.

She also remembered that when people were ill or in pain you brought them weak tea and aspirin and hot water bottles, and that they were usually in bed, wishing to suffer behind partly lowered shades, not just lying under a quilt with the fog pressing against darkening windows. But there was something here that did not belong in the land of tea and hot water bottles—a land that, indeed, now seemed on another planet. Joanna knew this, though she did not know what alternatives to offer, so she made no suggestions but just stood there, looking with shy politeness around the room. It was a cold, sparsely furnished place and it looked very bare to Joanna, most of whose life so far had been spent in comfortable, chintz-warmed interiors, with carpets that went from wall to wall. In this room, so obviously untouched for the past hundred years or more, was only the bed, a tall chest of drawers, a wash-hand-stand with a gold and white bowl and pitcher, two plain painted chairs, and a threadbare oval braided rug beside the bed. There were no curtains at the four windows, and practically no paint left on the uneven old floor. The fireplace was black and damp-smelling and filled with ashes and charred paper that rose high about the feet of the andirons. Joanna could not make out whether it was a guest room, or whose room it was, here and there were scattered possessions that might have been male or female—a bootjack, some framed snapshots, a comb, a dirty towel, some socks, a magazine on the floor. Chris's black coat was lying on a chair, and her bowler stood on the bureau. It was a blank room, bleak in the failing light.

Chris watched her from under her half-closed lids, waiting for her to speak, and presently Joanna said, "That was really an awful spill you had."

Chris moved her head on the pillow and said, "He's a brute of a horse. He'll never be fit to ride. I've schooled him for Mrs. Whittaker for a year now and ridden him in three shows and I thought he was pretty well over his troubles." She shrugged, and wrapped herself tighter in the quilt. "She's sunk so much money in him it's a crime, but he's just a brute and I don't think I can do anything more with him. Of course, if she wants to go on paying me to ride him, O.K., and her other horses are tops, so I haven't any kick, really. You can't have them all perfect."

"What does she bother with him for?" asked Joanna.

"Well, she's cracked, like most horse-show people," said Chris. "They can't resist being spectacular—exhibitionists, or whatever they call it. Got to have something startling, and then more startling, and so on. And I must say this horse is something to see. He's beautiful." Her somewhat bored little voice died away.

Joanna contemplated all this seriously. It seemed to her an arduous yet dramatic way of earning one's living; she did not notice that there was nothing in the least dramatic about the girl on the bed beside her. Chris, for her part, was speculating more directly about Joanna, watching her, appreciating her looks, wondering what she was doing with Phil. Then, because she was not unkind and sensed that Joanna was at loose ends in the strange house, she said to her, suddenly leaving the world of horses for the domestic scene where women cozily collaborate over the comforts of their men, "Is there a fire in the living room? I was too queasy to notice when I came in. If there isn't one why don't you light it so it'll be warm when they come in?"

"I'll look," said Joanna. "I didn't notice either. Can I get you anything?"

"No, I'll be down pretty soon," Chris said. "I've got to start supper."

Joanna went back down the little stairs. There was no fire in the living room, but a broken basket beside the fireplace was half full of logs, and she carefully laid these on the andirons and stuffed in some twigs and old comics and lit them. The tall flames sprang up into the black chimney, shiny with creosote. As they roared up, she sat on the floor and looked around the room. It was the same size as the bedroom above it, but it was comfortable and snug, with plain gray walls and white woodwork. A fat sofa, covered with dirty flowered linen, stood in front of the fire. There were some big wicker chairs and four little carved Victorian chairs and a round table with big bowed legs, covered with a red tablecoth; a high, handsome secretary stood against the long wall opposite the fire— its veneer was peeling, and it was filled with tarnished silver cups and ribbon rosettes. A guitar lay on a chair. There were dog hairs on the sofa and the floor was dirty, and outside the windows, there was nothingness. Joanna got up to look at the kitchen fire, put more wood on it, and returned to the living room. Overhead she heard Chris moving around quietly, and she pictured her walking about the barren, dusty bedroom, combing her short black hair, tying her necktie, folding up the quilt, looking in the gloom for a lipstick, and suddenly a dreadful, lonely sadness and longing came over her. The living room was growing dark too, and she would have lit the big nickel lamp standing on the table but she did not know how to, so she sat there dreaming in the hot golden firelight. Presently she heard the men's voices outside and they came into the kitchen and stopped there to talk, one of them rattling the stove lids. Sandy came to the door and, seeing Joanna, said to her, "Is Chris all right?"

"Yes, I think so," Joanna said. "She said she was, anyway."

"Guess I'll just see," he said, and went running up the stairs. The spaniel came in to the fire. Joanna stroked his back. His wavy coat was damp with fog and he smelled very strongly of dog; he sat down on the hearth facing the fire, raised his muzzle, and closed his eyes and gave a great sigh of comfort. Then all of a sudden he trotted away and went leaping up the stairs to the bedroom, and Joanna could hear his feet overhead.

Phil came in next, his hair sticking to his forehead. He hung his coat on a chair-back and said to Joanna, "How do you like it here?"

"It's wonderful," she said earnestly.

"It seems to me a queer place," he said, lifting the white fluted china shade off the lamp and striking a match. "Very queer—so far off. We're marooned. I don't feel there's any other place anywhere, do you?"

Joanna shook her head and watched him touch the match to the wick and stoop to settle the chimney on its base. When he put on the shade the soft yellow light caught becomingly on his red head and his narrow face with the sharp cheekbones and the small, deep-set blue eyes. Joanna had known him for years but she realized, looking at him in the yellow light, that she knew almost nothing about him. Before this, he had been Carol's elder brother, but there in the unfamiliar surroundings he was somebody real. She looked away from his lighted face, surprised and wondering. He took his pipe out of his coat pocket and came to the sofa and sat down with a sigh of comfort exactly like the dog's, sticking his long thin booted feet out to the fire, banishing the dark, making the fog retreat.

Sandy came down the stairs and went toward the kitchen, and Phil called after him, "Chris all right?"

"Yes," Sandy said, going out.

"She's a little crazy," Phil said. "Too much courage and no sense. But she's young. She'll settle down, maybe."

"Are she and Sandy engaged?" Joanna said.

"Well, no," said Phil. "Sandy's got a wife. She stays in Texas." He paused to light his pipe, and then he said, "That's where he raises his horses, you know—this place is only sort of a salesroom. But he and Chris know each other pretty well."

This seemed obvious to Joanna, who said, "Yes, I know." Phil smoked in silence.

"Doesn't his wife *ever* come here?" Joanna asked after a moment.

"I don't think so," Phil answered.

They could hear Sandy in the kitchen, whistling, and occasionally rattling pans. They heard the pump squeak as he worked the handle and the water splashed down into the black iron sink. Then he too came in to the fire and said to Joanna, smiling down at her, "Are you comfy, and all?"

"Oh, *yes*," she said and flushed with pleasure. "I love your house," she managed to say.

"I'm glad you do. It's kind of a barn of a place, but fine for the little I'm in it." He walked away, pulled the flowered curtains across the windows, and came back to stand before the fire. He looked very solid, small, and cheerful, with his shirt-sleeves rolled up and his collar unbuttoned with the gay printed tie loosened. He seemed to Joanna so smug and kind, so, somehow, sympathetic, that she could have leaned forward and hugged him round the knees—but at the idea of doing any such thing she blushed again and bent to pat the dog. Sandy took up the guitar and tuned it lazily.

As he began playing absent-mindedly, his stubby fingers straying across the strings as he stared into the fire, Chris came down the stairs. Instead of her long black boots she had on a pair of dilapidated Indian moccasins with a few beads remaining on the toes, and between these and the ends of her breeches legs were gay blue socks. The breeches were fawn-colored, and she had on a fresh white shirt with the sleeves rolled up. Her curly hair, cropped nearly as short as a boy's, was brushed and shining, and her hard, sallow little face was carefully made up and completely blank. Whether she was happy or disturbed, well or ill, Joanna could see no stranger would be able to tell.

"What about supper?" she asked Sandy.

"Calm yourself," he said. "I'm cook tonight. It's all started." He took her hand to draw her down on the sofa, but she moved away and pulled a cushion off a chair and lay down on the floor, her feet toward the fire and her hands folded like a child's on her stomach. Phil had gone into the next room and now he came back carrying a lighted lamp; it dipped wildly in his hand as he set it on the round table beside the other one. The room shone in the low, beneficent light. Sandy, leaning his head against the high, carved back of the sofa, humming and strumming, now sang aloud in a light, sweet voice,

> "For I'd rather hear your fiddle
> And the tone of one string
> Than watch the waters a-gliding,
> Hear the nightingales sing."

The soft strumming went on, and the soft voice, accompanied by Chris's gentle crooning. The fire snapped. Phil handed round some glasses and then went round with a bottle of whisky he had found in the kitchen. He paused at Joanna's glass, smiled at her, and poured her a very small portion.

> "If I ever return,
> It will be in the spring
> To watch the waters a-gliding,
> Hear the nightingales sing."

The old air died on a trailing chord.

"That's a lovely song," said Joanna, and then shrank at her sentimentality.

But Sandy said, "Yes, it's nice. My mother used to sing it. She knew an awful lot of old songs." He picked out the last bars again on the guitar. Joanna, sitting beside him on the floor, was swept with warmth and comfort.

"My God, the peas!" Sandy said suddenly in horror, as a loud sound of hissing came from the kitchen. Throwing the guitar down on the sofa, he rushed to rescue the supper.

Joanna and Chris picked their way toward the privy that adjoined the end of the barn nearer the house. They moved in a little circle of light from the kerosene lantern that Chris carried, the batteries of Sandy's big flashlight having turned out to be dead. They were both very full of food, and sleepy, and just a little tipsy. Chris had taken off her socks and moccasins and Joanna her leather sandals, and the soaking grass was cold indeed to their feet that had so lately been stretched out to the fire. Joanna had never been in a privy in her life and when Chris opened the door she was astonished at the four neatly covered holes, two large and—on a lower level—two small. Everything was whitewashed; there were pegs to hang things on, and a very strong smell of disinfectant. A few flies woke up and buzzed. Chris set the lantern down on the path and partly closed the door behind them.

There was something cozy about the privy, and they were in no particular hurry to go back to the house. Chris lit a cigarette, and they sat there comfortably in the semidarkness, and Chris talked. She told Joanna about her two years in college, to which she had been made to go by her family. But Chris's love was horses, not gaining an education, and finally she had left and begun to support herself as a professional rider.

"I'd known Sandy ever since I was little," she said. "I used to hang around him when I was a kid, and he let me ride his horses and everything, and when I left college he got me jobs and sort of looked after me."

"He's a darling, isn't he?" Joanna said dreamily, watching the dim slice of light from the open door, and the mist that drifted past it.

"Well, sometimes he is," said Chris. "And sometimes I wish I'd never seen him."

"Oh, *no!*" cried Joanna. "Why?"

"Because he's got so he takes charge too much of the time—you know?" Chris said. "At first I was so crazy about him I didn't care, but now it's gone on so long I'm beginning to see I'm handicapped in a way—or that's what I think, anyway. Everybody just assumes I'm his girl. And he's got a wife, you know, and he won't leave her, ever. And then he's not here a lot of the time. But the worst of all is that he's spoiled me—everybody else seems kind of tame and young. So you see it's a mixed pleasure."

Joanna pondered, a little fuzzily. She was not at all sure what it was that Chris was telling her, but she felt she was being talked to as by one worldly soul to another. Now Chris was saying, "He said that would happen, and I didn't care then. He said, 'I'm too *old* for you, Chris, even if I was single, and this way it's hopeless for you.' But I didn't care. I didn't want anybody or anything else and I just plain chased him. And now I don't want anything else either. So it *is* hopeless. . . . I hope you don't ever love anybody more than he loves you," said Chris.

"I've never really been in love," said Joanna bravely.

"Well, you will be," Chris said, lighting a second cigarette. The little white interior and their two young, drowsy faces shone for a second in the flash of the match. "First I thought you were coming here because you were Phil's girl, but I soon saw you weren't."

"Oh, *no!*" cried Joanna again. "He's just the brother of a friend of mine, that's all."

"Yes," said Chris, "he always picks racier types than you."

Racy, thought Joanna. I wish *I* was racy, but I'm too scared.

"I've seen some of his girls, and not one of them was as good-looking as you are," Chris went on. "But they were all very dizzy. He has to have that, I guess—he's so sort of restrained himself, with that family and all. I went to a cocktail party at his house once, and it was terrible. Jeepers!" She began to laugh.

Vulgarity is what he likes, then, said Joanna to herself. Perhaps I like it myself, though I don't know that I know what it is. Perhaps my mother would say Chris and Sandy were vulgar, but they don't seem vulgar to me, though I'm glad Mother isn't here to hear their language and some of Sandy's songs.

She gave it up, as Chris said with a yawn, "We'd better get back."

As they went toward the house it loomed up above them, twice its size, the kitchen windows throwing low beams of light out into the fog. Still there was no wind. In the heavy night air nothing was real, not even Chris and the lantern and the corner of the great wall near the house. Joanna was disembodied, moving through a dream on her bare, numb feet to a house of no substance.

"Let's walk around to the front," she said. "I love the fog."

"O.K.," said Chris, and they went around the corner and stopped by the lilac bushes to listen to the stillness.

But suddenly the dampness reached their bones, and they shivered and screeched and ran back to the back door, with the bobbing lantern smoking and smelling in Chris's hand.

When they came in, Phil looked at them fondly. "Dear little Joanna," he said. "She's all dripping and watery and vaporous, like Undine. What in God's name have you girls been doing?"

"Oh, talking," said Chris.

"Pull up to the fire," Sandy said. "What did you talk about? Us?"

"Yes, dear," said Chris. "We talked about you every single second."

"Joanna's very subdued," remarked Phil. "Did you talk her into a stupor, or what?"

"Joanna doesn't have to talk if she doesn't want to," said Sandy. "I like a quiet woman, myself."

"Do you now?" said Phil, laughing at Chris, who made a face at him and sat down beside Sandy and gave him a violent hug.

Joanna, blinking, sat on the floor with her wet feet tucked under her, and listened vaguely to the talk that ran to and fro above her. Her head was swimming, and she felt sleepy and wise, in the warm lamplight and with the sound of the bantering voices which she did not have to join unless she wanted to. Suddenly she heard Phil saying, "You know, Joanna, we've got to start along. It seems to me you made a rash promise to your family that you'd be home early and it's nearly ten now and we've got thirty miles to go." He yawned, stretched, and bent to knock out his pipe on the side of the fireplace.

"I don't want to go," said Joanna.

"Then stay," said Sandy. "There's plenty of room."

But Phil said, getting up, "No, we've got to go. They'd have the police out if we didn't come soon. Joanna's very carefully raised, you know."

"I *love* Joanna," said Chris, hugging Sandy again until he grunted. "I don't care how carefully she was raised, I love her."

"We all love her," Sandy said. "You haven't got a monopoly on her. Come again and stay longer, will you, Joanna? We love you, and you look so nice here in this horrible old house."

They really do like me, thought Joanna, pulling on her sandals. But not much as I like them. They have a lot of fun all the time, so it doesn't mean as much to them to find somebody they like. But I'll remember this evening as long as I live.

Sadly she went out with them to the station wagon, following the lantern, and climbed in and sat on the clammy leather seat beside Phil. Calling back, and being called to, they drove away, bumping slowly over the little road, and in a second Chris and Sandy and the lantern were gone in the fog.

Joanna let herself in the front door and turned to wave to Phil, who waved back and drove off down the leafy street, misty in the midnight silence. Inland, the fog was not as bad as it had been near the sea, but the trees dripped with the wetness and the sidewalk shone under the street light. She listened to the faraway, sucking sound of Phil's tires die away; then she sighed and closed the door and moved sleepily into the still house, dropping her key into the brass bowl on the hall table. The house was cool, and dark downstairs except for the hall light, and it smelled of the earth in her mother's little conservatory.

Joanna started up the stairs, slowly unfastening the belt of the old trench coat she had borrowed from Phil. The drive back had been a meaningless interval swinging in the night, with nothing to remember but the glow of the headlights blanketed by the fog so that they had had to creep around the curves and down the hills, peering out until their eyes ached. Soon after they had left the farm they had stopped in a small town while Joanna telephoned her family; through the open door of the phone booth she had watched Phil sitting on a spindly stool at the little marble counter next to the shelves full of Westerns, drinking a Coke—she had a Coke herself and sipped it as the telephone rang far away in her parent's house, while back of the counter a radio played dance music. And twice after that Phil had pulled off the road, once to light his pipe, and once for Joanna to put on his coat. But now, moving up the shallow, carpeted stairs, she was back in the great, cold, dusty house with the sound of Sandy's guitar and the smell of the oil lamps, and the night, the real night, wide and black and empty, only a step away outside.

Upstairs, there was a light in her own room and one in her mother's dressing room. It was a family custom that when she came in late she should put out her mother's light, so now she went into the small, bright room. With her hand on the light-chain she looked around her, at the chintz-covered chaise longue, the chintz-skirted dressing table with family snapshots, both old and recent, arranged under its glass top, at the polished furniture, the long mirror, the agreeable clutter of many years of satisfactory married life. On the walls were more family pictures covering quite a long period of time—enlargements of picnic photographs, of boats, of a few pets. There was Joanna at the age of twelve on a cowpony in Wyoming, her father and uncle in snow goggles and climbing boots on the lower slopes of Mont Blanc heaven knows how long ago, her sister and brother-in-law looking very young and carefree with their bicycles outside Salisbury Cathedral sometime in the early thirties, judging by her sister's clothes. The world of the pictures was as fresh and good and simple as a May morning; the sun shone and everyone was happy. She stared at the familiar little scenes on the walls with love—and with a sympathy for them she had never felt before—and then she put out the light and went back along the hall.

In her own room she kicked off her sandals and dropped Phil's coat on a chair. A drawn window shade moved inward and fell back again in the night breeze that rustled the thick, wet trees close outside; her pajamas lay on the turned-down bed with its tall, fluted posts. Joanna did not stop to brush her teeth or braid her hair; she was in bed in less than two minutes.

In the darkness she heard the wind rising around Sandy's house, breathing over the open hill, whistling softly in the wet, rusted window screens, stirring in the apple trees. She heard the last burning log in the fireplace tumble apart, and a horse kick at his stall out in the barn. If I'd stayed all night, she thought, in the morning when the fog burned off I'd have known how far you could see from the top of the hill.

For in the morning the hot sun would shine from a mild blue sky, the roofs would steam, the horses would gallop and squeal in the pastures between the great walls, and all the nightingales would rise singing out of the short tough grass.

Jeremy Larner

Oh, the Wonder!

In 1964, six years after his graduation from Brandeis, Jeremy Larner won the Delta Prize for his first novel, Drive, He Said, *and the Aga Kahn Prize given by* The Paris Review *for his story "Oh, the Wonder!" Since then he has been an editor of* Dissent *and a frequent commentator on social and political issues. A speech writer for Senator Eugene McCarthy during 1968, Larner wrote an account of his gradual disillusionment with McCarthy in* Nobody Knows: Reflections on the McCarthy Campaign of 1968. *In 1973 he won an Academy Award for the screenplay of the motion picture* The Candidate.

1

On a warm evening in May, Willie McBain telephoned his friend Lickens, who lived not far away on the Lower East Side of New York City.

"For me the worst time is after supper," he told Lickens. "It gets worse every minute. I try to keep from sleeping so I won't dream. I make sure that even if I do fall out I've got the lights and the radio on."

"But just what is it?" Lickens wanted to know.

"That's it, that's it: I don't know. Nothing! I'm going out of my box!"

"Afraid of getting married?"

"Of course! I'm afraid of everything. Oh the wonder of it, Lickens! Oh the wonder of it all. Life is unbearable. How can you be alive without going out of your box?"

"There are ways," Lickens said.

"Not with my stomach. I can't keep anything inside me, Lickens. I vomit before dinner and I vomit after dinner. I'm even afraid to go to the docaroony."

"Then that's what you're afraid of."

"Sure! But the reason I'm afraid is that if I keep talking to him I might really find out what I'm afraid of."

"So you're not only afraid, you're afraid of finding out what you're afraid of?"

"Oh the wonder of it all!"

"Me, too." Lickens sighed.

"Lickens!"

"Um?"

"Come over here and go me sock for sock!"

Lickens demurred. His arms had not yet recovered from the last time. He suggested they go for a beer.

"Can't," said Willie. "I've got to work."

"But you won't work. You know that. Take a break and then maybe things will be better."

"Then maybe things will be tomorrow, that's all! But why not? No, fuck it Lickens, this has got to be done tonight, so get thee the hell away from me. I've got to hang up.

"Good luck."

Willie McBain was a graduate student in Philosophy at Columbia University. He had set aside that night—just as he had set aside the eleven nights previous—to finish a paper that had been due in January. Within a week his extensions would be up on two more papers from the Fall semester, and he had not even begun research on one of them. When those were finished, he would have three fun-packed weeks in which to write his Master's paper and pass his language examinations. He complied with the mickeymouse because he wanted to teach; he thought he had a new way of teaching. Willie wanted to account for man's unpleasant psychology in philosophic terms. Specifically, he was impressed by the problem of aggression. From all that he felt and saw, he knew that to live was to hurt oneself. Could the pattern be undone? Could men come to know the score and do what they could for themselves? Or were his thoughts merely personal? These were the questions he would make his students answer, the very questions that had been neatly avoided by the spinners of spiritual and political systems. Because they were afraid: it's always so much easier to write things out neatly when you don't have to care how they really are. Willie was going to make them see. He would hunt them down remorselessly, cutting off every avenue of transcendental escape. He didn't have the answers, he knew; but he could make a start by insisting on the real questions.

But sooner or later he would have to write a book, and for the moment Willie McBain could not even manage to read a book. He would plot his time and settle carefully in the rubble of his railroad flat, only to find himself staring for hours at a single page. He could concentrate for a paragraph or two, then twenty minutes would disappear and he would come back to himself with a start, furious, without the slightest idea where he had been. The psychiatrist agreed that it was more than a matter of will-power. But still it made Willie angry. No matter what the doctor said, sooner or later he had to control himself, that was what it boiled down to, or else they might as well start padding the walls and removing sharp objects.

He pawed for the phone, and called Philadelphia where his fiancée was finishing her last year at college.

"I can't work," he told her. "I'm like that machine that turns itself off. Why don't you go out and find someone worthwhile?"

"Because I've got someone," she said. "Someone who turns *me* on. Willie, if you could only relax for a while. It doesn't make any difference if you can't do what you want right this minute. You'll do your work when you're really and truly ready, and tearing at yourself won't help."

"Sure I'll do my work! What if I don't? There's no law says I will. What's the difference between me and thousands of pretentious half-wits in this city who gas about what they are going to do some day?"

"There is a difference; I can't prove it to you but there is. I know it and so does everyone who ever met you."

Willie laughed. "Don't be a goddam girl-friend!"

She didn't answer. "What's the matter?" he said. "Are you hurt?"

"I guess so," she said. "I'm sorry."

"Look." he said. "I'm going to flunk out of school. I'll be drafted and you'll never see me again."

"I wouldn't like that. I'd go to the Army and make them give you back."

"What are you doing?" he asked her. "Get anything done tonight?"

She giggled. "Oh, I'm supposed to be studying for my Sosh finals tomorrow. But I think I know the material pretty well—I've just been sitting up talking with Francine . . ."

"Francine! That flaccid ass!"

"Shhhhhhhhh."

"Don't shhh me! I thought you promised not to see her anymore."

"I didn't promise."

"Oh, I get it, you just let me *think* you promised!"

"I can't talk about it now."

"Why not, 'cause she'll hear? Screw that! Who's more important to you anyway, me or her! Are you going to waste your whole life on namby-pamby gushing fawning half-wits? People who might challenge you you avoid like the plague! What's going to become of you, goddammit?"

He was nearly out of his box with rage. He shouted at her until she cried. When it was over he felt worse than ever. She promised to send Francine away and go back to studying, and he said, choking, that it didn't really matter what she did. He said if only he had her in his bed right that very instant—that was all that could make the difference. When he hung up he took a dish and slammed it against the wall.

Sarah was really not the girl for him. Perhaps he only loved her because she loved him. She was so utterly dependent on him, couldn't make a move without him, no plans, no ambitions, no nothing of her own . . . She wanted to be pregnant: he had to make damn sure every time that she got her diaphragm in. The ready-made identity! She would marry him and attach her life to his like a leech. But wasn't that what a woman was supposed to do? Was it wrong for a bright young girl to think of nothing but babies? Or was he so far out of his box he couldn't see straight?

But how would she become a person? Sarah wanted to think their life together was a lovey-dovey-ducky-wucky dreamaroony, and that wasn't what life was like! Life was too goddam unbearable, you had to be ready to fight! He, at least, had the guts to go to the doctor.

He paced the room thinking of his prize-fighting days. Maybe he should have turned pro. The new light-heavy-weight champ was a punk. Willie had a theory about how he could be set up. He cracked his fists into the porcelain of the fridgaroony, feeling it dent and spring out again. Neighbors pounded on the thin wall, loosening bits of plaster, and Willie pounded back, pound for pound, till the ceiling shook and he heard crashes on the other side.

He heard someone running down the stairs. Maybe the cops would come. Willie had never quite hit a cop. He coveted that pleasure: to sink a fist in one's massive blue frontage. He didn't care if they killed him.

He sat on the bed to watch a movie he had started in his mind. He was putting the slug to one cop after another while they pumped bullets into him and the whole block poured out to watch in love and fascination. Everyone loved him, he knew it—no matter if he brought the roach-infested house down. Even Sarah, whose teary face in the movie gave him a laugh. No babies now. No comfy for Sarah. Bitterly he thought how she would be the only one to miss the splendor of his gesture. She would feel cheated, and even think him foolish.

The hell with her, he would be dead. He laughed out loud and shook his head. He couldn't understand why when he was depressed he thought so little of dying. Normally the fear of death overtook him in every happiness, ran him down like a wolfhound. He was pondering this when the phone rang . . .

Ten minutes later he phoned Lickens.

"Luscious Louise called," he reported.

"Um," said Lickens.

"She wants me to come over. She's lonely. She wants me to talk to her. Let's be friends, she says."

"You going?"

"I shouldn't. But I was thinking what the hell I can't work anyway, maybe after this I'll come back, take a benny, stay up all night and it will be all out of my system, see?"

"So why call me?"

"You're supposed to talk me out of it."

"That's not fair. . . . but if you want, I'll go in your place."

"No," answered Willie still sad, though the fact was that Licken's offer had clinched it for him. "I'm going. Trouble is, I've got this itch in the old groinaroony . . ."

". . . and when Ah itches, Ah scratches!" Lickens drawled.

Luscious Louise made it difficult for about half an hour. She really did want to talk. She didn't know what to do with herself. She was too bright; she was tired of being a secretary. She had this idea that she would go to law school and she wanted Willie McBain to love her for it. Willie knew what her trouble was.

"I know what your trouble is," he said. "You want a penis. But you can't get one by going to law school. The only way is to use mine while you have a chance."

She tried to get on her high horse, but he wouldn't let her. He knew she wanted to.

"You know you want to," Willie said.

She sighed.

Making love to Louise was like riding the white horse in the circus. Where was she taking him, slick nervous antelope with such strange interior muscles?! She could play a tune on him like a piccolo. Sarah was tamer and didn't shriek so much—well, why should she? He loved her, she knew it . . . he wasn't even thinking of Luscious Louise except when she . . . wow! . . . she was going out of her box . . . he had never . . . now why couldn't Sarah be more like

this!

?

When she saw it was all up with him she snuggled close and closed her eyes in contentment. But Willie lay with his fists clenched and teeth jammed together like nails. He couldn't stand it; he wanted to get up and rush out on the fire escape and throw himself over. If he relaxed a single muscle he would plunge headfirst down the brickface wall and crunch powerfully through the sidewalk miles deep beneath the candy store.

Louise was clutching at his arms. "Willie, Willie-baby . . ."

"Let me go!"

He stood facing her, pathetic in his undershirt, his back against the wall while she made absurd calming motions.

"Get out of bed and I'll slam you one!"

She lay where she was. As he pulled on his clothes he heard her sniffling. Only when he was safely down in the street and running did he realize he had been tearing his hair and ears.

He ran six blocks down Avenue B and thumped three-at-a-time up the wooden steps of Licken's tenement.

He knocked and from within heard the sounds of Lickens grumbling and rolling out of bed. Then the striking of a match.

"You!" said Lickens. "G'morning, silly bastard!"

Willie saw that Lickens' eyes were not quite open.

"Now Lickens, sorry to wake you, man, just get back in bed, fall out, land of nod, forget and forgive, Lickens, that's it, easy there . . ."

"Peckerhead!" Lickens mumbled, as Willie eased him back onto his mattress. The keys were on the night table where Willie could palm them without any trouble. He stood for a while watching Lickens drop back to sleep and right next to him Lickens' beautiful wife sleeping in a band of moonlight, her face calm and womanly, her long hair strewn lightly on the pillow. Her features were more relaxed than in her waking hours. And her mouth closed. He bent close to admire her full lips and long dark lashes. She breathed sweetly as a doe. And look at Lickens lying there, snorting and twisting! What a jackass to be thumping himself around so and sticking his silly head under the pillow! Lickens didn't have any problems. His only problem was he thought he had problems. Lucky Lickens!

But no luckier than he, Willie McBain, might be! He had no debts, no job, no cancer. Nothing to lose but worry and time.

The junkpiley Lickensmobile sat right around the corner. Willie unlocked it, started it up and set off for Philadelphia.

He bit his nails at eighty miles an hour down the New Jersey turnpike. He didn't know it, but he was worried that he would arrive to find Sarah gone. Hung around his mind like an albatross was a picture of her with Roger Stennis. Stennis was the most respected student in Sarah's graduating class—an alert young man with quick lips and clean eyes. Stennis was going to be an historian, and one of the best: he had won a fellowship to Oxford and Willie was certain that Roger would like nothing better than to take Willie's Sarah along with him. And it was logical—why shouldn't she go? Wouldn't a cottage on the green and a well-bordered life and a creative, productive, attentive husband be far, far preferable to a stinking slum-hole in New York and a hung-up, hateful husband off screwing with Luscious Louise and even when with her flailing and cursing, climbing up by tearing her down, desperately clutching and snapping at every weakness in sight in his last-ditch efforts to punish the world for his own shortcomings? A sweet, bright girl like her, so long abused? She should have been long gone already. Without seeing it he saw in his mind a bed with Sarah and Roger Stennis well-sheeted together.

He would never forget what had happened when he took off on his canoe trip the summer before. On principle he had insisted that Sarah not refuse dates with other men, but when she wrote him she had gone out with Roger Stennis, he nearly went out of his box. Stennis had been in love with her a long time—no doubt about that. Sure, going out he didn't mind, but Stennis was a betrayal! He would kill the bastard. He would blast his head open with a hard right.

There was blood in his mouth from where he had chewed into his cheek. Glancing at his gas gauge, he saw the needle stuck on empty, and, dressed hurriedly as he was in workshirt and jeans, his rummagings produced a mere quarter. His headlights picked up a sign announcing a rest stop. He had to think of something. Fifteen minutes later he found himself sitting over an empty coffee cup in a Howard Johnson's. He tried to remember the waitress bringing him the coffee: had she been friendly? Perhaps he had gotten it himself. He was sitting alone at a little table, and the only other people in the place were a clutch of fifteen-sixteen-year-old boys at the counter.

Damned if they weren't giggling!

They were staring at him and trying to puzzle him out and giggling because they had never seen anything like him in their part of New Jersey.

Willie glared back with a vicious eyeblast intensity utterly unequal to their intentions and sending them into gales of laughter.

Willie's standing silenced them, until a brave one voiced the single word they knew for him: "Hey Mister, you a beatnik or sompin!"

Willie said, "No, are you?" A volcano of giggles.

"What's your name?" Willie said. "You!"

The boy was stumped for a second. "Puddentane!" he said triumphantly, and put his comrades in convulsions.

"Well look, Puddentane, you look like a beatnik to me, with all that acne and that grease on your hair. How about it?"

"I'm just a normal American boy," Puddentane replied. The laughter this time was uneasy; the boys poked each other, shifted, whispered.

"What do normal American boys do with themselves, Puddentane? Hang around Howard Johnson's all night and stare at customers?"

"If we feel like it," said Puddentane. "We're not bigtime like you."

"Don't you masturbate?"

The boys giggled in shock and broke out in very loud laughter and finally hoots. "Oh, brother!" said Puddentane. "You *are* a weird one!"

"It's weird to talk about sex, isn't it? You normal American boys don't like it, do you? It embarrasses you, huh?"

"Oh sure," someone said. No one was laughing.

"If it doesn't embarrass you, why are you turning red, Puddentane?"

Puddentane didn't know why he was turning red, but he did know, at last, that he hated Willie's guts the moment he saw him. The boys shrunk back like snakes, their eyes fixed on Willie.

"Why don't you go back to Russia?" one of them inquired.

"You want to fight?" said Willie instantly.

He caught them unprepared. The five of them working together could have taken him, but separately they couldn't decide. Time out for consultation.

"I'll leave you normal American boys to your circle-jerk." Willie took his departure.

As he went out the door, he heard behind him the shout, "Goodbye, beatnik!"—and then a chorus of shouts: "Goodbye, Communist, Goodbye, orang-utang, Goodbye, pigpen!" The five trailed behind as he walked toward the Lickensmobile and came close as he started it, shouting, jeering, thumping on the fenders and windows.

A mile later Willie remembered his gas gauge. Since traffic was light he was able to back carefully up the turnpike till he reached the Howard Johnson's again. There was a souped-up Ford in back which obviously belonged to the blackhead set. Willie took Lickens' always-ready rubber tube from the back seat and siphoned off the gasoline from the jutting Fordaroony into the thirsty tank of the Lickensmobile. As he was finishing the boys came out and spotted him. The Ford gave hot pursuit and undoubtedly would have caught him had it not run out of gas in three minutes.

But Willie had forgotten his new-found enemies in two minutes. He was remembering Sarah: "Roger? Why, he's only a *boy!*"

"Did you kiss him?" he had asked.

"Yes," she had said, flaring up. "I think so. So what?" *I think so? So what!* How had he put up with her solid brass evasiveness? He was eating on his tongue. It was obvious she was gone; he knew it now. He was driving full speed ahead into a tunnel that receded as fast as he came. But if he could encounter anything at all in the tunnel he would destroy it, or destroy himself trying.

He swung into Philadelphia and drove straight to the apartment where Sarah lived with her roommate, charged up the stairs and knocked three hard knocks at the door. In a matter of seconds he expected to be back in the Lickensmobile, racing for every last inch of justice he could extract. There was no answer to his knock. But he had forgotten that it was six o'clock in the morning. He had stormed down two landings when he heard the door open; he rushed back up and there was the anxious, bewildered, asleep face of his Sarah peering out from behind the door. There was no question of her not being there; it did not even occur to him. They sat in the kitchen having breakfast, she delighted and asleep, he at last relaxed. He had not remembered the depth or the sureness of her brown eyes, the charming rumple of her cotton bathrobe, her little breasts peeping out at him like baby birds. Relaxed: the new sun rippled on the kitchen wall, toilets flushed, radios came on. The dread night had vanished and Willie might curl the warm day around him and sleep.

Sarah tucked him into her bed all odorous of woman and he tumbled down a well, his thoughts behind him. He was up by noon, before she got back from her last final exam, in time to shower and wash all the Lusciousness of Louise from his stomach, chest and groin. Sarah's roommate was up and made bacon-lettuce-and-tomato sandwiches smothered in mayonnaise and rye bread (because she loved Willie, too, naturally—it was a problem). Willie ate two huge BLT's, laughed, joked, drank his beer, pinched Sarah's ass and the roommate's too. After lunch he went into Sarah's room and into bed with Sarah, quickly, voraciously, because the instant he was through Willie jumped up and sat down at the typewriter and from memory resumed his paper at the point where he had left off and finished it without even stopping to hesitate. There was no doubt in his mind, nor of anything else at the moment. If he did not go out of his box at an early age, he was going to be quite a man.

In only an hour he was through, and out of steam anyway, and collapsed back in bed with Sarah, where for a full five minutes he watched her sweet, spirited eyes dart back and forth along the book she was reading. Then his watching was too much for her and she turned to him. Until suppertime they stuck close, each to the other's skin, and talked about what they would make of their life together. Willie stretched out as he talked, and watched the afternoon sun come bouncing off the upturned venetian blinds and sparkle slowly across the ceiling.

More than anything, Sarah wanted to be his and to bear his children. But she had decided to take a degree in Social Psychology; for she had to be a person in her own right, and this meant having work of her own to last her whole life long and keep her from bringing to her children that desperate clutch which her own mother even now could not relax. Willie nodded, basked in her completeness. There was nothing unbeautiful in her, she fitted together in every part and thought: when he was not out of his box he saw this truly and wondered at his incredible luck in having her. What had he done, he whispered, caressing her trim thigh, interrupting her, to deserve someone so perfect? Just being you, she answered to his most private ear, pulling him close and delighting him with a gesture they had never before dared or even imagined.

Their final plans, as the light wobbled orange on the ceiling: in the morning they would drive to New York, take out a license and get married by a justice of the peace. Or why get married at all? he wondered idly—but she shyly confessed it meant something to her, she still had that much of the middle class in her. Or maybe it really wasn't that at all, she insisted, growing more confident, but simply that she wanted to feel him hers, the full weight of their promise to each other. Promise? Willie laughed, but he was flattered, pleased, touched . . . She thought him capable of keeping a promise!

Even so her parents would be shocked, but never mind . . . they would get over it, and she would never in all eternity get over him. Her parents would say how can you live? But what did they know about living? Willie and Sarah would live all right, just watch them.

They did not need the things their parents had needed. They would be too alive for the buying-earning routine through which they were expected to stumble and excuse their lives away. They had no use for empty job-working. They would live simply in an old barn in the country, changing it over with the love of their own hands, making it belong to them and the pulsing life they would bring to it. Life was possible, really possible, for those who had the gift of loving.

2

Willie came back to himself like an object sucking into a vacuum. Without warning, the room was dark. Night had pushed the sun down out of the sky and crept over the land looking for Willie. It got worse every minute, as it had the day before and the day before that, as it did on days when he loved and days when he was removed from his love. Sarah was sleeping nestled in his shoulder; he looked at her, felt of her . . . and could not stand her breathing there. He stroked her hair, trying, trying—he thrust her roughly away. He did not wake her. She looked like a goddamn child. What had she ever done in her life to make him believe she could be a woman? He couldn't have a woman, not him, not yet: he was too weak and too young. They made an absurd spectacle, Sarah and he—two overgrown babies hugging each other and playing big people in a dream world. Disgusting! She was so soft he could hardly fuck her. Why did he need this? His moment with Luscious Louise seemed infinitely more honest.

It was getting worse and he couldn't face it. Headlights shot into the room and raced across the ceiling. He lay petrified. He wanted to sleep, to conk out and stay out—but he was afraid of his dreams. His fists clamped tight to his groin, he tried grimly to focus on the hayloft in that mythical barn, where he would have rigged a punching-bag. Of course there would be no barn. No morning, either, nothing but a grubby, scroungy life of night after night. The doctor couldn't cure him—what nonsense for her to count on that! There was nothing to cure him of, his sickness was life. He was not out of his box; it was just that he could not fool himself. He was not a woman, he could not lie all warm and smelly and dream of babies and houses: the night was there and he saw it, and there was nothing he or anyone could do about it.

If he could not sleep he had to act, to move. Or else it would all be up. He must rise now and turn on the lights and the radio. Get up, get out of bed, turn on lights and radio. He strained against his body until he broke out in a violent sweat. Lying paralyzed and unblinking in the soaking sheets he saw himself pulled as if by a magnet, sucked to the window and through the slats of the venetian blinds, through the shivered glass and through the crusted streets like so many sheets of paper, cutting clean as a knife-blade into the grave.

He rose at last, lurching heavily, a landlubber coming on deck in a hurricane and stumbling for the rail . . . arms stiff as boards, he snapped on the lights, snapped on the radio.

Got to the bathroom as his insides came rushing out, and lay with his head in the toilet-bowl while his lungs and stomach heaved in dry spasms. He was dying, surely dying, oh merciful God, just let it be quick, he prayed to himself. Later he knew that Sarah must have woken up; she clung to his back, soothing him, still asleep and moaning for his hurt. With a twitch of his shoulders he shrugged her away, so that she banged her head on the sink and cried like a little girl. He threw up again, this time with relief; lay weak with his head in the toilet, purged, subsiding; and he loved her and everyone with all his heart, mixing his own happy tears with the vomit.

They went out to eat—showered, dressed up, holding hands and feeling large and good as an opera. It should have worked. The restaurant was something special: linen napkins, silver three-foot menus, two kinds of waiters, and so many plates there was no room for your elbows. Maybe it was too much for them. They ate extremely well, but there was nothing to say. Sarah simply sat there. Willie made a few remarks on his work, then hers, and she made routine answers, but she had nothing to say, nothing to start on her own. She was nervous and did not want to talk at all, just sit there and enjoy being with him. He saw she felt only for him; it was he who had to begin any thought that might connect them to the outside world, to life. She was competent to follow; it was up to him to begin and she would follow wherever he led. Willie saw more clearly than ever that his love for Sarah could bring him into no new relations with the world. Hardly! Difficult as it was to keep himself alive he would henceforth be expected to pull for two.

He sat on the back of his neck with his meat and potatoes, bread and tomatoes bombing him to his chair, while the chair itself sank slowly to the bottom of the ocean. As the depths closed over him he saw her smile, waveringly. Oh the tentativity of her; she could scarcely keep herself afloat! Her hand drifted toward him apologetically. Hardly daring to touch, she walked her fingers on the back of his hand.

"You have nothing to say for yourself, do you?"

She was hurt. "Am I on trial?"

He belched. "Oh what the hell!" he said.

"Look, it's been a long day," she said, biting her lip. If only she would lose her temper!

"And a hard day?" he needled hopefully.

"A hard day but a very good day," she said quietly. "Willie, I'm so tired. Please don't be hard on me."

He couldn't even bring himself to look at her. "I'm not being *hard* on you," he muttered. He ordered a globular heap of ice creams, which impacted themselves together about halfway down.

They walked down one of the streets bordering campus, where all the little stores were still open and brightly lit. Neat pressed suits could be had, and notebooks. He shoveled through a used-book stack while she looked on absently, as though all books were alike to her. He walked her rapidly down the street to one of the movie-houses. They were playing a sophisticated comedy with titillating risqué dialogue, the kind of picture he would see only in an emergency. He stopped with her in front of the posters.

"Well?" he said. She smiled, ready to go either way. "Do you want to see it?"

"If you do, Willie."

"The hell with whether I do! You're a person! This is a movie—either you want to see it, deep down *here* (poking her), or you don't. But don't do it just for me, baby—don't let yourself get away with that!"

She stuck her lip out and walked away. He ran after her, grabbed her roughly.

"No, goddammit! I'm not going to let you be hurt. That's too easy, Sarah. I just want to know a simple thing: do you or don't you want to see the movie? It's only a decision, baby, it's got nothing to do with me. You just say yes or no and it's all over."

She tried to jerk away, hatefully, but he held her fast. "You absolute bastard!" she cried. She began to weep. Willie relaxed. She was his small, tender girl, and he wanted only to love her and soothe her hurt. While he held her and caressed her she blubbered that she didn't know, didn't care about the movie—she knew he was nervous and would be happy doing anything that helped him relax, that's all, because she loved him. She didn't think of going to a harmless movie as a decision, she wasn't thinking of wasting her valuable time or building her valuable life. She was with him, and did it make much difference what they did?

Okay, okay, he said. Please don't cry. Here: he kissed away a tear. She cried happily now, with her head sniffling on his chest. People were looking. I feel so foolish, she said, standing like this in the middle of the sidewalk.

They walked on; he couldn't blame her. It was his twisted-up way of seeing things. Had they really said all they ever had to say in one afternoon? They walked on in silence past the little shops and the dressy college people, and Willie wanted desperately to be alone.

He felt like dashing up the street and around the corner. Just standing there by himself in his own body would be so free and fine. No little one to tow along beside him. Just to be himself in his own skin, smelling the night air and doing whatever, moving wherever, his desires took him. Himself alone.

But that was not to be. They met some friends of Sarah's on the street and had to stand babbling. Willie said little—the people were schmucks as far as he was concerned. He watched Sarah; she was giggling of all things, like a teenager. That was because the people had joked about marriage, and she didn't know what to say: she was giggling and looking up at him. He scowled and saw her eyes fill up with hurt. The inquiring young man & woman, when they got no reply from Sarah and no attention from Willie, smiled as if to shrug, and moved on.

"Maybe next week!" he called after them, like a fool.

Once more in a pinch she had lapsed into girlishness and made him look the brute.

"I only want you to respect yourself," he said.

She turned in anger—"Must you *watch* me like that!"—but the anger soon faded into a kind of bewilderment that was exasperating but really, when he thought about it, did her credit. She knew what he meant, why he was forced to watch. She was not by any means dead or done.

She took his arm.

"I'm sorry," she said. "I don't know what gets into me. My poor Willie, you certainly have a lot to put up with . . ."

But it was too late, Roger Stennis was upon them, looking five years older, bolstered by two grinning sycophants, handsome as the devil and dressed like the Duke of Wales. "Sarah!" he announced, in his bulletin-board baritone. He shook Willie's hand with a single pump, European style. He introduced his entourage, who followed suit.

"Well, old man!" Roger said.

"Well, old man!" mocked Willie.

Roger took the mockery fondly. Good old basically lovable, irascible Willie. We know you.

"How are things down at Columbia? Department all right?"

Okay, Willie guessed.

"Be through in another year, I suppose?"

"Through?"

"Phd, I mean. The old union card."

"Well, I don't know," Willie said, though he knew very well and the answer was no. "Three years would be a pretty short trip."

But it seemed that Roger would have it in three. After his year at Oxford on the Fulbright, he would enter the new three-year program at Harvard. He had an understanding with the department there.

"Nice," Willie said.

"Yes, but it's just the externals," Roger confessed.

"What really matters is what you do with it."

"Yes."

There was a difficult pause, as though Roger had inquired what Willie had done with his two years since college, and Willie had not been able to answer. But Roger didn't have to ask. Willie would have been almost brilliant, if he were not so hopelessly hungup . . .

They all shook hands again.

"I envy you Paris," said Willie, honestly. What he might not learn in Paris!

"I envy you something more than Paris, Willie." Roger smiled down at Sarah, the sad, knowing smile of one who has loved well and lost, but lost only after the loving was finished and he had moved on to better things. Dear old Sarah, his smile was saying, how I hope you'll be happy. I'm really quite fond of you, you know.

And Sarah, to Willie's horror, was blushing, grinnning like a little half-wit, nestling into his lapels!

Roger shook Willie's hand one more time. "Good luck, old man . . . the best." He meant it, too, really meant it, and Willie liked him, always had, for at least a full second.

"Oh the wonder of it all!" Willie mumbled inanely, then swung with all his might, smashing Roger Stennis right in the smile, knocking him off his feet and dribbling blood into his costly tie.

Sarah clung petrified to his right arm as he stood with fists clenched, waiting for Stennis to rise so he could knock him down again. But Stennis was in no hurry to rise. His friends dragged him away, heels trailing, Stennis holding a folded handkerchief to his lips and shaking his head groggily at the madness of Willie McBain, who watched after him ferocious, fists cocked, rigid and trembling in rage.

Willie and Sarah went home weeping and ashamed, and might have been good to one another had it not been for the cops waiting at the door. It seemed that the maniac Lickens had reported the Lickensmobile stolen, and suggested that the police might inquire for the thief in Philadelphia. Was this his idea of a joke? As Willie was led off furious between two brass bellies he thought for a moment of burying his elbows one to a pot and making a break for it. Alone at last! But why die? Life was awful but he was damned if he would give them the satisfaction.

Betrayed twice over, he stewed two hours in a jail cell before the stately Lickens phoned to confirm his identity. He was thinking mostly of Sarah by that time, and his thoughts swung round and round on a well-worn track. He wasn't sorry about Roger Stennis—why should he be? That had been his first clean act in months. No, it was Sarah—there was something wrong, deeper than tears could plumb, and this time he meant to have it out with her.

When he got back she was in her room with the lights out. She was still as stone but he could tell by her breathing she was not asleep. All the better. He snapped on the light and saw her stare back dry-eyed and cold, not moving a muscle.

"You're a coward," he said.

No answer.

"Well? Have anything to say for yourself? Has it been a long day?"

"It's been a miserable day." She was glaring at him as if she'd never seen him before.

"It's always a miserable day when you have to humiliate yourself at every opportunity."

"What do you want from me!" she burst out. "Humiliate! Yes, I was humiliated all right. I've never been so humiliated in my life. I was humiliated by a man who can no more control himself . . . no more . . . who strikes out like a little boy!"

"You mean, who strikes out to protect his so-called woman when she lets herself be turned into a ten-year-old girl, and likes it, revels in it! Is this what I have to expect from you? That every time there's a test you'll snuggle away like a child! Is it? Is it?"

She was crying now and yelling through her tears. "I a child! I a child! Why I felt sorry for that boy, I felt sorry and embarrassed for him! He was trying his hardest to impress you, don't you see, but you thought it was a test. You think everything's a test. You're still back in grade school, taking tests. That's what you want life to be for me, one test after another. Well I can't stand it, you hear? I don't want that kind of life! I want someone I can love and who loves me and who can live with me and be proud of me; yes, and take care of me too. I'm a woman, I'm not your boxing-partner!"

"Boxing-partner?! What does that mean? Shit! What in God's name does that mean? You want someone to be proud? Listen to me! I'll be proud of you when you can be proud of yourself. Take care of you, sure, you telling me I don't take care of you? But as a man takes care of his woman, not as a father his baby girl! I'll respect you when you have something to say for yourself, as one adult to another, when you can stand up and look people in the eye!"

"You mean *punch* people in the eye!"

"I MEAN WHAT I SAY! AND THAT'S ALL! I'M UPSET. I'M UPSET, I'M TERRIFICALLY UPSET AND YOU'RE DISTORTING EVERYTHING I SAY!"

He stepped back. He thought he was through shouting. "It's really very simple," he said. "God, how you upset me . . ."

She sat on the edge of the bed. She had stopped crying, and sat looking at him, eyes narrowed with hate.

"Get out," she said.

He stopped pacing. "What's that?"

"I said get out. I don't love you anymore. I loathe you. You're not a man, you're a bad tempered little boy. You don't want me as a woman, you want me as a roughneck sidekick to help you bully the other kids on the block."

"Listen," he said. "Some of what you say is right. OK. But what I say is very simple. I want you to be yourself. I want you to be your best. I want you to be proud so I can be proud too, of us. Because I love you. Believe me. I love you."

"You love yourself. You're talking to yourself now, you've got it all worked out. Get out of here. You disgust me." Suddenly she lost control. "I LOATHE YOU I LOATHE YOU I LOATHE YOU," she screamed, and fell weeping hysterically to the floor.

Her hysteria calmed him. He leaned to take her shoulder in his gentle hand and cupping her head smoothed her hair but she screamed GET AWAY FROM ME GET AWAY I LOATHE YOU GET AWAY!

And she twisted from him, squirmed violently, ugly, her face contorted, crawling for the door . . . A red screen came down before his eyes.

"DON'T YOU TALK TO ME THAT WAY!" he yelled. "DON'T YOU DARE, DON'T YOU EVER!" Before he knew he would he hit her, then when he knew hit her again, not out of malice but pure blind rage: clubbed the crawling girl clumsy blows on the head and then to the ribs, knocking her over.

He leaned back against the wall and screamed. She lay on the floor and screamed. She got to her feet, flashed him a look of indomitable hatred, ran to the bathroom and locked herself in.

When next he could speak he bellowed COME OUT OF THERE OR

I'LL KNOCK YOUR GODDAM DOOR IN! At which she shouted, vulgar as a whore, FUCK YOU YOU BASTARD GO AWAY I HATE YOU. And he said, choking, "How lovely you are!"

Then, in a little while, he called to her, "Please come out, Sarah. I'm sorry. I do love you, very much. I'm sorry for what I said." He heard no sound but her desperate weeping.

Methodically, in a cold fury, he began to pummel the wall. And even as he smashed one ruined fist after the other weeping and swearing he knew she would love him again, she would forgive him, they would love and be together for the rest of their lives and oh how he would hate her for it.

Isak Dinesen

The Old Chevalier

Isak Dinesen is the pseudonym that Baroness Karen Blixen adopted in 1934 when she published Seven Gothic Tales, *the first of several books she wrote in English. Born in Rungsted, Denmark, Ms. Dinesen studied literature at Oxford and painting at the Royal Academy in Copenhagen before marrying in 1914 and moving to British East Africa to run a coffee plantation with her husband. After their divorce in 1921, she managed the plantation alone for the next ten years, then had to give it up for economic reasons and returned to Denmark.* Out of Africa, *her extraordinary memoir of the years she had spent in Africa, was published in 1937.*

My father had a friend, old Baron von Brackel, who had in his day traveled much and known many cities and men. Otherwise he was not at all like Odysseus, and could least of all be called ingenious, for he had shown very little skill in managing his own affairs. Probably from a sense of failure in this respect he carefully kept from discussing practical matters with an efficient younger generation, keen on their careers and success in life. But on theology, the opera, moral right and wrong, and other unprofitable pursuits he was a pleasant talker.

He had been a singularly good-looking young man, a sort of ideally handsome youth, and although no trace of his past beauty could be found in his face, the history of it could be traced in a certain light-hearted dignity and self-reliance which are the product of a career of good looks, and which will be found, unaccountably, in the carriage of those shaking ruins who used to look into the mirrors of the last century with delight. In this way one should be able to point out, at a *danse macabre,* the skeletons of the real great beauties of their time.

One night he and I came to discuss an old theme, which has done its duty in the literature of the past: namely, whether one is ever likely to get any real benefit, any lasting moral satisfaction, out of forsaking an inclination for the sake of principle, and in the course of our talk he told me the following story:

On a rainy night in the winter of 1874, on an avenue in Paris, a drunken young girl came up and spoke to me. I was then, as you will understand, quite a young man. I was very upset and unhappy, and was sitting bareheaded in the rain on a seat along the avenue because I had just parted from a lady whom, as we said then, I did adore, and who had within this last hour tried to poison me.

This, though it has nothing to do with what I was going to tell you, was in itself a curious story. I had not thought of it for many years until, when I was last in Paris, I saw the lady in her box at the opera, now a very old woman, with two charming little girls in pink who were, I was told, her great-granddaughters. She was lovely no more, but I had never, in the time that I have known her, seen her look so contented. I was sorry afterward that I had not gone up and called on her in her box, for though there had been but little happiness for either of us in that old love affair of ours, I think that she would have been as pleased to be reminded of the beautiful young woman, who made men unhappy, as I had been to remember, vaguely as it was, the young man who had been so unhappy that long time ago.

Her great beauty, unless some rare artist has been able to preserve it in color or clay, now probably exists only within a few very old brains like mine. It was in its day something very wonderful. She was a blonde, the fairest, I think, that I have ever seen, but not one of your pink-and-white beauties. She was pale, colorless, all through, like an old pastel or the image of a woman in a dim mirror. Within that cool and frail form there was an unrivaled energy, and a distinction such as women have no more, or no more care to have.

I had met her and had fallen in love with her in the autumn, at the château of a friend where we were both staying together with a large party of other gay young people who are now, if they are alive, faded and crooked and deaf. We were there to hunt, and I think that I shall be able to remember to the last of my days how she used to look on a big bay horse that she had, and that autumn air, just touched with frost, when we came home in the evenings, warm in cold clothes, tired, riding side by side over an old stone bridge. My love was both humble and audacious, like that of a page for his lady, for she was so much admired, and her beauty had in itself a sort of disdain which might well give sad dreams to a boy of twenty, poor and a stranger in her set. So that every hour of our rides, dances and *tableaux vivants* was exuberant with ecstasy and pain, the sort of thing you will know yourself: a whole orchestra in the heart. When she made me happy, as one says, I thought that I was happy indeed. I remembered smoking a cigar on the terrace one morning, looking out over the large view of low, wood-covered blue hills, and giving the Lord a sort of receipt for all the happiness that I should ever have any claim to in my life. Whatever would happen to me now, I had had my due, and declared myself satisfied.

Love, with very young people, is a heartless business. We drink at that age from thirst, or to get drunk; it is only later in life that we occupy ourselves with the individuality of our wine. A young man in love is essentially enraptured by the forces within himself. You may come back to that view again, in a second adolescence. I knew a very old Russian in Paris, enormously rich, who used to keep the most charming young dancers, and who when once asked whether he had, or needed to have, any illusions as to their feelings for him, thought the question over and said: "I do not think, if my chef succeeds in making me a good omelette, that I bother much whether he loves me or not." A young man could not have put his answer into those words, but he might say that he did not care whether his wine merchant was of his own religion or not, and imagine that he had got close to the truth of things. In middle age, though, you arrive at a deeper humility, and you come to consider it of importance that the person who sells or grows your wine shall be of the same religion as you yourself. In this case of my own, of which I am telling you, my youthful vanity, if I had too much of it, was to be taught a lesson very soon. For during the months of that winter, while we were both living in Paris, where her house was the meeting place of many *bel-esprits,* and she herself the admired dilettante in music and arts, I began to think that she was making use of me, or of her own love for me, if such can be said, to make her husband jealous. This has happened, I suppose, to many young men down through the ages, without the total sum of their experience being much use to the young man who finds himself in the same position today. I began to wonder what the relations between those two were really like, and what strange forces there might be in her or in him, to toss me about between them in this way, and I think that I began to be afraid. She was jealous of me, too, and would scold me with a sort of moral indignation, as if I had been a groom failing in his duties. I thought that I could not live without her, and also that she did not want to live without me, but exactly what she wanted me for I did not know. Her contact hurt me as one is hurt by touching iron on a winter day: you do not know whether the pain comes from heat or from cold.

Before I had ever met her I had read about her family, whose name ran down for centuries through the history of France, and learned that there used to be werewolves amongst them, and I sometimes thought that I should have been happier to see her really go down on all fours and snarl at me, for then I should have known where I was. And even up to the end we had hours together of a particular charm, for which I shall always be thankful to her. During my first year in Paris, before I knew any people there, I had taken up studying the history of the old hotels of the town, and this hobby of mine appealed to her, so that we used to dive into old quarters and ages of Paris, and dwell together in the age of Abélard or of Molière, and while we were playing in this way she was serious and gentle with me, like a little girl. But at other times I thought that I could stand it no longer, and would try to get away from her, and any suspicion of this was enough, I imagine, to make her lie awake at night thinking out new methods of punishing me. It was between us the old game of the cat and the mouse—probably the original model of all the games of the world. But because the cat has more passion in it, and the mouse only the plain interest of existence, the mouse is bound to become tired first. Toward the end I thought that she wished us to be found out, she was so careless in this *liaison* of ours; and in those days a love affair had to be managed with prudence.

I remember during this period coming to her hotel on the night of a ball to which she was going, while I had not been asked, disguised as a hairdresser. In the 'seventies ladies had large chignons and the work of a *coiffeur* took time. And through everything the thought of her husband would follow me, like, I thought, the gigantic shadow, upon the white back-curtain, of an absurd little punchinello. I began to feel so tired—not exactly of her, but really exhausted in myself—that I was making up my mind to have a scene and an explanation from her, even if I should lose her by it, when suddenly, on the night of which I am telling you, she herself produced both the scene and the explanation, such a hurricane as I have never again been out in; and all with exactly the same weapons as I had myself had ready: with the accusation that I thought more of her husband than I did of her. And when she said this to me, in that pale blue boudoir of hers that I knew so well—the silk-lined, upholstered and scented box, such as the ladies of that time liked to keep themselves in, with, I remember, some paintings of flowers on the walls, and very soft silk cushions everywhere, and a lot of lilacs in the corner behind me, with the lamp subdued by a large red shade—I had no reply, for I knew that she was right.

You would know his name if I told you, for he is still talked about, though he has been dead for many years. Or you would find it in any of the memoirs of that period, for he was the idol of our generation. Later on, great unhappiness came upon him, but at that moment—I believe that he was then thirty-three years old—he was walking quietly in the full splendor of his strange power. I once, about that time, heard two old men talk about his mother, who had been one of the beauties of the Restoration, and one of them said of her that she carried all her famous jewels as lightly and gracefully as other young ladies would wear garlands of field flowers. "Yes," the other said after he had thought it over for a moment, "and she scattered them about her, in the end, like flowers, *à la* Ophelia." Therefore I think that this rare lightness of his must have been, together with the weakness, a family trait. Even in his wildest whims, and in a sort of mannerism which we then named *fin de siècle* and were rather proud of, he had something of *le grand siècle* about him: a straight nobility that belonged to the old France.

I have looked since at those great buildings of the seventeenth century which seem altogether inexpedient as dwellings for human beings, and have thought that they must have been built for him—and his mother, I suppose—to live in. He had a confidence in life, independent of the successes which we envied him, as if he knew that he could draw upon greater forces, unknown to us, if he wanted to. It gave me much to think about, on the fate of man, when many years later I was told how this young man had, toward the end of his tragic destiny, answered the friends who implored him in the name of God, in the words of Sophocles's Ajax: "You worry me too much, woman. Do you not know that I am no longer a debtor of the gods?"

I see that I ought not to have started talking about him, even after all these years; but an ideal of one's youth will always be a landmark amongst happenings and feelings long gone. He himself has nothing to do with this story.

I told you that I myself felt it to be true that my feelings for the lovely young woman, whom I adored, were really light of weight compared to my feelings for the young man. If he had been with her when we first met, or if I had known him before I met her, I do not think that I should ever have dreamed of falling in love with his wife.

But his wife's love for him, and her jealousy, were indeed of a strange nature. For that she was in love with him I knew from the moment that she began to speak of him. Probably I had known it a long time before. And she was jealous. She suffered, she cried—she was, as I have told you, ready to kill if nothing else would help her—and all the time that fight, which was very likely the only reality in her life, was not a struggle for possession, but a competition. She was jealous of him as if he had been another young woman of fashion, her rival, or as if she herself had been a young man who envied him his triumphs. I think that she was, in herself, always alone with him in a world that she despised. When she rode so madly, when she surrounded herself with admirers, she had her eye on him, as a competitor in a chariot race would have his eyes only on the driver just beside him. As for the rest of us, we only existed for her in so far as we were to belong to her or to him, and she took her lovers as she took her fences, to pile up more conquests than the man with whom she was in love.

I cannot, of course, know how this had begun between them. Afterward I tried to believe that it must have arisen from a desire for revenge, on her side, for something that he had done to her in the past. But I had the feeling that it was this barren passion which had burned all the color out of her.

Now you will know that all this happened in the early days of what we called then the "emancipation of woman." Many strange things took place then. I do not think that at the time the movement went very deep down in the social world, but here were the young women of the highest intelligence, and the most daring and ingenious of them, coming out of the chiaroscuro of a thousand years, blinking at the sun and wild with desire to try their wings. I believe that some of them put on the armor and the halo of St. Joan of Arc, who was herself an emancipated virgin, and became like white-hot angels. But most women, when they feel free to experiment with life, will go straight to the witches' Sabbath. I myself respect them for it, and do not think that I could ever really love a woman who had not, at some time or other, been up on a broomstick.

I have always thought it unfair to woman that she has never been alone in the world. Adam had a time, whether long or short, when he could wander about on a fresh and peaceful earth, among the beasts, in full possession of his soul, and most men are born with a memory of that period. But poor Eve found him there, with all his claims upon her, the moment she looked into the world. That is a grudge that woman has always had against the Creator: she feels that she is entitled to have that epoch of paradise back for herself. Only, worse luck, when chasing a time that has gone, one is bound to get hold of it by the tail, the wrong way. Thus these young witches got everything they wanted as in a catoptric image.

Old ladies of those days, patronesses of the church and of home, said that emancipation was turning the heads of the young women. Probably there were more young ladies than my mistress galloping high up above the ground, with their fair faces at the backs of their necks, after the manner of the wild huntsman in the tale. And in the air there was a theory, which caught hold of them there, that the jealousy of lovers was an ignoble affair, and that no woman should allow herself to be possessed by any male but the devil. On their way to him they were proud of being, according to Doctor Faust, always a hundred steps ahead of man. But the jealousy of competition was, as between Adam and Lilith, a noble striving. So there you would find, not only the old witches of Macbeth, of whom one might have expected it, but even young ladies with faces smooth as flowers, wild and mad with jealousy of their lovers' mustachios. All this they got from reading—in the orthodox witches' manner—the book of Genesis backwards. Left to themselves, they might have got a lot out of it. It was the poor, tame, male preachers of emancipation, cutting, as warlocks always will, a miserable figure at the Sabbath, who spoiled the style and flight of the whole thing by bringing it down to earth and under laws of earthly reason. I believe, though, that things have changed by now, and that at the present day, when males have likewise emancipated themselves, you may find the young lover on the hearth, following the track of the witch's shadow along the ground, and, with infinitely less imagination, blending the deadly brew for his mistress, out of envy of her breasts.

The part which had been granted to me, in the story of my emancipated young witch, was not in itself flattering. Still I believe that she was desperately fond of me, probably with the kind of passion which a little girl has for her favorite doll. And as far as that goes I was really the central figure of our drama. If she would be Othello, it was I, and not her husband, who must take the part of

Desdemona, and I can well imagine her sighing, "Oh, the pity of it, the pity of it, Iago," over this unfortunate business, even wanting to give me a kiss and yet another before finishing it altogether. Only she did not want to kill me out of a feeling of justice or revenge. She wished to destroy me so that she should not have to lose me and to see a very dear possession belong to her rival, in the manner of a determined general, who will blow up a fortress which he can no longer hold, rather than see it in the hands of the enemy.

It was toward the end of our interview that she tried to poison me. I believe that this was really against her program, and that she had meant to tell me what she thought of me when I already had the poison in me, but had been unable to control herself for so long. There was, as you will understand, something unnatural in drinking coffee at that stage of our dialogue. The way in which she insisted upon it, and sudden deadly silence as I raised the cup to my mouth, gave her away. I can still, although I only just touched it, recall the mortal, insipid taste of the opium, and had I emptied the cup, it could not have made my stomach rise and the marrow in my bones turn to water more than did the abrupt and fatal conviction that she wanted me to die. I let the cup drop, faint as a drowning man, and stood and stared at her, and she made one wild movement, as if she meant to throw herself at me still. Then we stood quite immovable for a minute, both knowing that all was lost. And after a little while she began to rock and whimper, with her hands at her mouth, suddenly changed into a very old woman. For my own part, I was not able to utter a sound, and I think that I just ran from the house as soon as I had strength enough to move. The air, the rain, and the street itself met me like old forgotten friends, faithful still in the hour of need.

And there I sat on a seat of the Avenue Montaigne, with the entire building of my pride and happiness lying around me in ruins, sick to death with horror and humiliation, when this girl, of whom I was telling you, came up to me.

I think that I must have been sitting there for some time, and that she must have stood and watched me before she could summon up her courage to approach. She probably felt herself in sympathy with me, thinking that I was drunk too, as sensible people do not sit without a hat in the rain, perhaps also because I was so near her own age. I did not hear what she said, neither the first nor the second time. I was not in a mood to enter into talk with a little girl of the streets. I think that it must have been from sheer instinct of self-preservation that I did in the end come to look at her and to listen. I had to get away from my own thoughts, and any human being was welcome to assist me. But there was at the same time something extraordinarily graceful and expressive about the girl, which may have attracted my attention. She stood there in the rain, highly rouged, with radiant eyes like stars, very erect though only just steady on her legs. When I kept on staring at her, she laughed at me, a low, clear laughter. She was very young. She was holding up her dress with one hand—in those days ladies wore long trains in the streets. On her head she had a black hat with ostrich feathers drooping sadly in the rain and overshadowing her forehead and eyes. The firm gentle curve of her chin, and her round young neck shone in the light of the gas lamp. Thus I can see her still, though I have another picture of her as well.

What impressed me about her was that she seemed altogether so strangely moved, intoxicated by the situation. Hers was not the conventional advance. She looked like a person out on a great adventure, or someone keeping a secret. I think that on looking at her I began to smile, some sort of bitter and wild smile, known only to young people, and that this encouraged her. She came nearer. I fumbled in my pocket for some money to give her, but I had no money on me. I got up and started to walk, and she came on, walking beside me. There was, I remember, a certain comfort in having her near me, for I did not want to be alone. In this way it happened that I let her come with me.

I asked her what her name was. She told me that it was Nathalie.

At this time I had a job at the Legation, and I was living in an apartment on the Place François I, so we had not far to go. I was prepared to come back late, and in those days, when I would come home at all sorts of hours, I used to keep a fire and a cold supper waiting for me. When we came into the room it was lighted and warm, and the table was laid for me in front of the fire. There was a bottle of champagne on ice. I used to keep a bottle of champagne to drink when I returned from my shepherd's hours.

The young girl looked around the room with a contented face. Here in the light of my lamp I could see how she really looked. She had soft brown curls and blue eyes. Her face was round, with a broad forehead. She was wonderfully pretty and graceful. I think that I just wondered at her, as one would wonder at finding a fresh bunch of roses in a gutter, no more. If I had been normally balanced I suppose I should have tried to get from her some explanation of the sort of mystery that she seemed to be, but now I do not think that this occurred to me at all.

The truth was that we must both have been in quite a peculiar sort of mood, such as will hardly ever have repeated itself for either of us. I knew as little of what moved her as she could have known about my state of mind, but, highly excited and strained, we met in a special sort of sympathy. I, partly stunned and partly abnormally wide awake and sensitive, took her quite selfishly, without any thought of where she came from or where she would disappear to again, as if she were a gift to me, and her presence a kind and friendly act of fate at this moment when I could not be alone. She seemed to me to have come as a little wild spirit from the great town outside—Paris—which may at any moment bestow unexpected favors on one, and which had in the right moment sent her to me. What she thought of me or what she felt about me, of that I can say nothing. At the moment I did not think about it, but on looking back now I should say that I must also have symbolized something to her, and that I hardly existed for her as an individual.

I felt it as a great happiness, a warmth all through me, that she was so young and lovely. It made me laugh again after those weird and dismal hours. I putled off her hat, lifted her face up, and kissed her. Then I felt how wet she was. She must have walked for a long time on the streets in the rain, for her clothes were like the feathers of a wet hen. I went over and opened the bottle on the table, poured her out a glass, and handed it to her. She took it, standing in front of the fire, her tumbled wet curls falling down over her forehead. With her red cheeks and shining eyes she looked like a child that has just awakened from sleep, or like a doll. She drank half the glass of wine quite slowly, with her eyes on my face, and, as if this half-glass of champagne had brought her to a point where she could no longer be silent, she started to sing, in a low, gentle voice, hardly moving her lips, the first lines of a song, a waltz, which was then sung in all the music halls. She broke it off, emptied her glass, and handed it back to me. *A votre santé,* she said.

Her voice was so merry, so pure, like the song of a bird in a bush, and of all things music at that time went most directly to my heart. Her song increased the feeling I had, that something special and more than natural had been sent to me. I filled her glass again, put my hand on her round white neck, and brushed the damp ringlets back from her face. "How on earth have you come to be so wet, Nathalie?" I said, as if I had been her grandmother. "You must take off your clothes and get warm." As I spoke my voice changed. I began to laugh again. She fixed her starlike eyes on me. Her face quivered for a moment. Then she started to unbutton her cloak, and let it fall onto the floor. Underneath this cloak of black lace, badly suited for the season and faded at the edges into a rusty brown, she had a black silk frock, tightly fitted over the bust, waist and hips, and pleated and draped below, with flounces and ruffles such as ladies wore at that time, in the early days of the bustle. Its folds shone in the light of my fire. I began to undress her, as I might have undressed a doll, very slowly and clumsily, and she stood up straight and let me do it. Her fresh face had a grave and childlike expression. Once or twice she colored under my hands, but as I undid her tight bodice and my hands touched her cool shoulders and bosom, her face broke into a gentle and wide smile, and she lifted up her hand and touched my fingers.

The old Baron von Brackel made a long pause. "I think that I must explain to you," he said, "so that you may be able to understand this tale aright, that to undress a woman was then a very different thing from what it must be now. What are the clothes that your ladies of these days are wearing? In themselves as little as possible—a few perpendicular lines, cut off again before they have had time to develop any sense. There is no plan about them. They exist for the sake of the body, and have no career of their own, or, if they have any mission at all, it is to reveal.

"But in those days a woman's body was a secret which her clothes did their utmost to keep. We would walk about in the streets in bad weather in order to catch a glimpse of an ankle, the sight of which must be as familiar to you young men of the present day as the stems of these wineglasses of ours. Clothes then had a being, an idea of their own. With a serenity that it was not easy to look through, they made it their object to transform the body which they encircled, and to create a silhouette so far from its real form as to make it a mystery which it was a divine privilege to solve. The long tight stays, the whalebones, skirts and petticoats, bustle and draperies, all that mass of material under which the women of my day were buried where they were not laced together as tightly as they could possibly stand it—all aimed at one thing: to disguise.

"Out of a tremendous froth of trains, pleatings, lace, and flounces which waved and undulated, *secundum artem,* at every movement of the bearer, the waist would shoot up like the chalice of a flower, carrying the bust, high and rounded as a rose, but imprisoned in whalebone up to the shoulder. Imagine now how different life must have appeared and felt to creatures living in those tight corsets within which they could just manage to breathe, and in those fathoms of clothes which they dragged along with them wherever they walked or sat, and who never dreamed that it could be otherwise, compared to the existence of your young women, whose clothes hardly touch them and take up no room. A woman was then a work of art, the product of centuries of civilization, and you talked of her figure as you talked of her salon, with the admiration which one gives to the achievement of a skilled and untiring artist.

"And underneath all this Eve herself breathed and moved, to be indeed a revelation to us every time she stepped out of her disguise, with her waist still delicately marked by the stays, as with a girdle of rose petals.

"To you young people who laugh at the ideas, as at the bustles, of the 'seventies, and who will tell me that in spite of all our artificiality there can have been but little mystery left to any of us, may I be allowed to say that you do not, perhaps, quite understand the meaning of the word? Nothing is mysterious until it symbolizes something. The bread and wine of the church itself has to be baked and bottled, I suppose. The women of those days were more than a collection of individuals. They symbolized, or represented, Woman. I understand that the word itself, in that sense, has gone out of the language. Where we talked of woman— pretty cynically, we liked to think—you talk of women, and all the difference lies there.

"Do you remember the scholars of the middle ages who discussed the question of which had been created first: the idea of a dog, or the individual dogs? To you, who are taught statistics in your kindergartens, there is no doubt, I suppose. And it is but justice to say that your world does in reality look as if it had been made experimentally. But to us even the ideas of old Mr. Darwin were new and strange. We had our ideas from such undertakings as symphonies and ceremonials of court, and had been brought up with strong feelings about the distinction between legitimate and illegitimate birth. We had faith in purpose. The idea of Woman—of *das ewig weibliche,* about which you yourself will not deny that there is some mystery—had to us been created in the beginning, and our women made it their mission to represent it worthily, as I suppose the mission of the individual dog must have been worthily to represent the Creator's idea of a dog.

"You could follow, then, the development of this idea in a little girl, as she was growing up and was gradually, no doubt in accordance with very ancient rules, inaugurated into the rites of the cult, and finally ordained. Slowly the center of gravity of her being would be shifted from individuality to symbol, and you would be met with that particular pride and modesty characteristic of the representative of the great powers—such as you may find again in a really great artist. Indeed, the haughtiness of the pretty young girl, or the old ladies' majesty, existed no more on account of personal vanity, or on any personal account whatever, than did the pride of Michelangelo himself, or the Spanish Ambassador to France. However much greeted at the banks of the Styx by the indignation of his individual victims with flowing hair and naked breasts, Don Giovanni would have been acquitted by a board of women of my day, sitting in judgment on him, for the sake of his great faith in the idea of Woman. But they would have agreed with the masters of Oxford in condemning Shelley as an atheist; and they managed to master Christ himself only by representing him forever as an infant in arms, dependent upon the Virgin.

"The multitude outside the temple of mystery is not very interesting. The real interest lies with the priest inside. The crowd waiting at the porch for the fulfillment of the miracle of the boiling blood of St. Pantaleone—that I have seen many times and in many places. But very rarely have I had admittance to the cool vaults behind, or the chance of seeing the priests, old and young, down to the choirboys, who feel themselves to be the most important persons at the ceremony, and are both scared and impudent, occupying themselves, in a measure of their own, with the preparations, guardians of a mystery that they know all about. What was the cynicism of Lord Byron, or of Baudelaire, whom we were just reading then with the *frisson nouveau,* to the cynicism of these little priestesses, augurs all of them, performing with the utmost conscientiousness all the rites of a religion which they knew all about and did not believe in, upholding, I feel sure, the doctrine of their mystery even amongst themselves. Our poets of those days would tell us how a party of young beauties, behind the curtains of the bathing-machine, would blush and giggle as they 'put lilies in water.'

"I do not know if you remember the tale of the girl who saves the ship under mutiny by sitting on the powder barrel with her lighted torch, threatening to put fire to it, and all the time knowing herself that it is empty? This has seemed to me a charming image of the women of my time. There they were, keeping the world in order, and preserving the balance and rhythm of it, by sitting upon the mystery of life, and knowing themselves that there was no mystery. I have heard you young people saying that the women of old days had no sense of humor. Thinking of the face of my young girl upon the barrel, with severely downcast eyes, I have wondered if our famous male humor be not a little insipid compared to theirs. If we were more thankful to them for existing than you are to your women of the present day, I think that we had good reason for it.

"I trust that you will not mind," he said, "an old man lingering over these pictures of an age gone by. It will be, I suppose, like being detained a little in a museum, before a *montre* showing its fashions. You may laugh at them, if you like."

The old chevalier then resumed his story:

As I then undressed this young girl, and the layers of clothes which so severely dominated and concealed her fell one by one there in front of my fire, in the light of my large lamp, itself swathed in layers of silk—all, my dear, was thus draped in those days, and my large chairs had, I remember, long silk fringes all around them and on the tops of those little velvet pompons. Otherwise they would not have been thought really pretty—until she stood naked, I had before me the greatest masterpiece of nature that my eyes have ever been privileged to rest upon, a sight to take away your breath. I know that there may be something very lovable in the little imperfections of the female form, and I have myself worshiped a knock-kneed Venus, but this young figure was pathetic, was heart-piercing, by reason of its pure faultlessness. She was so young that you felt, in the midst of your deep admiration, the anticipation of a still higher perfection, and that was all there was to be said.

All her body shone in the light, delicately rounded and smooth as marble. One straight line ran through it from neck to ankle, as through the heaven-aspiring column of a young tree. The same character was expressed in the high instep of the foot, as she pushed off her old shoes, as in the curve of the chin, as in the straight, gentle glance of her eyes, and the delicate and strong lines of her shoulder and wrist.

The comfort of the warmth of the fire on her skin, after the clinging of her wet and tumbled clothes, made her sigh with pleasure and turn a little, like a cat. She laughed softly, like a child who quits the doorstep of school for a holiday. She stood up erect before the fire; her wet curls fell down over her forehead and she did not try to push them back; her bright painted cheeks looked even more like a doll's above her fair naked body.

I think that all my soul was in my eyes. Reality had met me, such a short time ago, in such an ugly shape, that I had no wish to come into contact with it again. Somewhere in me a dark fear was still crouching, and I took refuge within the fantastic like a distressed child in his book of fairy tales. I did not want to look ahead, and not at all to look back. I felt the moment close over me, like a wave. I drank a large glass of wine to catch up with her, looking at her.

I was so young then that I could no more than other young people give up the deep faith in my own star, in a power that loved me and looked after me in preference to all other human beings. No miracle was incredible to me as long as it happened to myself. It is when this faith begins to wear out, and when you conceive the possiblity of being in the same position as other people, that youth is really over. I was not surprised or suspicious of this act of favor on the part of the gods, but I think that my heart was filled with a very sweet gratitude toward them. I thought it after all only reasonable, only to be expected, that the great friendly power of the universe should manifest itself again, and send me, out of the night, as a help and consolation, this naked and drunk young girl, a miracle of gracefulness.

We sat down to supper, Nathalie and I, high up there in my warm and quiet room, with the great town below us and my heavy silk curtains drawn upon the wet night, like two owls in a ruined tower within the depth of the forest, and nobody in the world knew about us. She leaned one arm on the table and rested her head on it. I think that she was very hungry, under the influence of the food. We had some caviar, I remember, and a cold bird. She began to beam on me, to laugh, to talk to me, and to listen to what I said to her.

I do not remember what we talked about. I think we were very openhearted, and that I told her, what I could not have mentioned to anybody else, of how I had come near to being poisoned just before I met her. I also think that I must have told her about my country, for I know that at a time afterwards the idea came to me that she would write to me there, or even come to look for me. I remember that she told me, rather sadly to begin with, a story of a very old monkey which could do tricks, and had belonged to an Armenian organ-grinder. Its master had died, and now it wanted to do its tricks and was always waiting for the catchword, but nobody knew it. In the course of this tale she imitated the monkey in the funniest and most gracefully inspired manner that one can imagine. But I remember most of her movements. Sometimes I have thought that the understanding of some pieces of music for violin and piano has come to me through the contemplation of the contrast, or the harmony, between her long slim hand and her short rounded chin as she held the glass to her mouth.

I have never in any other love affair—if this can be called a love affair—had the same feeling of freedom and security. In my last adventure I had all the time been worrying to find out what my mistress really thought of me, and what part I was playing in the eyes of the world. But no such doubts or fears could possibly penetrate into our little room here. I believe that this feeling of safety and perfect freedom must be what happily married people mean when they talk about the two being one. I wonder if that understanding can possibly, in marriage, be as harmonious as when you meet as strangers; but this, I suppose, is a matter of taste.

One thing did play in to both of us, though we were not conscious of it. The world outside was bad, was dreadful. Life had made a very nasty face at me, and must have made a worse at her. But this room and this night were ours, and were faithful to us. Although we did not think about it, ours was in reality a supper of the Girondists.

The wine helped us. I had not drunk much, but my head was fairly light before I began. Champagne is a very kind and friendly thing on a rainy night. I remember an old Danish bishop's saying to me that there are many ways to the recognition of truth, and that Burgundy is one of them. This is, I know, very well for an old man within his paneled study. But young people, who have seen the devil face to face, need a stronger helping hand. Over our softly hissing glasses we were brought back to seeing ourselves and this night of ours as a great artist might have seen us and it, worthy of the genius of a god.

I had a guitar lying on my sofa, for I was to serenade, in a *tableau vivant,* a romantic beauty—in real life an American woman from the Embassy who could not have given you an echo back from whatever angle you would have cried to her. Nathalie reached out for it, a little later in our supper. She shuddered slightly at the first sound, for I had not had time or thought for playing it, and crossing her knees, in my large low chair, she began to tune it. Then she sang two little songs to me. In my quiet room her low voice, a little hoarse, was clear as a bell, faintly giddy with happiness, like a bee's in a flower. She sang first a song from the music halls, a gay tune with a striking rhythm. Then she thought for a moment and changed over into a strange plaintive little song in a language that I did not understand. She had a great sense of music. That strong and delicate personality which showed itself in all her body came out again in her voice. The light metallic timbre, the straightness and ease of it, corresponded with her eyes, knees, and fingers. Only it was a little richer and fuller, as if it had grown up faster or had stolen a march somehow upon her body. Her voice knew more than she did herself, as did the bow of Mischa Elman when he played as a *Wunderkind.*

All my balance, which I had kept somehow while looking at her, suddenly left me at the sound of her voice. These words that I did not understand seemed to me more directly meaningful than any I have ever understood. I sat in another low chair, opposite her. I remember the silence when her song was finished, and that I pushed the table away, and how I came slowly down on one knee before her. She looked at me with such a clear, severe, wild look as I think that a hawk's eye must have when they lift off his hood. I went down on my other knee and put my arms around her legs. I do not know what there was in my face to convince her, but her own face changed and lighted up with a kind of heroic gentleness. Altogether there had been from the beginning something heroic about her. That was, I think, what had made her put up with the young fool that I was. For *du ridicule jusqu'au sublime,* surely, *il n'y a qu'un pas.*

My friend, she was as innocent as she looked. She was the first young girl who had been mine. There is a theory that a very young man should not make love to a virgin, but ought to have a more experienced partner. That is not true; it is the only natural thing.

It must have been an hour or two later in the night that I woke up to the feeling that something was wrong, or dangerous. We say when we turn suddenly cold that someone is walking over our grave—the future brings itself into memory. And as *l'on meurt en plein bonheur de ses malheurs passés,* so do we let go our hold of our present happiness on account of coming misfortune. It was not the *omne animal* affair only; it was a distrust of the future as if I had heard myself asking it: "I am to pay for this; what am I to pay?" But at the time I may have believed that what I felt was only fear of her going away.

Once before she had sat up and moved as if to leave me, and I had dragged her back. Now she said: "I must go back," and got up. The lamp was still burning, the fire was smoldering. It seemed to me natural that she should be taken away by the same mysterious forces which had brought her, like Cinderella, or a little spirit out of the *Arabian Nights*. I was waiting for her to come up and let me know when she would come back to me, and what I was to do. All the same I was more silent now.

She dressed and got back into her black shabby disguise. She put on her hat and stood there just as I had seen her first in the rain on the avenue. Then she came up to me where I was sitting on the arm of my chair, and said: "And you will give me twenty francs, will you not?" As I did not answer, she repeated her question and said: "Marie said that—she said that I should get twenty francs."

I did not speak. I sat there looking at her. Her clear and light eyes met mine.

A great clearness came upon me then, as if all the illusions and arts with which we try to transform our world, coloring and music and dreams, had drawn aside, and reality was shown to me, waste as a burnt house. This was the end of the play. There was no room for any superfluous word.

This was the first moment, I think, since I had met her those few hours ago, in which I saw her as a human being, within an existence of her own, and not as a gift to me. I believe that all thoughts of myself left me at the sight, but now it was too late.

We two had played. A rare jest had been offered me and I had accepted it; now it was up to me to keep the spirit of our game until the end. Her own demand was well within the spirit of the night. For the palace which he builds, for four hundred white and four hundred black slaves all loaded with jewels, the djinn asks for an old copper lamp; and the forest-witch who moves three towns and creates for the woodcutter's son an army of horse-soldiers demands for herself the heart of a hare. The girl asked me for her pay in the voice and manner of the djinn and the forest-witch, and if I were to give her twenty francs she might still be safe within the magic circle of her free and graceful and defiant spirit. It was I who was out of character, as I sat there in silence, with all the weight of the cold and real world upon me, knowing well that I should have to answer her or I might, even within these few seconds, pass it on to her.

Later on I reflected that I might have had it in me to invent something which would have kept her safe, and still have allowed me to keep her. I thought then that I should only have had to give her twenty francs and to have said: "And if you want another twenty, come back tomorrow night." If she had been less lovely to me, if she had not been so young and so innocent, I might perhaps have done it. But this young girl had called, during our few hours, on all the chivalrousness that I had in my nature. And chivalrousness, I think, means this: to love, or cherish, the pride of your partner, or of your adversary, as you will define it, as highly, or higher than, your own. Or if I had been as innocent of heart as she was, I might perhaps have thought of it, but I had kept company with this deadly world of reality. I was practiced in its laws and had the mortal bacilli of its ways in my blood. Now it did not enter my head any more than it ever has to alter my answers in church. When the priest says: "O God, make clean our hearts within us," I have never thought of telling him that it is not needed, or to answer anything whatever but, "And take not your holy spirit from us."

So, as if it were the only natural and reasonable thing to do, I took out twenty francs and gave them to her.

Before she went she did a thing that I have never forgotten. With my note in her left hand she stood close to me. She did not kiss me or take my hand to say good-by, but with the three fingers of her right hand she lifted my chin up a little and looked at me, gave me an encouraging, consoling glance, such as a sister might give her brother in farewell. Then she went away.

In the days that followed—not the first days, but later—I tried to construct for myself some theory and explanation of my adventure.

This happened only a short time after the fall of the Second Empire, that strange sham millennium, and the Commune of Paris. The atmosphere had been filled with catastrophe. A world had fallen. The Empress herself, whom, on a visit to Paris as a child, I had envisaged as a female deity resting upon clouds, smilingly conducting the ways of humanity, had flown in the night, in a carriage with her American dentist, miserable for the lack of a handkerchief. The members of her court were crowded into lodgings in Brussels and London while their country houses served as stables for the Prussians' horses. The Commune had followed, and the massacres in Paris by the Versailles army. A whole world must have tumbled down within these months of disaster.

This was also the time of Nihilism in Russia, when the revolutionaries had lost all and were fleeing into exile. I thought of them because of the little song that Nathalie had sung to me, of which I had not understood the words.

Whatever it was that had happened to her, it must have been a castastrophe of an extraordinarily violent nature. She must have gone down with a unique swiftness, or she would have known something of the resignation, the dreadful reconciliation to fate which life works upon us when it gets time to impress us drop by drop.

Also, I thought, she must have been tied to, and dragged down with, somebody else, for if she had been alone it could not have happened. It would have been, I reflected, somebody who held her, and yet was unable to help her, someone either very old, helpless from shock and ruin, or very young, children or a child, a little brother or sister. Left to herself she would have floated, or she would have been picked up near the surface by someone who would have valued her rare beauty, grace, and charm and have congratulated himself upon acquiring them; or, lower down, by somebody who might not have understood them, but whom they would still have impressed. Or, near the bottom, by people who would have thought of turning them to their own advantage. But she must have gone straight down from the world of beauty and harmony in which she had learned that confidence and radiance of hers, where they had taught her to sing, and to move and laugh as she did, where they had loved her, to a world where beauty and grace are of no account, and where the facts of life look you in the face, quite straight to ruin, desolation and starvation. And there, on the last step of the ladder, had been Marie, whoever she was, a friend who out of her narrow and dark knowledge of the world had given her advice, and lent her the miserable clothes, and poured some sort of spirit into her, to give her courage.

About all this I thought much, and for a long time; but of course I could not know.

As soon as she had gone and I was alone—so strange are the automatic movements which we make within the hands of fate—I had no thought but to go after her and get her back. I think that I went, in those minutes, through the exact experience, even to the sensation of suffocation, of a person who has been buried alive. But I had no clothes on. When I got into some clothes and came down to the street it was empty. I walked about in the streets for a long time. I came back, in the course of the early morning, to the seat on which I had been sitting when she first spoke to me, and to the hotel of my former mistress. I thought what a strange thing is a young man who runs about, within the selfsame night, driven by the mad passion and loss of two women. Mercutio's words to Romeo about it came into my mind, and, as if I had been shown a brilliant caricature of myself or of all young men, I laughed. When the day began to spring I walked back to my room, and there was the lamp, still burning, and the supper table.

This state of mine lasted for some time. During the first days it was not so bad, for I lived then in the thought of going down, at the same hour, to the same place where I had met her first. I thought that she might come there again. I attached much hope to this idea, which only slowly died away.

I tried many things to make it possible to live. One night I went to the opera, because I had heard other people talk about going there. It was clear that it was done, and there might be something in it. It happened to be a performance of *Orpheus*. Do you remember the music where he implores the shadows in Hades, and where Euridice is for such a short time given back to him? There I sat, in the brilliant light of the *entr'actes,* a young man in a white tie and lavender gloves, with bright people who smiled and talked all around, some of them nodding to me, closely covered and wrapped up in the huge black wings of the Eumenides.

At this time I developed also another theory. I thought of the goddess Nemesis, and I believed that had I not had the moment of doubt and fear in the night, I might have felt, in the morning, the strength in me, and the right, to move her destiny and mine. It is said about the highwaymen who in the old days haunted the forests of Denmark that they used to have a wire stretched across the road with a bell attached. The coaches in passing would touch the wire and the bell would ring within their den and call out the robbers. I had touched the wire and a bell had rung somewhere. The girl had not been afraid, but I had been afraid. I had asked: "What am I to pay for this?" and the goddess herself had answered: "Twenty francs," and with her you cannot bargain. You think of many things, when you are young.

All this is now a long time ago. The Eumenides, if they will excuse me for saying so, are like fleas, by which I was also much worried as a child. They like young blood, and leave us alone later in life. I have had, however, the honor of having them on me once more, not very many years ago. I had sold a piece of my land to a neighbor, and when I saw it again, he had cut down the forest that had been on it. Where were now the green shades, the glades and the hidden footpaths? And when I then heard again the whistle of their wings in the air, it gave me, with the pain, also a strange feeling of hope and strength—it was, after all, music of my youth.

"And did you never see her again?" I asked him.

"No," he said, and then, after a little while, "but I had a fantasy about her, a *fantaisie macabre,* if you like.

"Fifteen years later, in 1889, I passed through Paris on my way to Rome, and stayed there for a few days to see the exhibition and the Eiffel Tower which they had just built. One afternoon I went to see a friend, a painter. He had been rather wild as a young artist, but later had turned about completely, and was at the time studying anatomy with great zeal, after the example of Leonardo. I stayed there over the evening, and after we had discussed his pictures, and art in general, he said that he would show me the prettiest thing that he had in his studio. It was a skull from which he was drawing. He was keen to explain its rare beauty to me. 'It is really,' he said, 'the skull of a young woman, but the skull of Antinoüs must have looked like that, if one had been able to get hold of it.'

"I had it in my hand, and as I was looking at the broad, low brow, the clear and noble line of the chin, and the clean deep sockets of the eyes, it seemed suddenly familiar to me. The white polished bone shone in the light of the lamp, so pure. And safe. In those few seconds I was taken back to my room in the Place François I, with the silk fringes and the heavy curtains, on a rainy night of fifteen years before."

"Did you ask your friend anything about it?" I said.

"No," said the old man, "what would have been the use? He would not have known."

Bernard Malamud

The Magic Barrel

Born in Brooklyn, Bernard Malamud received a B.A. from the City College of New York and an M.A. from Columbia University. From 1940 to 1949 he taught evening classes in New York high schools, and from 1949 to 1961 was a member of the English Department at Oregon State University. His first novel, The Natural *(1952) was followed in 1957 by* The Assistant *and in 1958 by an outstanding collection of short stories,* The Magic Barrel, *for which he received the National Book Award in fiction. He won it again—and also the Pulitzer Prize—in 1967 for his fourth novel,* The Fixer. *Since 1961 Bernard Malamud has taught at Bennington College in Vermont.*

Not long ago there lived in uptown New York, in a small, almost meager room, though crowded with books, Leo Finkle, a rabbinical student in the Yeshivah University. Finkle, after six years of study, was to be ordained in June and had been advised by an acquaintance that he might find it easier to win himself a congregation if he were married. Since he had no present prospects of marriage, after two tormented days of turning it over in his mind, he called in Pinye Salzman, a marriage broker whose two-line advertisement he had read in the *Forward*.

The matchmaker appeared one night out of the dark fourth-floor hallway of the graystone rooming house where Finkle lived, grasping a black, strapped portfolio that had been worn thin with use. Salzman, who had been long in the business, was of slight but dignified build, wearing an old hat, and an overcoat too short and tight for him. He smelled frankly of fish, which he loved to eat, and although he was missing a few teeth, his presence was not displeasing, because of an amiable manner curiously contrasted with mournful eyes. His voice, his lips, his wisp of beard, his bony fingers were animated, but give him a moment of repose and his mild blue eyes revealed a depth of sadness, a characteristic that put Leo a little at ease although the situation, for him, was inherently tense.

He at once informed Salzman why he had asked him to come, explaining that his home was in Cleveland, and that but for his parents, who had married comparatively late in life, he was alone in the world. He had for six years devoted himself almost entirely to his studies, as a result of which, understandably, he had found himself without time for a social life and the company of young women. Therefore he thought it the better part of trial and error—of embarrassing fumbling—to call in an experienced person to advise him on these matters. He remarked in passing that the function of the marriage broker was ancient and honorable, highly approved in the Jewish community, because it made practical the necessary without hindering joy. Moreover, his own parents had been brought together by a matchmaker. They had made, if not a financially profitable marriage—since neither had possessed any worldly goods to speak of—at least a successful one in the sense of their everlasting devotion to each other. Salzman listened in embarrassed surprise, sensing a sort of apology. Later, however, he experienced a glow of pride in his work, an emotion that had left him years ago, and he heartily approved of Finkle.

The two went to their business. Leo had led Salzman to the only clear place in the room, a table near a window that overlooked the lamp-lit city. He seated himself at the matchmaker's side but facing him, attempting by an act of will to suppress the unpleasant tickle in his throat. Salzman eagerly unstrapped his portfolio and removed a loose rubber band from a thin packet of much-handled cards. As he flipped through them, a gesture and sound that physically hurt Leo, the student pretended not to see and gazed steadfastly out the window. Although it was still February, winter was on its last legs, signs of which he had for the first time in years begun to notice. He now observed the round white moon, moving high in the sky through a cloud menagerie, and watched with half-open mouth as it penetrated a huge hen, and dropped out of her like an egg laying itself. Salzman, though pretending through eyeglasses he had just slipped on, to be engaged in scanning the writing on the cards, stole occasional glances at the young man's distinguished face, noting with pleasure the long, severe scholar's nose, brown eyes heavy with learning, sensitive yet ascetic lips, and a certain, almost hollow quality of the dark cheeks. He gazed around at shelves upon shelves of books and let out a soft, contented sigh.

When Leo's eyes fell upon the cards, he counted six spread out in Salzman's hand.

"So few?" he asked in disappointment.

"You wouldn't believe me how much cards I got in my office," Salzman replied. "The drawers are already filled to the top, so I keep them now in a barrel, but is every girl good for a new rabbi?"

Leo blushed at this, regretting all he had revealed of himself in a curriculum vitae he had sent to Salzman. He had thought it best to acquaint him with his strict standards and specifications, but in having done so, felt he had told the marriage broker more than was absolutely necessary.

He hesitantly inquired, "Do you keep photographs of your clients on file?"

"First comes family, amount of dowry, also what kind promises," Salzman replied, unbuttoning his tight coat and settling himself in the chair. "After comes pictures, rabbi."

"Call me Mr. Finkle. I'm not yet a rabbi."

Salzman said he would, but instead called him doctor, which he changed to rabbi when Leo was not listening too attentively.

Salzman adjusted his horn-rimmed spectacles, gently cleared his throat and read in an eager voice the contents ot the top card:

"Sophie P. Twenty-four years. Widow one year. No children. Educated high school and two years college. Father promises eight thousand dollars. Has wonderful wholesale business. Also real estate. On the mother's side comes teachers, also one actor. Well known on Second Avenue."

Leo gazed up in surprise. "Did you say a widow?"

"A widow don't mean spoiled, rabbi. She lived with her husband maybe four months. He was a sick boy she made a mistake to marry him."

"Marrying a widow has never entered my mind."

"This is because you have no experience. A widow, especially if she is young and healthy like this girl, is a wonderful person to marry. She will be thankful to you the rest of her life. Believe me, if I was looking now for a bride, I would marry a widow."

Leo reflected, then shook his head.

Salzman hunched his shoulders in an almost imperceptible gesture of disappointment. He placed the card down on the wooden table and began to read another:

"Lily H. High school teacher. Regular. Not a substitute. Has savings and new Dodge car. Lived in Paris one year. Father is successful dentist thirty-five years. Interested in professional man. Well Americanized family. Wonderful opportunity."

"I knew her personally," said Salzman. "I wish you could see this girl.

She is a doll. Also very intelligent. All day you could talk to her about books and theyater and what not. She also knows current events."

"I don't believe you mentioned her age?"

"Her age?" Salzman said, raising his brows. "Her age is thirty-two years."

Leo said after a while, "I'm afraid that seems a little too old."

Salzman let out a laugh. "So how old are you, rabbi?"

"Twenty-seven."

"So what is the difference, tell me, between twenty-seven and thirty-two? My own wife is seven years older than me. So what did I suffer?—Nothing. If Rothschild's daughter wants to marry you, would you say on account her age, no?"

"Yes," Leo said dryly.

Salzman shook off the no in the yes. "Five years don't mean a thing. I give you my word that when you will live with her for one week you will forget her age. What does it mean five years—that she lived more and knows more than somebody who is younger? On this girl, God bless her, years are not wasted. Each one that it comes makes better the bargain."

"What subject does she teach in high school?"

"Languages. If you heard the way she speaks French, you will think it is music. I am in the business twenty-five years, and I recommend her with my whole heart. Believe me, I know what I'm talking, rabbi."

"What's on the next card?" Leo said abruptly.

Salzman reluctantly turned up the third card:

"Ruth K. Nineteen years. Honor student. Father offers thirteen thousand cash to the right bridegroom. He is a medical doctor. Stomach specialist with marvelous practice. Brother in law owns own garment business. Particular people."

Salzman looked as if he had read his trump card.

"Did you say nineteen?" Leo asked with interest.

"On the dot."

"Is she attractive?" He blushed. "Pretty?"

Salzman kissed his finger tips. "A little doll. On this I give you my word. Let me call the father tonight and you will see what means pretty."

But Leo was troubled. "You're sure she's that young?"

"This I am positive. The father will show you the birth certificate."

"Are you positive there isn't something wrong with her?" Leo insisted.

"Who says there is wrong?"

"I don't understand why an American girl her age should go to a marriage broker."

A smile spread over Salzman's face.

"So for the same reason you went, she comes."

Leo flushed. "I am pressed for time."

Salzman, realizing he had been tactless, quickly explained. "The father came, not her. He wants she should have the best, so he looks around himself. When we will locate the right boy he will introduce him and encourage. This makes a better marriage than if a young girl without experience takes for herself. I don't have to tell you this."

"But don't you think this young girl believes in love?" Leo spoke uneasily.

Salzman was about to guffaw but caught himself and said soberly, "Love comes with the right person, not before."

Leo parted dry lips but did not speak. Noticing that Salzman had snatched a glance at the next card, he cleverly asked, "How is her health?"

"Perfect," Salzman said, breathing with difficulty. "Of course, she is a little lame on her right foot from an auto accident that it happened to her when she was twelve years, but nobody notices on account she is so brilliant and also beautiful."

Leo got up heavily and went to the window. He felt curiously bitter and upbraided himself for having called in the marriage broker. Finally, he shook his head.

"Why not?" Salzman persisted, the pitch of his voice rising.

"Because I detest stomach specialists."

"So what do you care what is his business? After you marry her do you need him? Who says he must come every Friday night in your house?"

Ashamed of the way the talk was going, Leo dismissed Salzman, who went home with heavy, melancholy eyes.

Though he had felt only relief at the marriage broker's departure, Leo was in low spirits the next day. He explained it as arising from Salzman's failure to produce a suitable bride for him. He did not care for his type of clientele. But when Leo found himself hesitating whether to seek out another matchmaker, one more polished than Pinye, he wondered if it could be—his protestations to the contrary, and although he honored his father and mother—that he did not, in essence, care for the matchmaking institution? This thought he quickly put out of mind yet found himself still upset. All day he ran around in the woods—missed an important appointment, forgot to give out his laundry, walked out of a Broadway cafeteria without paying and had to run back with the ticket in his hand; had even not recognized his landlady in the street when she passed with a friend and courteously called out, "A good evening to you, Doctor Finkle." By nightfall, however, he had regained sufficient calm to sink his nose into a book and there found peace from his thoughts.

Almost at once there came a knock on the door. Before Leo could say enter, Salzman, commercial cupid, was standing in the room. His face was gray and meager, his expression hungry, and he looked as if he would expire on his feet. Yet the marriage broker managed, by some trick of the muscles, to display a broad smile.

"So good evening. I am invited?"

Leo nodded, disturbed to see him again, yet unwilling to ask the man to leave.

Beaming still, Salzman laid his portfolio on the table. "Rabbi, I got for you tonight good news."

"I've asked you not to call me rabbi. I'm still a student."

"Your worries are finished. I have for you a first-class bride."

"Leave me in peace concerning this subject." Leo pretended lack of interest.

"The world will dance at your wedding."

"Please, Mr. Salzman, no more."

"But first must come back my strength," Salzman said weakly. He fumbled with the portfolio straps and took out of the leather case an oily paper bag, from which he extracted a hard, seeded roll and a small, smoked white fish. With a quick motion of his hand he stripped the fish out of its skin and began ravenously to chew. "All day in a rush," he muttered.

Leo watched him eat.

"A sliced tomato you have maybe?" Salzman hesitantly inquired.

"No."

The marriage broker shut his eyes and ate. When he had finished he carefully cleaned up the crumbs and rolled up the remains of the fish, in the paper bag. His spectacled eyes roamed the room until he discovered, amid some piles of books, a one-burner gas stove. Lifting his hat he humbly asked, "A glass of tea you got, rabbi?"

Conscience-stricken, Leo rose and brewed the tea. He served it with a chunk of lemon and two cubes of lump sugar, delighting Salzman.

After he had drunk his tea, Salzman's strength and good spirits were restored.

"So tell me, rabbi," he said amiably, "you considered some more the three clients I mentioned yesterday?"

"There was no need to consider."

"Why not?"

"None of them suits me."

"What then suits you?"

Leo let it pass because he could give only a confused answer.

Without waiting for a reply, Salzman asked, "You remember this girl I talked to you—the high school teacher?"

"Age thirty-two?"

But, surprisingly, Salzman's face lit in a smile. "Age twenty-nine."

Leo shot him a look. "Reduced from thirty-two?"

"A mistake," Salzman avowed. "I talked today with the dentist. He took me to his safety deposit box and showed me the birth certificate. She was twenty-nine years last August. They made her a party in the mountains where she went for her vacation. When her father spoke to me the first time I forgot to write the age and I told you thirty-two, but now I remember this was a different client, a widow."

"The same one you told me about? I thought she was twenty-four?"

"A different. Am I responsible that the world is filled with widows?"

"No, but I'm not interested in them, nor for that matter, in school teachers."

Salzman pulled his clasped hand to his breast. Looking at the ceiling he devoutly exclaimed, "Yiddishe kinder, what can I say to somebody that he is not interested in high school teachers? So what then you are interested?"

Leo flushed but controlled himself.

"In what else will you be interested," Salzman went on, "if you not interested in this fine girl that she speaks four languages and has personally in the bank ten thousand dollars? Also her father guarantees further twelve thousand. Also she has a new car, wonderful clothes, talks on all subjects and she will give you a first-class home and children. How near do we come in our life to paradise?"

"If she's so wonderful, why wasn't she married ten years ago?"

"Why?" said Salzman with a heavy laugh. "—Why? Because she is *partikiler*. This is why. She wants the *best*."

Leo was silent, amused at how he had entangled himself. But Salzman had aroused his interest in Lily H., and he began seriously to consider calling on her. When the marriage broker observed how intently Leo's mind was at work on the facts he supplied, he felt certain they would soon come to an agreement.

Late Saturday afternoon, conscious of Salzman, Leo Finkle walked with Lily Hirschorn along Riverside Drive. He walked briskly and erectly, wearing with distinction the black fedora he had that morning taken with trepidation out of the dusty hat box on his closet shelf, and the heavy black Saturday coat he had thoroughly whisked clean. Leo also owned a walking stick, a present from a distant relative, but quickly put temptation aside and did not use it. Lily, petite and not unpretty, had on something signifying the approach of spring. She was au courant, animatedly, with all sorts of subjects, and he weighed her words and found her surprisingly sound—score another for Salzman, whom he uneasily sensed to be somewhere around, hiding perhaps high in a tree along the street, flashing the lady signals with a pocket mirror; or perhaps a cloven-hoofed Pan, piping nuptial ditties as he danced his invisible way before them, strewing wild buds on the walk and purple grapes in their path, symbolizing fruit of a union, though there was of course still none.

Lily startled Leo by remarking, "I was thinking of Mr. Salzman, a curious figure, wouldn't you say?"

Not certain what to answer, he nodded.

She bravely went on, blushing, "I for one am grateful for his introducing us. Aren't you?"

He courteously replied, "I am."

"I mean," she said with a little laugh—and it was all in good taste, or at least gave the effect of being not in bad—"do you mind that we came together so?"

He was not displeased with her honesty, recognizing that she meant to set the relationship aright, and understanding that it took a certain amount of experience in life, and courage, to want to do it quite that way. One had to have some sort of past to make that kind of beginning.

He said that he did not mind. Salzman's function was traditional and honorable—valuable for what it might achieve, which, he pointed out, was frequently nothing.

Lily agreed with a sigh. They walked on for a while and she said after a long silence, again with a nervous laugh, "Would you mind if I asked you something a little bit personal? Frankly, I find the subject fascinating." Although Leo shrugged, she went on half embarrassedly, "How was it that you came to your calling? I mean was it a sudden passionate inspiration?"

Leo, after a time, slowly replied. "I was always interested in the Law."

"You saw revealed in it the presence of the Highest?"

He nodded and changed the subject. "I understand that you spent a little time in Paris, Miss Hirschorn?"

"Oh, did Mr. Salzman tell you, Rabbi Finkle?" Leo winced but she went on, "It was ages ago and almost forgotten. I remember I had to return for my sister's wedding."

And Lily would not be put off. "When," she asked in a trembly voice, "did you become enamored of God?"

He stared at her. Then it came to him that she was talking not about Leo Finkle, but of a total stranger, some mystical figure, perhaps even passionate prophet that Salzman had dreamed up for her—no relation to the living or dead. Leo trembled with rage and weakness. The trickster had obviously sold her a bill of goods, just as he had him, who'd expected to become acquainted with a young lady of twenty-nine, only to behold, the moment he laid eyes upon her strained and anxious face, a woman past thirty-five and aging rapidly. Only his self control had kept him this long in her presence.

"I am not," he said gravely, "a talented religious person," and in seeking words to go on, found himself possessed by shame and fear. "I think," he said in a strained manner, "that I came to God not because I loved Him, but because I did not."

This confession he spoke harshly because its unexpectedness shook him.

Lily wilted. Leo saw a profusion of loaves of bread go flying like ducks high over his head, not unlike the winged loaves by which he had counted himself to sleep last night. Mercifully, then, it snowed, which he would not put past Salzman's machinations.

He was infuriated with the marriage broker and swore he would throw him out of the room the minute he reappeared. But Salzman did not come that night, and when Leo's anger had subsided, an unaccountable despair grew in its place. At first he thought this was caused by his disappointment in Lily, but before long it became evident that he had involved himself with Salzman without a true knowledge of his own intent. He gradually realized—with an emptiness that seized him with six hands—that he had called in the broker to find him a bride because he was incapable of doing it himself. This terrifying insight he had derived as a result of his meeting and conversation with Lily Hirschorn. Her probing questions had somehow irritated him into revealing—to himself more than her—the true nature of his relationship to God, and from that it had come upon him, with shocking force, that apart from his parents, he had never loved anyone. Or perhaps it went the other way, that he did not love God so well as he might, because he had not loved man. It seemed to Leo that his whole life stood starkly revealed and he saw himself for the first time as he truly was—unloved and loveless. This bitter but somehow not fully unexpected revelation brought him to a point of panic, controlled only by extraordinary effort. He covered his face with his hands and cried.

The week that followed was the worst of his life. He did not eat and lost weight. His beard darkened and grew ragged. He stopped attending seminars and almost never opened a book. He seriously considered leaving the Yeshivah, although he was deeply troubled at the thought of the loss of all his years of study—saw them like pages torn from a book, strewn over the city—and at the devastating effect of his decision upon his parents. But he had lived without knowledge of himself, and never in the Five Books and all the Commentaries—mea culpa—had the truth been revealed to him. He did not know where to turn, and in all this desolating loneliness there was no *to whom*, although he often thought of Lily but not once could bring himself to go downstairs and make the call. He became touchy and irritable, especially with his landlady, who asked him all manner of personal questions; on the other hand, sensing his own disagreeableness, he waylaid her on the stairs and apologized abjectly, until mortified, she ran from him. Out of this, however, he drew the consolation that he was a Jew and that a Jew suffered. But gradually, as the long and terrible week drew to a close, he regained his composure and some idea of purpose in life: to go on as planned. Although he was imperfect, the ideal was not. As for his quest for a bride, the thought of continuing afflicted him with anxiety and heartburn, yet perhaps with this new knowledge of himself he would be more successful than in the past. Perhaps love would now come to him and a bride to that love. And for this sanctified seeking who needed a Salzman?

The marriage broker, a skeleton with haunted eyes, returned that very night. He looked, withal, the picture of frustrated expectancy—as if he had steadfastly waited the week at Miss Lily Hirschorn's side for a telephone call that never came.

Casually coughing, Salzman came immediately to the point: "So how did you like her?"

Leo's anger rose and he could not refrain from chiding the matchmaker: "Why did you lie to me, Salzman?"

Salzman's pale face went dead white, the world had snowed on him.

"Did you not state that she was twenty-nine?" Leo insisted.

"I give you my word—"

"She was thirty-five, if a day. *At least* thirty-five."

"Of this don't be too sure. Her father told me—"

"Never mind. The worst of it was that you lied to her."

"How did I lie to her, tell me?"

"You told her things about me that weren't true. You made me out to be more, consequently less than I am. She had in mind a totally different person, a sort of semi-mystical Wonder Rabbi."

"All I said, you was a religious man."

"I can imagine."

Salzman sighed. "This is my weakness that I have," he confessed. "My wife says to me I shouldn't be a salesman, but when I have two fine people that they would be wonderful to be married, I am so happy that I talk too much." He smiled wanly. "This is why Salzman is a poor man."

Leo's anger left him. "Well, Salzman, I'm afraid that's all."

The marriage broker fastened hungry eyes on him.

"You don't want any more a bride?"

"I do," said Leo, "but I have decided to seek her in a different way. I am no longer interested in an arranged marriage. To be frank, I now admit the necessity of premarital love. That is, I want to be in love with the one I marry."

"Love?" said Salzman, astounded. After a moment he remarked, "For us, our love is our life, not for the ladies. In the ghetto they—"

"I know, I know," said Leo. "I've thought of it often. Love, I have said to myself, should be a by-product of living and worship rather than its own end. Yet for myself I find it necessary to establish the level of my need and fulfill it."

Salzman shrugged but answered, "Listen, rabbi, if you want love, this I can find for you also. I have such beautiful clients that you will love them the minute your eyes will see them."

Leo smiled unhappily. "I'm afraid you don't understand."

But Salzman hastily unstrapped his portfolio and withdrew a manila packet from it.

"Pictures," he said, quickly laying the envelope on the table.

Leo called after him to take the pictures away, but as if on the wings of the wind, Salzman had disappeared.

March came. Leo had returned to his regular routine. Although he felt not quite himself yet—lacked energy—he was making plans for a more active social life. Of course it would cost something, but he was an expert in cutting corners; and when there were no corners left he would make circles rounder. All the while Salzman's pictues had lain on the table, gathering dust. Occasionally as Leo sat studying, or enjoying a cup of tea, his eyes fell on the manila envelope, but he never opened it.

The days went by and no social life to speak of developed with a member of the opposite sex—it was difficult, given the circumstances of his situation. One morning Leo toiled up the stairs to his room and stared out the window at the city. Although the day was bright his view of it was dark. For some time he watched the people in the street below hurrying along and then turned with a heavy heart to his little room. On the table was the packet. With a sudden relentless gesture he tore it open. For a half-hour he stood by the table in a state of excitement, examining the photographs of the ladies Salzman had included. Finally, with a deep sigh he put them down. There were six, of varying degrees of attractiveness, but look at them long enough and they all became Lily Hirschorn: all past their prime, all starved behind bright smiles, not a true personality in the lot. Life, despite their frantic yoohooings, had passed them by; they were pictures in a brief case that stank of fish. After a while, however, as Leo attempted to return the photographs into the envelope, he found in it another, a snapshot of the type taken by a machine for a quarter. He gazed at it a moment and let out a cry.

Her face deeply moved him. Why, he could at first not say. It gave him the impression of youth—spring flowers, yet age—a sense of having been used to the bone, wasted; this came from the eyes, which were hauntingly familiar, yet absolutely strange. He had a vivid impression that he had met her before, but try as he might he could not place her although he could almost recall her name, as if he had read it in her own handwriting. No, this couldn't be; he would have remembered her. It was not, he affirmed, that she had extraordinary beauty—no, though her face was attractive enough; it was that *something* about her moved him. Feature for feature, even some of the ladies of the photographs could do better; but she leaped forth to his heart—had *lived,* or wanted to—more than just wanted, perhaps regretted how she had lived—had somehow deeply suffered: it could be seen in the depths of those reluctant eyes, and from the way the light enclosed and shone from her, and within her, opening realms of possibility: this was her own. Her he desired. His head ached and eyes narrowed with the intensity of his gazing, then as if an obscure fog had blown up in the mind, he experienced fear of her and was aware that he had received an impression, somehow, of evil. He shuddered, saying softly, it is thus with us all. Leo brewed some tea in a small pot and sat sipping it without sugar, to calm himself. But before he had finished drinking, again with excitement he examined the face and found it good: good for Leo Finkle. Only such a one could understand him and help him seek whatever he was seeking. She might, perhaps love him. How she had happened to be among the discards in Salzman's barrel he could never guess, but he knew he must urgently find her.

Leo rushed downstairs, grabbed up the Bronx telephone book, and searched for Salzman's home address. He was not listed, nor was his office. Neither was he in the Manhattan book. But Leo remembered having written down the address on a slip of paper after he had read Salzman's advertisement in the "personals" column of the *Forward.* He ran up to his room and tore through his papers, without luck. It was exasperating. Just when he needed the matchmaker he was nowhere to be found. Fortunately Leo remembered to look in his wallet. There on a card he found his name written and a Bronx address. No phone number was listed, the reason—Leo now recalled—he had originally communicated with Salzman by letter. He got on his coat, put a hat on over his skull cap and hurried to the subway station. All the way to the far end of the Bronx he sat on the edge of his seat. He was more than once tempted to take out the picture and see if the girl's face was as he remembered it, but he refrained, allowing the snapshot to remain in his inside coat pocket, content to have her so close. When the train pulled into the station he was waiting at the door and bolted out. He quickly located the street Salzman had advertised.

The building he sought was less than a block from the subway, but it was not an office building, nor even a loft, nor a store in which one could rent office space. It was a very old tenement house. Leo found Salzman's name in pencil on a soiled tag under the bell and climbed three dark flights to his apartment. When he knocked, the door was opened by a thin, asthmatic, gray-haired woman, in felt slippers.

"Yes?" she said, expecting nothing. She listened without listening. He could have sworn he had seen her, too, before but knew it was an illusion.

"Salzman—does he live here? Pinye Salzman," he said, "the matchmaker?"

She stared at him a long minute. "Of course."

He felt embarrassed. "Is he in?"

"No." Her mouth, though left open, offered nothing more.

"The matter is urgent. Can you tell me where his office is?"

"In the air." She pointed upward.

"You mean he has no office?" Leo asked.

"In his socks."

He peered into the apartment. It was sunless and dingy, one large room divided by a half-open curtain, beyond which he could see a sagging metal bed. The near side of a room was crowded with rickety chairs, old bureaus, a three-legged table, racks of cooking utensils, and all the apparatus of a kitchen. But there was no sign of Salzman or his magic barrel, probably also a figment of the imagination. An odor of frying fish made Leo weak to the knees.

"Where is he?" he insisted. "I've got to see your husband."

At length she answered, "So who knows where he is? Every time he thinks a new thought he runs to a different place. Go home, he will find you."

"Tell him Leo Finkle."

She gave no sign she had heard.

He walked downstairs, depressed.

But Salzman, breathless, stood waiting at his door.

Leo was astounded and overjoyed. "How did you get here before me?"

"I rushed."

"Come inside."

They entered. Leo fixed tea, and a sardine sandwich for Salzman. As they were drinking he reached behind him for the packet of pictures and handed them to the marriage broker.

Salzman put down his glass and said expectantly, "You found somebody you like?"

"Not among these."

The marriage broker turned away.

"Here is the one I want." Leo held forth the snapshot.

Salzman slipped on his glasses and took the picture into his trembling hand. He turned ghastly and let out a groan.

"What's the matter?" cried Leo.

"Excuse me. Was an accident this picture. She isn't for you."

Salzman frantically shoved the manila packet into his portfolio. He thrust the snapshot into his pocket and fled down the stairs.

Leo, after momentary paralysis, gave chase and cornered the marriage broker in the vestibule. The landlady made hysterical outcries but neither of them listened.

"Give me back the picture, Salzman."

"No." The pain in his eyes was terrible.

"Tell me who she is then."

"This I can't tell you. Excuse me."

He made to depart, but Leo forgetting himself, seized the matchmaker by his tight coat and shook him frenziedly.

"Please," sighed Salzman. "*Please.*"

Leo ashamedly let him go. "Tell me who she is," he begged. "It's very important for me to know."

"She is not for you. She is a wild one—wild, without shame. This is not a bride for a rabbi."

"What do you mean wild?"

"Like an animal. Like a dog. For her to be poor was a sin. This is why to me she is dead now."

"In God's name, what do you mean?"

"Her I can't introduce to you," Salzman cried.

"Why are you so excited?"

"Why, he asks," Salzman said, bursting into tears. "This is my baby, my Stella, she should burn in hell."

Leo hurried up to bed and hid under the covers. Under the covers he thought his life through. Although he soon fell asleep he could not sleep her out of his mind. He woke, beating his breast. Though he prayed to be rid of her, his prayers went unanswered. Through days of torment he endlessly struggled not to love her; fearing success, he escaped it. He then concluded to convert her to goodness, himself to God. The idea alternately nauseated and exalted him.

He perhaps did not know that he had come to a final decision until he encountered Salzman in a Broadway cafeteria. He was sitting alone at a rear table, sucking the bony remains of a fish. The marriage broker appeared haggard, and transparent to the point of vanishing.

Salzman looked up at first without recognizing him. Leo had grown a pointed beard and his eyes were weighted with wisdom.

"Salzman," he said, "love has at last come to my heart."

"Who can love from a picture?" mocked the marriage broker.

"It is not impossible."

"If you can love her, then you can love anybody. Let me show you some new clients that they just sent me their photographs. One is a little doll."

"Just her I want," Leo murmured.

"Don't be a fool, doctor. Don't bother with her."

"Put me in touch with her, Salzman," Leo said humbly. "Perhaps I can be of service."

Salzman had stopped eating and Leo understood with emotion that it was now arranged.

Leaving the cafeteria, he was, however, afflicted by a tormenting suspicion that Salzman had planned it all to happen this way.

***

Leo was informed by letter that she would meet him on a certain corner, and she was there one spring night, waiting under a street lamp. He appeared carrying a small bouquet of violets and rosebuds. Stella stood by the lamp post, smoking. She wore white with red shoes, which fitted his expectations, although in a troubled moment he had imagined the dress red, and only the shoes white. She waited uneasily and shyly. From afar he saw that her eyes—clearly her father's—were filled with desperate innocence. He pictured, in her, his own redemption. Violins and lit candles revolved in the sky. Leo ran forward with flowers outthrust.

Around the corner, Salzman, leaning against a wall, chanted prayers for the dead.

2 marriages

Peter Taylor

Reservations: A Love Story

Peter Taylor was born in Tennessee, grew up in Nashville and St. Louis, and graduated from Kenyon College in 1940. His first book, a collection of short stories entitled A Long Fourth, *was published in 1948, followed two years later by his only novel,* A Woman of Means. *Since then he has published four more collections of short stories, including his* Collected Stories *(1969), and a number of plays. In 1959 he won the O. Henry Prize for the best short story of the year. Throughout his career Peter Taylor has taught at many colleges and universities, among them Harvard, Kenyon, and the University of North Carolina at Greensboro. Since 1967 he has been a Professor of English at the University of Virginia.*

It was arranged, of all things, that the bride and groom should make their escape from the country club through the little boys' locker room! But this was very reasonable, really. At nine o'clock on a night in January, the exit from the little boys' locker room to the swimming-pool terrace was the exit least likely to be congested. It was the exit also most likely to be overlooked by mischievous members of the wedding party. Every precaution had to be taken! No one was to be trusted!

In the lounge of the women's locker room, the bride got out of her gown in exactly thirty seconds. (She had taken an hour, more or less, to get into it.) She pushed the wedding dress into the hands of one of the club's maids and from the hands of another accepted the tweed travelling suit—puce-brown tweed trimmed with black velvet. Because it was imperative that no suspicion of her departure be roused among the guests, the bride was not attended by her mother or by her maid of honor. Her mother and all the bridal attendants remained upstairs at the party, where there was dancing, and where waiters moved about balancing trays of stemmed glasses. At two minutes to nine, the bride ran on tiptoe along a service passageway that connected most of the rooms on the ground floor. She was accompanied now by the elder of the two maids who had assisted in the change from white satin to tweed. This woman was one of the club's veteran maids, a large, rather middle-aged person who, though she dyed her hair a lemon yellow and rouged her cheeks excessively, was known for her stalwart character and her incorruptibility. In the passageway, the bride chattered nervously to this companion who had been assigned to her. She told how she had written her name in the club's bride's book as "Franny Crowell," having forgotten momentarily that she was now Mrs. Miles Miller. The maid was not a very responsive sort, and said nothing. But this didn't bother Franny; she went on to say, sometimes laughing while she spoke, that somehow she could not shake off the feeling that it was a pity and a shame to be slipping away from a party given in your own honor.

In one hand the maid held the key to a door down the passageway that would let the bride into the little boys' locker room. In the other hand she carried a pair of fur-trimmed galoshes. As they approached the locked door, the maid interrupted Franny's chatter.

"Your father said tell you your fur coat's in the car, with your corsage pinned to it. He said be careful you don't sit on it." Simultaneously the maid held out the galoshes, giving them a little shake that indicated Franny should take them.

"What are those?" Franny chirped. "They're not mine."

"No, they're not yours, Mrs. Miller," said the maid, still pressing them on her.

"Well, I don't believe I'll want them," Franny said politely.

"Yes, your mother said so. It's snowing outside now—a nasty, wet snow, Mrs. Miller."

"But they're not mine, and they're not Mother's either. . . . How long has it been snowing?" She hoped to change the subject.

"Two hours off and on, Mrs. Miller. Ever since you got here from the church. It's not sticking, but there'll be slush underfoot."

"Well, whose are they?"

"Your mother snitched them from one of the guests—out of the cloakroom. She told me, 'Something borrowed.' "

Franny burst into laughter and took the galoshes. But she resolved not to put on the ugly things until after Miles had seen her and got the effect of her outfit.

While the maid fitted the key into the lock, Franny stood with her eyes lifted to the low basement ceiling. She heard the sound of the dancing overhead, and she speculated about which of the dancers upstairs these boots might belong to and thought of the pleasure it was sure to give some childhood friend of hers, or possibly some aunt or some woman friend of her parents, to learn that *she* had provided the bride with the one item that had been overlooked—the something borrowed.

Presently the door before her stood open. But Franny's eyes and thoughts were still directed toward the ceiling. "There you are," said the maid, obviously provoked by the bride's inattention.

Franny lowered her eyes. She looked at the woman beside her with a startled expression. Then she glanced briefly into the shadows of the unlighted locker room. And in the next moment she was clutching frantically at the starched sleeve of the maid's uniform. "But he is not here!" she exclaimed. Her tone was accusing; she eyed the maid suspiciously. Then, as if on further reflection, she spoke in a bewailing whisper: "He isn't hee-er!" According to the plan, he was to have been admitted to the little boys' locker room through a door from the adjoining men's locker room. But had he ever intended to be there? *He was gone! Of course he was! How else would it be?* Already Franny was thinking of what kind of poison she would administer to herself, of how she would manage to obtain the poison, of how she would look when they found her.

"What do you mean 'not here'?" said the maid, jerking her sleeve free.

Franny smiled coolly. She knew how she must carry it off. "Maybe I'll stay on for the party, after all," she said.

"What do you mean 'not here'?" the maid repeated. "He's standing there before your eyes."

Franny looked again, and of course there her bridegroom stood. "I didn't see him, it's so dark," she stammered.

But, instead of going to the bridegroom, suddenly the bride threw her arms about the woman with the lemon-yellow hair who had delivered her to him. This trustworthy woman had been known to Franny during most of her young life, but she was by no means a favorite of Franny's. And almost certainly Franny had never been a favorite of the woman's, either. . . . But still it seemed the thing to do. Somehow it was like embracing the whole wedding party or even the whole club membership, or possibly just simply her own mother. And, no doubt, in that moment this woman forgave Franny many an old score—forgave a little girl's criticism of sandwiches served toasted when they had been ordered untoasted, complaints about a bathing suit's not having been hung out to dry, and many another complaint besides. At any rate, the woman responded and returned the warm embrace. Then for an instant the two of them smiled at each other through the general mist of tears.

"Goodbye, little Miss 'Franny Crowell,'" the woman said.

"Goodbye, Bernice," said Franny, "and thanks for everything." Yes, the woman's name was Bernice. What a bother it had always been, trying to remember it, but now it had come out without Franny's having to try to think of it even.

Bernice took several steps backward, as if quitting a royal presence. At a respectful distance she turned her back, and in her white gum-soled shoes she retreated silently down the long service passageway.

While waiting for the bride to come through the doorway to him, the bridegroom had literally stood dangling his little narrow-brimmed hat, shifting it from one hand to the other. He did not know what to make of that blank look she had given him at first, didn't know what to make of her saying "He is not here," didn't know what to make of her throwing herself into the arms of the hired help instead of into his own. . . . The embrace perhaps he understood better than the look. But anyway, she had come to him at last, which was what he wanted most in the world at the moment. Presently he had seated her on one of the rough wooden benches in the locker room and, on his knees before her, he was struggling to push her feet into the borrowed galoshes. Franny had held on to the galoshes through both her embraces, and as soon as she had handed them to Miles and was seated on the bench, she began to chatter again—about the galoshes now, about how her mother had positively stolen "the ugly things" from somebody upstairs.

It wasn't easy getting the galoshes on. They were a near-perfect fit, but Franny seemed incapable of being any help. Her little ankles had gone limp, like an absent-minded child's. But finally Miles managed to force both galoshes on. He zipped them up neatly, and then lifted his face to Franny and smiled. Franny extended one of her tiny gloved hands to him, as if she were going to pull him to his feet. Miles seized it, but he remained on one knee before her, pressing the hand firmly between the two of his. While he knelt there, Franny made a vague gesture with her free hand, a gesture that indicated the whole of the dark locker room. "I've never been in here before, Miles," she said.

"Neither have I, you know," Miles said playfully.

"Oh," Franny breathed, thoughtfully. "No, you probably haven't, have you."

Now she felt she understood. . . . *That* was why she had not been able to see him there at first. She had never *imagined* him there. It was because Miles Miller was not one of the local boys she had grown up with, wasn't one of that familiar group from whose number she had always assumed she would someday accept a husband. He was better than any of *those,* of course; he was her own, beloved, blue-eyed, black-haired, fascinating Miles Miller, whom she had recognized the first moment she ever saw him as the best-looking man she had ever laid eyes on (or ever would), as the man she must have for *hers*—and the very same Miles, of course, that at least half a dozen other girls of her year had thought they must have for *theirs*. Moreover, he was the young man who doesn't turn up in *every*body's year: the young bachelor from out of town, brought in from a distant region by one of the big corporations to fill a place in its local office, a young man without any local history of teenage romances to annoy and perhaps worry the bride. And in Miles' case the circumstances were enhanced still further. He was an only child, and his parents had died while he was still in college. For his bride there would be no parents or brothers and sisters to be visited and adjusted to, and, since he had lived always on the West Coast and gone to Stanford, no prep-school friends, not even—at such a distance—a college roommate to be won over. Once they were married, Franny's family would be *their* family, her friends *their* friends. Besides all this, her Miles was at once the most modest and most self-assured human being imaginable. With one gentle look—gentle and yet reasonable and terribly penetrating—he could make her aware of the utter absurdity of something she said or did, and make her simultaneously aware of how little such absurdities mattered to someone who loved you.

Franny bent forward and kissed her husband gently on his smiling lips. He came up beside her on the bench, no longer smiling, and took Franny in his arms. For Franny it was as it had always been before—every time he had ever held her in his tender, confident way. It was as though she possessed at last, or was about to possess at last, what she had always wanted above everything else and had never dreamed she wanted—or, that is, never dreamed she wanted in quite the same way she wanted everything else. That was what seemed so incredible to her about it: *This* desire and *this* happiness differed only in degree from the other longings and other satisfactions one experienced. There was nothing at all unreal about it. And somehow the most miraculous part was that the man she was going to marry was not the man she had ever imagined herself marrying. On the contrary, he was the frightening stranger of her girlish daydreams—the dark, handsome man she was always going to meet on a train coming home from boarding school at Christmas or during the summer at Lake Michigan. In her daydreams she sometimes even bore that man a child, but there had always had to be a barrier to their marrying. The man was already married (perhaps to an invalid!) or he was a Jew, he was a Catholic—a French Canadian—or he was the foreign agent of a country committed to the destruction of her own country, or (when she was still younger) there was insanity or even a strain of Negro blood in his family! Yet the stranger had turned up after all—after she had almost forgotten him—and there was no barrier.

Still holding Franny close to him, Miles got to his feet and for a moment lifted his bride completely off the floor. "Franny, oh, 'little Miss Franny,' let's go!" he said. Franny laughed aloud. And to Miles she sounded for all the world like a delighted little girl of four or five. "Let's be on our way," he said, still holding her there. "Let's get out of here."

"Carry me to the car, Miles," she whispered.

"I will," he said. "You bet I will. Not this way, though. I'll set you down and get a good hold and then we'll dash."

But just as Franny's feet touched the floor, there came a great rattling sound from over toward the door to the terrace. Franny gave a little shriek that came out almost "Aha!" And then, in a quiet voice, in a tone of utter resignation, she said, "They've found us." She meant, of course, that the mischief-makers had found them. "We'll *never* get away."

"No, they haven't darling," Miles said impatiently.

Franny turned away from him. At the far end of the room she saw a man's figure silhouetted against the glass door to the terrace. She realized at once that the man must be one of the club's waiters. It was he, she surmised, who had let Miles in from the men's locker room. He had been present all the while, and actually he was now holding the terrace door a little way open. The rattling noise had, plainly, come from the long Venetian blind on that door. But the source of the rattling no longer interested Franny; she was too angry with Miles for not having told her they weren't alone.

Suddenly her impulse was to turn back and deliver Miles a slap across the face. His inference that the waiter's presence hadn't mattered was insulting both to herself and to this man who had so faithfully performed his duties assigned to him. But before she could turn or speak, Miles had seized her by the hand and the waiter had thrown open the door. Hand in hand, the bride and groom ran the length of the little boys' locker room. In the excitement of the moment, Miles had forgotten that he was going to carry Franny to the car. It was well for him that he had. Franny consented to let him hold her hand only in order to keep from embarrassing the waiter. Halfway to the door she made out just which of the club's waiters he was, and she could easily have called him by name. But instead she dropped her eyes, and she kept them lowered even when Miles paused in the doorway to slip a bill into the hand at the end of the white sleeve. In her pique with Miles, she wondered if the bill was of as large a denomination as it ought to be.

Outside, they ran along the edge of the gaping swimming pool and on in the direction of the tennis courts. Beyond the courts, Miles' new car was hidden. The wet snow was falling heavily, and it was beginning to stick now. It seemed to Franny that the snow might fill the empty swimming pool before the night was over. They went through the gate into the area of the tennis courts. From there Franny glanced back once at the lighted windows of the low, sprawling clubhouse. Through the snow it seemed miles away. They ran across the courts and through the white shrubbery. Neither of them spoke until they were in the car. By then their rendezvous in the locker room seemed like something that happened too long ago to mention. As Miles was helping her into her coat, and she was carefully protecting the big white orchid that she knew her father had pinned on the coat with his own hands, Franny said, "What are we going to do, Miles? I'm terrified. I hate snow. We can't get even as far as Bardstown tonight."

"Of course we can't, honey," he said. He had switched on the car lights and was starting the motor. "We'll have to stay here in town tonight. I telephoned the hotel a while ago. We'll have to stay there."

They had planned to spend the first night at Bardstown, which in good weather was only a few hours away, down in Kentucky, and where there was an attractive old inn. They had planned to make it to Natchez by the second night, and to be at the Gulf Coast by the third. Franny's father had urged them to fly down, or to take a train. But they were able to think only what fun it would be to have their own car once they got to Biloxi. It had been silly of them, they acknowledged now, driving into town through the snow, but they did have the satisfaction of knowing that all planes would be grounded on such a night, anyway. And to both of them the idea of spending their wedding night in a Pullman berth seemed grotesque.

It took Miles three-quarters of an hour to get them through the snow and the traffic to the downtown hotel where he had managed to make reservations. Along the way, he apologized to Franny for putting them up at this particular hotel—the hotel, that is, where he had himself been living during the past year and a half. "As luck would have it," he explained. "there are two big conventions in town this week. I was lucky to find a room anywhere at all. I hope you don't mind too much."

"Why in the world should I mind?" Franny laughed. "We're a bona-fide married couple now."

Yet the moment she had passed through the revolving door into the marble-pillared lobby of the hotel, Franny rested a gloved hand on the sleeve of Miles' overcoat and said, "I *do* feel a little funny about it, after all."

"I was afraid you might feel funny about it." Miles said. They stood there a moment waiting for the boy with their luggage to follow them through the revolving door, and Miles began to apologize all over again. "The other hotels were all full up," he said. "It's only because I happen to hit it off so well with Bill Carlisle that I was able to get a room here. It wasn't easy for him even; he's just the assistant manager. Your father, or almost any of the guys in the wedding, might have found us something better. But it seemed worse, somehow, to have any of them—even your father—know exactly where we're spending the night, since we can't get out of town. I guessed you would feel the same way about it."

But Franny was not listening to Miles. She had become aware that she was the only woman in the lobby, and the mention of the assistant manager's name had further distracted her. Bill Carlisle had been invited to the wedding—she recalled addressing his invitation—but he had not been invited to the reception and supper dance. As for her own acquaintance with him, it was very slight. She had known him for a long time, however, and she knew that he knew just about everyone that she did. She interrupted Miles' apologies to say, "Do we have to see Bill Collier?"

"Who?" asked Miles.

"You know—the assistant manager."

"Of course we don't, darling," he said. "We don't even have to register. That's all set."

The boy with their luggage had joined them now. Another boy had appeared with their key and was beckoning them to follow him to the elevator. As they crossed the lobby, Franny began laughing to herself. Miles noticed, and asked what was funny.

"I was wondering," she said, "do you think he'll have put us in your room?"

"Will who have?"

"You know, your friend Bill—the assistant manager."

"At least it won't be that," said Miles. "There was someone waiting to take it over when I got the last of my possessions out this morning."

"What a shame," Franny whispered. "It would have been kind of interesting, and no one but Bill Cook need ever have known."

"Bill Carlisle's his name," Miles said rather petulantly. Then he added, "He's a pretty nice fellow, in case you don't know."

"Certainly he is," Franny said with a wink. "I've known him for years."

Franny stepped into the elevator, followed by Miles. Then the boy with the luggage got in, then the one with the key. Franny observed that both the boys were mature men, and the key boy was even bald-headed. They kept their heads bowed, very courteously, not even looking up when presently they had occasion to speak to each other.

"Where's Jack?" the luggage boy asked quietly.

"He's coming," said the key boy.

"Who's Jack?" Franny asked Miles.

Thinking the question was directed to him, the luggage boy replied, "He's the elevator boy." As he spoke, he glanced up at Franny. Probably he thought it was demanded of him. Unlike the key boy, he had a heavy head of hair, as dark and thick as Miles' own, and the face he lifted was youthful, almost handsome even, with a broad jaw and black, rather cruel eyes that seemed brimming with energy. As soon as he looked up he realized his mistake and bent his head again. But he had reminded Franny of someone—someone she didn't like. Or *did* like. Which was it? She couldn't think who it was, and felt vaguely that she didn't want to. And what would Jack, the elevator operator, be like, she wondered, when he turned up? Somehow she was sure he would be a redhead. Presently he would come running; he would hop into the elevator, close the door, push the button, and there she would be, locked in the elevator with Miles and with the three men in their dark-green livery and with the heap of luggage, and the elevator would shoot them up to their floor and stop with a sickening little bounce. She wished Miles would *say* something!

"Jack seems to have gotten lost," Miles said. Franny burst out laughing.

Immediately, Jack appeared, as if from nowhere. He was a Negro boy, but with light skin and a reddish tint to his hair.

Franny was conscious of Jack's arrival, and conscious of the color of his hair, but at the same time her real attention had been caught by a figure out in the lobby. It was the figure of a woman, and she was moving swiftly across the lobby toward this elevator, making her way between the heavier figures of the conventioners in their tweed overcoats and gray fedoras. (Most of them, it seemed to Franny, were smoking cigars, the way conventioners were supposed to.) The woman was wearing a navy-blue topcoat and hat, and carried an oversize handbag. "Wait!" Franny said to the elevator boy.

"What do you mean, 'Wait'?" Miles asked.

"Don't you see who that is trying to catch us?" Franny said, rising on her toes.

"I see who it is, but you don't know her, and I can promise you I don't either."

One of the hotel boys snorted, but he cut it off so short Franny couldn't tell for sure which of them it was. She suspected the bald-headed one.

"It's Bernice! The maid from the club!" Franny tried to recall whether she had forgotten anything essential. No, the woman must have an urgent message for her. Her father or her mother had been taken ill, or there had been some disaster at the club—a fire perhaps. She remembered distinctly having left a cigarette burning in the women's lounge.

"It's no such thing," Miles was saying. "Let's go, Jack!"

The woman was close enough now for Franny to see it was not Bernice. The long stride and the yellow hair sticking out from under the hat had deceived her. But she should have known, shouldn't she, that Bernice could not have worn such heels.

The elevator door was closing right in the woman's face, and even if the woman wasn't Bernice, this was more than Franny could bear. "Stop it!" she commanded, utterly outraged by the ungallant behavior of these men. "There's room for another person, easily!"

The boys looked at Miles. "Let the lady in," Miles thundered.

Jack slid the door open. But the woman hesitated. With a swift glance she seemed to have taken in every aspect of the situation—that it was a bride and groom she was intruding upon, that the bride had insisted upon holding the car for her, that the groom had protested. She now signalled Jack to go on without her, but with Miles' thundering command still in his ears Jack made no move to do so. Miles kept silent. And so did Franny, who in a last-minute glance as swift as the woman's had taken in *her* total situation—that she was a middle-aged prostitute late for an engagement. There was but one solution to the awful silence and to the irresolution of the elevator boy. The woman stepped into the elevator and abruptly turned her back to the other passengers.

As the car shot upward, Jack asked with easy nonchalance, "Your floor, please?"

Again there was silence. Finally Miles said, "What's our floor?"

The key boy looked up, showing his full face for the first time—eyes set close together, a small, puffy nose, ears flat against the bald head. Franny thought it the stupidest, most brutal face she had ever set eyes on. "*Your* floor is eight, Mr. Miller," he said, barely opening his swollen lips when he spoke.

After a moment Jack repeated,"Your floor, please?"

The woman now turned her face toward the elevator boy so that Franny saw her profile. Her face was plain—neither homely nor otherwise, really—and seemed devoid of expression. Only the fact that she had turned her face toward him showed that she knew the boy expected an answer from her. It occurred to Franny that in her agitation this poor creature had forgotten what floor she was going to. At last, and as if with great effort, she did speak. "Seven for me," she said.

With a long, bony forefinger Jack stabbed the seventh-floor button. The elevator stopped almost at once, and the door slid open. The woman stepped out into the hallway, where there was a broad mirror facing her between two metal cigarette urns. Instead of turning to left or right she stopped here just outside the elevator, for one instant her pale eyes met Franny's in the glass. Then the door closed quietly between them.

Franny had not been aware of a bouncing sensation when the elevator stopped at that floor. But when it stopped at the floor above, the sensation so upset her equilibrium that she felt positively faint. Her two feet in their fur-trimmed galoshes seemed chilled to numbness. She felt that if she tried to take one step down the hallway in the direction of the bridal chamber her knees might buckle underneath her. She wondered how she would ever manage it.

To Miles Miller, his bride had seemed not herself at all, from the time they met in the shadows of the locker room at the country club until at last they were alone in the hotel room. But her confusion and nervousness were very understandable, he reasoned, in view of the upsetting change in their plans. And once they were alone in the room, she was indeed very much herself again. She was once again the vivacious, unaffected, ingenuous little being he had decided to marry after talking to her for five minutes during an intermission at a big début party last year. From the beginning, Miles had felt that he appreciated her special brand of innocence and even artlessness as no one else ever before had. One thing he had determined when he left college and entered upon his career in business was that he would not be the sort—the type—to marry the boss's daughter and further his career that way. He detested that type. He extended his pledge to himself even to include the daughters of prominent and influential men who might indirectly help him in his career. He extended it even to cover all the débutantes he had ever met or would ever meet. He had had no definite ideas about where he *would* find his wife, except one idea that was so childish he laughed at himself: He had thought of meeting a perfectly unspoiled girl while vacationing in an unspoiled countryside—perhaps in the highland South, perhaps even somewhere in Europe. He had thought particularly of Switzerland. But when thinking more realistically Miles told himself simply that he would not marry for the sake of his business or social advancement. His marriage and his family life must be something altogether apart from his career.

And then, in his twenty-sixth year, he had met Franny Crowell and had had a wonderful insight. Franny was, in a most important sense, as beautifully innocent and provincial as any little mountain girl might have been. She delighted in her surroundings, accepted her relation to them without question, and would be content to remain where she was and as she was for the rest of her life. She had been practically nowhere away from home. For two years she went to boarding school in Virginia but hated dormitory life and thought it silly of girls to go East to college when they could be so much more comfortable staying at home. She had herself attended the local city university for two years and had relished meeting different kinds of people from her own home town. True, she had spent most of her summers at a resort on Lake Michigan, but even there most of her companions had been the same people she went to school with at home during the winter. Miles Miller recognized in Franny Crowell the flaxen-haired mountain girl of his childish imaginings. Her outward appearance might deceive the world but never him. She arranged her golden-brown hair always in the lastest, most sophisticated fashions. Last summer she had even let the beauty parlor put a blond streak in her hair. She plucked her eye brows, even pencilled them. The shade of her lipstick paled or darkened according to whatever was newest. But Miles perceived that all of this was as innocent and natural in his Franny as plaiting flaxen pigtails might have been.

Miles and Franny had agreed in advance that they should each have only one glass of champagne at the club on their wedding night. But among the bags that they had had brought into the hotel was Miles' genuine Gucci liquor case—a present from the men at his office. Packed with ice in the plastic compartment of the elaborate leather case were two bottles of champagne of a somewhat earlier and better year than that offered the guests by the bride's father. And into Franny's makeup bag she had managed to fit two of their very own champagne glasses. Together they had thought of everything.

In their hotel room, they spent the first half hour making toasts. They drank to Betty Manville's début ball, where they had met, drank to their first date, to their first kiss, to the night he first proposed, to the night she accepted, to the night of the announcement party. Each toast had to be followed by a kiss. Each kiss inspired and motivated another reminiscence. Finally they turned to toasting people whom they associated with events of their courtship. Since Franny was a talented and tireless mimic, Miles encouraged her to "do" each of these people. She "did" Betty Manville's mother, her own father, and then one of her bridesmaids, who had once upon a time imagined *she* was going to have Miles Miller for herself. This last was the funniest of all to Miles. He was seated on the side of the bed, leaning on one elbow, and when he had witnessed Franny's version of that poor, misguided girl he set his champagne glass on the floor and fell back on the bed in a spasm of laughter. He threshed about, still laughing aloud, and all the while wiping tears from his eyes and begging Franny to stop.

When Franny promised to stop, Miles got control of himself and sat up in the center of the bed. Wiping his eyes with his handkerchief, he looked up again and found Franny sitting on the side of the bed with her thumb pressed against her nose so hard that her little nose was flattened on her face. Her eyes were squinted up and her mouth, which was normally small and tight, was stretched and spread into a wide ribbon across her face. "You know who this is?" she asked, barely moving her lips.

"I'm glad to say I don't," Miles said, as if offended by her ugliness.

"Oh, you do," Franny insisted.

"I don't, and it's not very attractive."

"Of course it's not attractive," said Franny, keeping the thumb pressed against her nose. "It's that bald-headed bellboy, the one with the key."

"What's wrong with him?" Miles said, swinging his feet around to the other side of the bed and thus momentarily turning his back to Franny.

"You don't have to turn your back," Franny said. "See, it's still only me."

Miles looked around and smiled apologetically. Franny's face was her own again, and she was looking down at her hands very seriously. "Weren't all three of those bellboys grotesque?" she said.

"I don't think so," Miles said. "They're perfectly normal-looking human beings. I see them every day."

"Normal-looking!" Franny exclaimed, lifting her eyes to his. "How can you say so? The bald-headed one was really monstrous. And the one with the mop of hair had a really mad look in his eyes. And that pale Negro boy with the kinky red hair! How blind you are to people, Miles. You don't really *see* them."

"Maybe not," said Miles, meaning to dismiss the subject, since Franny seemed so emotional about it. Turning now, he let himself fall across the bed toward her, and again he took one of her hands between the two of his. But before he could speak the endearment he intended, something else occurred to him that he felt must be said first. It was in defense of his vision, or—he couldn't define it—in defense of something even more specially his own that had been disparaged. "Anyway," he said, "you must admit that not one of those bellhops was half as weird-looking as that painted-up creature you had your hug fest with when we were leaving the club. After the elevator ride, I don't have to tell you what *she* looked like." Though they had been in the room for more than half an hour, this was the first reference either of them had made to the woman in the elevator.

Franny withdrew her hand and stood up.

Miles said, "We're not going to quarrel about something so silly on our wedding night, are we?"

Franny was silent for a moment. Her eyes moved about the room as if taking it in for the first time. Then she bent over and kissed Miles on the top of his head. "We aren't *ever* going to quarrel again, are we, Miles?"

"Never," he said. He reached out a hand, but she pulled away. "Come back," he said in a whisper.

"Not until I've slipped into something more—more right." She smiled vaguely.

Miles lay with his head propped on one hand and watched her go to her little overnight bag and take out the folds of lace and peach silk that were her negligee and gown. Suddenly he leaped from the bed with outstretched arms. But the bride dashed through the open doorway to the bathroom and closed the door.

Miles had long since changed into his blue silk pajamas with the white monogram on the pocket when he saw the first turning and twisting of the doorknob. When Franny failed to appear at once—that is, when the knob ceased its twisting and the bathroom door didn't open—his vexation showed itself momentarily in one little horizontal crease in his smooth forehead. But the moment was so brief that even his eyes didn't reflect it, and soon a sly little smile came to his lips. . . . He would give her a signal that all was ready and waiting, and at the same time give her motivation and courage. Stepping over to the dresser he uncorked the second bottle of champagne. He managed it very expertly, taking satisfaction in his expertness. The pop was loud enough for Franny to hear and comprehend, yet there was not one bubble of wasteful overflow. The tiny golden bubbles came just to the mouth of the champagne bottle and no further. Miles had not even taken the precaution of having the two glasses handy. He was expert and he was confident of his expertness.

He watched the first bubbles appear and then shot a glance across the room at the doorknob. It was turning again. He stepped over to where the two glasses were, on the bedside table, filled them, and then returned the bottle to its ice. Still no Franny. But the doorknob was now turning back and forth rather rapidly. Miles watched it as if hypnotized. Finally he uttered a tentative "Franny?" There was no response except in the acceleration of the knob's turning. "Franny?" he repeated, striding toward the door. "What's the matter?" Still no answer. The turning was frenzied now. "Franny, do you hear me? What are you doing?"

"Of course I hear you!" Franny exclaimed through the door. "I'm trying to get out of here, you fool!"

Miles seized the knob and gave it a forceful twist.

"That's not going to help," said Franny, resentful of the overpowering yank to the knob she had been holding on to.

"The thing must be locked," Miles said, astonished. "Why did you lock it?"

Franny was silent. Then she said, "*I* didn't lock it."

"Well, *I* didn't." Miles laughed. "Anyway, try unlocking it."

"Do you think I haven't already?"

"What kind of lock is it? Is there a key?"

"No. It's one of those damned little eggs you turn."

"But why on earth would you have locked it?"

"If I did it, Miles, I did it without thinking."

Miles was now trying to see the bolt through the crack of the door. "But why would you?" he said absently.

"Why would I what?"

"Lock it without thinking?"

"All decent people lock bathroom doors," she said with conviction.

"We didn't at our house," Miles said. He could definitely see the bolt through the crack. "My father used to throw away the key to the bathroom door as soon as we moved into a place."

"Don't start on your father *now*, Miles."

"My father was all right."

"Who said he wasn't? *Do* something, Miles, for God's sake."

"There's nothing to do but call the desk and have them take down the door."

Franny, who had for a moment been leaning against the rim of the washbowl, now straightened and grasped the doorknob again. "Miles, you *wouldn't!*"

"Don't go to pieces, Franny."

"You'd let them send up those three stooges—"

Miles burst into laughter.

"How coarse you are, Miles," Franny said, her voice deepening.

"Oh, honey, there's a regular maintenance crew, and—"

"Maybe so," she broke in, her voice climbing the scale till it was much higher than Miles had ever heard it before. "But don't you know, Miles, that Bill Carlisle would certainly know about it? Oh, God, everybody in this town would know about it before tomorrow morning!"

"In God's name, Franny, what do you propose I do?"

"What kind of man are you, Miles? Take the door down yourself. You've been living in this hotel so long you depend on them for everything. You seem to think the world's just one big hotel and that you call in the maintenance crew for any and every thing."

"O.K., Franny, I'll try," Miles said amiably. "But have you ever tried taking down a locked door?"

"Why did you have to bring me to this dump?" Franny wailed.

"And why did you have to lock the door?" he countered.

Now they were both silent as Miles went to the closet door where his Valpak hung, and dug out a small gold pocketknife. His first effort to remove the pin in the upper door hinge was fruitless. The pin wouldn't budge. Neither would the pin in the lower hinge. He decided he needed a hammer to drive the knife blade upward against the heads of the pins, and he was just turning to go and fetch his shoe for that purpose when Franny spoke again.

"Miles," she began, speaking very slowly and in a tone so grave that it stopped him, "do you remember that night at Cousin Jane Thompson's party?"

He listened, waiting for her to continue. Then he realized she expected some response from him. "Yes, Franny," he said.

"That night at Cousin Jane's," she now went on in the same sepulchral tone, "when you said Sue Maynard's date was drunk and that she asked you to take her home." Sue Maynard was the bridesmaid who had thought *she* would have Miles for herself. Miles had been a stag at the party that night.

"Yes, I remember."

"You were lying."

"In a way, Franny—"

"In the worst way," she said flatly. "You thought I would think it was just Sue's lie and that you didn't know better, or that you knew better but were too honorable to give her away."

"Maybe."

"That's how you *thought* I would think. But I knew even that night, Miles Miller, that you engineered it all. Her date was Puss Knowlton, and you had no trouble giving *him* the shove. And don't you think I know it's more than just necking that Sue Maynard goes in for? . . . And, Miles, the night last summer, *after* we were engaged, when you couldn't come for dinner at our house with Daddy's Aunt Caroline because of the report you had to write up—you didn't have any report to write up, Miles. You went someplace out on the South Side with a little creature named Becky Louise Johnson."

By the time Franny had finished, Miles had silently crossed the room to the bedside table and downed one of the two waiting glassfuls of champagne. He had listened intently to what she said, and the more he heard the more intent he had become on getting that damned door down. In his liquor case he found a bottle opener that he decided would work better than his knife. He returned to the door with his shoe and the bottle opener, and in no time he had the top pin out of its hinge.

"Miles—" Franny began again, still in the same tone.

"Shut up, Franny!" Miles said, and at once began hammering at the lower pin. It offered a little more resistance than the other, but was soon dislodged. The door was still firmly in place however. Twice Miles jabbed the bottle opener into the crack on the hinge side, as though he might prize the door open. Then he laughed aloud at himself.

Franny heard him laugh, of course. "Is it funny? Is it really funny to you, Miles?" she said.

"Try giving it a push from in there, on the hinge side of the door," said Miles. Franny pushed. The door creaked, but that was all.

"Miles," Franny began once again, in a whisper now, and he could tell that she was leaning against the door and speaking into the crack. "I've thought of something else I've never confronted you with."

Miles felt the blood rush to his face. Suddenly he banged on the door with his fist. "Will you shut up, you little bitch! You know, I'm not above socking you in earnest if ever I get you out of there!"

"You would sock me just one time, Miles Miller."

"It would be the second time. Don't you forget that," he said.

They were really at it now, for he was reminding her of an occasion two days after their announcement party when he had found her kissing a college kid whose name he did not even know. He had struck her with his open hand on the back of her neck—not while she was kissing the kid but afterward, as he pushed her along the terrace there at the Polo Club. He had had too much to drink that night, and that was what saved them. Franny could claim that he had deserted her in favor of the bar. She also claimed that she had not really been kissing the boy and added that, anyway, he was an old, old, old friend and therefore meant nothing to her. They hardly spoke to each other during the week following, though of course they continued going about together. And until now they had neither of them ever referred to the incident, as if by mutual agreement.

"You're no gentleman, Miles," Franny pronounced, carefully keeping away from the door now. "As Daddy said of you to start with, you have all the outward signs of a gentleman but that's no evidence you're one inside."

"I've already settled your father's hash, Franny."

"You mean he's settled yours."

It was an unfortunate word—"settled." And both of them were aware of it immediately. It quieted both of them for some time. It referred to another incident that was assumed to be closed. Franny's father had apparently suspected Miles of being a fortune hunter, and before the engagement was announced he had asked Miles frankly what kind of "settlement" he expected. Miles had stormed out of the house, and was reconciled with Mr. Crowell only after having it hammered home to him by Franny that what her father had done was merely the conventional, old-fashioned thing for a man in Mr. Crowell's position to do. Miles had finally accepted Franny's explanation, but only a few weeks ago he had had another stormy session over a similar matter. This time it was both the bride's parents. At that very date he had learned about certain letters of inquiry that had been sent out concerning his "background." The letters had been written to various family friends and relatives of the Crowells who had lived for many years in Santa Barbara and Laguna Beach. When Miles learned of these letters through a remark of Franny's, it was many months after the letters had been written and replied to. The revelation sent Miles into a rage. He was in such a state that Franny feared he might do real violence to her father, or even to her mother, who had actually written the letters.

She had let the cat out of the bag inadvertently. She and he were just going out to a movie one night, Franny had come down to the living room already wearing her coat and even with her gloves on, but Miles had wanted to linger and talk awhile. Before she came down, he had wandered about the room studying some family photographs taken thirty years before. These "portraits," in their upright frames on the mantelshelf and on the various tables, had reminded him of pictures in his own family's living room when he was growing up. He commenced talking to Franny about how his mother always placed the same pictures on the same tables and bureaus no matter where they were living, and then he went on to speak, as he had on several previous occasions, of how restless his father had been after he left the service. (Miles' father had been a West Point graduate and had remained in the Army until he had his first heart attack, just a few months before Pearl Harbor.) And now, as Miles had already done several times before, he began listing for Franny the towns they had lived in during and after the war. Franny, who was impatient to get on to the movie, didn't listen very carefully. When Miles hesitated, trying to think of which town it was he had omitted from his list, Franny absent-mindly supplied "Palo Alto." But it was not Palo Alto he was trying to think of it: it was San Jose.

"Palo Alto?" said Miles. "How did you know we ever lived in Palo Alto?"

"You've told me all this before," she answered.

But he had not told her about the spring in Palo Alto! It was then that his parents had quarreled so endlessly, though he—and probably they—had never known just why. At any rate, he was always careful to leave Palo Alto out of his catalogue of towns. And he was not content now until he had wrung a confession of the whole business of the letters of inquiry out of Franny. Once she had confessed, he insisted upon taking the matter up with her parents that very night; he insisted upon *seeing* the letters. For a time, Mrs. Crowell maintained that she had already thrown away the letters. But at last she broke down. She went upstairs and returned with the packet of letters, all of which Miles read, sitting there in the family circle. He had known there couldn't be anything really bad in them, because just as there was nothing very good that could be said of his parents, there was nothing very bad, either. The worst the letters said of them was that they were "rootless people and apparently of restricted means." Miles found he could not even resent one lady's description of his mother as a "harmless little woman—pleasant enough—with a vague Southern background." The letters repeated each other with phrases like "thoroughly nice" and "well bred" and "well behaved." The sole reference to Palo Alto was "I think they lived at Palo Alto for a time. John's sister Laura met them there. She thought Major Miller very handsome. He had a small black mustache, if I recall."

The memory of all this and of the "settlement" episode occupied Miles' mind as he crossed the hotel room and picked up the glass of champagne that he had poured for Franny. The champagne had gone flat already, but he relished its flatness. He sipped it slowly, as if tasting in each sip a different unpleasant incident or aspect of their courtship and engagement—tasting all they had not tasted and toasted with the first bottle. Suddenly he put down the glass, leaving still a sip or two in the bottle, and stepped quickly over to the bathroom door. "Franny," he said, "it has just occurred to me! It wasn't your father's idea to talk about a settlement with me. You put him up to it! It was you who thought I might be after your family's money! If it had been your father's idea, he wouldn't have been so meek and mild when I called his hand. And, by God, you put your mother up to writing those letters, or she never would have given in and shown them to me."

He waited for Franny's denial, but none came. "And, Franny," he went on after a moment, "there's one more thing I know that you didn't know I knew. Your father went down to my office and asked about the likelihood of my staying on here or being transferred."

"I knew he did that, Miles."

"Darn right you knew it. You put him up to that, too. You didn't even want to take a chance on my moving you away from here." But before he had finished his last sentence, Miles heard the water running full force into the bathtub. "Franny, I'm not finished!" he shouted. "What are you doing?"

"If you don't get this door down within ten minutes"—she was speaking through the crack again—"and get it down without having Bill Carlisle up here to witness it, I'm going to drown myself in the damned bathtub."

As a matter of fact, she had begun running the water to drown out Miles' accusations, but as she spoke she became convinced that suicide really had been her original intention.

"Yes," Miles boomed, "you drown yourself in the bathtub and I'll jump out our eighth-floor window! Romeo and Juliet, that's us!"

Franny shut off the water. She opened her mouth to reply, but no words came. She burst into tears. And the poor little bride could not herself have said whether her tears were brought on by the heavy irony and sarcasm of her groom or by the thought of her dear Miles and her dear self lying dead in their caskets with their love yet unfulfilled.

Almost at once Miles began pleading with her not to cry. But it seemed that his every word brought increased volume to the wailing beyond the bathroom door. It was as if she had decided she could more effectively drown out the sound of his voice with tears than with the rush of bath water. But actually it wasn't the sound of her bridegroom's voice alone that she wished not to hear. There was the sound of another voice—other voices. She had first become aware of the other voices during one of hers and Miles' silences. Which silence she couldn't have said, because for some time afterward she tried to believe that she had only imagined hearing the other voices, or at least imagined that they sounded as near to her as they did. Finally, though, the persistence of the voices drew her attention to the fact of the other door. The other door, she finally acknowledged, must certainly lead into an adjoining room. And the voices—a man's and a woman's—came to her from that room. And now the ever-increasing volume of her own wailing was meant to conceal from herself that the woman's voice was addressing her directly through that door.

"Honey, I think we can help you." The offer was unmistakable.

"No, you can't, no, you can't!" Franny wailed.

"The gentleman in here thinks he is pretty good with locks."

"No, no, please don't come in here," Franny begged, too frightened, too perplexed for more tears now.

"Franny, what's going on?" Miles seemed on the verge of tears himself. "Darling, I'll get a doctor, you'll be all right!"

"Miles, there's another door."

"Yes?"

"And there's someone over there. Oh, Miles, make them go away."

"Keep your head, Franny, What do they want?"

"It's a woman. She says there's a man in there who can get me out of here."

"You do want to get out, don't you, Franny?" It was as though he were speaking to someone on a window ledge.

"Not that way, I don't," said Franny. Now she was whispering through the door crack. "Miles, their voices sound familiar!"

"Now, Franny, cut it out!" scolded Miles, and Franny understood his full meaning. For a moment she listened to the other voices. From the start the man's voice had been no more than a low mumbling. He didn't want his voice recognized! The woman spoke more distinctly. Franny could hear them now discussing the problem. Presently the man said something and laughed. And the woman said, "Hush, the kid will hear you." Somehow this gave Franny courage. She stepped over to the other door and said bravely, "*Will* you help me?"

Hearing her, Miles gave a sigh of relief. Then he said. "Ask them to let me come around into their room—and help."

"Will you let my—my husband come around into your room?"

She heard them deliberating. The man was opposed. Finally, the woman said, "No. He can come and meet you outside our hall door if we get this one open."

She repeated this to Miles.

"Tell them O.K." he commanded.

"O.K.," said Franny softly.

Now the man and woman were at the door. The man was still mumbling. "Is there a latch on your side?" the woman asked.

"Yes," said Franny. "A little sort of knob."

"Tell her to turn it," the man muttered.

"Turn it," said the woman.

Franny turned it. It moved easily. "I have," she said. She watched the big doorknob revolving, but the door didn't open. There was more discussion on the other side of the door.

"It's locked with a key," said the woman to Franny. "But that's how he's going to make hisself useful." Franny's deliverer was hard at work. She couldn't tell whether it was a skeleton key or some makeshift instrument he was using. Presently, she heard the click of the lock and heard the man say, "That's got it."

"Miles!" Franny called out. But Miles didn't answer. He was already waiting at their neighbor's hall door. There was the sound of footsteps hurriedly retreating, and then the door opened. The room itself was in darkness, but in the light from the bathroom Franny could see the man's figure outlined on the bed.

The sheet was pulled up over his face. Franny looked at the woman. She was fully dressed, though barefoot, and she stood smiling at the ridiculous sight in the bed and probably at the memory of the male figure's racing across the room and jumping into the bed and pulling the sheet over his head.

"You're an angel," Franny said, without having known she was going to say it.

The woman acknowledged the compliment only by allowing the smile to fade from her lips. "He'll get up from there and try to open the other door for you in a minute," she said.

Franny gave her a grateful smile, and then she turned and walked with perfect poise toward the hall door. Her peach negligee was floor-length and its little train of lace swept gracefully along the dark carpet. When her hand was on the doorknob, she turned and said simply, "Good night." She might have been at home, turning to say a casual good night to her mother.

In the hallway, Miles had waited, fully expecting to have to carry his bride back to their room in his arms. When she appeared he was stunned by her radiance and self-possession. He had never seen her so beautiful. And Franny was equally stunned by Miles' manly beauty as he stood before her in his blue silk pajamas. For a moment they stood there beaming at one another. Finally Miles slipped his arm gently about his bride's waist and hurried her off to their room.

They found their bathroom door standing half open, and the door beyond it tightly closed. The two heavy pins still lay on the floor, but Miles quickly slipped them into the hinges. The door was now in perfect working order. Miles stood a moment gazing into the bright bathroom where Franny's clothes were heaped in one corner like a child's. "Well," he said at last, "that fellow worked fast."

"Miles," said Franny, also looking into the bathroom but with her eyes focussed on the door opposite, "did you see who it was?"

"What do you mean?"

"The woman over there—she was the woman on the elevator."

"Franny, Franny! . . . She got off at the seventh floor! How could you forget?"

"And the man—" Franny began.

"Franny, Franny, Franny," Miles interrupted, already having left her side to fetch the champagne glasses and refill them. "The man in that room is one of the conventioners from out of town. You never heard his voice or saw him before in your life."

She had been going to say that the man in the bed was Bill Carlisle. But she saw it was useless. And she knew she would never say it now. Miles came toward her slowly with the two glasses filled to the brim. They sipped their champagne, looking at one another over the glasses. In their hearts both of them were glad they had said all the things that they said through the door. As they gazed deep into each other's eyes, they believed that they had got all of that off their chests once and for all. There was nothing in the world to come between them now. They believed, really and truly, that neither of them would ever deceive or mistrust the other again. Silently they were toasting their own bliss and happiness, confident that it would never again be shadowed by the irrelevances of the different circumstances of their upbringings or by the possibly impure and selfish motives that had helped to bring them together.

D. H. Lawrence

The White Stocking

The son of a coal miner, D. H. Lawrence was born and raised in the English Midlands. Encouraged by his mother, he began to write and draw early in life and attended the Nottingham high school on scholarship. In 1908 he received a teaching certificate from University College, Nottingham, and that fall he took a position in a school near London. Writing at night and during vacations, within a year Lawrence had published his first poems and stories and completed his first novel, The White Peacock *(1910). After his mother's death in the winter of 1911, Lawrence became seriously ill, gave up teaching, and began writing his highly autobiographical novel,* Sons and Lovers.

1

"I'm getting up, Teddilinks," said Mrs. Whiston, and she sprang out of bed briskly.

"What the Hanover's got you?" asked Whiston.

"Nothing. Can't I get up?" she replied animatedly.

It was about seven o'clock, scarcely light yet in the cold bedroom. Whiston lay still and looked at his wife. She was a pretty little thing, with her fleecy, short black hair all tousled. He watched her as she dressed quickly, flicking her small, delightful limbs, throwing her clothes about her. Her slovenliness and untidiness did not trouble him. When she picked up the edge of her petticoat, ripped off a torn string of white lace, and flung it on the dressing-table, her careless abandon made his spirit glow. She stood before the mirror and roughly scrambled together her profuse little mane of hair. He watched the quickness and softness of her young shoulders, calmly, like a husband, and appreciatively.

"Rise up," she cried, turning to him with a quick wave of her arm—"and shine forth."

They had been married two years. But still, when she had gone out of the room, he felt as if all his light and warmth were taken away, he became aware of the raw, cold morning. So he rose himself, wondering casually what had roused her so early. Usually she lay in bed as late as she could.

Whiston fastened a belt round his loins and went downstairs in shirt and trousers. He heard her singing in her snatchy fashion. The stairs creaked under his weight. He passed down the narrow little passage, which she called a hall, of the seven and sixpenny house which was his first home.

He was a shapely young fellow of about twenty-eight, sleepy now and easy with well-being. He heard the water drumming into the kettle, and she began to whistle. He loved the quick way she dodged the supper cups under the tap to wash them for breakfast. She looked an untidy minx, but she was quick and handy enough.

"Teddilinks," she cried.

"What?"

"Light a fire, quick."

She wore an old, sack-like dressing-jacket of black silk pinned across her breast. But one of the sleeves, coming unfastened, showed some delightful pink upper-arm.

"Why don't you sew your sleeve up?" he said, suffering from the sight of the exposed soft flesh.

"Where?" she cried, peering round. "Nuisance," she said, seeing the gap, then with light fingers went on drying the cups.

The kitchen was of fair size, but gloomy. Whiston poked out the dead ashes.

Suddenly a thud was heard at the door down the passage.

"I'll go," cried Mrs. Whiston, and she was gone down the hall.

The postman was a ruddy-faced man who had been a soldier. He smiled broadly, handing her some packages.

"They've not forgot you," he said impudently.

"No—lucky for them," she said, with a toss of the head. But she was interested only in her envelopes this morning. The postman waited inquisitively, smiling in an ingratiating fashion. She slowly, abstractedly, as if she did not know anyone was there, closed the door in his face, continuing to look at the addresses on her letters.

She tore open the thin envelope. There was a long, hideous, cartoon valentine. She smiled briefly and dropped it on the floor. Struggling with the string of a packet, she opened a white cardboard box, and there lay a white silk handkerchief packed neatly under the paper lace of the box, and her initial worked in heliotrope, fully displayed. She smiled pleasantly, and gently put the box aside. The third envelope contained another white packet—apparently a cotton handkerchief neatly folded. She shook it out. It was a long white stocking, but there was a little weight in the toe. Quickly, she thrust down her arm, wriggling her fingers into the toe of the stocking, and brought out a small box. She peeped inside the box, then hastily opened a door on her left hand, and went into the little cold sitting-room. She had her lower lip caught earnestly between her teeth.

With a little flash of triumph, she lifted a pair of pearl earrings from the small box, and she went to the mirror. There, earnestly, she began to hook them through her ears, looking at herself sideways in the glass. Curiously concentrated and intent she seemed as she fingered the lobes of her ears, her head bent on one side.

Then the pearl earrings dangled under her rosy, smail ears. She shook her head sharply, to see the swing of the drops. They went chill against her neck, in little, sharp touches. Then she stood still to look at herself, bridling her head in the dignified fashion. Then she simpered at herself. Catching her own eye, she could not help winking at herself and laughing.

She turned to look at the box. There was a scrap of paper with this posy:

"Pearls may be fair, but thou art fairer.
Wear these for me, and I'll love the wearer."

She made a grimace and a grin. But she was drawn to the mirror again, to look at her earrings.

Whiston had made the fire burn, so he came to look for her. When she heard him, she started round quickly, guiltily. She was watching him with intent blue eyes when he appeared.

He did not see much, in his morning-drowsy warmth. He gave her, as ever, a feeling of warmth and slowness. His eyes were very blue, very kind, his manner simple.

"What ha' you got?" he asked.

"Valentines," she said briskly, ostentatiously turning to show him the silk handkerchief. She thrust it under his nose. "Smell how good," she said.

"Who's that from?" he replied, without smelling.

"It's a valentine," she cried. "How do I know who it's from?"

"I'll bet you know," he said.

"Ted!—I don't!" she cried, beginning to shake her head, then stopping because of the earrings.

He stood still a moment, displeased.

"They've no right to send you valentines now," he said.

"Ted!—Why not? You're not jealous, are you? I haven't the least idea who it's from. Look—there's my initial"—she pointed with an emphatic finger at the heliotrope embroidery——

> "E for Elsie,
> Nice little gelsie,"

she sang.

"Get out," he said. "You know who it's from."

"Truth, I don't," she cried.

He looked round, and saw the white stocking lying on a chair.

"Is this another?" he said.

"No, that's a sample," she said. "There's only a comic." And she fetched in the long cartoon.

He stretched it out and looked at it solemnly.

"Fools!" he said, and went out of the room.

She flew upstairs and took off the earrings. When she returned, he was crouched before the fire blowing the coals. The skin of his face was flushed, and slightly pitted, as if had had small-pox. But his neck was white and smooth and goodly. She hung her arms round his neck as he crouched there, and clung to him. He balanced on his toes.

"This fire's a slow-coach," he said.

"And who else is a slow-coach?" she said.

"One of us two, I know," he said, and he rose carefully. She remained clinging round his neck, so that she was lifted off her feet.

"Ha!—swing me." she cried.

He lowered his head, and she hung in the air, swinging from his neck, laughing. Then she slipped off.

"The kettle is singing," she sang, flying for the teapot. He bent down again to blow the fire. The veins in his neck stood out, his shirt collar seemed too tight.

> "Doctor Wyer,
> Blow the fire,
> Puff! puff! puff!"

she sang, laughing.

He smiled at her.

She was so glad because of her pearl earrings.

Over the breakfast she grew serious. He did not notice. She became portentous in her gravity. Almost it penetrated through his steady good-humor to irritate him.

"Teddy!" she said at last.

"What?" he asked.

"I told you a lie," she said, humbly tragic.

His soul stirred uneasily.

"Oh aye?" he said casually.

She was not satisfied. He ought to be more moved.

"Yes," she said.

He cut a piece of bread.

"Was it a good one?" he asked.

She was piqued. Then she considered—was it a good one? Then she laughed.

"No," she said, "it wasn't up to much."

"Ah!" he said easily, but with a steady strength of fondness for her in his tone. "Get it out then."

It became a little more difficult.

"You know that white stocking," she said earnestly. "I told you a lie. It wasn't a sample. It was a valentine."

A little frown came on his brow.

"Then what did you invent it as a sample for?" he said. But he knew this weakness of hers. The touch of anger in his voice frightened her.

"I was afraid you'd be cross," she said pathetically.

"I'll bet you were vastly afraid," he said.

"I *was*, Teddy."

There was a pause. He was resolving one or two things in his mind.

"And who sent it?" he asked.

"I can guess," she said, "though there wasn't a word with it—except——"

She ran to the sitting-room and returned with a slip of paper.

"Pearls may be fair, but thou art fairer.
Wear these for me, and I'll love the wearer."

He read it twice, then a dull red flush came on his face.

"And *who* do you guess it is?" he asked, with a ringing of anger in his voice.

"I suspect it's Sam Adams," she said, with a little virtuous indignation.

Whiston was silent for a moment.

"Fool!" he said. "An' what's it got to do with pearls?—and how can he say 'wear these for me' when there's only one? He hasn't got the brain to invent a proper verse."

He screwed the slip of paper into a ball and flung it into the fire.

"I suppose he thinks it'll make a pair with the one last year," she said.

"Why, did he send one then?"

"Yes. I thought you'd be wild if you knew."

His jaw set rather sullenly.

Presently he rose, and went to wash himself, rolling back his sleeves and pulling open his shirt at the breast. It was as if his fine, clear-cut temples and steady eyes were degraded by the lower, rather brutal part of his face. But she loved it. As she whisked about, clearing the table, she loved the way in which he stood washing himself. He was such a man. She liked to see his neck glistening with water as he swilled it. It amused her and pleased her and thrilled her. He was so sure, so permanent, he had her so utterly in his power. It gave her a delightful, mischievous sense of liberty. Within his grasp, she could dart about excitingly.

He turned round to her, his face red from the cold water, his eyes fresh and very blue.

"You haven't been seeing anything of him, have you?" he asked roughly.

"Yes," she answered, after a moment, as if caught guilty. "He got into the tram with me, and he asked me to drink a coffee and a Benedictine in the Royal."

"You've got it off fine and glib," he said sullenly. "And did you?"

"Yes," she replied, with the air of a traitor before the rack.

The blood came up into his neck and face, he stood motionless, dangerous.

"It was cold, and it was such fun to go into the Royal," she said.

"You'd go off with a nigger for a packet of chocolate," he said, in anger and contempt, and some bitterness. Queer how he drew away from her, cut her off from him.

"Ted—how beastly!" she cried. "You know quite well—" She caught her lip, flushed, and the tears came to her eyes.

He turned away, to put on his necktie. She went about her work, making a queer pathetic little mouth, down which occasionally dripped a tear.

He was ready to go. With his hat jammed down on his head, and his overcoat buttoned up to his chin, he came to kiss her. He would be miserable all the day if he went without. She allowed herself to be kissed. Her cheek was wet under his lip, and his heart burned. She hurt him so deeply. And she felt aggrieved, and did not quite forgive him.

In a moment she went upstairs to her earrings. Sweet they looked nestling in the little drawer—sweet! She examined them with voluptuous pleasure, she threaded them in her ears, she looked at herself, she posed and postured and smiled and looked sad and tragic and winning and appealing, all in turn before the mirrror. And she was happy, and very pretty.

She wore her earrings all morning, in the house. She was self-conscious, and quite brilliantly winsome, when the baker came, wondering if he would notice. All the tradesmen left her door with a glow in them, feeling elated, and unconsciously favoring the delightful little creature, though there had been nothing to notice in her behavior.

She was stimulated all the day. She did not think about her husband. He was the permanent basis from which she took these giddy little flights into nowhere. At night, like chickens and curses, she would come home to him, to roost.

Meanwhile Whiston, a traveller and confidential support of a small firm, hastened about his work, his heart all the while anxious for her, yearning for surety, and kept tense by not getting it.

2

She had been a warehouse girl in Adams's lace factory before she was married. Sam Adams was her employer. He was a bachelor of forty, growing stout, a man well dressed and florid, with a large brown moustache and thin hair. From the rest of his well-groomed, showy appearance, it was evident his baldness was a chagrin to him. He had a good presence, and some Irish blood in his veins.

His fondness for the girls, or the fondness of the girls for him, was notorious. And Elsie, quick, pretty, almost witty little thing—she *seemed* witty, although, when her sayings were repeated, they were entirely trivial—she had a great attraction for him. He would come into the warehouse dressed in a rather sporting reefer coat, of fawn color, and trousers of fine black-and-white check, a cap with a big peak and scarlet carnation in his button-hole, to impress her. She was only half impressed. He was too loud for her good taste. Instinctively perceiving this, he sobered down to navy blue. Then a well-built man, florid, with large brown whiskers, smart navy blue suit, fashionable boots, and manly hat, he was the irreproachable. Elsie was impressed.

But meanwhile Whiston was courting her, and she made splendid little gestures, before her bedroom mirror, of the constant-and-true sort.

"True, true till death——"

That was her song. Whiston was made that way, so there was no need to take thought for him.

Every Christmas Sam Adams gave a party at his house, to which he invited his superior work-people—not factory hands and laborers, but those above. He was a generous man in his way, with a real warm feeling for giving pleasure.

Two years ago Elsie had attended this Christmas-party for the last time. Whiston had accompanied her. At that time he worked for Sam Adams.

She had been very proud of herself, in her close-fitting, full-skirted dress of blue silk. Whiston called for her. Then she tripped beside him, holding her large cashmere shawl across her breast. He strode with long strides, his trousers handsomely strapped under his boots, and her silk shoes bulging the pocket of his full-skirted overcoat.

They passed through the park gates, and her spirits rose. Above them the

Castle Rock loomed grandly in the night, the naked trees stood still and dark in the frost, along the boulevard.

They were rather late. Agitated with anticipation, in the cloak-room she gave up her shawl, donned her silk shoes, and looked at herself in the mirror. The loose bunches of curls on either side her face danced prettily, her mouth smiled.

She hung a moment in the door of the brilliantly lighted room. Many people were moving within the blaze of lamps, under the crystal chandeliers, the full skirts of women balancing and floating, the side-whiskers and white cravats of the men bowing above. Then she entered the light.

In an instant Sam Adams was coming forward, lifting both his arms in boisterous welcome. There was a constant red laugh on his face.

"Come late, would you," he shouted, "like royalty."

He seized her hands and led her forward. He opened his mouth wide when he spoke, and the effect of the warm, dark opening behind the brown whiskers was disturbing. But she was floating into the throng on his arm. He was very gallant.

"Now then," he said, taking her card to write down the dances, "I've got *carte blanche,* haven't I?"

"Mr. Whiston doesn't dance," she said.

"I am a lucky man!" he said, scribbling his initials. "I was born with an *amourette* in my mouth."

He wrote on, quietly. She blushed and laughed, not knowing what it meant.

"Why, what is that?" she said.

"It's you, even littler than you are, dressed in little wings," he said.

"I should have to be pretty small to get in your mouth," she said.

"You think you're too big, do you!" he said easily.

He handed her her card, with a bow.

"Now I'm set up, my darling, for this evening," he said.

Then, quick, always at his ease, he looked over the room. She waited in front of him. He was ready. Catching the eye of the band, he nodded. In a moment, the music began. He seemed to relax, giving himself up.

"Now then, Elsie," he said, with a curious caress in his voice that seemed to lap the outside of her body in a warm glow, delicious. She gave herself to it. She liked it.

He was an excellent dancer. He seemed to draw her close in to him by some male warmth of attraction, so that she became all soft and pliant to him, flowing to his form, whilst he united her with him and they lapsed along in one movement. She was just carried in a kind of strong, warm flood, her feet moved of themselves, and only the music threw her away from him, threw her back to him, to his clasp, in his strong form moving against her, rhythmically, deliciously.

When it was over, he was pleased and his eyes had a curious gleam which thrilled her and yet had nothing to do with her. Yet it held her. He did not speak to her. He only looked straight into her eyes with a curious, gleaming look that disturbed her fearfully and deliciously. But also there was in his look some of the automatic irony of the *roué*. It left her partly cold. She was not carried away.

She went, driven by an opposite, heavier impulse, to Whiston. He stood looking gloomy, trying to admit that she had a perfect right to enjoy herself apart from him. He received her with rather grudging kindliness.

"Aren't you going to play whist?" she asked.

"Aye," he said. "Directly."

"I do wish you could dance."

"Well, I can't," he said. "So you enjoy yourself."

"But I should enjoy it better if I could dance with you."

"Nay, you're all right," he said. "I'm not made that way."

"Then you ought to be!" she cried.

"Well, it's my fault, not yours. You enjoy yourself," he bade her. Which she proceeded to do, a little bit irked.

She went with anticipation to the arms of Sam Adams, when the time came to dance with him. It *was* so gratifying, irrespective of the man. And she felt a little grudge against Whiston, soon forgotten when her host was holding her near to him, in a delicious embrace. And she watched his eyes, to meet the gleam in them, which gratified her.

She was getting warmed right through, the glow was penetrating into her, driving away everything else. Only in her heart was a little tightness, like conscience.

When she got a chance, she escaped from the dancing-room to the card-room. There in a cloud of smoke, she found Whiston playing cribbage. Radiant, roused, animated, she came up to him and greeted him. She was too strong, too vibrant a note in the quiet room. He lifted his head, and a frown knitted his gloomy forehead.

"Are you playing cribbage? Is it exciting? How are you getting on?" she chattered.

He looked at her. None of these questions needed answering, and he did not feel in touch with her. She turned to the cribbage-board.

"Are you white or red?" she asked.

"He's red," replied the partner.

"Then you're losing," she said, still to Whiston. And she lifted the red peg from the board. "One—two—three—four—five—six—seven—eight—— Right up there you ought to jump——"

"Now put it back in its right place," said Whiston.

"Where was it?" she asked gaily, knowing her transgression. He took the little red peg away from her and stuck it in its hole.

The cards were shuffled.

"What a shame you're losing," said Elsie.

"You'd better cut for him," said the partner.

She did so hastily. The cards were dealt. She put her hand on his shoulder, looking at his cards.

"It's good," she cried, "isn't it?"

He did not answer, but threw down two cards. It moved him more strongly than was comfortable, to have her hand on his shoulder, her curls dangling and touching his ears, whilst she was roused to another man. It made the blood flame over him.

At that moment Sam Adams appeared, florid and boisterous, intoxicated more with himself, with the dancing, than with wine. In his eye the curious, impersonal light gleamed.

"I thought I should find you here, Elsie," he cried boisterously, a disturbing, high note in his voice.

"What made you think so?" she replied, the mischief rousing in her.

The florid, well-built man narrowed his eyes to a smile.

"I should never look for you among the ladies," he said, with a kind of intimate, animal call to her. He laughed, bowed, and offered her his arm.

"Madam, the music waits."

She went almost helplessly, carried along with him, unwilling, yet delighted.

That dance was an intoxication to her. After the first few steps, she felt herself slipping away from herself. She almost knew she was going, she did not even want to go. Yet she must have chosen to go. She lay in the arm of the steady, close man with whom she was dancing, and she seemed to swim away out of contact with the room, into him. She had passed into another, denser element of him, an essential privacy. The room was all vague around her, like an atmosphere, like under sea, with a flow of ghostly, dumb movements. But she herself was held real against her partner, and it seemed she was connected with him, as if the movements of his body and limbs were her own movements, yet not her own movements—and oh, delicious! He also was given up, oblivious, concentrated, into the dance. His eye was unseeing. Only his large, voluptuous body gave off a subtle activity. His fingers seemed to search into her flesh. Every moment, and every moment, she felt she would give way utterly, and sink molten: the fusion point was coming when she would fuse down into perfect unconsciousness at his feet and knees. But he bore her round the room in the dance, and he seemed to sustain all her body with his limbs, his body, and his warmth seemed to come closer into her, nearer, till it would fuse right through her, and she would be as liquid to him as an intoxication only.

It was exquisite. When it was over, she was dazed, and was scarcely breathing. She stood with him in the middle of the room as if she were alone in a remote place. He bent over her. She expected his lips on her bare shoulder, and waited. Yet they were not alone, they were not alone. It was cruel.

" 'Twas good, wasn't it, my darling?" he said to her, low and delighted. There was a strange impersonality about his low, exultant call that appealed to her irresistably. Yet why was she aware of some part shut off in her? She pressed his arm, and he led her towards the door.

She was not aware of what she was doing, only a little grain of resistant trouble was in her. The man, possessed, yet with a superficial presence of mind, made way to the dining-room, as if to give her refreshment, cunningly working his own escape with her. He was molten hot, filmed over with presence of mind, and bottomed with cold disbelief. In the dining-room was Whiston, carrying coffee to the plain, neglected ladies. Elsie saw him, but felt as if he could not see her. She was beyond his reach and ken. A sort of fusion existed between her and the large man at her side. She ate her custard, but an incomplete fusion all the while sustained and contained within the being of her employer.

But she was growing cooler. Whiston came up. She looked at him, and saw him with different eyes. She saw his slim, young man's figure real and enduring before her. That was he. But she was in the spell with the other man, fused with him, and she could not be taken away.

"Have you finished your cribbage?" she asked, with hasty evasion of him.

"Yes," he replied. "Aren't you getting tired of dancing?"

"Not a bit," she said.

"Not she," said Adams heartily. "No girl with any spirit gets tired of dancing. Have something else, Elsie. Come—sherry. Have a glass of sherry with us, Whiston."

Whilst they sipped the wine, Adams watched Whiston almost cunningly, to find his advantage.

"We'd better be getting back—there's the music," he said. "See the women get something to eat, Whiston, will you, there's a good chap."

And he began to draw away. Elsie was drifting helplessly with him. But Whiston put himself beside them, and went along with them. In silence they passed through to the dancing-room. There Adams hesitated, and looked round the room. It was as if he could not see.

A man came hurrying forward, claiming Elsie, and Adams went to his other partner. Whiston stood watching during the dance. She was conscious of him standing there observant of her, like a ghost, or a judgment, or a guardian angel. She was also conscious, much more intimately and impersonally, of the body of the other man moving somewhere in the room. She still belonged to him, but a feeling of distraction possessed her, and helplessness. Adams danced on, adhering to Elsie, waiting his time, with the persistence of cynicism.

The dance was over. Adams was detained. Elsie found herself beside Whiston. There was something shapely about him as he sat, about his knees and his distinct figure, that she clung to. It was as if he had enduring form. She put her hand on his knee.

"Are you enjoying yourself?" he asked.

"*Ever* so," she replied, with a fervent, yet detached tone.

"It's going on for one o'clock," he said.
"Is it?" she answered. It meant nothing to her.
"Should we be going?" he said.

She was silent. For the first time for an hour or more an inkling of her normal consciousness returned. She resented it.

"What for?" she said.
"I thought you might have had enough," he said.

A slight soberness came over her, an irritation at being frustrated of her illusion.

"Why?" she said.
"We've been here since nine," he said.

That was no answer, no reason. It conveyed nothing to her. She sat detached from him. Across the room Sam Adams glanced at her. She sat there exposed for him.

"You don't want to be too free with Sam Adams," said Whiston cautiously, suffering. "You know what he is."

"How free?" she asked.
"Why—you don't want to have too much to do with him."

She sat silent. He was forcing her into consciousness of her position. But he could not get hold of her feelings, to change them. She had a curious, perverse desire that he should not.

"I like him," she said.
"What do you find to like in him?" he said, with a hot heart.
"I don't know—but I like him," she said.

She was immutable. He sat feeling heavy and dulled with rage. He was not clear as to what he felt. He sat there unliving whilst she danced. And she, distracted, lost to herself between the opposing forces of the two men, drifted. Between the dances, Whiston kept near to her. She was scarcely conscious. She glanced repeatedly at her card, to see then she would dance again with Adams, half in desire, half in dread. Sometimes she met his steady, glaucous eye as she passed him in the dance. Sometimes she saw the steadiness of his flank as he danced. And it was always as if she rested on his arm, were borne along, up-borne by him, away from herself. And always there was present the other's antagonism. She was divided.

The time came for her to dance with Adams. Oh, the delicious closing of contact with him, of his limbs touching her limbs, his arm supporting her. She seemed to resolve. Whiston had not made himself real to her. He was only a heavy place in her consciousness.

But she breathed heavily, beginning to suffer from the closeness of strain. She was nervous. Adams also was constrained. A tightness, a tension was coming over them all. And he was exasperated, feeling something counteracting physical magnetism, feeling a will stronger with her than his own, intervening in what was becoming a vital necessity to him.

Elsie was almost lost to her own control. As she went forward with him to take her place at the dance, she stooped for her pocket handkerchief. The music sounded for quadrilles. Everybody was ready. Adams stood with his body near her, exerting his attraction over her. He was tense and fighting. She stooped for her pocket handkerchief, and shook it as she rose. It shook out and fell from her hand. With agony, she saw she had taken a white stocking instead of a handkerchief. For a second it lay on the floor, a twist of white stocking. Then, in an instant, Adams picked it up, with a little, surprised laugh of triumph.

"That'll do for me," he whispered—seeming to take possession of her. And he stuffed the stocking in his trousers pocket, and quickly offered her his handkerchief.

The dance began. She felt weak and faint, as if her will were turned to water. A heavy sense of loss came over her. She could not help herself any more. But it was peace.

When the dance was over, Adams yielded her up. Whiston came to her.

"What was it as you dropped?" Whiston asked.

"I thought it was my handkerchief—I'd taken a stocking by mistake," she said, detached and muted.

"And he's got it?"

"Yes."

"What does he mean by that?"

She lifted her shoulders.

"Are you going to let him keep it?" he asked.

"I don't let him."

There was a long pause.

"Am I to go and have it out with him?" he asked, his face flushed, his blue eyes going hard with opposition.

"No," she said, pale.

"Why?"

"No—I don't want you to say anything about it."

He sat exasperated and nonplussed.

"You'll let him keep it, then?" he asked.

She sat silent and made no form of answer.

"What do you mean by it?" he said, dark with fury. And he started up.

"No!" she cried. "Ted!" And she caught hold of him, sharply detaining him.

It made him black with rage.

"Why?" he said.

The something about her mouth was pitiful to him. He did not understand, but he felt she must have her reasons.

"Then I'm not stopping here," he said. "Are you coming with me?"

She rose mutely, and they went out of the room. Adams had not noticed. In a few moments they were in the street.

"What the hell do you mean?" he said, in a black fury.

She went at his side, in silence, neutral.

"That great hog, an' all," he added.

Then they went a long time in silence through the frozen, deserted darkness of the town. She felt she could not go indoors. They were drawing near her house.

"I don't want to go home," she suddenly cried in distress and anguish. "I don't want to go home."

He looked at her.

"Why don't you?" he said.

"I don't want to go home," was all she could sob.

He heard somebody coming.

"Well, we can walk a bit farther," he said.

She was silent again. They passed out of the town into the fields. He held her by the arm—they could not speak.

"What's a-matter?" he asked at length, puzzled.

She began to cry again.

At last he took her in his arms, to soothe her. She sobbed by herself, almost unaware of him.

"Tell me what's a-matter, Elsie," he said. "Tell me what's a-matter—my dear—tell me, then——"

He kissed her wet face, and caressed her. She made no response. He was puzzled and tender and miserable.

At length she became quiet. Then he kissed her, and she put her arms round him, and clung to him very tight, as if for fear and anguish. He held her in his arms, wondering.

"Ted!" she whispered, frantic. "Ted!"

"What, my love?" he answered, becoming also afraid.

"Be good to me," she cried. "Don't be cruel to me."

"No, my pet," he said, amazed and grieved. "Why?"

"Oh, be good to me," she sobbed.

And he held her very safe, and his heart was white-hot with love for her. His mind was amazed. He could only hold her against his chest that was white-hot with love and belief in her. So she was restored at last.

3

She refused to go to her work at Adams's any more. Her father had to submit and she sent in her notice—she was not well. Sam Adams was ironical. But he had a curious patience. He did not fight.

In a few weeks, she and Whiston were married. She loved him with passion and worship, a fierce little abandon of love that moved him to the depths of his being, and gave him a permanent surety and sense of realness in himself. He did not trouble about himself any more: he felt he was fulfilled and now he had only the many things in the world to busy himself about. Whatever troubled him, at the bottom was surety. He had found himself in this love.

They spoke once or twice of the white stocking.

"Ah!" Whiston exclaimed. "What does it matter?"

He was impatient and angry, and could not bear to consider the matter. So it was left unresolved.

She was quite happy at first, carried away by her adoration of her husband. Then gradually she got used to him. He always was the ground of her happiness, but she got used to him, as to the air she breathed. He never got used to her in the same way.

Inside of marriage she found her liberty. She was rid of the responsibility of herself. Her husband must look after that. She was free to get what she could out of her time.

So that, when, after some months, she met Sam Adams, she was not quite as unkind to him as she might have been. With a young wife's new and exciting knowledge of men, she perceived he was in love with her, she knew he had always kept an unsatisfied desire for her. And, sportive, she could not help playing a little with this, though she cared not one jot for the man himself.

When Valentine's day came, which was near the first anniversary of her wedding day, there arrived a white stocking with a little amethyst brooch. Luckily Whiston did not see it, so she said nothing of it to him. She had not the faintest intention of having anything to do with Sam Adams, but once a little brooch was in her possession, it was hers, and she did not trouble her head for a moment how she had come by it. She kept it.

Now she had the pearl earrings. They were a more valuable and a more conspicuous present. She would have to ask her mother to give them to her, to explain their presence. She made a little plan in her head. And she was extraordinarily pleased. As for Sam Adams, even if he saw her wearing them, he would not give her away. What fun, if he saw her wearing his earrings! She would pretend she had inherited them from her grandmother, her mother's mother. She laughed to herself as she went down-town in the afternoon, the pretty drops dangling in front of her curls. But she saw no one of importance.

Whiston came home tired and depressed. All day the male in him had been uneasy, and this had fatigued him. She was curiously against him, inclined, as she sometimes was nowadays, to make mock of him and jeer at him and cut him off. He did not understand this, and it angered him deeply. She was uneasy before him.

She knew he was in a state of suppressed irritation. The veins stood out on the backs of his hands, his brow was drawn stiffly. Yet she could not help goading him.

"What did you do wi' that white stocking?" he asked, out of a gloomy silence, his voice strong and brutal.

"I put it in a drawer—why?" she replied flippantly.

"Why didn't you put it on the fire-back?" he said harshly. "What are you hoarding it up for?"

"I'm not hoarding it up," she said. "I've got a pair."

He relapsed into gloomy silence. She, unable to move him, ran away upstairs, leaving him smoking by the fire. Again she tried on the earrings. Then another little inspiration came to her. She drew on the white stockings, both of them.

Presently she came down in them. Her husband still sat immovable and glowering by the fire.

"Look!" she said. "They'll do beautifully."

And she picked up her skirts to her knees, and twisted round, looking at her pretty legs in the neat stockings.

He filled with unreasonable rage, and took the pipe from his mouth.

"Don't they look nice?" she said. "One from last year and one from this, they just do. Save you buying a pair."

And she looked over her shoulders at her pretty calves, and at the dangling frills of her knickers.

"Put your skirts down and don't make a fool of yourself," he said.

"Why a fool of myself?" she asked.

And she began to dance slowly round the room, kicking up her feet half reckless, half jeering, in ballet-dancer's fashion. Almost fearful, yet in defiance, she kicked up her legs at him, singing as she did so. She resented him.

"You little fool, ha' done with it," he said. "And you'll backfire them stockings, I'm telling you." He was angry. His face flushed dark, he kept his head bent. She ceased to dance.

"I shan't," she said. "They'll come in very useful."

He lifted his head and watched her, with lighted, dangerous eyes.

"You'll put 'em on the fire-back, I tell you," he said.

It was a war now. She bent forward, in a ballet-dancer's fashion, and put her tongue between her teeth.

"I shan't back-fire them stockings," she sang, repeating his words, "I shan't, I shan't, I shan't."

And she danced round the room doing a high kick to the tune of her words. There was a real biting indifference in her behavior.

"We'll see whether you will or not," he said, "Trollops! You'd like Sam Adams to know you was wearing 'em, wouldn't you? That's what would please you."

"Yes, I'd like him to see how nicely they fit me, he might give me some more then."

And she looked down at her pretty legs.

He knew somehow that she *would* like Sam Adams to see how pretty her legs looked in the white stockings. It made his anger go deep, almost to hatred.

"Yer nasty trolley," he cried. "Put yer petticoats down, and stop being so foul-minded."

"I'm not foul-minded," she said. "My legs are my own. And why shouldn't Sam Adams think they're nice?"

There was a pause. He watched her with eyes glittering to a point.

"Have you been havin' owt to do with him?" he asked.

"I've just spoken to him when I've seen him," she said. "He's not as bad as you would make out."

"Isn't he?" he cried, a certain wakefulness in his voice. "Them who has anything to do wi' him is too bad for me, I tell you."

"Why, what are you frightened of him for?" she mocked.

She was rousing all his uncontrollable anger. He sat glowering. Every one of her sentences stirred him up like a red-hot iron. Soon it would be too much. And she was afraid herself; but she was neither conquered nor convinced.

A curious little grin of hate came on his face. He had a long score against her.

"What am I frightened of him for?" he repeated automatically. "What am I frightened of him for? Why, for you, you stray-running little bitch."

She flushed. The insult went deep into her, right home.

"Well, if you're so dull——" she said, lowering her eyelids, and speaking coldly, haughtily.

"If I'm so dull I'll break your neck the first word you speak of him," he said, tense.

"Pf!" she sneered. "Do you think I'm frightened of you?" She spoke coldly, detached.

She was frightened, for all that, white round the mouth.

His heart was getting hotter.

"You *will* be frightened of me, the next time you have anything to do with him," he said.

"Do you think *you'd* ever be told—ha!"

Her jeering scorn made him go white-hot, molten. He knew he was incoherent, scarcely responsible for what he might do. Slowly, unseeing, he rose and went out of doors, stifled, moved to kill her.

He stood leaning against the garden fence, unable either to see or hear. Below him, far off, fumed the lights of the town. He stood still, unconscious with a black storm of rage, his face lifted to the night.

Presently, still unconscious of what he was doing, he went indoors again. She stood, a small, stubborn figure with tight-pressed lips and big, sullen, childish eyes, watching him, white with fear. He went heavily across the floor and dropped into his chair.

There was a silence.

"*You're* not going to tell me everything I shall do, and everything I shan't," she broke out at last.

He lifted his head.

"I tell you *this*," he said, low and intense. "Have anything to do with Sam Adams, and I'll break your neck."

She laughed, shrill and false.

"How I hate your word 'break you neck,' " she said, with a grimace of the mouth. "It sounds so common and beastly. Can't you say something else—"

There was a dead silence.

"And besides," she said, with a queer chirrup of mocking laughter, "what do you know about anything? He sent me an amethyst brooch and a pair of pearl earrings."

"He what?" said Whiston, in a suddenly normal voice. His eyes were fixed on her.

"Sent me a pair of pearl earrings, and an amethyst brooch," she repeated, mechanically, pale to the lips.

And her big, black, childish eyes watched him, fascinated, held in her spell.

He seemed to thrust his face and his eyes forward at her, as he rose slowly and came to her. She watched transfixed in terror. Her throat made a small sound, as she tried to scream.

Then, quick as lightning, the back of his hand struck her with a crash across the mouth, and she was flung back blinded against the wall. The shock shook a queer sound out of her. And then she saw him still coming on, his eyes holding her, his fist drawn back, advancing slowly. At any instant the blow might crash into her.

Mad with terror, she raised her hands with a queer clawing movement to cover her eyes and her temples, opening her mouth in a dumb shriek. There was no sound. But the sight of her slowly arrested him. He hung before her, looking at her fixedly, as she stood crouched against the wall with open, bleeding mouth, and wide-staring eyes, and two hands clawing over her temples. And his lust to see her bleed, to break her and destroy her, rose from an old source against her. It carried him. He wanted satisfaction.

But he had seen her standing there, a piteous, horrified thing, and he turned his face aside in shame and nausea. He went and sat heavily in his chair, and a curious ease, almost like sleep, came over his brain.

She walked away from the wall towards the fire, dizzy, white to the lips, mechanically wiping her small, bleeding mouth. He sat motionless. Then, gradually, her breath began to hiss, she shook, and was sobbing silently, in grief for herself. Without looking, he saw. It made his mad desire to destroy her come back.

At length he lifted his head. His eyes were glowing again, fixed on her.

"And what did he give them you for?" he asked, in a steady, unyielding voice.

Her crying dried up in a second. She also was tense.

"They came as valentines," she replied, still not subjugated, even if beaten.

"When, today?"

"The pearl earrings today—the amethyst brooch last year."

"You've had it a year?"

"Yes."

She felt that now nothing would prevent him if he rose to kill her. She could not prevent him any more. She was yielded up to him. They both trembled in the balance, unconscious.

"What have you had to do with him?" he asked, in a barren voice.

"I've not had anything to do with him," she quavered.

"You just kept 'em because they were jewelry?" he said.

A weariness came over him. What was the worth of speaking any more of it? He did not care any more. He was dreary and sick.

She began to cry again, but he took no notice. She kept wiping her mouth on her handkerchief. He could see it, the blood-mark. It made him only more sick and tired of the responsibility of it, the violence, the shame.

When she began to move about again, he raised his head once more from his dead, motionless position.

"Where are the things?" he said.

"They are upstairs," she quavered. She knew the passion had gone down in him.

"Bring them down," he said.

"I won't," she wept, with rage. "You're not going to bully me and hit me like that on the mouth."

And she sobbed again. He looked at her in contempt and compassion and in rising anger.

"Where are they?" he said.

"They're in the little drawer under the looking-glass," she sobbed.

He went slowly upstairs, struck a match, and found the trinkets. He brought them downstairs in his hand.

"These?" he said, looking at them as they lay in his palm.

She looked at them without answering. She was not interested in them any more.

He looked at the little jewels. They were pretty.

"It's none of their fault," he said to himself.

And he searched round slowly, persistently, for a box. He tied the things up and addressed them to Sam Adams. Then he went out in his slippers to post the little package.

When he came back she was still sitting crying.

"You'd better go to bed," he said.

She paid no attention. He sat by the fire. She still cried.

"I'm sleeping down here," he said. "Go you to bed."

In a few moments she lifted her tear-stained, swollen face and looked at him with eyes all forlorn and pathetic. A great flash of anguish went over his body. He went over, slowly, and very gently took her in his hands. She let herself be taken. Then as she lay against his shoulder, she sobbed aloud:

"I never meant——"

"My love—my little love——" he cried, in anguish of spirit, holding her in his arms.

Katherine Anne Porter

Rope

Katherine Anne Porter was born in Texas and educated at Southern girls' schools. Though she lived mainly in New York during the 1920's and thirties, she spent a great deal of time in Mexico and Europe and used a voyage she took from Veracruz to Bremerhaven in 1931 as the scene of her only full-length novel, Ship of Fools *(1962). Known primarily for the immense craftsmanship of her short stories and novellas—especially* Noon Wine *(1937) and* Pale Horse, Pale Rider *(1939)—Katherine Anne Porter has long been considered one of America's finest writers. In 1966 she won both a Pulitzer Prize and National Book Award for her* Collected Short Stories.

On the third day after they moved to the country he came walking back from the village carrying a basket of groceries and a twenty-four-yard coil of rope. She came out to meet him, wiping her hands on her green smock. Her hair was tumbled, her nose was scarlet with sunburn; he told her that already she looked like a born country woman. His gray flannel shirt stuck to him, his heavy shoes were dusty. She assured him he looked like a rural character in a play.

Had he brought the coffee? She had been waiting all day long for coffee. They had forgot it when they ordered at the store the first day.

Gosh, no, he hadn't. Lord, now he'd have to go back. Yes, he would if it killed him. He thought, though, he had everything else. She reminded him it was only because he didn't drink coffee himself. If he did he would remember it quick enough. Suppose they ran out of cigarettes? Then she saw the rope. What was that for? Well, he thought it might do to hang clothes on, or something. Naturally she asked him if he thought they were going to run a laundry? They already had a fifty-foot line hanging right before his eyes? Why, hadn't he noticed it, really? It was a blot on the landscape to her.

He thought there were a lot of things a rope might come in handy for. She wanted to know what, for instance. He thought a few seconds, but nothing occurred. They could wait and see, couldn't they? You need all sorts of strange odds and ends around a place in the country. She said, yes, that was so; but she thought just at that time when every penny counted, it seemed funny to buy more rope. That was all. She hadn't meant anything else. She hadn't just seen, not at first, why he felt it was necessary.

Well, thunder, he had bought it because he wanted to, and that was all there was to it. She thought that was reason enough, and couldn't understand why he hadn't said so, at first. Undoubtedly it would be useful, twenty-four yards of rope, there were hundreds of things, she couldn't think of any at the moment, but it would come in handy. Of course. As he had said, things always did in the country.

But she was a little disappointed about the coffee, and oh, look, look, look at the eggs! Oh, my, they're all running! What had he put on top of them? Hadn't he known eggs mustn't be squeezed? Squeezed, who had squeezed them, he wanted to know. What a silly thing to say. He had simply brought them along in the basket with the other things. If they got broke it was the grocer's fault. He should know better than to put heavy things on top of eggs.

She believed it was the rope. That was the heaviest thing in the pack, she saw him plainly when he came in from the road, the rope was a big package on top of everything. He desired the whole wide world to witness that this was not a fact. He had carried the rope in one hand and the basket in the other, and what was the use of her having eyes, if that was the best they could do for her?

Well, anyhow, she could see one thing plain: no eggs for breakfast. They'd have to scramble them now, for supper. It was too damned bad. She had planned to have steak for supper. No ice, meat wouldn't keep. He wanted to know why she couldn't finish breaking the eggs in a bowl and set them in a cool place.

Cool place! if he could find one for her, she'd be glad to set them there. Well, then, it seemed to him they might very well cook the meat at the same time they cooked the eggs and then warm up the meat for tomorrow. The idea simply choked her. Warmed-over meat, when they might as well have had it fresh. Second best and scraps and makeshifts, even to the meat! He rubbed her shoulder a little. It doesn't really matter so much, does it, darling? Sometimes when they were playful, he would rub her shoulder and she would arch and purr. This time she hissed and almost clawed. He was getting ready to say that they could surely manage somehow when she turned on him and said, if he told her they could manage somehow she would certainly slap his face.

He swallowed the words red hot, his face burned. He picked up the rope and started to put it on the top shelf. She would not have it on the top shelf, the jars and tins belonged there; positively she would not have the top shelf cluttered up with a lot of rope. She had borne all the clutter she meant to bear in the flat in town, there was space here at least and she meant to keep things in order.

Well, in that case, he wanted to know what the hammer and nails were doing up there? And why had she put them there when she knew very well he needed the hammer and those nails upstairs to fix the window sashes? She simply slowed down everything and made double the work on the place with her insane habit of changing things around and hiding them.

She was sure she begged his pardon, and if she had had any reason to believe he was going to fix the sashes this summer she would have left the hammer and nails right where he put them; in the middle of the bedroom floor where they could step on them in the dark. And now if he didn't clear the whole mess out of there she would throw them down the well.

Oh, all right, all right—could he put them in the closet? Naturally not, there were brooms and mops and dustpans in the closet, and why couldn't he find a place for his rope outside her kitchen? Had he stopped to consider there were seven God-forsaken rooms in the house, and only one kitchen?

He wanted to know what of it? And did she realize she was making a complete fool of herself? And what did she take him for, a three-year-old idiot? The whole trouble with her was she needed something weaker than she was to heckle and tyrannize over. He wished to God now they had a couple of children she could take it out on. Maybe he'd get some rest.

Her face changed at this, she reminded him he had forgot the coffee and had bought a worthless piece of rope. And when she thought of all the things they actually needed to make the place even decently fit to live in, well, she could cry, that was all. She looked so forlorn, so lost and despairing he couldn't believe it was only a piece of rope that was causing all the racket. What *was* the matter, for God's sake?

Oh, would he please hush and go away, and *stay* away, if he could, for five minutes? By all means, yes, he would. He'd stay away indefinitely if she wished. Lord, yes, there was nothing he'd like better than to clear out and never come back. She couldn't for the life of her see what was holding him, then. It was a swell time. Here she was, stuck, miles from a railroad, with a half-empty house on her hands, and not a penny in her pocket, and everything on earth to do; it seemed the God-sent moment for him to get out from under. She was surprised he hadn't stayed in town as it was until she had come out and done the work and got things straightened out. It was his usual trick.

It appeared to him that this was going a little far. Just a touch out of bounds, if she didn't mind his saying so. Why the hell had he stayed in town the summer before? To do a half-dozen extra jobs to get the money he had sent her. That was it. She knew perfectly well they couldn't have done it otherwise. She had agreed with him at the time. And that was the only time so help him he had ever left her to do anything by herself.

Oh, he could tell that to his great-grandmother. She had her notion of what had kept him in town. Considerably more than a notion, if he wanted to know. So, she was going to bring all that up again, was she? Well, she could just think what she pleased. He was tired of explaining. It may have looked funny but he had simply got hooked in, and what could he do? It was impossible to believe that she was going to take it seriously. Yes, yes, she knew how it was with a man: if he was left by himself a minute, some woman was certain to kidnap him. And naturally he couldn't hurt her feelings by refusing!

Well, what was she raving about? Did she forget she had told him those two weeks alone in the country were the happiest she had known for four years? And how long had they been married when she said that? All right, shut up! If she thought that hadn't stuck in his craw.

She hadn't meant she was happy because she was away from him. She meant she was happy getting the devilish house nice and ready for him. That was what she had meant, and now look! Bringing up something she had said a year ago simply to justify himself for forgetting her coffee and breaking the eggs and buying a wretched piece of rope they couldn't afford. She really thought it was time to drop the subject, and now she wanted only two things in the world. She wanted him to get that rope from underfoot, and go back to the village and get her coffee, and if he could remember it, he might bring a metal mitt for the skillets, and two more curtain rods, and if there were any rubber gloves in the village, her hands were simply raw, and a bottle of milk of magnesia from the drugstore.

He looked out at the dark blue afternoon sweltering on the slopes, and mopped his forehead and sighed heavily and said, if only she could wait a minute for *anything*, he was going back. He had said so, hadn't he, the very instant they found he had overlooked it?

Oh, yes, well ... run along. She was going to wash windows. The country was so beautiful! She doubted they'd have a moment to enjoy it. He meant to go, but he could not until he had said that if she wasn't such a hopeless melancholiac she might see that this was only for a few days. Couldn't she remember anything pleasant about the other summers? Hadn't they ever had any fun? She hadn't time to talk about it, and now would he please not leave that rope lying around for her to trip on? He picked it up, somehow it had toppled off the table, and walked out with it under his arm.

Was he going this minute? He certainly was. She thought so. Sometimes it seemed to her he had second sight about the precisely perfect moment to leave her ditched. She had meant to put the mattresses out to sun, if they put them out this minute they would get at least three hours, he must have heard her say that morning she meant to put them out. So of course he would walk off and leave her to it. She supposed he thought the exercise would do her good.

Well, he was merely going to get her coffee. A four-mile walk for two pounds of coffee was ridiculous, but he was perfectly willing to do it. The habit was making a wreck of her, but if she wanted to wreck herself there was nothing he could do about it. If he thought it was coffee that was making a wreck of her, she congratulated him: he must have a damned easy conscience.

Conscience or no conscience, he didn't see why the mattresses couldn't very well wait until tomorrow. And anyhow, for God's sake, were they living *in* the house, or were they going to let the house ride them to death? She paled at this, her face grew livid about the mouth, she looked quite dangerous, and reminded him that housekeeping was no more her work than it was his: she had other work to do as well, and when did he think she was going to find time to do it at this rate?

Was she going to start on that again? She knew as well as he did that his work brought in the regular money, hers was only occasional, if they depended on what *she* made—and she might as well get straight on this question once for all!

That was positively not the point. The question was, when both of them were working on their own time, was there going to be a division of the housework, or wasn't there? She merely wanted to know, she had to make her plans. Why, he thought that was all arranged. It was understood that he was to help. Hadn't he always, in summers?

Hadn't he, though? Oh, just hadn't he? And when, and where, and doing what? Lord, what an uproarious joke!

It was such a very uproarious joke that her face turned slightly purple, and she screamed with laughter. She laughed so hard she had to sit down, and finally a rush of tears spurted from her eyes and poured down into the lifted corners of her mouth. He dashed towards her and dragged her up to her feet and tried to pour water on her head. The dipper hung by a string on a nail and he broke it loose. Then he tried to pump water with one hand while she struggled in the other. So he gave it up and shook her instead.

She wrenched away, crying out for him to take his rope and go to hell, she had simply given him up: and ran. He heard her high-heeled bedroom slippers clattering and stumbling on the stairs.

He went out around the house and into the lane; he suddenly realized he had a blister on his heel and his shirt felt as if it were on fire. Things broke so suddenly you didn't know where you were. She could work herself into a fury about simply nothing. She was terrible, damn it: not an ounce of reason. You might as well talk to a sieve as that woman when she got going. Damned if he'd spend his life humoring her! Well, what to do now? He would take back the rope and exchange it for something else. Things accumulated, things were mountainous, you couldn't move them or sort them out or get rid of them. They just lay and rotted around. He'd take it back. Hell, why should he? He wanted it. What was it anyhow? A piece of rope. Imagine anybody caring more about a piece of rope than about a man's feelings. What earthly right had she to say a word about it? He remembered all the useless, meaningless things she bought for herself: Why? because I wanted it, that's why! He stopped and selected a large stone by the road. He would put the rope behind it. He would put it in the tool-box when he got back. He'd heard enough about it to last him a life-time.

When he came back she was leaning against the post box beside the road waiting. It was pretty late, the smell of broiled steak floated nose high in the cooling air. Her face was young and smooth and fresh-looking. Her unmanageable funny black hair was all on end. She waved to him from a distance, and he speeded up. She called out that supper was ready and waiting, was he starved?

You bet he was starved. Here was the coffee. He waved it at her. She looked at his other hand. What was that he had there?

Well, it was the rope again. He stopped short. He had meant to exchange it but forgot. She wanted to know why he should exchange it, if it was something he really wanted. Wasn't the air sweet now, and wasn't it fine to be here?

She walked beside him with one hand hooked into his leather belt. She pulled and jostled him a little as he walked, and leaned against him. He put his arm clear around her and patted her stomach. They exchanged wary smiles. Coffee, coffee for the Ootsum-Wootsums! He felt as if he were bringing her a beautiful present.

He was a love, she firmly believed, and if she had had her coffee in the morning, she wouldn't have behaved so funny. . . . There was a whippoorwill still coming back, imagine, clear out of season, sitting in the crab-apple tree calling all by himself. Maybe his girl stood him up. Maybe she did. She hoped to hear him once more, she loved whippoorwills. . . . He knew how she was, didn't he?

Sure, he knew how she was.

Doris Lessing

A Man and Two Women

Born in Persia of English parents, Doris Lessing grew up on a large farm in central Rhodesia to which the family moved when she was five. At the age of fourteen she quit school and spent the next four years reading and writing; by the age of eighteen she had written and destroyed two novels. From 1937 to 1949 Ms. Lessing lived mainly in Salisbury, marrying twice, having three children, supporting herself with ordinary jobs (telephone operator, secretary, typist), and writing and tearing up four more novels. In 1949 she divorced her second husband and moved from Salisbury to London, taking her infant son with her.

Stella's friends the Bradfords had taken a cheap cottage in Essex for the summer, and she was going down to visit them. She wanted to see them, but there was no doubt there was something of a letdown (and for them too) in the English cottage. Last summer Stella had been wandering with her husband around Italy; had seen the English couple at a café table, and found them sympathetic. They all liked each other, and the four went about for some weeks, sharing meals, hotels, trips. Back in London the friendship had not, as might have been expected, fallen off. Then Stella's husband departed abroad, as he often did, and Stella saw Jack and Dorothy by herself. There were a great many people she might have seen, but it was the Bradfords she saw most often, two or three times a week, at their flat or hers. They were at ease with each other. Why were they? Well, for one thing they were all artists—in different ways. Stella designed wallpapers and materials; she had a name for it.

The Bradfords were real artists. He painted, she drew. They had lived mostly out of England in cheap places around the Mediterranean. Both from the North of England, they had met at art school, married at twenty, had taken flight from England, then returned to it, needing it, then off again: and so on, for years, in the rhythm of so many of their kind, needing, hating, loving England. There had been seasons of real poverty, while they lived on *pasta* or bread or rice, and wine and fruit and sunshine, in Majorca, southern Spain, Italy, North Africa.

A French critic had seen Jack's work, and suddenly he was successful. His show in Paris, then one in London, made money; and now he charged in the hundreds where a year or so ago he charged ten or twenty guineas. This had deepened his contempt for the values of the markets. For a while Stella thought that this was the bond between the Bradfords and herself. They were so very much, as she was, of the new generation of artists (and poets and playwrights and novelists) who had one thing in common, a cool derision about the racket. They were so very unlike (they felt) the older generation with their Societies and their Lunches and their salons and their cliques: their atmosphere of connivance with the snobberies of success. Stella, too, had been successful by a fluke. Not that she did not consider herself talented; it was that others as talented were unfêted, and unbought. When she was with the Bradfords and other fellow spirits, they would talk about the racket, using each other as yardsticks or fellow consciences about how much to give in, what to give, how to use without being used, how to enjoy without becoming dependent on enjoyment.

Of course Dorothy Bradford was not able to talk in quite the same way, since she had not yet been "discovered"; she had not "broken through." A few people with discrimination bought her unusual delicate drawings, which had a strength that was hard to understand unless one knew Dorothy herself. But she was not at all, as Jack was, a great success. There was a strain here, in the marriage, nothing much; it was kept in check by their scorn for their arbitrary rewards of "the racket." But it was there, nevertheless.

Stella's husband had said: "Well, I can understand that, it's like me and you—you're creative, whatever that may mean. I'm just a bloody TV journalist." There was no bitterness in this. He was a good journalist, and besides he sometimes got the chance to make a good small film. All the same, there was that between him and Stella, just as there was between Jack and his wife.

After a time Stella saw something else in her kinship with the couple. It was that the Bradfords had a close bond, bred of having spent so many years together in foreign places, dependent on each other because of their poverty. It had been a real love marriage, one could see it by looking at them. It was now. And Stella's marriage was a real marraige. She understood she enjoyed being with the Bradfords because the two couples were equal in this. Both marriages were those of strong, passionate, talented individuals; they shared a battling quality that strengthened them, not weakened them.

The reason why it had taken Stella so long to understand this was that the Bradfords had made her think about her own marriage, which she was beginning to take for granted, sometimes even found exhausting. She had understood, through them, how lucky she was in her husband; how lucky they all were. No marital miseries; nothing of (what they saw so often in friends) one partner in a marriage victim to the other, resenting the other; no claiming of outsiders as sympathizers or allies in an unequal battle.

There had been a plan for these four people to go off again to Italy or Spain, but then Stella's husband departed, and Dorothy got pregnant. So there was the cottage in Essex instead, a bad second choice, but better, they all felt, to deal with a new baby on home ground, at least for the first year. Stella, telephoned by Jack (on Dorothy's particular insistence, he said), offered and received commiserations on its being only Essex and not Majorca or Italy. She also received sympathy because her husband had been expected back this weekend, but had wired to say he wouldn't be back for another month, probably—there was trouble in Venezuela. Stella wasn't really forlorn; she didn't mind living alone, since she was always supported by knowing her man would be back. Besides, if she herself were offered the chance of a month's "trouble" in Venezuela, she wouldn't hesitate, so it wasn't fair . . . fairness characterized their relationship. All the same, it was nice that she could drop down (or up) to the Bradfords, people with whom she could always be herself, neither more nor less.

She left London at midday by train, armed with food unobtainable in Essex: salamis, cheeses, spices, wine. The sun shone, but it wasn't particularly warm. She hoped there would be heating in the cottage, July or not.

The train was empty. The little station seemed stranded in a green nowhere. She got out, cumbered by bags full of food. A porter and a stationmaster examined, then came to succor her. She was a tallish, fair woman, rather ample; her soft hair, drawn back, escaped in tendrils, and she had great helpless-looking blue eyes. She wore a dress made in one of the materials she had designed. Enormous green leaves laid hands all over her body, and fluttered about her knees. She stood smiling, accustomed to men running to wait on her, enjoying them enjoying her. She walked with them to the barrier where Jack waited, appreciating the scene. He was a smallish man, compact, dark. He wore a blue-green summer shirt, and smoked a pipe and smiled, watching. The two men delivered her into the hands of the third, and departed, whistling, to their duties.

Jack and Stella kissed, then pressed their cheeks together.

"Food," he said, "food," relieving her of the parcels.

"What's it like here, shopping?"

"Vegetables all right, I suppose."

Jack was still Northern in this: he seemed brusque, to strangers; he wasn't shy, he simply hadn't been brought up to enjoy words. Now he put his arm briefly around Stella's waist, and said: "Marvellous, Stella, marvellous." They walked on, pleased with each other. Stella had with Jack, her husband had with Dorothy, these moments, when they said to each other wordlessly: If I were not married to my husband, if you were not married to your wife, how delightful it would be to be married to you. These moments were not the least of the pleasures of this four-sided friendship.

"Are you liking it down here?"

"It's what we bargained for."

There was more than his usual shortness in this, and she glanced at him to find him frowning. They were walking to the car, parked under a tree.

"How's the baby?"

"Little bleeder never sleeps, he's wearing us out, but he's fine."

The baby was six weeks old. Having the baby was a definite achievement: getting it safely conceived and born had taken a couple of years. Dorothy, like most independent women, had had divided thoughts about a baby. Besides, she was over thirty and complained she was set in her ways. All this—the difficulties, Dorothy's hesitations—had added up to an atmosphere which Dorothy herself described as "like wondering if some damned horse is going to take the fence." Dorothy would talk, while she was pregnant, in a soft staccato voice: "Perhaps I don't really want a baby at all? Perhaps I'm not fitted to be a mother? Perhaps . . . and if so . . . and how . . . ?"

She said: "Until recently Jack and I were always with people who took it for granted that getting pregnant was a disaster, and now suddenly all the people we know have young children and baby-sitters and . . . perhaps . . . If . . ."

Jack said: "You'll feel better when it's born."

Once Stella had heard him say, after one of Dorothy's long troubled dialogues with herself: "Now that's enough, that's enough, Dorothy." He had silenced her, taking the responsibility.

They reached the car, got in. It was a second-hand job recently bought. "They" (being the press, the enemy generally) "wait for us" (being artists or writers who have made money) "to buy flashy cars." They had discussed it, decided that *not* to buy an expensive car if they felt like it would be allowing themselves to be bullied; but bought a second-hand one after all. Jack wasn't going to give *them* so much satisfaction, apparently.

"Actually we could have walked," he said, as they shot down a narrow lane, "but with these groceries, it's just as well."

"If the baby's giving you a tough time, there can't be much time for cooking." Dorothy was a wonderful cook. But now again there was something in the air as he said: "Food's definitely not too good just now. You can cook supper, Stell, we could do with a good feed."

Now Dorothy hated anyone in her kitchen, except, for certain specified jobs, her husband; and this was surprising.

"The truth is, Dorothy's worn out," he went on, and now Stella understood he was warning her.

"Well, it is tiring," said Stella soothingly.

"You were like that?"

Like that was saying a good deal more than just worn out, or tired, and Stella understood that Jack was really uneasy. She said, plaintively humorous: "You two always expect me to remember things that happened a hundred years ago. Let me think. . . ."

She had been married when she was eighteen, got pregnant at once. Her husband had left her. Soon she had married Philip, who also had a small child from a former marriage. These two children, her daughter, seventeen, his son, twenty, had grown up together.

She remembered herself at nineteen, alone, with a small baby. "Well, I was alone," she said. "That makes a difference. I remember I was exhausted. Yes, I was definitely irritable and unreasonable."

"Yes," said Jack, with a brief reluctant look at her.

"All right, don't worry," she said, replying aloud as she often did to things that Jack had not said aloud.

"Good," he said.

Stella thought of how she had seen Dorothy, in the hospital room, with the new baby. She had sat up in bed, in a pretty bed jacket, the baby beside her in a basket. He was restless. Jack stood between basket and bed, one large hand on his son's stomach. "Now, you just shut up, little bleeder," he had said, as he grumbled. Then he had picked him up, as if he'd been doing it always, held him against his shoulder, and, as Dorothy held her arms out, had put the baby into them. "Want your mother, then? Don't blame you."

That scene, the ease of it, the way the two parents were together, had, for Stella, made nonsense of all the months of Dorothy's self-questioning. As for Dorothy, she had said, parodying the expected words but meaning them: "He's the most beautiful baby ever born. I can't imagine why I didn't have him before."

"There's the cottage," said Jack. Ahead of them was a small laborer's cottage, among full green trees, surrounded by green grass. It was painted white, had four sparkling windows. Next to it a long shed or structure that turned out to be a greenhouse.

"The man grew tomatoes," said Jack. "Fine studio now."

The car came to rest under another tree.

"Can I just drop in to the studio?"

"Help yourself." Stella walked into the long, glass-roofed shed. In London Jack and Dorothy shared a studio. They had shared huts, sheds, any suitable building, all around the Mediterranean. They always worked side by side. Dorothy's end was tidy, exquisite, Jack's lumbered with great canvases, and he worked in a clutter. Now Stella looked to see if this friendly arrangement continued, but as Jack came in behind her he said: "Dorothy's not set herself up yet. I miss her, I can tell you."

The greenhouse was still partly one: trestles with plants stood along the ends. It was lush and warm.

"As hot as hell when the sun's really going, it makes up. And Dorothy brings Paul in sometimes, so he can get used to decent climate young."

Dorothy came in, at the far end, without the baby. She had recovered her figure. She was a small dark woman, with neat, delicate limbs. Her face was white, with scarlet rather irregular lips, and black glossy brows, a little crooked. So while she was not pretty, she was lively and dramatic-looking. She and Stella had their moments together, when they got pleasure from contrasting their differences, one woman so big and soft and blond, the other so dark and vivacious.

Dorothy came forward through shafts of sunlight, stopped, and said: "Stella, I'm glad you've come." Then forward again, to a few steps off, where she stood looking at them. "You two look good together," she said, frowning. There was something heavy and overemphasized about both statements, and Stella said: "I was wondering what Jack had been up to."

"Very good, I think," said Dorothy, coming to look at the new canvas on the easel. It was of sunlit rocks, brown and smooth, with blue sky, blue water, and people swimming in spangles of light. When Jack was in the South he painted pictues that his wife described as "dirt and grime and misery"—which was how they both described their joint childhood background. When he was in England he painted scenes like these.

"Like it? It's good, isn't it?" said Dorothy.

"Very much," said Stella. She always took pleasure from the contrast between Jack's outward self—the small, self-contained little man who could have vanished in a moment into a crowd of factory workers in, perhaps Manchester, and the sensuous bright pictures like these.

"And you?" asked Stella.

"Having a baby's killed everything creative in me—quite different from being pregnant," said Dorothy, but not complaining of it. She had worked like a demon while she was pregnant.

"Have a heart," said Jack, "he's only just got himself born."

"Well, I don't care," said Dorothy. "That's the funny thing, I *don't* care." She said this flat, indifferent. She seemed to be looking at them both again from a small troubled distance. "You two look good together," she said, and again there was the small jar.

"Well, how about some tea?" said Jack, and Dorothy said at once: "I made it when I heard the car. I thought better inside, it's not really hot in the sun." She led the way out of the greenhouse, her white linen dress dissolving in lozenges of yellow light from the glass panes above, so that Stella was reminded of the white limbs of Jack's swimmers disintegrating under sunlight in his new picture. The work of these two people was always reminding one of each other, or each other's work, and in all kinds ways: they were so much married, so close.

The time it took to cross the space of rough grass to the door of the little house was enough to show Dorothy was right: it was really chilly in the sun. Inside two electric heaters made up for it. There had been two little rooms downstairs, but they had been knocked into one fine low-ceilinged room, stone-floored, white-washed. A tea table, covered with a purple checked cloth, stood waiting near a window where flowering bushes and trees showed through clean panes. Charming. They adjusted the heaters and arranged themselves so they could admire the English countryside through glass. Stella looked for the baby; Dorothy said: "In the pram at the back." Then she asked: "Did yours cry a lot?"

Stella laughed and said again: "I'll try to remember."

"We expect you to guide and direct, with all your experience," said Jack.

"As far as I can remember, she was a little demon for about three months, for no reason I could see, then suddenly she became civilized."

"Roll on the three months," said Jack.

"Six weeks to go," said Dorothy, handling teacups in a languid indifferent manner Stella found new in her.

"Finding it tough going?"

"I've never felt better in my life," said Dorothy at once, as if being accused.

"You look fine."

She looked a bit tired, nothing much; Stella couldn't see what reason there was for Jack to warn her. Unless he meant the languor, a look of self-absorption? Her vivacity, a friendly aggressiveness that was the expression of her lively intelligence, was dimmed. She sat leaning back in a deep armchair, letting Jack manage things, smiling vaguely.

"I'll bring him in in a minute," she remarked, listening to the silence from the sunlit garden at the back.

"Leave him," said Jack. "He's quiet seldom enough. Relax, woman, and have a cigarette."

He lit a cigarette for her, and she took it in the same vague way, and sat breathing out smoke, her eyes half closed.

"Have you heard from Philip?" she asked, not from politeness, but with sudden insistence.

"Of course she has, she got a wire," said Jack.

"I want to know how she feels," said Dorothy. "How do you feel, Stell?" She was listening for the baby all the time.

"Feel about what?"

"About his not coming back."

"But he is coming back, it's only a month," said Stella, and heard, with surprise, that her voice sounded edgy.

"You see?" said Dorothy to Jack, meaning the words, not the edge of them.

At this evidence that she and Philip had been discussed, Stella felt, first, pleasure: because it was pleasurable to be understood by two such good friends; then she felt discomfort, remembering Jack's warning.

"See what?" she asked Dorothy, smiling.

"That's enough now," said Jack to his wife in a flash of stubborn anger, which continued the conversation that had taken place.

Dorothy took direction from her husband, and kept quiet a moment, then seemed impelled to continue: "I've been thinking it must be nice, having your husband go off, then come back. Do you realize Jack and I haven't been separated since we married? That's over ten years. Don't you think there's something awful in two grown people stuck together all the time like Siamese twins?" This ended in a wail of genuine appeal to Stella.

"No, I think it's marvellous."

"But you don't mind being alone so much?"

"It's not *so* much, it's two or three months in a year. Well of course I mind. But I enjoy being alone, really. But I'd enjoy it too if we were together all the time. I envy you two." Stella was surprised to find her eyes wet with self-pity because she had to be without her husband another month.

"And what does he think?" demanded Dorothy, "What does Philip think?"

Stella said: "Well, I think he likes getting away from time to time—yes. He likes intimacy, he enjoys it, but it doesn't come as easily to him as it does to me." She had never said this before because she had never thought about it. She was annoyed with herself that she had had to wait for Dorothy to prompt her. Yet she knew that getting annoyed was what she must not do, with the state Dorothy was in, whatever it was. She glanced at Jack for guidance, but he was determinedly busy on his pipe.

"Well, I'm like Philip," announced Dorothy. "Yes, I'd love it if Jack went off sometimes. I think I'm being stifled being shut up with Jack day and night, year in year out."

"Thanks," said Jack, short but good-humored.

"No, but I mean it. There's something humiliating about two adult people never for one second out of each other's sight."

"Well," said Jack, "when Paul's a bit bigger, you buzz off for a month or so and you'll appreciate me when you get back."

"It's not that I don't appreciate you, it's not that at all," said Dorothy, insistent, almost strident, apparently fevered with restlessness. Her languor had quite gone, and her limbs jerked and moved. And now the baby, as if he had been prompted by his father's mentioning him, let out a cry. Jack got up, forestalling his wife, saying: "I'll get him."

Dorothy sat, listening for her husband's movements with the baby, until he came back, which he did, supporting the infant sprawled against his shoulder with a competent hand. He sat down, let his son slide onto his chest, and said: "There now, you shut up and leave us in peace a bit longer." The baby was looking up into his face with the astonished expression of the newly born, and Dorothy sat smiling at both of them. Stella understood that her restlessness, her repeated curtailed movements, meant that she longed—more, needed—to have the child in her arms, have its body against hers. And Jack seemed to feel this, because Stella could have sworn it was not a conscious decision that made him rise and slide the infant into his wife's arms. Her flesh, her needs, had spoken direct to him without words, and he had risen at once to give her what she wanted. This silent instinctive conversation between husband and wife made Stella miss her own husband violently, and with resentment against fate that kept them apart so often. She ached for Philip.

Meanwhile Dorothy, now the baby was sprawled softly against her chest, the small feet in her hand, seemed to have lapsed into good humor. And Stella, watching, remembered something she really had forgotten: the close, fierce physical tie between herself and her daughter when she had been a tiny baby. She saw this bond in the way Dorothy stroked the small head that trembled on its neck as the baby looked up into his mother's face. Why, she remembered it was like being in love, having a new baby. All kinds of forgotten or unused instincts woke in Stella. She lit a cigarette, took herself in hand; set herself to enjoy the other woman's love affair with her baby instead of envying her.

The sun, dropping into the trees, struck the windowpanes; and there was a dazzle and a flashing of yellow and white light into the room, particularly over Dorothy in her white dress and the baby. Again Stella was reminded of Jack's picture of the white-limbed swimmers in sun-dissolving water. Dorothy shielded the baby's eyes with her hand and remarked dreamily: "This is better than any man, isn't it, Stell? Isn't it better than any man?"

"Well—no," said Stella laughing. "No, not for long."

"If you say so, you should know . . . but I can't imagine ever . . . tell me, Stell, does your Philip have affairs when he's away?"

"For God's sake!" said Jack, angry. But he checked himself.

"Yes, I am sure he does."

"Do you mind?" asked Dorothy, loving the baby's feet with her enclosing palm.

And now Stella was forced to remember, to think about having minded, minding, coming to terms, and the ways in which she now did not mind.

"I don't think about it," she said.

"Well, I don't think I'd mind," said Dorothy.

"Thanks for letting me know," said Jack, short despite himself. Then he made himself laugh.

"And you, do you have affairs while Philip's away?"

"Sometimes. Not really."

"Do you know, Jack was unfaithful to me this week," remarked Dorothy, smiling at the baby.

"That's *enough*," said Jack, really angry.

"No it isn't enough, it isn't. Because what's awful is, I don't care."

"Well why should you care, in the circumstances?" Jack turned to Stella. "There's a silly bitch Lady Edith lives across that field. She got all excited, real live artists living down her lane. Well Dorothy was lucky, she had an excuse in the baby, but I had to go to her silly party. Booze flowing in rivers, and the most incredible people—you know. If you read about them in a novel you'd never believe . . . but I can't remember much after about twelve."

"Do you know what happened?" said Dorothy. "I was feeding the baby, it was terribly early. Jack sat straight up in bed and said: 'Jesus, Dorothy, I've just remembered, I screwed that silly bitch Lady Edith on her brocade sofa.' "

Stella laughed. Jack let out a snort of laughter. Dorothy laughed, an unscrupulous chuckle of appreciation. Then she said seriously: "But that's the point, Stella—the thing is, I don't care a tuppenny damn."

"But why should you?" asked Stella.

"But it's the first time he ever has, and surely I should have minded?"

"Don't you be too sure of that," said Jack, energetically puffing his pipe. "Don't be too sure." But it was only for form's sake, and Dorothy knew it, and said: "Surely I should have cared, Stell?"

"No. You'd have cared if you and Jack weren't so marvellous together. Just as I'd care if Philip and I weren't. . . ." Tears came running down her face. She let them. These were her good friends; and besides, instinct told her tears weren't a bad thing, with Dorothy in this mood. She said, sniffling: "When Philip gets home, we always have a flaming bloody row in the first day or two, about something unimportant, but what it's really about, and we know it, is that I'm jealous of any affair he's had and vice versa. Then we go to bed and make up." She wept, bitterly, thinking of this happiness, postponed for a month, to be suceeded by the delightful battle of their day to day living.

"Oh Stella," said Jack. "Stell . . ." He got up, fished out a handkerchief, dabbed her eyes for her. "There, love, he'll be back soon."

"Yes, I know. It's just that you two are so good together and whenever I'm with you I miss Philip."

"Well, I suppose we're good together?" said Dorothy, sounding surprised. Jack, bending over Stella with his back to his wife, made a warning grimace, then stood up and turned, commanding the situation. "It's nearly six. You'd better feed Paul. Stella's going to cook supper."

"Is she? How nice," said Dorothy. "There's everything in the kitchen, Stella. How lovely to be looked after."

"I'll show you our mansion," said Jack.

Upstairs were two small white rooms. One was the bedroom, with their things and the baby's in it. The other was an overflow room, jammed with stuff. Jack picked up a large leather folder off the spare bed and said: "Look at these,

Stell." He stood at the window, back to her, his thumb at work in his pipe bowl, looking into the garden. Stella sat on the bed, opened the folder and at once exclaimed: "When did she do these?"

"The last three months she was pregnant. Never seen anything like it, she just turned them out one after the other."

There were a couple of hundred pencil drawings, all of two bodies in every kind of balance, tension, relationship. The two bodies were Jack's and Dorothy's, mostly unclothed, but not all. The drawings startled, not only because they marked a real jump forward in Dorothy's achievement, but because of their bold sensuousness. They were a kind of chant, or exaltation about the marriage. The instinctive closeness, the harmony of Jack and Dorothy, visible in every movement they made towards or away from each other, visible even when they were not together, was celebrated here with a frank, calm triumph.

"Some of them are pretty strong," said Jack, the Northern working-class boy reviving in him for a moment's puritanism.

But Stella laughed, because the prudishness masked pride: some of the drawings were indecent.

In the last few of the series the woman's body was swollen in pregnancy. They showed her trust in her husband, whose body, commanding hers, stood or lay in positions of strength and confidence. In the very last Dorothy stood turned away from her husband, her two hands supporting her big belly, and Jack's hands were protective on her shoulders.

"They are marvellous," said Stella.

"They are, aren't they."

Stella looked, laughing, and with love, towards Jack; for she saw that his showing her the drawings was not only pride in his wife's talent; but that he was using this way of telling Stella not to take Dorothy's mood too seriously. And to cheer himself up. She said, impulsively: "Well that's all right then, isn't it?"

"What? Oh yes, I see what you mean, yes, I think it's all right."

"Do you know what?" said Stella, lowering her voice. "I think Dorothy's guilty because she feels unfaithful to you."

"*What?*"

"No, I mean, with the baby, and that's what it's all about."

He turned to face her, troubled, then slowly smiling. There was the same rich unscrupulous quality of appreciation in that smile as there had been in Dorothy's laugh over her husband and Lady Edith. "You think so?" They laughed together, irrepressibly and loudly.

"What's the joke?" shouted Dorothy.

"I'm laughing because your drawings are so good," shouted Stella.

"Yes, they are, aren't they?" But Dorothy's voice changed to flat incredulity: "The trouble is, I can't imagine how I ever did them, I can't imagine ever being able to do it again."

"Downstairs," said Jack to Stella and they went down to find Dorothy nursing the baby. He nursed with his whole being, all of him in movement. He was wrestling with the breast, thumping Dorothy's plump pretty breast with his fists. Jack stood looking down at the two of them, grinning. Dorothy reminded Stella of a cat, half closing her yellow eyes to stare over her kittens at work on her side, while she stretched out a paw where claws sheathed and unsheathed themselves, making a small rip-rip-rip on the carpet she lay on.

"You're a savage creature," said Stella, laughing.

Dorothy raised her small vivid face and smiled. "Yes, I am," she said, and looked at the two of them calm, and from a distance, over the head of her energetic baby.

Stella cooked supper in a stone kitchen, with a heater brought by Jack to make it tolerable. She used the good food she had brought with her, taking trouble. It took some time, then the three ate slowly over a big wooden table. The baby was not asleep. He grumbled for some minutes on a cushion on the floor, then his father held him briefly, before passing him over, as he had done earlier, in response to his mother's need to have him close.

"I'm supposed to let him cry," remarked Dorothy. "But why should he? If he were an Arab or an African baby he'd be plastered to my back."

"And very nice too," said Jack. "I think they come out too soon into the light of day, they should just stay inside for about eighteen months, much better all around."

"Have a heart," said Dorothy and Stella together, and they all laughed; but Dorothy added, quite serious: "Yes, I've been thinking so too."

This good nature lasted through the long meal. The light went cool and thin outside; and inside they let the summer dusk deepen, without lamps.

"I've got to go quite soon," said Stella, with regret.

"Oh, no, you've got to stay!" said Dorothy, strident. It was sudden, the return of the woman who made Jack and Dorothy tense themselves to take strain.

"We all thought Philip was coming. The children will be back tomorrow night, they've been on holiday."

"Then stay till tomorrow, I *want* you," said Dorothy, petulant.

"But I can't," said Stella.

"I never thought I'd want another woman around, cooking in my kitchen, looking after me, but I do," said Dorothy, apparently about to cry.

"Well, love, you'll have to put up with me," said Jack.

"Would you mind, Stell?"

"Mind *what?*" asked Stella, cautious.

"Do you find Jack attractive?"

"Very."

"Well I know you do. Jack, do you find Stella attractive?"

"Try me," said Jack, grinning; but at the same time signalling warnings to Stella.

"Well, then!" said Dorothy.

"A *ménage à trois?*" asked Stella laughing. "And how about my Philip? Where does he fit in?"

"Well, if it comes to that, I wouldn't mind Philip myself," said Dorothy, knitting her sharp black brows and frowning.

"I don't blame you," said Stella, thinking of her handsome husband.

"Just for a month, till he comes back," said Dorothy. "I tell you what, we'll abandon this silly cottage, we must have been mad to stick ourselves away in England in the first place. The three of us'll just pack up and go off to Spain or Italy with the baby."

"And what else?" enquired Jack, good-natured at all costs, using his pipe as a safety valve.

"Yes, I've decided I approve of polygamy," announced Dorothy. She had opened her dress and the baby was nursing again, quietly this time, relaxed against her. She stroked his head, softly, softly, while her voice rose and insisted at the other two people: "I never understood it before, but I do now. I'll be the senior wife, and you two can look after me."

"Any other plans?" enquired Jack, angry now. "You just drop in from time to time to watch Stella and me have a go, is that it? Or are you going to tell us when we can go off and do it, give us your gracious permission?"

"Oh I don't care what you do, that's the point," said Dorothy, sighing, sounding forlorn, however.

Jack and Stella, careful not to look at each other, sat waiting.

"I read something in the newspaper yesterday, it struck me," said Dorothy, conversational. "A man and two women living together—here, in England. They are both his wives, they consider themselves his wives. The senior wife has a baby, and the younger wife sleeps with him—well, that's what it looked like, reading between the lines."

"You'd better stop reading between lines," said Jack. "It's not doing you any good."

"No, I'd like it," insisted Dorothy. "I think our marriages are silly. Africans and people like that, they know better, they've got some sense."

"I can just see if I did make love to Stella," said Jack.

"Yes!" said Stella, with a short laugh which, against her will, was resentful.

"But I wouldn't mind," said Dorothy, and burst into tears.

"Now, Dorothy, that's enough," said Jack. He got up, took the baby, whose sucking was mechanical now, and said: "Now listen, you're going right upstairs and you're going to sleep. This little stinker's full as a tick, he'll be asleep for hours, that's my bet."

"I don't feel sleepy," said Dorothy, sobbing.

"I'll give you a sleeping pill, then."

Then started a search for sleeping pills. None to be found.

"That's just like us," wailed Dorothy, "we don't even have a sleeping pill in the place. . . . Stella, I wish you'd stay, I really do. Why can't you?"

"Stella's going in just a minute, I'm taking her to the station," said Jack. He poured some Scotch into a glass, handed it to his wife and said: "Now drink that, love, and let's have an end of it. I'm getting fed-up." He sounded fed-up.

Dorothy obediently drank the Scotch, got unsteadily from her chair and went slowly upstairs. "Don't let him cry," she demanded, as she disappeared.

"Oh you silly bitch," he shouted after her. "When have I let him cry? Here, you hold on a minute," he said to Stella, handing her the baby. He ran upstairs.

Stella held the baby. This was almost for the first time, since she sensed how much another woman's holding her child made Dorothy's fierce new possessiveness uneasy. She looked down at the small, sleepy, red face and said softly: "Well, you're causing a lot of trouble, aren't you?"

Jack shouted from upstairs: "Come up a minute, Stell." She went up, with the baby. Dorothy was tucked up in bed, drowsy from the Scotch, the bedside light was turned away from her. She looked at the baby, but Jack took it from Stella.

"Jack says I'm a silly bitch," said Dorothy, apologetic, to Stella.

"Well, never mind, you'll feel different soon."

"I suppose so, if you say so. All right, I *am* going to sleep," said Dorothy, in a stubborn, sad little voice. She turned over, away from them. In the last flare of her hysteria she said: "Why don't you two walk to the station together? It's a lovely night."

"We're going to," said Jack, "don't worry."

She let out a weak giggle, but did not turn. Jack carefully deposited the now sleeping baby in the bed, about a foot from Dorothy. Who suddenly wriggled over until her small, defiant white back was in contact with the blanketed bundle that was her son.

Jack raised his eyebrows at Stella: but Stella was looking at mother and baby, the nerves of her memory filling her with sweet warmth. What right had this woman, who was in possession of such delight, to torment her husband, to torment her friend, as she had been doing—what right had she to rely on their decency as she did?

Surprised by these thoughts, she walked away downstairs, and stood at the door into the garden, her eyes shut, holding herself rigid against tears.

She felt a warmth on her bare arm—Jack's hand. She opened her eyes to see him bending towards her, concerned.

"It'd serve Dorothy right if I did drag you off into the bushes. . . ."

"Wouldn't have to drag me," he said; and while the words had the measure of facetiousness the situation demanded, she felt his seriousness envelop them both in danger.

The warmth of his hand slid across her back, and she turned towards him under its pressure. They stood together, cheeks touching, scents of skin and hair mixing with the smells of warmed grass and leaves.

She thought: What is going to happen now will blow Dorothy and Jack and that baby sky-high; it's the end of my marriage; I'm going to blow everything to bits. There was almost uncontrollable pleasure in it.

She saw Dorothy, Jack, the baby, her husband, the two half-grown children, all dispersed, all spinning downwards through the sky like bits of debris after an explosion.

Jack's mouth was moving along her cheek towards her mouth, dissolving her whole self in delight. She saw, against closed lids, the bundled baby upstairs, and pulled back from the situation, exclaiming energetically: "Damn Dorothy, damn her, damn her, I'd like to kill her. . . ."

And he, exploding into reaction, said in a low furious rage: "Damn you both! I'd like to wring both your bloody necks. . . ."

Their faces were at a foot's distance from each other, their eyes staring hostility. She thought that if she had not had the vision of the helpless baby they would now be in each other's arms—generating tenderness and desire like a couple of dynamos, she said to herself, trembling with dry anger.

"I'm going to miss my train if I don't go," she said.

"I'll get your coat," he said, and went in, leaving her defenseless against the emptiness of the garden.

When he came out, he slid the coat around her without touching her, and said: "Come on, I'll take you by car." He walked away in front of her to the car, and she followed meekly over rough lawn. It really was a lovely night.

Cyrus Colter

The Beach Umbrella

Cyrus Colter was born in Noblesville, Indiana, and educated at Youngstown College, Ohio State University, and the Chicago-Kent College of Law. At the age of fifty he began writing in his spare time, and ten years later, in 1970, his first book, The Beach Umbrella, *won the Iowa School of Letters Award for the best collection of short fiction by an unpublished writer. Mr. Colter has since published two novels,* The River of Eros *(1972) and* The Hippodrome *(1973), and now teaches creative writing in the Department of African-American Studies at Northwestern University.*

The Thirty-first Street beach lay dazzling under a sky so blue that Lake Michigan ran to the horizon like a sheet of sapphire silk, studded with little barbed white sequins for sails; and the heavy surface of the water lapped gently at the boulder "sea wall" which had been cut into, graded, and sanded to make the beach. Saturday afternoons were always frenzied: three black lifeguards, giants in sunglasses, preened in their towers and chaperoned the bathers—adults, teen-agers, and children—who were going through every physical gyration of which the human body is capable. Some dove, swam, some hollered, rode inner tubes, or merely stood waistdeep and pummeled the water; others—on the beach—sprinted, did handsprings and somersaults, sucked Eskimo pies, or just buried their children in the sand. Then there were the lollers—extended in their languor under a garish variety of beach umbrellas.

Elijah lolled too—on his stomach in the white sand, his chin cupped in his palm; but under no umbrella. He had none. By habit, though, he stared in awe at those who did, and sometimes meddled in their conversation: "It's gonna be gettin' *hot* pretty soon—if it ain't careful," he said to a Bantu-looking fellow and his girl sitting near by with an older woman. The temperature was then in the nineties. The fellow managed a negligent smile. "Yeah," he said, and persisted in listening to the women. Buoyant still, Elijah watched them. But soon his gaze wavered, and then moved on to other lollers of interest. Finally he got up, stretched, brushed sand from his swimming trunks, and scanned the beach for a new spot. He started walking.

He was not tall. And he appeared to walk on his toes—his walnut-colored legs were bowed and skinny and made him hobble like a jerky little spider. Next he plopped down near two men and two girls—they were hilarious about something—sitting beneath a big purple-and-white umbrella. The girls, chocolate brown and shapely, emitted squeals of laughter at the wisecracks of the men. Elijah was enchanted. All summer long the rambunctious gaiety of the beach had fastened on him a curious charm, a hex, that brought him gawking and twiddling to the lake each Saturday. The rest of the week, save Sunday, he worked. But Myrtle, his wife, detested the sport and stayed away. Randall, the boy, had been only twice and then without little Susan, who during the summer was her mother's own midget reflection. But Elijah came regularly, especially whenever Myrtle was being evil, which he felt now was almost always. She was getting worse, too—if that was possible. The woman was money-*crazy.*

"You gotta sharp-lookin' umbrella there!" he cut in on the two laughing couples. They studied him—the abruptly silent way. Then the big-shouldered fellow smiled and lifted his eyes to their spangled roof. "Yeah? . . . Thanks," he said. Elijah carried on: "I see a lot of 'em out here this summer—much more'n last year." The fellow meditated on this, but was noncommittal. The others went on gabbing, mostly with their hands. Elijah, squinting in the hot sun, watched them. He didn't see how they could be married; they cut the fool too much, acted like they'd itched to get together for weeks and just now made it. He pondered going back in the water, but he'd already had an hour of that. His eyes traveled the sweltering beach. Funny about his folks; they were every shape and color a God-made human could be. Here was a real sample of variety—pink white to jetty black. Could you any longer call that a *race* of people? It was a complicated complication—for some real educated guy to figure out. Then another thought slowly bore in on him: the beach umbrellas blooming across the sand attracted people—slews of friends, buddies; and gals, too. Wherever the loudest-racket tore the air, a big red, or green, or yellowish umbrella—bordered with white fringe maybe—flowered in the middle of it all and gave shade to the happy good-timers.

Take, for instance, that tropical-looking pea-green umbrella over there, with the Bikinied brown chicks under it, and the portable radio jumping. A real beach party! He got up, stole over, and eased down in the sand at the fringe of the jubilation—two big thermos jugs sat in the shade and everybody had a paper cup in hand as the explosions of buffoonery carried out to the water. Chief provoker of mirth was a bulging-eyed old gal in a white bathing suit who, encumbered by big flabby overripe thighs, cavorted and pranced in the sand. When, perspiring from the heat, she finally fagged out, she flopped down almost on top of him. So far, he had gone unnoticed. But now, as he craned in at closer range, she brought him up: "Whatta *you* want, Pops?" She grinned, but with a touch of hostility.

Pops! Where'd she get that stuff? He was only forty-one, not a day older than that boozy bag. But he smiled. "Nothin'," he said brightly, "but you sure got one goin' here." He turned and viewed the noise-makers.

"An' you wanta get in on it!" she wrangled.

"Oh, I was just lookin'—"

"—You was just lookin'. Yeah, you was just lookin' at them young chicks there!" She roared a laugh and pointed at the sexy-looking girls under the umbrella.

Elijah grinned weakly.

"Beat it!" she catcalled, and turned back to the party.

He sat like a rock—the hell with her. But soon he relented, and wandered down to the water's edge—remote now from all inhospitality—to sit in the sand and hug his raised knees. Far out, the sailboats were pinned to the horizon and, despite all the close-in fuss, the wide miles of lake lay impassive under a blazing calm; far south and east down the long-curving lake shore, miles in the distance, the smoky haze of the Whiting plant of the Youngstown Sheet and Tube Company hung ominously in an otherwise bright sky. And so it was that he turned back and viewed the beach again—and suddenly caught his craving. Weren't they something—the umbrellas! The flashy colors of them! And the swank! No wonder folks ganged round them. Yes . . . yes, he too must have one. The thought came slow and final, and scared him. For there stood Myrtle in his mind. She nagged him now night and day, and it was always money that got her started; there was never enough—for Susan's shoes, Randy's overcoat, for new kitchen linoleum, Venetian blinds, for a better car than the old Chevy. "I just don't understand you!" she had said only night before last. "Have you got any plans at all for your family? You got a family, you know. If you could only bear to pull yourself away from that deaf old tightwad out at that warehouse, and go get yourself a *real* job. . . . But no! Not *you*!"

She was talking about old man Schroeder, who owned the warehouse where he worked. Yes, the pay could be better, but it still wasn't as bad as she made out. Myrtle could be such a fool sometimes. He had been with the old man nine years now; had started out as a freight handler, but worked up to doing inventories and a little paper work. True, the business had been going down recently, for the old man's sight and hearing were failing and his key people had left. Now he depended on *him,* Elijah—who of late wore a necktie on the job, and made his inventory rounds with a ball-point pen and clipboard. The old man was friendlier, too—almost "hat in hand" to him. He liked everything about the job now—except the pay. And that was only because of Myrtle. She just wanted so much; even talked of moving out of their rented apartment and buying out in the Chatham area. But one thing had to be said for her: she never griped about anything for herself; only for the family, the kids. Every payday he endorsed his check and handed it over to her, and got back in return only gasoline and cigarette money. And this could get pretty tiresome. About six weeks ago he'd gotten a thirty-dollar-a-month raise out of the old man, but that had only made her madder than ever. He'd thought about looking for another job all right; but where would he go to get another white-collar job? There weren't many of them for him. *She* wouldn't care if he went back to the steel mills, back to pouring that white-hot ore out at Youngstown Sheet and Tube. It would be okay with *her*—so long as his pay check was fat. But that kind of work was no good, undignified; coming home on the bus you were always so tired you went to sleep in your seat, with your lunch pail in your lap.

Just then two wet boys, chasing each other across the sand, raced by him into the water. The cold spray on his skin made him jump, jolting him out of his thoughts. He turned and slowly scanned the beach again. The umbrellas were brighter, gayer, bolder than ever—each a hiving center of playful people. He stood up finally, took a long last look, and then started back to the spot where he had parked the Chevy.

The following Monday evening was hot and humid as Elijah sat at home in their plain living room and pretended to read the newspaper; the windows were up, but not the slightest breeze came through the screens to stir Myrtle's fluffy curtains. At the moment she and nine-year-old Susan were in the kitchen finishing the dinner dishes. For twenty minutes now he had sat waiting for the furtive chance to speak to Randall. Randall, at twelve, was a serious, industrious boy, and did deliveries and odd jobs for the neighborhood grocer. Soon he came through—intent, absorbed—on his way back to the grocery store for another hour's work.

"Gotta go back, eh, Randy?" Elijah said.

"Yes, sir." He was tall for his age, and wore glasses. He paused with his hand on the doorknob.

Elijah hesitated. Better wait, he thought—wait till he comes back. But Myrtle might be around then. Better ask him now. But Randall had opened the door. "See you later, Dad," he said—and left.

Elijah, shaken, again raised the newspaper and tried to read. He should have called him back, he knew, but he had lost his nerve—because he couldn't tell how Randy would take it. Fifteen dollars was nothing really—Randy probably had fifty or sixty stashed away somewhere in his room. Then he thought of Myrtle, and waves of fright went over him—to be even thinking about a beach umbrella was bad enough; and to buy one, especially now, would be to her some kind of crime; but to borrow even a part of the money for it from Randy . . . well, Myrtle would go out of her mind. He had never lied to his family before. This would be the first time. And he had thought about it all day long. During the morning, at the warehouse, he had gotten out the two big mail-order catalogues, to look at the beach umbrellas; but the ones shown were all so small and dinky-looking he was contemptuous. So at noon he drove the Chevy out to a sporting-goods store on West Sixty-third Street. There he found a gorgeous assortment of yard and beach umbrellas. And there he found his prize. A beauty, a big beauty, with wide red and white stripes, and a white fringe. But oh the price! Twenty-three dollars! And he with nine.

"What's the matter with you?" Myrtle had walked in the room. She was thin, and medium brown-skinned with a saddle of freckles across her nose, and looked harried in her sleeveless housedress with her hair unkempt.

Startled, he lowered the newspaper. "Nothing," he said.

"How can you read looking *over* the paper?"

"Was I?"

Not bothering to answer, she sank in a chair. "Susie," she called back into the kitchen, "bring my cigarettes in here, will you, baby?"

Soon Susan, chubby and solemn, with the mist of perspiration on her forehead, came in with the cigarettes. "Only three left, Mama," she said, peering into the pack.

"Okay," Myrtle sighed, taking the cigarettes. Susan started out. "Now, scour the sink good, honey—and then go take your bath. You'll feel cooler."

Before looking at him again, Myrtle lit a cigarette. "School starts in three weeks," she said, with a forlorn shake of her head. "Do you realize that?"

"Yeah? . . . Jesus, time flies." He could not look at her.

"Susie needs dresses, and a couple of pairs of *good* shoes—and she'll need a coat before it gets cold."

"Yeah, I know." He patted the arm of the chair.

"Randy—bless his heart—has already made enough to get most of *his* things. That boy's something; he's all business—I've never seen anything like it." She took a drag on her cigarette. "And old man Schroeder giving you a thirty-dollar raise! What was you thinkin' about? What'd you *say* to him?"

He did not answer at first. Finally he said, "Thirty dollars are thirty dollars, Myrtle. *You* know business is slow."

"*I'll* say it is! And there won't be any business before long—and then where'll you be? I tell you over and over again, you better start looking for something *now!* I been preachin' it to you for a year."

He said nothing.

"Ford and International Harvester are hiring every man they can lay their hands on! And the mills out in Gary and Whiting are going full blast—you see the red sky every night. The men make *good* money."

"They earn every nickel of it, too," he said in gloom.

"But they *get* it! Bring it home! It spends! Does that mean anything to you? Do you know what some of them make? Well, ask Hawthorne—or ask Sonny Milton. Sonny's wife says his checks some weeks run as high as a hundred sixty, hundred eighty, dollars. One week! Take-home pay!"

"Yeah? . . . And Sonny told me he wished he had a job like mine."

Myrtle threw back her head with a bitter gasp. "Oh-h-h, God! Did you tell him what you made? Did you tell him that?"

Suddenly Susan came back into the muggy living room. She went straight to her mother and stood as if expecting an award. Myrtle absently patted her on the side of the head. "Now, go and run your bath water, honey," she said.

Elijah smiled at Susan. "Susie," he said, "d'you know your tummy is stickin' way out—you didn't eat too much, did you?" He laughed.

Susan turned and observed him; then looked at her mother. "No," she finally said.

"Go on, now, baby," Myrtle said. Susan left the room.

Myrtle resumed. "Well, there's no use going through all this again. It's plain as the nose on your face. You got a family—a good family, *I* think. The only question is, do you wanta get off your hind end and do somethin' for it. It's just that simple."

Elijah looked at her. "You can talk real crazy sometimes, Myrtle."

"I think it's that old man!" she cried, her freckles contorted. "He's got you answering the phone, and taking inventory—wearing a necktie and all that. You wearing a necktie and your son mopping in a grocery store, so he can buy his own clothes." She snatched up her cigarettes, and walked out of the room.

His eyes did not follow her, but remained off in space. Finally he got up and went back into the kitchen. Over the stove the plaster was thinly cracked, and, in spots, the linoleum had worn through the pattern; but everything was immaculate. He opened the refrigerator, poured a glass of cold water, and sat down at the kitchen table. He felt strange and weak, and sat for a long time sipping the water.

Then after a while he heard Randall's key in the front door, sending tremors of dread through him. When Randall came into the kitchen, he seemed to him as tall as himself; his glasses were steamy from the humidity outside, and his hands were dirty.

"Hi, Dad," he said gravely without looking at him, and opened the refrigerator door.

Elijah chuckled. "Your mother'll get after you about going in there without washing your hands."

But Randall took out the water pitcher and closed the door.

Elijah watched him. Now was the time to ask him. His heart was hammering. Go on—now! But instead he heard his husky voice saying, "What'd they have you doing over at the grocery tonight?"

Randall was drinking the glass of water. When he finished he said, "Refilling shelves."

"Pretty hot job tonight, eh?"

"It wasn't so bad." Randall was matter-of-fact as he set the empty glass over the sink, and paused before leaving.

"Well . . . you're doing fine, son. Fine. Your mother sure is proud of you. . . ." Purpose had lodged in his throat.

The praise embarrassed Randall. "Okay, Dad," he said, and edged from the kitchen.

Elijah slumped back in his chair, near prostration. He tried to clear his mind of every particle of thought, but the images became only more jumbled, oppressive to the point of panic.

Then before long Myrtle came into the kitchen—ignoring him. But she seemed not so hostile now as coldly impassive, exhibiting a bravado he had not seen before. He got up and went back into the living room and turned on the television. As the TV-screen lawmen galloped before him, he sat oblivious, admitting the failure of his will. If only he could have gotten Randall to himself long enough—but everything had been so sudden, abrupt; he couldn't just ask him out of the clear blue. Besides, around him, Randall always seemed so busy, too busy to talk. He couldn't understand that; he had never mistreated the boy, never whipped him in his life; had shaken him a time or two, but that was long ago, when he was little.

He sat and watched the finish of the half-hour TV show. Myrtle was in the bedroom now. He slouched in his chair, lacking the resolve to get up and turn off the television.

Suddenly he was on his feet.

Leaving the television on, he went back to Randall's room in the rear. The door was open and Randall was asleep, lying on his back on the bed, perspiring, still dressed except for his shoes and glasses. He stood over the bed and looked at him. He was a good boy; his own son. But how strange—he thought for the first time—there was no resemblance between them. None whatsoever. Randy had a few of his mother's freckles on his thin brown face, but he could see none of himself in the boy. Then his musings were scattered by the return of his fear. He dreaded waking him. And he might be cross. If he didn't hurry, though, Myrtle or Susie might come strolling out any minute. His bones seemed rubbery from the strain. Finally he bent down and touched Randall's shoulder. The boy did not move a muscle, except to open his eyes. Elijah smiled at him. And he slowly sat up.

"Sorry, Randy—to wake you up like this."

"What's the matter?" Randall rubbed his eyes.

Elijah bent down again, but did not whisper. "Say, can you let me have fifteen bucks—till I get my check? . . . I need to get some things—and I'm a little short this time." He could hardly bring the words up.

Randall gave him a slow, queer look.

"I'll get my check a week from Friday," Elijah said, ". . . and I'll give it back to you then—sure."

Now instinctively Randall glanced toward the door, and Elijah knew Myrtle had crossed his thoughts. "You don't have to mention anything to your mother," he said with casual suddenness.

Randall got up slowly off the bed, and, in his socks, walked to the little table where he did his homework. He pulled the drawer out, fished far in the back a moment, and brought out a white business envelope secured by a rubber band. Holding the envelope close to his stomach, he took out first a ten-dollar bill, and then a five, and, sighing, handed them over.

"Thanks, old man," Elijah quivered, folding the money. "You'll get this back the day I get my check. . . . That's for sure."

"Okay," Randall finally said.

Elijah started out. Then he could see Myrtle on payday—her hand extended for his check. He hesitated, and looked at Randall, as if to speak. But he slipped the money in his trousers pocket and hurried from the room.

The following Saturday at the beach did not begin bright and sunny. By noon it was hot, but the sky was overcast and angry, the air heavy. There was no certainty whatever of a crowd, raucous or otherwise, and this was Elijah's chief concern as, shortly before twelve o'clock, he drove up in the Chevy and parked in the bumpy, graveled stretch of high ground that looked down eastward over the lake and was used for a parking lot. He climbed out of the car, glancing at the lake and clouds, and prayed in his heart it would not rain—the water was murky and restless, and only a handful of bathers had showed. But it was early yet. He stood beside the car and watched a bulbous, brown-skinned woman, in bathing suit and enormous straw hat, lugging a lunch basket down toward the beach, followed by her brood of children. And a fellow in swimming trunks, apparently the father, took a towel and sandals from his new Buick and called petulantly to his family to "just wait a minute, please." In another car, two women sat waiting, as yet fully clothed and undecided about going swimming. While down at the water's edge there was the usual cluster of dripping boys who, brash and boisterous, swarmed to the beach every day in fair weather or foul.

Elijah took off his shirt, peeled his trousers from over his swimming trunks, and started collecting the paraphernalia from the back seat of the car: a frayed pink rug filched from the house, a towel, sunglasses, cigarettes, a thermos jug filled with cold lemonade he had made himself, and a dozen paper cups. All this he stacked on the front fender. Then he went around to the rear and opened the trunk. Ah, there it lay—encased in a long, slim package trussed with heavy twine, and barely fitting athwart the spare tire. He felt prickles of excitement as he took the knife from the tool bag, cut the twine, and pulled the wrapping paper away. Red and white stripes sprang at him. It was even more gorgeous than when it had first seduced him in the store. The white fringe gave it style; the wide red fillets were cardinal and stark, and the white stripes glared. Now he opened it over his head, for the full thrill of its colors, and looked around to see if anyone else agreed. Finally after a while he gathered up all his equipment and headed down for the beach, his short, nubby legs seeming more bowed than ever under the weight of their cargo.

When he reached the sand, a choice of location became a pressing matter. That was why he had come early. From past observation it was clear that the center of the gaiety shifted from day to day; last Saturday it might have been nearer the water, this Saturday, well back; or up, or down, the beach a ways. He must pick the site with care, for he could not move about the way he did when he had no umbrella; it was too noticeable. He finally took a spot as near the center of the beach as he could estimate, and dropped his gear in the sand. He knelt down and spread the pink rug, then moved the thermos jug over onto it, and folded the towel and placed it with the paper cups, sunglasses and cigarettes down beside the jug. Now he went to find a heavy stone or brick to drive down the spike for the hollow umbrella stem to fit over. So it was not until the umbrella was finally up that he again had time for anxiety about the weather. His whole morning's effort had been an act of faith, for, as yet, there was no sun, although now and then a few azure breaks appeared in the thinning cloud mass. But before very long this brighter texture of the sky began to grow and spread by slow degrees, and his hopes quickened. Finally he sat down under the umbrella, lit a cigarette, and waited.

It was not long before two small boys came by—on their way to the water. He grinned, and called to them, "Hey, fellas, been in yet?"—their bathing suits were dry.

They stopped, and observed him. Then one of them smiled, and shook his head.

Elijah laughed. "Well, whatta you waitin' for? Go on in there and get them suits wet!" Both boys gave him silent smiles. And they lingered. He thought this a good omen—it had been different the Saturday before.

Once or twice the sun burst through the weakening clouds. He forgot the boys now in watching the skies, and soon they moved on. His anxiety was not detectable from his lazy posture under the umbrella, with his dwarfish, gnarled legs extended and his bare heels on the little rug. But then soon the clouds began to fade in earnest, seeming not to move away laterally, but slowly to recede into a lucent haze, until at last the sun came through hot and bright. He squinted at the sky and felt delivered. They would come, the folks would come!—were coming now; the beach would soon be swarming. Two other umbrellas were up already, and the diving board thronged with wet, acrobatic boys. The lifeguards were in their towers now, and still another launched his yellow rowboat. And up on the Outer Drive, the cars, one by one, were turning into the parking lot.

The sun was bringing them out all right; soon he'd be in the middle of a field day. He felt a low-key, welling excitement, for the water was blue, and far out the sails were starched and white.

Soon he saw the two little boys coming back. They were soaked. Their mother—a thin, brown girl in a yellow bathing suit—was with them now, and the boys were pointing to his umbrella. She seemed dignified for her youth, as she gave him a shy glance and then smiled at the boys.

"Ah, ha!" he cried to the boys. "You've been in *now* all right!" And then laughing to her, "I was kiddin' them awhile ago about their dry bathing suits."

She smiled at the boys again. "They like for me to be with them when they go in," she said.

"I got some lemonade here," he said abruptly, slapping the thermos jug. "Why don't you have some?" His voice was anxious.

She hesitated.

He jumped up. "Come on, sit down." He smiled at her and stepped aside.

Still she hesitated. But her eager boys pressed close behind her. Finally she smiled and sat down under the umbrella.

"You fellas can sit down under here too—in the shade," he said to the boys, and pointed under the umbrella. The boys flopped down quickly in the shady sand. He started at once serving them cold lemonade in the paper cups.

"Whew! I thought it was goin' to rain there for a while," he said, making conversation after passing out the lemonade. He had squatted on the sand and lit another cigarette. "Then there wouldn't a been much goin' on. But it turned out fine after all—there'll be a mob here before long."

She sipped the lemonade, but said little. He felt she had sat down only because of the boys, for she merely smiled and gave short answers to his questions. He learned the boys' names, Melvin and James; their ages, seven and nine; and that they were still frightened by the water. But he wanted to ask *her* name, and inquire about her husband. But he could not capture the courage.

Now the sun was hot and the sand was hot. And an orange-and-white umbrella was going up right beside them—two fellows and a girl. When the fellow who had been kneeling to drive the umbrella spike in the sand stood up, he was stringbean tall, and black, with his glistening hair freshly processed. The girl was a lighter brown, and wore a lilac bathing suit, and, although her legs were thin, she was pleasant enough to look at. The second fellow was medium, really, in height, but short beside his tall, black friend. He was yellow-skinned, and fast getting bald, although still in his early thirties. Both men sported little shoestring mustaches.

Elijah watched them in silence as long as he could. "You picked the right spot all right!" he laughed at last, putting on his sunglasses.

"How come, man?" The tall, black fellow grinned, showing his mouthful of gold teeth.

"You see *every*body here!" happily rejoined Elijah. "They all come here!"

"Man, I been coming here for years," the fellow reproved, and sat down in his khaki swimming trunks to take off his shoes. Then he stood up. "But right now, in the water I goes." He looked down at the girl. "How 'bout you, Lois, baby?"

"No, Caesar," she smiled, "not yet; I'm gonna sit here awhile and relax."

"Okay, then—you just sit right there and relax. And Little Joe"—he turned and grinned to his shorter friend—"you sit there an' relax right along with her. You all can talk with this gentleman here"—he nodded at Elijah—"an' his nice wife." Then, pleased with himself, he trotted off toward the water.

The young mother looked at Elijah, as if he should have hastened to correct him. But somehow he had not wanted to. Yet too, Ceasar's remark seemed to amuse her, for she soon smiled. Elijah felt the pain of relief—he did not want her to go; he glanced at her with a furtive laugh, and then they both laughed. The boys had finished their lemonade now, and were digging in the sand. Lois and Little Joe were busy talking.

Elijah was not quite sure what he should say to the mother. He did not understand her, was afraid of boring her, was desperate to keep her interested. As she sat looking out over the lake, he watched her. She was not pretty; and she was too thin. But he thought she had poise; he liked the way she treated her boys—tender, but casual; how different from Myrtle's frantic herding.

Soon she turned to the boys. "Want to go back in the water?" she laughed.

The boys looked at each other, and then at her. "Okay," James said finally, in resignation.

"Here, have some more lemonade," Elijah cut in.

The boys, rescued for the moment, quickly extended their cups. He poured them more lemonade, as she looked on smiling.

Now he turned to Lois and Little Joe sitting under their orange-and-white umbrella. "How 'bout some good ole cold lemonade?" he asked with a mushy smile. "I got plenty of cups." He felt he must get something going.

Lois smiled back, "No, thanks," she said, fluttering her long eyelashes, "not right now."

He looked anxiously at Little Joe.

"*I'll* take a cup!" said Little Joe, and turned and laughed to Lois: "Hand me that bag there, will you?" He pointed to her beach bag in the sand. She passed it to him, and he reached in and pulled out a pint of gin. "We'll have some *real* lemonade," he vowed, with a daredevilish grin.

Lois squealed with pretended embarrassment. "Oh, *Joe!*"

Elijah's eyes were big now; he was thinking of the police. But he handed Little Joe a cup and poured the lemonade, to which Joe added gin. Then Joe, grinning, thrust the bottle at Elijah. "How 'bout yourself, chief?" he said.

Elijah, shaking his head, leaned forward and whispered, "You ain't supposed to drink on the beach, y'know."

"*This* ain't a drink, man—it's a taste!" said Little Joe, laughing and waving the bottle around toward the young mother. "How 'bout a little taste for your wife here?" he said to Elijah.

The mother laughed and threw up both her hands. "No, not for me!"

Little Joe gave her a rakish grin. "What'sa matter? You *'fraid* of that guy?" He jerked his thumb toward Elijah. "You 'fraid of gettin' a whippin', eh?"

"No, not exactly," she laughed.

Elijah was so elated with her his relief burst up in hysterical laughter. His laugh became strident and hoarse and he could not stop. The boys gaped at him, and then at their mother. When finally recovered, Little Joe asked him, "Whut's so funny 'bout *that?*" Then Little Joe grinned at the mother. "You beat *him* up sometimes, eh?"

This started Elijah's hysterics all over again. The mother looked concerned now, and embarrassed; her laugh was nervous and shadowed. Little Joe glanced at Lois, laughed, and shrugged his shoulders. When Elijah finally got control of himself again he looked spent and demoralized.

Lois now tried to divert attention by starting a conversation with the boys. But the mother showed signs of restlessness and seemed ready to go. At this moment Caesar returned. Glistening beads of water ran off his long, black body; and his hair was unprocessed now. He surveyed the group and then flashed a wide, gold-toothed grin. "One big, happy family, like I said." Then he spied the paper cup in Little Joe's hand. "Whut you got there, man?"

Little Joe looked down into his cup with a playful smirk. "Lemonade, lover boy, lemonade."

"Don't hand me that jive, Joey. You ain't never had any straight lemonade in your life."

This again brought uproarious laughter from Elijah. "I got the straight lemonade *here!*" He beat the thermos jug with his hand. "Come on—have some!" He reached for a paper cup.

"Why, sure," said poised Caesar. He held out the cup and received the lemonade. "Now, gimme that gin," he said to Little Joe. Joe handed over the gin, and Caesar poured three fingers into the lemonade and sat down in the sand with his legs crossed under him. Soon he turned to the two boys, as their mother watched him with amusement. "Say, ain't you boys goin' in any more? Why don't you tell your daddy there to take you in?" He nodded toward Elijah.

Little Melvin frowned at him. "My daddy's workin'," he said.

Caesar's eyebrows shot up. "Ooooh, la, la!" he crooned. "Hey, now!" And he turned and looked at the mother and then at Elijah, and gave a clownish little snigger.

Lois tittered before feigning exasperation at him. "There you go again," she said, "talkin' when you shoulda been listening."

Elijah laughed along with the rest. But he felt deflated. Then he glanced at the mother, who was laughing too. He could dectect in her no sign of dismay.

Why then had she gone along with the gag in this first place, he thought—if now she didn't hate to see it punctured?

"*Hold the phone!*" softly exclaimed Little Joe. "Whut is *this?*" He was staring over his shoulder. Three women, young, brown, and worldly-looking, wandered toward them, carrying an assortment of beach paraphernalia and looking for a likely spot. They wore very scant bathing suits, and were followed, but slowly, by an older woman with big, unsightly thighs. Elijah recognized her at once. She was the old gal who, the Saturday before, had chased him away from her beach party. She wore the same white bathing suit, and one of her girls carried the pea-green umbrella.

Caesar forgot his whereabouts ogling the girls. The older woman, observing this, paused to survey the situation. "How 'bout along in here?" she finally said to one of the girls. The girl carrying the thermos jug set it in the sand so close to Caesar it nearly touched him. He was rapturous. The girl with the umbrella had no chance to put it up, for Caesar and Little Joe instantly encumbered her with help. Another girl turned on their radio, and grinning, feverish Little Joe started snapping his fingers to the music's beat.

Within a half hour, a boisterous party was in progress. The little radio, perched on a hump of sand, blared out hot jazz, as the older woman—whose name turned out to be Hattie—passed around some cold, rum-spiked punch; and before long she went into her dancing-prancing act—to the riotous delight of all, especially Elijah. Hattie did not remember him from the Saturday past, and he was glad, for everything was so different today! As different as milk and ink. He knew no one realized it, but this was *his* party really—the wildest, craziest, funniest, and best he had ever seen or heard of. Nobody had been near the water—except Caesar, and the mother and boys much earlier. It appeared Lois was Caesar's girl friend, and she was hence more capable of reserve in face of the come-on antics of Opal, Billie, and Quanita—Hattie's girls. But Little Joe, to Caesar's tortured envy, was both free and aggressive. Even the young mother, who now volunteered her name to be Mrs. Green, got frolicsome, and twice jabbed Little Joe in the ribs.

Finally Caesar proposed they all go in the water. This met with instant, tipsy acclaim; and Little Joe, his yellow face contorted from laughing, jumped up, grabbed Billie's hand, and made off with her across the sand. But Hattie would not budge. Full of rum, and stubborn, she sat sprawled with her flaccid thighs spread in an obscene V, and her eyes half shut. Now she yelled at her departing girls: "You all watch out, now! Dont'cha go in too far. . . . Just wade! None o' you can swim a lick!"

Elijah now was beyond happiness. He felt a floating, manic glee. He sprang up and jerked Mrs. Green splashing into the water, followed by her somewhat less ecstatic boys. Caesar had to paddle about with Lois and leave Little Joe unassisted to caper with Billie, Opal, and Quanita. Billie was the prettiest of the three, and despite Hattie's contrary statement, she could swim; and Little Joe, after taking her out in deeper water, waved back to Caesar in triumph. The sun was brazen now, and the beach and lake thronged with a variegated humanity. Elijah, a strong, but awkward, country-style swimmer, gave Mrs. Green a lesson in floating on her back, and, though she too could swim, he often felt obligated to place both his arms under her young body and buoy her up.

And sometimes he would purposely let her sink to her chin, whereupon she would feign a happy fright and utter faint simian screeches. Opal and Quanita sat in the shallows and kicked up their heels at Caesar, who, fully occupied with Lois, was a grinning water-threshing study in frustration.

Thus the party went—on and on—till nearly four o'clock. Elijah had not known the world afforded such joy; his homely face was a wet festoon of beams and smiles. He went from girl to girl, insisting she learn to float on his outstretched arms. Once begrudgingly Caesar admonished him, "Man, you gonna *drown* one o' them pretty chicks in a minute." And Little Joe bestowed his highest accolade by calling him "lover boy," as Elijah nearly strangled from laughter.

At last, they looked up to see old Hattie as she reeled down to the water's edge, coming to fetch her girls. Both Caesar and Little Joe ran out of the water to meet her, seized her by the wrists, and, despite her struggles and curses, dragged her in. "Turn me loose! You big galoots!" she yelled and gasped as the water hit her. She was in knee-deep before she wriggled and fought herself free and lurched out of the water. Her breath reeked of rum. Little Joe ran and caught her again, but she lunged backwards, and free, with such force she sat down in the wet sand with a thud. She roared a laugh now, and spread her arms for help, as her girls came sprinting and splashing out of the water and tugged her to her feet. Her eyes narrowed to vengeful, grinning slits as she turned on Caesar and Little Joe: "*I* know whut you two're up to!" She flashed a glance around toward her girls. "I been watchin' both o' you studs! Yeah, yeah, but your eyes may shine, an' your teeth may grit. . . ." She went limp in a sneering, raucous laugh. Everybody laughed now—except Lois and Mrs. Green.

They had all come out of the water now, and soon the whole group returned to their three beach umbrellas. Hattie's girls immediately prepared to break camp. They took down their pea-green umbrella, folded some wet towels, and donned their beach sandals, as Hattie still bantered Caesar and Little Joe.

"Well, you sure had *yourself* a ball today," she said to Little Joe, who was sitting in the sand.

"Comin' back next Saturday?" asked grinning Little Joe.

"I jus' might at that," surmised Hattie. "We wuz here last Saturday."

"Good! Good!" Elijah broke in. "Let's *all* come back—next Saturday!" He searched every face.

"*I'll* be here," chimed Little Joe, grinning to Caesar. Captive Caesar glanced at Lois, and said nothing.

Lois and Mrs. Green were silent. Hattie, insulted, looked at them and started swelling up. "Never mind," she said pointedly to Elijah, "you jus' come on anyhow. You'll run into a slew o' folks lookin' for a good time. You don't need no *certain* people." But a little later, she and her girls all said friendly goodbyes and walked off across the sand.

The party now took a sudden downturn. All Elijah's efforts at resuscitation seemed unavailing. The westering sun was dipping toward the distant buildings of the city, and many of the bathers were leaving. Caesar and Little Joe had become bored; and Mrs. Green's boys, whining to go, kept a reproachful eye on their mother.

"Here, you boys, take some more lemonade," Elijah said quickly, reaching for the thermos jug. "Only got a little left—better get while gettin's good!" He laughed. The boys shook their heads.

On Lois he tried cajolery. Smiling, and pointing to her wet, but trim bathing suit, he asked, "What color would you say that is?"

"Lilac," said Lois, now standing.

"It sure is pretty! Prettiest on the beach!" he whispered.

Lois gave him a weak smile. Then she reached down for her beach bag, and looked at Caesar.

Caesar stood up. "Let's cut," he turned and said to Little Joe, and began taking down their orange-and-white umbrella.

Elijah was desolate. "Whatta you goin' for? It's gettin' cooler! Now's the time to *enjoy* the beach!"

"I've got to go home," Lois said.

Mrs. Green got up now; her boys had started off already. "Just a minute, Melvin," she called, frowning. Then, smiling, she turned and thanked Elijah.

He whirled around to them all. "Are we comin' back next Saturday? Come on—let's all come back! Wasn't it great! It was *great!* Don't you think? Whatta you say?" He looked now at Lois and Mrs. Green.

"We'll see," Lois said, smiling, "Maybe."

"Can *you* come?" He turned to Mrs. Green.

"I'm not sure," she said. "I'll try."

"Fine! Oh, that's fine!" He turned on Caesar and Little Joe. "I'll be lookin' for you guys, hear?"

"Okay, chief," grinned Little Joe. "An' put somethin' in that lemonade, will ya?"

Everybody laughed . . . and soon they were gone.

Elijah slowly crawled back under his umbrella, although the sun's heat was almost spent. He looked about him. There was only one umbrella on the spot now, his own; where before there had been three. Cigarette butts and paper cups lay strewn where Hattie's girls had sat, and the sandy imprint of Caesar's enormous street shoes marked his site. Mrs. Green had dropped a bobby pin. He too was caught up now by a sudden urge to go. It was hard to bear much longer—the lonesomeness. And most of the people were leaving anyway. He stirred and fidgeted in the sand, and finally started an inventory of his belongings. . . . Then his thoughts flew home, and he reconsidered. Funny—he hadn't thought of home all afternoon. Where had the time gone anyhow? . . . It seemed he'd just pulled up in the Chevy and unloaded his gear; now it was time to go home again. Then the image of solemn Randy suddenly formed in his mind, sending waves of guilt through him. He forgot where he was as the duties of his existence leapt on his back—where would he ever get Randy's fifteen dollars? He felt squarely confronted by a great blank void. It was an awful thing he had done—all for a day at the beach . . . with some sporting girls. He thought of his family and felt tiny—and him itching to come back next Saturday! Maybe Myrtle was right about him after all. Lord, if she knew what he had done. . . .

He sat there for a long time. Most of the people were gone now. The lake was quiet save for a few boys still in the water. And the sun, red like blood, had settled on the dark silhouettes of the housetops across the city. He sat beneath the umbrella just as he had at one o'clock . . . and the thought smote him. He was jolted. Then dubious. But there it was—quivering, vital, swelling inside his skull like an unwanted fetus. So this was it. He mutinied inside. So he must sell it . . . his *umbrella*. Sell it for anything—only as long as it was enough to pay back Randy. For fifteen dollars even, if necessary. He was dogged; he couldn't do it; that wasn't the answer anyway. But the thought clawed and clung to him, rebuking and coaxing him by turns, until it finally became conviction. He must do it; it was the right thing to do; the only thing to do. Maybe then the awful weight would lift, the dull commotion in his stomach cease. He got up and started collecting his belongings; placed the thermos jug, sunglasses, towel, cigarettes, and little rug together in a neat pile, to be carried to the Chevy later. Then he turned to face his umbrella. Its red and white stripes stood defiant against the wide, churned-up sand. He stood for a moment mooning at it. Then he carefully let it down and, carrying it in his right hand, went off across the sand.

The sun now had gone down behind the vast city in a shower of crimson-golden glints, and on the beach only a few stragglers remained. For his first prospects, he approached two teen-age boys, but suddenly realizing they had no money, he turned away and went over to an old woman, squat and black, in street clothes—a spectator—who stood gazing eastward out across the lake. She held in her hand a little black book, with red-edged pages, which looked like the *New Testament.* He smiled at her. "Wanna buy a nice new beach umbrella?" He held out the collapsed umbrella toward her.

She gave him a beatific smile, but shook her head. "No, son," she said, "that ain't what *I* want." And she turned to gaze out on the lake again.

For a moment he still held the umbrella out, with a question mark on his face. "Okay, then," he finally said, and went on.

Next he hurried to the water's edge, where he saw a man and two women preparing to leave. "Wanna buy a nice new beach umbrella?" His voice sounded high-pitched, as he opened the umbrella over his head. "It's brand-new. I'll sell it for fifteen dollars—it cost a lot more'n that."

The man was hostile, and glared. Finally he said, "Whatta you take me for—a fool?"

Elijah looked bewildered, and made no answer. He observed the man for a moment. Finally he let the umbrella down. As he moved away, he heard the man say to the women, "It's hot—he stole it somewhere."

Close by, another man sat alone in the sand. Elijah started toward him. The man wore trousers, but was stripped to the waist, and bent over intent on some task in his lap. When Elijah reached him, he looked up from half a hatful of cigarette butts he was breaking open for the tobacco he collected in a little paper bag. He grinned at Elijah, who meant now to pass on.

"No, I ain't interested either, buddy," the man insisted as Elijah passed him. "Not me. I jus' got *outa* jail las' week—an' ain't goin' back for no umbrella." He laughed, as Elijah kept on.

Now he saw three women, still in their bathing suits, sitting together near the diving board. They were the only people he had not tried—except the one lifeguard left. As he approached them, he saw that all three wore glasses and were sedate. Some schoolteachers maybe, he thought, or office workers. They were talking—until they saw him coming; then they stopped. One of them was plump, but a smooth dark brown, and sat with a towel around her shoulders. Elijah addressed them through her: "Wanna buy a nice beach umbrella?" And again he opened the umbrella over his head.

"Gee! It's beautiful," the plump woman said to the others. "But where'd you get it?" she suddenly asked Elijah, polite mistrust entering her voice.

"I bought it—just this week."

The three women looked at each other. "Why do you want to sell it so soon, then?" a second woman said.

Elijah grinned. "I need the money."

"Well!" The plump woman was exasperated. "*No,* we don't want it." And they turned from him. He stood for a while, watching them; finally he let the umbrella down and moved on.

Only the lifeguard was left. He was a huge youngster, not over twenty, and brawny and black, as he bent over cleaning out his beached rowboat. Elijah approached him so suddenly he looked up startled.

"Would you be interested in this umbrella?" Elijah said, and proffered the umbrella. "It's brand-new—I just bought it Tuesday. I'll sell it cheap." There was urgency in his voice.

The lifeguard gave him a queer stare; and then peered off toward the Outer Drive, as if looking for help. "You're lucky as hell," he finally said. "The cops just now cruised by—up on the Drive. I'd have turned you in so quick it'd make your head swim. Now you get the hell outa here." He was menacing.

Elijah was angry. "Whatta you mean? I *bought* this umbrella—it's mine."

The lifeguard took a step toward him. "I said you better get the hell outa here! An' I mean it! *You thievin' bastard, you!*"

Elijah, frightened now, gave ground. He turned and walked away a few steps; and then slowed up, as if an adequate answer had hit him. He stood for a moment. But finally he walked on, the umbrella drooping in his hand.

He walked up the gravelly slope now toward the Chevy, forgetting his little pile of belongings left in the sand. When he reached the car, and opened the trunk, he remembered; and went back down and gathered them up. He returned, threw them in the trunk and, without dressing, went around and climbed under the steering wheel. He was scared, shaken; and before starting the motor sat looking out on the lake. It was seven o'clock; the sky was waning pale, the beach forsaken, leaving a sense of perfect stillness and approaching night; the only sound was a gentle lapping of the water against the sand—one moderate *hallo-o-o-o* would have carried across to Michigan. He looked down at the beach. Where were they all now—the funny, proud, laughing people? Eating their dinners, he supposed, in a variety of homes. And all the beautiful umbrellas—where were they? Without their colors the beach was so deserted. Ah, the beach . . . after pouring hot ore all week out at the Youngstown Sheet and Tube, he would probably be too fagged out for the beach. But maybe he wouldn't—who knew? It was great while it lasted . . . great. And his umbrella . . . he didn't know what he'd do with that . . . he might never need it again. He'd keep it, though—and see. Ha! . . . hadn't he sweat to get it! . . . and they thought he had stolen it . . . stolen it . . . ah . . . and maybe they were right. He sat for a few moments longer. Finally he started the motor, and took the old Chevy out onto the Drive in the pink-hued twilight. But down on the beach the sun was still shining.

Grace Paley

An Interest in Life

A native New Yorker, Grace Paley has said that she writes sometimes on the subway. And indeed, it is the gritty intelligence and joke-cracking quickness of her style that has in recent years won her the admiration of many critics and fellow writers. The recipient of a Guggenheim fellowship and a grant from the National Council on the Arts, Mrs. Paley has published two collections of short stories, The Little Disturbances of Man *(1959, reissued 1968) and* Enormous Changes at the Last Minute *(1974). Since the mid-sixties she has been militantly engaged in some of the social and political issues of our time, and describes herself as an "Anarchist, if that's politics."*

My husband gave me a broom one Christmas. This wasn't right. No one can tell me it was meant kindly.

"I don't want you not to have anything for Christmas while I'm away in the Army," he said. "Virginia, please look at it. It comes with this fancy dustpan. It hangs off a stick. Look at it, will you? Are you blind or crosseyed?"

"Thanks, chum," I said. I had always wanted a dustpan hooked up that way. It was a good one. My husband doesn't shop in bargain basements or January sales.

Still and all, in spite of the quality, it was a mean present to give a woman you planned on never seeing again, a person you had children with and got onto all the time, drunk or sober, even when everybody had to get up early in the morning.

I asked him if he could wait and join the Army in a half hour, as I had to get the groceries. I don't like to leave kids alone in a three-room apartment full of gas and electricity. Fire may break out from a nasty remark. Or the oldest decides to get even with the youngest.

"Just this once," he said. "But you better figure out how to get along without me."

"You're a handicapped person mentally," I said. "You should've been institutionalized years ago." I slammed the door. I didn't want to see him pack his underwear and ironed shirts.

I never got further than the front stoop, though, because there was Mrs. Raftery, ringing her hands, tears in her eyes as though she had a monopoly on all the good news.

"Mrs. Raftery!" I said, putting my arm around her. "Don't cry." She leaned on me because I am such a horsy build. "Don't cry, Mrs. Raftery, please!" I said.

"That's like you, Virginia. Always looking at the ugly side of things. 'Take in the wash. It's rainin'!' That's you. You're the first one knows it when the dumb-waiter breaks."

"Oh, come on now, that's not so. It just isn't so," I said. "I'm the exact opposite."

"Did you see Mrs. Cullen yet?" she asked, paying no attention.

"Where?"

"Virginia!" she said, shocked. "She's passed away. The whole house knows it. They've got her in white like a bride and you never saw a beautiful creature like that. She must be eighty. Her husband's proud."

"She was never more than an acquaintance; she didn't have any children," I said.

"Well, I don't care about that. Now, Virginia, you do what I say now, you go downstairs and you say like this—listen to me—say, 'I hear, Mr. Cullen, your wife's passed away. I'm sorry.' Then ask him how he is. Then you ought to go around the corner and see her. She's in Witson & Wayde. Then you ought to go over to the church when they carry her over."

"It's not my church," I said.

"That's no reason, Virginia. You go up like this," she said, parting from me to do a prancy dance. "Up the big front steps, into the church you go. It's beautiful in there. You can't help kneeling only for a minute. Then round to the right. Then up the other stairway. Then you come to a great oak door that's arched above you, then," she said, seizing a deep, deep breath, for all the good it would do her, "and then turn the knob slo-owly and open the door and see for yourself: Our Blessed Mother is in charge. Beautiful. Beautiful. Beautiful."

I sighed in and I groaned out, so as to melt a certain pain around my heart. A steel ring like arthritis, at my age.

"You are a groaner," Mrs. Raftery said, gawking into my mouth.

"I am not," I said. I got a whiff of her, a terrible cheap wine lush.

My husband threw a penny at the door from the inside to take my notice from Mrs. Raftery. He rattled the glass door to make sure I looked at him. He had a fat duffel bag on each shoulder. Where did he acquire so much worldly possession? What was in them? My grandma's goose feathers from across the ocean? Or all the diaper-service diapers? To this day the truth is shrouded in mystery.

"What the hell are you doing, Virginia?" he said, dumping them at my feet. "Standing out here on your hind legs telling everybody your business? The Army gives you a certain time, for God's sakes, they're not kidding." Then he said, "I beg your pardon," to Mrs. Raftery. He took hold of me with his two arms as though in love and pressed his body hard against mine so that I could feel him for the last time and suffer my loss. Then he kissed me in a mean way to nearly split my lip. Then he winked and said, "That's all for now," and skipped off into the future, duffel bags full of rags.

He left me in an embarrassing situation, nearly fainting, in front of that old widow, who can't even remember the half of it. "He's a crock," said Mrs. Raftery. "Is he leaving for good or just temporarily, Virginia?"

"Oh, he's probably deserting me," I said, and sat down on the stoop, pulling my big knees up to my chin.

"If that's the case, tell the Welfare right away," she said. "He's a bum, leaving you just before Christmas. Tell the cops," she said. "They'll provide the toys for the little kids gladly. And don't forget to let the grocer in on it. He won't be so hard on you expecting payment."

She saw that sadness was stretched world-wide across my face. Mrs. Raftery isn't the worst person. She said, "Look around for comfort, dear." With a nervous finger she pointed to the truckers eating lunch on their haunches across the street, leaning on the loading platforms. She waved her hand to include in all the men marching up and down in search of a decent luncheonette. She didn't leave out the six longshoremen loafing under the fish-market marquee. "If their lungs and stomachs ain't crushed by overwork, they disappear somewhere in the world. Don't be disappointed, Virginia. I don't know a man living'd last you a lifetime."

Ten days later Girard asked, "Where's Daddy?"

"Ask me no questions, I'll tell you no lies." I didn't want the children to know the facts. Present or past, a child should have a father.

"Where *is* Daddy?" Girard asked the week after that.

"He joined the Army," I said.

"He made my bunk bed," said Phillip.

"The truth shall make ye free," I said.

Then I sat down with pencil and pad to get in control of my resources. The facts, when I added and subtracted them, were that my husband had left me with fourteen dollars, and the rent unpaid, in an emergency state. He'd claimed he was sorry to do this, but my opinion is out of sight, out of mind. "The city won't let you starve," he'd said. "After all, you're half the population. You're keeping up the good work. Without you the race would die out. Who'd pay the taxes? Who'd keep the streets clean? There wouldn't be no Army. A man like me wouldn't have no place to go."

I sent Girard right down to Mrs. Raftery with a request about the whereabouts of Welfare. She responded RSVP with an extra comment in left-handed script: "Poor Girard. . . he's never the boy my John was!"

Who asked her?

I called on Welfare right after the new year. In no time I discovered that they're rigged up to deal with liars, and if you're truthful it's disappointing to them. They may even refuse to handle your case if you're too truthful.

They asked sensible questions at first. They asked where my husband had enlisted. I didn't know. They put some letter writers and agents after him. "He's not in the United States Army," they said. "Try the Brazilian Army," I suggested.

They have no sense of kidding around. They're not the least bit lighthearted and they tried. "Oh no," they said. "That was incorrect. He is not in the Brazilian Army."

"No?" I said. "How strange! He must be in the Mexican Navy."

By law, they had to hound his brothers. They wrote to his brother who has a first-class card in the Teamsters and owns an apartment house in California. They asked his two brothers in Jersey to help me. They have large families. Rightfully they laughed. Then they wrote to Thomas, the oldest, the smart one (the one they all worked so hard for years to keep him in college until his brains could pay off). He was the one who sent ten dollars immediately, saying, "What a bastard! I'll send something time to time, Ginny, but whatever you do, don't tell the authorities." Of course I never did. Soon they began to guess they were better people than me, that I was in trouble because I deserved it, and then they liked me better.

But they never fixed my refrigerator. Every time I called I said patiently, "The milk is sour . . ." I said, "Corn beef went bad." Sitting in that beer-stinking phone booth in Felan's for the sixth time (sixty cents) with the baby on my lap and Barbie tapping at the glass door with an American flag, I cried into the secretary's hardhearted ear, "I bought real butter for the holiday, and it's rancid . . ." They said, "You'll have to get a better bid on the repair job."

While I waited indoors for a man to bid, Girard took to swinging back and forth on top of the bathroom door, just to soothe himself, giving me the laugh, dreamy, nibbling calcimite off the ceiling. On first sight Mrs. Raftery said, "Whack the monkey, he'd be better off on arsenic."

But Girard is my son and I'm the judge. It means a terrible thing for the future, though I don't know what to call it.

It was from constantly thinking of my foreknowledge on this and other subjects, it was from observing when I put my lipstick on daily, how my face was just curling up to die, that John Raftery came from Jersey to rescue me.

On Thursdays, anyway, John Raftery took the tubes in to visit his mother. The whole house knew it. She was cheerful even before breakfast. She sang out loud in a girlish brogue that only came to tongue for grand occasions. Hanging out the wash, she blushed to recall what a remarkable boy her John had been. "Ask the sisters around the corner," she said to the open kitchen windows. "They'll never forget John."

That particular night after supper Mrs. Raftery said to her son, "John, how come you don't say hello to your old friend Virginia? She's had hard luck and she's gloomy."

"Is that so, Mother?" he said, and immediately climbed two flights to knock at my door.

"Oh, John," I said at the sight of him, hat in hand in a white shirt and blue-striped tie, spick-and-span, a Sunday-school man. "Hello!"

"Welcome, John!" I said. "Sit down. Come right in. How are you? You look awfully good. You do. Tell me, how've you been all this time, John?"

"How've I been?" he asked thoughtfully. To answer within reason, he described his life with Margaret, marriage, work, and children up to the present day.

I had nothing good to report. Now that he had put the subject around before my very eyes, every burnt-up day of my life smoked in shame, and I couldn't even get a clear view of the good half hours.

"Of course," he said, "you do have lovely children. Noticeable-looking, Virginia. Good looks is always something to be thankful for."

"Thankful?" I said. "I don't have to thank anything but my own foolishness for four children when I'm twenty-six years old, deserted, and poverty-struck, regardless of looks. A man can't help it, but I could have behaved better."

"Don't be so cruel on yourself, Ginny," he said. "Children come from God."

"You're still great on holy subjects, aren't you? You know damn well where children come from."

He did know. His red face reddened further. John Raftery has had that color coming out on him boy and man from keeping his rages so inward.

Still he made more sense in his conversation after that, and I poured fresh tea to tell him how my husband used to like me because I was a passionate person. That was until he took a look around and saw how in the long run this life only meant more of the same thing. He tried to turn away from me once he came to this understanding, and make me hate him. His face changed. He gave up his brand of cigarettes, which we had in common. He threw out the two pairs of socks I knitted by hand. "If there's anything I hate in this world, it's navy blue," he said. Oh, I could have dyed them. I would have done anything for him, if he were only not too sorry to ask me.

"You were a nice kid in those days," said John, referring to certain Saturday nights. "A wild, nice kid."

"Aaah," I said, disgusted. Whatever I was then, was on the way to where I am now. "I was fresh. If I had a kid like me, I'd slap her cross-eyed."

The very next Thursday John gave me a beautiful radio with a record player. "Enjoy yourself," he said. That really made Welfare speechless. We didn't own any records, but the investigator saw my burden was lightened and he scribbled a dozen pages about it in his notebook.

On the third Thursday he brought a walking doll (twenty-four inches) for Linda and Barbie with a card inscribed, "A baby doll for a couple of dolls." He had also had a couple of drinks at his mother's and this made him want to dance. "La-la-la," he sang, a ramrod swaying in my kitchen chair. "La-la-la, let yourself go . . ."

"You gotta give a little," he sang, "live a little . . ." He said, "Virginia, may I have this dance?"

"Sssh, we finally got them asleep. Please, turn the radio down. Quiet. Deathly silence, John Raftery."

"Let me do your dishes, Virginia."

"Don't be silly, you're a guest in my house," I said. "I still regard you as a guest."

"I want to do something for you, Virginia."

"Tell me I'm the most gorgeous thing," I said, dipping my arm to the funny bone in dish soup.

He didn't answer. "I'm having a lot of trouble at work," was all he said. Then I heard him push the chair back. He came up behind me, put his arms around my waistline, and kissed my cheek. He whirled me around and took my hands. He said, "An old friend is better than rubies." He looked me in the eye. He held my attention by trying to be honest. And he kissed me a short sweet kiss on my mouth.

"Please sit down, Virginia," he said. He kneeled before me and put his head in my lap. I was stirred by so much activity. Then he looked up at me and, as though proposing marriage for life, he offered—because he was drunk—to place his immortal soul in peril to comfort me.

First I said, "Thank you." Then I said, "No."

I was sorry for him, but he's devout, a leader of the Fathers' Club at his church, active in all the lay groups for charities, orphans, etc. I knew that if he stayed late to love with me, he would not do it lightly but would in the end pay terrible penance and ruin his long life. The responsibility would be on me.

So I said no.

And Barbie is such a light sleeper. All she has to do, I thought, is to wake up and wander in and see her mother and her new friend John with his pants around his knees, wrestling on the kitchen table. A vision like that could affect a kid for life.

I said no.

Everyone in this building is so goddamn nosy. That evening I had to say no.

But John came to visit, anyway, on the fourth Thursday. This time he brought the discarded dresses of Margaret's daughters, organdy party dresses and glazed cotton for every day. He gently admired Barbara and Linda, his blue eyes rolling to back up a couple of dozen oohs and ahs.

Even Phillip, who thinks God gave him just a certain number of hellos and he better save them for the final judgment, Phillip leaned on John and said, "Why don't you bring your boy to play with me? I don't have nobody who to play with." (Phillip's a liar. There must be at least seventy-one children in this house, pale pink to medium brown, English-talking and gibbering in Spanish, rough-and-tough boys, the Lone Ranger's bloody pals, or the exact picture of Supermouse. If a boy wanted a friend, he could pick the very one out of his neighbors.)

Also, Girard is a cold fish. He was in a lonesome despair. Sometimes he looked in the mirror and said, "How come I have such an ugly face? My nose is funny. Mostly people don't like me." He was a liar too. Girard has a face like his father's. His eyes are the color of those little blue plums in August. He looks like an advertisement in a magazine. He could be a child model and make a lot of money. He is my first child, and if he thinks he is ugly, I think I am ugly.

John said, "I can't stand to see a boy mope like that. . . . What do the sisters say in school?"

"He doesn't pay attention is all they say. You can't get much out of them."

"My middle boy was like that," said John. "Couldn't take an interest. Aaah, I wish I didn't have all that headache on the job. I'd grab Girard by the collar and make him take notice of the world. I wish I could ask him out to Jersey to play in all that space."

"Why not?" I said.

"Why, Virginia, I'm surprised you don't know why not. You know I can't take your children out to meet my children."

I felt a lot of strong arthritis in my ribs.

"My mother's the funny one, Virginia." He felt he had to continue with the subject matter. "I don't know. I guess she likes the idea of bugging Margaret. She says, 'You goin' up, John?' 'Yes, Mother,' I say. 'Behave yourself, John,' she says. 'That husband might come home and hack-saw you into hell. You're a Catholic man, John,' she says. But I figured it out. She likes to know I'm in the building. I swear, Virginia, she wishes me the best of luck."

"I do too, John," I said. We drank a last glass of beer to make sure of a peaceful sleep. "Good night, Virginia," he said, looping his muffler neatly under his chin. "Don't worry. I'll be thinking of what to do about Girard."

I got into the big bed that I share with the girls in the little room. For once I had no trouble falling asleep. I only had to worry about Linda and Barbara and Phillip. It was a great relief to me that John had taken over the thinking about Girard.

John was sincere. That's true. He paid a lot of attention to Girard, smoking out all his sneaky sorrows. He registered him into a wild pack of cub scouts that went up to the Bronx once a week to let off steam. He gave him a Junior Erector Set. And sometimes when his family wasn't listening he prayed at great length for him.

One Sunday, Sister Veronica said in her sweet voice from another life, "He's not worse. He might even be a little better. How are *you*, Virginia?" putting her hand on mine. Everybody around here acts like they know everything.

"Just fine," I said.

"We ought to start on Phillip," John said, "if it's true Girard's improving."

"You should've been a social worker, John."

"A lot of people have noticed that about me," said John.

"Your mother was always acting so crazy about you, how come she didn't knock herself out a little to see you in college? Like we did for Thomas?"

"Now, Virginia, be fair. She's a poor old woman. My father was a weak earner. She had to have my wages, and I'll tell you, Virginia, I'm not sorry. Look at Thomas. He's still in school. Drop him in this jungle and he'd be devoured. He hasn't had a touch of real life. And here I am with a good chunk of a family, a home of my own, a name in the building trades. One thing I have to tell you, the poor old woman is sorry. I said one day (oh, in passing—years ago) that I might marry you. She stuck a knife in herself. It's a fact. Not more than an eighth of an inch. You never saw such a gory Sunday. One thing—you would have been a better daughter-in-law to her than Margaret."

"Marry me?" I said.

"Well, yes. . . . Aaah—I always liked you, then . . . Why do you think I'd sit in the shade of this kitchen every Thursday night? For God's sakes, the only warm thing around here is this teacup. Yes, sir, I did want to marry you, Virginia."

"No kidding, John? Really?" It was nice to know. Better late than never, to learn you were desired in youth.

I didn't tell John, but the truth is, I would never have married him. Once I met my husband with his winking looks, he was my only interest. Wild as I had been with John and others, I turned all my wildness over to him and then there was no question in my mind.

Still, face facts, if my husband didn't budge on in life, it was my fault. On me, as they say, be it. I greeted the morn with a song. I had a hello for everyone but the landlord. Ask the people on the block, come or go—even the Spanish ones, with their sad dark faces—they have to smile when they see me.

But for his own comfort, he should have done better lifewise and moneywise. I was happy, but I am now in possession of knowledge that this is wrong. Happiness isn't so bad for a woman. She gets fatter, she gets older, she could lie down, nuzzling a regiment of men and little kids, she could just die of the pleasure. But men are different, they have to own money, or they have to be famous, or everybody on the block has to look up to them from the cellar stairs.

A woman counts her children and acts snotty, like she invented life, but men *must* do well in the world. I know that men are not fooled by being happy.

"A funny guy," said John, guessing where my thoughts had gone. "What stopped him up? He was nobody's fool. He had a funny thing about him, Virginia, if you don't mind my saying so. He wasn't much distance up, but he was all set and ready to be looking down on us all."

"He was very smart, John. You don't realize that. His hobby was crossword puzzles, and I said to him real often, as did others around here, that he ought to go out on the '$64 Question.' Why not? But he laughed. You know what he said? He said, 'That proves how dumb you are if you think I'm smart.' "

"A funny guy," said John. "Get it all off your chest," he said. "Talk it out, Virginia; it's the only way to kill the pain."

By and large, I was happy to oblige. Still I could not carry through about certain cruel remarks. It was like trying to move back into the dry mouth of a nightmare to remember that the last day I was happy was the middle of a week in March, when I told my husband I was going to have Linda. Barbara was five months old to the hour. The boys were three and four. I had to tell him. It was the last day with anything happy about it.

Later on he said, "Oh, you make me so sick, you're so goddamn big and fat, you look like a goddamn brownstone, the way you're squared off in front."

"Well, where are you going tonight?" I asked.

"How should I know?" he said. "Your big ass takes up the whole goddamn bed," he said. "There's no room for me." He bought a sleeping bag and slept on the floor.

I couldn't believe it. I would start every morning fresh. I couldn't believe that he would turn against me so, while I was still young and even his friends still liked me.

But he did, he turned absolutely against me and became no friend of mine. "All you ever think about is making babies. This place stinks like the men's room in the BMT. It's a fucking *pissoir*." He was strong on truth all through the year. "That kid eats more than the five of us put together," he said. "Stop stuffing your face, you fat dumbbell," he said to Phillip.

Then he worked on the neighbors. "Get that nosy old bag out of here," he said. "If she comes on once more with 'my son in the building trades' I'll squash her for the cat."

Then he turned on Spielvogel, the checker, his oldest friend, who only visited on holidays and never spoke to me (shy, the way some bachelors are). "That sonofabitch, don't hand me that friendship crap, all he's after is your ass. That's what I need—a little shitmaker of his using up the air in this flat."

And then there was no one else to dispose of. We were left alone fair and square, facing each other.

"Now, Virginia," he said, "I come to the end of my rope. I see a black wall ahead of me. What the hell am I supposed to do? I only got one life. Should I lie down and die? I don't know what to do anymore. I'll give it to you straight, Virginia, if I stick around, you can't help it, you'll hate me . . ."

"I hate you right now," I said. "So do whatever you like."

"This place drives me nuts," he mumbled. "I don't know what to do around here. I want to get you a present. Something."

"I told you, do whatever you like. Buy me a rattrap for rats."

That's when he went down to the House Appliance Store, and he brought back a new broom and a classy dustpan.

"A new broom sweeps clean," he said. "I got to get out of here," he said. "I'm going nuts." Then he began to stuff the duffel bags, and I went to the grocery store but was stopped by Mrs. Raftery, who had to tell me what she considered so beautiful—death—then he kissed and went to join some army somewhere.

I didn't tell John any of this, because I think it makes a woman look too bad to tell on how another man has treated her. He begins to see her through the other man's eyes, a sitting duck, a skinful of flaws. After all, I had come to depend on John. All my husband's friends were strangers now, though I had always said to them, "Feel welcome."

And the family men in the building looked too cunning, as though they had all personally deserted me. If they met me on the stairs, they carried the heaviest groceries up and helped bring Linda's stroller down, but they never asked me a question worth answering at all.

Besides that, Girard and Phillip taught the girls the days of the week: Monday, Tuesday, Wednesday, Johnday, Friday. They waited for him once a week, under the hallway lamp, half asleep like bugs in the sun, sitting in their little chairs with their names on in gold, a birth present from my mother-in-law. At fifteen after eight he punctually came, to read a story, pass out some kisses, and tuck them into bed.

But one night, after a long Johnday of them squealing my eardrum split, after a rainy afternoon with brother constantly raising up his hand against brother, with the girls near ready to go to court over the proper ownership of Melinda Lee, the twenty-four-inch walking doll, the doorbell rang three times. Not any of those times did John's face greet me.

I was too ashamed to call down to Mrs. Raftery, and she was too mean to knock on my door and explain.

He didn't come the following Thursday either. Girard said sadly, "He must've run away, John."

I had to give him up after two weeks' absence and no word. I didn't know how to tell the children: something about right and wrong, goodness and meanness, men and women. I had it all at my finger tips, ready to hand over. But I didn't think I ought to take mistakes and truth away from them. Who knows? They might make a truer friend in this world somewhere than I have ever made. So I just put them to bed and sat in the kitchen and cried.

In the middle of my third beer, searching my mind for the next step, I found the decision to go on "Strike It Rich." I scrounged some paper and pencil from the toy box and I listed all my troubles, which must be done in order to qualify. The list when complete could have brought tears to the eye of God if He had a minute. At the sight of it my bitterness began to improve. All that is really necessary for survival of the fittest, it seems, is an interest in life, good, bad, or peculiar.

As always happens in these cases where you have begun to help yourself with plans, news comes from an opposite direction. The doorbell rang, two short and two long—meaning John.

My first thought was to wake the children and make them happy. "No! No!" he said. "Please don't put yourself to that trouble. Virginia, I'm dog-tired," he said. "Dog-tired. My job is a damn headache. It's too much. It's all day and it scuttles my mind at night, and in the end who does the credit go to?"

"Virginia," he said, "I don't know if I can come any more. I've been wanting to tell you. I just don't know. What's it all about? Could you answer me if I asked you? I can't figure this whole thing out at all."

I started the tea steeping because his fingers when I touched them were cold. I didn't speak. I tried looking at it from his man point of view, and I thought he had to take a bus, the tubes, and a subway to see me; and then the subway, the tubes, and a bus to go back home at 1 A.M. It wouldn't be any trouble at all for him to part with us forever. I thought about my life, and I gave strongest consideration to my children. If given the choice, I decided to choose not to live without him.

"What's that?" he asked, pointing to my careful list of troubles. "Writing a letter?"

"Oh no," I said, "it's for 'Strike It Rich.' I hope to go on the program."

"Virginia, for goodness' sakes," he said, giving it a glance, "you don't have a ghost. They'd laugh you out of the studio. Those people really suffer."

"Are you sure, John?" I asked.

"No question in my mind at all," said John. "Have you ever seen that program? I mean, in addition to all of this—the little disturbances of man"—he waved a scornful hand at my list—"they *suffer*. They live in the forefront of tornadoes, their lives are washed off by floods—catastrophes of God. Oh, Virginia."

"Are you sure, John?"

"For goodness' sake . . ."

Sadly I put my list away. Still, if things got worse, I could always make use of it.

Once that was settled, I acted on an earlier decision. I pushed his cup of scalding tea aside. I wedged myself onto his lap between his hard belt buckle and the table. I put my arms around his neck and said, "How come you're so cold, John?" He has a kind face and he knew how to look astonished. He said, "Why, Virginia, I'm getting warmer." We laughed.

John became a lover to me that night.

Mrs. Raftery is sometimes really silly and sick from her private source of cheap wine. She expects John often. "Honor your mother, what's the matter with you, John?" she complains. "Honor. Honor."

"Virginia dear," she says. "You never would've taken John away to Jersey like Margaret. I wish he'd've married you."

"You didn't like me much in those days."

"That's a lie," she says. I know she's a hypocrite, but no more than the rest of the world.

What is remarkable to me is that it doesn't seem to conscience John as I thought it might. It is still hard to believe that a man who sends out the Ten Commandments every year for a Christmas card can be so easy buttoning and unbuttoning.

Of course we must be very careful not to wake the children or disturb the neighbors who will enjoy another person's excitement just so far, and then the pleasure enrages them. We must be very careful for ourselves, too, for when my husband comes back, realizing the babies are in school and everything easier, he won't forgive me if I've started it all up again—noisy signs of life that are so much trouble to a man.

We haven't seen him in two and a half years. Although people have suggested it, I do not want the police or Intelligence or a private eye or anyone to go after him to bring him back. I know that if he expected to stay away forever he would have written and said so. As it is, I just don't know what evening, any time, he may appear. Sometimes, stumbling over a blockbuster of a dream at midnight, I wake up to vision his soft arrival.

He comes in the door with his old key. He gives me a strict look and says, "Well, you look older, Virginia." "So do you," I say, although he hasn't changed a bit.

He settles in the kitchen because the children are asleep all over the rest of the house. I unknot his tie and offer him a cold sandwich. He raps my backside, paying attention to the bounce. I walk around him as though he were a Maypole, kissing as I go.

"I didn't like the Army much," he says. "Next time I think I might go join the Merchant Marine."

"What army?" I say.

"It's pretty much the same everywhere," he says.

"I wouldn't be a bit surprised," I say.

"I lost my cuff link, goddamnit," he says, and drops to the floor to look for it. I go down too on my knees, but I know he never had a cuff link in his life. Still I would do a lot for him.

"Got you off your feet that time," he says, laughing. "Oh yes I did." And before I can even make myself half comfortable on that polka-dotted linoleum, he got onto me right where we were, and the truth is, we were so happy, we forgot the precautions.

3
exploitations

Doris Lessing

One off the Short List

Doris Lessing's first novel, The Grass Is Singing, *was published in 1950, less than a year after her arrival in London. With its immediate success she was able to devote her full time to writing, and over the next decade published ten books, beginning with* Martha Quest *(1952), the first of five novels in the* Children of Violence *series. After a visit to Rhodesia in 1956, the government declared her a " prohibited immigrant." That same year Ms. Lessing withdrew from a four-year membership in the Communist Party, an ideological sympathy that had begun many years earlier with her observation of the racial tensions and social inequalities of south Africa.*

When he had first seen Barbara Coles, some years before, he only noticed her because someone said: "That's Johnson's new girl." He certainly had not used of her the private erotic formula: *Yes, that one.* He even wondered what Johnson saw in her. "She won't last long," he remembered thinking, as he watched Johnson, a handsome man, but rather flushed with drink, flirting with some unknown girl while Barbara stood by a wall looking on. He thought she had a sullen expression.

She was a pale girl, not slim, for her frame was generous, but her figure could pass as good. Her straight yellow hair was parted on one side in a way that struck him as gauche. He did not notice what she wore. But her eyes were all right, he remembered: large, and solidly green, square-looking because of some trick of the flesh at their corners. Emeraldlike eyes in the face of a schoolgirl, or young schoolmistress who was watching her lover flirt and would later sulk about it.

Her name sometimes cropped up in the papers. She was a stage decorator, a designer, something on those lines.

Then a Sunday newspaper had a competition for stage design and she won it. Barbara Coles was one of the "names" in the theatre, and her photograph was seen about. It was always serious. He remembered having thought her sullen.

One night he saw her across the room at a party. She was talking with a well-known actor. Her yellow hair was still done on one side, but now it looked sophisticated. She wore an emerald ring on her right hand that seemed deliberately to invite comparison with her eyes. He walked over and said: "We have met before, Graham Spence." He noted, with discomfort, that he sounded abrupt. "I'm sorry, I don't remember, but how do you do?" she said, smiling. And continued her conversation.

He hung around a bit, but soon she went off with a group of people she was inviting to her home for a drink. She did not invite Graham. There was about her an assurance, a carelessness, that he recognized as the signature of success. It was then, watching her laugh as she went off with her friends, that he used the formula: "*Yes, that one.*" And he went home to his wife with enjoyable expectation, as if his date with Barbara Coles were already arranged.

His marriage was twenty years old. At first it had been stormy, painful, tragic—full of partings, betrayals and sweet reconciliations. It had taken him at least a decade to realize that there was nothing remarkable about this marriage that he had lived through with such surprise of the mind and the senses. On the contrary, the marriages of most of the people he knew, whether they were first, second or third attempts, were just the same. His had run true to form even to the serious love affair with the young girl for whose sake he had *almost* divorced his wife—yet at the last moment had changed his mind, letting the girl down so that he must have her for always (not unpleasurably) on his conscience. It was with humiliation that he had understood that this drama was not at all the unique thing he had imagined. It was nothing more than the experience of everyone in his circle. And presumably in everybody else's circle too?

Anyway, round about the tenth year of his marriage he had seen a good many things clearly, a certain kind of emotional adventure went from his life, and the marriage itself changed.

His wife had married a poor youth with a great future as a writer. Sacrifices had been made, chiefly by her, for that future. He was neither unaware of them, nor ungrateful; in fact he felt permanently guilty about it. He at last published a decently successful book, then a second which now, thank God, no one remembered. He had drifted into radio, television, book reviewing.

He understood he was not going to make it; that he had become—not a hack, no one could call him that—but a member of that army of people who live by their wits on the fringes of the arts. The moment of realization was when he was in a pub one lunchtime near the B.B.C. where he often dropped in to meet others like himself: he understood that was why he went there—they *were* like him. Just as that melodramatic marriage had turned out to be like everyone else's—except that it had been shared with one woman instead of with two or three—so it had turned out that his unique talent, his struggles as a writer had led him here, to this pub and the half dozen pubs like it, where all the men in sight had the same history. They all had their novel, their play, their book of poems, a moment of fame, to their credit. Yet here they were, running television programs about which they were cynical (to each other or to their wives) or writing reviews about other people's books. Yes, that's what he had become, an impresario of other people's talent. These two moments of clarity, about his marriage and about his talent, had roughly coincided with his wife's decision to leave him for a man younger than himself who had a future, she said, as a playwright. Well, he had talked her out of it. For her part she had to understand he was not going to be the T. S. Eliot or Graham Greene of our time—but after all, how many were? She must finally understand this, for he could no longer bear her awful bitterness. For his part he must stop coming home drunk at five in the morning, and starting a new romantic affair every six months which he took so seriously that he made her miserable because of her implied deficiencies. In short he was to be a good husband. (He had always been a dutiful father.) And she a good wife. And so it was: the marriage became stable, as they say.

The formula: *Yes, that one* no longer implied a necessarily sexual relationship. In its more mature form, it was far from being something he was ashamed of. On the contrary, it expressed a humorous respect for what he was, for his real talents and flair, which had turned out to be not artistic after all, but to do with emotional life, hard-earned experience. It expressed an ironical dignity, a proving to himself not only: I can be honest about myself, but also: I have earned the best in *that* field whenever I want it.

He watched the field for the women who were well known in the arts, or in politics; looked out for photographs, listened for bits of gossip. He made a point of going to see them act, or dance, or orate. He built up a not unshrewd picture of them. He would either quietly pull strings to meet her or—more often, for there was a gambler's pleasure in waiting—bide his time until he met her in the natural course of events, which was bound to happen sooner or later. He would be seen out with her a few times in public, which was in order, since his work meant he had to entertain well-known people, male and female. His wife always knew, he told her. He might have a brief affair with this woman, but more often than not it was the appearance of an affair. Not that he didn't get pleasure from other people envying him—he would make a point, for instance, of taking this woman into the pubs where his male colleagues went. It was that his real pleasure came when he saw her surprise at how well she was understood by him. He enjoyed the atmosphere he was able to set up between an intelligent woman and himself: a humorous complicity which had in it much that was unspoken, and which almost made sex irrelevant.

Onto the list of women with whom he planned to have this relationship went Barbara Coles. There was no hurry. Next week, next month, next year, they would meet at a party. The world of well-known people in London is a small one. Big and little fishes, they drift around, nose each other, flirt their fins, wriggle off again. When he bumped into Barbara Coles, it would be time to decide whether or not to sleep with her.

Meanwhile he listened. But he didn't discover much. She had a busband and children, but the husband seemed to be in the background. The children were charming and well brought up, like everyone else's children. She had affairs, they said; but while several men he met sounded familiar with her, it was hard to determine whether they had slept with her, because none directly boasted of her. She was spoken of in terms of her friends, her work, her house, a party she had given, a job she had found someone. She was liked, she was respected, and Graham Spence's self-esteem was flattered because he had chosen her. He looked forward to saying in just the same tone: "Barbara Coles asked me what I thought about the set and I told her quite frankly. . . ."

Then by chance he met a young man who did boast about Barbara Coles; he claimed to have had the great love affair with her, and recently at that; and he spoke of it as something generally known. Graham realized how much he had already become involved with her in his imagination because of how perturbed he was now, on account of the character of this youth, Jack Kennaway. He had recently become successful as a magazine editor—one of those young men who, not as rare as one might suppose in the big cities, are successful from sheer impertinence, effrontery. Without much talent or taste, yet he had the charm of his effrontery. "Yes, I'm going to succeed, because I've decided to; yes, I may be stupid; but not so stupid that I don't know my deficiencies. Yes, I'm going to be successful because you people with integrity, etc., etc., simply don't believe in the possibility of people like me. You are too cowardly to stop me. Yes, I've taken your measure and I'm going to succeed because I've got the courage, not only to be unscrupulous, but to be quite frank about it. And besides, you admire me, you must, or otherwise you'd stop me. . . ." Well, that was young Jack Kennaway, and he shocked Graham. He was a tall, languishing young man, handsome in a dark melting way, and, it was quite clear, he was either asexual or homosexual. And this youth boasted of the favors of Barbara Coles; boasted, indeed, of her love. Either she was a raving neurotic with a taste for neurotics; or Jack Kennaway was a most accomplished liar; or she slept with anyone.

Graham was intrigued. He took Jack Kennaway out to dinner in order to hear him talk about Barbara Coles. There was no doubt the two were pretty close—all those dinners, theatres, weekends in the country—Graham Spence felt he had put his finger on the secret pulse of Barbara Coles; and it was intolerable that he must wait to meet her; he decided to arrange it.

It became unnecessary. She was in the news again, with a run of luck. She had done a successful historical play, and immediately afterwards a modern play, and then a hit musical. In all three, the sets were remarked on. Graham saw some interviews in newspapers and on television. These all centered around the theme of her being able to deal easily with so many different styles of theatre; but the real point was, of course, that she was a woman, which naturally added piquancy to the thing. And now Graham Spence was asked to do a half-hour radio interview with her. He planned the questions he would ask her with care, drawing on what people had said of her, but above all on his instinct and experience with women. The interview was to be at nine-thirty at night; he was to pick her up at six from the theatre where she was currently at work, so that there would be time, as the letter from the B.B.C. had put it, "for you and Miss Coles to get to know each other."

At six he was at the stage door, but a message from Miss Coles said she was not quite ready, could he wait a little. He hung about, then went to the pub opposite for a quick one, but still no Miss Coles. So he made his way backstage, directed by voices, hammering, laughter. It was badly lit, and the group of people at work did not see him. The director, James Poynter, had his arm around Barbara's shoulders. He was newly well-known, a carelessly good-looking young man reputed to be intelligent. Barbara Coles wore a dark blue overall, and her flat hair fell over her face so that she kept pushing it back with the hand that had the emerald on it. These two stood close, side by side. Three young men, stagehands, were on the other side of a trestle which had sketches and drawings on it. They were studying some sketches. Barbara said, in a voice warm with energy: "Well, so I thought if we did *this*—do you see, James? What do you think, Steven?" "Well, love," said the young man she called Steven, "I see your idea, but I wonder if . . ." "I think you're right, Babs," said the director. "Look," said Barbara, holding one of the sketches towards Steven, "look, let me show you." They all leaned forward, the five of them, absorbed in the business.

Suddenly Graham couldn't stand it. He understood he was shaken to his depths. He went off stage; and stood with his back against a wall in the dingy passage that led to the dressing rooms. His eyes were filled with tears. He was seeing what a long way he had come from the crude, uncompromising, admirable young egomaniac he had been when he was twenty. That group of people there—working, joking, arguing, yes, that's what he hadn't known for years. What bound them was the democracy of respect for each other's work, a confidence in themselves and in each other. They looked like people banded together against a world which they—no, not despised, but which they measured, understood, would fight to the death, out of respect for what *they* stood for, for what *it* stood for. It was a long time since he felt part of that balance. And he understood that he had seen Barbara Coles when she was most herself, at ease with a group of people she worked with. It was then, with the tears drying on his eyelids, which felt old and ironic, that he decided he would sleep with Barbara Coles. It was a necessity for him. He went back through the door onto the stage, burning with this single determination.

The five were still together. Barbara had a length of blue gleaming stuff which she was draping over the shoulder of Steven, the stagehand. He was showing it off, and the others watched. "What do you think, James?" she asked the director. "We've got that sort of dirty green, and I thought . . ." "Well," said James, not sure at all, "well, Babs, well . . ."

Now Graham went forward so that he stood beside Barbara, and said: "I'm Graham Spence, we've met before." For the second time she smiled socially and said: "Oh I'm sorry, I don't remember." Graham nodded at James, whom he had known or at least had met off and on, for years. But it was obvious James didn't remember him either.

"From the B.B.C," said Graham to Barbara, again sounding abrupt, against his will. "Oh I'm sorry, I'm so sorry, I forgot all about it. I've got to be interviewed," she said to the group. "Mr. Spence is a journalist." Graham allowed himself a small smile ironical of the word journalist, but she was not looking at him. She was going on with her work. "We should decide tonight," she said. "Steven's right." "Yes, I am right," said the stagehand. "She's right, James, we need that blue with that sludge-green everywhere." "James," said Barbara, "James, what's wrong with it? You haven't said." She moved forward to James, passing Graham. Remembering him again, she became contrite. "I'm sorry," she said, "we can none of us agree. Well, look"—she turned to Graham—"you advise us, we've got so involved with it that . . ." At which James laughed, and so did the stagehands. "No, Babs," said James, "of course Mr. Spence can't advise. He's just this moment come in. We've got to decide. Well I'll give you till tomorrow morning. Time to go home, it must be six by now."

"It's nearly seven," said Graham, taking command.

"It isn't!" said Barbara, dramatic. "My God, how terrible, how appalling, how could I have done such a thing. . . ." She was laughing at herself. "Well, you'll have to forgive me, Mr. Spence, because you haven't got any alternative."

They began laughing again: this was clearly a group joke. And now Graham took his chance. He said firmly, as if he were her director, in fact copying James Poynter's manner with her: "No, Miss Coles, I won't forgive you, I've been kicking my heels for nearly an hour." She grimaced, then laughed and accepted it. James said: "There, Babs, that's how you ought to be treated. We spoil you." He kissed her on the cheek, she kissed him on both his, the stagehands moved off. "Have a good evening, Babs," said James, going, and nodding to Graham. Who stood concealing his pleasure with difficulty. He knew, because he had had the courage to be firm, indeed, peremptory, with Barbara, that he had saved himself hours of maneuvering. Several drinks, a dinner—perhaps two or three evenings of drinks and dinners—had been saved because he was now on this footing with Barbara Coles, a man who could say: "No, I won't forgive you, you've kept me waiting."

She said: "I've just got to . . ." and went ahead of him. In the passage she hung her overall on a peg. She was thinking, it seemed, of something else, but seeing him watching her, she smiled at him, companionably: he realized with triumph it was the sort of smile she would offer one of the stagehands, or even James. She said again: "Just one second . . ." and went to the stage-door office. She and the stage doorman conferred. There was some problem. Graham said, taking another chance: "What's the trouble, can I help?"—as if he could help, as if he expected to be able to. "Well . . ." she said, frowning. Then, to the man: "No, it'll be all right. Good night." She came to Graham. "We've got ourselves into a bit of a fuss because half the set's in Liverpool and half's here and—but it will sort itself out." She stood, at ease, chatting to him, one colleague to another. All this was admirable, he felt; but there would be a bad moment when they emerged from the special atmosphere of the theatre into the street. He took another decision, grasped her arm firmly, and said: "We're going to have a drink before we do anything at all, it's a terrible evening out." Her arm felt resistant, but remained within his. It was raining outside, luckily. He directed her, authoritative: "No, not that pub, there's a nicer one around the corner." "Oh, but I like this pub," said Barbara, "we always use it."

"Of course you do," he said to himself. But in that pub there would be the stagehands, and probably James, and he'd lose contact with her. He'd become a *journalist* again. He took her firmly out of danger around two corners, into a pub he picked at random. A quick look around—no, they weren't there. At least, if there were people from the theatre, she showed no sign. She asked for a beer. He ordered her a double Scotch, which she accepted. Then, having won a dozen preliminary rounds already, he took time to think. Something was bothering him—what? Yes, it was what he had observed backstage, Barbara and James Poynter. Was she having an affair with him? Because if so, it would all be much more difficult. He made himself see the two of them together, and thought with a jealousy surprisingly strong: *Yes, that's it*. Meantime he sat looking at her, seeing himself look at her, *a man gazing in calm appreciation at a woman:* waiting for her to feel it and respond. She was examining the pub. Her white woollen suit was belted and had a not unprovocative suggestion of being a uniform. Her flat yellow hair, hastily pushed back after work, was untidy. Her clear white skin, without any color, made her look tired. Not very exciting, at the moment, thought Graham, but maintaining his appreciative pose for when she would turn and see it. He knew what she would see: he was relying not only on the "warm kindly" beam of his gaze, for this was merely a reinforcement of the impression he knew he made. He had black hair, a little greyed. His clothes were loose and bulky—masculine. His eyes were humorous and appreciative. He was not, never had been, concerned to lessen the impression of being settled, dependable: the husband and father. On the contrary, he knew women found it reassuring.

When she at last turned she said, almost apologetic: "Would you mind if we sat down? I've been lugging great things around all day." She had spotted two empty chairs in a corner. So had he, but rejected them, because there were other people at the table. "But my dear, of course!" They took the chairs, and then Barbara said: "If you'll excuse me a moment." She had remembered she needed makeup. He watched her go off, annoyed with himself. She was tired; and he could have understood, protected, sheltered. He realized that in the other pub, with the people she had worked with all day, she would not have thought: "I must make myself up, I must be on show." That was for outsiders. She had not, until now, considered Graham an outsider, because of his taking his chance to seem one of the working group in the theatre; but now he had thrown this opportunity away. She returned armored. Her hair was sleek, no longer defenseless. And she had made up her eyes. Her eyebrows were untouched, pale gold streaks above the brilliant green eyes whose lashes were blackened. Rather good, he thought, the contrast. Yes, but the moment had gone when he could say: Did you know you had a smudge on your cheek? Or—my dear girl!—pushing her hair back with the edge of a brotherly hand. In fact, unless he was careful, he'd be back at starting point.

He remarked: "That emerald is very cunning"—smiling into her eyes.

She smiled politely, and said: "It's not cunning, it's an accident, it was my grandmother's." She flirted her hand lightly by her face, though, smiling. But that was something she had done before, to a compliment she had had before, and often. It was all social, she had become social entirely. She remarked: "Didn't you say it was half past nine we had to record?"

"My dear Barbara, we've got two hours. We'll have another drink or two, then I'll ask you a couple of questions, then we'll drop down to the studio and get it over, and then we'll have a comfortable supper."

"I'd rather eat now, if you don't mind. I had no lunch, and I'm really hungry."

"But my dear, of course." He was angry. Just as he had been surprised by his real jealousy over James, so now he was thrown off balance by his anger: he had been counting on the long quiet dinner afterwards to establish intimacy. "Finish your drink and I'll take you to Nott's." Nott's was expensive. He glanced at her assessingly as he mentioned it. She said: "I wonder if you know Butler's? It's good and it's rather close." Butler's was good, and it was cheap, and he gave her a good mark for liking it. But Nott's it was going to be. "My dear, we'll get into a taxi and be at Nott's in a moment, don't worry."

She obediently got to her feet: the way she did it made him understand how badly he had slipped. She was saying to herself: Very well, he's like that, then all right, I'll do what he wants and get it over with. . . .

Swallowing his own drink he followed her, and took her arm in the pub doorway. It was polite within his. Outside it drizzled. No taxi. He was having bad luck now. They walked in silence to the end of the street. There Barbara glanced into a side street where a sign said: BUTLER'S. Not to remind him of it, on the contrary, she concealed the glance. And here she was, entirely at his disposal, they might never have shared the comradely moment in the theatre.

They walked half a mile to Nott's. No taxis. She made conversation: this was, he saw, to cover any embarrassment he might feel because of a half-mile walk through rain when she was tired. She was talking about some theory to do with the theatre, with designs for theatre building. He heard himself saying, and repeatedly: Yes, yes, yes. He thought about Nott's, how to get things right when they reached Nott's. There he took the headwaiter aside, gave him a pound, and instructions. They were put in a corner. Large Scotches appeared. The menus were spread. "And now, my dear," he said, "I apologize for dragging you here, but I hope you'll think it's worth it."

"Oh, it's charming, I've always liked it. It's just that . . ." She stopped herself saying: it's such a long way. She smiled at him, raising her glass, and said: "It's one of my very favorite places, and I'm glad you dragged me here." Her voice was flat with tiredness. All this was appalling; he knew it; and he sat thinking how to retrieve his position. Meanwhile she fingered the menu. The headwaiter took the order, but Graham made a gesture which said: Wait a moment. He wanted the Scotch to take effect before she ate. But she saw his silent order; and, without annoyance or reproach, leaned forward to say, sounding patient: "Graham, please, I've got to eat, you don't want me drunk when you interview me, do you?"

"They are bringing it as fast as they can," he said, making it sound as if she were greedy. He looked neither at the headwaiter nor at Barbara. He noted in himself, as he slipped further and further away from contact with her, a cold determination growing in him; one apart from, apparently, any conscious act of will, that come what may, if it took all night, he'd be in her bed before morning. And now, seeing the small pale face, with the enormous green eyes, it was for the first time that he imagined her in his arms. Although he had said: *Yes, that one*, weeks ago, it was only now that he imagined her as a sensual experience. Now he did, so strongly that he could only glance at her, and then away towards the waiters who were bringing food.

"Thank the Lord," said Barbara, and all at once her voice was gay and intimate. "Thank heavens. Thank every power that is. . . ." She was making fun of her own exaggeration; and, as he saw, because she wanted to put him at his ease after his boorishness over delaying the food. (She hadn't been taken in, he saw, humiliated, disliking her.) "Thank all the gods of Nott's," she went on, "because if I hadn't eaten inside five minutes I'd have died, I tell you." With which she picked up her knife and fork and began on her steak. He poured wine, smiling with her, thinking that *this* moment of closeness he would not throw away. He watched her frank hunger as she ate, and thought:

Sensual—it's strange I hadn't wondered whether she would be or not.

"Now," she said, sitting back, having taken the edge off her hunger: "Let's get to work."

He said: "I've thought it over very carefully—how to present you. The first thing seems to me, we must get away from that old chestnut: Miss Coles, how extraordinary for a woman to be so versatile in her work . . . I hope you agree?" This was his trump card. He had noted, when he had seen her on television, her polite smile when this note was struck. (The smile he had seen so often tonight.) This smile said: All right, if you *have* to be stupid, what can I do?

Now she laughed and said: "What a relief. I was afraid you were going to do the same thing."

"Good, now you eat and I'll talk."

In his carefully prepared monologue he spoke of the different styles of theatre she had shown herself mistress of, but not directly: he was flattering her on the breadth of her experience; the complexity of her character, as shown in her work. She ate, steadily, her face showing nothing. At last she asked: "And how did you plan to introduce this?"

He had meant to spring that on her as a surprise, something like: Miss Coles, a surprisingly young woman for what she has accomplished (she was thirty? thirty-two?) and a very attractive one. . . . "Perhaps I can give you an idea of what she's like if I say she could be taken for the film star Marie Carletta. . . ." The Carletta was a strong earthy blonde, known to be intellectual. He now saw he could not possibly say this: he could imagine her cool look if he did. She said: "Do you mind if we get away from all that—my manifold talents, et cetera. . . ." He felt himself stiffen with annoyance; particularly because this was not an accusation, he saw she did not think him worth one. She had assessed him: This is the kind of man who uses this kind of flattery and therefore. . . . It made him angrier that she did not even trouble to say: Why did you do exactly what you promised you wouldn't? She was being invincibly polite, trying to conceal her patience with his stupidity.

"After all," she was saying, "it is a stage designer's job to design what comes up. Would anyone take, let's say Johnnie Cranmore" (another stage designer) "onto the air or television and say: How very versatile you are because you did that musical about Java last month and a modern play about Irish laborers this?"

He battened down his anger. "My dear Barbara, I'm sorry. I didn't realize that what I said would sound just like the mixture as before. So what shall we talk about?"

"What I was saying as we walked into the restaurant: can we get away from the personal stuff?"

Now he almost panicked. Then, thank God, he laughed from nervousness, for she laughed and said: "You didn't hear one word I said."

"No, I didn't. I was frightened you were going to be furious because I made you walk so far when you were tired."

They laughed together, back to where they had been in the theatre. He leaned over, took her hand, kissed it. He said: "Tell me again." He thought: Damn, now she's going to be earnest and intellectual.

But he understood he had been stupid. He had forgotten himself at twenty—or, for that matter, at thirty; forgotten one could live inside an idea, a set of ideas, with enthusiasm. For in talking about her ideas (also the ideas of people she worked with) for a new theatre, a new style of theatre, she was as she had been with her colleagues over the sketches or the blue material. She was easy, informal, almost chattering. This was how, he remembered, one talked about ideas that were a breath of life. The ideas, he thought, were intelligent enough; and he would agree with them, with her, if he believed it mattered a damn one way or another, if any of these enthusiasms mattered a damn. But at least he now had the key, he knew what to do. At the end of not more than half an hour, they were again two professionals, talking about the ideas they shared, for he remembered caring about all this himself once. *When? How many years ago was it that he had been able to care?*

At last he said: "My dear Barbara, do you realize the impossible position you're putting me in? Margaret Ruyen who runs this program is determined to do you personally, the poor woman hasn't got a serious thought in her head."

Barbará frowned. He put his hand on hers, teasing her for the frown: "No, wait, trust me, we'll circumvent her." She smiled. In fact Margaret Ruyen had left it all to him, had said nothing about Miss Coles.

"They aren't very bright—the brass," he said. "Well, never mind: we'll work out what we want, do it, and it'll be a *fait accompli.*"

"Thank you, what a relief. How lucky I was to be given you to interview me." She was relaxed now, because of the whiskey, the food, the wine, above all because of this new complicity against Margaret Ruyen. It would all be easy. They worked out five or six questions, over coffee, and took a taxi through rain to the studios. He noted that the cold necessity to have her, to make her, to beat her down, had left him. He was even seeing himself, as the evening ended, kissing her on the cheek and going home to his wife. This comradeship was extraordinarily pleasant. It was balm to the wound he had not known he carried until that evening, when he had had to accept the justice of the word *journalist*. He felt he could talk forever about the state of the theatre, its finances, the stupidity of the government, the philistinism of . . .

At the studios he was careful to make a joke so that they walked in on the laugh. He was careful that the interview began at once, without conversation with Margaret Ruyen; and that from the moment the green light went on, his voice lost its easy familiarity. He made sure that not one personal note was struck during the interview. Afterwards, Margaret Ruyen, who was pleased, came forward to say so; but he took her aside to say that Miss Coles was tired and needed to be taken home at once; for he knew this must look to Barbara as if he were squaring a producer who had been expecting a different interview. He led Barbara off, her hand held tight in his against his side. "Well," he said, "we've done it, and I don't think she knows what hit her."

"Thank you," she said, "it really was pleasant to talk about something sensible for once."

He kissed her lightly on the mouth. She returned it, smiling. By now he felt sure that the mood need not slip again, he could hold it.

"There are two things we can do," he said. "You can come to my club and have a drink. Or I can drive you home and you can give me a drink. I have to go past you."

"Where do you live?"

"Wimbledon." He lived, in fact, at Highgate; but she lived in Fulham. He was taking another chance, but by the time she found out, they would be in a position to laugh over his ruse.

"Good," she said. "You can drop me home then. I have to get up early." He made no comment. In the taxi he took her hand; it was heavy in his, and ne asked: "Does James slave-drive you?"

"I didn't realize you knew him—no, he doesn't."

"Well I don't know him intimately. What's he like to work with?"

"Wonderful," she said at once. "There's no one I enjoy working with more."

Jealousy spurted in him. He could not help himself: "Are you having an affair with him?"

She looked: what's it to do with you? but said: "No, I'm not."

"He's very attractive," he said, with a chuckle of worldly complicity. She said nothing, and he insisted: "If I were a woman I'd have an affair with James."

It seemed she might very well say nothing. But she remarked: "He's married."

His spirits rose in a swoop. It was the first stupid remark she had made. It was a remark of such staggering stupidity that . . . he let out a humoring snort of laughter, put his arm around her, kissed her, said: "My dear little Babs."

She said: "Why Babs?"

"Is that the prerogative of James. And of the stagehands?" he could not prevent himself adding.

"I'm only called that at work." She was stiff inside his arm.

"My dear Barbara, then . . ." He waited for her to enlighten and explain, but she said nothing. Soon she moved out of his arm, on the pretext of lighting a cigarette. He lit it for her. He noted that his determination to lay her, and at all costs, had come back. They were outside her house. He said quickly: "And now, Barbara, you can make me a cup of coffee and give me a brandy." She hesitated; but he was out of the taxi, paying, opening the door for her. The house had no lights on, he noted. He said: "We'll be very quiet so as not to wake the children."

She turned her head slowly to look at him. She said, flat, replying to his real question: "My husband is away. As for the children, they are visiting friends tonight." She now went ahead of him to the door of the house. It was a small house, in a terrace of small and not very pretty houses. Inside a little, bright, intimate hall, she said: "I'll go and make some coffee. Then, my friend, you must go home because I'm very tired."

The *my friend* struck him deep, because he had become vulnerable during their comradeship. He said, gabbling: "You're annoyed with me—oh, please don't, I'm sorry."

She smiled, from a cool distance. He saw, in the small light from the ceiling, her extraordinary eyes. "Green" eyes are hazel, are brown with green flecks, are even blue. Eyes are checkered, flawed, changing. Hers were solid green, but really, he had never seen anything like them before. They were like very deep water. They were like—well, emeralds; or the absolute clarity of green in the depths of a tree in summer. And now, as she smiled almost perpendicularly up at him, he saw a darkness come over them. Darkness swallowed the clear green. She said: "I'm not in the least annoyed." It was as if she had yawned with boredom. "And now I'll get the things . . . in there." She nodded at a white door and left him. He went into a long, very tidy white room, that had a narrow bed in one corner, a table covered with drawings, sketches, pencils. Tacked to the walls with drawing pins were swatches of colored stuffs. Two small chairs stood near a low round table; an area of comfort in the working room. He was thinking: I wouldn't like it if my wife had a room like this. I wonder what Barbara's husband . . . ? He had not thought of her till now in relation to her husband, or to her children. Hard to imagine her with a frying pan in her hand, or for that matter, cosy in the double bed.

A noise outside: he hastily arranged himself, leaning with one arm on the mantelpiece. She came in with a small tray that had cups, glasses, brandy, coffeepot. She looked abstracted. Graham was on the whole flattered by this: it probably meant she was at ease in his presence. He realized he was a little tight and rather tired. Of course, she was tired, too, that was why she was vague. He remembered that earlier in the evening he had lost a chance by not using her tiredness. Well now, if he were intelligent . . . She was about to pour coffee. He firmly took the coffeepot out of her hand, and nodded at a chair. Smiling, she obeyed him. "That's better," he said. He poured coffee, poured brandy, and pulled the table towards her. She watched him. Then he took her hand, kissed it, patted it, laid it down gently. Yes, he thought, I did that well.

Now, a problem. He wanted to be closer to her, but she was fitted into a damned silly little chair that had arms. If he were to sit by her on the floor . . . ? But no, for him, the big bulky reassuring man, there could be no casual gestures, no informal postures. Suppose I scoop her out of the chair onto the bed? He drank his coffee as he plotted. Yes, he'd carry her to the bed, but not yet.

"Graham," she said, setting down her cup. She was, he saw with annoyance, looking tolerant. "Graham, in about half an hour I want to be in bed and asleep."

As she said this, she offered him a smile of amusement at this situation—man and woman maneuvering, the great comic situation. And with part of himself he could have shared it. Almost, he smiled with her, laughed. (Not till days later he exclaimed to himself: Lord what a mistake I made, not to share the joke with her then: that was where I went seriously wrong.) But he could not smile. His face was frozen, with a stiff pride. Not because she had been watching him plot; the amusement she now offered him took the sting out of that; but because of his revived determination that he was going to have his own way, he was going to have her. He was not going home. But he felt that he held a bunch of keys, and did not know which one to choose.

He lifted the second small chair opposite to Barbara, moving aside the coffee table for this purpose. He sat in this chair, leaned forward, took her two hands, and said: "My dear, don't make me go home yet, don't, I beg you." The trouble was, nothing had happened all evening that could be felt to lead up to these words and his tone—simple, dignified, human being pleading with human being for surcease. He saw himself leaning forward, his big hands swallowing her small ones; he saw his face, warm with the appeal. And he realized he had meant the words he used. They were nothing more than what he felt. He wanted to stay with her because she wanted him to, because he was her colleague, a fellow worker in the arts. He needed this desperately. But she was examining him, curious rather than surprised, and from a critical distance. He heard himself saying: "If James were here, I wonder what you'd do?" His voice was aggrieved; he saw the sudden dark descend over her eyes, and she said: "Graham, would you like some more coffee before you go?"

He said: "I've been wanting to meet you for years. I know a good many people who know you."

She leaned forward, poured herself a little more brandy, sat back, holding the glass between her two palms on her chest. An odd gesture: Graham felt that this vessel she was cherishing between her hands was herself. A patient, long-suffering gesture. He thought of the various men who had mentioned her. He thought of Jack Kennaway, wavered, panicked, said: "For instance, Jack Kennaway."

And now, at the name, an emotion lit her eyes—what was it? He went on, deliberately testing this emotion, adding to it: "I had dinner with him last week—oh, quite by chance!—and he was talking about you."

"Was he?"

He remembered he had thought her sullen, all those years ago. Now she seemed defensive, and she frowned. He said: "In fact he spent most of the evening talking about you."

She said in short, breathless sentences, which he realized were due to anger: "I can very well imagine what he says. But surely you can't think I enjoy being reminded that . . ." She broke off, resenting him, he saw, because he forced her down onto a level she despised. But it was not his level either: it was all her fault, all hers! He couldn't remember not being in control of a situation with a woman for years. Again he felt like a man teetering on a tightrope. He said, trying to make good use of Jack Kennaway, even at this late hour: "Of course, he's a charming boy, but not a man at all."

She looked at him, silent, guarding her brandy glass against her breasts.

"Unless appearances are totally deceptive, of course." He could not resist probing, even though he knew it was fatal.

She said nothing.

"Do you know you are supposed to have had the great affair with Jack Kennaway?" he exclaimed, making this an amused expostulation against the fools who could believe it.

"So I am told." She set down her glass. "And now," she said, standing up, dismissing him. He lost his head, took a step forward, grabbed her in his arms, and groaned: "Barbara!"

She turned her face this way and that under his kisses. He snatched a diagnostic look at her expression—it was still patient. He placed his lips against her neck, groaned "Barbara" again, and waited. She would have to do something. Fight free, respond, something. She did nothing at all. At last she said: "For the Lord's sake, Graham!" She sounded amused: he was again being offered amusement. But if he shared it with her, it would be the end of this chance to have her. He clamped his mouth over hers, silencing her. She did not fight him off so much as blow him off. Her mouth treated his attacking mouth as a woman blows and laughs in water, puffing off waves or spray with a laugh, turning aside her head. It was a gesture half annoyance, half humor. He continued to kiss her while she moved her head and face under the kisses as if they were small attacking waves.

And so began what, when he looked back on it afterwards, was the most embarrassing experience of his life. Even at the time he hated her for his ineptitude. For he held her there for what must have been nearly half an hour. She was much shorter than he, he had to bend, and his neck ached. He held her rigid, his thighs on either side of hers, her arms clamped to her side in a bear's hug. She was unable to move, except for her head. When his mouth ground hers open and his tongue moved and writhed inside it, she still remained passive. And he could not stop himself. While with his intelligence he watched this ridiculous scene, he was determined to go on, because sooner or later her body must soften in wanting his. And he could not stop because he could not face the horror of the moment when he set her free and she looked at him. And he hated her more, every moment. Catching glimpses of her great green eyes, open and dismal beneath his, he knew he had never disliked anything more than those "jeweled" eyes. They were repulsive to him. It occurred to him at last that even if by now she wanted him, he wouldn't know it, because she was not able to move at all. He cautiously loosened his hold so that she had an inch or so leeway. She remained quite passive. As if, he thought derisively, she had read or been told that the way to incite men maddened by lust was to fight them. He found he was thinking: Stupid cow, so you imagine I find you attractive, do you? You've got the conceit to think that!

The sheer, raving insanity of this thought hit him, opened his arms, his thighs, and lifted his tongue out of her mouth. She stepped back, wiping her mouth with the back of her hand, and stood dazed with incredulity. The embarrassment that lay in wait for him nearly engulfed him, but he let anger postpone it. She said positively apologetic, even, at this moment, humorous: "You're crazy, Graham. What's the matter, are you drunk? You don't seem drunk. You don't even find me attractive."

The blood of hatred went to his head and he gripped her again. Now she had got her face firmly twisted away so that he could not reach her mouth, and she repeated steadily as he kissed the parts of her cheeks and neck that were available to him: "Graham, let me go, do let me go, Graham." She went on saying this; he went on squeezing, grinding, kissing and licking. It might go on all night: it was a sheer contest of wills, nothing else. He thought: It's only a really masculine woman who wouldn't have given in by now out of sheer decency of the flesh! One thing he knew, however: that she would be in that bed, in his arms, and very soon. He let her go, but said: "I'm going to sleep with you tonight, you know that, don't you?"

She leaned with hand on the mantelpiece to steady herself. Her face was colorless, since he had licked all the makeup off. She seemed quite different: small and defenseless with her large mouth pale now, her smudged green eyes fringed with gold. And now, for the first time, he felt what it might have been supposed (certainly by her) he felt hours ago. Seeing the small damp flesh of her face, he felt kinship, intimacy with her, he felt intimacy of the flesh, the affection and good humor of sensuality. He felt she was flesh of his flesh, his sister in the flesh. He felt desire for her, instead of the will to have her; and because of this, was ashamed of the farce he had been playing. Now he desired simply to take her into bed in the affection of his senses.

She said: "What on earth am I supposed to do? Telephone the police, or what?" He was hurt that she still addressed the man who had ground her into sulky apathy; she was not addressing *him* at all.

She said: "Or scream for the neighbors is that what you want?"

The gold-fringed eyes were almost black, because of the depth of the shadow of boredom over them. She was bored and weary to the point of falling to the floor, he could see that.

He said: "I'm going to sleep with you."

"But how can you possibly want to?"—a reasonable, a civilized demand addressed to a man who (he could see) she believed would respond to it. She said: "You know I don't want to, and I know you don't really give a damn one way or the other."

He was stung back into being the boor because she had not the intelligence to see that the boor no longer existed; because she could not see that this was a man who wanted her in a way which she must respond to.

There she stood, supporting herself with one hand, looking small and white and exhausted, and utterly incredulous. She was going to turn and walk off out of simple incredulity, he could see that. "Do you think I don't mean it?" he demanded, grinding this out between his teeth. She made a movement—she was on the point of going away. His hand shot out on its own volition and grasped her wrist. She frowned. His other hand grasped her other wrist. His body hove up against hers to start the pressure of a new embrace. Before it could, she said: "Oh Lord no, I'm not going through all that again. Right, then."

"What do you mean—right, then?" he demanded.

She said: "You're going to sleep with me. O.K. Anything rather than go through that again. Shall we get it over with?"

He grinned, saying in silence: "No darling, oh no you don't, I don't care what words you use, I'm going to have you now and that's all there is to it."

She shrugged. The contempt, the weariness of it, had no effect on him, because he was now again hating her so much that wanting her was like needing to kill something or someone.

She took her clothes off, as if she were going to bed by herself: her jacket, skirt, petticoat. She stood in white bra and panties, a rather solid girl, brown-skinned still from the summer. He felt a flash of affection for the brown girl with her loose yellow hair as she stood naked. She got into bed and lay there, while the green eyes looked at him in civilized appeal: Are you really going through with this? Do you have to? Yes, his eyes said back: I do have to. She shifted her gaze aside, to the wall, saying silently: Well, if you want to take me without any desire at all on my part, then go ahead, if you're not ashamed. He was not ashamed, because he was maintaining the flame of hate for her which he knew quite well was all that stood between him and shame. He took off his clothes, and got into bed beside her. As he did so, knowing he was putting himself in the position of raping a woman who was making it elaborately clear he bored her, his flesh subsided completely sad, and full of reproach because a few moments ago it was reaching out for his sister whom he could have made happy. He lay on his side by her, secretly at work on himself, while he supported himself across her body on his elbow, using the free hand to manipulate her breasts. He saw that she gritted her teeth against his touch. At least she could not know that after all this fuss he was not potent.

In order to incite himself, he clasped her again. She felt his smallness, writhed free of him, sat up and said: "Lie down."

While she had been lying there, she had been thinking: The only way to get this over with is to make him big again, otherwise I've got to put up with him all night. His hatred of her was giving him a clairvoyance: he knew very well what went on through her mind. She had switched on, with the determination to *get it all over with*, a sensual good humor, a patience. He lay down. She squatted beside him, the light from the ceiling blooming on her brown shoulders, her flat fair hair falling over her face. But she would not look at his face. Like a bored, skilled wife, she was; or like a prostitute. She administered to him, she was setting herself to please him. Yes, he thought, she's sensual, or she could be.

Meanwhile she was succeeding in defeating the reluctance of his flesh, which was the tender token of a possible desire for her, by using a cold skill that was the result of her contempt for him. Just as he decided: Right, it's enough, now I shall have her properly, she made him come. It was not a trick, to hurry or cheat him, what defeated him was her transparent thought: Yes, that's what he's worth.

Then, having succeeded, and waited for a moment or two, she stood up, naked, the fringes of gold at her loins and in her armpits speaking to him a language quite different from that of her green, bored eyes. She looked at him and thought, showing it plainly: What sort of man is it who . . . ? He watched the slight movement of her shoulders: a just-checked shrug. She went out of the room: then the sound of running water. Soon she came back in a white dressing gown, carrying a yellow towel. She handed him the towel, looking away in politeness as he used it. "Are you going home now?" she enquired hopefully, at this point.

"No, I'm not." He believed that now he would have to start fighting her again, but she lay down beside him, not touching him (he could feel the distaste of her flesh for his) and he thought: Very well, my dear, but there's a lot of the night left yet. He said aloud: "I'm going to have you properly tonight." She said nothing, lay silent, yawned. Then she remarked consolingly, and he could have laughed outright from sheer surprise: "Those were hardly conducive circumstances for making love." She was *consoling* him. He hated her for it. A proper little slut: I force her into bed, she doesn't want me, but she still has to make me feel good, like a prostitute. But even while he hated her he responded in kind, from the habit of sexual generosity. "It's because of my admiration for you, because . . . after all, I was holding in my arms one of the thousand women."

A pause. "The thousand?" she enquired carefully.

"The thousand especial women."

"In Britain or in the world? You choose them for their brains, their beauty—what?"

"Whatever it is that makes them outstanding," he said, offering her a compliment.

"Well," she remarked at last, inciting him to be amused again: "I hope that at least there's a short list you can say I am on, for politeness' sake."

He did not reply for he understood he was sleepy. He was still telling himself that he must stay awake when he was slowly waking and it was morning. It was about eight. Barbara was not there. He thought: My God! What on earth shall I tell my wife? Where was Barbara? He remembered the ridiculous scenes of last night and nearly succumbed to shame. Then he thought, reviving anger: If she didn't sleep beside me here I'll never forgive her. . . . He sat up, quietly, determined to go through the house until he found her and having found her, to possess her, when the door opened and she came in. She was fully dressed in a green suit, her hair done, her eyes made up.

She carried a tray of coffee, which she set down beside the bed. He was conscious of his big loose hairy body, half uncovered. He said to himself that he was not going to lie in bed, naked, while she was dressed. He said: "Have you got a gown of some kind?" She handed him, without speaking, a towel, and said: "The bathroom's second on the left." She went out. He followed, the towel around him. Everything in this house was gay, intimate—not at all like her efficient working room. He wanted to find out where she had slept, and opened the first door. It was the kitchen, and she was in it, putting a brown earthenware dish into the oven. "The next door," said Barbara. He went hastily past the second door, and opened (he hoped quietly) the third. It was a cupboard full of linen. "This door," said Barbara, behind him.

"So all right then, where did you sleep?"

"What's it to do with you? Upstairs in my own bed. Now, if you have everything, I'll say goodbye, I want to get to the theatre."

"I'll take you," he said at once.

He saw again the movement of her eyes, the dark swallowing the light in deadly boredom. "I'll take you," he insisted.

"I'd prefer to go by myself," she remarked. Then she smiled: "However, you'll take me. Then you'll make a point of coming right in, so that James and everyone can see—that's what you want to take me for, isn't it?"

He hated her, finally, and quite simply, for her intelligence; that not once had he got away with anything, that she had been watching, since they had met yesterday, every movement of his campaign for her. However, some fate or inner urge over which he had no control made him say sentimentally: "My dear, you must see that I'd like at least to take you to your work."

"Not at all, have it on me," she said, giving him the lie direct. She went past him to the room he had slept in. "I shall be leaving in ten minutes," she said.

He took a shower fast. When he returned, the workroom was already tidied, the bed made, all signs of the night gone. Also, there were no signs of the coffee she had brought in for him. He did not like to ask for it, for fear of an outright refusal. Besides, she was ready, her coat on, her handbag under her arm. He went, without a word, to the front door, and she came after him, silent.

He could see that every fibre of her body signalled a simple message: Oh God, for the moment when I can be rid of this boor! She was nothing but a slut, he thought.

A taxi came. In it she sat as far away from him as she could. He thought of what he should say to his wife.

Outside the theatre she remarked: "You could drop me here, if you liked." It was not a plea, she was too proud for that. "I'll take you in," he said, and saw her thinking: Very well, I'll go through with it to shame him. He was determined to take her in and hand her over to her colleagues, he was afraid she would give him the slip. But far from playing it down, she seemed determined to play it his way. At the stage door, she said to the doorman: "This is Mr.

Spence, Tom—do you remember, Mr. Spence from last night?" "Good morning, Babs," said the man, examining Graham, politely, as he had been ordered to do.

Barbara went to the door of the stage, opened it, held it open for him. He went in first, then held it open for her. Together they walked into the cavernous, littered, badly lit place and she called out: "James, James!" A man's voice called out from the front of the house: "Here, Babs, why are you so late?"

The auditorium opened before them, darkish, silent, save for an early-morning busyness of charwomen. A vacuum cleaner roared, smally, somewhere close. A couple of stagehands stood looking up at a drop which had a design of blue and green spirals. James stood with his back to the auditorium, smoking. "You're late, Babs," he said again. He saw Graham behind her, and nodded. Barbara and James kissed. Barbara said, giving allowance to every syllable: "You remember Mr. Spence from last night?" James nodded: How do you do? Barbara stood beside him, and they looked together up at the blue-and-green backdrop. Then Barbara looked again at Graham, asking silently: All right now, isn't that enough? He could see her eyes, sullen with boredom.

He said: "Bye, Babs Bye, James. I'll ring you, Babs." No response, she ignored him. He walked off slowly, listening for what might be said. For instance: "Babs, for God's sake, what are you doing with him?" Or she might say: "Are you wondering about Graham Spence? Let me explain."

Graham passed the stagehands who, he could have sworn, didn't recognize him. Then at last he heard Jame's voice to Barbara: "It's no good, Babs, I know you're enamored of that particular shade of blue, but do have another look at it, there's a good girl. . . ." Graham left the stage, went past the office where the stage doorman sat reading a newspaper. He looked up, nodded, went back to his paper. Graham went to find a taxi, thinking: I'd better think up something convincing, then I'll telephone my wife.

Luckily he had an excuse not to be at home that day, for this evening he had to interview a young man (for television) about his new novel.

John Cheever
The Five-forty-eight

John Cheever's formal education ended at the age of seventeen when he was expelled from Thayer Academy. But that same year he also had his first publication, a short story in The New Republic. *For several years he was a handyman at Yaddo, an artist's colony; he then served in the U.S. Army during World War II. Virtually the archetype of the "*New Yorker *writer," Cheever is known for the urbanity and wit with which he describes life in the affluent suburbs. Though primarily a short story writer, John Cheever has published three novels, winning the National Book Award in 1958 for his first,* The Wapshot Chronicle.

When Blake stepped out of the elevator, he saw her. A few people, mostly men waiting for girls, stood in the lobby watching the elevator doors. She was among them. As he saw her, her face took on a look of such loathing and purpose that he realized she had been waiting for him. He did not approach her. She had no legitimate business with him. They had nothing to say. He turned and walked toward the glass doors at the end of the lobby, feeling that faint guilt and bewilderment we experience when we by-pass some old friend or classmate who seems threadbare, or sick, or miserable in some other way. It was five-eighteen by the clock in the the Western Union office. He could catch the express. As he waited his turn at the revolving doors, he saw that it was still raining. It had been raining all day, and he noticed now how much louder the rain made the noises of the street. Outside, he started walking briskly east toward Madison Avenue. Traffic was tied up, and horns were blowing urgently on a crosstown street in the distance. The sidewalk was crowded. He wondered what she had hoped to gain by a glimpse of him coming out of the office building at the end of the day. Then he wondered if she was following him.

Walking in the city, we seldom turn and look back. The habit restrained Blake. He listened for a minute—foolishly—as he walked, as if he could distinguish her footsteps from the worlds of sound in the city at the end of a rainy day. Then he noticed, ahead of him on the other side of the street, a break in the wall of buildings. Something had been torn down; something was being put up, but the steel structure had only just risen above the sidewalk fence and daylight poured through the gap. Blake stopped opposite here and looked into a store window. It was a decorator's or an auctioneer's. The window was arranged like a room in which people live and entertain their friends. There were cups on the coffee table, magazines to read, and flowers in the vases, but the flowers were dead and the cups were empty and the guests had not come. In the plate glass, Blake saw a clear reflection of himself and the crowds that were passing, like shadows, at his back. Then he saw her image—so close to him that it shocked him. She was standing only a foot or two behind him. He could have turned then and asked her what she wanted, but instead of recognizing her, he shied away abruptly from the reflection of her contorted face and went along the street. She might be meaning to do him harm—she might be meaning to kill him.

The suddenness with which he moved when he saw the reflection of her face tipped the water out of his hatbrim in such a way that some of it ran down his neck. It felt unpleasantly like the sweat of fear. Then the cold water falling into his face and onto his bare hands, the rancid smell of the wet gutters and pavings, the knowledge that his feet were beginning to get wet and that he might catch cold—all the common discomforts of walking in the rain—seemed to heighten the menace of his pursuer and to give him a morbid consciousness of his own physicalness and of the ease with which he could be hurt. He could see ahead of him the corner of Madison Avenue, where the lights were brighter. He felt that if he could get to Madison Avenue he would be all right. At the corner, there was a bakery shop with two entrances, and he went in by the door on the crosstown street, bought a coffee ring, like any other commuter, and went out the Madison Avenue door. As he started down Madison Avenue, he saw her waiting for him by a hut where newspapers were sold.

She was not clever. She would be easy to shake. He could get into a taxi by one door and leave by the other. He could speak to a policeman. He could run—although he was afraid that if he did run, it might precipitate the violence he now felt sure she had planned. He was approaching a part of the city that he knew well and where the maze of street-level and underground passages, elevator banks, and crowded lobbies made it easy for a man to lose a pursuer. The thought of this, and a whiff of sugary warmth from the coffee ring, cheered him. It was absurd to imagine being harmed on a crowded street. She was foolish, misled, lonely perhaps—that was all it could amount to. He was an insignificant man, and there was no point in anyone's following him from his office to the station. He knew no secrets of any consequence. The reports in his brief case had no bearing on war, peace, the dope traffic, the hydrogen bomb, or any of the other international skulduggeries that he associated with pursuers, men in trench coats, and wet sidewalks. Then he saw ahead of him the door of a men's bar. Oh, it was so simple!

He ordered a Gibson and shouldered his way in between two other men at the bar, so that if she should be watching from the window she would lose sight of him. The place was crowded with commuters putting down a drink before the ride home. They had brought in on their clothes—on their shoes and umbrellas—the rancid smell of the wet dusk outside, but Blake began to relax as soon as he tasted his Gibson and looked around at the common, mostly not-young faces that surrounded him and that were worried, if they were worried at all, about tax rates and who would be put in charge of merchandising. He tried to remember her name—Miss Dent, Miss Bent, Miss Lent—and he was surprised to find that he could not remember it, although he was proud of the retentiveness and reach of his memory and it had only been six months ago.

Personnel had sent her up one afternoon—he was looking for a secretary. He saw a dark woman—in her twenties, perhaps—who was slender and shy. Her dress was simple, her figure was not much, one of her stockings was crooked, but her voice was soft and he had been willing to try her out. After she had been working for him a few days, she told him that she had been in the hospital for eight months and that it had been hard after this for her to find work, and she wanted to thank him for giving her a chance. Her hair was dark, her eyes were dark; she left him with a pleasant impression of darkness. As he got to know her better, he felt that she was oversensitive and, as a consequence, lonely. Once, when she was speaking to him of what she imagined his life to be—full of friendships, money, and a large and loving family—he had thought he recognized a peculiar feeling of deprivation. She seemed to imagine the lives of the rest of the world to be more brilliant than they were. Once, she had put a rose on his desk, and he had dropped it into the wastebasket. "I don't like roses," he told her.

She had been competent, punctual, and a good typist, and he had found only one thing in her that he could object to—her handwriting. He could not associate the crudeness of her handwriting with her appearance. He would have expected her to write a rounded backhand, and in her writing there were intermittent traces of this, mixed with clumsy printing. Her writing gave him the feeling that she had been the victim of some inner—some emotional—conflict that had in its violence broken the continuity of the lines she was able to make on paper. When she had been working for him three weeks—no longer—they stayed late one night and he offered, after work, to buy her a drink. "If you really want a drink," she said, "I have some whiskey at my place."

She lived in a room that seemed to him like a closet. There were suit boxes and hatboxes piled in a corner, and although the room seemed hardly big enough to hold the bed, the dresser, and the chair he sat in, there was an upright piano against one wall, with a book of Beethoven sonatas on the rack. She gave him a drink and said that she was going to put on something more comfortable. He urged her to; that was, after all, what he had come for. If he had had any qualms, they would have been practical. Her diffidence, the feeling of deprivation in her point of view, promised to protect him from any consequences. Most of the many women he had known had been picked for their lack of self-esteem.

When he put on his clothes again, an hour or so later, she was weeping. He felt too contented and warm and sleepy to worry much about her tears. As he was dressing, he noticed on the dresser a note she had written to a cleaning woman. The only light came from the bathroom—the door was ajar—and in this half light the hideously scrawled letters again seemed entirely wrong for her, and as if they must be the handwriting of some other and very gross woman. The next day, he did what he felt was the only sensible thing. When she was out for lunch, he called personnel and asked them to fire her. Then he took the afternoon off. A few days later, she came to the office, asking to see him. He told the switchboard girl not to let her in. He had not seen her again until this evening.

Blake drank a second Gibson and saw by the clock that he had missed the express. He would get the local—the five-forty-eight. When he left the bar the sky was still light; it was still raining. He looked carefully up and down the street and saw that the poor woman had gone. Once or twice, he looked over his shoulder, walking to the station, but he seemed to be safe. He was still not quite himself, he realized, because he had left his coffee ring at the bar, and he was not a man who forgot things. This lapse of memory pained him.

He bought a paper. The local was only half full when he boarded it, and he got a seat on the river side and took off his raincoat. He was a slender man with brown hair—undistinguished in every way, unless you could have divined in his pallor or his gray eyes his unpleasant tastes. He dressed—like the rest of us—as if he admitted the existence of sumptuary laws. His raincoat was the pale buff color of a mushroom. His hat was dark brown; so was his suit. Except for the few bright threads in his necktie, there was a scrupulous lack of color in his clothing that seemed protective.

He looked around the car for neighbors. Mrs. Compton was several seats in front of him, to the right. She smiled, but her smile was fleeting. It died swiftly and horribly. Mr. Watkins was directly in front of Blake. Mr. Watkins needed a haircut, and he had broken the sumptuary laws; he was wearing a corduroy jacket. He and Blake had quarreled, so they did not speak.

The swift death of Mrs. Compton's smile did not affect Blake at all. The Comptons lived in the house next to the Blakes, and Mrs. Compton had never understood the importance of minding her own business. Louise Blake took her troubles to Mrs. Compton, Blake knew, and instead of discouraging her crying jags, Mrs. Compton had come to imagine herself a sort of confessor and had developed a lively curiosity about the Blakes' intimate affairs. She had probably been given an account of their most recent quarrel. Blake had come home one night, overworked and tired, and had found that Louise had done nothing about getting supper. He had gone into the kitchen, followed by Louise, and he had pointed out to her that the date was the fifth. He had drawn a circle around the date on the kitchen calendar. "One week is the twelfth," he said. "Two weeks will be the nineteenth." He drew a circle around the nineteenth. "I'm not going to speak to you for two weeks," he had said. "That will be the nineteenth." She had wept, she had protested, but it had been eight or ten years since she had been able to touch him with her entreaties. Louise had got old. Now the lines in her face were ineradicable, and when she clapped her glasses onto her nose to read the evening paper she looked to him like an unpleasant stranger. The physical charms that had been her only attraction were gone. It had been nine years since Blake had built a bookshelf in the doorway that connected their rooms and had fitted into the bookshelf wooden doors that could be locked, since he did not want the children to see his books. But their prolonged estrangement didn't seem remarkable to Blake. He had quarreled with his wife, but so did every other man born of woman. It was human nature. In any place where you can hear their voices—a hotel courtyard, an air shaft, a street on a summer evening—you will hear harsh words.

The hard feeling between Blake and Mr. Watkins also had to do with Blake's family, but it was not as serious or as troublesome as what lay behind Mrs. Compton's fleeting smile. The Watkinses rented. Mr. Watkins broke the sumptuary laws day after day—he once went to the eight-fourteen in a pair of sandals—and he made his living as a commercial artist. Blake's oldest son—Charles was fourteen—had made friends with the Watkins boy. He had spent a lot of time in the sloppy rented house where the Watkinses lived. The friendship had affected his manners and his neatness. Then he had begun to take some meals with the Watkinses, and to spend Saturday nights there. When he had moved most of his possessions over to the Watkinses' and had begun to spend more than half his nights there, Blake had been forced to act. He had spoken not to Charlie but to Mr. Watkins, and had, of necessity, said a number of things that must have sounded critical. Mr. Watkins' long and dirty hair and his corduroy jacket reassured Blake that he had been in the right.

But Mrs. Compton's dying smile and Mr. Watkins' dirty hair did not lessen the pleasure Blake took in settling himself in an uncomfortable seat on the five-forty-eight deep underground. The coach was old and smelled oddly like a bomb shelter in which whole families had spent the night. The light that spread from the ceiling down onto their heads and shoulders was dim. The filth on the window glass was streaked with rain from some other journey, and clouds of rank pipe and cigarette smoke had begun to rise from behind each newspaper, but it was a scene that meant to Blake that he was on a safe path, and after his brush with danger he even felt a little warmth toward Mrs. Compton and Mr. Watkins.

The train traveled up from underground into the weak daylight, and the slums and the city reminded Blake vaguely of the woman who had followed him. To avoid speculation or remorse about her, he turned his attention to the evening paper. Out of the corner of his eye he could see the landscape. It was industrial and, at that hour, sad. There were machine sheds and warehouses, and above these he saw a break in the clouds—a piece of yellow light. "Mr. Blake," someone said. He looked up. It was she. She was standing there holding one hand on the back of the seat to steady herself in the swaying coach. He remembered her name then—Miss Dent. "Hello, Miss Dent," he said.

"Do you mind if I sit here?"

"I guess not."

"Thank you. It's very kind of you. I don't like to inconvenience you like this. I don't want to . . ." He had been frightened when he looked up and saw her, but her timid voice rapidly reassured him. He shifted his hams—that futile and reflexive gesture of hospitality—and she sat down. She sighed. He smelled her wet clothing. She wore a formless black hat with a cheap crest stitched onto it. Her coat was thin cloth, he saw, and she wore gloves and carried a large pocketbook.

"Are you living out in this direction now, Miss Dent?"

"No."

She opened her purse and reached for her handerchief. She had begun to cry. He turned his head to see if anyone in the car was looking, but no one was. He had sat beside a thousand passengers on the evening train. He had noticed their clothes, the holes in their gloves; and if they fell asleep and mumbled he had wondered what their worries were. He had classified almost all of them briefly before he buried his nose in the paper. He had marked them as rich, poor, brilliant or dull, neighbors or strangers, but no one of the thousands had ever wept. When she opened her purse, he remembered her perfume. It had clung to his skin the night he went to her place for a drink.

"I've been very sick," she said. "This is the first time I've been out of bed in two weeks. I've been terribly sick."

"I'm sorry that you've been sick, Miss Dent," he said in a voice loud enough to be heard by Mr. Watkins and Mrs. Compton. "Where are you working now?"

"What?"

"Where are you working now?"

"Oh, don't make me laugh," she said softly.

"I don't understand."

"You poisoned their minds."

He straightened his back and braced his shoulders. These wrenching movements expressed a brief—and hopeless—longing to be in some other place. She meant trouble. He took a breath. He looked with deep feeling at the half-filled, half-lighted coach to affirm his sense of actuality, of a world in which there was not very much bad trouble after all. He was conscious of her heavy breathing and the smell of her rain-soaked coat. The train stopped. A nun and a man in overalls got off. When it started again, Blake put on his hat and reached for his raincoat.

"Where are you going?" she said.

"I'm going up to the next car."

"Oh, no," she said. "No, no, no." She put her white face so close to his ear that he could feel her warm breath on his cheek. "Don't do that," she whispered. "Don't try and escape me. I have a pistol and I'll have to kill you and I don't want to. All I want to do is to talk with you. Don't move or I'll kill you. Don't, don't, don't!"

Blake sat back abruptly in his seat. If he had wanted to stand and shout for help, he would not have been able to. His tongue had swelled to twice its size, and when he tried to move it, it stuck horribly to the roof of his mouth. His legs were limp. All he could think to do then was to wait for his heart to stop its hysterical beating, so that he could judge the extent of his danger. She was sitting a little sidewise, and in her pocketbook was the pistol, aimed at his belly.

"You understand me now, don't you?" she said. "You understand that I'm serious?" He tried to speak but he was still mute. He nodded his head. "Now we'll sit quietly for a little while," she said. "I got so excited that my thoughts are all confused. We'll sit quietly for a little while, until I can get my thoughts in order again."

Help would come, Blake thought. It was only a question of minutes. Someone, noticing the look on his face or her peculiar posture, would stop and interfere, and it would all be over. All he had to do was to wait until someone noticed his predicament. Out of the window he saw the river and the sky. The rain clouds were rolling down like a shutter, and while he watched, a streak of orange light on the horizon became brilliant. Its brilliance spread—he could see it move—across the waves until it raked the banks of the river with a dim firelight. Then it was put out. Help would come in a minute, he thought. Help would come before they stopped again; but the train stopped, there were some comings and goings, and Blake still lived on, at the mercy of the woman beside him. The possibility that help might not come was one that he could not face. The possibility that his predicament was not noticeable, that Mrs. Compton would guess that he was taking a poor relation out to dinner at Shady Hill, was something he would think about later. Then the saliva came back into his mouth and he was able to speak.

"Miss Dent?"

"Yes."

"What do you want?"

"I want to talk with you."

"You can come to my office."

"Oh, no. I went there every day for two weeks."

"You could make an appointment."

"No," she said. "I think we can talk here. I wrote you a letter but I've been too sick to go out and mail it. I've put down all my thoughts. I like to travel. I like trains. One of my troubles has always been that I could never afford to travel. I suppose you see this scenery every night and don't notice it any more, but it's nice for someone who's been in bed a long time. They say that He's not in the river and the hills but I think He is. 'Where shall wisdom be found,' it says. 'Where is the place of understanding? The depth saith it is not in me; the sea saith it is not with me. Destruction and death say we have heard the force with our ears.'

"Oh, I know what you're thinking," she said. "You're thinking that I'm crazy, and I have been very sick again but I'm going to be better. It's going to make me better to talk with you. I was in the hospital all the time before I came to work for you but they never tried to cure me, they only wanted to take away my self-respect. I haven't had any work now for three months. Even if I did have to kill you, they wouldn't be able to do anything to me except put me back in the hospital, so you see I'm not afraid. But let's sit quietly for a little while longer. I have to be calm."

The train continued its halting progress up the bank of the river, and Blake tried to force himself to make some plans for escape, but the immediate threat to his life made this difficult, and instead of planning sensibly, he thought of the many ways in which he could have avoided her in the first place. As soon as he had felt these regrets, he realized their futility. It was like regretting his lack of suspicion when she first mentioned her months in the hospital. It was like regretting his failure to have been warned by her shyness, her diffidence, and the handwriting that looked like the marks of a claw. There was no way now of rectifying his mistakes, and he felt—for perhaps the first time in his mature life—the full force of regret. Out of the window, he saw some men fishing on the nearly dark river, and then a ramshackle boat club that seemed to have been nailed together out of scraps of wood that had been washed up on the shore.

Mr. Watkins had fallen asleep. He was snoring. Mrs. Compton read her paper. The train creaked, slowed, and halted infirmly at another station. Blake could see the southbound platform, where a few passengers were waiting to go into the city. There was a workman with a lunch pail, a dressed-up woman, and a man with a suitcase. They stood apart from one another. Some advertisements were posted on the wall behind them. There was a picture of a couple drinking a toast in wine, a picture of a Cat's Paw rubber heel, and a picture of a Hawaiian dancer. Their cheerful intent seemed to go no farther than the puddles of water on the platform and to expire there. The platform and the people on it looked lonely. The train drew away from the station into the scattered lights of a slum and then into the darkness of the country and the river.

"I want you to read my letter before we get to Shady Hill," she said. "It's on the seat. Pick it up. I would have mailed it to you, but I've been too sick to go out. I haven't gone out for two weeks. I haven't had any work for three months. I haven't spoken to anybody but the landlady. Please read my letter."

He picked up the letter from the seat where she had put it. The cheap paper felt abhorrent and filthy to his fingers. It was folded and refolded. "Dear Husband," she had written, in that crazy, wandering hand, "they say that human love leads us to divine love, but is this true? I dream about you every night. I have such terrible desires. I have always had a gift for dreams. I dreamed on Tuesday of a volcano erupting with blood. When I was in the hospital they said they wanted to cure me but they only wanted to take away my self-respect. They only wanted me to dream about sewing and basketwork but I protected my gift for dreams. I'm clairvoyant. I can tell when the telephone is going to ring. I've never had a true friend in my whole life. . . ."

The train stopped again. There was another platform, another picture of the couple drinking a toast, the rubber heel, and the Hawaiian dancer. Suddenly she pressed her face close to Blake's again and whispered in his ear. "I know what you're thinking. I can see it in your face. You're thinking you can get away from me in Shady Hill, aren't you? Oh, I've been planning this for weeks. It's all I've had to think about. I won't harm you if you'll let me talk. I've been thinking about devils. I mean if there are devils in the world, if there are people in the world who represent evil, is it our duty to exterminate them? I know that you always prey on weak people. I can tell. Oh, sometimes I think that I ought to kill you. Sometimes I think you're the only obstacle between me and my happiness. Sometimes . . ."

She touched Blake with the pistol. He felt the muzzle against his belly. The bullet, at that distance, would make a small hole where it entered, but it would rip out of his back a place as big as a soccer ball. He remembered the unburied dead he had seen in the war. The memory came in a rush: entrails, eyes, shattered bone, ordure, and other filth.

"All I've ever wanted in life is a little love," she said. She lightened the pressure of the gun. Mr. Watkins still slept. Mrs. Compton was sitting calmly with her hands folded in her lap. The coach rocked gently, and the coats and mushroom-colored raincoats that hung between the windows swayed a little as the car moved. Blake's elbow was on the window sill and his left shoe was on the guard above the steampipe. The car smelled like some dismal classroom. The passengers seemed asleep and apart, and Blake felt that he might never escape the smell of heat and wet clothing and the dimness of the light. He tried to summon the calculated self-deceptions with which he sometimes cheered himself, but he was left without any energy for hope or self-deception.

The conductor put his head in the door and said "Shady Hill, next, Shady Hill."

"Now," she said. "Now you get out ahead of me."

Mr. Watkins waked suddenly, put on his coat and hat, and smiled at Mrs. Compton, who was gathering her parcels to her in a series of maternal gestures. They went to the door. Blake joined them, but neither of them spoke to him or seemed to notice the woman at his back. The conductor threw open the door, and Blake saw on the platform of the next car a few other neighbors who had missed the express, waiting patiently and tiredly in the wan light for their trip to end. He raised his head to see through the open door the abandoned mansion outside of town, a NO TRESPASSING sign nailed to a tree, and then the oil tanks. The concrete abutments of the bridge passed, so close to the open door that he could have touched them. Then he saw the first of the lampposts on the northbound platform, the sign SHADY HILL in black and gold, and the little lawn and flower bed kept up by the Improvement Association, and then the cab stand and a corner of the old-fashioned depot. It was raining again; it was pouring. He could hear the splash of water and see the lights reflected in puddles and in the shining pavement, and the idle sound of splashing and dripping formed in his mind a conception of shelter, so light and strange that it seemed to belong to a time of his life that he could not remember.

He went down the steps with her at his back. A dozen or so cars were waiting by the station with their motors running. A few people got off from each of the other coaches; he recognized most of them, but none offered to give him a ride. They walked separately or in pairs—purposefully out of the rain to the shelter of the platform, where the car horns called to them. It was time to go home, time for a drink, time for love, time for supper, and he could see the lights on the hill—lights by which children were being bathed, meat cooked, dishes washed—shining in the rain. One by one, the cars picked up the heads of families, until there were only four left. Two of the stranded passengers drove off in the only taxi the village had. "I'm sorry, darling," a woman said tenderly to her husband when she drove up a few minutes later. "All our clocks are slow." The last man looked at his watch, looked at the rain, and then walked off into it, and Blake saw him go as if they had some reason to say good-by—not as we say good-by to friends after a party but as we say good-by when we are faced with an inexorable and unwanted parting of the spirit and the heart. The man's footsteps sounded as he crossed the parking lot to the sidewalk, and then they were lost. In the station, a telephone began to ring. The ringing was loud, plaintive, evenly spaced, and unanswered. Someone wanted to know about the next train to Albany, but Mr. Flanagan, the stationmaster, had gone home an hour ago. He had turned on all his lights before he went away. They burned in the empty waiting room. They burned, tin-shaded, at intervals up and down the platform and with the peculiar sadness of dim and purposeless light. They lighted the Hawaiian dancer, the couple drinking a toast, the rubber heel.

"I've never been here before," she said. "I thought it would look different. I didn't think it would look so shabby. Let's get out of the light. Go over there."

His legs felt sore. All his strength was gone. "Go on," she said.

North of the station there were a freight house and a coalyard and an inlet where the butcher and the baker and the man who ran the service station moored the dinghies from which they fished on Sundays, sunk now to the gunwales with the rain. As he walked toward the freight house, he saw a movement on the ground and heard a scraping sound, and then he saw a rat take its head out of a paper bag and regard him. The rat seized the bag in its teeth and dragged it into a culvert.

"Stop," she said. "Turn around. Oh, I ought to feel sorry for you. Look at your poor face. But you don't know what I've been through. I'm afraid to go out in the daylight. I'm afraid the blue sky will fall down on me. I'm like poor Chicken-Licken. I only feel like myself when it begins to get dark. But still and all I'm better than you. I still have good dreams sometimes. I dream about picnics and Heavèn and the brotherhood of man, and about castles in the moonlight and a river with willow trees all along the edge of it and foreign cities, and after all I know more about love than you."

He heard from off the dark river the drone of an outboard motor, a sound that drew slowly behind it across the dark water such a burden of clear, sweet memories of gone summers and gone pleasures that it made his flesh crawl, and he thought of dark in the mountains and the children singing. "They never wanted to cure me," she said. "They . . ." The noise of a train coming down from the north drowned out her voice, but she went on talking. The noise filled his ears, and the windows where people ate, drank, slept, and read flew past. When the train had passed beyond the bridge, the noise grew distant, and he heard her screaming at him, "*Kneel down!* Kneel down! Do what I say. *Kneel down!*"

He got to his knees. He bent his head. "There," she said. "You see, if you do what I say, I won't harm you, because I really don't want to harm you, I want to help you, but when I see your face it sometimes seems to me that I can't help you. Sometimes it seems to me that if I were good and loving and sane—oh, much better than I am—sometimes it seems to me that if I were all these things and young and beautiful, too, and if I called to show you the right way, you wouldn't heed me. Oh, I'm better than you, I'm better than you, and I shouldn't waste my time or spoil my life like this. Put your face in the dirt. *Put your face in the dirt!* Do what I say. Put your face in the dirt."

He fell forward in the filth. The coal skinned his face. He stretched out on the ground, weeping. "Now I feel better," she said. "Now I can wash my hands of you, I can wash my hands of all this, because you see there is some kindness some saneness in me that I can find again and use. I can wash my hands." Then he heard her footsteps go away from him, over the rubble. He heard the clearer more distant sound they made on the hard surface of the platform. He heard them diminish. He raised his head. He saw her climb the stairs of the wooden footbridge and cross it and go down to the other platform, where her figure in the dim light looked small, common, and harmless. He raised himself out of the dust—warily at first, until he saw by her attitude, her looks, that she had forgotten him; that she had completed what she had wanted to do, and that he was safe. He got to his feet and picked up his hat from the ground where it had fallen and walked home.

Joyce Carol Oates

Accomplished Desires

Born in Lockport, New York, Joyce Carol Oates received a B.A. from Syracuse University and her Masters degree from the University of Wisconsin. Her first book was a collection of short stories, By the North Gate, *published in 1963 when she was 25. Since then she has published six novels, three volumes of poetry, two books of literary criticism, and three more short story collections. Her stories are regularly selected for inclusion in the annual anthologies of best short stories, and in 1970 she won a National Book Award for her novel* Them. *Since 1967 Ms. Oates has been a member of the English Department at the University of Windsor, Ontario.*

There was a man she loved with a violent love, and she spent much of her time thinking about his wife.

No shame to it, she actually followed the wife. She followed her to Peabody's Market, which was a small, dark, crowded store, and she stood in silence on the pavement as the woman appeared again and got into her station wagon and drove off. The girl, Dorie, would stand as if paralyzed, and even her long fine blond hair seemed paralyzed with thought—her heart pounded as if it too was thinking, planning—and then she would turn abruptly as if executing one of the steps in her modern dance class and cross through Peabody's alley and out to the Elks' Club parking lot and so up toward the campus, where the station wagon was bound.

Hardly had the station wagon pulled into the driveway when Dorie, out of breath, appeared a few houses down and watched. How that woman got out of a car!—you could see the flabby expanse of her upper leg, white flesh that should never be exposed, and then she turned and leaned in, probably with a grunt, to get shopping bags out of the back seat. Two of her children ran out to meet her, without coats or jackets. They had nervous, darting bodies—Dorie felt sorry for them—and their mother rose, straightening, a stout woman in a colorless coat, either scolding them or teasing them, one bag in either muscular arm—and so—so the mother and children went into the house and Dorie stood with nothing to stare at except the battered station wagon, and the small snowy wilderness that was the Arbers' front yard, and the house itself. It was a large, ugly, peeling Victorian home in a block of similar homes, most of which had been fixed up by the faculty members who rented them. Dorie, who had something of her own mother's shrewd eye for hopeless, cast-off things, believed that the house could be remodeled and made presentable—but as long as he remained married to *that woman* it would be slovenly and peeling and ugly.

She loved that woman's husband with a fierce love that was itself a little ugly. Always a rather stealthy girl, thought to be simply quiet, she had entered his life by no accident—had not appeared in his class by accident—but every step of her career, like every outfit she wore and every expression on her face, was planned and shrewd and desperate. Before her twenties she had not thought much about herself; now she thought about herself continuously. She was leggy, long-armed, slender, and had a startled look—but the look was stylized now, and attractive. Her face was denuded of make-up and across her soft skin a galaxy of freckles glowed with health. She looked like a girl about to bound onto the tennis courts—and she did play tennis, though awkwardly. She played tennis with *him*. But so confused with love was she that the game of tennis, the relentless slamming of the ball back and forth, had seemed to her a disguise for something else, the way everything in poetry or literature was a disguise for something else—for love?—and surely he must know, or didn't he know? Didn't he guess? There were many other girls he played tennis with, so that was nothing special, and her mind worked and worked while she should have slept, planning with the desperation of youth that has never actually been young —planning how to get him, how to get him, for it seemed to her that she would never be able to overcome her desire for this man.

The wife was as formidable as the husband. She wrote narrow volumes of poetry Dorie could not understand and he, the famous husband, wrote novels and critical pieces. The wife was a big, energetic, high-colored woman; the husband, Mark Arber, was about her size though not so high-colored—his complexion was rather putty-colored, rather melancholy. Dorie thought about the two of them all the time, awake or asleep, and she could feel the terrible sensation of blood flowing through her body, a flowing of desire that was not just for the man but somehow for the woman as well, a desire for her accomplishments, her fame, her children, her ugly house, her ugly body, her very life. She had light, frank blue eyes and people whispered that she drank; Dorie never spoke of her.

The college was a girls' college, exclusive and expensive, and every girl who remained there for more than a year understood a peculiar, even freakish kinship with the place—as if she had always been there and the other girls, so like herself with their sleepy unmade-up faces, the skis in winter and the bicycles in good weather, the excellent expensive professors, and the excellent air—everything, everything had always been there, had existed for centuries. They were stylish and liberal in their cashmere sweaters with soiled necks; their fingers were stained with ballpoint ink; and like them, Dorie understood that most of the world was wretched and would never come to this college, never, would be kept back from it by armies of helmeted men. She, Dorie Weinheimer, was not wretched but supremely fortunate, and she must be grateful always for her good luck, for there was no justification for her existence any more than there was any justification for the wretched lots of the world's poor. And there would flash to her mind's eye a confused picture of dark-faced starving mobs, or emaciated faces out of an old-fashioned Auschwitz photograph, or something—some dreary horror from the *New York Times'* one hundred neediest cases in the Christmas issue— She had, in the girls' soft, persistent manner, an idealism-turned-pragmatism under the influence of the college faculty, who had all been idealists at Harvard and Yale as undergraduates but who were now in their forties, and as impatient with normative values as they were with their students' occasional lockets-shaped-into-crosses; Mark Arber was the most disillusioned and the most eloquent of the Harvard men.

In class he sat at the head of the seminar table, leaning back in his leather-covered chair. He was a rather stout man. He had played football once in a past Dorie could not quite imagine, though she wanted to imagine it, and he had been in the war—one of the wars—she believed it had been World War II. He had an ugly, arrogant face and discolored teeth. He read poetry in a raspy, hissing, angry voice. "Like Marx, I believe that poetry has had enough of love; the hell with it. Poetry should now cultivate the whip," he would say grimly, and Dorie would stare at him to see if he was serious. There were four senior girls in this class and they sometimes asked him questions or made observations of their own, but there was no consistency in his reaction. Sometimes he seemed not to hear, sometimes he nodded enthusiastically and indifferently, sometimes he opened his eyes and looked at them, not distinguishing among them, and said: "A remark like that is quite characteristic." So she sat and stared at him and her heart seemed to turn to stone, wanting him, hating his wife and envying her violently, and the being that had been Dorie Weinheimer for twenty-one years changed gradually through the winter into another being, obsessed with jealousy. She did not know what she wanted most, this man or the victory over his wife.

She was always bringing poems to him in his office. She borrowed books from him and puzzled over every annotation of his. As he talked to her he picked at his fingernails, settled back in his chair, and he talked on in his rushed, veering, sloppy manner, as if Dorie did not exist or were a crowd, or a few intimate friends, it hardly mattered, as he raved about frauds in contemporary poetry, naming names, "that bastard with his sonnets," "that cow with her daughter-poems," and getting so angry that Dorie wanted to protest, no, no, why are you angry? Be gentle. Love me and be gentle.

When he failed to come to class six or seven times that winter the girls were all understanding. "Do you think he really is a genius?" they asked. His look of disintegrating, decomposing recklessness, his shiny suit and bizarre loafer shoes, his flights of language made him so different from their own fathers that it was probable he was a genius; these were girls who believed seriously in the existence of geniuses. They had been trained by their highly paid, verbose professors to be vaguely ashamed of themselves, to be silent about any I.Q. rated under 160, to be uncertain about their talents within the school and quite confident of them outside it—and Dorie, who had no talent and only adequate intelligence, was always silent about herself. Her talent perhaps lay in her faithfulness to an obsession, her cunning patience, her smile, her bared teeth that were a child's teeth and yet quite sharp. . . .

One day Dorie had been waiting in Dr. Arber's office for an hour, with some new poems for him. He was late but he strode into the office as if he had been hurrying all along, sitting heavily in the creaking swivel chair, panting; he looked a little mad. He was the author of many reviews in New York magazines and papers and in particular the author of three short, frightening novels, and now he had a burned-out, bleached-out look. Like any of the girls at this college, Dorie would have sat politely if one of her professors set fire to himself, and so she ignored his peculiar stare and began her rehearsed speech about—but what did it matter what it was about? The poems of Emily Dickinson or the terrible yearning of Shelley or her own terrible lust, what did it matter?

He let his hand fall onto hers by accident. She stared at the hand, which was like a piece of meat—and she stared at him and was quite still. She was pert and long-haired, in the chair facing him, an anonymous student and a minor famous man, and every wrinkle of his sagging, impatient face was bared to her in the winter sunlight from the window—and every thread of blood in his eyes—and quite calmly and politely she said, "I guess I should tell you, Dr. Arber, that I'm in love with you. I've felt that way for some time."

"You what, you're what?" he said. He gripped her feeble hand as if clasping it in a handshake. "What did you say?" He spoke with an amazed, slightly irritated urgency, and so it began.

2

His wife wrote her poetry under an earlier name, Barbara Scott. Many years before she had had a third name, a maiden name—Barbara Cameron—but it belonged to another era about which she never thought except under examination from her analyst. She had a place cleared in the dirty attic of her house and she liked to sit up there, away from the children, and look out the small octagon of a window, and think. People she saw from her attic window looked bizarre and helpless to her. She herself was a hefty, perspiring woman, and all her dresses—especially her expensive ones—were stained under the arms with great lemon-colored half-moons no dry cleaner could remove. Because she was so large a woman, she was quick to see imperfection in others, as if she used a magnifying glass. Walking by her window on an ordinary morning were an aged tottering woman, an enormous Negro woman—probably someone's cleaning lady—and a girl from the college on aluminum crutches, poor brave thing, and the white-blond child from up the street who was precocious and demonic. Her own children were precocious and only slightly troublesome. Now two of them were safe in school and the youngest, the three-year-old, was asleep somewhere.

Barbara Scott had won the Pulitzer Prize not long before with an intricate sonnet series that dealt with the "voices" of many people; her energetic, coy line was much imitated. This morning she began a poem that her agent was to sell, after Barbara's death, to the *New Yorker:*

> *What awful wrath*
> *what terrible betrayal*
> *and these aluminum crutches, rubber-tipped. . . .*

She had such a natural talent that she let words take her anywhere. Her decade of psychoanalysis had trained her to hold nothing back; even when she had nothing to say, the very authority of her technique carried her on. So she sat that morning at her big, nicked desk—over the years the children had marred it with sharp toys—and stared out the window and waited for more inspiration. She felt the most intense kind of sympathy when she saw someone deformed—she was anxious, in a way, to see deformed people because it released such charity in her. But apart from the girl on the crutches she saw nothing much. Hours passed and she realized that her husband had not come home; already school was out and her two boys were running across the lawn.

When she descended the two flights of stairs to the kitchen, she saw that the three-year-old Geoffrey, had opened a white plastic bottle of ammonia and had spilled it on the floor and on himself; the stench was sickening. The two older boys bounded in the back door as if spurred on by the argument that raged between them, and Barbara whirled upon them and began screaming. The ammonia had spilled onto her slacks. The boys ran into the front room and she remained in the kitchen, screaming. She sat down heavily on one of the kitchen chairs. After half an hour she came to herself and tried to analyze the situation. Did she hate these children, or did she hate herself? Did she hate Mark? Or was her hysteria a form of love, or was it both love and hate together . . . ? She put the ammonia away and made herself a drink.

When she went into the front room she saw that the boys were playing with their mechanical inventors' toys and had forgotten about her. Good. They were self-reliant. Slight, cunning children, all of them dark like Mark and prematurely aged, as if by the burden of their prodigious intelligences, they were not always predictable: they forgot things, lost things, lied about things, broke things, tripped over themselves and each other, mimicked classmates, teachers, and their parents, and often broke down into pointless tears. And yet sometimes they did not break down into tears when Barbara punished them, as if to challenge her. She did not always know what she had given birth to: they were so remote, even in their struggles and assaults, they were so fictional, as if she had imagined them herself. It had been she who'd imagined them, not Mark. Their father had no time. He was always in a hurry, he had three aged typewriters in his study and paper in each one, an article or a review or even a novel in progress in each of the machines, and he had no time for the children except to nod grimly at them or tell them to be quiet. He had been so precocious himself, Mark Arber, that after his first, successful novel at the age of twenty-four he had had to whip from place to place, from typewriter to typewriter, in a frantic attempt to keep up with—he called it keeping up with his "other self," his "real self," evidently a kind of alter ego who was always typing and creating, unlike the real Mark Arber. The real Mark Arber was now forty-five and he had made the transition from "promising" to "established" without anything in between, like most middle-aged critics of prominence.

Strachey, the five-year-old, had built a small machine that was both a man and an automobile, operated by the motor that came with the set of toys. "This is a modern centaur," he said wisely, and Barbara filed that away, thinking perhaps it would do well in a poem for a popular, slick magazine. . . . She sat, unbidden, and watched her boys' intense work with the girders and screws and bolts, and sluggishly she thought of making supper, or calling Mark at school to see what had happened . . . that morning he had left the house in a rage and when she went into his study, prim and frowning, she had discovered four or five crumpled papers in his wastebasket. It was all he had accomplished that week.

Mark had never won the Pulitzer Prize for anything. People who knew him spoke of his slump, familiarly and sadly; if they disliked Mark they praised Barbara, and if they disliked Barbara they praised Mark. They were "established" but it did not mean much, younger writers were being discovered all the time who had been born in the mid- or late forties, strangely young, terrifyingly young, and people the Arbers' age were being crowded out, hustled toward the exits. . . . Being "established" should have pleased them, but instead it led them to long spiteful bouts of eating and drinking in the perpetual New England winter.

She made another drink and fell asleep in the chair. Sometime later her children's fighting woke her and she said, "Shut up," and they obeyed at once. They were playing in the darkened living room, down at the other end by the big brick fireplace that was never used. Her head ached. She got to her feet and went out to make another drink.

Around one o'clock Mark came in the back door. He stumbled and put the light on. Barbara, in her plaid bathrobe, was sitting at the kitchen table. She had a smooth, shiny, bovine face, heavy with fatigue. Mark said, "What the hell are you doing here?"

She attempted a shrug of her shoulders. Mark stared at her. "I'm getting you a housekeeper," he said. "You need more time for yourself, for your work. For your work," he said, twisting his mouth at the word to show what he thought of it. "You shouldn't neglect your poetry so we're getting in a housekeeper, not to do any heavy work, just to sort of watch things—in other words—a kind of external consciousness. You should be freed from ordinary considerations."

He was not drunk but he had the appearance of having been drunk, hours before, and now his words were muddled and dignified with the air of words spoken too early in the morning. He wore a dirty tweed overcoat, the same coat he'd had when they were married, and his necktie had been pulled off and stuffed somewhere, and his puffy, red face looked mean. Barbara thought of how reality was too violent for poetry and how poetry, and the language itself, shimmered helplessly before the confrontation with living people and their demands. "The housekeeper is here. She's outside," Mark said "I'll go get her."

He returned with a college girl who looked like a hundred other college girls. "This is Dorie, this is my wife Barbara, you've met no doubt at some school event, here you are," Mark said. He was carrying a suitcase that must have belonged to the girl. "Dorie has requested room and board with a faculty family. The Dean of Women arranged it. Dorie will babysit or something—we can put her in the spare room. Let's take her up."

Barbara had not yet moved. The girl was pale and distraught; she looked about sixteen. Her hair was disheveled. She stared at Barbara and seemed about to speak.

"Let's take her up, you want to sit there all night?" Mark snarled.

Barbara indicated with a motion of her hand that they should go up without her. Mark, breathing heavily, stomped up the back steps and the girl followed at once. There was no indication of her presence because her footsteps were far too light on the stairs. She said nothing, and only a slight change in the odor of the kitchen indicated something new—a scent of cologne, hair scrubbed clean, a scent of panic. Barbara sat listening to her heart thud heavily inside her and she recalled how, several years before, Mark had left her and had turned up at a friend's apartment in Chicago—he'd been beaten up by someone on the street, an accidental event—and how he had blackened her eye once in an argument over the worth of Samuel Richardson, and how—there were many other bitter memories—and of course there had been other women, some secret and some known—and now this—

So she sat thinking with a small smile of how she would have to dismiss this when she reported it to their friends: *Mark has had this terrible block for a year now, with his novel, and so . . .*

She sat for a while running through phrases and explanations, and when she climbed up the stairs to bed she was grimly surprised to see him in their bedroom, asleep, his mouth open and his breath raspy and exhausted. At the back of the house, in a small oddly shaped maid's room, slept the girl; in their big dormer room slept the three boys, or perhaps they only pretended to sleep; and only she, Barbara, stood in the dark and contemplated the bulk of her own body, wondering what to do and knowing that there was nothing she would do, no way for her to change the process of events any more than she could change the heavy fact of her body itself. There was no way to escape what the years had made her.

3

From that time on they lived together like a family. Or it was as Mark put it: "Think of a babysitter here permanently. Like the Lunt girl, staying on here permanently to help, only we won't need that one any more." Barbara made breakfast for them all, and then Mark and Dorie drove off to school and returned late, between six and six-thirty, and in the evenings Mark worked hard at his typewriters, going to sit at one and then the next and then the next, and the girl, Dorie helped Barbara with the dishes and odd chores and went up to her room, where she studied . . . or did something, she must have done something.

Of the long afternoons he and the girl were away, Mark said nothing. He was evasive and jaunty; he looked younger. He explained carefully to Dorie that when he and Mrs. Arber were invited somewhere she must stay home and watch the children, that she was not included in these invitations; and the girl agreed eagerly. She did so want to help around the house! She had inherited from her background a dislike for confusion—so the mess of the Arber house upset her and she worked for hours picking things up, polishing tarnished objects Barbara herself had forgotten were silver, cleaning, arranging, fixing. As soon as the snow melted she was to be seen outside, raking shyly through the flower beds. How to explain her to the neighbors? Barbara said nothing.

"But I didn't think we lived in such a mess. I didn't think it was so bad,"

Barbara would say to Mark in a quiet, hurt voice, and he would pat her hand and say, "It isn't a mess, she just likes to fool around. *I* don't think it's a mess."

It was fascinating to live so close to a young person. Barbara had never been young in quite the way Dorie was young. At breakfast—they ate crowded around the table—everyone could peer into everyone else's face, there were no secrets, stale mouths and bad moods were inexcusable, all the wrinkles of age or distress that showed on Barbara could never be hidden, and not to be hidden was Mark's guilty enthusiasm, his habit of saying "*We* should go to . . . ," *We* are invited . . ." and the "we" meant either him and Barbara, or him and Dorie, but never all three; he had developed a new personality. But Dorie was fascinating. She awoke to the slow gray days of spring with a panting, wondrous expectation, her blond hair shining, her freckles clear as dabs of clever paint on her heartbreaking skin, her teeth very, very white and straight, her pert little lips innocent of lipstick and strangely sensual . . . yes, it was heartbreaking. She changed her clothes at least twice a day while Barbara wore the same outfit—baggy black slacks and a black sweater—for weeks straight. Dorie appeared downstairs in cashmere sweater sets that were the color of birds' eggs, or of birds' fragile legs, and white trim blouses that belonged on a genteel hockey field, and bulky pink sweaters big as jackets, and when she was dressed casually she wore stretch slacks that were neatly secured by stirrups around her long, narrow, white feet. Her eyes were frankly and emptily brown, as if giving themselves up to every observer. She was so anxious to help that it was oppressive; "No, I can manage, I've been making breakfast for eight years by myself," Barbara would say angrily, and Dorie, a chastised child, would glance around the table not only at Mark but at the children for sympathy. Mark had a blackboard set up in the kitchen so that he could test the children's progress in languages, and he barked out commands for them—French or Latin or Greek—and they responded with nervous glee, clacking out letters on the board, showing off for the rapt, admiring girl who seemed not to know if they were right or wrong.

"Oh, how smart they are—how wonderful everything is," Dorie breathed.

Mark had to drive to Boston often because he needed his prescription for tranquilizers refilled constantly, and his doctor would not give him an automatic refill. But though Barbara had always looked forward to these quick trips, he rarely took her now. He went off with Dorie, now his "secretary," who took along a notebook decorated with the college's insignia to record his impressions in, and since he never gave his wife warning she could not get ready in time, and it was such an obvious trick, so crudely cruel, that Barbara stood in the kitchen and wept as they drove out. . . . She called up friends in New York but never told them what was going on. It was so ludicrous, it made her seem such a fool. Instead she chatted and barked with laughter; her conversations with these people were always so witty that nothing, nothing seemed very real until she hung up the receiver again; and then she became herself, in a drafty college-owned house in New England, locked in this particular body.

She stared out the attic window for hours, not thinking. She became a state of being, a creature. Downstairs the children fought, or played peacefully, or rifled through their father's study, which was forbidden, and after a certain amount of time something would nudge Barbara to her feet and she would descend slowly, laboriously, as if returning to the real world where an ugliness was possible. When she slapped the boys for being bad, they stood in meek defiance and did not cry. "Mother, you're out of your mind," they said. "Mother, you're losing control of yourself."

"It's your father who's out of his mind!" she shouted.

She had the idea that everyone was talking about them, everyone. Anonymous, worthless people who had never published a line gloated over her predicament; high-school baton twirlers were better off than Barbara Scott, who had no dignity. Dorie, riding with Mark Arber on the expressway to Boston, was at least young and stupid, anonymous though she was, and probably she too had a slim collection of poems that Mark would manage to get published . . . and who knew what would follow, who could tell? Dorie Weinheimer was like any one of five hundred or five thousand college girls and was no one, had no personality, and yet Mark Arber had somehow fallen in love with her, so perhaps everyone would eventually fall in love with her . . . ? Barbara imagined with panic the parties she knew nothing about to which Mark and his new girl went: Mark in his slovenly tweed suits, looking like his own father in the thirties, and Dorie chic as a Vogue model in her weightless bones and vacuous face.

"Is Dorie going to stay here long?" the boys kept asking.

"Why, don't you like her?"

"She's nice. She smells nice. Is she going to stay long?"

"Go ask your father that," Barbara said angrily.

The girl was officially boarding with them; it was no lie. Every year certain faculty families took in a student or two, out of generosity or charity, or because they themselves needed the money, and the Arbers' themselves had always looked down upon such hearty liberalism. But now they had Dorie, and in Peabody's Market Barbara had to rush up and down the aisles with her shopping cart, trying to avoid the wives of other professors who were sure to ask her about the new boarder; and she had to buy special things for the girl, spinach and beets and artichokes, while Barbara and Mark liked starches and sweets and fat, foods that clogged up the blood vessels and strained the heart and puffed out the stomach. While Barbara ate and drank hungrily, Dorie sat chaste with her tiny forkfuls of food, and Barbara could eat three platefuls to Dorie's one; her appetite increased savagely just in the presence of the girl. (The girl was always asking politely, "Is it the boys who get the bathroom all dirty?" or "Could I take the vacuum cleaner down and have it fixed?" and these questions, polite as they were, made Barbara's appetite increase savagely.)

In April, after Dorie had been boarding with them three and a half months, Barbara was up at her desk when there was a rap on the plywood door. Unused to visitors, Barbara turned clumsily and looked at Mark over the top of her glasses. "Can I come in?" he said. "What are you working on?"

There was no paper in her typewriter. "Nothing," she said.

"You haven't shown me any poems lately. What's wrong?"

He sat on the window ledge and lit a cigarette. Barbara felt a spiteful satisfaction to see how old he looked—he hadn't her fine, fleshed-out skin, the smooth complexion of an overweight woman; he had instead the bunched, baggy complexion of an overweight man whose weight keeps shifting up and down. Good. Even his fingers shook as he lit the cigarette.

"This is the best place in the house," he said.

"Do you want me to give it up to Dorie?"

He stared at her. "Give it up—why? Of course not."

"I thought you might be testing my generosity."

He shook his head, puzzled. Barbara wondered if she hated this man or if she felt a writer's interest in him. Perhaps he was insane. Or perhaps he had been drinking again; he had not gone out to his classes this morning and she'd heard him arguing with Dorie. "Barbara, how old are you?" he said.

"Forty-three. You know that."

He looked around at the boxes and other clutter as if coming to an important decision. "Well, we have a little problem here."

Barbara stared at her blunt fingernails and waited.

"She got herself pregnant. It seems on purpose."

"She what?"

"Well," Mark said uncomfortably, "she did it on purpose."

They remained silent. After a while, in a different voice he said, "She claims she loves children. She loves our children and wants some of her own. It's a valid point, I can't deny her her rights . . . but . . . I thought you should know about it in case you agree to help."

"What do you mean?"

"Well, I have something arranged in Boston," he said, not looking at her, "and Dorie has agreed to it . . . though reluctantly . . . and unfortunately I don't think I can drive her myself . . . you know I have to go to Chicago. . . ."

Barbara did not look at him.

"I'm on this panel at the University of Chicago, with John Ciardi. You know, it's been set up for a year, it's on the state of contemporary poetry—you know—I can't possibly withdraw from it now—"

"And so?"

"If you could drive Dorie in—"

"If I could drive her in?"

"I don't see what alternative we have," he said slowly.

"Would you like a divorce so you can marry her?"

"I have never mentioned that," he said.

"Well, would you?"

"I don't know."

"Look at me. Do you want to marry her?"

A nerve began to twitch in his eye. It was a familiar twitch—it had been with him for two decades. "No, I don't think so. I don't know—you know how I feel about disruption."

"Don't you have any courage?"

"Courage?"

"If you want to marry her, go ahead. I won't stop you."

"Do you want a divorce yourself?"

"I'm asking you. It's up to you. Then Dorie can have her baby and fulfill herself," Barbara said with a deathly smile. "She can assert her rights as a woman twenty years younger than I. She can become the third Mrs. Arber and become automatically envied. Don't you have the courage for it?"

"I had thought," Mark said with dignity, "that you and I had an admirable marriage. It was different from the marriages of other people we know—part of it is that we don't work in the same area, yes, but the most important part lay in our understanding of each other. It has taken a tremendous generosity on your part, Barbara, over the last three months and I appreciate it," he said, nodding slowly, "I appreciate it and I can't help asking myself whether . . . whether I would have had the strength to do what you did, in your place. I mean, if you had brought in—"

"I know what you mean."

"It's been an extraordinary marriage. I don't want it to end on an impulse, anything reckless or emotional," he said vaguely. She thought that he did look a little mad, but quietly mad; his ears were very red. For the first time she began to feel pity for the girl who was, after all, nobody, and who had no personality, and who was waiting in the ugly maid's room for her fate to be decided.

"All right, I'll drive her to Boston," Barbara said.

4

Mark had to leave the next morning for Chicago. He would be gone, he explained, about a week—there was not only the speaking appearance but other things as well. The three of them had a kind of farewell party the night before. Dorie sat with her frail hand on her flat, child's stomach and drank listlessly, while Barbara and Mark argued about the comparative merits of two English novelists—their literary arguments were always witty, superficial, rapid, and very enjoyable. At two o'clock Mark woke Dorie to say good-by and Barbara, thinking herself admirably discreet, went upstairs alone.

She drove Dorie to Boston the next day. Dorie was a mother's child, the kind of girl mothers admire—clean, bright, passive—and it was a shame for her to be so frightened. Barbara said roughly, "I've known lots of women who've had abortions. They lived."

"Did you ever have one?"

"No."

Dorie turned away as if in reproach.

"I've had children and that's harder, maybe. It's thought to be harder," Barbara said, as if offering the girl something.

"I would like children, maybe three of them," Dorie said.

"Three is a good number, yes."

"But I'd be afraid . . . I wouldn't know what to do. . . . I don't know what to do now. . . ."

She was just a child herself, Barbara thought with a rush of sympathy; of all of them it was Dorie who was most trapped. The girl sat with a scarf around her careless hair, staring out the window. She wore a camel's hair coat like all the girls and her fingernails were colorless and uneven, as if she had been chewing them.

"Stop thinking about it. Sit still."

"Yes," the girl said listlessly.

They drove on. Something began to weigh at Barbara's heart, as if her flesh were aging moment by moment. She had never liked her body. Dorie's body was so much more prim and chaste and stylish and her own body belonged to another age, a hearty nineteenth century where fat had been a kind of virtue. Barbara thought of her poetry, which was light and sometimes quite clever, the poetry of a girl, glimmering with half-seen visions and echoing the peculiar off-rhymes—and truly it ought to have been Dorie's poetry and not hers. She was not equal to her own writing. And, on the highway like this, speeding toward some tawdry destination, she had the sudden terrible conviction that language itself did not matter and that nothing mattered ultimately except the body, the human body and the bodies of other creatures and objects: what else existed?

Her own body was the only real fact about her. Dorie, huddled over in her corner, was another real fact and they were going to do something about it, defeat it. She thought of Mark already in Chicago, at a cocktail party, the words growing like weeds in his brain and his wit moving so rapidly through the brains of others that it was, itself, a kind of lie. It seemed strange to her that the two of them should move against Dorie, who suffered because she was totally real and helpless and gave up nothing of herself to words.

They arrived in Boston and began looking for the street. Barbara felt clumsy and guilty and did not dare to glance over at the girl. She muttered aloud as they drove for half an hour, without luck. Then she found the address. It was a small private hospital with a blank gray front. Barbara drove past it and circled the block and approached it again. "Come on, get hold of yourself!" she said to Dorie's stiff profile, "this is no picnic for me either."

She stopped the car and she and Dorie stared out at the hospital, which looked deserted. The neighborhood itself seemed deserted. Finally Barbara said, with a heaviness she did not understand, "Let's find a place to stay tonight first. Let's get that settled." She took the silent girl to a motel on a boulevard and told her to wait in the room, she'd be back shortly. Dorie stared in a drugged silence at Barbara, who could have been her mother—there flashed between them the kind of camaraderie possible only between mother and daughter—and then Barbara left the room. Dorie remained sitting in a very light chair of imitation wood and leather. She sat so that she was staring at the edge of the bureau; occasionally her eye was attracted by the framed picture over the bed, of a woman in a red evening gown and a man in a tuxedo observing a waterfall by moonlight. She sat like this for quite a while, in her coat. A nerve kept twitching in her thigh but it did not bother her; it was a most energetic thumping twitch, as if her very flesh were doing a dance. But it did not bother her. She remained there for a while, waking to the morning light, and it took her several panicked moments to remember where she was and who had brought her here. She had the immediate thought that she must be safe—if it was morning she must be safe—and someone had taken care of her, had seen what was best for her and had carried it out.

5

And so she became the third Mrs. Arber, a month after the second one's death. Barbara had been found dead in an elegant motel across the city, the Paradise Inn, which Mark thought was a brave, cynical joke; he took Barbara's death with an alarming rhetorical melodrama, an alcoholic melancholy Dorie did not like. Barbara's "infinite courage" made Dorie resentful. The second Mrs. Arber had taken a large dose of sleeping pills and had died easily, because of the strain her body had made upon her heart; so that was that. But somehow it wasn't—because Mark kept talking about it, speculating on it, wondering: "She did it for the baby; to preserve life. It's astonishing, it's exactly like something in a novel," he said. He spoke with a perpetual guilty astonishment.

She married him and became Mrs. Arber, which surprised everyone. It surprised even Mark. Dorie herself was not very surprised, because a daydreamer is prepared for most things and in a way she had planned even this, though she had not guessed how it would come about. Surely she had rehearsed the second Mrs. Arber's suicide and funeral already a year before, when she'd known nothing, could have guessed nothing, and it did not really surprise her. Events lost their jagged edges and became hard and opaque and routine, drawing her into them. She was still a daydreamer, though she was Mrs. Arber. She sat at the old desk up in the attic and leaned forward on her bony elbows to stare out the window, contemplating the hopeless front yard and the people who strolled by, some of them who—she thought—glanced toward the house with a kind of amused contempt, as if aware of her inside. She was almost always home.

The new baby was a girl, Carolyn. Dorie took care of her endlessly and she took care of the boys; she hadn't been able to finish school. In the evening when all the children were at last asleep Mark would come out of his study and read to her in his rapid, impatient voice snatches of his new novel, or occasionally poems of his late wife's, and Dorie would stare at him and try to understand. She was transfixed with love for him and yet—and yet she was unable to locate this love in this particular man, unable to comprehend it. Mark was invited everywhere that spring; he flew all the way out to California to take part in a highly publicized symposium with George Steiner and James Baldwin, and Dorie stayed home. Geoffrey was seeing a psychiatrist in Boston and she had to drive him in every other day, and there was her own baby, and Mark's frequent visitors who arrived often without notice and stayed a week—sleeping late, staying up late, drinking, eating, arguing—it was exactly the kind of life she had known would be hers, and yet she could not adjust to it. Her baby was somehow mixed up in her mind with the other wife, as if it had been that woman's and only left to her, Dorie, for safekeeping. She was grateful that her baby was a girl because wasn't there always a kind of pact or understanding between women?

In June two men arrived at the house to spend a week, and Dorie had to cook for them. They were long, lean, gray-haired young men who were undefinable, sometimes very fussy, sometimes reckless and hysterical with wit, always rather insulting in a light, veiled manner Dorie could not catch. They were both vegetarians and could not tolerate anyone eating meat in their presence. One evening at a late dinner Dorie began to cry and had to leave the room, and the two guests and Mark and even the children were displeased with her. She went up to the attic and sat mechanically at the desk. It did no good to read Barbara Scott's poetry because she did not understand it. Her understanding had dropped to tending the baby and the boys, fixing meals, cleaning up and shopping, and taking the station wagon to the garage perpetually . . . and she had no time to go with the others to the tennis courts, or to accompany Mark to New York . . . and around her were human beings whose lives consisted of language, the grace of language, and she could no longer understand them. She felt strangely cheated, a part of her murdered, as if the abortion had taken place that day after all and something had been cut permanently out of her.

In a while Mark climbed the stairs to her. She heard him coming, she heard his labored breathing. "Here you are," he said, and slid his big beefy arms around her and breathed his liquory love into her face, calling her his darling, his beauty. After all, he did love her, it was real and his arms were real, and she still loved him although she had lost the meaning of that word. "Now will you come downstairs and apologize, please?" he said gently. "You've disturbed them and it can't be left like this. You know how I hate disruption."

She began weeping again, helplessly, to think that she had disturbed anyone, that she was this girl sitting at a battered desk in someone's attic, and no one else, no other person who might confidently take upon herself the meaning of this man's words—she was herself and that was a fact, a final fact she would never overcome.

Ernest Hemingway
The Short Happy Life of Francis Macomber

Ernest Hemingway was born in Oak Park, Illinois, learned to hunt and fish in the woods of northern Michigan as a boy, was wounded on the Italian front in World War I, and lived in Paris during the 1920's. There he wrote two novels, The Sun Also Rises *(1926) and* A Farewell to Arms *(1929), and two collections of short stories,* In Our Time *(1924) and* Men Without Women *(1927). These works, which established him as one of the most important writers of the twentieth century, have continued to influence writers for five decades. In 1954 Hemingway was awarded the Nobel Prize for Literature.*

It was now lunch time and they were all sitting under the double green fly of the dining tent pretending that nothing had happened.

"Will you have lime juice or lemon squash?" Macomber asked.

"I'll have a gimlet," Robert Wilson told him.

"I'll have a gimlet too. I need something," Macomber's wife said.

"I suppose it's the thing to do," Macomber agreed. "Tell him to make three gimlets."

The mess boy had started them already, lifting the bottles out of the canvas cooling bags that sweated wet in the wind that blew through the trees that shaded the tents.

"What had I ought to give them?" Macomber asked.

"A quid would be plenty," Wilson told him. "You don't want to spoil them."

"Will the headman distribute it?"

"Absolutely."

Francis Macomber had, half an hour before, been carried to his tent from the edge of the camp in triumph on the arms and shoulders of the cook, the personal boys, the skinner and the porters. The gun-bearers had taken no part in the demonstration. When the native boys put him down at the door of his tent, he had shaken all their hands, received their congratulations, and then gone into the tent and sat on the bed until his wife came in. She did not speak to him when she came in and he left the tent at once to wash his face and hands in the portable wash basin outside and go over to the dining tent to sit in a comfortable canvas chair in the breeze and the shade.

"You've got your lion," Robert Wilson said to him, "and a damned fine one too."

Mrs. Macomber looked at Wilson quickly. She was an extremely handsome and well-kept woman of the beauty and social psoition which had, five years before, commanded five thousand dollars as the price of endorsing, with photographs, a beauty product which she had never used. She had been married to Francis Macomber for eleven years.

"He is a good lion, isn't he?" Macomber said. His wife looked at him now. She looked at both these men as though she had never seen them before.

One, Wilson, the white hunter, she knew she had never truly seen before. He was about middle height with sandy hair, a stubby mustache, a very red face and extremely cold blue eyes with faint white wrinkles at the corners that grooved merrily when he smiled. He smiled at her now and she looked away from his face at the way his shoulders sloped in the loose tunic he wore with the four big cartridges held in loops where the left breast pocket should have been, at his big brown hands, his old slacks, his very dirty boots and back to his red face again. She noticed where the baked red of his face stopped in a white line that marked the circle left by his Stetson hat that hung now from one of the pegs of the tent pole.

"Well, here's to the lion," Robert Wilson said. He smiled at her again, and, not smiling, she looked curiously at her husband.

Francis Macomber was very tall, very well built if you did not mind that length of bone, dark, his hair cropped like an oarsman, rather thin-lipped, and was considered handsome. He was dressed in the same sort of safari clothes that Wilson wore except that his were new, he was thirty-five years old, kept himself very fit, was good at court games, had a number of big-game fishing records, and had just shown himself, very publicly, to be a coward.

"Here's to the lion," he said. "I can't ever thank you for what you did."

Margaret, his wife, looked away from him and back to Wilson.

"Let's not talk about the lion," she said.

Wilson looked over at her without smiling and now she smiled at him.

"It's been a very strange day," she said. "Hadn't you ought to put your hat on even under the canvas at noon? You told me that, you know."

"Might put it on," said Wilson.

"You know you have a very red face, Mr. Wilson," she told him and smiled again.

"Drink," said Wilson.

"I don't think so," she said. "Francis drinks a great deal, but his face is never red."

"It's red today," Macomber tried a joke.

"No," said Margaret. "It's mine that's red today. But Mr. Wilson is always red."

"Must be racial," said Wilson. "I say, you wouldn't like to drop my beauty as a topic, would you?"

"I've just started on it."

"Let's chuck it," said Wilson.

"Conversation is going to be so difficult," Margaret said.

"Don't be silly, Margot," her husband said.

"No difficulty," Wilson said. "Got a damn fine lion."

Margot looked at them both and they both saw that she was going to cry. Wilson had seen it coming for a long time and he dreaded it. Macomber was past dreading it.

"I wish it hadn't happened. Oh, I wish it hadn't happened," she said and started for her tent. She made no noise of crying but they could see that her shoulders were shaking under the rose-colored, sun-proofed shirt she wore.

"Women upset," said Wilson to the tall man. "Amounts to nothing. Strain on the nerves and one thing'n another."

"No," said Macomber. "I suppose that I rate that for the rest of my life now."

"Nonsense. Let's have a spot of the giant killer," said Wilson. "Forget the whole thing. Nothing to it anyway."

"We might try," said Macomber. "I won't forget what you did for me though."

"Nothing," said Wilson. "All nonsense."

So they sat there in the shade where the camp was pitched under some wide-topped acacia trees with a boulder-strewn cliff behind them, and a stretch of grass that ran to the bank of a boulder-filled stream in front with forest beyond it, and drank their just-cool lime drinks and avoided one another's eyes while the boys set the table for lunch. Wilson could tell that the boys all knew about it now and when he saw Macomber's personal boy looking curiously at his master while he was putting dishes on the table he snapped at him in Swahili. The boy turned away with his face blank.

"What were you telling him?" Macomber asked.

"Nothing. Told him to look alive or I'd see he got about fifteen of the best."

"What's that? Lashes?"

"It's quite illegal," Wilson said. "You're supposed to fine them."

"Do you still have them whipped?"

"Oh, yes. They could raise a row if they chose to complain. But they don't. They prefer it to the fines."

"How strange!" said Macomber.

"Not strange, really," Wilson said. "Which would you rather do? Take a good birching or lose your pay?"

Then he felt embarrassed at asking it and before Macomber could answer he went on, "We all take a beating every day, you know, one way or another."

This was no better. "Good God," he thought. "I am a diplomat, aren't I?"

"Yes, we take a beating," said Macomber, still not looking at him. "I'm awfully sorry about that lion business. It doesn't have to go any further, does it? I mean no one will hear about it, will they?"

"You mean will I tell it at the Mathaiga Club?" Wilson looked at him now coldly. He had not expected this. So he's a bloody four-letter man as well as a bloody coward, he thought. I rather liked him too until today. But how is one to know about an American?

"No," said Wilson. "I'm a professional hunter. We never talk about our clients. You can be quite easy on that. It's supposed to be bad form to ask us not to talk though."

He had decided now that to break would be much easier. He would eat, then, by himself and could read a book with his meals. They would eat by themselves. He would see them through the safari on a very formal basis—what was it the French called it? Distinguished consideration—and it would be a damn sight easier than having to go through this emotional trash. He'd insult him and make a good clean break. Then he could read a book with his meals and he'd still be drinking their whisky. That was the phrase for it when a safari went bad. You ran into another white hunter and you asked, "How is everything going?" and he answered, "Oh, I'm still drinking their whisky," and you knew everything had gone to pot.

"I'm sorry," Macomber said and looked at him with his American face that would stay adolescent until it became middle-aged, and Wilson noted his crew-cropped hair, fine eyes only faintly shifty, good nose, thin lips and handsome jaw. "I'm sorry I didn't realize that. There are lots of things I don't know."

So what could he do, Wilson thought. He was all ready to break it off quickly and neatly and here the beggar was apologizing after he had just insulted him. He made one more attempt. "Don't worry about me talking," he said. "I have a living to make. You know in Africa no woman ever misses her lion and no white man ever bolts."

"I bolted like a rabbit," Macomber said.

Now what in hell were you going to do about a man who talked like that, Wilson wondered.

Wilson looked at Macomber with his flat, blue, machine-gunner's eyes and the other smiled back at him. He had a pleasant smile if you did not notice how his eyes showed when he was hurt.

"Maybe I can fix it up on buffalo," he said. "We're after them next, aren't we?"

"In the morning if you like," Wilson told him. Perhaps he had been wrong. This was certainly the way to take it. You most certainly could not tell a damned thing about an American. He was all for Macomber again. If you could forget the morning. But, of course, you couldn't. The morning had been about as bad as they come.

"Here comes the Memsahib," he said. She was walking over from her tent looking refreshed and cheerful and quite lovely. She had a very perfect oval face, so perfect that you expected her to be stupid. But she wasn't stupid, Wilson thought, no, not stupid.

"How is the beautiful red-faced Mr. Wilson? Are you feeling better, Francis, my pearl?"

"Oh, much," said Macomber.

"I've dropped the whole thing," she said, sitting down at the table. "What importance is there to whether Francis is any good at killing lions? That's not his trade. That's Mr. Wilson's trade. Mr. Wilson is really very impressive killing anything. You do kill anything, don't you?"

"Oh, anything," said Wilson. "Simply anything." They are, he thought, the hardest in the world; the hardest, the cruelest, the most predatory and the most attractive and their men have softened or gone to pieces nervously as they have hardened. Or is it that they pick men they can handle? They can't know that much at the age they marry, he thought. He was grateful that he had gone through his education on American women before now because this was a very attractive one.

"We're going after buff in the morning," he told her.

"I'm coming," she said.

"No, you're not."

"Oh, yes, I am. Mayn't I, Francis?"

"Why not stay in camp?"

"Not for anything," she said. "I wouldn't miss something like today for anything."

When she left, Wilson was thinking, when she went off to cry, she seemed a hell of a fine woman. She seemed to understand, to realize, to be hurt for him and for herself and to know how things really stood. She is away for twenty minutes and now she is back, simply enamelled in that American female cruelty. They are the damnedest women. Really the damnedest.

"We'll put on another show for you tomorrow," Francis Macomber said.

"You're not coming," Wilson said.

"You're very mistaken," she told him. "And I want *so* to see you perform again. You were lovely this morning. That is if blowing things' heads off is lovely."

"Here's the lunch," said Wilson. "You're very merry, aren't you?"

"Why not? I didn't come out here to be dull."

"Well, it hasn't been dull," Wilson said. He could see the boulders in the river and the high bank beyond with the trees and he remembered the morning.

"Oh, no," she said. "It's been charming. And tomorrow. You don't know how I look forward to tomorrow."

"That's eland he's offering you," Wilson said.

"They're the big cowy things that jump like hares, aren't they?"

"I suppose that describes them," Wilson said.

"It's very good meat," Macomber said.

"Did you shoot it, Francis?" she asked.

"Yes."

"They're not dangerous, are they?"

"Only if they fall on you," Wilson told her.

"I'm so glad."

"Why not let up on the bitchery just a little, Margot," Macomber said, cutting the eland steak and putting some mashed potato, gravy and carrot on the down-turned fork that tined through the piece of meat.

"I suppose I could," she said, "since you put it so prettily."

"Tonight we'll have champagne for the lion," Wilson said. "It's a bit too hot at noon."

"Oh, the lion," Margot said. "I'd forgotten the lion!"

So Robert Wilson thought to himself, she *is* giving him a ride, isn't she? Or do you suppose that's her idea of putting up a good show? How should a woman act when she discovers her husband is a bloody coward? She's damn cruel but they're all cruel. They govern, of course, and to govern one has to be cruel sometimes. Still, I've seen enough of their damn terrorism.

"Have some more eland," he said to her politely.

That afternoon, late, Wilson and Macomber went out in the motor car with the native driver and the two gun-bearers. Mrs. Macomber stayed in the camp. It was too hot to go out, she said, and she was going with them in the early morning. As they drove off Wilson saw her standing under the big tree, looking pretty rather than beautiful in her faintly rosy khaki, her dark hair drawn back off her forehead and gathered in a knot low on her neck. her face as fresh, he thought, as though she were in England. She waved to them as the car went off through the swale of high grass and curved around through the trees into the small hills of orchard bush.

In the orchard bush they found a herd of impala, and leaving the car they stalked one old ram with long, wide-spread horns and Macomber killed it with a very creditable shot that knocked the buck down at a good two hundred yards and sent the herd off bounding wildly and leaping over one another's backs in long, leg-drawn-up leaps as unbelievable and as floating as those one makes sometimes in dreams.

"That was a good shot," Wilson said. "They're a small target."

"Is it a worth-while head?" Macomber asked.

"It's excellent," Wilson told him. "You shoot like that and you'll have no trouble."

"Do you think we'll find buffalo tomorrow?"

"There's a good chance of it. They feed out early in the morning and with luck we may catch them in the open."

"I'd like to clear away that lion business," Macomber said. "It's not very pleasant to have your wife see you do something like that."

I should think it would be even more unpleasant to do it, Wilson thought, wife or no wife, or to talk about it having done it. But he said, "I wouldn't think about that any more. Any one could be upset by his first lion. That's all over."

But that night after dinner and a whisky and soda by the fire before going to bed, as Francis Macomber lay on his cot with the mosquito bar over him and listened to the night noises it was not all over. It was neither all over nor was it beginning. It was there exactly as it happened with some parts of it indelibly emphasized and he was miserably ashamed at it. But more than shame he felt cold, hollow fear in him. The fear was still there like a cold slimy hollow in all the emptiness where once his confidence had been and it made him feel sick. It was still there with him now.

It had started the night before when he had wakened and heard the lion roaring somewhere up along the river. It was a deep sound and at the end there were sort of coughing grunts that made him seem just outside the tent, and when Francis Macomber woke in the night to hear it he was afraid. He could hear his wife breathing quietly, asleep. There was no one to tell he was afraid, nor to be afraid with him, and, lying alone, he did not know the Somali proverb that says a brave man is always frightened three times by a lion; when he first sees his track, when he first hears him roar and when he first confronts him. Then while they were eating breakfast by lantern light out in the dining tent, before the sun was up, the lion roared again and Francis thought he was just at the edge of camp.

"Sounds like an old-timer," Robert Wilson said, looking up from his kippers and coffee. "Listen to him cough."

"Is he very close?"

"A mile or so up the stream."

"Will we see him?"

"We'll have a look."

"Does his roaring carry that far? It sounds as though he were right in camp."

"Carries a hell of a long way," said Robert Wilson. "It's strange the way it carries. Hope he's a shootable cat. The boys said there was a very big one about here."

"If I get a shot, where should I hit him," Macomber asked, "to stop him?"

"In the shoulders," Wilson said. "In the neck if you can make it. Shoot for bone. Break him down."

"I hope I can place it properly," Macomber said.

"You shoot very well," Wilson told him. "Take your time. Make sure of him. The first one in is the one that counts."

"What range will it be?"

"Can't tell. Lion has something to say about that. Don't shoot unless it's close enough so you can make sure."

"At under a hundred yards?" Macomber asked.

Wilson looked at him quickly.

"Hundred's about right. Might have to take him a bit under. Shouldn't chance a shot at much over that. A hundred's a decent range. You can hit him wherever you want at that. Here comes the Memsahib."

"Good morning," she said. "Are we going after that lion?"

"As soon as you deal with your breakfast," Wilson said. "How are you feeling?"

"Marvellous," she said. "I'm very excited."

"I'll just go and see that everything is ready," Wilson went off. As he left the lion roared again.

"Noisy beggar," Wilson said. "We'll put a stop to that."

"What's the matter, Francis?" his wife asked him.

"Nothing," Macomber said.

"Yes, there is," she said. "What are you upset about?"

"Nothing," he said.

"Tell me," she looked at him. "Don't you feel well?"

"It's that damned roaring," he said. "It's been going on all night, you know."

"Why didn't you wake me," she said. "I'd love to have heard it."

"I've got to kill the damned thing," Macomber said miserably.

"Well, that's what you're out here for, isn't it?"

"Yes. But I'm nervous. Hearing the thing roar gets on my nerves."

"Well, then, as Wilson said, kill him and stop his roaring."

"Yes, darling," said Francis Macomber. "It sounds easy, doesn't it?"

"You're not afraid, are you?"

"Of course not. But I'm nervous from hearing him roar all night."

"You'll kill him marvellously," she said. "I know you will. I'm awfully anxious to see it."

"Finish your breakfast and we'll be starting."

"It's not light yet," she said. "This is a ridiculous hour."

Just then the lion roared in a deep-chested moaning, suddenly guttural, ascending vibration that seemed to shake the air and ended in a sigh and a heavy, deep-chested grunt.

"He sounds almost here," Macomber's wife said.

"My God," said Macomber. "I hate that damned noise."

"It's very impressive."

"Impressive. It's frightful."

Robert Wilson came up then carrying his short, ugly, shockingly big-bored .505 Gibbs and grinning.

"Come on," he said. "Your gun-bearer has your Springfield and the big gun. Everything's in the car. Have you solids?"

"Yes."

"I'm ready," Mrs. Macomber said.

"Must make him stop that racket," Wilson said. "You get in front. The Memsahib can sit back here with me."

They climbed into the motor car and, in the gray first daylight, moved off up the river through the trees. Macomber opened the breech of his rifle and saw he had metal-cased bullets, shut the bolt and put the rifle on safety. He saw his hand was trembling. He felt in his pockets for more cartridges and moved his fingers over the cartridges in the loops of his tunic front. He turned back to where Wilson sat in the rear seat of the doorless, box-bodied motor car beside his wife, them both grinning with excitement, and Wilson leaned forward and whispered.

"See the birds dropping. Means the old boy has left his kill."

On the far bank of the stream Macomber could see, above the trees, vultures circling and plummeting down.

"Chances are he'll come to drink along here," Wilson whispered. "Before he goes to lay up. Keep an eye out."

They were driving slowly along the high bank of the stream which here cut deeply to its boulder-filled bed, and they wound in and out through big trees as they drove. Macomber was watching the opposite bank when he felt Wilson take hold of his arm. The car stopped.

"There he is," he heard the whisper. "Ahead and to the right. Get out and take him. He's a marvellous lion."

Macomber saw the lion now. He was standing almost broadside, his great head up and turned toward them. The early morning breeze that blew toward them was just stirring his dark mane, and the lion looked huge, silhouetted on the rise of bank in the gray morning light, his shoulders heavy, his barrel of a body bulking smoothly.

"How far is he?" asked Macomber, raising his rifle.

"About seventy-five. Get out and take him."

"Why not shoot from where I am?"

"You don't shoot them from cars," he heard Wilson saying in his ear. "Get out. He's not going to stay there all day."

Macomber stepped out of the curved opening at the side of the front seat, onto the step and down onto the ground. The lion still stood looking majestically and coolly toward this object that his eyes only showed in silhouette, sulking like some super-rhino. There was no man smell carried toward him and he watched the object, moving his great head a little from side to side. Then watching the object, not afraid, but hesitating before going down the bank to drink with such a thing opposite him, he saw a man figure detach itself from it and he turned his heavy head and swung away toward the cover of the trees as he heard a cracking crash and felt the slam of a .30-06 220-grain solid bullet that bit his flank and ripped in sudden hot scalding nausea through his stomach. He trotted, heavy, big-footed, swinging wounded full-bellied, through the trees toward the tall grass and cover, and the crash came again to go past him ripping the air apart. Then it crashed again and he felt the blow as it hit his lower ribs and ripped on through, blood sudden hot and frothy in his mouth, and he galloped toward the high grass where he could crouch and not be seen and make them bring the crashing thing close enough so he could make a rush and get the man that held it.

Macomber had not thought how the lion felt as he got out of the car. He only knew his hands were shaking and as he walked away from the car it was almost impossible for him to make his legs move. They were stiff in the thighs, but he could feel the muscles fluttering. He raised the rifle, sighted on the junction of the lion's head and shoulders and pulled the trigger. Nothing happened though he pulled until he thought his finger would break. Then he knew he had the safety on and as he lowered the rifle to move the safety over he moved another frozen pace forward, and the lion seeing his silhouette now clear of the silhouette of the car, turned and started off at a trot, and, as Macomber fired, he heard a whunk that meant the bullet was home; but the lion kept on going. Macomber shot again and everyone saw the bullet throw a spout of dirt beyond the trotting lion. He shot again, remembering to lower his aim, and they all heard the bullet hit, and the lion went into a gallop and was in the tall grass before he had the bolt pushed forward.

Macomber stood there, feeling sick at his stomach, his hands that held the Springfield still cocked, shaking, and his wife and Robert Wilson were standing by him. Beside him too were the two gun-bearers chattering in Wakamba.

"I hit him," Macomber said. "I hit him twice."

"You gut-shot him and you hit him somewhere forward," Wilson said without enthusiasm. The gun-bearers looked very grave. They were silent now.

"You may have killed him," Wilson went on. "We'll have to wait a while before we go in to find out."

"What do you mean?"

"Let him get sick before we follow him up."

"Oh," said Macomber.

"He's a hell of a fine lion," Wilson said cheerfully. "He's gotten into a bad place though."

"Why is it bad?"

"Can't see him until you're on him."

"Oh," said Macomber.

"Come on," said Wilson. "The Memsahib can stay here in the car. We'll go to have a look at the blood spoor."

"Stay here, Margot," Macomber said to his wife. His mouth was very dry and it was hard for him to talk.

"Why?" she asked.

"Wilson says to."

"We're going to have a look," Wilson said. "You stay here. You can see even better from here."

"All right."

Wilson spoke in Swahili to the driver. He nodded and said, "Yes, Bwana."

Then they went down the steep bank and across the stream, climbing over and around the boulders and up the other bank, pulling up by some projecting roots, and along it until they found where the lion had been trotting when Macomber first shot. There was dark blood on the short grass that the gun-bearers pointed out with grass stems, and that ran away behind the river bank trees.

"What do we do?" asked Macomber.

"Not much choice," said Wilson. "We can't bring the car over. Bank's too steep. We'll let him stiffen up a bit and then you and I'll go and have a look for him."

"Can't we set the grass on fire?" Macomber asked.

"Too green."

"Can't we send beaters?"

Wilson looked at him appraisingly. "Of course we can," he said. "But it's just a touch murderous. You see we know the lion's wounded. You can drive an unwounded lion—he'll move on ahead of a noise—but a wounded lion's going to charge. You can't see him until you're right on him. He'll make himself perfectly flat in cover you wouldn't think would hide a hare. You can't very well send boys in there to that sort of a show. Somebody bound to get mauled."

"What about the gun-bearers?"

"Oh, they'll go with us. It's their *shauri* [agreement]. You see, they signed on for it. They don't look too happy though, do they?"

"I don't want to go in there," said Macomber. It was out before he knew he'd said it.

"Neither do I," said Wilson very cheerily. "Really no choice though."

Then, as an afterthought, he glanced at Macomber and saw suddenly how he was trembling and the pitiful look on his face.

"You don't have to go in, of course," he said. "That's what I'm hired for, you know. That's why I'm so expensive."

"You mean you'd go in there by yourself? Why not leave him there?"

Robert Wilson, whose entire occupation had been with the lion and the problem he presented, and who had not been thinking about Macomber except to note that he was rather windy, suddenly felt as though he had opened the wrong door in a hotel and seen something shameful.

"What do you mean?"

"Why not just leave him?"

"You mean pretend to ourselves he hasn't been hit?"

"No. Just drop it."

"It isn't done."

"Why not?"

"For one thing, he's certain to be suffering. For another, some one else might run onto him."

"I see."

"But you don't have to have anything to do with it."

"I'd like to," Macomber said. "I'm just scared, you know."

"I'll go ahead when we go in," Wilson said, "with Kongoni tracking. You keep behind me and a little to one side. Chances are we'll hear him growl. If we see him we'll both shoot. Don't worry about anything. I'll keep you backed up. As a matter of fact, you know, perhaps you'd better not go. It might be much better. Why don't you go over and join the Memsahib while I just get it over with?"

"No, I want to go."

"All right," said Wilson. "But don't go in if you don't want to. This is my *shauri* now, you know."

"I want to go," said Macomber.

They sat under a tree and smoked.

"Want to go back and speak to the Memsahib while we're waiting?" Wilson asked.

"No."

"I'll just step back and tell her to be patient."

"Good," said Macomber. He sat there, sweating under his arms, his mouth dry, his stomach hollow feeling, wanting to find courage to tell Wilson to go on and finish off the lion without him. He could not know that Wilson was furious because he had not noticed the state he was in earlier and sent him back to his wife. While he sat there Wilson came up. "I have your big gun," he said. "Take it. We've given him time, I think. Come on."

Macomber took the big gun and Wilson said:

"Keep behind me and about five yards to the right and do exactly as I tell you." Then he spoke in Swahili to the two gun-bearers who looked the picture of gloom.

"Let's go," he said.

"Could I have a drink of water?" Macomber asked. Wilson spoke to the older gun-bearer, who wore a canteen on his belt, and the man unbuckled it, unscrewed the top and handed it to Macomber, who took it noticing how heavy it seemed and how hairy and shoddy the felt covering was in his hand. He raised it to drink and looked ahead at the high grass with the flat-topped trees behind it. A breeze was blowing toward them and the grass rippled gently in the wind. He looked at the gun-bearer and he could see the gun-bearer was suffering too with fear.

Thirty-five yards into the grass the big lion lay flattened out along the ground. His ears were back and his only movement was a slight twitching up and down of his long, black-tufted tail. He had turned at bay as soon as he had reached this cover and he was sick with the wound through his belly, and weakening with the wound through his lungs that brought a thin foamy red to his mouth each time he breathed. His flanks were wet and hot and flies were on the little openings the solid bullets had made in his tawny hide, and his big yellow eyes, narrowed with hate, looked straight ahead, only blinking when the pain came as he breathed, and his claws dug in the soft baked earth. All of him, pain, sickness, hatred and all of his remaining strength, was tightening into an absolute concentration for a rush. He could hear the men talking and he waited, gathering all of himself into this preparation for a charge as soon as the men would come into the grass. As he heard their voices his tail stiffened to twitch up and down, and, as they came into the edge of the grass, he made a coughing grunt and charged.

Kongoni, the old gun-bearer, in the lead watching the blood spoor, Wilson watching the grass for any movement, his big gun ready, the second gun-bearer looking ahead and listening, Macomber close to Wilson, his rifle cocked, they had just moved into the grass when Macomber heard the blood-choked coughing grunt, and saw the swishing rush in the grass. The next thing he knew he was running; running wildly, in panic in the open, running toward the stream.

He heard the *ca-ra-wong!* of Wilson's big rifle, and again in a second crashing *carawong!* and turning saw the lion, horrible-looking now, with half his head seeming to be gone, crawling toward Wilson in the edge of the tall grass while the red-faced man worked the bolt on the short ugly rifle and aimed carefully as another blasting *carawong!* came from the muzzle, and the crawling, heavy, yellow bulk of the lion stiffened and the huge, mutilated head slid forward and Macomber, standing by himself in the clearing where he had run, holding a loaded rifle, while two black men and a white man looked back at him in contempt, knew the lion was dead. He came toward Wilson, his tallness all seeming a naked reproach, and Wilson looked at him and said:

"Want to take pictures?"

"No," he said.

That was all any one had said until they reached the motor car. Then Wilson had said:

"Hell of a fine lion. Boys will skin him out. We might as well stay here in the shade."

Macomber's wife had not looked at him nor he at her and he had sat by her in the back seat with Wilson sitting in the front seat. Once he had reached over and taken his wife's hand without looking at her and she had removed her hand from his. Looking across the stream to where the gun-bearers were skinning out the lion he could see that she had been able to see the whole thing. While they sat there his wife had reached forward and put her hand on Wilson's shoulder. He turned and she had leaned forward over the low seat and kissed him on the mouth.

"Oh, I say," said Wilson, going redder than his natural baked color.

"Mr. Robert Wilson," she said. "The beautiful red-faced Mr. Robert Wilson."

Then she sat down beside Macomber again and looked away across the stream to where the lion lay, with uplifted, white-muscled, tendon-marked naked forearms, and white bloating belly, as the black men fleshed away the skin. Finally the gun-bearers brought the skin over, wet and heavy, and climbed in behind with it, rolling it up before they got in, and the motor car started. No one had said anything more until they were back in camp.

That was the story of the lion. Macomber did not know how the lion had felt before he started his rush, nor during it when the unbelievable smash of the .505 with a muzzle velocity of two tons had hit him in the mouth, nor what kept him coming after that, when the second ripping crash had smashed his hind quarters and he had come crawling on toward the crashing, blasting thing that had destroyed him. Wilson knew something about it and only expressed it by saying, "Damned fine lion," but Macomber did not know how Wilson felt about things either. He did not know how his wife felt except that she was through with him.

His wife had been through with him before but it never lasted. He was very wealthy, and would be much wealthier, and he knew she would not leave him ever now. That was one of the few things he really knew. He knew about that, about motor cycles—that was earliest—about motor cars, about duck-shooting, about fishing, trout, salmon and big-sea, about sex in books, many books, too many books, about all court games, about dogs, not much about horses, about hanging on to his money, about most of the other things his world dealt in, and about his wife not leaving him. His wife had been a great beauty and she was still a great beauty in Africa, but she was not a great enough beauty any more at home to be able to leave him and better herself and she knew it and he knew it. She had missed the chance to leave him and he knew it. If he had been better with women she would probably have started to worry about him getting another new, beautiful wife; but she knew too much about him to worry about him either. Also, he had always had a great tolerance which seemed the nicest thing about him if it were not the most sinister.

All in all they were known as a comparatively happily married couple, one of those whose disruption is often rumored but never occurs, and as the society columnist put it, they were adding more than a spice of *adventure* to their much envied and ever-enduring *Romance* by a *Safari* in what was known as *Darkest Africa* until the Martin Johnsons lighted it on so many silver screens where they were pursuing *Old Simba* the lion, the buffalo, *Tembo* the elephant and as well collecting specimens for the Museum of Natural History. This same columnist had reported them *on the verge* at least three times in the past and they had been. But they always made it up. They had a sound basis of union. Margot was too beautiful for Macomber to divorce her and Macomber had too much money for Margot ever to leave him.

It was now about three o'clock in the morning and Francis Macomber, who had been asleep a little while after he had stopped thinking about the lion, wakened and then slept again, woke suddenly, frightened in a dream of the bloody-headed lion standing over him, and listening while his heart pounded, he realized that his wife was not in the other cot in the tent. He lay awake with that knowledge for two hours.

At the end of that time his wife came into the tent, lifted her mosquito bar and crawled cozily into bed.

"Where have you been?" Macomber asked in the darkness.

"Hello," she said. "Are you awake?"

"Where have you been?"

"I just went out to get a breath of air."

"You did, like hell."

"What do you want me to say, darling?"

"Where have you been?"

"Out to get a breath of air."

"That's a new name for it. You *are* a bitch."

"Well, you're a coward."

"All right," he said. "What of it?"

"Nothing as far as I'm concerned. But please let's not talk, darling, because I'm very sleepy."

"You think that I'll take anything."

"I know you will, sweet."

"Well, I won't."

"Please, darling, let's not talk. I'm so very sleepy."

"There wasn't going to be any of that. You promised there wouldn't be."

"Well, there is now," she said sweetly.

"You said if we made this trip that there would be none of that. You promised."

"Yes, darling. That's the way I meant it to be. But the trip was spoiled yesterday. We don't have to talk about it do we?"

"You don't wait long when you have an advantage, do you?"

"Please let's not talk. I'm so sleepy, darling."

"I'm going to talk."

"Don't mind me then, because I'm going to sleep." And she did.

At breakfast they were all three at the table before daylight and Francis Macomber found that, of all the many men he had hated, he hated Robert Wilson the most.

"Sleep well?" Wilson asked in his throaty voice, filling a pipe.

"Did you?"

"Topping," the white hunter told him.

You bastard, thought Macomber, you insolent bastard.

So she woke him when she came in, Wilson thought, looking at them both with his flat, cold eyes. Well, why doesn't he keep his wife where she belongs? What does he think I am, a bloody plaster saint? Let him keep her where she belongs. It's his own fault.

"Do you think we'll find buffalo?" Margot asked, pushing away a dish of apricots.

"Chance of it," Wilson said and smiled at her. "Why don't you stay in camp?"

"Not for anything," she told him.

"Why not order her to stay in camp?" Wilson said to Macomber.

"You order her," said Macomber coldly.

"Let's not have any ordering, nor," turning to Macomber, "any silliness, Francis," Margot said quite pleasantly.

"Are you ready to start?" Macomber asked.

"Any time," Wilson told him. "Do you want the Memsahib to go?"

"Does it make any difference whether I do or not?"

The hell with it, thought Robert Wilson. The utter complete hell with it. So this is what it's going to be like. Well, this is what it's going to be like, then.

"Make's no difference," he said.

"You're sure you wouldn't like to stay in camp with her yourself and let me go out and hunt the buffalo?" Macomber asked.

"Can't do that," said Wilson. "Wouldn't talk rot if I were you."

"I'm not talking rot. I'm disgusted."

"Bad word, disgusted."

"Francis, will you please try to speak sensibly!" his wife said.

"I speak too damned sensibly," Macomber said. "Did you ever eat such filthy food?"

"Something wrong with the food?" asked Wilson quietly.

"No more than with everything else."

"I'd pull yourself together, laddybuck," Wilson said very quietly. "There's a boy waits at table that understands a little English."

"The hell with him."

Wilson stood up and puffing on his pipe strolled away, speaking a few words in Swahili to one of the gun-bearers who was standing waiting for him. Macomber and his wife sat on at the table. He was staring at his coffee cup.

"If you make a scene I'll leave you, darling," Margot said quietly.

"No, you won't."

"You can try it and see."

"You won't leave me."

"No," she said. "I won't leave you and you'll behave yourself."

"Behave myself? That's a way to talk. Behave myself."

"Yes. Behave yourself."

"Why don't *you* try behaving?"

"I've tried it for so long. So very long."

"I hate that red-faced swine," Macomber said. "I loathe the sight of him."

"He's really *very* nice."

"Oh, *shut up*," Macomber almost shouted. Just then the car came up and stopped in front of the dining tent and the driver and the two gun-bearers got out. Wilson walked over and looked at the husband and wife sitting there at the table.

"Going shooting?" he asked.

"Yes," said Macomber, standing up. "Yes."

"Better bring a woolly. It will be cool in the car," Wilson said.

"I'll get my leather jacket," Margot said.

"The boy has it," Wilson told her. He climbed into the front with the driver and Francis Macomber and his wife sat, not speaking, in the back seat.

Hope the silly beggar doesn't take a notion to blow the back of my head off, Wilson thought to himself. Women *are* a nuisance on safari.

The car was grinding down to cross the river at a pebbly ford in the gray daylight and then climbed, angling up the steep bank, where Wilson had ordered a way shovelled out the day before so they could reach the parklike wooded rolling country on the far side.

It was a good morning, Wilson thought. There was a heavy dew and as the wheels went through the grass and low bushes he could smell the odor of the crushed fronds. It was an odor like verbena and he liked this early morning smell of the dew, the crushed bracken and the look of the tree trunks showing black through the early morning mist, as the car made its way through the untracked, parklike country. He had put the two in the back seat out of his mind now and was thinking about buffalo. The buffalo that he was after stayed in the daytime in a thick swamp where it was impossible to get a shot, but in the night they fed out into an open stretch of country and if he could come between them and their swamp with the car, Macomber would have a good chance at them in the open. He did not want to hunt buff with Macomber in thick cover. He did not want to hunt buff or anything else with Macomber at all, but he was a professional hunter and he had hunted with some rare ones in his time. If they got buff today there would only be rhino to come and the poor man would have gone through his dangerous game and things might pick up. He'd have nothing more to do with the woman and Macomber would get over that too. He must have gone through plenty of that before by the look of things. Poor beggar. He must have a way of getting over it. Well, it was the poor sod's own bloody fault.

He, Robert Wilson, carried a double size cot on safari to accommodate any windfalls he might receive. He had hunted for a certain clientele, the international, fast, sporting set, where the women did not feel they were getting their money's worth unless they had shared that cot with the white hunter. He despised them when he was away from them although he liked some of them well enough at the time, but he made his living by them; and their standards were his standards as long as they were hiring him.

They were his standards in all except the shooting. He had his own standards about the killing and they could live up to them or get someone else to hunt them. He knew, too, that they all respected him for this. This Macomber was an odd one though. Damned if he wasn't. Now the wife. Well, the wife. Yes, the wife. Hm, the wife. Well he'd dropped all that. He looked around at them. Macomber sat grim and furious. Margot smiled at him. She looked younger today, more innocent and fresher and not so professionally beautiful. What's in her heart God knows, Wilson thought. She hadn't talked much last night. At that it was a pleasure to see her.

The motor car climbed up a slight rise and went on through the trees and then out into a grassy prairie-like opening and kept in the shelter of the trees along the edge, the driver going slowly and Wilson looking carefully out across the prairie and along its far side. He stopped the car and studied the opening with his field glasses. Then he motioned to the driver to go on and the car moved slowly along, the driver avoiding wart-hog holes and driving around the mud castles ants had built. Then, looking across the opening, Wilson suddenly turned and said,

"By God, there they are!"

And looking where he pointed, while the car jumped forward and Wilson spoke in rapid Swahili to the driver, Macomber saw three huge, black animals looking almost cylindrical in their long heaviness, like big black tank cars, moving at a gallop across the far edge of the open prairie. They moved at a stiff-necked, stiff-bodied gallop and he could see the upswept wide black horns on their heads as they galloped heads out; the heads not moving.

"They're three old bulls," Wilson said. "We'll cut them off before they get to the swamp."

The car was going a wild forty-five miles an hour across the open and as Macomber watched, the buffalo got bigger and bigger until he could see the gray, hairless, scabby look of one huge bull and how his neck was a part of his shoulders and the shiny black of his horns as he galloped a little behind the others that were strung out in that steady plunging gait; and then, the car swaying as though it had just jumped a road, they drew up close and he could see the plunging hugeness of the bull, and the dust in his sparsely haired hide, the wide boss of horn and his outstretched wide-nostrilled muzzle, and he was raising his rifle when Wilson shouted, "Not from the car, you fool!" and he had no fear, only hatred of Wilson, while the brakes clamped on and the car skidded, plowing sideways to an almost stop and Wilson was out on one side and he on the other, stumbling as his feet hit the still speeding-by of the earth, and then he was shooting at the bull as he moved away, hearing the bullets whunk into him, emptying his rifle at him as he moved steadily away, finally remembering to get his shots forward into the shoulder, and as he fumbled to reload, he saw the bull was down. Down on his knees, his big head tossing, and seeing the other two still galloping he shot the leader and hit him. He shot again and missed and he heard the *carawonging* roar as Wilson shot and saw the leading bull slide forward onto his nose.

"Get that other," Wilson said. "Now you're shooting!"

But the other bull was moving steadily at the same gallop and he missed, throwing a spout of dirt, and Wilson missed and the dust rose in a cloud and Wilson shouted, "Come on. He's too far!" and grabbed his arm and they were in the car again, Macomber and Wilson hanging on the sides and rocketing swayingly over the uneven ground, drawing up on the steady, plunging, heavy-necked, straight-moving gallop of the bull.

They were behind him and Macomber was filling his rifle, dropping shells onto the ground, jamming it, clearing the jam, then they were almost up with the bull when Wilson yelled "Stop," and the car skidded so that it almost swung over and Macomber fell forward onto his feet, slammed his bolt forward and fired as far forward as he could aim into the galloping, rounded black back, aimed and shot again, then again, then again, and the bullets, all of them hitting, had no effect on the buffalo that he could see. Then Wilson shot, the roar deafening him, and he could see the bull stagger. Macomber shot again, aiming carefully, and down he came, onto his knees.

"All right," Wilson said. "Nice work. That's the three."

Macomber felt a drunken elation.

"How many times did you shoot?" he asked.

"Just three," Wilson said. "You killed the first bull. The biggest one. I helped you finish the other two. Afraid they might have got into cover. You had them killed. I was just mopping up a little. You shot damn well."

"Let's go to the car," said Macomber. "I want a drink."

"Got to finish off that buff first," Wilson told him. The buffalo was on his knees and he jerked his head furiously and bellowed in a pig-eyed, roaring rage as they came toward him.

"Watch he doesn't get up," Wilson said. Then, "Get a little broadside and take him in the neck just behind the ear."

Macomber aimed carefully at the center of the huge, jerking, rage-driven neck and shot. At the shot the head dropped forward.

"That does it," said Wilson. "Got the spine. They're a hell of a looking thing, aren't they?"

"Let's get the drink," said Macomber. In his life he had never felt so good.

In the car Macomber's wife sat very white faced. "You were marvellous, darling," she said to Macomber. "What a ride."

"Was it rough?" Wilson asked.

"It was frightful. I've never been more frightened in my life."

"Let's all have a drink," Macomber said.

"By all means," said Wilson. "Give it to the Memsahib." She drank the neat whisky from the flask and shuddered a little when she swallowed. She handed the flask to Macomber who handed it to Wilson.

"It was frightfully exciting," she said. "It's given me a dreadful headache. I didn't know you were allowed to shoot them from cars though."

"No one shot from cars," Wilson said coldly.

"I mean chase them from cars."

"Wouldn't ordinarily," Wilson said. "Seemed sporting enough to me though while we were doing it. Taking more chance driving that way across the plain full of holes and one thing and another than hunting on foot. Buffalo could have charged us each time we shot if he liked. Gave him every chance. Wouldn't mention it to any one though. It's illegal if that's what you mean."

"It seemed very unfair to me," Margot said, "chasing those big helpless things in a motor car."

"Did it?" said Wilson.

"What would happen if they heard about it in Nairobi?"

"I'd lose my license for one thing. Other unpleasantnesses," Wilson said, taking a drink from the flask. "I'd be out of business."

"Really?"

"Yes, really."

"Well," said Macomber, and he smiled for the first time all day. "Now she has something on you."

"You have such a pretty way of putting things, Francis," Margot Macomber said. Wilson looked at them both. If a four-letter man marries a five-letter woman, he was thinking, what number of letters would their children be? What he said was, "We lost a gun-bearer. Did you notice it?"

"My God, no," Macomber said.

"Here he comes," Wilson said. "He's all right. He must have fallen off when we left the first bull."

Approaching them was the middle-aged gun-bearer, limping along in his knitted cap, khaki tunic, shorts and rubber sandals, gloomy-faced and disgusted looking. As he came up he called out to Wilson in Swahili and they all saw the change in the white hunter's face.

"What does he say?" asked Margot.

"He says the first bull got up and went into the bush," Wilson said with no expression in his voice.

"Oh," said Macomber blankly.

"Then it's going to be just like the lion," said Margot, full of anticipation.

"It's not going to be a damned bit like the lion," Wilson told her. "Did you want another drink, Macomber?"

"Thanks, yes," Macomber said. He expected the feeling he had had about the lion to come back but it did not. For the first time in his life he really felt wholly without fear. Instead of fear he had a feeling of definite elation.

"We'll go and have a look at the second bull," Wilson said. "I'll tell the driver to put the car in the shade."

"What are you going to do?" asked Margaret Macomber.

"Take a look at the buff," Wilson said.

"I'll come."

"Come along."

The three of them walked over to where the second buffalo bulked blackly in the open, head forward on the grass, the massive horns swung wide.

"He's a very good head," Wilson said. "That's close to a fifty-inch spread."

Macomber was looking at him with delight.

"He's hateful looking," said Margot. "Can't we go into the shade?"

"Of course," Wilson said. "Look," he said to Macomber, and pointed. "See that patch of bush?"

"Yes."

"That's where the first bull went in. The gun-bearer said when he fell off the bull was down. He was watching us helling along and the other two buff galloping. When he looked up there was the bull up and looking at him. Gun-bearer ran like hell and the bull went off slowly into that bush."

"Can we go in after him now?" asked Macomber eagerly.

Wilson looked at him appraisingly. Damned if this isn't a strange one, he thought. Yesterday he's scared sick and today he's a ruddy fire-eater.

"No, we'll give him a while."

"Let's please go into the shade," Margot said. Her face was white and she looked ill.

They made their way to the car where it stood under a single, wide-spreading tree and all climbed in.

"Chances are he's dead in there," Wilson remarked. "After a little we'll have a look."

Macomber felt a wild unreasonable happiness that he had never known before.

"By God, that was a chase," he said. "I've never felt any such feeling. Wasn't it marvellous, Margot?"

"I hated it."

"Why?"

"I hated it," she said bitterly. "I loathed it."

"You know I don't think I'd ever be afraid of anything again," Macomber said to Wilson. "Something happened in me after we first saw the buff and started after him. Like a dam bursting. It was pure excitement."

"Cleans out your liver," said. Wilson. "Damn funny things happen to people."

Macomber's face was shining. "You know something did happen to me," he said. "I feel absolutely different."

His wife said nothing and eyed him strangely. She was sitting far back in the seat and Macomber was sitting forward talking to Wilson who turned sideways talking over the back of the front seat.

"You know, I'd like to try another lion," Macomber said. "I'm really not afraid of them now. After all, what can they do to you?"

"That's it," said Wilson. "Worst one can do is kill you. How does it go? Shakespeare. Damned good. See if I can remember. Oh, damned good. Used to quote it to myself at one time. Let's see. 'By my troth, I care not; a man can die but once; we owe God a death and let it go which way it will he that dies this year is quit for the next.' Damned fine, eh?"

He was very embarrassed, having brought out this thing he had lived by, but he had seen men come of age before and it always moved him. It was not a matter of their twenty-first birthday.

It had taken a strange chance of hunting, a sudden precipitation into action without opportunity for worrying beforehand, to bring this about with Macomber, but regardless of how it had happened it had most certainly happened. Look at the beggar now, Wilson thought. It's that some of them stay little boys so long, Wilson thought. Sometimes all their lives. Their figures stay boyish when they're fifty. The great American boy-men. Damned strange people. But he liked this Macomber now. Damned strange fellow. Probably meant the end of cuckoldry too. Well, that would be a damned good thing. Damned good thing. Beggar had probably been afraid all of his life. Don't know what started it. But over now. Hadn't had time to be afraid with the buff. That and being angry too. Motor car too. Motor cars made it familiar. Be a damn fire eater now. He'd seen it in the war work the same way. More of a change than any loss of virginity. Fear gone like an operation. Something else grew in its place. Main thing a man had. Made him into a man. Women knew it too. No bloody fear.

From the far corner of the seat Margaret Macomber looked at the two of them. There was no change in Wilson. She saw Wilson as she had seen him the day before when she had first realized what his great talent was. But she saw the change in Francis Macomber now.

"Do you have that feeling of happiness about what's going to happen?" Macomber asked, still exploring his new wealth.

"You are not supposed to mention it," Wilson said, looking in the other's face. "Much more fashionable to say you're scared. Mind you, you'll be scared too, plenty of times."

"But you *have* a feeling of happiness about action to come?"

"Yes," said Wilson. "There's that. Doesn't do to talk too much about all this. Talk the whole thing away. No pleasure in anything if you mouth it up too much."

"You're both talking rot," said Margot. "Just because you've chased some helpless animals in a motor car you talk like heroes."

"Sorry," said Wilson. "I have been gassing too much." She's worried about it already, he thought.

"If you don't know what we're talking about why not keep out of it?" Macomber asked his wife.

"You've gotten awfully brave, awfully suddenly," his wife said contemptuously, but her contempt was not secure. She was very afraid of something.

Macomber laughed, a very natural hearty laugh. "You know I *have*," he said. "I really have."

"Isn't it sort of late?" Margot said bitterly. Because she had done the best she could for many years back and the way they were together now was no one person's fault.

"Not for me," said Macomber.

Margot said nothing but sat back in the corner of the seat.

"Do you think we've given him time enough?" Macomber asked Wilson cheerfully.

"We might have a look," Wilson said. "Have you any solids left?"

"The gun-bearer has some."

Wilson called in Swahili and the older gun-bearer, who was skinning out one of the heads, straightened up, pulled a box of solids out of his pocket and brought them over to Macomber, who filled his magazine and put the remaining shells in his pocket.

"You might as well shoot the Springfield," Wilson said. "You're used to it. We'll leave the Mannlicher in the car with the Memsahib. Your gun-bearer can carry your heavy gun. I've this damned cannon. Now let me tell you about them." He had saved this until the last because he did not want to worry Macomber. "When a buff comes he comes with his head high and thrust straight out. The boss of the horns covers any sort of a brain shot. The only shot is straight into the nose. The only other shot is into his chest or, if you're to one side, into the neck or the shoulders. After they've been hit once they take a hell of a lot of killing. Don't try anything fancy. Take the easiest shot there is. They've finished skinning out that head now. Should we get started?"

He called to the gun-bearers, who came up wiping their hands, and the older one got into the back.

"I'll only take Kongini," Wilson said. "The other can watch to keep the birds away."

As the car moved slowly across the open space toward the island of brushy trees that ran in a tongue of foliage along a dry water course that cut the open swale, Macomber felt his heart pounding and his mouth was dry again, but it was excitement, not fear.

"Here's where he went in," Wilson said. Then to the gun-bearer in Swahili, "Take the blood spoor."

The car was parallel to the patch of bush. Macomber, Wilson and the gun-bearer got down. Macomber, looking back, saw his wife, with the rifle by her side, looking at him. He waved to her and she did not wave back.

The brush was very thick ahead and the ground was dry. The middle-aged gun-bearer was sweating heavily and Wilson had his hat down over his eyes and his red neck showed just ahead of Macomber. Suddenly the gun-bearer said something in Swahili to Wilson and ran forward.

"He's dead in there," Wilson said. "Good work" and he turned to grip Macomber's hand and as they shook hands, grinning at each other, the gun-bearer shouted wildly and they saw him coming out of the bush sideways, fast as a crab, and the bull coming, nose out, mouth tight closed, blood dripping, massive head straight out, coming in a charge, his little pig eyes bloodshot as he looked at them. Wilson, who was ahead was kneeling shooting, and Macomber, as he fired, unhearing his shot in the roaring of Wilson's gun, saw fragments like slate burst from the huge boss of the horns, and the head jerked, he shot again at the wide nostrils and saw the horns jolt again and fragments fly, and he did not see Wilson now and, aiming carefully, shot again with the buffalo's huge bulk almost on him and his rifle almost level with the on-coming head, nose out, and he could see the wicked little eyes and the head started to lower and he felt a sudden white-hot, blinding flash explode inside his head and that was all he ever felt.

Wilson had ducked to one side to get in a shoulder shot. Macomber had stood solid and shot for the nose, shooting a touch high each time and hitting the heavy horns, splintering and chipping them like hitting a slate roof, and Mrs. Macomber, in the car, had shot at the buffalo with the 6.5 Mannlicher as it seemed about to gore Macomber and had hit her husband about two inches up and a little to one side of the base of his skull.

Francis Macomber lay now, face down, not two yards from where the buffalo lay on his side and his wife knelt over him with Wilson beside her.

"I wouldn't turn him over," Wilson said.

The woman was crying hysterically.

"I'd get back in the car," Wilson said. "Where's the rifle?"

She shook her head, her face contorted. The gun-bearer picked up the rifle.

"Leave it as it is," said Wilson. Then, "Go get Abdulla so that he may witness the manner of the accident."

He knelt down, took a handkerchief from his pocket, and spread it over Francis Macomber's crew-cropped head where it lay. The blook sank into the dry, loose earth.

Wilson stood up and saw the buffalo on his side, his legs out, his thinly-haired belly crawling with ticks. "Hell of a good bull," his brain registered automatically. "A good fifty inches, or better. Better." He called to the driver and told him to spread a blanket over the body and stay by it. Then he walked over to the motor car where the woman sat crying in the corner.

"That was a pretty thing to do," he said in a toneless voice. "He *would* have left you too."

"Stop it," she said.

"Of course it's an accident," he said. "I know that."

"Stop it," she said.

"Don't worry," he said. "There will be a certain amount of unpleasantness but I will have some photographs taken that will be very useful at the inquest. There's the testimony of the gun-bearers and the driver too. You're perfectly all right."

"Stop it," she said.

"There's a hell of a lot to be done," he said. "And I'll have to send a truck off to the lake to wireless for a plane to take the three of us into Nairobi. Why didn't you poison him? That's what they do in England."

"Stop it. Stop it. Stop it," the woman cried.

Wilson looked at her with his flat blue eyes.

"I'm through now," he said. "I was a little angry. I'd begun to like your husband."

"Oh, please stop it," she said. "Please, please stop it."

"That's better," Wilson said. "Please is much better. Now I'll stop."

William Melvin Kelley

The Dentist's Wife

William Melvin Kelley grew up in New York City, graduated from Harvard (where he was a student of Archibald MacLeish and John Hawkes), and has taught at the New School for Social Research and the State University of New York at Geneseo. His first novel, A Different Drummer *(1962), received wide critical acclaim; he has since published* Dancers on the Shore *(1964), a collection of short stories, and three other novels:* A Drop of Patience *(1965),* dem *(1967), and* Dunfords Travels Everywheres *(1970), which has been called "a Black equivalent to James Joyce's* Finnegan's Wake.*" Currently residing in New York, Kelley has lived for brief periods in Paris, Rome, and Jamaica.*

In Harlem, there once lived a dentist who didn't love his wife. In fact, he was sure she was insane. Even though he'd given her a fantastic wardrobe, a brownstone on the Hill and a cottage on Long Island, she still wasn't satisfied. She wanted one more thing—to cruise around the world. And so he asked her for a divorce.

She refused to give it to him.

He kept asking; she kept refusing; he began to feel trapped. He imagined himself cutting her face up or pouring lye under each eyelid while she slept. He imagined ridding himself of her in many ways, but realized finally only one way was open: He would have to catch her committing adultery.

Not that he was certain she was cheating on him. But he was certain she might be; long before he asked for his divorce, he'd stopped making love to her. Common sense told him that if he was not between her legs, then some other black man could be.

But he could not catch her at it and so decided to hire someome to get under his wife's clothes and to have pictures taken of the event. Someone was Carlyle Bedlow.

Carlyle was sitting in the dentist's chair—two small leather pillows messing his straightened hair—when the dentist made his proposal. Carlyle's mind said yes immediately, but he wanted to see if the dentist was serious and just how much he was offering. He pretended reluctance and also that such a job was beneath him. "Man, you must be crazy. I don't do no shit like that." He pretended to be someone else so well that, for a moment, he forgot the dentist had just pulled his tooth.

"You didn't let me finish." The dentist stood over him, Carlyle's molar clamped between the prongs of his silver pliers. He inspected the tooth, held it so Carlyle could look into its black hole. "You got to take better care of your mouth, Carlyle." He shook his head. "This is a disgrace." He put the pliers and the tooth into a metal dish. "Look, I'm in a spot and it's my only ex-cape. Besides, I ain't mentioned money yet."

"You're hurting me, man, but don't mention it. I don't go in for that kind of stuff. I stick to numbers and warm fur coats." He leaned forward, as if to get up, but the dentist pushed him deeper into his great chair, fingered Carlyle's wound and inserted fresh cotton between cheek and gum.

"The bleeding's stopping." He paused. "Did you ever realize I ain't asking you to do anything illegal?" He smiled now; the dentist himself had a good dentist. "It's got to be done by somebody and I was just throwing the money your way. All you do is get her clothes off and someone to break in and take pictures."

"Why don't you just ask her for a divorce?" Of course, Carlyle knew, the dentist had already done that.

"You think I hasn't? She won't hear nothing like that. Look, man, I'm in prison with a crazy warden, trying to get me to do all kinds of crazy things." Then he told about his wife's obsession with sailing all around the world.

Carlyle agreed. That did sound crazy. But he still pretended hesitation. "Suppose she really ain't got nobody else? Some women wait. I heard about them. Besides, it ain't my thing."

"She ain't waiting. She's getting some from somewhere. You don't understand how bad it is." He went to the glass door and opened it. "Jean, come in here, will you, baby?"

Entering the office, hand against jaw, Carlyle had noticed Jean's legs even through his pain. He had tried his smile on her, but her lips had not softened, had remained stretched across her teeth. Now she came in almost suspiciously, but smiled at the dentist after she'd closed the door.

"This is my girl."

"Pleased to meet you." Her eyes were black. She was younger, darker and much better built up than the dentist's wife, whom Carlyle had seen once or twice, with the dentist, in Jack O'Gee's Silver Goose Bar and Restaurant.

"I want to marry Jean." The dentist sat down. "And I thought you might help me, out of friendship."

Carlyle nodded, leaned into the small basin beside him and spat. He did not consider the dentist his friend. He did not even have his home phone number. And if he'd had it, Carlyle would never have listed it among his first five choices as a number to call when he was being arrested. He and the dentist met two or three times a month, by accident only, in the Silver Goose.

The dentist waited for Carlyle to straighten up before he continued. "Now I found me a sane woman and can't live with a crazy one no more. I need those grounds!"

Carlyle glanced at Jean to see if the scheme was new to her. She leaned against the wall near the door, her face empty except for make-up, which was lighter than her skin. "How much you paying?"

"We ain't got no kids." The dentist hesitated and Carlyle knew this, too, was part of the trouble. Carlyle wasn't married, but already he had two children and visited their mothers when he had some money. "That means no support," the dentist hadn't stopped, "and if I get her on adultery, I can cut the alimony down low. So it's worth a thousand if I get my pictures."

It was a better offer than he had expected, but he didn't tell that to the dentist. "Will you throw in my teeth?"

The dentist agreed.

Carlyle climbed out of the dentist's leather chair. "Then, I guess I'll turn legal for a while."

They agreed to meet that night in the Silver Goose. The dentist would bring his wife. Carlyle would sit at their table. After that, they could only hope that the dentist's wife was ready for another new man.

. . .

Carlyle was standing at the bar, over his second drink, when they came in. He had seen her only a few times before and his memory had been kind: She looked even less appetizing than he remembered her—in a dull pink dress that hung loosely from narrow shoulders, drowned high, hard breasts and sharp-edged hips. Her face was the color of milk mixed with orange juice, the features squeezed into its center.

Passing by him on the way to the booths at the rear of the Goose, the dentist had not spoken or nodded. But after helping her into a seat and ordering her drink, he returned to the bar and Carlyle. "Bitch didn't want to come, but I told her I sure didn't want to stare at her all night."

Carlyle looked beyond the dentist at his wife. The glass in front of her, a brandy alexander, was already half empty. "What happens to her when she gets drunk?"

"She cries."

Carlyle told the dentist the truth: It couldn't hurt him. "I like your money, but we'll never make it."

"Well, go ahead and try. One thousand dollars is a lot of money."

"You're right." He pushed away from the bar, leaving his drink, which had been stinging the dentist's work, and started toward the booth, the dentist close behind him.

She looked up at them, light-brown eyes in her light-orange face, but she did not speak.

"I ain't seen this nigger in years, Robena." The dentist suddenly pretended great excitement. "We was in the Army together." He introduced them.

Carlyle smiled. "Pleased to meet you." Her hand was cold, filled with tiny bones.

"Have a seat." The dentist motioned him into the booth next to his wife. As Carlyle was getting settled, she finished her drink, pushed the foamed glass a few inches across the table.

"You want another?" After she nodded the dentist went on selling Carlyle. "We was in Asia. Right, Carlyle?"

"That's right." But, so far, Carlyle had been lucky enough to avoid wearing any uniforms.

She looked at him now, seemed not to believe him.

"So how you been, Carlyle?" The dentist did not let him answer. "You do want another drink, don't you?"

She nodded, continuing to study Carlyle.

"What you been doing, man?"

"A little of a lot of things." He reached for his cigarettes, wishing he had smoked for this meeting, trying to decide what to say if she wanted a more precise definition of his livelihood. But then she turned away.

The dentist did not give up. "Carlyle was a male nurse in the dental corps, even pulled some teeth when we had lots of work. He was pretty good at it. I remember the first time I asked him to swing the hammer while I held the chisel. Cat's tooth'd broken off at the root." He started to laugh. "I had to keep telling Carlyle to hit harder. Finally got that sucker out, though. Right, Carlyle?"

"That's right."

The waiter came with her drink. She drained half right away.

"She drinks that like lemonade, huh, Carlyle?"

He did not know what to answer. The dentist had been stupid to ask it. But he forced himself to speak, watching her eyes. "Some people take it better than others."

"And some get falling-down nasty drunk."

She snorted, a short laugh, leaving Carlyle with a silence to fill. "Your wife doesn't look like that kind." He tried a broad smile.

"Yeah." The dentist finished his drink, put ten dollars on the table and stood up. "I'll be right back." He went toward the rest rooms; but when, 15 minutes later, he had not returned, Carlyle realized he was on his own.

Weather did not interest her, nor Asia, nor even hemlines. She would not speak, gave him no handle. When the ten-dollar bill had dwindled to seven pennies and a dime, he helped her out of the booth, up the stairs to the street and into a taxi.

On the Hill, she handed him a key and he opened her door. He stepped aside, knowing in this situation she would have to ask him inside. "Can you make it all right?"

She nodded and started into the dark house, with his $1000. Then her heels stopped and turned back, but he could not see her pinched face. "You seem too nice to be his friend, Mr. Bedlow." She closed the door in his face.

. . .

The next day, he paid the dentist a visit. "Man, that was the wrongest thing you could've did, leaving like that. I got to sell myself under your nose."

Bent over his worktable, the dentist was inspecting his tools. "What happened?"

"Nothing. She just sat there and filled up on that ten you left." He was in the dentist's chair, and his jaw, remembering, began to throb. "We worse off than when we started."

"How you figure that?"

"Because now she connects me with an unhappy time. I got to have a chance to sympathize with her. But she didn't tell me nothing. I didn't have the chance to call you a bastard."

The dentist turned around, a small knife in his hand. "I couldn't sit there with that crazy bitch no more. I went to Jean's."

"You have to hold that back if you want this to work. You educated and all, but that was dumb."

"I couldn't help it." He looked unhappy. "So you didn't make progress?"

"Nothing, man. As a matter of fact, I think she knows we ain't Army buddies, because at the end, she sticks her head out the door and tells me I'm too nice to be your friend—Mr. Bedlow."

"She did?" The dentist brightened. "Goddamn! You made it, Carlyle." He jumped, the knife shining in his fist. "Why didn't you tell me that before?"

Carlyle cleared his throat. "Remember you said you wanted to get out before you got crazy, too?" He shook his head. "You too late."

"Listen." The dentist came toward him, waving the knife. "You're too nice to be my friend. That's a compliment."

Just then, Carlyle very much wished he was on his way to a steady customer with a fur coat fresh from some white woman's unlocked car, perfume still strong in its silk lining. "That ain't no compliment. Not the way she said it. She was just getting you."

"You're wrong. I know my wife, man. I'm a bad guy. But you're too nice to be my friend. She's going for it. Time for stage number two." The weekend was coming, he went on. Friday night, Carlyle, Jean, the dentist and his wife would go down to the cottage at the end of Long Island. Jean would pretend to be Carlyle's date. But once they had arrived, Jean and the dentist would have lots of paperwork. Carlyle would be free to seduce the dentist's wife. He was so sure it would work that he told Carlyle to arrange to have someone there to take pictures on Saturday night. He would put the photographer up at a small motel nearby.

There was no arguing with him. Carlyle agreed to come to the office at six that Friday with a suitcase full of attractive sports clothes, the better to trap the dentist's wife.

. . .

The dentist owned a very big automobile. Carlyle and Jean—her big, beautiful thighs crossed—sat in the back. The dentist's wife stared out of the open right front window at cemeteries, airports, rows of pink and gray houses and, finally, sandy hills covered with stubby Christmas trees and hard, dull-green bushes. Two hours from Harlem, they turned onto a dirt road. Then, even over the engine, Carlyle heard the music, as if they had made a giant circle and returned to the summer jukeboxes of the Avenue.

The community was crowded in the dusk light around a small, bright bay. It did not look like Harlem, but if he had come on it by accident, Carlyle would've known that black people lived there. The music was loud and there was the smell of good food, barbecuing ribs, frying chickens. Carlyle had always believed that black people like the dentist and his wife tried very hard to act white. If so, their music and food gave them away.

The dentist's house was glass and lacquered wood, 30 yards from the beach. They sat around an empty yellow-brick fireplace, flicking their ashes into ceramic trays, while the dentist's wife fixed dinner. Behind her back, the dentist winked, smiled, waved at Jean. Carlyle read a magazine, trying to give them privacy—and wondered if the dentist's wife actually did not know about Jean and the dentist. They ate, drank two or three Scotches apiece, tried to talk and, at 11, gave up and went to bed.

Carlyle had not been in bed at 11 in years, and he awoke in the middle of the night. Listening to the waves, he missed Harlem: cars racing lights on the Avenue, drunks indicting the white man, someone still up and playing music. Unable to get sleep back, he climbed out of bed, removed his black pressing rag and went out into the front yard. Something made him look up and he discovered the stars. In Harlem, he could see only the brightest, strongest ones. But now he saw more stars than sequins on a barmaid's dress, and liked them. He sat, then lay down, careful to keep his hands between the wet grass and his hair.

At first he did not hear her thumping toward him. Then her pinched orange-gray face was peering down at him, her hair wrapped around tiny spiked metal rollers. "You didn't like your bed?" She wore only a nightgown, drab in the starlight.

He sat up quickly. "I couldn't sleep, not enough noise." That sounded funny to him and he laughed quietly.

"I know what you mean." She hesitated for a moment, then sat down next to him. It was going to work, after all. The man did know his wife. Maybe she had some men but was very careful about it.

Lowering herself down beside him, she'd gathered up the nightgown to show him knees as square and hard as fist-sized ivory dice. "It's a nice night, though."

"Yeah." He had not finished judging her legs.

"They're not much, are they? Maybe that's why—" She stopped. "No, that's not why." Then she looked at him. "Mr. Bedlow—"

He did not let her finish, had pushed her onto her back while his name was still soft in the air. It was business, like opening a car door, going through a glove compartment, tossing the road maps aside, hoping to find a portable radio or a wallet. She wrapped her thin arms and legs around him, gasping as if in pain.

On hands and knees, he pulled away from her and discovered she had begun to cry. "Oh, this is bad. This is bad. But . . . I was so hot!" She rolled onto her stomach, muffling sobs in the grass. "This is really bad. I can't do *this*."

He patted her shoulder blades, pulled her nightgown over her buttocks, realizing, as he tried to comfort her, that the dentist had lied to him. If she had been cheating, Carlyle could hope to be the President of the United States. Of course, it did not matter, only that he did not want it known that he believed everything people told him.

Finally, he got her to stop crying and sit up. She would not look at him but huddled on the grass, her back to him. "I'm sorry, Mr. Bedlow. I guess you could tell we was having troubles. But I didn't mean to bring you into it."

"Come on, Robena, the sky won't fall down. And call me Carlyle. Mr. Bedlow don't make it now." He moved closer to her, spoke over her shoulder. "What kind of trouble you people got? You own everything, two houses, a big car and all that. So it can't be money." He believed what he said but had asked because now he wanted to know the dentist's weaknesses.

She lowered her chin to her chest. "No, it's not money. Yes, it's money." She raised her head and turned toward him. "How old are you?"

He gave himself a few years.

"I'm thirty-six." She waited, let the number die. "Me and my husband, when we went to school in Washington, it was different, even from your time. We always thought, at least I did—I mean, now I don't know what he really thought—I mean, we thought it was enough for him to be a dentist. You know what I mean?"

All this had little to do with marriage, the kind he knew. He had expected the usual story, the dentist in the street, running after the many Jeans he'd had before this one. Or perhaps she would think the dentist cheap. He waited.

"But that's not enough anymore. I mean, he's a good dentist, he really is, but they don't care if he's good or not. I always thought they'd care."

They? Carlyle thought. Then he realized she was talking about white people.

"But they don't. It took me a long time to see that; and after, I didn't want to believe it." She paused. "We was raised to believe we had to be best. My momma was always telling me, you got to be best in your class."

Carlyle, too, remembered those words.

"But I was a girl and was only supposed to be the best wife I could be. So when we got married, I worked so he could go to school full time. He's a good dentist, but it didn't do any good. When he should've been on the staff of a good clinic, he ended up in Harlem. And when he should've—" She stopped, shook her head. "This isn't very interesting, is it?"

One quality Carlyle had developed in his work was patience; he told her to go on, still hoping she would give him something important.

"The point is, when I saw they was lying about caring, I looked into everything they said, and you know what? They lied about everything." She spoke as if still bewildered by her discovery.

"Hell, I known that since I was seven."

She shook her head several times. "No, listen, everything. Even about food. You ever read the small print on a box of ice cream? It's not even ice cream."

"You sound like my little brother." He started to laugh. "He's a Black Jesuit. And you know they crazy."

She ignored him. "What I want is for him to stop working for a year and go around the world. I want to see if what I think is true really is. And I want him to see it. And if it is, maybe we can do just something small. It's not enough for us to sit out here on a little pile of money. I mean, we was supposed to do something good for our race, too." She stopped talking then, sat with her chin on her knees, her nightgown bunched around her thighs, leaving Carlyle disappointed.

Then she stood up. "Well, that's my sad tale. Maybe you'll tell me yours one time." She smiled, for the first time.

In the kitchen, she gave him a cup of instant coffee. He read the label and wondered what kind of chemicals the X's and Y's were, and what they did to his stomach. When he had finished the coffee, he returned to his room, retied his head and climbed into bed.

. . .

The dentist knocked at his door at nine the next morning but did not wait for Carlyle to ask him in. "You made it, didn't you? I knew you could crack it open. Been done before. I hope your man is a good picture taker. My prints got to come out clear!"

Carlyle propped himself against the bed's headboard. "She may not do it again." He had decided he would let the dentist think himself still in charge.

"Go on, man. Everybody knows the first nut is the hardest."

"Maybe so. How you know, anyway?"

"I woke up at three and she wasn't in bed. And neither was you. I figured you was together someplace. What'd you think of it?"

"Ain't the best I ever had."

"Me, too." The dentist came to the bed's foot. "But with the money, you can buy something better." The dentist smiled, good even white teeth, one gold covered—then closed his lips. "You better drive over to that motel and tell your friend to load his camera."

Carlyle nodded. "What's your plan for today?"

"We're invited to a party. In the late afternoon. We get her drunk, you bring her home, naked, and in bed. I'll make sure you got the house to yourselves." He smiled again. "Me and my Jean'll make sure, someplace." He laughed, turning to the door. "Get your hook in deep."

"I might toss this one back."

He opened the door. "Not in my creek, you won't."

But Carlyle was not so sure.

As he dressed—in short-sleeved pink silk shirt, white bell-bottoms—he tried to decide exactly what to do. Obviously, he wanted to come out the other end with the dentist's $1000. But then the dentist would have to get his pictures. What Carlyle most wanted was to get his money but leave the dentist married to his crazy wife. That would sound good when told in the bars. "That dentist thought he had Carlyle, but then Carlyle Bedlow got down to business, do you hear, business!" That meant he had to get the money before the dentist saw the pictures, bad ones. Pictures in which the woman's face was not quite clear. When he paid the money, the dentist would have to believe the pictures were good. Carlyle heard himself talking: "She passed out, man. I just sat there beside her in my shorts: we pulled back the covers and Hondo snapped away. They so good we might even sell some." But the pictures wouldn't show a thing. He rehearsed his speech while he finished dressing.

He avoided breakfast, wanting the dentist to suffer through a morning with both of his women, imagining that as he drove between the trees on his way to see his friend, the photographer, Hondo Johnson.

"Wait a minute. You saying you don't want the pictures to come out?"

"Right."

"Well, why don't you just give him a blank roll?" Hondo was still in his pajamas, a pullover top, shorts. They were lemon yellow and his legs were brown and shiny. He was sitting on the edge of his motel bed.

"Because, if he ever finds me, I can tell him it was a surprise to me, too. I'll offer to do it again." He was looking into Hondo's mirror, checking his hair. "But he won't go for it, because no man could do it two times to the same woman. And I'm sorry, Doc, but I already spent that money. He ain't got no boys to send after me."

"Come on, man. Why can't we just do it simple? Take the pictures and get the money." Once Hondo thought it was going one way, he did not like to change his plans. He couldn't improvise. But if he knew exactly what to do, it was done. "We'll mess up, man. And I could've used the money."

"We won't lose the money. We'll take insurance pictures. Good ones, with her legs open and all. I know a man downtown'll buy them." And it would be good to have the pictures, just in case the dentist did have some boys. "You satisfied now?"

Hondo nodded but did not look happy. His lips were poked out under his mustache. "Tell me the signal."

"When I turn out the lights." Carlyle hadn't really thought about it.

Hondo started to laugh. "And how'm I supposed to shoot pictures in the dark?" He was pleased to have caught Carlyle.

"You're all right, man." He adjusted his shirt, turned from the mirror. "What about the blinds?"

"That's good. Pull down the blinds, and if they already down, pull them up. Just do something with them blinds." He stood up. "You got that?"

"OK." He liked Hondo. "But I'll try to get her falling-down, so we'll have plenty of time and she won't know nothing. Then we leave. I don't like no drunken broads, anyway."

. . .

It was working. She might even pass out before he got her off the dirt road, into the house and out of her clothes. The party had started at five and now, at ten, was still going. They had eaten—potato salad, fried chicken and greens, on paper plates—drinking steadily. The doctors, lawyers, dentists, big-time hustlers got very loud about baseball, the white man, Harlem after the War, when they were all starting careers. Their children, teenagers, had finally gained control of the phonograph and were dancing hard on the lawn. Carlyle had filled her empty glasses. Finally, he asked her if she wanted to go home. Winking at the dentist, he led her out of the house.

In the moonlight, the dirt of the road, half sand, shone gray. He was supporting her with a hand on her bony rib cage. "How you doing?" He did not really want her to answer and disturb herself.

"I'm doing fine. What did you say?"

"Nothing." They were on the dentist's grass now, circling a clump of lawn chairs and an umbrella table, a few steps from the porch. He saw the bushes move and waved at Hondo.

Taking her straight to her bedroom, he turned on the dim table lamp and began to undress her. She did not resist but was so still that he was not sure she was awake. He put her clothes onto a chair, returned to the bed and pulled the bedcovers from under her. "Thanks, baby." It sounded strange the way she said it. It was meant not for him but for the dentist.

He undressed to his shorts, went to the window and pulled down the blinds.

"What's that?" She raised her head, but it weighed too much.

He tried to imitate the dentist. "Nothing, baby. We need some air, is all."

Hondo was coming. He had banged open the front door, was making his way through the living room, bumping into things. He slid the coffee table out of his way, Carlyle went to the bedroom door. "Hey, man, quiet down. Follow my voice."

"Why didn't you turn on some lights, nigger?" He had almost reached the hallway. Carlyle was at the other end.

"Follow my voice, man."

Now Hondo ran toward him, appeared, in Bermuda shorts and sneakers. Carlyle backed into the room.

Hondo popped into the doorway, stopped. "You expect me to take pictures in this light?" He was disgusted.

"Quiet down, man." Carlyle whispered. "She ain't out yet."

"I got to have more light. I ain't got no infra-red attachment." He began to focus his camera on the dentist's naked wife.

"Baby?" She rolled to her side, then back. "Who's that?"

"Ain't nobody. Close your eyes. I'm turning on the top light."

She did not answer. He waited, then switched it on. It was very bright. For a few seconds, he could not see Hondo. "OK now?"

"I think so." He put the camera to his face again. "But I can't be sure until I read the meter."

"Come on, man. We ain't got time for that." She was going to wake up. Somehow he knew it.

"Always got time. What if we ain't got our insurance pictures?" He took a light meter from his pocket, advanced on her, held it over her navel.

Carlyle sat down on the bed. "How you doing, baby?" He patted her shoulder.

Her eyes were closed. "Who was that just now?"

"Just a guy." He leaned over, kissed her cheek.

"I got it now, man." Hondo had moved to the foot of the bed. "One point four. But I got to do it in seconds, so you can't move."

"Who's that voice?" She raised herself to her elbows, looked up into Hondo's lens. "Who's he?"

"OK, now hold it."

But she was already moving, realizing she was with Carlyle, scrambling to the edge of the bed. "He got you to do this."

Carlyle reached out for her, but she broke away and jumped for the closet. "He'll never get one now." She pulled the door behind her.

Carlyle did not follow her. He could easily open the closet door, but that would be useless. She had to be in bed with a man, looking either surprised or happy, but not struggling. "You better come out of there, Robena." He put a threat into his voice but did not mean it. She had to imprison herself while he thought. He knew what he had to do now: convince her to pose for the pictures.

He looked at Hondo, still busy with final adjustments, then stood up. "Listen, baby, you can't stay in there all night. And nobody's coming to rescue you." His mouth was close to the door.

"And nobody's getting a divorce, either." She started to scold him. "I thought you was nice."

"I am. We ain't even into how nice I really am. Come on out."

Hondo sat on the bed, camera waiting.

"You're not nice." She paused, cleared her nose. "You make love to women for money." She sniffled again.

"That ain't the way it is. I came out here with Jean. Your husband's nurse?"

"I know her. She got a crush on him."

"No, she don't." He waited; she did not speak. "She's with me, but then last night you and me got into something special. But your husband found out. And he said he'd make a lot of trouble for me if I didn't get his pictures. He got me in a terrible spot."

She paused for a moment. "First of all, you didn't even talk to Jean all the way out in the car. And second, where did you get a cameraman so fast?"

The dentist's wife was very smart. "You being real stupid. What you want with a man who don't want you?"

"He does so want me." She did not believe herself.

"No, he don't. He wants Jean. He wants to marry Jean." His voice was cold, the way he talked to white policemen as long as their guns were buried under blue winter coats. "And he's paying me lots of money to get him a divorce."

She waited again, crying behind the closet door. "Well, he's not getting one."

"Listen to me, Robena." He bent closer, softened his tone. "Face it, baby. He don't want anything about you. He don't want to go around the world with you. He thinks you're crazy to want to do that. Give the man his pictures."

And she did.

. . .

They were the clearest pictures any judge would ever see. The woman on the bed, bare to the waist. She looked sad, her infidelity uncovered. The young black hoodlum, his hair shiny and slightly waved, was certainly not her husband.

Hondo took no others. Carlyle had decided against trying for the extra money. One thousand was enough. The dentist paid him in cash, the following Monday evening.

Carlyle had long since turned the money into clothes, a good camel's-hair overcoat, shoes, a few suits, when next he heard from the dentist's wife. She had mailed a postcard to him, care of the Silver Goose. It came from Europe:

Hello. We're here on our honeymoon. My husband is a dentist from [the ink had been smudged] in Africa. Best wishes, Robena (the dentist's wife, remember?).

At first Carlyle did not remember. When he did, he thought about it for a while. . . .

'4
reassessments

Joyce Cary

A Good Investment

Joyce Cary was born in Donegal, Ireland, educated at Trinity College, Oxford, and studied art in Edinburgh and Paris. From 1913 to 1920 he was in Africa with the Nigerian Political Service, first as a military officer, then as magistrate of the remote Borgu district. In 1920 he retired because of ill health, returned to England, and began writing. Ten years later, at the age of 42, he published his first novel. By the time of his death Joyce Cary had published fifteen more novels—among them Mister Johnson *(1939),* The Horse's Mouth *(1944), and* Prisoner of Grace *(1952)—and was recognized as one of the major English writers of the twentieth century.*

Old Mrs. Bill of Hunter's Green had three daughters, Daisy, Letty, and Francie, the youngest. Daisy is a spinster of fifty who travels round the world from one friend's house to another on cargo boats, buses, hitch-hikes, and has, she says, a gorgeous time. She drinks a good deal when she can get it free, eats enormously, and loves a noise. Letty is married to a lawyer called Gordon Todd with a taste for archaeology which, it is said, has damaged his practice. They have two children, boy and girl, and Letty complains very much of their wildness, of all her housekeeping troubles and expenses. She spends much of her time in bed, and whenever the children or the husband are too much for her nerves, she telephones to her mother for Francie, who duly rushes over and takes charge of house, husband, and children for as long as Letty can keep her, that is, as long as her mother is ready to spare her. This is usually four days at the most.

Letty complains bitterly of her mother's selfishness when she recalls Francie even after a week. "What does she want with Francie—she has Mrs. Jones, and there's only herself to look after. And after all, Mother is a good deal stronger than I am."

Mrs. Bill says that Letty is a poor spoiled lily and that she preys on Francie. But she does not excuse Francie for deserting her because she blames Francie for having spoiled Letty at the beginning. "There's no need for Francie to rush away at a word from Letty and it's very bad for Letty. But it's Francie's affair. I never interfere."

Francie says nothing. She has no time between her various duties of keeping Mrs. Jones the housekeeper in a good temper, managing her mother's parties; and she knows too that anything she said would only irritate Letty and bring from her mother the remark, "But why all the fuss? I never fuss, life is too short."

Francie Bill is a very small woman, about thirty-five years of age, with a big round forehead, deeply lined, small grey eyes, and a rather prominent round chin. Her mouth is good and it has a very serious expression, except when she laughs. She laughs with her whole face, causing her eyes to disappear and her wrinkles to deepen.

Some time ago Francie had a love affair, but for months no one even realized it except the lover. He was a widower with a daughter of nine. His name was Catto, aged forty-eight, partner in a printing firm, moderately well off, and, as he considered, good at life. That is to say, he knew how to make a success of most things. His marriage had been successful, but he was not at all afraid, like so many prudent citizens who have had lucky marriages, of taking another chance. He realized very well how much luck had gone into his first choice—his wife, actually on the honeymoon, had changed into a different woman with exceedingly strong views on such delicate questions as where to live, how to decorate and manage a house, and which of her husband's friends were worth keeping up with. It was pure luck that he had agreed with her.

But he considered that a man of his age and experience would have more foresight in a second choice. He began to look round almost as soon as his wife was buried. He wanted above all a good housekeeper and a companion for his daughter—he was accustomed to good housekeeping and he distrusted nurses, even the most expensive. And he told himself that even from a financial point of view, the plan was justified. "With wages at their highest and service at its worst, a competent wife is actually a first-class investment."

And one day, by good luck, as he said afterwards, he met Daisy Bill at Wimbledon. He had barely settled himself on his stool in the morning queue, when a tall brown girl in a man's shirt, about three yards further down the row, called out loudly, "Bill, Bill," and then, "Daisy."

Catto as a small boy had known the Bill family very well. For three summers running they had shared the same lodgings at the seaside, and he had got on very well with Daisy especially, nearest to him in age. He had even fallen a good deal in love with Daisy at fifteen, during their last holiday together.

He thought, even before he identified the girl, "Daisy Bill, could it be the old Daisy, and not married? If Daisy really isn't married, then what about her? The right age, too old for babies. I don't want a rival to poor little Jean, and Daisy was really a very nice girl in a very nice way—good-natured, healthy, and she would probably have money too. As far as I can remember, all the Bill girls had something coming from the aunt who married into toothpaste."

He looked round him, half stood up, and after a moment recognized Daisy. "She must be that huge red-faced woman with the cigarette-holder shaped like a pipe. She couldn't be anyone else with that nose and those eyes. Yes, there she is waving to her friend."

He excused himself to the neighbors and edged past them to present himself. Daisy knew him at once. She cried out in a voice to be heard ten yards away, "Good Lord, Tommy, Tom Cat!" and wrung his fingers in a powerful clasp. "But how wonderful, you haven't changed a bit. How extraordinary. What a bit of luck. You must join us." The neighbors in the queue, discreetly interested and pleased, with that almost family feeling which belongs to the Wimbledon queue, made way for his stool, and he joined the Bill party. It consisted now of Daisy, a little, thin, sharp woman who turned out to be a celebrated authoress, and the brown girl in the man's shirt who was a tennis star, a county champion.

Catto had been shocked by the change in Daisy's looks, but her greeting reassured him. He was reminded again of his old love, her easy good nature, her freedom from all those airs which in a girl of sixteen he most detested, touchiness and sudden changes of mood. He had told himself then that, with all her charm, she was as reliable a friend as any of the boys at school.

"Good heavens," Daisy said, breathing tobacco in his face, "do you remember those walks along the shore? And how you hated the kids for trailing after us?" She gave a loud laugh and then, dropping his hand, turned to the champion and exclaimed in a serious tone, as one who takes up again the more important affairs of life, "So you don't think much of Seixas' service?"

And the pair continued their tennis gossip with enthusiasm. Catto might not have existed for either of them.

The authoress, having glared at the champion for some time, dismissed Catto with a single glance, and then, with a twist of her little pursed mouth and a droop of her eyelids, fell into a gloomy meditation which made her all at once ten years older and gave her a sad but distinguished beauty.

Catto had no recollection of his jealousy; Daisy seemed to have a more accurate memory of the affair. But he was already sorry that he had so impulsively presented himself. He observed his old friend with a rueful amusement. "Yes, steady as a boy and now a regular fellow." He recoiled from this bluff Daisy. It was obvious why she had never married. And neither of her sisters, even if they were unmarried, had ever attracted him. The languid, fragile, lovely Letty, always being rescued from crabs and wrapped up from the cold; the rat-tailed Francie, at six, with her red button of a nose, hurling herself into the seas and making love to the very fishermen.

But just before the party, having obtained its tickets, dispersed for lunch, Daisy recalled her manners and became even more hearty, asked after his family, expressed a manly sympathy for his loss, and told of her own father's death. But her mother was still at the old place, she would so like to see him again. Why not come out next weekend? There was to be quite an amusing party to dinner.

Catto accepted these attentions in their own spirit and resolved not to go to dinner on any account. Why waste time on the Bills if Daisy was not a suitable prospect? He was put out when Mrs. Bill wrote to him. She also expressed her sympathy, a cheerful sympathy: "These things must happen, one has to take them," and she pressed him to come to dinner. "You remember Hunter's? It's just the same, and Daisy tells me so are you. Isn't that nice? It's quite encouraging in these days when everything else seems to get worse and worse, including the people. But poor things, I suppose they can't be blamed for being so flat when the newspapers are so full of bombs. Though I can't imagine why everyone should go off so terribly before the bombs even tick, or whatever they do when they drop."

And in a postscript she wrote, "Quite a small party, about eight, don't dress. Mrs. Mair is coming, who lost her husband last year in that plane crash, and the Offer girl who used to be so fond of you."

Catto seemed to hear a voice, rattling little voice like a cracked dinner bell. He had not heard it for thirty years, in fact since his last holiday with the Dills, before he had gone to the university and they had gone to Switzerland for Letty's health. He had not paid much attention to it then. Mrs. Bill had not talked much with boys of his age, nor, indeed, with her own children. She had been preoccupied with her handsome husband and the half-dozen other men, much older than herself, who frequented the house. Even at the seaside her life had been a series of parties, chiefly on yachts. The Bills had taken rooms at Clarksfoot, small and remote, unfashionable and even uncouth, with its mining workers, its Welsh Bethels singing hymns on the beach, because of her friend, Lord S., who kept his big yacht there.

S. asked her to his parties in harbor but did not expect her to go cruising. Mrs. Bill was a very bad sailor. Her stories of her own feelings on the sea were among her most amusing. The voice tinkled with laughter in the background of Catto's mind. But now that it came back to him in the cadences of the note, so neatly written in a minute, precise hand, he found, to his surprise, that he liked his memory of Mrs. Bill, as of someone always gay, lively, good-tempered, and tolerant. "Perhaps she did not trouble much with us children, but she never worried us either. She understood how to make things pleasant and comfortable. And then this widow, Mrs. Mair? I know Mrs. Bill was a bit of a match-maker. But why not—a widow might be the answer for me. She'd know the ropes and wouldn't have fantastic expectations, and yet she would appreciate the solid advantages of a husband and being on good terms with him. And this Offer girl too, she must be somewhere near my age if she was fond of me thirty years ago."

He accepted Mrs. Bill's invitation; and it was true that the house had not changed. But the neighborhood had. The place had been a farm, and Theodore Bill had even kept it as a farm, without a bailiff, losing money every year. Now the farmhouse with its garden stood incongruously in a vast new suburb which was actually named after it, Hunter's Green.

Catto, opening the old wooden gate, a farm gate still, had the sense of one who finds an unexpected treasure and, at the same moment, sees it fall into the dust, as the bodies of the old saints are said to do when you dig them up. He had loved Hunter's Green where he had ridden his first pony, and had his first passionate love, with the slim, lovely girl who had put him over the jumps. With Daisy, in short, And where was that Daisy now? She was less than an existence, for the actual Daisy was already making faint and unreliable even that sweet memory that had been a vivid existence. And now Hunter's Green, the old Hunter's Green, the solid bricks, the immense elms, the coachhouse with its dovecot, mysteriously disintegrated before his very eyes.

Hunter's Green had never pretended to beauty. It had always been a plain house—square, three-storied, with a slate roof a little too small, and a long lean-to conservatory.

In the farm among its trees, with the cows grazing opposite the windows, this plainness had been a charm. It seemed to say, "I am the unpretending home of plain country people." True, Theodore and Tottie Bill were anything but plain country people. But for that very reason, they had appreciated Hunter's Green, and carefully preserved its honest want of make-up.

But now the rough five-bar gate, the coarse grass in the lawn which was much too small for a paddock, a minute haycock in one corner of it, and the rusty pump at the angle of the wall, looked false, stagey. They had indeed become false by being preserved into a different age.

Catto went in expecting more disappointment of the same kind, relics of the past that spoiled and obscured the past by their meretricious survival. He was delighted, therefore, by Mrs. Bill. The little woman seemed no older. She was the same—pretty, vivacious, with her fine thin nose, her dead white skin, her black eyes that sparkled all the more for the contrast of her cheeks, her cracked voice, her high Edwardian handshake.

"Ah, but this is an occasion—don't you feel the sand between your toes? Don't you smell the stairs on the *Naiad?* I have never been able to use rubber since poor S. died. It makes me cry and it makes me seasick, and those are two things that simply can't go together. Some people drink claret with oysters, yes I know, I met such a man and he wasn't a character part. In fact, it was old Roger Kent.''. And turning to another guest, "Do you remember Roger in *Mrs. Tanqueray?*"

She had turned from Catto, as Daisy had turned from him, to a more responsive audience, and seeing her white curly head from behind, he reflected, "But she was dark then—she must be seventy. I think she hasn't changed because I've been getting old too. And certainly she's kept her features."

The dinner was quite good, the company distinguished, if not of the first distinction. A well-known Shakespearian actor, scholarly and earnest like all those who have never been stars; an ugly, amusing old critic with a broken nose, like a boxer's nose; and the vicar, a big red-faced man, full of good stories, and, Catto would have said, old port, a type that he had not met for years, and enjoyed. "A sensible stout fellow," he thought, "and probably a fine preacher. I wish we had more of them in the Church. Good fellows with their feet on the ground."

Mrs. Mair, a well-known women's editor under her maiden name, arrived late with a new husband, and the Offer girl, a thin pale creature of about seventeen, enthusiastic about ballet, had never even heard of Catto. He remembered that Mrs. Bill was celebrated for her inconsequence. It had been one of her charms and, because it had been a charm, he enjoyed it again.

Francie was the eighth at the table. That is to say, she did not appear till after the soup, when, flushed, hot, with damp hair and red shiny nose, she slipped into her place between the young bridegroom and the critic's wife.

As the vicar sat opposite Mrs. Bill it was impossible to alternate the sexes, and Catto, on her left, sat next to the critic. No one explained Francie, or her sudden appearance. Catto was left to infer, after some reflection, that this thick-set woman, with grey streaks in her hair, must be the youngest Bill daughter, Frank, Frankie, Francie. He could not recognize her at all. But when she disappeared again with the chickens, and came in soon after the ice pudding, he perceived that she was acting as cook. The maid who waited was no doubt a daily woman, possibly a waiter hired only for the party. And when the party moved to the veranda, overlooking the bogus paddock and the decorator's haycock, he noticed that Francie not only arranged her mother's cushions but mixed the vicar's whisky and fetched the actor's pipe from his room.

The actor, Maxton, was staying in the house. He seemed like an old family friend, and when Francie, noticing that he fumbled in his pocket, silently disappeared and brought the pipe, he did not interrupt his description of Bernhardt's absurd masterpiece in *L'Aiglon,* he received the pipe with his fingers as a man at table who has dropped a fork takes a new one from the waiter.

"Or a father from a daughter." Catto thought. "But she calls him Mr. Maxton. He can't be so familiar. Yet she knew what he wanted and where to find it."

And suddenly he had a new recollection of the old Francie, the child of six who had always been so dirty, noisy, always falling into the water, tearing her frocks, so often in the way when he had wanted to be alone with the lovely, so friendly Daisy. He recalled a general cry of, "Frankie, Frankie," and the small girl with flying tangled hair tearing madly along the corridor; his brain lighted up a snapshot of Mrs. Bill at her prettiest in a white serge frock, standing on the stairs above a group of men and saying with a charming bend of her head, "But don't bother, I'm absolutely fated to lose things. Frankie will find it for me," and then again, "Frankie is the practical one, aren't you, Frankie?"

And again he saw, at forty-eight, an angle of his old friends that, at eighteen, had made only an impression on his memory, none on his observation. Daisy had been so easy, so friendly, yes, and Mrs. Bill's tinkling voice had usually been heard by the children in these cheerful laments. She was always needing something fetched or found. Her good-humor confessed, "I'm a nuisance, I know, but you'll forgive me because I forgive everyone else."

And Frankie had been the practical one. Had they given her the character and made her a family slave, was she really fit for nothing else? And looking at the girl's face as she sat, silent as usual, half hidden behind her mother's chair, listening to the actor and the critic discussing Bernhardt, he thought, amused by the recollection, "Yes, how she trailed after me—after anything in trousers. How she would throw herself into my arms and say, 'But Tom, you haven't kissed me good night.' And I should think she's a real woman still—rather shy and dull perhaps but the tomboy has quite disappeared." And suddenly he thought, "Why not Francie, could I do better? A kind soul, modest, simple, pretty capable, too, if she cooked that dinner. Of course, she's a bit young—she can't be more than thirty-six. There could be a baby, and that's a complication I particularly wanted to avoid. Of course, one could make a bargain—babies barred. It's common enough in second marriages."

He reflected a moment on this tricky point. But like many steady, careful fellows who look for a fair deal in life, he had also a strong sense of what is fair in dealing with others. "No," he thought, "if she wanted a baby I should have to give her one. On the other hand, youth does have some advantages. She'd stand up better to the job."

He looked again at Francie, and caught her at a plainer moment. The lamp shone on her nose and the prominent forehead, a strand of damp hair, well steamed from the kitchen, was lying limp against her cheek. But Catto rallied. "Damn it, I'm not a boy. What do looks matter? What I need is a good home-maker—someone to take an interest in Jean—domestic competence and peace."

He sought some private talk with her, but this was difficult to manage. Rain was falling in thick heavy lines and the cars could not come down to the door because at Hunter's Green, as in a proper farm-house, there was a little front garden full of old-fashioned flowers, with a narrow brick path to the front porch. The party stood crowded in the hall, looking out disgustedly, while Francie was busy with hats and coats.

When she brought him his coat he turned smiling and said, "Frances, Frankie, do you remember Clarksfoot?"

But Mrs. Bill interrupted with a remark to the world, "Dear me, there used to be a carriage umbrella in the hall. But it seems to have lost itself. Everything in this house gets itself lost."

Francie, still silent, ran for the carriage umbrella in the back passage and escorted the guests to their cars.

Catto, who had come by train and taxi, had a lift in the critic's car. He made one more attempt to speak to Francie from the back window. "Thank you, Francie, do you remember how you used to go round at bedtime and wish us all good night?"

The girl had turned away at a call from the house. Someone had dropped a scarf. She did not even hear him. But Catto was a determined man. He wrote to Mrs. Bill, thanking her for a delightful evening, and asked her to the theatre "with my old friend, Francie."

And when Mrs. Bill refused on account of an engagement, he took the train again to Hunter's Green and called.

He was lucky. Mrs. Bill was out, and Frances was weeding the garden. In an old pair of trousers, gardening boots, a plaid shirt, and a handkerchief tied over her hair, she looked like a picture of slave labor in a Soviet camp. But she received Catto with something of Daisy's frankness. "I'm sorry Mother's out, but she'll be in at six. Do wait. She'll be so upset to miss you."

"Thanks, I should like to. And how are you, Francie? I didn't really see you last week."

"Do you mind if I finish this border—I've got so behind with the weeds."

"No—let me help you."

"Oh, you couldn't—you'll get filthy."

"I can wash."

"Are you sure you know which are weeds?"

"I see you're still practical."

The woman looked at him in surprise. He explained his point, as a joke, but she did not smile. She reflected and said at last, "I wonder——"

"You were a quaint little thing at six."

But she was weeding again, he saw only the short broad back.

"You don't remember me at all."

"Not really." She stood up again and looked at him intently. She was obviously curious, she felt that his visit had some purpose beyond a mere call.

She shook her head, "Mother says that you were Daisy's great friend."

"I like to think I was yours too. You never let me leave the house without a kiss."

"Oh well, at six." She dismissed this carelessly. She was not at all embarrassed, as Catto had expected. She showed no shyness. Indeed, now that he had been able to talk to her, he felt that she had grown up with something of the Bill poise. She asked him abruptly, "What do you do, Mr. Catto? Tell me about yourself."

"That's a very dull story. I'm a printer, a widower, with a young daughter—forty-eight years old. Really, there's nothing more to tell."

"Is it long since you—" she hesitated.

"Lost my wife? No, eighteen months. But it seems a very long time indeed. We were very happy—I am a lonely man, Francie—a very lonely man. Men like me who have been happily married and then widowed, suffer a very special kind of loneliness."

The woman looked at him and the wrinkles in her forehead were very noticeable. "Yes, I can imagine it. I'm sorry. But then you did have all that happiness."

"It's a danger."

"Yes, it's a danger. But worth it. Or don't you think so? Perhaps now——"

"Oh yes, tremendously worth it."

"In fact, in spite of everything, you've been——"

"Yes, I've been lucky. I was always rather lucky. I was lucky to know you when I was a boy."

"Me——"

"I mean the family as a whole. Yes, you too. You were rather an important part of the experience."

The woman looked at him and her expression was critical. She was taking a new view of this middle-aged man who made such rapid advances. Then she said that she must really get the weeding done, and set to work. No word was said for twenty minutes and the silence itself was expressive. It said plainly that there was a situation.

"I've been too sudden," Catto said to himself. "She doesn't seem shy—at thirty-six, she knows how to manage her feelings. But she's timid and wary."

The bed finished, they straightened up together face to face, and the girl smiled in a broad and frank manner. Her whole face expressed a personal interest. She had settled something with herself. "Come, Mr. Catto, you need tea, or a drink."

"Why Mr. Catto?"

"Well, what did I call you?"

"I was Tom to you all."

"Come, Tom, we'll have tea." She blushed as she spoke and stooped to gather her basket.

For the moment, Catto was afraid that he had been too enterprising. He did not want to commit himself to the girl before he knew her better. He had, as we have seen, as well as prudence, a strong sense of responsibility.

But the woman at once recovered her practical air. She had placed Catto to her satisfaction as a nice middle-aged man eager to renew his childhood memories. They talked of the days at Clarksfoot, they exchanged news. She told how Mrs. Bill after her husband's death had lost most of her memory and sold the land, how Daisy loved travelling and seldom appeared at home, how Letty needed special treatment and how much it cost.

He told her about his marriage, about Jean, and how hard he thought it for a girl of nine to lose her mother. That he had seriously considered remarrying again, on her account alone.

"I'm sure you're right," Francie said, "if you can find the right person."

"That's the problem."

"A widow perhaps, without children, who wanted a child to care for."

"I'm not so sure. A younger woman might be a better companion."

"A widow could be quite young. There are lots of young widows. What about war widows?"

"It's the person that matters. I don't see why she need be a widow."

"Oh no, of course."

"Or why I shouldn't have another baby if she were young enough."

There was a pause, and Catto again thought that he had been indiscreet. But the woman was only reflecting. "You'd have to discuss that with the new wife." In fact, it was not till three months later, when Catto actually proposed in so many words that Francie understood him.

"You really want to marry me?"

"Yes, yes. I've been trying to tell you so for the last fortnight."

"Well, I did wonder sometimes but I didn't like to think——"

"But you haven't answered me yet."

"But don't you see?"

"What?"

"Why I didn't like to think. Why, Tom," and she laughed that tomboyish broad laugh which brought all her wrinkles and made her little eyes disappear, "of course I'll marry you."

The laugh disappeared and she looked suddenly very serious. All at once Catto understood that the headlong Francie of thirty years before was still there. He was much startled. He had not expected so passionate a kiss, so eager an embrace.

Mrs. Bill was greatly amused by the news. She congratulated Catto and said, laughing. "Sir Galahad to the rescue, or is it Perseus? But I'm not really a monster, you know, and Francie loves her chains. She adores a fuss." Catto, taken by surprise, found himself turning red. He did not know what to answer. But Mrs. Bill had dashed on at once. "Letty will hate you, but it won't do Letty any harm to take a little exercise."

He received a most friendly letter from Daisy in Venezuela, who said how glad she was to see that her darling Francie was to get away from home at last and have some life of her own. She wanted Catto to "keep mother at bay, for Francie's sake, or you'll have no peace."

The wedding was quiet. Mrs. Bill forgot to provide linen and Francie bought her own wedding dress, but Catto presented his bride with the latest refrigerator, freezer, enamelled stove, and double sink in a completely remodeled kitchen, and all Mrs. Bill's old friends sent autographed copies of their works—published twenty or thirty years before, period sensations now wearing as strange a look as the hats and skirts of that ancient world in which they had achieved their distinction.

Catto had already arranged for a honeymoon in Paris. His first honeymoon had been in Paris. Francie had hoped for Italy, but she enjoyed Paris enormously as a bride. And she was deeply apologetic when the month they had planned was cut a week short because Daisy came back from Jamaica, in a banana boat, with a mysterious illness called Daisy's fever, and the Cattos had to hurry home to look after her. But Catto could not complain that Daisy looked upon his home as a refuge in time of trouble.

Francie nursed her for six weeks before Catto got a hint, from Mrs. Bill, that Daisy's fever came on only when she was broke. "Don't let her kill Francie," she wrote. "Daisy has always treated Francie as her private and personal slave. Have you tried the gold cure for fever? A check, I've found, is far the best prescription."

Daisy had been complaining every day of all the wonderful holidays she was missing by this unlucky illness, and Catto now offered her a loan of twenty pounds to take advantage of an invitation to Finland. She left the next morning by milk-float to catch a trawler whose captain was an old Bombay friend. Catto, relieved, told himself that Daisy would not come very often. But he protested when Francie confessed that she had engaged herself to stay three days at Hunter's Green in order to cook for her mother's traditional Easter party. He wrote to Mrs. Bill suggesting that she should advertise for a temporary cook. But she answered none was required.

"Francie seems to think she ought to come but it's quite unnecessary—Mrs. Jones is quite lazy enough as it is. She does just as little as she dares." She addressed the note to Galahad Catto Esq., and signed herself "the monster."

Catto took it to Francie and said, "You see, your mother doesn't even want you."

"But it was Mummy told me that Mrs. Jones threatened to give notice if she asked five people to stay. And now she's asked seven people. And you know if we lose Mrs. Jones we'll never get another up to Mummy's standards."

"Then she'll have to change her standards—like other people."

Francie was silent, as usual, in these arguments. But a certain obstinate desperation in her forehead and chin seemed to ask, "How? It's easy to say, but how do you do it?" And she went to the work—Mrs. Bill's celebrated party was again a great success, for which she received much praise, even a graceful notice in a Sunday newspaper. And for three months afterwards she did not send for Francie; either she did not need her or she had been offended by Catto's note.

Francie believed she was offended, and it worried her. "Mummy is so sensitive about being a nuisance," she said. "And of course she'll never tell you when she's hurt."

"She's no right to be hurt."

Francie's wrinkles deepened. "It's not very nice for her, living alone. I should hate it."

Catto did not answer that Francie was off the point. He told himself that women have their own methods of argument and that, above all, he must not start a quarrel with Francie about her mother. That situation was too foolish as well as too vulgar. How easy for a sensible man to avoid it. And it seemed that Mrs. Bill, hurt or not, meant to leave Francie alone.

Francie's first baby was born in December, a very cold December; and on the day before she got up there was a note from Letty asking if she could take the elder girl to school, she herself had a migraine; and on the day after she got up, Mrs. Bill telephoned. She did not ask for help. Mrs. Bill's claim that she never sought Francie's help, was perfectly justified. Her method was to send news of trouble, as a joke, or to ask advice. This time she did both.

"I've got three people for the weekend and of course Mrs. Jones has sprained her ankle. You can rely on Mrs. Jones's ankle, it's never failed her yet when there's some real work to do. But meanwhile I have to find an experienced daily. Should I advertise? I'm so bad at these things. And I simply must get someone by this evening."

Catto, running in from the works in the mid-morning, to have a glimpse of his wife, finds her up and dressed. She is at the telephone, nursing the baby through her opened coat and arguing with Letty about school clothes. Jean, with an expression of reserved disapproval which comically reproduces her father's look in the same kind of crisis, stands looking on. Jean, a sensible Catto, is already devoted, in her sensible way, to her stepmother. She knows how to value her practical good nature, and quite agrees with her father about the Bill relations.

"But Letty," Francie's voice implores her sister to be reasonable. "She simply must have four face towels. It may be ridiculous but you know there was trouble last time when she went with only two, and it upsets a child so much to be different."

Catto, furious, tries to take the telephone out of Francie's hands. Startled, she turns crimson and fights him.

"No—what are you doing?"

And he, equally surprised by this strong resistance, gives way. She says hastily to Letty, "It's all right, darling. Nothing. I'll be round in ten minutes," and hangs up. She smiles nervously at Catto and says, "I can do Letty on the way to Mother's. How lucky that I was going anyhow."

"You're not going to do Letty, or your mother either. This is where we stop. You're not fit." And seeing the obstinate look in her face, he begins to storm. Her mother and Letty are two of the most selfish people on earth. And has she no consideration for her baby, not to speak of her husband?

Francie, flustered, tries to interrupt. Suddenly she bursts into tears. Catto, alarmed by her violent agitation, sits down beside her and puts an arm around her.

"My darling, you see how it is. Someone has to make a stand. Let me do it for you if you're afraid."

"But you can't, you can't. No one can."

"But that's nonsense."

"You don't understand. Letty would simply let that poor child go off again with all the wrong things, and of course Mother won't get a daily in time for dinner this evening. There isn't a hope. She'll leave everything to settle itself, and Mrs. Jones will limp about and get up a grievance till she gives notice. She loves a real grievance. And if Mother loses Mrs. Jones I'd have to go every day. Either that or Mother would have to live with us. And you'd hate that. Oh dear, there's Gordon in the car." And still nursing, while her brother-in-law, chattering about Letty's headache, gathers her bag, she hurries out.

Six months later Mrs. Bill did lose Mrs. Jones, and she has failed to keep another housekeeper. She is very cheerful and says that on the whole she prefers to manage without Mrs. Jones who had no humor.

Francie has her second baby, and she lives a still more distracted life, dashing over three times a week to manage her mother's household. It has been proposed that Mrs. Bill should live with the Cattos, but she absolutely refuses to give up her dear old house, with its glorious memories of William Archer, E. F. Benson, and George Alexander. And as for the proposal that the Cattos should live with her, taking half the house for their separate apartment, which is Mrs. Bill's solution to the problem, Catto can't bring himself to leave his home. He points out that the kitchen was especially designed for Francie's convenience.

So that he too lives a distracted life. See him now at ten o'clock at night waiting at Hunter's Green to take Francie home. It is raining but he is so angry that he won't leave the car to go into the house. This, of course, is stupid, for Mrs. Bill is always good-natured with him and says, "My dear Tom, I don't ask Francie to run my show, it's Francie who insists on it. She's so practical—she hates a muddle. Now, I don't mind muddle a bit."

For Mrs. Bill has never suffered from a muddle—Francie sees to that. And Catto thinks bitterly, "Practical and affectionate—how true that was—and is."

Suddenly the house door opens and Francie comes running through the rain. He starts the engine, before he realizes that she has neither hat nor coat. She comes to the driver's side, pulls open the door, and puts her arms round his neck. "Darling, only ten more minutes I swear."

"But you're getting wet."

"Yes, I saw the car from the window and I knew how you were feeling. Only ten more minutes. And then we'll be off. And I am so longing——"

She kisses him again and again, there is a cry from the house, "Francie," and she runs.

Catto falls back in his seat. He is excited, his heart is beating fast, there are tears in his eyes. For he adores his wife, it is an agony for him to see Francie used, worn out by people that, to him, are worthless beside her. And it seems that there is no cure. He suffers, he grumbles, he quarrels with the amused Mrs. Bill, he makes a fool of himself, he does not know if he is more happy or more wretched. All he knows is this passionate love, a thing he has never imagined before—that devours him with anxiety, with anger, with despair.

Katherine Mansfield

A Dill Pickle

Born and raised in Wellington, New Zealand, Katherine Mansfield settled in England in 1908. Three years later, at the age of twenty-three, she published her first collection of short stories, In a German Pension. *That same year she met John Middleton Murry, and in 1918 they were married. Between 1918 and 1923 four more collections of her stories were published. Gravely ill with tuberculosis throughout this period, Katherine Mansfield died at the age of thirty-four in Fontainebleau, France. A few years later Murry edited and published her journal and the letters she had written him during their frequent and lengthy separations.*

And then, after six years, she saw him again. He was seated at one of those little bamboo tables decorated with a Japanese vase of paper daffodils. There was a tall plate of fruit in front of him, and very carefully, in a way she recognized immediately as his "special" way, he was peeling an orange.

He must have felt that shock of recognition in her for he looked up and met her eyes. Incredible! He didn't know her! She smiled; he frowned. She came towards him. He closed his eyes an instant, but opening them his face lit up as though he had struck a match in a dark room. He laid down the orange and pushed back his chair, and she took her little warm hand out of her muff and gave it to him.

"Vera!" he exclaimed. "How strange. Really, for a moment I didn't know you. Won't you sit down? You've had lunch? Won't you have some coffee?"

She hesitated, but of course she meant to.

"Yes, I'd like some coffee." And she sat down opposite him.

"You've changed. You've changed very much," he said, staring at her with that eager, lighted look. "You look so well. I've never seen you look so well before."

"Really?" She raised her veil and unbuttoned her high fur collar. "I don't feel very well. I can't bear this weather, you know."

"Ah, no. You hate the cold. . . ."

"Loathe it." She shuddered. "And the worst of it is that the older one grows . . ."

He interrupted her. "Excuse me," and tapped on the table for the waitress. "Please bring some coffee and cream." To her: "You are sure you won't eat anything? Some fruit, perhaps. The fruit here is very good."

"No, thanks. Nothing."

"Then that's settled." And smiling just a hint too broadly he took up the orange again. "You were saying—the older one grows—"

"The colder," she laughed. But she was thinking how well she remembered that trick of his—the trick of interrupting her—and of how it used to exasperate her six years ago. She used to feel then as though he, quite suddenly, in the middle of what she was saying, put his hands over her lips, turned from her, attended to something different, and then took his hand away, and with just the same slightly too broad smile, gave her his attention again. . . . Now we are ready. That is settled.

"The colder!" He echoed her words, laughing too. "Ah, ah. You still say the same things. And there is another thing about you that is not changed at all—your beautiful voice—your beautiful way of speaking." Now he was very grave; he leaned towards her, and she smelled the warm, stinging scent of the orange peel. "You have only to say one word and I would know your voice among all other voices. I don't know what it is—I've often wondered—that makes your voice such a—haunting memory. . . . Do you remember that first afternoon we spent together at Kew Gardens? You were so surprised because I did not know the names of any flowers. I am still just as ignorant for all your telling me. But whenever it is very fine and warm, and I see some bright colors—it's awfully strange—I hear your voice saying: 'Geranium, marigold and verbena.' And I feel those three words are all I recall of some forgotten, heavenly language. . . . You remember that afternoon?"

"Oh, yes, very well." She drew a long, soft breath, as though the paper daffodils between them were almost too sweet to bear. Yet, what had remained in her mind of that particular afternoon was an absurd scene over the tea table. A great many people taking tea in a Chinese pagoda, and he behaving like a maniac about the wasps—waving them away, flapping at them with his straw hat, serious and infuriated out of all proportion to the occasion. How delighted the sniggering tea drinkers had been. And how she had suffered.

But now, as he spoke, that memory faded. His was the truer. Yes, it had been a wonderful afternoon, full of geranium and marigold and verbena, and—warm sunshine. Her thoughts lingered over the last two words as though she sang them.

In the warmth, as it were, another memory unfolded. She saw herself sitting on a lawn. He lay beside her, and suddenly, after a long silence, he rolled over and put his head in her lap.

"I wish," he said, in a low, troubled voice, "I wish that I had taken poison and were about to die—here now!"

At that moment a little girl in a white dress, holding a long, dripping water lily, dodged from behind a bush, stared at them, and dodged back again. But he did not see her. She leaned over him.

"Ah, why do you say that? I could not say that."

But he gave a kind of soft moan, and taking her hand he held it to his cheek.

"Because I know I am going to love you too much—far too much. And I shall suffer terribly, Vera, because you never, never will love me."

He was certainly far better looking now than he had been then. He had lost all that dreamy vagueness and indecision. Now he had the air of a man who has found his place in life, and fills it with a confidence and an assurance which was, to say the least, impressive. He must have made money too. His clothes were admirable, and at that moment he pulled a Russian cigarette case out of his pocket.

"Won't you smoke?"

"Yes, I will." She hovered over them. "They look very good."

"I think they are. I get them made for me by a little man in St. James's Street. I don't smoke very much. I'm not like you—but when I do, they must be delicious, very fresh cigarettes. Smoking isn't a habit with me; it's a luxury—like perfume. Are you still so fond of perfumes? Ah, when I was in Russia . . ."

She broke in: "You've really been to Russia?"

"Oh, yes. I was there for over a year. Have you forgotten how we used to talk of going there?"

"No, I've not forgotten."

He gave a strange half laugh and leaned back in his chair. "Isn't it curious. I have really carried out all those journeys that we planned. Yes, I have been to all those places that we talked of, and stayed in them long enough to—as you used to say, 'air oneself' in them. In fact, I have spent the last three years of my life travelling all the time. Spain, Corsica, Siberia, Russia, Egypt. The only country left is China, and I mean to go there, too, when the war is over."

As he spoke, so lightly, tapping the end of his cigarette against the ash-tray, she felt the strange beast that had slumbered so long within her bosom stir, stretch itself, yawn, prick up its ears, and suddenly bound to its feet, and fix its longing, hungry stare upon those far away places. But all she said was, smiling gently: "How I envy you."

He accepted that. "It has been," he said, "very wonderful—especially Russia. Russia was all that we had imagined, and far, far more. I even spent some days on a river boat on the Volga. Do you remember that boatman's song that you used to play?"

"Yes." It began to play in her mind as she spoke.

"Do you ever play it now?"

"No, I've no piano."

He was amazed at that. "But what has become of your beautiful piano?"

She made a little grimace. "Sold. Ages ago."

"But you were so fond of music," he wondered.

"I've no time for it now," said she.

He let it go at that. "That river life," he went on, "is something quite special. After a day or two you cannot realize that you have ever known another. And it is not necessary to know the language—the life of the boat creates a bond between you and the people that's more than sufficient. You eat with them, pass the day with them, and in the evening there is that endless singing."

She shivered, hearing the boatman's song break out again loud and tragic, and seeing the boat floating on the darkening river with melancholy trees on either side. . . . "Yes, I should like that," said she, stroking her muff.

"You'd like almost everything about Russian life," he said warmly. "It's so informal, so impulsive, so free without question. And then the peasants are so splendid. They are such human beings—yes, that is it. Even the man who drives your carriage has—has some real part in what is happening. I remember the evening a party of us, two friends of mine and the wife of one of them, went for a picnic by the Black Sea. We took supper and champagne and ate and drank on the grass. And while we were eating the coachman came up. 'Have a dill pickle,' he said. He wanted to share with us. That seemed to me so right, so—you know what I mean?"

And she seemed at that moment to be sitting on the grass beside the mysteriously Black Sea, black as velvet, and rippling against the banks in silent, velvet waves. She saw the carriage drawn up to one side of the road, and the little group on the grass, their faces and hands white in the moonlight. She saw the pale dress of the woman outspread and her folded parasol, lying on the grass like a huge pearl crochet hook. Apart from them, with his supper in a cloth on his knees, sat the coachman. "Have a dill pickle," said he, and although she was not certain what a dill pickle was, she saw the greenish glass jar with a red chili like a parrot's beak glimmering through. She sucked in her cheeks; the dill pickle was terribly sour. . . .

"Yes, I know perfectly what you mean," she said.

In the pause that followed they looked at each other. In the past when they had looked at each other like that they had felt such a boundless understanding between them that their souls had, as it were, put their arms round each other and dropped into the same sea, content to be drowned, like mournful lovers. But now, the surprising thing was that it was he who held back. He who said:

"What a marvellous listener you are. When you look at me with those wild eyes I feel that I could tell you things that I would never breathe to another human being."

Was there just a hint of mockery in his voice or was it her fancy? She could not be sure.

"Before I met you," he said, "I had never spoken of myself to anybody. How well I remember one night, the night that I brought you the little Christmas tree, telling you all about my childhood. And of how I was so miserable that I ran away and lived under a cart in our yard for two days without being discovered. And you listened, and your eyes shone, and I felt that you had even made the little Christmas tree listen too, as in a fairy story."

But of that evening she had remembered a little pot of caviar. It had cost seven and sixpence. He could not get over it. Think of it—a tiny jar like that costing seven and sixpence. While she ate it he watched her, delighted and shocked.

"No, really, that is eating money. You could not get seven shillings into a little pot that size. Only think of the profit they must make. . . ." And he had begun some immensely complicated calculations. . . . But now good-bye to the caviar. The Christmas tree was on the table, and the little boy lay under the cart with his head pillowed on the yard dog.

"The dog was called Bosun," she cried delightedly.

But he did not follow. "Which dog? Had you a dog? I don't remember a dog at all."

"No, no. I mean the yard dog when you were a little boy." He laughed and snapped the cigarette case to.

"Was he? Do you know I had forgotten that. It seems such ages ago. I cannot believe that it is only six years. After I had recognized you today—I had to take such a leap—I had to take a leap over my whole life to get back to that time. I was such a kid then." He drummed on the table. "I've often thought how I must have bored you. And now I understand so perfectly why you wrote to me as you did—although at the time that letter nearly finished my life. I found it again the other day, and I couldn't help laughing as I read it. It was so clever—such a true picture of me." He glanced up. "You're not going?"

She had buttoned her collar again and drawn down her veil.

"Yes, I am afraid I must," she said, and managed a smile. Now she knew that he had been mocking.

"Ah, no please," he pleaded. "Don't go just for a moment," and he caught up one of her gloves from the table and clutched at it as if that would hold her. "I see so few people to talk to nowadays, that I have turned into a sort of barbarian," he said. "Have I said something to hurt you?"

"Not a bit," she lied. But as she watched him draw her glove through his fingers, gently, gently, her anger really did die down, and besides, at the moment he looked more like himself of six years ago. . . .

"What I really wanted then," he said softly, "was to be a sort of carpet—to make myself into a sort of carpet for you to walk on so that you need not be hurt by the sharp stones and the mud that you hated so. It was nothing more positive than that—nothing more selfish. Only I did desire, eventually, to turn into a magic carpet and carry you away to all those lands you longed to see."

As he spoke she lifted her head as though she drank something; the strange beast in her bosom began to purr. . . .

"I felt that you were more lonely than anybody else in the world," he went on, "and yet, perhaps, that you were the only person in the world who was really, truly alive. Born out of your time," he murmured, stroking the glove, "fated."

Ah, God! What had she done! How had she dared to throw away her happiness like this. This was the only man who had ever understood her. Was it too late? Could it be too late? *She* was that glove that he held in his fingers. . . .

"And then the fact that you had no friends and never had made friends with people. How I understood that, for neither had I. Is it just the same now?"

"Yes," she breathed. "Just the same. I am as alone as ever."

"So am I," he laughed gently, "just the same."

Suddenly with a quick gesture he handed her back the glove and scraped his chair on the floor. "But what seemed to me so mysterious then is perfectly plain to me now. And to you, too, of course. . . . It simply was that we were such egoists, so self-engrossed, so wrapped up in ourselves that we hadn't a corner in our hearts for anybody else. Do you know," he cried, naive and hearty, and dreadfully like another side of that old self again, "I began studying a Mind System when I was in Russia, and I found that we were not peculiar at all. It's quite a well known form of . . ."

She had gone. He sat there, thunder-struck, astounded beyond words. . . . And then he asked the waitress for his bill.

"But the cream has not been touched," he said. "Please do not charge me for it."

Kay Boyle

Astronomer's Wife

Born in St. Paul, Minnesota, Kay Boyle has published over a dozen novels and a great many short stories, the best of which appear in her collections, The White Horses of Vienna, and Other Stories *(1936) and* Thirty Stories *(1946). She lived in England, France, and Austria during the 1920's and thirties, spent the war years in New York, and then returned to Germany in 1946 as a correspondent for* The New Yorker. *Since the early sixties Ms. Boyle, who has six children, has lived in the United States and taught writing at several colleges and universities. Her stories have appeared frequently in the annual O. Henry collections; she won the best story award in 1934 and 1941.*

There is an evil moment on awakening when all things seem to pause. But for women, they only falter and may be set in action by a single move: a lifted hand and the pendulum will swing, or the voice raised and through every room the pulse takes up its beating. The astronomer's wife felt the interval gaping and at once filled it to the brim. She fetched up her gentle voice and sent it warily down the stairs for coffee, swung her feet out upon the oval mat, and hailed the morning with her bare arms' quivering flesh drawn taut in rhythmic exercise: left, left, left my wife and fourteen children, right, right, right in the middle of the dusty road.

The day would proceed from this, beat by beat, without reflection, like every other day. The astronomer was still asleep, or feigning it; and she, once out of bed, had come into her own possession. Although scarcely ever out of sight of the impenetrable silence of his brow, she would be absent from him all the day in being clean, busy, kind. He was a man of other things, a dreamer. At times he lay still for hours, at others he sat upon the roof behind his telescope, or wandered down the pathway to the road and out across the mountains. This day, like any other, would go on from the removal of the spot left there from dinner on the astronomer's vest to the severe thrashing of the mayonnaise for lunch. That man might be each time the new arching wave, and woman the undertow that sucked him back, were things she had been told by his silence were so.

In spite of the earliness of the hour, the girl had heard her mistress's voice and was coming up the stairs. At the threshold of the bedroom she paused, and said: "Madame, the plumber is here."

The astronomer's wife put on her white and scarlet smock very carefully and buttoned it at the neck. Then she stepped carefully around the motionless spread of water in the hall.

"Tell him to come right up," she said. She laid her hands on the bannisters and stood looking down the wooden stairway. "Ah, I am Mrs. Ames," she said softly as she saw him mounting. "I am Mrs. Ames," she said softly, softly down the flight of stairs. "I am Mrs. Ames," spoken soft as a willow weeping. "The professor is still sleeping. Just step this way."

The plumber himself looked up and saw Mrs. Ames with her voice hushed, speaking to him. She was a youngish woman, but this she had forgotten. The mystery and silence of her husband's mind lay like a chiding finger on her lips. Her eyes were gray; for the light had been extinguished in them. The strange dim halo of her yellow hair was still uncombed and sideways on her head.

For all of his heavy boots, the plumber quieted the sound of his feet, and together they went down the hall, picking their way around the still lake of water that spread as far as the landing and lay docile there. The plumber was a tough, hardy man; but he took off his hat when he spoke to her and looked her fully, almost insolently in the eye.

"Does it come from the wash-basin," he said, "or from the other. . . ?"

"Oh, from the other," said Mrs. Ames without hesitation.

In this place the villas were scattered out few and primitive and although beauty lay without there was no reflection of her face within. Here all was awkward and unfit; a sense of wrestling with uncouth forces gave everything an austere countenance. Even the plumber, dealing as does a woman with matters under hand, was grave and stately. The mountains round about seemed to have cast them into the shadow of great dignity.

Mrs. Ames began speaking of their arrival that summer in the little villa, mourned each event as it followed on the other.

"Then, just before going to bed last night," she said, "I noticed something was unusual."

The plumber cast down a folded square of sack-cloth on the brimming floor and laid his leather apron on it. Then he stepped boldly onto the heart of the island it shaped and looked long into the overflowing bowl.

"The water should be stopped from the meter in the garden," he said at last.

"Oh, I did that," said Mrs. Ames, "The very first thing last night. I turned it off at once, in my nightgown, as soon as I saw what was happening. But all this had already run in."

The plumber looked for a moment at her red kid slippers. She was standing just at the edge of the clear, pure-seeming tide.

"It's no doubt the soil lines," he said severely. "It may be that something has stopped them, but my opinion is that the water seals aren't working. That's the trouble often enough in such cases. If you had a valve you wouldn't be caught like this."

Mrs. Ames did not know how to meet this rebuke. She stood, swaying a little, looking into the plumber's blue relentless eye.

"I'm sorry—I'm sorry that my husband," she said, "is still—resting and cannot go into this with you. I'm sure it must be very interesting. . . ."

"You'll probably have to have the traps sealed," said the plumber grimly, and at the sound of this Mrs. Ames' hand flew in dismay to the side of her face. The plumber made no move, but the set of his mouth as he looked at her seemed to soften. "Anyway, I'll have a look from the garden end," he said.

"Oh, do," said the astronomer's wife in relief. Here was a man who spoke of action and object as simply as women did! But however hushed her voice had been, it carried clearly to Professor Ames who lay, dreaming and solitary, upon his bed. He heard their footsteps come down the hall, pause, and skip across the pool of overflow.

"Katherine!" said the astronomer in a ringing tone. "There's a problem worthy of your mettle!"

Mrs. Ames did not turn her head, but led the plumber swiftly down the stairs. When the sun in the garden struck her face, he saw there was a wave of color in it, but this may have been anything but shame.

"You see how it is," said the plumber, as if leading her mind away. "The drains run from these houses right down the hill, big enough for a man to stand upright in them, and clean as a whistle too." There they stood in the garden with the vegetation flowering in disorder all about. The plumber looked at the astronomer's wife. "They come out at the torrent on the other side of the forest beyond there," he said.

But the words the astronomer had spoken still sounded in her despair. The mind of man, she knew, made steep and sprightly flights, pursued illusion, took foothold in the nameless things that cannot pass between the thumb and forefinger. But whenever the astronomer gave voice to the thoughts that soared within him, she returned in gratitude to the long expanses of his silence. Desert-like they stretched behind and before the articulation of his scorn.

Life, life is an open sea, she sought to explain it in sorrow, and to survive women cling to the floating débris on the tide. But the plumber had suddenly fallen upon his knees in the grass and had crooked his fingers through the ring of the drains' trap-door. When she looked down she saw that he was looking up into her face, and she saw too that his hair was as light as gold.

"Perhaps Mr. Ames," he said rather bitterly, "would like to come down with me and have a look around?"

"Down?" said Mrs. Ames in wonder.

"Into the drains," said the plumber brutally. "They're a study for a man who likes to know what's what."

"Oh, Mr. Ames," said Mrs. Ames in confusion. "He's still—still in bed, you see."

The plumber lifted his strong, weathered face and looked curiously at her. Surely it seemed to him strange for a man to linger in bed, with the sun pouring yellow as wine all over the place. The astronomer's wife saw his lean cheeks, his high, rugged bones, and the deep seams in his brow. His flesh was as firm and clean as wood, stained richly tan with the climate's rigor. His fingers were blunt, but comprehensible to her, gripped in the ring and holding the iron door wide. The backs of his hands were bound round and round with ripe blue veins of blood.

"At any rate," said the astronomer's wife, and the thought of it moved her lips to smile a little, "Mr. Ames would never go down there alive. He likes going up," she said. And she, in her turn, pointed, but impudently, towards the heavens. "On the roof. Or on the mountains. He's been up on the tops of them many times."

"It's a matter of habit," said the plumber, and suddenly he went down the trap. Mrs. Ames saw a bright little piece of his hair still shining, like a star, long after the rest of him had gone. Out of the depths, his voice, hollow and dark with foreboding, returned to her. "I think something has stopped the elbow," was what he said.

This was speech that touched her flesh and bone and made her wonder. When her husband spoke of height, having no sense of it, she could not picture it nor hear. Depth or magic passed her by unless a name were given. But madness in a daily shape, as elbow stopped, she saw clearly and well. She sat down on the grasses, bewildered that it should be a man who had spoken to her so.

She saw the weeds springing up, and she did not move to tear them up from life. She sat powerless, her senses veiled, with no action taking shape beneath her hands. In this way some men sat for hours on end, she knew, tracking a single thought back to its origin. The mind of man could balance and divide, weed out, destroy. She sat on the full, burdened grasses, seeking to think, and dimly waiting for the plumber to return.

Whereas her husband had always gone up, as the dead go, she knew now that there were others who went down, like the corporeal being of the dead. That men were then divided into two bodies now seemed clear to Mrs. Ames. This knowledge stunned her with its simplicity and took the uneasy motion from her limbs. She could not stir, but sat facing the mountains' rocky flanks, and harking in silence to lucidity. Her husband was the mind, this other man the meat, of all mankind.

After a little, the plumber emerged from the earth: first the light top of his head, then the burnt brow, and then the blue eyes fringed with whitest lash. He braced his thick hands flat on the pavings of the garden-path and swung himself completely from the pit.

"It's the soil lines," he said pleasantly. "The gasses," he said as he looked down upon her lifted face, "are backing up the drains."

"What in the world are we going to do?" said the astronomer's wife softly. There was a young and strange delight in putting questions to which true answers would be given. Everything the astronomer had ever said to her was a continuous query to which there could be no response.

"Ah, come now," said the plumber, looking down and smiling. "There's a remedy for every ill, you know. Sometimes it may be that," he said as if speaking to a child, "or sometimes the other thing. But there's always a help for everything a-miss."

Things come out of herbs and make you young again, he might have been saying to her; or the first good rain will quench any drought; or time of itself will put a broken bone together.

"I'm going to follow the ground pipe out right to the torrent," the plumber was saying. "The trouble's between here and there and I'll find it on the way. There's nothing at all that can't be done over for the caring," he was saying, and his eyes were fastened on her face in insolence, or gentleness, or love.

The astronomer's wife stood up, fixed a pin in her hair, and turned around towards the kitchen. Even while she was calling the servant's name, the plumber began speaking again.

"I once had a cow that lost her cud," the plumber was saying. The girl came out on the kitchen-step and Mrs. Ames stood smiling at her in the sun.

"The trouble is very serious, very serious," she said across the garden. "When Mr. Ames gets up, please tell him I've gone down."

She pointed briefly to the open door in the pathway, and the plumber hoisted his kit on his arm and put out his hand to help her down.

"But I made her another in no time," he was saying, "out of flowers and things and what-not."

"Oh," said the astronomer's wife in wonder as she stepped into the heart of the earth. She took his arm, knowing that what he said was true.

Elizabeth Bowen

Songs My Father Sang Me

Born in Dublin, Elizabeth Bowen spent most of her life in Ireland, writing novels, stories, biographies, and literary criticism. In the more than fifty years of her active literary career, she was often compared to Henry James and Virginia Woolf as a novelist, and to Chekhov and Katherine Mansfield as a short story writer. The Death of the Heart *(1938) is generally considered her best novel. In 1949 Trinity College, Dublin, honored her with a D. Litt. degree, as did Oxford University in 1956. She died in 1973.*

"*What's* the matter," he asked, "have I said something?"

Not troubling to get him quite into focus, she turned her head and said, "No, why—did you say anything?"

"Or p'r'aps you don't like this place?"

"I don't mind it—why?" she said, looking round the night club, which was not quite as dark as a church, as though for the first time. At some tables you had to look twice, to see who was there; what lights there were were dissolved in a haze of smoke; the walls were rather vaultlike, with no mirrors; on the floor dancers drifted like pairs of vertical fish. He, meanwhile, studied her from across their table with neither anxiety nor acute interest, but with a dreamlike caricature of both. Then he raised the bottle between them and said, "Mm-mm?" to which she replied by placing the flat of her hand mutely, mulishly, across the top of her glass. Not annoyed, he shrugged, filled up his own and continued, "Then anything isn't really the matter, then?"

"This tune, this song, is the matter."

"Oh—shall we dance?"

"No." Behind her agelessly girlish face, sleekly framed by the cut of her fawn-blonde hair, there passed a wave of genuine trouble for which her features had no vocabulary. "It's what they're playing—this tune."

"It's pre-war," he said knowledgeably.

"It's last war."

"Well, last war's pre-war."

"It's the tune my father remembered he used to dance to; it's the tune I remember him always trying to sing."

"Why, is your father dead?"

"No, I don't suppose so; why?"

"Sorry," he said quickly, "I mean, if . . ."

"Sorry, why are you sorry?" she said, raising her eyebrows. "Didn't I ever tell you about my father? I always thought he made me rather a bore. Wasn't it you I was telling about my father?"

"No. I suppose it must have been someone else. One meets so many people."

"Oh, what," she said, "have I hurt your feelings? But you haven't got any feelings about me."

"Only because you haven't got any feelings about me."

"Haven't I?" she said, as though really wanting to know. "Still, it hasn't seemed all the time as though we were quite a flop."

"Look," he said, "don't be awkward. Tell me about your father."

"He was twenty-six."

"When?"

"How do you mean, 'when'? Twenty-six was my father's age. He was tall and lean and leggy, with a casual sort of way of swinging himself about. He was fair, and the shape of his face was a rather long narrow square. Sometimes his eyes faded in until you could hardly see them; sometimes he seemed to be wearing a blank mask. You really only quite got the plan of his face when it was turned halfway between a light and a shadow—*then* his eyebrows and eyehollows, the dints just over his nostrils, the cut of his upper lip and the cleft in his chin, and the broken in-and-out outline down from his temple past his cheekbone into his jaw all came out at you, like a message you had to read in a single flash."

She paused and lighted a cigarette. He said, "You sound as though you had never got used to him."

She went on, "My father was one of the young men who were not killed in the last war. He was a man in the last war until that stopped; then I don't quite know what he was, and I don't think he ever quite knew either. He got his commission and first went out to France about 1915, I think he said. When he got leaves he got back to London and had good times, by which I mean something larky but quite romantic, in the course of one of which, I don't know which one, he fell in love with my mother and they used to go dancing, and got engaged in that leave and got married the next. My mother was a flapper, if you knew about flappers? They were the pinups *de ses jours*, and at the same time inspired idealistic feeling. My mother was dark and fluffy and as slim as a wraith; a great *glacé* ribbon bow tied her hair back and stood out like a calyx behind her face, and her hair itself hung down in a plume so long that it tickled my father's hand while he held her while they were dancing and while she sometimes swam up at him with her violet eyes. Each time he had to go back to the front again she was miserable, and had to put her hair up, because her relations said it was high time. But sometimes when he got back again on leave she returned to being a flapper again, to please him. Between his leaves she had to go back to live with her mother and sisters in West Kensington; and her sisters had a whole pack of business friends who had somehow never had to go near the front, and all these combined in an effort to cheer her up, but, as she always wrote to my father, nothing did any good. I suppose everyone felt it was for the best when they knew there was going to be the patter of little feet. I wasn't actually *born* till the summer of 1918. If you remember, I told you my age last night.

"The first thing *I* remember, upon becoming conscious, was living in one of those bungalows on the flats near Staines. The river must have been somewhere, but I don't think I saw it. The only point about that region is that it has no point and that it goes on and on. I think there are floods there sometimes, there would be nothing to stop them; a forest fire would be what is needed really, but that would not be possible as there are no trees. It would have looked better, really, just as primeval marsh, but someone had once said, 'Let there be bungalows.' If you ever motored anywhere near it you probably asked yourself who lives there, and why. Well, my father and mother and I did, and why?—because it was cheap, and there was no one to criticize how you were getting on. Our bungalow was tucked well away in the middle, got at by a sort of maze of in those days unmade roads. I'm glad to say I've forgotten which one it was. Most of our neighbors kept themselves to themselves for, probably, like ours, the best reasons, but most of them kept hens also; we didn't even do that. All around us, nature ran riot between corrugated iron, clothes-lines and creosoted lean-to sheds.

"I know that our bungalow had been taken furnished; the only things we seemed to have of our own were a number of satin cushions with satin fruits stitched on. In order to dislodge my biscuit crumbs from the satin apples my mother used to shake the cushions out of the window on to the lawn. Except for the prettiness of the dandelions, our lawn got to look and feel rather like a hearth-rug; I mean, it got covered with threads and cinders and shreds; once when I was crawling on it I got a pin in my hand, another time I got sharp glass beads in my knee. The next-door hens used to slip through and pick about; never, apparently, quite in vain. At the far end, some Dorothy Perkins roses tried to climb up a pergola that was always falling down. I remember my father reaching up in his shirt-sleeves, trying to nail it up. Another thing he had to do in our home was apply the whole of his strength to the doors, french window and windows, which warped until they would not open nor shut. I used to come up behind him and push too.

"The war by now, of course, had been over for some years; my father was out of the British Army and was what was called taking his time and looking around. For how long he had been doing so I can't exactly tell you. He not only read all the 'post vacant' advertisements every day but composed and succeeded in getting printed an advertisement of himself, which he read aloud to me: it said he was prepared to go anywhere and try anything. I said, 'But what's an ex-officer?', and he said, 'I am.' Our dining room table, which was for some reason, possibly me, sticky, was always spread with the newspapers he had just brought home, and he used to be leaning over them on his elbows, biting harder and harder on the stem of his pipe. I don't think I discovered for some years later that the principal reason for newspapers is news. My father never looked at them for that reason—just as he always lost interest in any book in which he had lost his place. Or perhaps he was not in the mood for world events. My mother had never cared much for them at the best of times. 'To think of all we expected after the war,' she used to say to my father, from day to day.

"My mother, by this time, had had her hair shingled—in fact, *I* never remember her any other way than with a dark shaved point tapered down the back of her neck. I don't know when she'd begun to be jealous of him and me. Every time he came back from an interview that hadn't come to anything, he used to bring me back something, to cheer himself up, and the wheels off all the mechanical toys got mixed with the beads and the threads and the cinders into our lawn. What my mother was really most afraid of was that my father would bundle us all off into the great open spaces, in order to start fresh somewhere and grow something. I imagine he knew several chaps who had, or were going to. After one or two starts on the subject he shut up, but I could see she could see he was nursing it. It frustrated her from nagging at him all out about not succeeding in getting a job in England: she was anxious not to provide an opening for him to say, 'Well, there's always one thing we *could* do . . .' The hard glassy look her eyes got made them look like dolls' eyes, which may partly have been what kept me from liking dolls. So they practically never talked about anything. I don't think she even knew he minded about her hair.

"You may be going to ask when my father sang. He often *began* to sing—when he hammered away at the pergola, when something he thought of suddenly struck him as good, when the heave he gave at the warped french window sent it flying open into the garden. He was constantly starting to sing, but he never got very far—you see, he had no place where he could sing unheard. The walls were thin and the lawn was tiny and the air round the bungalow was so silent and heavy that my mother was forced to listen to every note. The lordly way my father would burst out singing, like the lordly way he cocked his hat over one eye, had come to annoy her, in view of everything else. But the still more unfortunate thing was that my father only knew, or else only liked, two tunes out of the bygone years which made him think of the war and being in love. Yes, they were dance tunes; yes, we have just heard one; yes, they also reminded my mother of war and love. So when he had got to the fourth or fifth bar of either, she would call out to know if he wanted to drive her mad. He would stop and say, 'Sorry,' but if he was in the mood he'd be well away, the next minute, with the alternative tune, and she would be put to the trouble of stopping that.

"Mother did not know what to look like now she was not a flapper. Mostly she looked like nothing—I wonder whether she knew. Perhaps that was what she saw in the satin cushions: they looked like something—at least, to her. The day she and I so suddenly went to London to call on her sister's friend she did certainly manage, however, to look like something. My father, watching us down the garden path, ventured no comment on her or my appearance. However, which ought to have cheered me up, we created quite a furore in the train. We went sailing into the richly-appointed office of mother's sister's friend, who was one of those who, during the war, had felt mother should be cheered up. Can I, need I, describe him? The usual kind of business pudge, in a suit. He looked in a reluctant way at my mother, and reluctantly, slightly morbidly, at me. I don't know how I got the impression mother held all the cards. The conversation, of course, flowed over my head—I just cruised round and round the room, knocking objects over. But the outcome—as I gathered when we got home—was that my mother's sister's friend said he'd give my father a job. He had said he could use an ex-officer, provided it was an ex-officer with charm. What my father would have to do was to interest housewives, not in himself but in vacuum cleaners. If it helped to interest some housewives in vacuum cleaners, he could interest them just a little bit in himself. Mother's sister's friend called this, using judgment of character.

"When my mother, that evening, put all this to my father, he did not say anything but simply stood and stared. *She* said, 'Then I suppose you want us to starve?'

"So my father stopped being a problem and became a travelling salesman. The best part was that the firm allowed him a car.

"I must say for my mother that she did not ask my father how he was getting on. At least she had much less trouble about the singing: sometimes he'd be away for two or three days together; when he was home he simply sprawled in his chair, now and then asking when there'd be something to eat, as unmusical as a gramophone with the spring broken. When I came filtering in he sometimes opened one eye and said, 'And what have *you* been doing?'—as though he'd just finished telling me what he'd been doing himself. He garaged the car some way down the next road, and in the mornings when he was starting off I used to walk with him to the garage. He used to get into the car, start up the engine, back out, then look round at me and say, 'Like to come out on the job?—yes, I bet you would,' then let the clutch in and whizz off. Something about this always made me feel sick.

"I don't of course clearly remember when this began, or how long it went on for; but I know when it stopped. The night before my seventh birthday was a June night, because my birthdays are in June. The people who lived all round us were sitting out, on the verandas or on their lawns, but my mother had sent me to bed early because she was having a party for me next day and did not want to get me over-excited. My birthday cake which had arrived from the shop was on the dining-room sideboard, with a teacloth over it to keep the flies off, and my father and mother were in the lounge with the french window shut, because she had several things to say to him that she did not want the people all round to hear. The heat travelled through the roof into all the rooms, so that I could not sleep: also, my bed was against the wall of my room, and the lounge was the other side of the wall. My mother went on like someone who had been saving up—just some touch, I suppose, had been needed to set her off. She said she would like to know why there was not more money—my father's job, I suppose now, was on a commission basis. Or, she said, was he keeping another woman?—a thing she had heard that most travelling salesmen did. She said she really felt quite ashamed of having foisted my father on to her sister's friend, and that she only wondered how long the firm would stand for it. She said her sisters pitied her, though she had tried to conceal from them that her life was hell. My father, who had as usual got home late and as usual had not yet had any supper, could not be heard saying anything. My mother then said she wished she knew why she had married him, and would like still more to know why he had married her.

"My father said, 'You were so lovely—you've no idea.'

"Next morning there was a heat-haze over everything. I bustled into the dining-room to see if there was anything on my plate. I forget what my mother had given me, but her richest sister had sent me a manicure-set in a purple box: all the objects had purple handles and lay in grooves on white velvet. While I was taking them out and putting them back again, my father suddenly looked up from his coffee and said *his* present for me was in the car, and that I'd have to come out and fetch it. My mother could hardly say no to this, though of course I saw her opening her mouth. So out we set, I gripping the manicure-set. I don't think my father seemed odder than usual, though he was on the point of doing an unexpected thing—when he had got the car started and backed out he suddenly held open the other door and said, 'Come on, nip in, look sharp; my present to you is a day trip.' So then I nipped in and we drove off, as though this were the most natural thing in the world.

"The car was a two-seater, with a let-down hood . . . No, of course I cannot remember what make it was. That morning, the hood was down. Locked up in the dickie behind my father kept the specimen vacuum cleaner he interested women in. He drove fast, and as we hit the bumps in the road I heard the parts of the cleaner clonking about. As we drove, the sun began to burn its way through the haze, making the roses in some of the grander gardens look almost impossibly large and bright. My bare knees began to grill on the leather cushion, and the crumples eased out of the front of my cotton frock.

"I had never been with my father when he was driving a car—it felt as though speed and power were streaming out of him, and as if he and I were devouring everything that we passed. I sat slumped round with my cheek against the hot cushion and sometimes stared at his profile, sometimes stared at his wrists, till he squinted round and said, 'Anything wrong with *me*?' Later on, he added, 'Why not look at the scenery?' By that time there *was* some scenery, if that means grass and trees; in fact, these had been going on for some time, in a green band streaming behind my father's face. When I said, 'Where are we going?' he said, 'Well, where *are* we going?' At that point I saw quite a large hill, in fact a whole party of them, lapping into each other as though they would never stop, and never having seen anything of the kind before I could not help saying, 'Oh, I say, look!'

"My father gave a nod, without stopping singing—I told you he had begun to sing? He had not only started but gone on: when he came to the end of his first tune he said, 'Pom-*pom*,' like a drum, then started through it again; after that he worked around to the second, which he sang two or three times, with me joining in. We both liked the second still better, and how right we were—and it's worn well, hasn't it? That's what this band's just played."

"Oh, what they've just played?" he said, and looked narrowly at the band; while, reaching round for the bottle on the table between them he lifted it to replenish her glass and his. This time she did not see or did not bother to stop him: she looked at her full glass vaguely, then vaguely drank. After a minute she went on:

"Ginger beer, sausage rolls, chocolate—that was what we bought when we stopped at the village shop. Also my father bought a blue comb off a card of combs, with which he attempted to do my hair, which had blown into tags and ratstails over my eyes and face. He looked at me while he combed in a puzzled way, as though something about me that hadn't struck him became a problem to him for the first time. I said, 'Aren't we going to sell any vacuum cleaners?' and he said, 'We'll try and interest the Berkshire Downs.' I thought that meant, meet a family; but all we did was turn out of the village and start up a rough track, to where there could not be any people at all. The car climbed with a slow but exciting roar: from the heat of the engine and the heat of the sun the chocolate in the paper bag in my hands was melting by the time we came to the top.

"From the top, where we lay on our stomachs in the shade of the car, we could see—oh well, can't you imagine, can't you? It was an outsize June day.

The country below us looked all colors, and was washed over in the most reckless way with light; going on and on into the distance the clumps of trees and the roofs of villages and the church towers had quivering glimmers round them; but most of all there was space, sort of moulded space, and the blue of earth ran into the blue of sky.

"My father's face was turned away from me, propped up on his hand. I finally said to him, 'What's that?'

" 'What's what?' he said, startled.

" 'What we're looking at.'

" 'England,' he said, 'that's England. I thought I'd like to see her again.'

" 'But don't we live in England?'

"He took no notice. 'How I loved her,' he said.

" 'Oh, but don't you now?'

" 'I've lost her,' he said, 'or she's lost me; I don't quite know which; I don't understand what's happened.' He rolled round and looked at me and said, 'But *you* like it, don't you? I thought I'd like you to see, if just once, what I once saw.'

"I was well into the third of my sausage rolls: my mouth was full, I could only stare at my father. He said, 'And there's something else down there—see it?' I screwed my eyes up but still only saw the distance. 'Peace,' he said. 'Look hard at it; don't forget it.'

" 'What's peace?' I said.

" 'An idea you have when there's a war on, to make you fight well. An idea that gets lost when there isn't a war.'

"I licked pastry-crumbs off my chin and began on chocolate. By this time my father lay on his back, with his fingers thatched together over his eyes: he talked, but more to the sky than me. None of the things he was saying now went anywhere near my brain—a child's brain, how could they?—his actual words are gone as though I had never heard them, but his meaning lodged itself in some part of my inside, and is still there and has grown up with me. He talked about war and how he had once felt, and about leaves and love and dancing and going back to the war, then the birth of me—'Seven years ago to-day,' he said, 'seven years; I remember how they brought me the telegram.'

"Something else, on top of the sausage and heat and chocolate suddenly made me feel sick and begin to cry. 'Oh please, oh please don't,' I said, 'it' my birthday.'

" 'Don't what?' he said. I, naturally, didn't know. My father again looked at me, with the same expression he had worn when attempting to comb my hair. Something about me—my age?—was a proposition. Then he shut his eyes, like—I saw later, not at the time—somebody finally banishing an idea. 'No; it wouldn't work,' he said. 'It simply couldn't be done. You can wait for me if you want. I can't wait for you.'

"Then he began acting like somebody very sleepy: he yawned and yawned at me till I yawned back at him. I didn't feel sick any more, but the heat of the afternoon came down like a grey-blue blanket over my head. 'What you and I want,' my father said, watching me, 'is a good sleep.'

"I wish I could tell you at *which* moment I fell asleep, and stopped blurrily looking at him between my eyelids, because *that* was the moment when I last saw my father.

"When I woke, there was no more shadow on my side of the car; the light had changed and everything looked bright yellow. I called to my father but he did not answer, for the adequate reason that he was not there. He was gone. For some reason I wasn't at all frightened; I thought he must have gone to look for something for us for tea. I remembered that I was not at my birthday party, and I must say I thought twice about that pink cake. I was more bored than anything, till I remembered my manicure-set, which owing to the funniness of the day I had not been able to open a second time. I took the objects out of their velvet bedding and began to prod at my nails, as I'd seen my mother do. Then I got up and walked, once more, all the way round the car. It was then that I noticed what I had missed before: a piece of white paper twisted into the radiator. I couldn't read handwriting very well, but did at last make out what my father had put. *'The car and the vacuum cleaner are the property of Messrs. X and X''* (the firm of my mother's sister's friend), *'the child is the property of Mrs. So-and-so, of Such-and-such'* (I needn't bother to give you my mother's name and the name of our bungalow), *'the manicure-set, the comb and anything still left in the paper bags are the property of the child. Signed—'* It was signed with my father's name.

"The two dots I saw starting zigzag up the side of the down turned out to be two sweating policemen. What happened when they came to where I was was interesting at the moment but is not interesting now. They checked up on the message on the front of the car, then told me my father had telephoned to the police station, and that I was to be a good girl and come with them. When they had checked up on the cleaner, we all drove down. I remember the constable's knobbly, sticky red hands looked queer on the wheel where my father's had lately been. . . . At the police station, someone or other's wife made quite a fuss about me and gave me tea, then we piled into another car and drove on again. I was soon dead asleep; and I only woke when we stopped in the dark at the gate of the bungalow.

"Having tottered down the path, in the light from the front door, my mother clawed me out of the car, sobbing. I noticed her breath smelt unusual. We and the policeman then trooped into the lounge, where the policeman kept nodding and jotting things on a pad. To cheer up my mother he said that England was very small—'And he's not, so far as you know, in possession of a passport?' I sucked blobs of chocolate off the front of my frock while my mother described my father to the policeman. 'But no doubt,' the policeman said, 'he'll be thinking better of this. A man's home is a man's home, I always say.'

"When my mother and I were left alone in the lounge, we stared at each other in the electric light. While she asked if I knew how unnatural my father was, she kept pouring out a little more from the bottle: she said she had to have medicine to settle her nerves, but it seemed to act on her nerves just the opposite way. That I wouldn't say what my father had said and done set her off fairly raving against my father. To put it mildly, she lost all kind of control. She finished up with: 'And such a fool, too—a fool, a fool!'

" 'He is not a fool,' I said, 'he's my father.'

" 'He is not your father,' she screamed, 'and he is a fool!'

"That made me stare at her, and her stare at me.

" 'How do you mean,' I said, 'my father is not my father?'

"My mother's reaction to this was exactly like as if someone had suddenly pitched a pail of cold water over her. She pulled herself up and something jumped in her eyes. She said she had not said anything of the sort, and that if I ever said she had I was a wicked girl. I said I hadn't said she had, but she had said so. She put on a worried look and put a hand on my forehead and said she could feel I'd got a touch of the sun. A touch of the sun, she said, would make me imagine things—and no wonder, after the day I'd had.

"All next day I was kept in bed; not as a punishment but as a kind of treat. My mother was ever so nice to me; she kept coming in to put a hand on my forehead. The one thing she did not do was get the doctor. And afterwards, when I was let get up, nothing was good enough for me; until really anyone would have thought that my mother felt she was in my power. Shortly after, her rich sister came down, and my mother then had a fine time, crying, talking and crying; the sister then took us back with her to London, where my mother talked and cried even more. Of course I asked my aunt about what my mother had said, but my aunt said that if I imagined such wicked things they would have to think there was something wrong with my brain. So I did not re-open the subject, and am not doing so now. In the course of time my mother succeeded in divorcing my father for desertion; she was unable to marry her sister's friend because he was married and apparently always had been, but she did marry a friend of her sister's friend's, and was soon respectably settled in Bermuda, where as far as I know she still is."

"But your father?" he said.

"Well, what about my father?"

"You don't mean you never heard anything more of him?"

"I never said so—he sent me two picture postcards. The last"—she counted back—"arrived fourteen years ago. But there probably have been others that went astray. The way I've always lived, I'm not long at any address."

He essayed, rashly, "Been a bit of a waif?"

The look he got back for this was halfway between glass and ice. "A waif's the first thing I learned not to be. No, more likely my father decided, better leave it at that. People don't, on the whole, come back, and I've never blamed them. No, why should he be dead? Why should not he be—any place?"

"Here, for instance?"

"Tonight, you mean?"

"Why not?" he said. "Why not—as you say?"

"Here?" She looked round the tables, over which smoke thickened, round which khaki melted into the khaki gloom. Then her eyes returned, to fix, with unsparing attention, an addled trio of men round the fifty-five mark. "Here?" she repeated, "my father?—I hope not."

"But I thought," he said, watching the old buffers, "I thought we were looking for someone of twenty-six?"

"Give me a cigarette," she said, "and, also, don't be cruel."

"I wouldn't be," he said, as he lighted the cigarette, "if you had any feeling for me."

Claude McKay

Truant

Claude McKay was born in Jamaica but emigrated to the United States in 1912 in order to study and write. He attended Tuskegee Institute and Kansas State University for brief periods, then moved to Harlem and supported himself with menial jobs while publishing a great deal of poetry. From 1915 to 1944 he lived mainly in Europe—first in England, then for short periods in Russia, Germany, Spain, and Morocco. He finally settled in the south of France, where he wrote Home to Harlem (1928), Banjo (1929), Gingertown (1932), a collection of short stories, and Banana Bottom (1933). In 1944 Claude McKay returned to the United States and spent the last years of his life in Chicago.

The warbling of a mother's melody had just ended, and the audience was in a sentimental state and ready for the scene that the curtain, slowly drawn, disclosed. A mother in calico print jigged on her knee a little baby, crooning the while some Gaelic folk-words. A colleen sat on a red-covered box, mending a chemise; sitting at her feet, a younger sister with a picture book. Three boys in shirt sleeves and patched pantaloons playing with a red-and-green train on a lacquer-black railroad. A happy family. An antique sitting room, torn wallpaper, two comic chairs, and the Holy Virgin on the mantelpiece. A happy family. Father, fat and round like a chianti bottle, skips into the picture and up leaps boys and girls and mother with baby. The Merry Mulligans!

The orchestra starts at the pointing baton. Squeaky-burlesque family singing. Dancing. Stunting. A performing wonder, that little baby. Charming family of seven. American-famous. The Merry Mulligans, beloved of all lovers of clean vaudeville.

With them the show finished. Barclay Oram and his wife Rhoda descended from Nigger Heaven, walked up to 50th Street, and caught the local subway train for Harlem. He took the slower train, hoping there would be seats and the passengers not jammed together as always.

Perhaps others had hoped for the same thing. The cars were packed. Rhoda broke up a piece of chewing gum and chewed. She had a large mouth, and she chewed the gum as if she were eating food, opening her mouth so wide that people could see the roof. When they were first married, Barclay had detested her way of chewing gum and told her so. But she replied that it was absurd to let a little thing like chewing gum irritate him.

"Oh, you brown baby!" she had cried, taking his face in her hands and kissing him with the perfumed flavor of her favorite chewing gum on her breath. . . .

"The show was pretty nice, eh?" said Rhoda.

"I am fed up with them; a cabaret in Harlem is better," replied Barclay.

"I don't think so. Anything downtown for a change is preferable to the cheap old colored shows. I'm dead sick of them."

She chewed the gum vigorously, dropping a few pointless phrases that were half-swallowed up in the roar of the train though the enormous gut of the city and the strange staccato talk of voices half-lifted above and half-caught in the roar. Barclay gazed moodily at the many straphangers who were jammed together. None seemed standing on his feet. All seemed like fat bags and lean boxes piled up indiscriminately in a warehouse. Penned up like cattle, the standing closely pressing the seated passengers, kneading them with their knees and blotting out their sight, so that those who had been fortunate to find seats were as uncomfortable as those who had not.

"I thought we'd have a little air in this local box," he said.

"It'll be better at 72nd Street," she said.. "Some of them will get out."

"And others will push in. New York City is swarming with people like a beehive."

"Getting thicker and thicker every day," she agreed.

At 135th Street they left the train. Rhoda, as usual, put her hand through her husband's arm as they walked home. The saloons, restaurants, candy stores of the Avenue were crowded. The Chop Suey Palace was doing a good after-theater business.

"Might have some chop suey," suggested Barclay.

"Not tonight," she said. "Betsy's with the Howlands, and they might want to go to bed."

"Ah yes!" He had forgotten about Betsy, their four-year-old child. Always he forgot about her. Never could he quite realize that he was the father of a family. A railraod waiter, although he was thirty-six, he always felt himself just a boy—a servant boy. His betters whom he served treated him always as a boy—often as a nice dog. And when he grew irritated and snapped, they turned on him as upon a bad dog. It was better for him, then, that, although he was a husband and father, he should feel like an irresponsible boy. Even when sometimes he grew sad, sullen, and disquieted, these were the moods of a boy. Rhoda bossed him a little and never took his moods seriously. . . .

They went straight home. Barclay lighted up the three-room apartment. Rhoda went across the hall to the Howlands' for Betsy. She brought the child in, sleeping on her breast, and bent down that Barclay might kiss her. Then she put her to bed in her little cot beside the dresser.

They had a little supper, cold chicken and beer. . . . They went to bed in the front room that they had made their bedroom. Another room was let to a railroad porter, and the dining room served for eating and sitting room.

Rhoda undressed, rubbed her face and her limbs with cold cream, slipped on a long white gown with pink ribbon around the neck, and lay down against the wall. Barclay laid himself down beside her in his underclothes. During the first six months of their union he had slept regularly in pyjamas. Then he ignored them and began sleeping in his underclothes, returning to the habit of his village boyhood. Rhoda protested at first. Afterwards she accepted it quietly. . . .

Sleep, sweet sleep. . . .

The next morning Rhoda shook Barclay at five o'clock. "O God!" He stretched himself, turned over, and rested his head on her breast.

"Time to get up," she said.

"Yes," he sighed. "God! I feel tired." He stretched his arms, touched, fondled her face, and fell into a slight doze.

Ten minutes more. Rhoda gave him a dig in the back with her knee and cried, "You just must get up, Barclay."

"All right." He turned out of bed. Six o'clock in the Pennsylvania Station for duty, that was life itself. A dutiful black boy among proud and sure white men, so that he could himself be a man in Harlem with purchasing power for wife, child, flat, movie, food, liquor. . . .

He went to the bathroom and washed. Dressed, he entered the dining room, opened a cabinet, and poured out a glass of whisky. That peppered him up and opened his eyes wide. It was not necessary for Rhoda to make coffee. He would breakfast with the other waiters in the dining car. Mechanically he kissed her good-by. She heard him close the door, and she moved over into the middle of the bed, comfortably alone, for an early-morning nap.

It was a disastrous trip for Barclay. On the dining car he was the first waiter and in charge of the pantry. As pantryman he received five dollars a month more than the other waiters. It was his job to get the stores (with the steward and chef) from the commissary. He was responsible for the stuff kept in the pantry. There were some waiters and cooks addicted to petty stealing. Butter, cream, cheese, sugar, fruit. They stole for their women in New York. They stole for their women-on-the-side in the stopover cities. Always Barclay had to mount guard quietly. Between him and the raw-voiced, black-bull chef there was an understanding to watch out for the nimble-fingered among the crew. For if they were short in the checking up of the stores, the steward held them responsible. And the commissary held the steward responsible.

This trip Barclay had one of his moody-boy spells. He would not watch the pantry. Let the boys swipe the stuff. He had no pleasure waiting on the passengers. It was often a pleasure, something of an anticipated adventure, each day to meet new passengers, remark the temperature of their looks, and sometimes make casual conversation with a transient acquaintance. But today it was all wrong from the moment he observed them, impatient, crowding the corridor, and the rushing of the dining room as soon as the doors were opened. They filled him with loathing, made him sick of service. SERVICE. A beautiful word fallen upon bad days. No place for true human service in these automatic-serving days.

Mechanically Barclay picked up the dimes and quarters that were left for service. For Rhoda and Betsy. It pleasured him when Rhoda wore pretty clothes. And Betsy loved him more each time he remembered to bring home colored bonbons. What was he going to do with the child? He wondered if he would be able to give her a good education like her mother's. And what would she do? Perhaps marry a railroad waiter like her mother and raise up children to carry on that great tradition of black servitude.

Philadelphia, Harrisburg, Altoona, Pittsburgh. No dice, no coon-can, this trip. His workmates coaxed. Nothing could lift him out of himself. He was a moody boy this trip. The afternoon of the fourth day from New York brought the dining car to Washington. Washington reminded Barclay of a grave. He had sharp, hammering memories of his university days there. For there he had fallen in love. . . .

He went up to 7th Street, loitering through the Negro district, stopping curiously before a house, leaning against a stoop, sniffing here and there like a stray hound. He went into a barrel-house and drank a glass of whisky. The place was sour-smelling, full of black men, dim and smoky, close, but friendly warm.

The hour of his train's departure approached. Barclay continued drinking. He felt pleased with himself in doing something irregular. Oh, he had been regular for such a long time! A good waiter, an honest pantryman. Never once had he sneaked a packet of sugar nor a pound of butter for his flat. Rhoda would have flung it in the street. He had never given in to the colored girls who worked in the yards and visited the dining cars with their teasing smiles. Oh, it was hard to be responsible, hard to be regular.

What would the steward say about his being left in Washington? Maybe he would be drunk himself, for he was a regular souser. Barclay recalled the day when he got helplessly stewed on the Washington run, and the waiters managed the dining car, handed out checks, made change among themselves, and gave the best service they ever did as a crew. At Philadelphia an inspector hopped on the train and took charge of the service. The dining car was crowded. The steward half-roused himself out of his stupor and came lurching through the jam of passengers in the corridor into the diner, to dispute the stewardship with the inspector.

"I'm in charge of this diner," he said in a nerve-biting, imey-wimey voice. "Give a man a chance; treat me like a gen'leman."

Tears trickled down his cheeks. He staggered and swayed in the corridor, blocking the entrance and exit of the guests. Like a challenged mastiff, the inspector eyed him, at the same time glancing quickly from the waiters to the amazed guests. Then he gripped the steward by the scruff of the collar and, with the help of the Pullman conductor, locked him up in a drawing room until the train reached New York.

The crew did not like the steward and hoped they would be rid of him at last. But he was back with them the next trip. The inspector was known as a hard guy, quick to report a waiter if a flask of gin were discovered in his locker. But it was different with the steward. Both men were peers, the inspector being a promoted steward.

"Well, I'm off duty, anyhow," murmured Barclay. He smiled and ordered another drink. The train must have passed Baltimore by then, on its way to New York. What waiter was waiting on the first two tables? "I should worry." He had the warm, luxurious feelings of a truant. He drank himself drunk.

"Something for a change. I've been regular too long. Too awfully regular," he mused.

He rocked heavily out of the barrel-house to a little fried-chicken restaurant. He ate. His stomach appeased, his thoughts turned to a speakeasy. May as well finish the thing in style—be grandly irregular, he thought. He found a speakeasy. Bold-eyed chocolate girls, brown girls, yellow girls. Blues. Pianola blues, gramophone blues. Easy-queasy, daddy-mammy, honey-baby, brown-gal, black-boy, hot-dog blues. . . .

The next day he reported himself at the restaurant-car department in Washington, and was sent home to New York. There at the commissary the superintendent looked him over and said: "Well, you're a case. You wanted a little time off, eh? Well, take ten days."

That was his punishment—ten idle days. He left the commissary walking on air. For three years he had worked on the railroad without taking a holiday.

Why? He did not himself know. He had often yearned for a few entirely free days. But he had never had the courage to take them, not for fear of forfeiting the nominal wages, but the tips—his real wages. Nor had he wanted to lose his former dining car. He had liked his work-pals there. A good crew teaming splendidly along together, respectful to and respected by the steward, who was a decent-minded man. Moreover, there was the flat with Rhoda and Betsy. Every day was precious, every tip necessary. . . . Ten days gratuitously thrust upon him with malicious intent. No wages-and-food, no tips. Let him cool his heels and tighten his belt. Yet he was happy, happy like a truant suspended from school.

Freedom! Ten days. What would he do with them? There would be parties. Rhoda loved parties. She had friends in New York who knew her when she was a schoolteacher. Whist. Dancing. Movies.

He nosed around the tenderloin district. When he first came to New York he had lived in 40th Street.

He met a pal he had once worked with as elevator boy in a department store. They drank two glasses of beer each and walked up to San Juan Hill.

When Barclay got home, Rhoda, in an orange evening dress, was just leaving for a party. They embraced.

"I phoned up the commissary yesterday and they said you were left in Washington. Bad boy!" She laughed. "Guess I'll fix you something to eat."

"Don't bother. I'm not hungry," said Barclay.

"All right. I'm going on to Mame Dixon's for whist and a little dancing afterwards. You might dress up and come on down and have a little fun."

"Not tonight, honey. We'll have plenty of time to go around together. They gave me ten days."

"Ten days!" she cried. "The rent is due on Friday and the insurance on—on—Ten days! But why did you get left, Barclay?"

"I don't know. Felt rotten the whole trip—tired, blue. Been too punctual all along. Just had to break the habit. Feel a little irresponsible."

"But you might get in bad with the company. How could you, when there's Betsy and me to think of and our social position?"

She broke up a stick of chewing gum and vigorously chewed. "Well, anyway, come on along to Mame's if you feel like it." She rolled the gum with her tongue. "But if you don't you can bring Betsy over from the Howlands'."

Chewing, chewing, she went out.

"Kill-joy," murmured Barclay. Riding on the subway from San Juan Hill to Harlem, he had been guessing chucklingly at what she would say. Perhaps: "All right, honey-stick, why slave every day? Let's play around together for ten days."

Chewing, chewing. Always chewing. Yet that mouth was the enchanting thing about her. . . . Her mouth. It made me marry her. Her skin was brown and beautiful. Like cat's fur, soft to the fingers. But it was not her fruit-ripe skin. It was her mouth that made me.

Ordinary her face would have been, if it were not for the full, large mouth that was mounted on the ample plane of her features like an exquisite piece of bas-relief.

He went across the hall to the Howlands' and brought back Betsy.

"Candy, daddy, candy!" The happy brown thing clapped her hands and pulled at his pantaloons. He set her on his knee and gave her a little paper packet. He danced her up and down: "Betsy, wupsy, mupsy, pretsy, eatsy, plentsy candy."

She wriggled off his knee with the packet and dropped the candies one by one into a small glass jar, gurgling over the colors and popping one into her mouth at intervals. . . . She returned again to Barclay's knee, squeezing a brown rubber doll. For a little while she made a rocking horse of him. Then she scratched her head and yawned. Barclay undressed her and put her in the crib.

"Betsy and me and our social position." That social position! Alone he brooded, moody, unreasonable. Resentment gripped his heart. He hated his love of Rhoda's mouth. He hated the flat and his pitiable "social position." He hated fatherhood. He resented the sleeping child.

"Betsy and me and—" Should he go on forever like that? Round the circle of the Eastern field? New York, Boston, Buffalo, Pittsburgh, Harrisburg, Washington, Baltimore, Philadelphia, again New York.

Forever? Getting off nowhere?

Forever fated to the lifelong task of the unimaginative? Why was he, a West Indian peasant boy, held prisoner within the huge granite-gray walls of New York? Dreaming of tawny tasseled fields of sugar cane, and silver-gray John-tuhits among clusters of green and glossy-blue berries of pimento. The husbands and fathers of his village were not mechanically driven servant boys. They were hardy, independent tillers of the soil or struggling artisans.

What enchantment had lured him away from the green intimate life that clustered round his village—the simple African-transplanted life of the West Indian hills? Why had he hankered for the hard-slabbed streets, the vertical towers, the gray complex life of this steel-tempered city? Stone and steel! Steel and stone! Mounting in heavy-pursuing magnificence. Feet piled upon feet, miles circling miles, of steel and stone. A tree seemed absurd and a garden queer in this iron-gray majesty of man's imagination. He was a slave to it. A part of him was in love with this piling grandeur. And that was why he was a slave to it.

From the bedroom came a slight stirring and a sleepy murmur of child-language. Barclay was lost in the past. Step by step he retraced his life. . . . His fever-like hunger for book knowledge, for strange lands and great cities. His grand adolescent dream.

The evening of his departure from the village came back star-blue and clear. He had trudged many miles to the railroad with his bright-patterned carpet bag on his shoulder. For three years in the capital of his island he had worked in a rum warehouse. Happy. On the road to his beautiful dream. Later he had crossed over to Santiago in Cuba. And at twenty-five he had reached New York, found his strange land—a great city of great books.

Two years of elevator-running and switchboard-operating had glanced by like a magic arrow against the gaunt gray walls of the city. Time was a radiant servant working for his dream.

His dream, of course, was the Negro university. Now he remembered how he turned green cold like a cucumber when he was told that he could not enter the university course. Two years preparatory work was needed. Undaunted, he had returned to New York and crammed for a year. And the next fall he swept through the entrance examinations.

For Barclay then the highroad to wisdom led necessarily by way of a university. It had never occurred to him that he might have also attained his goal in his own free, informal way.

He had been enchanted by the words: University, Seat of Learning. He had seen young men of the insular island villages returned from the native colleges. They all brought back with them a new style of clothes, a different accent, a new gait, the exciting, intoxicating smell of the city—so much more intriguing than the ever-fresh accustomed smell of the bright-green hill-valley village. Style and accent and exotic smell—all those attractive fruits of college training, fundamental forms of the cultural life. Home study could not give him the stamp. . . . His disillusion had not embittered him. . . .

My college days were happy, he reflected. A symmetrical group of buildings, gray walls supporting in winter stout, dark-brown leafless creepers. An all-Negro body of students—men and women—of many complexions, all intensely active. The booklore was there, housed in a kind of Gothic building with a projecting façade resting on Grecian pillars. The names of Aristotle, Solon, Virgil, Shakespeare, Dante, and Longfellow were cut in the façade. The building was one of the many symbols, scattered over America and the world, summing up the dream of a great romantic king of steel.

Barclay found no romance in textbooks, of course. But he found plenty of it in the company of the jolly girls and chummy chaps of his widened acquaintance. And the barbaric steps of the turkey-trot and the bunny-hug (exciting dances of that period) he had found more enchanting than the library. He was amorously touched by the warm, intimate little dances he attended—the spontaneous outburst of group-singing when the dancers were particularly drunk on a rich, tintinnabulating melody.

Then one day he was abruptly pulled up in his fantastic steps. No more money in the box. He had to wheel round about and begin the heavy steps of working his way through college.

The next fall he met Rhoda. It was at one of those molasses-thick Aframerican affairs that had rendered university life so attractive to him, at the home of a very generous fawn-brown widow who enjoyed giving a few students a nice time at her flat. The widow entertained her guests in a free kind of way.

She did not belong to the various divisions that go to the making of nice Negro society, for she was merely the widow of a Pullman porter, who had saved up his tips and paid up on a good insurance policy. She had been too fine for the non-discriminating parlor-social sets, and too secular for the prayer-meeting black ladies. So she had cleverly gone in for the non-snobbish young intellectuals—poor students who could not afford to put on airs.

Barclay recalled the warm roomful of young Negro men and girls. Copper and chocolate and fine anthracite, with here and there a dash of cream, all warmly dancing. One night he was attracted to Rhoda. He danced with her all the time and she was warm to him, loving to him. She was the first American girl with whom he began a steady intimacy. All the ardors of him were stirred to her, and simply, impetuously he had rushed into deep love, like a bee that darts too far into the heart of a flower and, unable to withdraw, dies at the bottom of the juice.

Rhoda, who had been earning her own living as a teacher, helped him, and the problem of money was lifted from his mind. Oh, he was very happy then! Books and parties and Rhoda. . . .

In the middle of his junior year she told him she was with child. They discussed whether she should have the child or operate it away. If she had it without being married, she would lose her job. He remembered a schoolteaching girl of his village who had tried to conceal her pregnancy and died under an operation in the city. The other girls, the free peasant girls, always bore their children when they were gotten with child. Perhaps it was better that way.

Rhoda was pleased that Barclay wanted the thing to develop in the natural way. She desired a child. She was at that vague age when some women feel that marriage is more than the grim pursuit of a career. So they went to New York together and got married.

But Barclay did not fully realize the responsibility, perhaps could not, of marriage. Never fully understood its significance.

Barclay remembered now that he was as keen as Rhoda for the marriage. Carried away by the curiosity to take up a new role, there had been something almost of eagerness in his desire to quit the university. And it had seemed a beautiful gesture. Rhoda had helped him when he was in great need, and he felt splendid now to come to her support when she was incapacitated for work. He would have hated to see her drop down to menial tasks. As a Jack-of-all-trades he had met many refined colored girls having a rough time, jammed at the bottom of the common scramble to survive.

He had been happy that Rhoda was not pushed to leave Betsy in one of those dime dumps where poor colored children were guarded while their mothers worked, happy that from his job on the railroad he was earning enough for the family to live simply and comfortably.

About that job he had never taken serious thought. Where was it leading him? What was it making of his character? He had taken it as if he were acting in a play rather than working at a job. It met the necessary bill of being in love.

For he was really in love with Rhoda. The autumn-leaf mellowness of her body. Her ripe-ripe accent and richness of laughter. And her mouth: the full form of it, its strength and beauty, its almost unbearable sweetness, magnetic, drawing, sensuous, exquisite, a dark pagan piece of pleasure. . . . How fascinated and enslaved he had been to what was now stale with chewing gum and banal remarks on "socialposition."

Barclay's attitude to the railroad was about the same toward the modern world in general. He had entered light-heartedly into the whirl and crash and crush, the grand babel of building, the suction and spouting, groaning and whining and breaking of steel—all the riotous, contagious movement around him.

He had entered into the rough camaraderie of the railroad with all the hot energy of youth. It was a rugged, new experience that kindled his vagabonding mind and body. There was rude poetry in the roar and rush and rattle of trains, the sharp whistle of engines and racing landscapes, the charm of a desolate mining town and glimpses of faces lost as soon as seen. He had even tried to capture some of those fleeting piled-up images. Some he had read to his workmates, which they appreciated, but teased him for writing:

> *We are out in the field, the vast wide-open field,*
> *Thundering through from city to city*
> *Where factories grow like jungle trees*
> *Yielding new harvests for the world.*
> *Through Johnstown glowing like a world aflame,*
> *And Pittsburgh, Negro-black, brooding in iron smoke,*
> *Philly's Fifteenth street of wenches, speakeasies, and cops.*
> *Out in the field, new fields of life*
> *Where machines spin flowers like tropic trees*
> *And coal and steel are blazing suns—*
> *And darkly we wonder, night-wrapped in the light.*

The steel-framed poetry of cities did not crowd out but rather intensified in him the singing memories of his village life. He loved both, the one complementing the other. Against the intricate stone-and-steel flights of humanity's mass spirit, misty in space and time, hovered the green charm of his village. Yellow-eyed and white-lidded Spanish needles coloring the grassy hillsides, barefooted black girls, straight like young sweet-woods, tramping to market with baskets of mangoes or star-apples poised unsupported on their heads. The native cockish liquor juice of the sugar cane, fermented in bamboo joints for all-night carousal at wakes and tea meetings. Heavy drays loaded with new-made sugar, yams, and plantains, rumbling along the chalky country road away down and over the hills under the starshine and the hot-free love songs of the draymen.

He remembered all, regretting nothing, since his life was a continual fluxion from one state to another. His deepest regret was always momentary, arising from remaining in a rut after he had exhausted the experience.

Rhoda now seemed only another impasse into which he had drifted. Just a hole to pull out of again and away from the road, that arena of steel rushing him round and round in the same familiar circle. He had to evade it and be irresponsible again.

But there was the child and the Moral Law. The cold white law. Rhoda seemed more than he to be subject to it with her constant preoccupation about social position.

Spiritually he was subject to another law. Other gods of strange barbaric glory claimed his allegiance, and not the grim frock-coated gentleman of the Moral Law of the land. The Invisible Law that upheld those magnificent machines and steel-spired temples and new cathedrals erected to the steel-flung traffic plan of man. Oh, he could understand and love the poetry of them, but not their law that held humanity gripped in fear.

His thought fell to a whisper within him. He could never feel himself more than a stranger within these walls. His body went through the mechanical process, but untamed, for his spirit was wandering far. . . .

Rhoda at the party and the child asleep. He could hear her breathing and wondered if it were breath of his breath. For he had often felt to himself a breath of his own related to none. Suppose he should start now on the trail again with that strange burning thought. Related to none.

There was the Liberty Bonds in his trunk. Rhoda would need them. He remembered how he had signed for them. All the waiters herded together in one of the commissary rooms and lectured by one of the special war men.

"Buy a bond, boys. All you boys will buy a bond because you all believe in the Allied cause. We are in the war to make the world safe for Democracy. You boys on the railroad are enjoying the blessings of Democracy like all real Americans. Your service is inestimable. Keep on doing your part and do your best by buying a bond because you believe in the Allied cause and you want America to win the war and the banner of Democracy float over the world. Come on, take your bond."

For the Moral Law. Buy a bond.

Well it was all right; he had subscribed. One way of saving money, although the bonds were worth so much less now. There was the bankbook with a couple hundred dollars. Leave that, too. Insurance policies. Forget them.

He thought he heard the child stir. He dared not look. He clicked the door and stepped out. Where? Destination did not matter. Maybe his true life lay in eternal inquietude.

D.H. Lawrence

Samson and Delilah

*In the spring of 1912 Lawrence fell in love with Frieda von Richthofen, the wife of one of his former professors at Nottingham, and six weeks later they left together for the continent. Though the next eight years were a period of great productivity for Lawrence—*Sons and Lovers *was published in 1913,* The Rainbow *in 1915, and* Women in Love *in 1919—it was also a time of growing bitterness at the public censorship of his work and criticism of his life. In 1919 the Lawrences moved to Italy, hoping to find a place where they could be happier than they had been in England during the war years.*

A man got down from the motor-omnibus that runs from Penzance to St. Just-in-Penwith, and turned northwards, uphill towards the Polestar. It was only half-past six, but already the stars were out, a cold little wind was blowing from the sea, and the crystalline, three-pulse flash of the lighthouse below the cliffs beat rhythmically in the first darkness.

The man was alone. He went his way unhesitating, but looked from side to side with cautious curiosity. Tall, ruined power-houses of tin-mines loomed in the darkness from time to time, like remnants of some by-gone civilization. The lights of many miners' cottages scattered on the hilly darkness twinkled desolate in their disorder, yet twinkled with the lonely homeliness of the Celtic night.

He tramped steadily on, always watchful with curiosity. He was a tall, well-built man, apparently in the prime of life. His shoulders were square and rather stiff, he leaned forwards a little as he went, from the hips, like a man who must stoop to lower his height. But he did not stoop his shoulders: he bent his straight back from the hips.

Now and again short, stump, thick-legged figures of Cornish miners passed him, and he invariably gave them good night, as if to insist that he was on his own ground. He spoke with the West Cornish intonation. And as he went along the dreary road, looking now at the lights of the dwellings on land, now at the lights away to sea, vessels veering round in sight of the Longships Lighthouse, the whole of the Atlantic Ocean in darkness and space between him and America, he seemed a little excited and pleased with himself, watchful, thrilled, veering along in a sense of mastery and of power in conflict.

The houses began to close on the road, he was entering the straggling, formless, desolate mining village, that he knew of old. On the left was a little space set back from the road, and cozy lights of an inn. There it was. He peered up at the sign: 'The Tinners' Rest.' But he could not make out the name of the proprietor. He listened. There was excited talking and laughing, a woman's voice laughing shrilly among the men's.

Stooping a little, he entered the warmly-lit bar. The lamp table was burning, a buxom woman rose from the white-scrubbed deal table where the black and white and red cards were scattered, and several men, miners, lifted their faces from the game.

The stranger went to the counter, averting his face. His cap was pulled down over his brow.

"Good evening!" said the landlady, in her rather ingratiating voice.

"Good evening. A glass of ale."

"A glass of ale," repeated the landlady suavely. "Cold night—but bright."

"Yes," the man assented, laconically. Then he added, when nobody expected him to say any more: "Seasonable weather."

"Quite seasonable, quite," said the landlady. "Thank you."

The man lifted his glass straight to his lips, and emptied it. He put it down again on the zinc counter with a click.

"Let's have another," he said.

The woman drew the beer, and the man went away with his glass to the second table, near the fire. The woman, after a moment's hesitation, took her seat again at the table with the card-players. She had noticed the man: a big fine fellow, well dressed, a stranger.

But he spoke with that Cornish-Yankee accent she accepted as the natural twang among the miners.

The stranger put his foot on the fender and looked into the fire. He was handsome, well colored, with well-drawn Cornish eyebrows, and the usual dark, bright, mindless Cornish eyes. He seem abstracted in thought. Then he watched the card-party.

The woman was buxom and healthy, with dark hair and small, quick brown eyes. She was bursting with life and vigor, the energy she threw into the game of cards excited all the men, they shouted, and laughed, and the woman held her breast, shrieking with laughter.

"Oh, my, it'll be the death o' me," she panted. "Now, come on, Mr. Trevorrow, play fair. Play fair, I say, or I s'll put the cards down."

"Play fair! Why, who's played unfair?" ejaculated Mr. Trevorrow. "Do you mean t'accuse me, as I haven't played fair, Mrs. Nankervis?"

"I do. I say it, and I mean it. Haven't you got the Queen of Spades? Now, come on, no dodging round me. *I* know you've got that Queen, as well as I know my name's Alice."

"Well—if your name's Alice, you'll have to have it—"

"Ay, now—what did I say? Did ever you see such a man? My word, but your missus must be easy took in, by the looks of things."

And off she went into peals of laughter. She was interrupted by the entrance of four men in khaki, a short, stumpy sergeant of middle age, a young corporal, and two young privates. The woman leaned back in her chair.

"Oh, my!" she cried. "If there isn't the boys back: looking perished, I believe—"

"Perished, Ma!" exclaimed the sergeant. "Not yet."

"Near enough," said a young private uncouthly.

The woman got up.

"I'm sure you are, my dears. You'll be wanting your suppers, I'll be bound."

"We could do with 'em."

"Let's have a wet first," said the sergeant.

The woman bustled about getting the drinks. The soldiers moved to the fire, spreading out their hands.

"Have your suppers in here, will you?" she said. "Or in the kitchen?"

"Let's have it here," said the sergeant. "More cozier—if you don't mind."

"You shall have it where you like, boys, where you like."

She disappeared. In a minute a girl of about sixteen came in. She was tall and fresh, with dark, young, expressionless eyes, and well-drawn brows, and the immature softness and mindlessness of the sensuous Celtic type.

"Ho, Maryann! Evenin', Maryann! How's Maryann, now?" came the multiple greeting.

She replied to everybody in a soft voice, a strange, soft aplomb that was very attractive. And she moved round with rather mechanical, attractive movements, as if her thoughts were elsewhere. But she had always this dim far-awayness in her bearing: a sort of modesty. The strange man by the fire watched her curiously. There was an alert, inquisitive, mindless curiosity on his well-colored face.

"I'll have a bit of supper with you, if I might," he said.

She looked at him with her clear, unreasoning eyes, just like the eyes of some non-human creature.

"I'll ask mother," she said. Her voice was soft-breathing, gently sing-song.

When she came in again:

"Yes," she said, almost whispering. "What will you have?"

"What have you got?" he said, looking up into her face.

"There's cold meat—"

"That's for me, then."

The stranger sat at the end of the table, and ate with the tired, quiet soldiers. Now the landlady was interested in him. Her brow was knit rather tense, there was a look of panic in her large, healthy face, but her small brown eyes were fixed most dangerously. She was a big woman, but her eyes were small and tense. She drew near the stranger. She wore a rather loud-patterned flannelette blouse and a dark skirt.

"What will you have to drink with your supper?" she asked, and there was a new, dangerous note in her voice.

He moved uneasily.

"Oh, I'll go on with ale."

She drew him another glass. Then she sat down on the bench at the table with him and the soldiers, and fixed him with her attention.

"You've come from St. Just, have you?" she said.

He looked at her with those clear, dark, inscrutable Cornish eyes, and answered at length:

"No, from Penzance."

"Penzance!—but you're not thinking of going back there tonight?"

"No—no."

He still looked at her with those wide, clear eyes that seemed like very bright agate. Her anger began to rise. It was seen on her brow. Yet her voice was still suave and deprecating.

"I *thought* not—but you're not living in these parts, are you?"

"No—no, I'm not living here." He was always slow in answering, as if something intervened between him and any outside question.

"Oh, I see," she said. "You've got relations down here."

Again he looked straight into her eyes, as if looking her into silence.

"Yes," he said.

He did not say any more. She rose with a flounce. The anger was tight on her brow. There was no more laughing and card-playing that evening, though she kept up her motherly, suave, good-humored way with the men. But they knew her, they were all afraid of her.

The supper was finished, the table cleared, the stranger did not go. Two of the young soldiers went off to bed, with their cheery:

"Good night, Ma. Good night, Maryann."

The stranger talked a little to the sergeant about the war, which was in its first year, about the new army, a fragment of which was quartered in this district, about America.

The landlady darted looks at him from her small eyes, minute by minute the electric storm welled in her bosom, as still he did not go. She was quivering with suppressed, violent passion, something frightening and abnormal. She could not sit still for a moment. Her heavy form seemed to flash with sudden, involuntary movements as the minutes passed by, and still he sat there, and the tension on her heart grew unbearable. She watched the hands of the clock move on. Three of the soldiers had gone to bed, only the crop-haired, terrier-like old sergeant remained.

The landlady sat behind the bar fidgeting spasmodically with the newspaper. She looked again at the clock. At last it was five minutes to ten.

"Gentlemen—the enemy!" she said in her diminished, furious voice. "Time, please. Time, my dears. And good night, all!"

The men began to drop out, with a brief good night. It was a minute to ten. The landlady rose.

"Come," she said. "I'm shutting the door."

The last of the miners passed out. She stood, stout and menacing, holding the door. Still the stranger sat on by the fire, his black overcoat opened, smoking.

"We're closed now, sir," came the perilous, narrowed voice of the landlady.

The little, dog-like, hard-headed sergeant touched the arm of the stranger.

"Closing time," he said.

The stranger turned round in his seat, and his quick-moving, dark, jewel-like eyes went from the sergeant to the landlady.

"I'm stopping here tonight," he said, in his laconic Cornish-Yankee accent.

The landlady seemed to tower. Her eyes lifted strangely, frightening.

"Oh, indeed!" she cried. "Oh, indeed! And whose orders are those, may I ask?"

He looked at her again.

"My orders," he said.

Involuntarily she shut the door, and advanced like a great, dangerous bird. Her voice rose, there was a touch of hoarseness in it.

"And what might *your* orders be, if you please?" she cried. "Who might *you* be, to give orders, in the house?"

He sat still, watching her.

"You know who I am," he said. "At least, I know who you are."

"Oh, do you? Oh, do you? And who am *I* then, if you'll be so good as to tell me?"

He stared at her with his bright, dark eyes.

"You're my Missis, you are," he said. "And you know it, as well as I do."

She started as if something had exploded in her.

Her eyes lifted and flared madly.

"*Do* I know it, indeed!" she cried. "I know no such thing! I know no such thing! Do you think a man's going to walk into this bar, and tell me off-hand I'm his Missis, and I'm going to believe him? I say to you, whoever you may be, you're mistaken. I know myself for no Missis of yours, and I'll thank you to go out of this house, this minute, before I get those that will put you out."

The man rose to his feet, stretching his head towards her a little. He was a handsomely built Cornishman in the prime of life.

"What you say, eh? You don't know me?" he said in his sing-song voice, emotionless, but rather smothered and pressing: it reminded one of the girl's. "I should know you anywhere, you see. I should! I shouldn't have to look twice to know you, you see. You see, now, don't you?"

The woman was baffled.

"So you may say," she replied, staccato. "So you may say. That's easy enough. My name's known, and respected, by most people for ten miles round. But I don't know *you*."

Her voice ran to sarcasm. "I can't say I know *you*. You're a *perfect* stranger to me, and I don't believe I've ever set eyes on you before tonight."

Her voice was very flexible and sarcastic.

"Yes, you have. Your name's my name, and that girl Maryann is my girl; she's my daughter. You're my Missis right enough. As sure as I'm Willie Nankervis."

He spoke as if it were an accepted fact. His face was handsome, with a strange, watchful alertness and a fundamental fixity of intention that maddened her.

"You villain!" she cried. "You villain, to come to this house and dare to speak to me. You villain, you downright rascal!"

He looked at her.

"Ay," he said, unmoved. "All that." He was uneasy before her. Only he was not afraid of her. There was something impenetrable about him, like his eyes, which were as bright as agate.

She towered, and drew near to him menacingly.

"You're going out of this house, aren't you?" She stamped her foot in sudden madness. "*This minute!*"

He watched her. He knew she wanted to strike him.

"No," he said, with suppressed emphasis. "I've told you, I'm stopping here."

He was afraid of her personality, but it did not alter him. She wavered. Her small, tawny-brown eyes concentrated in a point of vivid, sightless fury, like a tiger's. The man was wincing, but he stood his ground. Then she bethought herself. She would gather her forces.

"We'll see whether you're stopping here," she said. And she turned, with a curious, frightening lifting of her eyes, and surged out of the room. The man, listening, heard her saying: "Do you mind coming down a minute, boys? I want you. I'm in trouble."

The man in the bar took off his cap and his black overcoat, and threw them on the seat behind him. His black hair was short and touched with grey at the temples. He wore a well-cut, well-fitting suit of dark grey, American in style, and a turn-down collar. He looked well-to-do, a fine, solid figure of a man. The rather rigid look of the shoulders came from his having had his collar-bone twice broken in the mines.

The little terrier of a sergeant, in dirty khaki, looked at him furtively.

"She's your Missis?" he asked, jerking his head in the direction of the departed woman.

"Yes, she is," barked the man. "She's that, sure enough."

"Not seen her for a long time, haven't ye?"

"Sixteen years come March month."

"Hm!"

And the sergeant laconically resumed his smoking.

The landlady was coming back, followed by the three young soldiers, who entered rather sheepishly, in trousers and shirt and stocking-feet. The woman stood histrionically at the end of the bar, and exclaimed:

"That man refuses to leave the house, claims he's stopping the night here. You know very well I have no bed, don't you? And this house doesn't accommodate travellers. Yet he's going to stop in spite of all! But not while I've a drop of blood in my body, that I declare with my dying breath. And not if you men are worth the name of men, and will help a woman as has no one to help her."

Her eyes sparkled, her face was flushed pink. She was drawn up like an Amazon.

The young soldiers did not quite know what to do. They looked at the man, they looked at the sergeant, one of them looked down and fastened his braces on the second button.

"What say, sergeant?" asked one whose face twinkled for a little devilment.

"Man says he's husband to Mrs. Nankervis," said the sergeant.

"He's no husband of mine. I declare I never set eyes on him before this night. It's a dirty trick, nothing else, it's a dirty trick."

"Why, you're a liar, saying you never set eyes on me before," barked the man near the hearth. "You're married to me, and that girl Maryann you had by me—well enough you know it."

The young soldier looked on in delight, the sergeant smoked imperturbed.

"Yes," sang the landlady, slowly shaking her head in supreme sarcasm, "it sounds very pretty, doesn't it? But you see we don't believe a word of it, and *how* are you going to prove it?" She smiled nastily.

The man watched in silence for a moment, then he said:

"It wants no proof."

"Oh, yes, but it does! Oh, yes, but it does, sir, it wants a lot of proving!" sang the lady's sarcasm. "We're not such gulls as all that, to swallow your words whole."

But he stood unmoved near the fire. She stood with one hand resting on the zinc-covered bar, the sergeant sat with legs crossed, smoking, on the seat half-way between them, the three young soldiers in their shirts and braces stood wavering in the gloom behind the bar. There was silence.

"Do you know anything of the whereabouts of your husband, Mrs. Nankervis? Is he still living?" asked the sergeant, in his judicious fashion.

Suddenly the landlady began to cry, great scalding tears, that left the young men aghast.

"I know nothing of him," she sobbed, feeling for her pocket handkerchief. "He left me when Maryann was a baby, went mining to America, and after about six months never wrote a line nor sent me a penny bit. I can't say whether he's alive or dead, the villain. All I've heard of him's the bad—and I've heard nothing for years an' all, now." She sobbed violently.

The golden-skinned, handsome man near the fire watched her as she wept. He was frightened, he was troubled, he was bewildered, but none of his emotions altered him underneath.

There was no sound in the room but the violent sobbing of the landlady. The men, one and all, were overcome.

"Don't you think as you'd better go, for tonight?" said the sergeant to the man, with sweet reasonableness. "You'd better leave it a bit, and arrange something between you. You can't have much claim on a woman, I should imagine, if it's how she says. And you've come down on her a bit too sudden-like."

The landlady sobbed heart-brokenly. The man watched her large breasts shaken. They seemed to cast a spell over his mind.

"How I've treated her, that's no matter," he replied. "I've come back, and I'm going to stop in my own home—for a bit, anyhow. There you've got it."

"A dirty action," said the sergeant, his face flushing dark. "A dirty action, to come, after deserting a woman for that number of years, and want to force yourself on her! A dirty action—as isn't allowed by the law."

The landlady wiped her eyes.

"Never you mind about law nor nothing," cried the man, in a strange, strong voice. "I'm not moving out of this public tonight."

The woman turned to the soldiers behind her, and said in a wheedling, sarcastic tone:

"Are we going to stand it, boys? Are we going to be done like this,

Sergeant Thomas, by a scoundrel and a bully as has led a life beyond *mention* in those American mining-camps, and then wants to come back and make havoc of a poor woman's life and savings, after having left her with a baby in arms to struggle as best she might? It's a crying shame if nobody will stand up for me—a crying shame——!"

The soldiers and the little sergeant were bristling. The woman stooped and rummaged under the counter for a minute. Then, unseen to the man away near the fire, she threw out a plaited grass rope, such as if used for binding bales, and left it lying hear the feet of the young soldiers, in the gloom at the back of the bar.

Then she rose and fronted the situation.

"Come now," she said to the man, in a reasonable, coldly-coaxing tone, "put your coat on and leave us alone. Be a man, and not worse than a brute of a German. You can get a bed easy enough in St. Just, and if you've nothing to pay for it, sergeant would lend you a couple of shillings, I'm sure he would."

All eyes were fixed on the man. He was looking down at the woman like a creature spell-bound or possessed by some devil's own intention.

"I've got money of my own," he said. "Don't you be frightened for your money, I've plenty of that, for the time."

"Well, then," she coaxed, in a cold, almost sneering propitiation, "put your coat on and go where you're wanted—be a *man*, not a brute of a German."

She had drawn quite near to him, in her challenging coaxing intentness. He looked down at her with his bewitched face.

"No, I shan't," he said. "I shan't do no such thing. *You'll* put me up for tonight."

"Shall I?" she cried. And suddenly she flung her arms round him, hung on to him with all her powerful weight, calling to the soldiers: "Get the rope, boys, and fasten him up. Alfred—John, quick now——"

The man reared, looked round with maddened eyes, and heaved his powerful body. But the woman was powerful also, and very heavy, and was clenched with the determination of death. Her face, with its exulting, horribly vindictive look, was turned up to him from his own breast; he reached back his head frantically, to get away from it. Meanwhile the young soldiers, after having watched this frightful Laocoon swaying for a moment, stirred, and the malicious one darted swiftly with the rope. It was tangled a little.

"Give me the end here," cried the sergeant.

Meanwhile the big man heaved and struggled, swung the woman round against the seat and the table, in his convulsive effort to get free. But she pinned down his arms like a cuttlefish wreathed heavily upon him. And he heaved and swayed, and they crashed about the room, the soldiers hopping, the furniture bumping.

The young soldier had got the rope once round, the brisk sergeant helping him. The woman sank heavily lower, they got the rope round several times. In the struggle the victim fell over against the table. The ropes tightened till they cut his arms. The woman clung to his knees. Another soldier ran in a flash of genius, and fastened the strange man's feet with the pair of braces. Seats had crashed over, the table was thrown against the wall, but the man was bound, his arms pinned against his sides, his feet tied. He lay half-fallen, sunk against the table, still for a moment.

The woman rose, and sank, faint, on to the seat against the wall. Her breast heaved, she could not speak, she thought she was going to die. The bound man lay against the overturned table, his coat all twisted and pulled up beneath the ropes, leaving the loins exposed. The soldiers stood around, a little dazed, but excited with the row.

The man began to struggle again, heaving instinctively against the ropes, taking great, deep breaths. His face, with its golden skin, flushed dark and surcharged. He heaved again. The great veins in his neck stood out. But it was no good, he went relaxed. Then again, suddenly, he jerked his feet.

"Another pair of braces, William," cried the excited soldier. He threw himself on the legs of the bound man, and managed to fasten the knees. Then again there was stillness. They could hear the clock tick.

The woman looked at the prostrate figure, the strong, straight limbs, the strong back bound in subjection, the wide-eyed face that reminded her of a calf tied in a sack in a cart, only its head stretched dumbly backwards. And she triumphed.

The bound-up body began to struggle again. She watched fascinated the muscles working, the shoulders, the hips, the large, clean thighs. Even now he might break the ropes. She was afraid. But the lively young soldier sat on the shoulders of the bound man, and after a few perilous moments, there was stillness again.

"Now," said the judicious sergeant to the bound man, "if we untie you, will you promise to go off and make no more trouble?"

"You'll not untie him in here," cried the woman. "I wouldn't trust him as far as I could blow him."

There was silence.

"We might carry him outside, and undo him there," said the soldier. "Then we could get the poliecman, if he made any more bother."

"Yes," said the sergeant. "We could do that." Then again, in an altered, almost severe tone, to the prisoner: "If we undo you outside, will you take your coat and go without creating any more disturbance?"

But the prisoner would not answer, he only lay with wide, dark, bright eyes, like a bound animal. There was a space of perplexed silence.

"Well, then, do as you say," said the woman irritably. "Carry him out amongst you, and let us shut up the house."

They did so. Picking up the bound man, the four soldiers staggered clumsily into the silent square in front of the inn, the woman followed with the cap and overcoat. The young soldiers quickly unfastened the braces from the prisoner's legs, and they hopped indoors. They were in their stocking-feet, and outside the stars flashed cold. They stood in the doorway watching. The man lay quite still on the cold ground.

"Now," said the sergeant, in a subdued voice, "I'll loosen the knot, and he can work himself free, if you go in, Missis."

She gave a last look at the dishevelled, bound man, as he sat on the ground. Then she went indoors, followed quickly by the sergeant. Then they were heard locking and barring the door.

The man seated on the ground outside worked and strained at the rope. But it was not so easy to undo himself even now. So, with hands bound, making an effort, he got on his feet, and went and worked the cord against the rough edge of an old wall. The rope, being of a kind of plaited grass, soon frayed and broke, and he freed himself. He had various contusions. His arms were hurt and bruised from the bonds. He rubbed them slowly. Then he pulled his clothes straight, stooped, put on his cap, struggled into his overcoat, and walked away.

The stars were very brilliant. Clear as crystal, the beam from the lighthouse under the cliffs struck rhythmically on the night. Dazed, the man walked along the road past the churchyard. Then he stood leaning up against a wall, for a long time.

He was roused because his feet were so cold. So he pulled himself together, and turned again in the silent night, back towards the inn.

The bar was in darkness. But there was a light in the kitchen. He hesitated. Then very quietly he tried the door.

He was surprised to find it open. He entered, and quietly closed it behind him. Then he went down the step past the bar-counter, and through to the lighted doorway of the kitchen. There sat his wife, planted in front of the range, where a furze fire was burning. She sat in a chair full in front of the range, her knees wide apart on the fender. She looked over her shoulder at him as he entered, but she did not speak. Then she stared in the fire again.

It was a small, narrow kitchen. He dropped his cap on the table that was covered with yellowish American cloth, and took a seat with his back to the wall, near the oven. His wife still sat with her knees apart, her feet on the steel fender and stared into the fire, motionless. Her skin was smooth and rosy in the firelight. Everything in the house was very clean and bright. The man sat silent, too, his head dropped. And thus they remained.

It was a question who would speak first. The woman leaned forward and poked the ends of the sticks in between the bars of the range. He lifted his head and looked at her.

"Others gone to bed, have they?" he asked.

But she remained closed in silence.

" 'S a cold night, out," he said, as if to himself.

And he laid his large, yet well-shapen workman's hand on the top of the stove, that was polished black and smooth as velvet. She would not look at him, yet she glanced out of the corners of her eyes.

His eyes were fixed brightly on her, the pupils large and electric like those of a cat.

"I should have picked you out among thousands," he said. "Though you're bigger than I'd have believed. Fine flesh you've made."

She was silent for some time. Then she turned in her chair upon him.

"What do you think of yourself," she said, "coming back on me like this after over fifteen year? You don't think I've not heard of you, neither, in Butte City and elsewhere?"

He was watching her with his clear, translucent, unchallenged eyes.

"Yes," he said. "Chaps comes an' goes—I've heard tell of you from time to time."

She drew herself up.

"And what lies have you heard about *me*?" she demanded superbly.

"I dunno as I've heard any lies at all—'cept as you was getting on very well, like."

His voice ran warily and detached. Her anger stirred again in her violently. But she subdued it, because of the danger there was in him, and more, perhaps, because of the beauty of his head and his level drawn brows, which she could not bear to forfeit.

"That's more than I can say of *you*," she said. "I've heard more harm than good about *you*."

"Ay, I dessay," he said looking in the fire. It was a long time since he had seen the furze burning, he said to himself. There was a silence, during which she watched his face.

"Do you call yourself a *man*?" she said, more in contemptuous reproach than in anger. "Leave a woman as you've left me, you don't care to what!—and then to turn up in *this* fashion, without a word to say for yourself."

He stirred in his chair, planted his feet apart, and resting his arms on his knees, looked steadily into the fire without answering. So near to her was his head, and the close black hair, she could scarcely refrain from starting away, as if it would bite her.

"Do you call that the action of a *man*?" she repeated.

"No," he said, reaching and poking the bits of wood into the fire with his fingers. "I didn't call it anything, as I know of. It's no good calling things by any names whatsoever, as I know of."

She watched him in his actions. There was a longer and longer pause between each speech, though neither knew it.

"I *wonder* what you think of yourself!" she exclaimed, with vexed emphasis. "I *wonder* what sort of a fellow you take yourself to be!" She was really perplexed as well as angry.

"Well," he said, lifting his head to look at her, "I guess I'll answer for my own faults, if everybody else'll answer for theirs."

Her heart beat fiery hot as he lifted his face to her. She breathed heavily, averting her face, almost losing her self-control.

"And what do you take *me* to be?" she cried, in real helplessness.

His face was lifted, watching her soft, averted face. And the softly heaving mass of her breasts.

"I take you," he said, with that laconic truthfulness which exercised such power over her, "to be the deuce of a fine woman—darn me if you're not as fine a built woman as I've seen, handsome with it as well. I shouldn't have expected you to put on such handsome flesh: 'struth I shouldn't."

Her heart beat fiery hot, as he watched her with those bright agate eyes, fixedly.

"Been very handsome to *you*, for fifteen years, my sakes!" she replied.

He made no answer to this, but sat with his bright, quick eyes upon her.

Then he rose. She started involuntarily. But he only said, in his laconic, measured way:

"It's warm in here now."

And he pulled off his overcoat, throwing it on the table. She sat as if slightly cowed, whilst he did so.

"Them ropes has given my arms something, by Ga-ard," he drawled, feeling his arms with his hands.

Still she sat in her chair before him, slightly cowed.

"You was sharp, wasn't you, to catch me like that, eh?" he smiled slowly. "By Ga-ard, you had me fixed proper—proper, you did."

He leaned forwards in his chair towards her.

"I don't think no worse of you for it, no, darned if I do. Fine pluck in a woman's what I admire. That I do, indeed."

She only gazed into the fire.

"We fet from the start, we did. And, my word, you begin again quick the minute you see me, you did. Darn me, you was too sharp for me. A darn fine woman, puts up a darn good fight. Darn me if I could find a woman in all the darn States as could get me down like that. Wonderful fine woman you be, truth to say, at this minute."

She only sat glowering into the fire.

"As grand a pluck as a man could wish to find in a woman, true as I'm here," he said, reaching forward his hand and tentatively touching her between her full, warm breasts, quietly.

She started, and seemed to shudder. But his hand insinuated itself between her breasts, as she continued to gaze in the fire.

"And don't you think I've come back here a-begging," he said. "I've more than *one* thousand pounds to my name, I have. And a bit of a fight for a how-de-do pleases me, that it do. But that doesn't mean as you're going to deny as you're my Missis . . ."

5
impasses

Anton Chekhov

The Lady with the Dog

Anton Chekhov began writing humorous sketches to help support his parents while he was studying medicine at the University of Moscow. After his graduation in 1884, he practiced medicine for only a few years and then devoted his full attention to fiction and the drama. By the time he was thirty Chekhov was one of the most celebrated short story writers in Russia. His first success as a dramatist came in 1898 with the Moscow Art Theatre's production of The Seagull, *which encouraged him to write three more plays:* Uncle Vanya *(1900),* The Three Sisters *(1901), and* The Cherry Orchard *(1904). In 1904 Chekhov died of tuberculosis at the age of 44.*

1

People were telling one another that a newcomer had been seen on the promenade—a lady with a dog. Dmitri Dmitrich Gurov had been a fortnight in Yalta, and was accustomed to its ways, and he, too, had begun to take an interest in fresh arrivals. From his seat in Vernet's outdoor café, he caught sight of a young woman in a toque, passing along the promenade; she was fair and not very tall; after her trotted a white pomeranian.

Later he encountered her in the municipal park, and in the square, several times a day. She was always alone, wearing the same toque, and the pomeranian always trotted at her side. Nobody knew who she was, and people referred to her simply as "the lady with the dog."

"If she's here without her husband, and without any friends," thought Gurov, "it wouldn't be a bad idea to make her acquaintance."

He was not yet forty, but had a twelve-year-old daughter and two schoolboy sons. He had been talked into marrying in his second year at college, and his wife now looked nearly twice as old as he was. She was a tall, black-browed woman, erect, dignified, imposing, and, as she said of herself, a "thinker." She was a great reader, omitted the "hard sign" at the end of words in her letters, and called her husband "Dimitri" instead of Dmitri; and though he secretly considered her shallow, narrow-minded, and dowdy, he stood in awe of her, and disliked being at home. It was long since he had first begun deceiving her and he was now constantly unfaithful to her, and this was no doubt why he spoke slightingly of women, to whom he referred as *the lower race*.

He considered that the ample lessons he had received from bitter experience entitled him to call them whatever he liked, but without this "lower race" he could not have existed a single day. He was bored and ill-at-ease in the company of men, with whom he was always cold and reserved, but felt quite at home among women, and knew exactly what to say to them, and how to behave; he could even be silent in their company without feeling the slightest awkwardness. There was an elusive charm in his appearance and disposition which attracted women and caught their sympathies. He knew this and was himself attracted to them by some invisible force.

Repeated and bitter experience had taught him that every fresh intimacy, while at first introducing such pleasant variety into everyday life, and offering itself as a charming, light adventure, inevitably developed, among decent people (especially in Moscow, where they are so irresolute and slow to move), into a problem of excessive complication leading to an intolerably irksome situation. But every time he encountered an attractive woman he forgot all about this experience, the desire for life surged up in him, and everything suddenly seemed simple and amusing.

One evening, then, while he was dining at the restaurant in the park, the lady in the toque came strolling up and took a seat at a neighboring table. Her expression, gait, dress, coiffure, all told him that she was from the upper classes, that she was married, that she was in Yalta for the first time, alone and bored. . . . The accounts of the laxity of morals among visitors to Yalta are greatly exaggerated, and he paid no heed to them, knowing that for the most part they were invented by people who would gladly have transgressed themselves, had they known how to set about it. But when the lady sat down at a neighboring table a few yards away from him, the stories of easy conquests, of excursions to the mountains, came back to him, and the seductive idea of a brisk transitory liaison, an affair with a woman whose very name he did not know, suddenly took possession of his mind.

He snapped his fingers at the pomeranian, and when it trotted up to him, shook his forefinger at it. The pomeranian growled. Gurov shook his finger again.

The lady glanced at him and instantly lowered her eyes.

"He doesn't bite," she said, and blushed.

"May I give him a bone?" he asked, and on her nod of consent added in friendly tones: "Have you been in Yalta long?"

"About five days."

"And I am dragging out my second week here."

Neither spoke for a few minutes.

"The days pass quickly, and yet one is so bored here," she said, not looking at him.

"It's the thing to say it's boring here. People never complain of boredom in God-forsaken holes like Belyev or Zhizdra, but when they get here it's: 'Oh, the dullness! Oh, the dust!' You'd think they'd come from Granada, to say the least."

She laughed. Then they both went on eating in silence, like complete strangers. But after dinner they left the restaurant together, and embarked upon the light, jesting talk of people free and contented, for whom it is all the same where they go, or what they talk about. They strolled along, remarking on the strange light over the sea. The water was a warm, tender purple. The moonlight lay on its surface in a golden strip. They said how close it was, after the hot day. Gurov told her he was from Moscow, that he was really a philologist, but worked in a bank; that he had at one time trained himself to sing in a private opera company, but had given up the idea; that he owned two houses in Moscow. . . . And from her he learned that she had grown up in Petersburg, but had got married in the town of S., where she had been living two years, that she would stay another month in Yalta, and that perhaps her husband, who also needed a rest, would join her. She was quite unable to explain whether her husband was a member of the gubernia council, or on the board of the Zemstvo, and was greatly amused at herself for this. Further, Gurov learned that her name was Anna Sergeyevna.

Back in his own room he thought about her, and felt sure he would meet her the next day. It was inevitable. As he went to bed he reminded himself that only a very short time ago she had been a schoolgirl, like his own daughter, learning her lessons; he remembered how much there was of shyness and constraint in her laughter, in her way of conversing with a stranger—it was probably the first time in her life that she found herself alone, and in a situation in which men could follow her and watch her, and speak to her, all the time with a secret aim she could not fail to divine. He recalled her slender, delicate neck, her fine gray eyes.

"And yet there's something pathetic about her," he thought to himself as he fell asleep.

2

A week had passed since the beginning of their acquaintance. It was a holiday. Indoors it was stuffy, but the dust rose in clouds out of doors, and people's hats blew off. It was a thirsty day and Gurov kept going to the outdoor café for fruit-drinks and ices to offer Anna Sergeyevna. The heat was overpowering.

In the evening, when the wind had dropped, they walked to the pier to see the steamer come in. There were a great many people strolling about the landing-place; some, bunches of flowers in their hands, were meeting friends. Two peculiarities of the smart Yalta crowd stood out distinctly—the elderly ladies all tried to dress very young, and there seemed to be an inordinate number of generals about.

Owing to the roughness of the sea the steamer arrived late, after the sun had gone down, and it had to maneuver for some time before it could get alongside the pier. Anna Sergeyevna scanned the steamer and passengers through her lorgnette, as if looking for someone she knew, and when she turned to Gurov her eyes were glistening. She talked a great deal, firing off abrupt questions and forgetting immediately what it was she had wanted to know. Then she lost her lorgnette in the crush.

The smart crowd began dispersing, features could no longer be made out, the wind had quite dropped, and Gurov and Anna Sergeyevna stood there as if waiting for someone else to come off the steamer. Anna Sergeyevna had fallen silent, every now and then smelling her flowers, but not looking at Gurov.

"It's turned out a fine evening," he said. "What shall we do? We might go for a drive."

She made no reply.

He looked steadily at her and suddenly took her in his arms and kissed her lips, and the fragrance and dampness of the flowers closed round him, but the next moment he looked behind him in alarm—had anyone seen them?

"Let's go to your room," he murmured.

And they walked off together, very quickly.

Her room was stuffy and smelled of some scent she had bought in the Japanese shop. Gurov looked at her, thinking to himself: "How full of strange encounters life is!" He could remember carefree, good-natured women who were exhilarated by love-making and grateful to him for the happiness he gave them, however short-lived; and there had been others—his wife among them—whose caresses were insincere, affected, hysterical, mixed up with a great deal of quite unnecessary talk, and whose expression seemed to say that all this was not just love-making or passion, but something much more significant; then there had been two or three beautiful, cold women, over whose features flitted a predatory expression, betraying a determination to wring from life more than it could give, women no longer in their first youth, capricious, irrational, despotic, brainless, and when Gurov had cooled to these, their beauty aroused in him nothing but repulsion, and the lace trimming on their underclothes reminded him of fish-scales.

But here the timidity and awkwardness of youth and inexperience were still apparent; and there was a feeling of embarrassment in the atmosphere, as if someone had just knocked at the door. Anna Sergeyevna, "the lady with the dog," seemed to regard the affair as something very special, very serious, as if she had become a fallen woman, an attitude he found odd and disconcerting. Her features lengthened and drooped, her long hair hung mournfully on either side of her face. She assumed a pose of dismal meditation, like a repentant sinner in some classical painting.

"It isn't right," she said. "You will never respect me anymore."

On the table was a watermelon. Gurov cut himself a slice from it and began slowly eating it. At least half an hour passed in silence.

Anna Sergeyevna was very touching, revealing the purity of a decent, naïve woman who had seen very little of life. The solitary candle burning on the table scarcely lit up her face, but it was obvious that her heart was heavy.

"Why should I stop respecting you?" asked Gurov. "You don't know what you're saying."

"May God forgive me!" she exclaimed, her eyes filled with tears. "It's terrible."

"No need to seek to justify yourself."

"How can I justify myself? I'm a wicked, fallen woman. I despise myself and have not the least thought of self-justification. It isn't my husband I have deceived, it's myself. And not only now, I have been deceiving myself for ever so long. My husband is no doubt an honest, worthy man, but he's a flunkey. I don't know what it is he does at his office, but I know he's a flunkey. I was only twenty when I married him, and I was devoured by curiosity, I wanted something higher. I told myself that there must be a different kind of life. I wanted to live, to live. . . . I was burning with curiosity . . . you'll never understand that, but I swear to God I could no longer control myself, nothing could hold me back, I told my husband I was ill, and I came here. . . . And I started going about like one possessed, like a madwoman . . . and now I have become an ordinary, worthless woman, and everyone has the right to despise me."

Gurov listened to her, bored to death. The naïve accents, the remorse, all was so unexpected, so out of place. But for the tears in her eyes, she might have been jesting or play-acting.

"I don't understand," he said gently. "What is it you want?"

She hid her face against his breast and pressed closer to him.

"Do believe me, I implore you to believe me," she said. "I love all that is honest and pure in life, vice is revolting to me, I don't know what I'm doing.

The common people say they are snared by the devil. And now I can say that I have been snared by the devil, too."

"Come, come," he murmured.

He gazed into her fixed, terrified eyes, kissed her, and soothed her with gentle affectionate words, and gradually she calmed down and regained her cheerfulness. Soon they were laughing together again.

When, a little later, they went out, there was not a soul on the promenade, the town and its cypresses looked dead, but the sea was still roaring as it dashed against the beach. A solitary fishing-boat tossed on the waves, its lamp blinking sleepily.

They found a droshky and drove to Oreanda.

"I discovered your name in the hall, just now," said Gurov, "written up on the board. Von Diederitz. Is your husband a German?"

"No. His grandfather was, I think, but he belongs to the Orthodox church himself."

When they got out of the droshky at Oreanda they sat down on a bench not far from the church, and looked down at the sea, without talking. Yalta could be dimly discerned through the morning mist, and white clouds rested motionless on the summits of the mountains. Not a leaf stirred, the grasshoppers chirruped, and the monotonous hollow roar of the sea came up to them, speaking of peace, of the eternal sleep lying in wait for us all. The sea had roared like this long before there was any Yalta or Oreanda, it was roaring now, and it would go on roaring, just as indifferently and hollowly, when we have passed away. And it may be that in this continuity, this utter indifference to life and death, lies the secret of our ultimate salvation, of the stream of life on our planet, and of its never-ceasing movement toward perfection.

Side by side with a young woman, who looked so exquisite in the early light, soothed and enchanted by the sight of all this magical beauty—sea, mountains, clouds and the vast expanse of the sky—Gurov told himself that, when you came to think of it, everything in the world is beautiful really, everything but our own thoughts and actions, when we lose sight of the higher aims of life, and of our dignity as human beings.

Someone approached them—a watchman, probably—looked at them and went away. And there was something mysterious and beautiful even in this. The steamer from Feodosia could be seen coming toward the pier, lit up by the dawn, its lamps out.

"There's dew on the grass," said Anna Sergeyevna, breaking the silence.

"Yes. Time to go home."

They went back to the town.

After this they met every day at noon on the promenade, lunching and dining together, going for walks, and admiring the sea. She complained of sleeplessness, of palpitations, asked the same questions over and over again, alternately surrendering to jealousy and the fear that he did not really respect her. And often, when there was nobody in sight in the square or the park, he would draw her to him and kiss her passionately. The utter idleness, these kisses in broad daylight, accompanied by furtive glances and the fear of discovery, the heat, the smell of the sea, and the idle, smart, well-fed people continually crossing their field of vision, seemed to have given him a new lease on life. He told Anna Sergeyevna she was beautiful and seductive, made love to her with impetuous passion, and never left her side, while she was always pensive, always trying to force from him the admission that he did not respect her, that he did not love her a bit, and considered her just an ordinary woman. Almost every night they drove out of town, to Oreanda, the waterfall, or some other beauty spot. And these excursions were invariably a success, each contributing fresh impressions of majestic beauty.

All this time they kept expecting her husband to arrive. But a letter came in which he told his wife that he was having trouble with his eyes, and implored her to come home as soon as possible. Anna Sergeyevna made hasty preparations for leaving.

"It's a good thing I'm going," she said to Gurov. "It's the intervention of fate."

She left Yalta in a carriage, and he went with her as far as the railway station. The drive took nearly a whole day. When she got into the express train, after the second bell had been rung, she said:

"Let me have one more look at you. . . . One last look. That's right."

She did not weep, but was mournful, and seemed ill, the muscles of her cheeks twitching.

"I shall think of you . . . I shall think of you all the time," she said. "God bless you! Think kindly of me. We are parting for ever, it must be so, because we ought never to have met. Good-bye—God bless you."

The train steamed rapidly out of the station, its lights soon disappearing, and a minute later even the sound it made was silenced, as if everything were conspiring to bring this sweet oblivion, this madness, to an end as quickly as possible. And Gurov, standing alone on the platform and gazing into the dark distance, listened to the shrilling of the grasshoppers and the humming of the telegraph wires, with a feeling that he had only just waked up. And he told himself that this had been just one more of the many adventures in his life, and that it, too, was over, leaving nothing but a memory. . . . He was moved and sad, and felt a slight remorse. After all, this young woman whom he would never again see had not been really happy with him. He had been friendly and affectionate with her, but in his whole behavior, in the tones of his voice, in his very caresses, there had been a shade of irony, the insulting indulgence of the fortunate male, who was, moreover, almost twice her age. She had insisted in calling him good, remarkable, high-minded. Evidently he had appeared to her different from his real self, in a word he had involuntarily deceived her. . . .

There was an autumnal feeling in the air, and the evening was chilly.

"It's time for me to be going north, too," thought Gurov, as he walked away from the platform. "High time!"

3

When he got back to Moscow it was beginning to look like winter, the stoves were heated every day, and it was still dark when the children got up to go to school and drank their tea, so that the nurse had to light the lamp for a short time. Frost had set in. When the first snow falls, and one goes for one's first sleigh-ride, it is pleasant to see the white ground, the white roofs; one breathes freely and lightly, and remembers the days of one's youth. The ancient lime-trees and birches, white with rime, have a good-natured look, they are closer to the heart than cypresses and palms, and beneath their branches one is no longer haunted by the memory of mountains and the sea.

Gurov had always lived in Moscow, and he returned to Moscow on a fine frosty day, and when he put on his fur-lined overcoat and thick gloves, and sauntered down Petrovka Street, and when, on Saturday evening, he heard the church bells ringing, his recent journey and the places he had visited lost their charm for him. He became gradually immersed in Moscow life, reading with avidity three newspapers a day, while declaring he never read Moscow newspapers on principle. Once more he was caught up in a whirl of restaurants, clubs, banquets, and celebrations, once more glowed with the flattering consciousness that well-known lawyers and actors came to his house, that he played cards in the Medical Club opposite a professor.

He had believed that in a month's time Anna Sergeyevna would be nothing but a vague memory, and that hereafter, with her wistful smile, she would only occasionally appear to him in dreams, like others before her. But the month was now well over and winter was in full swing, and all was as clear in his memory as if he had only parted with Anna Sergeyevna the day before. And his recollections grew ever more insistent. When the voices of his children at their lessons reached him in his study through the evening stillness, when he heard a song, or the sounds of a musical-box in a restaurant, when the wind howled in the chimney, it all came back to him: early morning on the pier, the misty mountains, the steamer from Feodosia, the kisses. He would pace up and down his room for a long time, smiling at his memories, and then memory turned into dreaming, and what had happened mingled in his imagination with what was going to happen. Anna Sergeyevna did not come to him in his dreams, she accompanied him everywhere, like his shadow, following him everywhere he went. When he closed his eyes, she seemed to stand before him in the flesh, still lovelier, younger, tenderer than she had really been, and looking back, he saw himself, too, as better than he had been in Yalta. In the evenings she looked out at him from the bookshelves, the fireplace, the corner; he could hear her breathing, the sweet rustle of her skirts. In the streets he followed women with his eyes, to see if there were any like her. . . .

He began to feel an overwhelming desire to share his memories with someone. But he could not speak of his love at home, and outside his home who was there for him to confide in? Not the tenants living in his house, and certainly not his colleagues at the bank. And what was there to tell? Was it love that he had felt? Had there been anything exquisite, poetic, anything instructive or even amusing about his relations with Anna Sergeyevna? He had to content himself with uttering vague generalizations about love and women, and nobody guessed what he meant, though his wife's dark eyebrows twitched as she said:

"The role of a coxcomb doesn't suit you a bit, Dimitri."

One evening, leaving the Medical Club with one of his card-partners, a government official, he could not refrain from remarking:

"If you only knew what a charming woman I met in Yalta!"

The official got into his sleigh, and just before driving off turned and called out:

"Dmitri Dmitrich!"

"Yes?"

"You were quite right, you know—the sturgeon was just a *leetle* off."

These words, in themselves so commonplace, for some reason infuriated Gurov, seemed to him humiliating, gross. What savage manners, what people! What wasted evenings, what tedious, empty days! Frantic card-playing, gluttony, drunkenness, perpetual talk always about the same thing. The greater part of one's time and energy went on business that was no use to anyone, and on discussing the same thing over and over again, and there was nothing to show for it all but a stunted, earth-bound existence and a round of trivialities, and there was nowhere to escape to, you might as well be in a madhouse or a convict settlement.

Gurov lay awake all night, raging, and went about the whole of the next day with a headache. He slept badly on the succeeding nights, too, sitting up in bed, thinking, or pacing the floor of his room. He was sick of his children, sick of the bank, felt not the slightest desire to go anywhere or talk about anything.

When the Christmas holidays came, he packed his things, telling his wife he had to go to Petersburg in the interests of a certain young man, and set off for the town of S. To what end? He hardly knew himself. He only knew that he must see Anna Sergeyevna, must speak to her, arrange a meeting, if possible.

He arrived at S. in the morning and engaged the best room in the hotel, which had a carpet of gray military frieze, and a dusty ink-pot on the table, surmounted by a headless rider, holding his hat in his raised hand. The hall porter told him what he wanted to know: von Diederitz had a house of his own in Staro-Goncharnaya Street. It wasn't far from the hotel, he lived on a grand scale, luxuriously kept carriage-horses, the whole town knew him. The hall porter pronounced the name "Drideritz."

Gurov strolled over to Staro-Goncharnaya Street and discovered the house. In front of it was a long gray fence with inverted nails hammered into the tops of the palings.

"A fence like that is enough to make anyone want to run away," thought Gurov, looking at the windows of the house and the fence.

He reasoned that since it was a holiday, her husband would probably be at home. In any case it would be tactless to embarrass her by calling at the house. And a note might fall into the hands of the husband, and bring about catastrophe. The best thing would be to wait about on the chance of seeing her. And he walked up and down the street, hovering in the vicinity of the fence, watching for his chance. A beggar entered the gate, only to be attacked by dogs; then, an hour later, the faint, vague sounds of a piano reached his ears. That would be Anna Sergeyevna playing. Suddenly the front door opened and an old woman came out, followed by a familiar white pomeranian. Gurov tried to call to it, but his heart beat violently, and in his agitation he could not remember its name.

He walked on, hating the gray fence more and more, and now ready to tell himself irately that Anna Sergeyevna had forgotten him, had already, perhaps, found distraction in another—what could be more natural in a young woman who had to look at this accursed fence from morning to night? He went back to his hotel and sat on the sofa in his room for some time, not knowing what to do, then he ordered dinner, and after dinner, had a long sleep.

"What a foolish, restless business," he thought, waking up and looking toward the dark windowpanes. It was evening by now. "Well, I've had my sleep out. And what am I to do in the night?"

He sat up in bed, covered by the cheap gray quilt, which reminded him of a hospital blanket, and in his vexation he fell to taunting himself.

"You and your lady with the dog . . . there's adventure for you! See what you get for your pains."

On his arrival at the station that morning he had noticed a poster announcing in enormous letters the first performance at the local theater of *The Geisha*. Remembering this, he got up and made for the theater.

"It's highly probable that she goes to first-nights," he told himself.

The theater was full. It was a typical provincial theater, with a mist collecting over the chandeliers, and the crowd in the gallery fidgeting noisily. In the first row of the stalls the local dandies stood waiting for the curtain to go up, their hands clasped behind them. There, in the front seat of the Governor's box, sat the Governor's daughter, wearing a boa, the Governor himself hiding modestly behind the drapes, so that only his hands were visible. The curtain stirred, the orchestra took a long time tuning up their instruments. Gurov's eyes roamed eagerly over the audience as they filed in and occupied their seats.

Anna Sergeyevna came in, too. She seated herself in the third row of the stalls and when Gurov's glance fell on her, his heart seemed to stop, and he knew in a flash that the whole world contained no one nearer or dearer to him, no one more important to his happiness. This little woman, lost in the provincial crowd, in no way remarkable, holding a silly lorgnette in her hand, now filled his whole life, was his grief, his joy, all that he desired. Lulled by the sounds coming from the wretched orchestra, with its feeble, amateurish violinists, he thought how beautiful she was . . . thought and dreamed. . . .

Anna Sergeyevna was accompanied by a tall, round-shouldered young man with small whiskers, who nodded at every step before taking the seat beside her and seemed to be continually bowing to someone. This must be her husband, whom, in a fit of bitterness, at Yalta, she had called a "flunkey." And there really was something of the lackey's servility in his lanky figure, his side-whiskers, and the little bald spot on the top of his head. And he smiled sweetly, and the badge of some scientific society gleaming in his buttonhole was like the number on a footman's livery.

The husband went out to smoke in the first interval, and she was left alone in her seat. Gurov, who had taken a seat in the stalls, went up to her and said in a trembling voice, with a forced smile: "How d'you do?"

She glanced up at him and turned pale, then looked at him again in alarm, unable to believe her eyes, squeezing her fan and lorgnette in one hand, evidently struggling to overcome a feeling of faintness. Neither of them said a word. She sat there, and he stood beside her, disconcerted by her embarrassment, and not daring to sit down. The violins and flutes sang out as they were tuned, and there was a tense sensation in the atmosphere, as if they were being watched from all the boxes. At last she got up and moved rapidly toward one of the exits. He followed her and they wandered aimlessly along corridors, up and down stairs; figures flashed by in the uniforms of legal officials, high-school teachers, and civil servants, all wearing badges; ladies' coats hanging on pegs, flashed by; there was a sharp draft, bringing with it an odor of cigarette stubs. And Gurov, whose heart was beating violently, thought:

"What on earth are all these people, this orchestra for? . . ."

The next minute he suddenly remembered how, after seeing Anna Sergeyevna off that evening at the station, he had told himself that all was over, and they would never meet again. And how far away the end seemed to be now!

She stopped on a dark narrow staircase over which was a notice bearing the inscription "To the upper circle."

"How you frightened me!" she said, breathing heavily, still pale and half-stunned. "Oh, how you frightened me! I'm almost dead! Why did you come? Oh, why?"

"But, Anna," he said, in low, hasty tones. "But, Anna. . . . Try to understand . . . do try. . . ."

She cast him a glance of fear, entreaty, love, and then gazed at him steadily, as if to fix his features in her memory.

"I've been so unhappy," she continued, taking no notice of his words. "I could think of nothing but you the whole time, I lived on the thoughts of you. I tried to forget—why, oh, why did you come?"

On the landing above them were two schoolboys, smoking and looking down, but Gurov did not care, and, drawing Anna Sergeyevna toward him, began kissing her face, her lips, her hands.

"What are you doing, oh, what are you doing?" she said in horror, drawing back. "We have both gone mad. Go away this very night, this moment. . . . By all that is sacred, I implore you. . . . Somebody is coming."

Someone was ascending the stairs.

"You must go away," went on Anna Sergeyevna in a whisper. "D'you hear me, Dmitri Dmitrich? I'll come to you in Moscow, I swear it! And now we must part! My dear one, my kind one, my darling, we must part."

She pressed his hand and hurried down the stairs, looking back at him continually, and her eyes showed that she was in truth unhappy. Gurov stood where he was for a short time, listening, and when all was quiet went to look for his coat, and left the theater.

4

And Anna Sergeyevna began going to Moscow to see him. Every two or three months she left the town of S., telling her husband that she was going to consult a specialist on female diseases, and her husband believed her and did not believe her. In Moscow she always stayed at the "Slavyanski Bazaar," sending a man in a red cap to Gurov the moment she arrived. Gurov went to her, and no one in Moscow knew anything about it.

One winter morning he went to see her as usual (the messenger had been to him the evening before, but had not found him at home). His daughter was with him for her school was on the way, and he thought he might as well see her to it.

"It is three degrees above zero," said Gurov to his daughter, "and yet it is snowing. You see it is only above zero close to the ground, the temperature in the upper layers of the atmosphere is quite different."

"Why doesn't it ever thunder in winter, Papa?"

He explained this, too. As he was speaking, he kept reminding himself that he was going to a rendezvous and that not a living soul knew about it, or, probably, ever would. He led a double life—one in public, in the sight of all whom it concerned, full of conventional truth and conventional deception, exactly like the lives of his friends and acquaintances, and another which flowed in secret. And, owing to some strange, possibly accidental chain of circumstances, everything that was important, interesting, essential, everything about which he was sincere and never deceived himself, everything that composed the kernel of his life, went on in secret, while everything that was false in him, everything that composed the husk in which he hid himself and the truth which was in him—his work at the bank, discussions at the club, his "lower race," his attendance at anniversary celebrations with his wife—was on the surface. He began to judge others by himself, no longer believing what he saw, and always assuming that the real, the only interesting life of every individual goes on as under cover of night, secretly. Every individual existence revolves around mystery, and perhaps that is the chief reason that all cultivated individuals insisted so strongly on the respect due to personal secrets.

After leaving his daughter at the door of her school Gurov set off for the "Slavyanski Bazaar." Taking off his overcoat in the lobby, he went upstairs and knocked softly on the door. Anna Sergeyevna, wearing the gray dress he liked most, exhausted by her journey and by suspense, had been expecting him since the evening before. She was pale and looked at him without smiling, but was in his arms almost before he was fairly in the room. Their kiss was lingering, prolonged, as if they had not met for years.

"Well, how are you?" he asked. "Anything new?"

"Wait. I'll tell you in a minute. . . . I can't. . . ."

She could not speak, because she was crying. Turning away, she held her handkerchief to her eyes.

"I'll wait till she's had her cry out," he thought, and sank into a chair.

He rang for tea, and a little later, while he was drinking it, she was still standing there, her face to the window. She wept from emotion, from her bitter consciousness of the sadness of their life; they could only see one another in secret, hiding from people, as if they were thieves. Was not their life a broken one?

"Don't cry," he said.

It was quite obvious to him that this love of theirs would not soon come to an end, and that no one could say when this end would be. Anna Sergeyevna loved him ever more fondly, worshipped him, and there would have been no point in telling her that one day it must end. Indeed, she would not have believed him.

He moved over and took her by the shoulders, intending to fondle her with light words, but suddenly he caught sight of himself in the looking-glass.

His hair was already beginning to turn gray. It struck him as strange that he should have aged so much in the last few years. The shoulders on which his hands lay were warm and quivering. He felt a pity for this life, still so warm and exquisite, but probably soon to fade and droop like his own. Why did she love him so? Women had always believed him different from what he really was, had loved in him not himself but the man their imagination pictured him, a man they had sought for eagerly all their lives. And afterwards when they discovered their mistake, they went on loving him just the same. And not one of them had ever been happy with him. Time had passed, he had met one woman after another, become intimate with each, parted with each, but had never loved. There had been all sorts of things between them, but never love.

And only now, when he was gray-haired, had he fallen in love properly, thoroughly, for the first time in his life.

He and Anna Sergeyevna loved one another as people who are very close and intimate, as husband and wife, as dear friends love one another. It seemed to them that fate had intended them for one another, and they could not understand why she should have a husband, and he a wife. They were like two migrating birds, the male and the female, who had been caught and put into separate cages. They forgave one another all that they were ashamed of in the past, in their present, and felt that this love of theirs had changed them both.

Formerly, in moments of melancholy, he had consoled himself by the first argument that came into his head, but now arguments were nothing to him, he felt profound pity, desired to be sincere, tender.

"Stop crying, my dearest," he said. "You've had your cry, now stop. . . Now let us have a talk, let us try and think what we are to do."

Then they discussed their situation for a long time, trying to think how they could get rid of the necessity for hiding, deception, living in different towns, being so long without meeting. How were they to shake off these intolerable fetters?

"How? How?" he repeated, clutching his head. "How?"

And it seemed to them that they were within an inch of arriving at a decision, and that then a new, beautiful life would begin. And they both realized that the end was still far, far away, and that the hardest, the most complicated part was only just beginning.

Doris Lessing

Winter in July

With the publication of The Golden Notebook *in 1962, Doris Lessing was recognized as one of the most remarkable writers of the twentieth century. Though she is greatly and deservedly admired by feminists, Ms. Lessing speaks of her ultimate objective as an attempt to describe "the intellectual and moral climate" of our time, to try to close "the terrible gap between the public and the private conscience." Ms. Lessing, who has written in all of the genres—including poetry and the drama—has published nineteen books since 1950. Her short stories have been published in four collections:* The Habit of Loving *(1957),* A Man and Two Women *(1963),* African Stories *(1965), and* The Temptation of Jack Orkney *(1973).*

The three of them were sitting at their evening meal on the verandah. From behind, the living-room shed light on to the table, where their moving hands, the cutlery, the food, showed dimly, but clear enough for efficiency. Julia liked the half-tones. A lamp or candles would close them into a soft illuminated space, but obliterate the sky, which now bent towards them through the pillars of the verandah, a full deep sky, holding a yellowy bloom from an invisible moon that absorbed the stars into a faint far glitter.

Sometimes Tom said, grumbling humorously: "Romantic, that's what she is"; and Kenneth would answer, but with an abrupt, rather grudging laugh: "I like to see what I am eating." Kenneth was altogether an abrupt person. That quick, quickly-checked laugh, the swift critical look he gave her (which she met with her own eyes, as critical as his) were part of the long dialogue between them. For Kenneth did not accept her. He resisted her. Tom accepted her, as he accepted everything. For Julia it was not a question of preference: the two men supported her in their different manners. And the things they said, the three of them, seemed hardly to matter. The real thing was the soft elastic tension that bound them close.

Her liking for the evening hour, before moving indoors to the brightly-lit room, was expression of her feeling for them. The mingling lights, half from the night-sky, half from the lamp, softened their faces and subdued their voices, and she was free to feel what they were, rather than rouse herself by listening. This state was a continuation of her day, spent by herself (for the men were most of the time on the lands) in an almost trance-like condition where the soft flowing of the hours was marked by no necessities of action strong enough to wake her. As for them, she knew that returning to her was an entrance into that condition. Their day was hard and vigorous, full of practical details and planning. At sundown they entered her country, and the evening meal, where the outlines of fact were blurred by her passivity no less than by the illusion of indistinctness created by sitting under a roof which projected shadow-like into the African night, was the gateway to it.

They used to say to her sometimes: "What do you do with yourself all day? Aren't you bored?" She could not explain how it was she could never become bored. All restlessness had died in her. She was content to do nothing for hours at a time; but it depended on her feeling of being held loosely in the tension between the two men. Tom liked to think of her content and peaceful in his life; Kenneth was irritated.

This particular evening, halfway through the meal, Kenneth rose suddenly and said: "I must fetch my coat." Dismay chilled Julia as she realized that she, too, was cold. She had been cold for several nights, but had put off the hour of recognizing the fact. Her thoughts were confirmed by Tom's remark: "It's getting too cold to eat outside now, Julia."

"What month is it?"

He laughed indulgently. "We are reaping."

Kenneth came back, shrugging himself quickly into his coat. He was a small, quick-moving, vital man; dark, dark-eyed, impatient; he did everything as if he resented the time he had to spend on it. Tom was large, fair, handsome, in every way Kenneth's opposite. He said with gentle persistence to Julia, knowing that she needed prodding: "Better tell the boys to move the table inside tomorrow."

"Oh, I suppose so," she grumbled. Her summer was over: the long luminous warm nights, broken by swift showers, or obscured suddenly by heavy driving clouds—the tumultuous magical nights—were gone and finished for this year. Now, for the three months of winter, they would eat indoors, with the hot lamp over the table, the cold shivering about their legs, and outside a parched country, roofed by dusty freezing stars.

Kenneth said briskly: "Winter, Julia, you'll have to face it."

"Well," she smiled, "tomorrow you'll be able to see what you are eating."

There was a slight pause; then Kenneth said: "I shan't be here tomorrow night. I'm taking the car into town in the morning."

Julia did not reply. She had not heard. That is to say, she felt dismay deepening in her at the sound of his voice; then she wondered at her own forebodings, and then the words: "Town. In the morning," presented themselves to her.

They very seldom went into the city, which was fifty miles away. A trip was always planned in advance, for it would be a matter of buying things that were not available at the local store. The three of them had made the journey only last week. Julia's mind was now confronting and absorbing the fact that on that day Kenneth had abruptly excused himself and gone off on some business of his own. She remembered teasing him, a little, in her fashion. To herself she would have said (disliking the knowledge) that she controlled jealousy, like many jealous women, by becoming an accomplice, as it were, in Kenneth's adventures: the tormenting curiosity was eased when she knew what he had been doing. Last week he had disliked her teasing.

Now she looked over at Tom for reassurance, and saw that his eyes were expressing disquiet as great as her own. Doubly deserted, she gazed clearly and deliberately at both men; and because Kenneth's bald statement of his intentions seemed to her so gross a betrayal of their real relations, chose to say nothing, but in a manner of waiting for an explanation. None was offered, though Kenneth appeared uneasy. They finished their meal in silence and went indoors, passing through the stripped dining-room, which tomorrow would appear in its winter guise of arranged furniture and candles and bowls of fruit, into the living-room.

The house was built for heat. In the winter cold struck up from the floor and out of the walls. This room was very bare, very high, of dull red brick, flagged with stone. Tomorrow she would put down rugs. There was a large stone fireplace, in which stood an earthenware jar filled with Christ-thorn. Julia unconsciously crossed to it, knelt, and bent to the little glowing red flowers, holding out her hands as if to the comfort of fire. Realizing what she was doing, she lifted her head, smiled wrily at the two men, who were watching her with the same small smile, and said: "I'll get a fire put in." Shaking herself into a knowledge of what she did by action, she walked purposefully to the door, and called to the servants. Soon the houseboy entered with logs and kindling materials, and the three stood drinking their coffee, watching him as he knelt to make the fire. They were silent, not because of any scruples against letting their lives appear falsely to servants, but because they knew speech was necessary, and that what must be said would break their life together. Julia was trembling; it was as if a support had been cut away beneath her. Held as she was by these men, her life made for her by them, her instincts were free to come straight and present themselves to her without the necessity for disapproval or approval. Now she found herself glancing alternatively from Tom, that large gentle man, her husband, whose very presence comforted her into peace, to Kenneth, who was frowning down at his coffee cup, so as not to meet her eyes. If he had simply laughed and said what was needed!—he did not. He drank what remained in the cup with two large gulps, seemed to feel the need of something to do, and then went over to the fireplace. The native still knelt there, his bare legs projecting loosely behind him, his hands hanging loose, his body free and loose save for head and shoulders, into which all his energy was concentrated for the purpose of blowing up the fire, which he did with steady, bellow-like breathing. "Here," said Kenneth, "I'll do that." The servant glanced at him, accepted the white man's whim, and silently left the room, leaving the feeling behind him that he had said: "White men can't make fires"; just as Julia could feel her cook saying, when she was giving orders in the kitchen: "I can make better pastry than you."

Kenneth knelt where the servant had knelt and began fiddling with the logs. But he was good with his hands, and in a moment the sparse beginnings of a fire flowered in the wall; while the crock of prickly red thorn blossoms, Julia's summer fire, was set to one side.

"Now," said Kenneth, rather offhand, rather too loudly: "You can warm your hands, Julia." He gave his quick, grudging laugh. Julia found it offensive; and met his eyes. They were hostile. She flushed, walked slowly over to the fireplace, and sat down. The two men followed her example. For a while they did nothing; that unoffered explanation hung in the air between them. After a while Kenneth reached for a magazine and began to read. Julia looked over at her husband, whose kind blue eyes had always accepted everything she was, and raised her brows humorously. He did not respond, for he had turned again to Kenneth's now purposely bent head.

The fact that Kenneth had not spoken, that Tom was troubled, made Julia, thrown back on herself, ask: "Why should you be so resentful? Surely he has a right to do as he pleases?" No, she answered herself. Not in this way. He shouldn't suddenly withdraw, shutting us out. Either one thing or the other. Doing it this way means that all our years together have been a lie; he simply repudiates them. But that *was* Kenneth, this continuous alternation between giving and withdrawal. Julia felt tears welling up inside her from a place that for a long time had remained dry. They were the tears of trembling insecurity. The thin, cold air in the great stone room, just beginning to be warmed by the small fire; was full of menace for Julia. But Kenneth did not speak: he was reading as if his future depended on the advertisements for tractors; and Tom soon began to read too, ignoring Julia.

She pulled herself together, and lay back in her chair, making herself think. She was thinking consciously of her life and what she was. There had been no need for her to consider herself for so long, and she hated having to do it.

She was the daughter of a small-town doctor in the North of England. To say that she had been ambitious would be false: the word ambition implies purpose; she was rather critical and curious, and her rebellion against the small-town atmosphere, and the prospect of marrying into it was no more conscious than the rebellion of most young people who think vaguely: Surely life can be better than this?

Yet she escaped. She was clever: at the end of her schooling she was better educated than most. She learned French and German because languages came easily to her, but mostly because at eighteen she fell in love with a French student, and at twenty became secretary to a man who had business connections in Germany, and she liked to please men. She was an excellent secretary, not merely because she was competent, but because of her peculiar fluid sympathy for the men she worked with. Her employers found that she quickly, intuitively, fitted herself in with what they wanted: it was a sort of directed passivity, a receptiveness towards people. So she earned well, and soon had the opportunity of leaving her home town and going to London.

Looking back now from the age she had reached (which was nearly forty) on the life she had lived (which had been varied and apparently adventurous) she could not put her finger on any point in her youth when she had said to herself: "I want to travel; I want to be free." Yet she had travelled widely, moving from one country to the next, from one job to the next; and all her relations with people, whether men or women, had been coloured by the brilliance of impermanence. When she left England she had not known it would be final. It was on a business trip with her employer, and her relations with him were almost those of a wife with a husband, excepting for sex: she could not work with a man unless she offered a friendly, delicate sympathy.

In France she fell in love, and stayed there for a year. When that came to an end, the mood took her to go to Italy—no, that is the wrong way of putting it. When she described it like that to herself, she scrupulously said: That's not the truth. The fact was that she had been very seriously in love; and yet could not bring herself to marry. Going to Italy (she had not wanted to go in the least) had been a desperate but final way of ending the affair. She simply could not face the idea of marriage. In Italy she worked in a travel agency; and there she met a man whom she grew to love. It was not the desperate passion of a year before, but serious enough to marry. Later, she moved to America. Why America? Why not?—she was offered a good job there at the time she was looking for some place to go.

She stayed there two years, and had, as they say, a wonderful time. She was now a little bit more cautious about falling in love; but nevertheless, there was a man who almost persuaded her to stay in New York. At the last moment a wild, trapped feeling came over her: what have I got to do with this country?

she asked herself. This time, leaving the man was a destroying effort; she did not want to leave him. But she went south to the Argentine, and her state of mind was not a pleasant one.

Also, she found she was not as efficient as she had been. This was because she had become more wary, less adaptable. Afraid of falling in love, she was conscious of pulling away from the people she worked for; she gave only what she was paid to give, and this did not satisfy her. What, then, was going to satisfy her? After all, she could not spend all her life moving from continent to continent; yet there seemed no reason why she should settle in one place rather than another, even why it should be one man rather than another. She was tired. She was very tired. The springs of her feeling had run dry. This particular malaise is not so easily cured.

And now, for the first time, she had an affair with a man for whom she cared nothing: this was a half-conscious choice, for she understood that she could not have chosen a man whom she would grow to love. And so it went on, for perhaps two years. She was associating only with people who moved her not at all; and this was because she did not want to be moved.

There came a point when she said to herself that she must decide now, finally, what she wanted, and make sacrifices to get it. She was twenty-eight. She had spent the years since leaving school moving from hotel to furnished flat, from one job to the next, from one country to another. She seemed to have a tired affectionate remembrance of so many people, men and women, who had once filled her life. Now it was time to make something permanent. But what?

She said to herself that she was getting hard; yet she was not hard; she was numbed and tired. She must be very careful, she decided; she must not fall in love, lightly, again. Next time, it must matter.

All this time she was leading a full social life: she was attractive, well-dressed, amusing. She had the reputation of being brilliant and cold. She was also very lonely and she had never been lonely before, since there had always been some man to whom she gave warmth, affection, sympathy.

There was one morning when she had a vision of evil. It was at the window of a large hotel, one warm summer's day, when she was looking down through the streets of the attractive modern city in South America, with the crowds of people and the moving traffic . . . it might have been almost any city, on a bright warm day, from a hotel window, with the people blowing like leaves across her vision, as rootless as she, as impermanent, their lives meaning as little. For the first time in her life, the word evil meant something to her: she looked at it, coldly, and rejected it. This was sentiment, she said; the result of being tired, and nearly thirty. The feeling was not related to anything. She could not feel—why should one feel? She disliked what she was—well, it was at any rate honest to accept oneself as unlikable. Her brain remarked dispassionately that if one lived without rules, one should be prepared to take the consequences, even if that meant moments of terror at hotel windows, with death beckoning below and whispering: Why live? Anyway, who was responsible for the way she was?

Had she ever planned it? Why should one be one thing rather than another?

It was chance that took her to Cape Town. At a party she met a man who offered her a job as his secretary on a business trip, and it was easy to accept, for she had come to hate South America.

During the trip over she found, with a groan, that she had never been more efficient, more responsible, more gently responsive. He was an unhappy man, who needed sympathy . . . she gave it. At the end of the trip he asked her to marry him; and she understood she would have felt much the same if he had asked her to dinner. She fled.

She had enough money saved to live without working, so for months she stayed by herself, in a small hotel high over Cape Town, where she could watch the ships coming and going in the harbor and think: they are as restless as I am. She lived gently, testing every emotion she felt, making no contact save the casual ones inevitable in a hotel, walking by herself for hours of every day, soaking herself in the sea and the sun as if the beautiful peninsula could heal her by the power of its beauty. And she ran away from any possibility of liking some other human being as if love itself were poisoned.

One warm afternoon when she was walking high along the side of a mountain, with the blue sea swinging and lifting below, and a low sun sending a sad red pathway from the horizon, she was overtaken by two other walkers. There was no one else in sight, and it was inevitable they should continue together. She found they were farmers on holiday from Rhodesia, half-brothers, who had worked themselves into prosperity; this was the first holiday they had taken for years, and they were in a loosened, warm, adventurous mood. She sensed they were looking for wives to take back with them.

She liked Tom from the first, though for a day or so she flirted with Kenneth. This was an automatic response to his laughing, challenging antagonism. It was Kenneth who spoke first, in his brusque, offhand way, and she felt attracted to him: theirs was the relationship of people moving towards a love affair. But she did not really want to flirt; with Kenneth it seemed anything else was impossible. She was struck by the way Tom, the elder brother, listened while they sparred, smiling uncritically, almost indulgently: his was an almost protective attitude. It was more than protective. A long while afterwards she told Tom that on that first afternoon he had reminded her of the peasant who uses a bird to catch fish for him. Yet there was a moment during the long hike back to the city through the deepening evening, when Julia glanced curiously at Tom and saw his warm blue glance resting kindly on her in a slow, speculative way, and she chose him, then, in her mind, even while she continued the exchange with Kenneth. Because of that kindness, she let herself sink towards the idea of marriage. It was what she wanted, really; and she did not care where she lived. Emotionally there was no country of which she could say: this is my home.

For several days the three of them went about together, and all the time she bantered with Kenneth and watched Tom. That defensive, grudging thing she could feel in Kenneth, which attracted her, against her will, was what she was afraid of: she was watching, half-fearfully, half-cynically, for its appearance in Tom. Then, slowly, Kenneth's treatment of her grew more offhand and brutal: he knew he was being made use of. There came a point when in his sarcastic frank way he shut himself off from her; and for a while the three of them were together without contact. It had been Kenneth and she, with Tom as urbane onlooker; now it was she, by herself, drifting alone, floating loose, waiting, as it were, to be gathered in; and it was possible to mark the point when Tom and Kenneth looked at each other sardonically, in understanding, before Tom moved into Kenneth's place in his warm and deliberate fashion, claiming her.

He was nicer than she had believed possible. There was suddenly no conflict. He listened to her tales about her life with detached interest, as if they could not possibly concern him. He remarked once, in his tender, protective way: "You must have been hurt hard at some time. That's the trouble with you independent women. Actually, you are quite a nice woman, Julia." She laughed at him scornfully, as an arrogant male who has to make some kind of a picture of a woman so as to be able to fit her into his life. He treated her laughter tolerantly. When she said things like this he found it merely a sort of piquancy, a sign of her wit. Half-laughingly, half-despairingly, she said to Kenneth: "You do realize that Tom hasn't an idea of what I'm like? Do you think it's fair to marry him?"

"Well, why not, if he wants to be married?" returned Kenneth briskly. "He's romantic. He sees you as a wanderer from city to city, and from bed to bed, because you are trying to heal a broken heart or something of the kind. That appeals to him."

Tom listened to this silently, smiling with disquiet. But there were times when Julia liked to think she had a broken heart; it certainly felt bruised. It was restful to accept Tom's idea of her. She said in a piqued way to Kenneth: "I suppose *you* understand perfectly easily why I've lived the way I have?"

Kenneth raised his brows. "Why? Because you enjoyed it of course. What better reason?"

She could not help laughing, even while she said crossly, feeling misunderstood: "The fact is, you are as bad as Tom. You make up stories about women, too, to suit yourself. You like thinking of women as hard and decided, cynically making use of men."

"Certainly," said Kenneth. "Much better than letting yourself be made use of. I like women to know what they want and get it."

This kind of conversation irritated and saddened Julia: it was rather like the froth whipping on the surface of the sea, with the currents underneath dark and unknown.

She did not like being reminded how much better Kenneth understood her than Tom did. She was pleased to get the business of the ceremony over. Tom married her in a purposeful, unhurrying way; but he remarked that it must be before a certain date because he wanted to start planting soon.

Kenneth attended as best man with a glint of malice in his eye, and the air of a well-wishing onlooker, interested to see how things would turn out. Julia and he exchanged a glance of pure understanding, very much against their wills, for their attitude towards each other now was one of brisk friendship. From the security of Tom's arms, she allowed herself to think that if Kenneth were not the kind of man to feel protective towards a woman simply because he enjoyed feeling protective, then it was so much the worse for him. This was slightly vindictive in her; but on the whole good-natured enough—good-nature was necessary; the three of them would be living together in one house, on the same farm, seeing other people seldom.

It was quite easy, after all. Kenneth did not have to efface himself. Tom effortlessly claimed Julia as his wife, from his magnificent, lazy self-assurance, and she was glad to be claimed. Kenneth and she maintained a humorous understanding. He was given three rooms to himself in one wing of the house; but it was not long before they became disused. It seemed silly for him to retire after dinner by himself. In the evenings, the fact that Julia was Tom's wife was marked by their two big chairs set side by side, with Kenneth's opposite. He used to sit there watching them with his observant, slightly sarcastic smile.

After a while Julia understood she was feeling uneasy; she put it down to the fact that she had expected subtle antagonism between the two men, which she would have to smooth over, while in fact there was no antagonism. It went deeper than that. Those first few nights, when Kenneth tactfully withdrew to his rooms, but looking amused, Tom was restless: he missed Kenneth badly. Julia watched them; and saw with a curious humorous sinking of the heart that they were so close to each other they could not bear to be apart for long. In the evenings it was they who talked, in the odd bantering manner they used even when serious: particularly when serious. Tom liked it when Kenneth sat there opposite, looking shrewd and sceptical about this marriage: they would tease each other in a way that, had they been man and woman, would have seemed positively flirtatious. Listening to them, Julia felt an extraordinary unease, as at a perversity. She chose not to think about it. Better to be affectionately amused at Tom's elder-brother attitude towards Kenneth; there was often something petulant, rebellious, childish, in Kenneth's attitude towards Tom. Why, Tom was even elder-brotherish to her, who had been managing her own life, so efficiently, for years all over the world. Well, and was not that why she had married him?

She accepted it. They all accepted it. They grew into a silent comfortable understanding. Tom, so to speak, was the head of the family, commanding, strong, perhaps a little obtuse, as authority has to be; and Julia and Kenneth deferred to him, with the slightest hint of mockery, to gloss the fact that they were glad to defer: how pleasant to let the responsibility rest on someone else!

Julia even learned to accept the knowledge that when Tom was busy, and she walked with Kenneth, or swam with Kenneth, or took trips into town with

Kenneth, it was not only with Tom's consent: more, he liked it, even needed it. Sometimes she felt as if he were urging her to be with his brother. Kenneth felt it and rebelled, shying away in his petulant younger-brother manner. He would exclaim: "Good Lord, man, Julia's your wife, not mine." And Tom would laugh uneasily and say: "I don't like the idea of being possessive." The thought of Tom being possessive was so absurd that Julia and Kenneth began giggling helplessly, like conspiring and wise children. And when Tom had departed, leaving them together, she would say to Kenneth, in her troubled serious fashion: "But I don't understand this. I don't understand any of it. It flies in the face of nature."

"So it does," Kenneth would return easily. He looked at her with a quizzical glint. "You must take things as they come, my dear sister-in-law." But Julia felt she had been doing just that: she had relaxed, without thinking, drifting warmly and luxuriously inside Tom's warm and comfortable grasp: which was also Kenneth's, and because Tom wanted it that way.

In spite of Tom, she maintained with Kenneth a slight but strong barrier, because they were people who could be too strongly attracted to each other. Once or twice, when they had been left alone together by Tom, Kenneth would fly off irritably: "Really, why I bother to be loyal in the circumstances I can't think."

"But what *are* the circumstances?" Julia asked, puzzied.

"Oh *Lord*, Julia . . ." Kenneth expostulated irritably.

Once, when he was brutal without irritability, he made the curious remark: "The fact is, it was just about time Tom and I had a wife." He began laughing, not very pleasantly.

Julia did not understand. She thought it sounded ugly.

Kenneth regarded her ironically and said: "Fortunately for Tom, he doesn't know anything at all about himself."

But Julia did not like this said about her husband, even though she felt it to be true. Instinctively this particular frontier in their mutual relations was avoided in future; and she was careful with Kenneth, refusing to discuss Tom with him.

From time to time during those two years before Tom left for the war, Kenneth investigated (his own word) the girls on surrounding farms, with a view to marrying. They bored him. He had a prolonged affair with a married woman whose husband bored her. To Julia and Tom he made witty remarks about his position as a lover. Sometimes the three of them would become helpless with laughter at his descriptions of himself being gallant: the lady was romantic, and liked being courted. Kenneth was not romantic, and his interest in the lady was confined to an end which he could not prevent himself describing in his pungent, sour, resigned fashion during those long evenings with the married couple. Again, Julia got the uneasy feeling that Tom was really too interested—no, that was not the word; it was not the easy-going interest of an amused outsider that Tom displayed; while he listened to Kenneth being witty about his affair, it was almost as if he were participating himself, as if he were silently urging Kenneth on to further revelations. On these occasions Julia felt a revulsion from Tom. She said to herself that she was jealous, and repressed the feeling.

When the war started Tom became restless; Julia knew that he would soon go. He volunteered before there was conscription; and she watched, with a humorous sadness, the scene (an uncomfortable one) between her two men, when it seemed that Tom felt impelled to apologize to Kenneth for taking the advantage of him in grasping a rare chance of happiness. Kenneth was unfit: the two brothers had come to Africa in the first place because of Kenneth's delicate lungs. Kenneth did not at all want to go to war. "Lord!" he exclaimed to Tom; "there's no need to sound so apologetic. You're welcome. I'm not a romantic. I don't like getting killed unless in a good cause. I can't see any point in the thing." In this way he appeared to dismiss the war and the world's turmoil. As for Tom, he didn't really care about the issues of the war, either. It was sufficient that there was a war. For both men it was axiomatic that it was impossible England could ever be beaten in a war; they might laugh at their own attitude (which they did, when Julia, from her liberal travelled internationalism, mocked at them), but that was what they felt, nevertheless.

As for Julia, she was more unhappy about the war than either of them. She had grown into security on the farm; now the world, which she had wanted to shut out, pressed in on her again; and she thought of her many friends, in so many countries, in the thick of things, feeling strange partisan emotions which seemed to her absurd. For she thought in terms of people, not of nations or issues; and the war, to her, was a question of mankind gone mad, killing each other pointlessly. Always the pointlessness of everything! And now she was not allowed to forget it.

To her credit, all her unhappiness and female resentment at being so lightly abandoned by Tom at the first sound of a bugle calling adventure down the wind was suppressed. She merely said scornfully to him: "What a baby you are! As if there hadn't been the last war! And look at all the men in the district, pleased as punch because something exciting is going to happen. If you really cared two hoots about the war, I might respect you. But you don't. Nor do most of the people we know."

Tom did not like this. The atmosphere of war had stirred him into a superficial patriotism. "You sound like a newspaper leader," Julia mocked him. "You don't really believe a word you say. The truth is that most people like us, in all the countries I've been in, haven't a notion what we believe about anything. We don't believe in the slogans and the lies. It makes me sick, to see the way you all get excited the moment war comes."

This made Tom angry, because it was true; and because he had suddenly remembered his sentimental attachment to England, in the Rupert Brooke fashion. They were on edge with each other, in the days before he left: he was glad to go; particularly as Kenneth was being no less caustic. This was the first time the two men had ever been separated; and Julia felt that Kenneth was as hurt as she because Tom left them so easily. In fact, they were all pleased when Tom was able to leave the farm, and put an end to the misery of their tormenting each other.

But after he had gone, Julia was very unhappy. She missed him badly. Marrying had been a greater peace than she had imagined possible for her. To let the restless critical part of one die; to drift; to relax; to enjoy Africa as a country, the way it looked and the way it felt; to enjoy the physical things slowly, without haste—learning all this had, she imagined, healed her. And now, without Tom, she was nothing. She was unsupported and unwarmed; and she knew that marrying had after all cured her of nothing. She was still floating rootlessly, without support; she belonged nowhere; and even Africa, which she had grown to love, meant nothing to her really: it was another country she had visited as lightly as a migrant bird.

And Kenneth was no help at all. With Tom on the farm she might have been able to drift with the current, to take the conventional attitude towards the war. But Kenneth used to switch on the wireless in the evenings and pungently translate the news of the war into the meaningless chaotic brutality which was how she herself saw it. He spoke with the callous cynicism that means people are suffering, and which she could hear in her own voice.

"It's all very well," she would say to him. "It's all very well for us. We sit here out of it all. Millions of people are suffering."

"People like suffering," he would retort, angrily. "Look at Tom. There he sits in the desert, bored as hell. He'll be talking about the best years of his life in ten years' time."

Julia could hear Tom's voice, nostalgically recalling adventure, only too clearly. At the same time Kenneth made her angry, because he expressed what she felt, and she did not like the way she felt. She joined the local women's groups and started knitting and helping with district functions; and flushed up when she saw Kenneth's cold angry eyes resting on her. "By God, Julia, you are as bad as Tom . . ."

"Well, surely, one must be part of it, Kenneth?" She tried hard to express what she was feeling.

"Just what are you fighting *for*?" he demanded. "Can you tell me that?"

"I feel we ought to find out . . ."

He wouldn't listen. He flounced off down the farm saying: "I'm going to make a new dam. Unless they bomb it, it's something useful done in all this waste and chaos. You can go and knit nice woollies for those poor devils who are getting themselves killed and listen to the dear women talking about the dreadful Nazis. My God, the hypocrisy. Just tell them to take a good look at South Africa, from me, will you?"

The fact was, he missed Tom. When he was approached to subscribe to war charities he gave generously, in Tom's name, sending the receipts carefully to Tom, with sarcastic intention. As the war deepened and the dragging weight of death and suffering settled in their minds, Julia would listen at night to the angry pacing footsteps up and down, up and down the long stone passages of the house, and, going out in her dressing-gown, would come on Kenneth, his eyes black with anger, his face tense and white: "Get out of my way, Julia. I shall kill you or somebody. I'd like to blow the whole thing up. Why not blow it up and be finished with it? It would be good riddance."

Julia would gently take him by the arm and lead him back to bed, shutting down her own cold terror at the world. It was necessary for one of them to remain sane. Kenneth at that time was not quite sane. He was working fourteen hours a day; up long before sunrise, hastening back up the road home after sundown, for an evening's studying: he read scientific stuff about farming. He was building dams, roads, bridges; he planted hundreds of acres of trees; he contour-ridged and drained. He would listen to the news of so many thousands killed and wounded, so many factories blown up, and turn to Julia, his face contracted with hate, saying: "At any rate I'm building not destroying."

"I hope it comforts you." Julia would remark, mildly sarcastic, though she felt bitter and futile.

He would look at her balefully and stride out again, away on some work for his hands.

They were quite alone in the house. For a short while after Tom left they discussed whether they would get an assistant, for conventional reasons. But they disliked the idea of a stranger, and the thing drifted. Soon, as the men left the farms to go off to the war, many women were left alone, doing the work themselves, or with assistants who were unfit for fighting, and there was nothing really outrageous in Kenneth and Julia living together by themselves. It was understood in the district, that for the duration of the war, this kind of situation should not be made a subject for gossip.

It was inevitable they should be lovers. From the moment Tom left they both knew it.

Tom was away three years. She was exhausted by Kenneth. His mood was so black and bitter and she knew that nothing she could do or say might help him, for she was as bad herself.

She became the kind of woman he wanted: he did not want a warm, consoling woman. She was his mistress. Their relationship was a complicating fencing game, conducted with irony, tact, and good sense—except when he boiled over into hatred and vented it on her. There were times when suddenly all vitality failed her, and she seemed to sink swiftly, unsupported, to lie helpless in the depths of herself, looking up undesirously at the life of emotion and warmth washing gently over her head. Then Kenneth used to leave her alone, whereas Tom would have gently coaxed her into life again.

"I wish Tom would come back, oh dear Christ, I wish he'd come back," she would sigh.

"Do you imagine I don't?" Kenneth would enquire bitterly. Then, a little piqued, but not much: "Don't I do?"

"Well enough, I suppose."

"What do you want then?" he enquired briefly, giving what small amount of attention he could spare from the farm to the problem of Julia, the woman.

"Tom," Julia replied simply.

He considered this critically. "The fact is, you and I have far more in common than you and Tom."

"I don't see what 'in common' has to do with it."

"You and I are the same kind of animal. Tom doesn't know the first thing about you. He never could."

"Perhaps that's the reason."

Dislike began welling between them, tempered, as always by patient irony. "You don't like women at all," complained Julia suddenly. "You simply don't like me. You don't trust me."

"Oh if it comes to liking . . ." He laughed, resentfully. "You don't trust me either, for that matter."

It was the truth; they didn't trust each other; they mistrusted the destructive nihilism that they had in common. Conversations like these, which became far more frequent as time went on, left them hardened against each other for days, in a condition of watchful challenge. This was part of their long, exhausting exchange, which was a continual resolving of mutual antagonism in tired laughter.

Yet, when Tom wrote saying he was being demobilized, Kenneth, in a mood of tenderness, asked Julia to marry him. She was shocked and astonished. "You know quite well you don't want to marry me," she expostulated. "Besides, how could you do that to Tom?" Catching his quizzical glance, she began laughing helplessly.

"I don't know whether I want to marry you or not," admitted Kenneth honestly, laughing with her.

"Well, I know. You don't."

"I've got used to you."

"I haven't got used to you. I never could."

"I don't understand what it is Tom gives you that I don't."

"Peace," said Julia simply. "You and I fight all the time, we never do anything else."

"We don't fight," protested Kenneth. "We have never, as they say, exchanged a cross word." He grimaced. "Except when I get wound up, and that's a different thing."

Julia saw that he could not imagine a relationship with a woman that was not based on antagonism. She said, knowing it was useless: "Everything is so easy with Tom."

"Of course it's easy," he said angrily. "The whole damn thing is a lie from the beginning to end. However, if that's what you like . . ." He shrugged, his anger evaporating. He said drily: "I imagined I was qualifying as a husband."

"Some men can't ever be husbands. They'll always be lovers."

"I thought women liked that?"

"I wasn't talking about women. I was talking about me."

"Well, I intend to get married, for all that."

After that they did not discuss it. Speaking of what they felt left them confused, angry, puzzled.

Before Tom came back Kenneth said: "I ought to leave the farm."

She did not trouble to answer, it was so insincere.

"I'll get a farm over the other side of the district."

She merely smiled. Kenneth had written long letters to Tom every week of those three years, telling him every detail of what was happening on the farm. Plans for the future were already worked out.

It was arranged that Julia should go and meet Tom in town, where they would spend some weeks before the three began life together again. As Kenneth said, sarcastically, to Julia: "It will be just like a second honeymoon."

It was. Tom returned from the desert toughened, sunburnt, swaggering a little because he was unsure of himself with Julia. But she was so happy to see him that in a few hours they were back where they had been. "About Kenneth . . ." began Tom warily, after they had edged around this subject for some days.

"Much better not talk about it," said Julia quickly.

Tom's blue eyes rested on her, not critically, but appealingly. "Is it going to be all right?" he asked after a moment. She could see he was terrified she might say that Kenneth had decided to go away. She said drily: "I didn't want you to go off to the wars like a hero, did I?"

"There's something in that," he admitted; admitting at the same time that they were quits. Actually, he was rather subdued because of his years as a soldier. He was quick to drop the subject. It would not be just yet that he would begin talking about the happiest years of his life. He had still to forget how bored he had been and how he had missed his farm.

For a few days there was awkwardness between the three. Kenneth was jealous because of the way Julia had gladly turned back to Tom. But there was so much work to do, and Kenneth and Tom were so pleased to be back together, that it was not long before everything was as easy as before. Julia thought it was easier: now that her attraction for Kenneth, and his for her, had been slaked, the restlessness that had always been between them would vanish. Perhaps not quite . . . Julia's and Kenneth's eyes would meet sometimes in that instinctive, laughing understanding that she could never have with Tom, and then she would feel guilty.

Sometimes Kenneth would "take out" a girl from a near farm; and they would afterwards discuss his getting married. "If only I could fall in love," he would complain humorously. "You are the only woman I can bear the thought of, Julia." He would say this before Tom, and Tom would laugh: they had reached such a pitch of complicity.

Very soon there were plans for expanding the farm. They bought several thousands of acres of land next door. They would grow tobacco on a large scale: this was the time of the tobacco boom. They were getting very rich.

There were two assistants on the new farm, but Tom spent most of his days there. Sometimes his nights, too. Julia, after three days spent alone with Kenneth, with the old attraction strong between them, said to him: "I wish you would let Kenneth run that farm."

Tom, who was absorbed and fascinated by the new problems, said rather impatiently: "Why?"

"Surely that's obvious."

"That's up to you, isn't it?"

"Perhaps it isn't, always."

It was the business of the war over again. He seemed a slow, deliberate man, without much fire. But he liked new problems to solve. He got bored. Kenneth, the quick, lively, impatient one, liked to be rooted in one place, liked to develop what he had.

Julia had the helpless feeling again that Tom simply didn't care about herself and Kenneth. She grew to accept the knowledge that really, it was Kenneth that mattered to him. Except for the war, they had never been separated. Tom's father had died, and his mother married Kenneth's father. Tom had always been with Kenneth, he could not remember a time when he had not been protectively guarding him. Once Julia asked him: "I suppose you must have been very jealous of him, that was it, wasn't it?" and she was astonished at his quick flare of rage at the suggestion. She dropped the thing: what did it matter now?

The two boys had gone through various schools and to university together. They had started farming in their early twenties, when they hadn't a penny between them, and had to borrow money to support their mother, for whom they shared a deep love, which was also half-exasperated admiration; she had apparently been a helpless, charming lady with many admirers who left her children to the care of nurses.

When Tom was away one evening, and would not be back till next day, Kenneth said brusquely, with the roughness that is the result of conflict: "Coming to my room tonight, Julia?"

"How can I?" she protested.

"Well, I don't like the idea of coming to the marriage bed," he said practically, and they began to laugh. To Julia, Kenneth would always be the laughter of inevitability.

Tom said nothing, though he must have known. When Julia again appealed that he should stay on this farm and send Kenneth to the other, he turned away, frowning, and did not reply. His manner to her did not change. And she still felt: this is my husband, and compared to that feeling, Kenneth was nothing. At the same time a grim anxiety was taking possession of her: it seemed that in some perverse way the two men were brought even closer together, for a time, by sharing the same woman. That was how Julia put it, to herself: the plain and brutal fact.

It was Kenneth who pulled away in the end. Not from Julia: from the situation. There came a time when it was possible for Kenneth to say, as he stood smiling sardonically opposite Julia and Tom, who were sitting like an old married couple on their side of the fire: "You know that it is quite essential I should get married. Things can't go on like this."

"But you can't marry without being in love," protested Julia; and immediately checked herself with an annoyed laugh—she realized that what she was protesting against was Kenneth going away from her.

"You must see that I should."

"I don't like the idea," said Tom, as if it were his marriage that was under discussion.

"Look at you and Tom," said Kenneth peaceably, but not without maliciousness. "A very satisfactory marriage. You weren't in love."

"Weren't we in love, Julia?" asked Tom, rather surprised.

"Actually, I was 'in love' with Kenneth," said Julia, with the sense that this was an unnecessary thing to say.

"You wanted a wife. Julia wanted a husband. All very sensible."

"One can be 'in love' once too often," said Julia, aiming this at Kenneth.

"Are you in love with Kenneth now?"

Julia did not answer; it annoyed her that Tom should ask it after virtually handing her over to Kenneth. After a moment she remarked: "I suppose you are right. You really ought to get married." Then, thoughtfully: "I couldn't be married to you, Kenneth. You destroy me." The word sounded heightened and absurd. She hurried on: "I didn't know it was possible to be as happy as I have been with Tom." She smiled at her husband and reached over and took his hand: he returned the pressure gratefully.

"Ergo, I have to get married," said Kenneth caustically.

"But you say so yourself."

"I don't seem to be feeling what I ought to feel," said Tom at last, laughing in a bewildered way.

"That's what's wrong with the three of us," said Julia; then, feeling as if she were on the edge of that dangerous thing that might destroy them, she stopped and said: "Let's not talk about it. It doesn't do any good to talk about it."

That conversation had taken place a month ago. Kenneth had not mentioned getting married since; and Julia had secretly hoped he had shelved it. Not long since, during that trip to town, he had spent a day away from Tom and herself—and with whom? Tomorrow he was making the trip again, and for the first time for years, since they had been together, it was not the three of them, close in understanding, but Tom and Julia, with Kenneth deliberately excluding himself and putting up barriers.

Kenneth did not open his mouth the whole evening; though both Tom and Julia waited for him to break the silence. Julia did not read; she moiled over the facts of her life unhappily; and from time to time looked over at Tom, who smiled back affectionately, knowing she wanted this of him.

In spite of the fire, that now roared and crackled in the wall, Julia was cold. The thin frosty air of the high veld was of an electric dryness in the big bare room. The roof was crackling with cold; every time the tin snapped overhead it evoked the arching, myriad-starred, chilly night outside, and the drying, browning leaves, the tall waving grass that was now a dull parched color. Julia's skin crinkled and stung with dryness.

Suddenly she said: "It won't do, Kenneth. You can't behave like this." She got up, and stood with her back to the fire, gazing levelly at them. She felt herself to be parching and withering within; she felt no heavier than a twig; the sap did not run in her veins. Because of Kenneth's betrayal, she was wounded in some place she could not name. She had no substance. That was how she felt.

What they saw was a tall, rather broad woman, big-framed, the bones of her face strongly supporting the flesh. Her eyes were blue and candid, now clouded by trouble, but still humorously troubled. She was forcing them to look at her; to make comparisons; she was challenging them. She was forcing them even to break the habit of loyalty which, blithely tender, continually recreative, blinds the eyes of lovers to change.

They saw this strong, ageing woman, the companion of their lives, standing there in front of them, still formed in the shape of beauty, for she was pleasant to look at, but with the light of beauty gone. They remembered her, perhaps, on that afternoon by the sea when they had first encountered her, or when she was newly arrived at the farm: young, vivid, a slender and rather boyish girl, with sleek, close-cropped hair and quick amused blue eyes.

Now, around the firm and bony face the soft hair fell in dressed waves, she wore a soft flowery dress: they saw a disquieting incongruity between this expression of feminity and what they knew her to be. They were irritated. To stand there, reminding them (when they did not want to be reminded) that she was facing the sorrowful abdication of middle age, and facing it alone, seemed to them irrelevant, even unfair.

Kenneth said resentfully: "Oh, Lord, you are very much a woman, after all, Julia. Must you make a scene?"

Her quick laugh was equally resentful. "Why shouldn't I make a scene. I feel entitled to it."

Kenneth said: "We all know there's got to be a change. Can't we go through with it without this sort of thing?"

"Surely," she said helplessly, "everything can't be changed without some sort of explanation . . ." She could not go on.

"Well, what sort of explanation do you want?"

She shrugged hoeplessly. After a moment she said, as if continuing an old conversation: "Perhaps I should have had children, after all?"

"I always said so," remarked Tom mildly.

"You are nearly forty," said Kenneth practically.

"I wouldn't make a good mother," she said. "I couldn't compete with yours. I wouldn't have the courage to take it on, knowing I should fail by comparison with your so perfect mother." She was being sarcastic, but there were tears in her voice.

"Let's leave our mother out of it," said Tom coldly.

"Of course, we always leave everything important out of it."

Neither of them said anything; they were closed away from her in hostility. She went on: "I often wonder, why did you want me at all, Tom? You didn't really want children particularly."

"Yes, I did," said Tom, rather bewildered.

"Not enough to make me feel you cared one way or the other. Surely a woman is entitled to that, to feel that her children matter. I don't know what it is you took me into your life *for*?"

After a moment Kenneth said lightly, trying to restore the comfortable surface of flippancy: "I have always felt that we ought to have children."

Neither Tom nor Julia responded to this appeal. Julia took a candle from the mantelpiece, bent to light it at the fire, and said: "Well, I'm off to bed. The whole situation is beyond me."

"Very well then," said Kenneth. "If you must have it: I'm getting married soon."

"Obviously," said Julia drily.

"What did you want me to say?"

"Who is it?" Tom sounded so resentful that it changed the weight of the conversation: now it was Tom and Kenneth as antagonists.

"Well, she's a girl from England. She came out here a few months ago in this scheme for importing marriageable women to the Colonies . . . well, that's what the scheme amounts to."

"Yes, but the girl?" asked Julia, amused in spite of herself at Kenneth's invincible distaste at the idea of marrying.

"Well . . ." Kenneth hesitated, his dark bright eyes on Julia's face, his mouth already beginning to twist into dry amusement. "She's fair. She's pretty. She seems capable. She wants to be married . . . what more do I want?" That last phrase was savage. They had come to a dead end.

"I'm going to bed!" exclaimed Julia suddenly, the tears pouring down her face. "I can't bear this."

Neither of them said anything to prevent her leaving. When she had gone, Kenneth made an instinctive defensive movement towards Tom. After a moment Tom said irritably, but commandingly: "It's absurd for you to get married when there's no need."

"Obviously there's a need," said Kenneth angrily. He rose, taking another candle from the mantelpiece. As he left the room—and it was clear then he left in order to forestall the scene Tom was about to make—he said: "I want to have children before I get an old man. It seems to be the only thing left."

When Tom went into the bedroom, Julia was lying dry-eyed on the pillow, waiting for him. She was waiting for him to comfort her into security of feeling.

He had never failed her. When he was in bed, she found herself comforting him: it gave her such a perverse, topsy-turvy feeling she could not sleep.

Soon after breakfast Kenneth left for town. He was dressed smartly: normally he did not care how he looked, and his clothes seemed to have been put on in the spirit of one picking up tools for a job. All three acknowledged his appearance with small, constricted smiles; and Kenneth reddened as he got into the car. "I might not be back tonight," he called back, driving away without looking back.

Tom and Julia watched the big car nose its way through the trees, and turned back to face each other. "Like to come down the lands with me?" he asked. "Yes, I would," she accepted gratefully. Then she saw, and was thrown back on to herself by the knowledge of it, that he was asking her, not for her comfort, but for his own.

It was a windy, sunlit morning, and very cold; winter had taken possession of the veld overnight.

The house was built on a slight ridge, with the country falling away on either side. The landscape was dulling for the dry season into olive green and thin yellows; there was that extraordinary contrast of limpid sparkling skies, with sunshine pouring down like a volatile spirit, and dry cold parching the face and hands that made Julia uneasy in winter. It was as if the dryness tightened the cold into rigid fetters on her, so that a perpetual inner shivering had to be suppressed. She walked beside Tom over the fields with hunched shoulders and arms crossed tight over her chest. Yet she was not cold, not in the physical sense. Around the house the mealie fields, now a gentle silvery-gold color, swept into runnels of light as the wind passed over them, and there was a dry tinkling of parched leaves moving together, like rat's feet over grass. Tom did not speak; but his face was heavy and furrowed. When she took his hand he responded, but listlessly. She wanted him to turn to her, to say: "Now he's going to make something of his own, you must come to me, and we'll build up again." She wanted him to claim her, heal her, make her whole. But he was uneasy and restless; and she said at last diffidently: "Why should you mind so much. It ought to be me who's unhappy."

"Don't you?" he asked, sounding like a person angry at dishonesty.

"Yes, of course," she said; and tried to find the words to say that if only he could take her gently into his own security, as he had years ago, things would be right for them.

But that security no longer existed in him.

All that day they hardly spoke, not because of animosity between them but because of a deep, sad helplessness. They could not help each other.

That night Kenneth did not come back from town. Next day Tom went off by himself to the second farm, leaving her with a gentle apologetic look as if to say: "Leave me alone, I can't help it."

Kenneth telephoned in the middle of the morning from town. His voice was offhand; it was also subtly defensive. That small voice coming from such a distance down the wires, conjured up such a clear vision of Kenneth himself, that she smiled tenderly.

"Well?" she asked warily.

"I'll be back sometime. I don't know when."

"That means it's definite?"

"I think so." A pause. Then the voice dropped into dry humor. "She's such a nice girl that things take a long time, don't you know." Julia laughed. Quickly he added: "But she really is, you know, Julia. She's awfully nice."

"Well, you must do as you think," she said cautiously.

"How's Tom?" he asked.

"I suddenly don't know anything about Tom," she answered.

There was such a long silence that she clicked the telephone.

"I'm still here," said Kenneth. "I was trying to think of the right things to say."

"Has it come to the point where we have to think of the right things?"

"Looks like it, doesn't it?"

"Goodbye," she said quickly, putting down the receiver. "Let me know when you're coming and I'll get your things ready."

As usual in the mornings, she passed on a tour of inspection from room to room of the big bare house, where the windows stood open all day, showing blocks of blue crystal round the walls, or views of veld, as if the building, the very bricks and iron, were compounded with sky and landscape to form a new kind of home. When she had made her formal inspection, and found everything cleaned and polished and arranged, she went to the kitchen. Here she ordered the meals, and discussed the state of the pantry with her cook. Then she went back to the verandah; at this hour she would normally read, or sew, till lunchtime.

The thought came into her mind, with a destroying force, that if she were not in the house, Tom would hardly notice it, from a physical point of view: the servants would create comfort without her. She suppressed an impulse to go into the kitchen and cook, or tidy a cupboard, to find some work for the hands: that was not what she sought, a temporary salve for feeling useless. She took her large light straw hat from the nail in the bare, stone-floored passage, and went out into the garden. As she did not care for gardening, the ground about the house was arranged with groups of shrubs, so that there would be patches of blossom at any time of the year. The garden boy kept the lawns fresh and green. Over the vivid emerald grass spread the flowers of dryness, the poinsettias, loose scattering shapes of bright scarlet, creamy pink, light yellow. On the fine, shiny-brown stems fluttered light green leaves. In a swift gusty wind the quickly moving blossoms and leaves danced and shook; they seemed to her the very essence of the time of year, the essence of dry cold, of light thin sunshine, of high cold-blue skies.

She passed quietly down the path through the lawns and flowers to the farm road, and turned to look back at the house. From the outside it appeared such a large, assertive, barn of a place, with its areas of shiny tin roof, the hard pink of the walls, the glinting angled shapes of the windows. Although shrubs grew sparsely around it, and it was shaded by a thick clump of trees, it looked naked, raw, crude. "That is my home," said Julia to herself, testing the word. She rejected it. In that house she had lived ten years—more. She turned away from it, walking lightly through the sifting pink dust of the roads like a stranger. There had always been times when Africa rejected her, when she felt like a critical ghost. This was one of those times. Through the known and loved scenes of the veld she saw Buenos Aires, Rome, Cape Town—a dozen cities, large and small, merging and mingling as the country rose and fell about her. Perhaps it is not good for human beings to live in so many places? But it was not that. She was suffering from an unfamiliar dryness of the senses, an unlocated, unfocussed ache that, if she were young, would have formed itself about a person or place, but now remained locked within her. "What am I?" she kept saying to herself as she walked through the veld, in the moving patch of shade that fell from the large drooping hat. On either side the long grass moved and whispered sibilantly; the doves throbbed gently from the trees; the sky was a flower-blue arch over her—it was, as they say, a lovely morning.

She passed like a revenant along the edges of the mealie fields, watching the working gangs of natives; at the well she paused to see the women with their groups of naked children; at the cattle sheds she leaned to touch the wet noses of the thrusting softheaded calves which butted and pushed at her legs. There she stayed for some time, finding comfort in these young creatures. She understood at last that it was nearly lunchtime. She must go home, and preside at the lunch-table for Tom, in case he should decide to return. She left the calves thinking: Perhaps I ought to have children? She knew perfectly well that she would not.

The road back to the house wound along the high hogs's-back between two vleis that fell away on either side. She walked slowly, trying to recover that soft wonder she had felt when she first arrived on the farm and learned how living in cities had cheated her of the knowledge of the shapes of sky and land. Above her, in the great bright bell of blue sky, the wind currents were marked by swirls of cloud, the backwaters of the air by heavy sculptured piles of sluggish white. Around her the skeleton of rock showed under the thin covering of living soil. The trees thickened with the fall or rise of the ground, with the running of underground rivers; the grass—the long blond hair of the grass—struggled always to heal and hold whatever wounds were made by hoof of beast or thoughtlessness of man. The sky, the land, the swirling air, closed around her in an exchange of water and heat, and the deep multitudinous murmuring of living substance sounded like a humming in her blood. She listened, half-passively, half-rebelliously, and asked: "What do I contribute to all this?"

That afternoon she walked again, for hours; and throughout the following day; returning to the house punctually for meals, and greeting Tom across the distance that puts itself between people who try to support themselves with the mental knowledge of a country, and those who work in it. Once Tom said, with tired concern, looking at her equally tired face: "Julia, I didn't know you would mind so much. I suppose it was conceit. I always thought I came first."

"You do," she said quickly, "believe me, you do."

She went to him, so that he could put his arms about her. He did, and there was no warmth in it for either of them. "We'll come right again," he promised her. But it was as though he listened to the sound of his own voice for a message of assurance.

Kenneth came back unexpectedly on the fourth evening. He was alone; and he appeared purposeful and decided. During dinner no one spoke much. After dinner, in the bare, gaunt, firelit room, the three waited for someone to speak.

At last Julia said: "Well, Kenneth?"

"We are getting married next month."

"Where?"

"In Church," he said. He smiled constrictedly. "She wants a proper wedding. I don't mind, if she likes it." Kenneth's attitude was altogether brisk, down-to-earth and hard. At the same time he looked at Julia and Tom uneasily: he hated his position.

"How old is she?" asked Julia.

"A baby. Twenty-three."

This shocked Julia. "Kenneth, you can't do that."

"Why not?"

Julia could not really see why not.

"Has she money of her own?" asked Tom practically, causing the other two to look at him in surprise. "After all," he said quickly, "we must know about her, before she comes?"

"Of course she hasn't," said Kenneth coldly. "She wouldn't be coming out to the Colonies on a subsidized scheme for importing marriageable women, would she?"

Tom grimaced. "You two are brutal," he remarked.

Kenneth and Julia glanced at each other; it was like a shrug. "I didn't mention money in the first place," he pointed out. "You did. Anyway, what's wrong with it? If I were a surplus woman in England I should certainly emigrate to find a husband. It's the only sensible thing to do."

"What is she living on now?" asked Julia.

"She has a job in an office. Some such nonsense." Kenneth dismissed this. "Anyway, why talk about money? Surely we have enough?"

"How much have we got?" asked Julia, who was always rather vague about money.

"A hell of a lot." said Tom, laughing. "The last three years we've made thousands."

"How many thousands?"

"Difficult to say, there's so much going back into the farms. Fifty thousand perhaps. We'll make a lot more this year."

Julia smiled. The words "fifty thousand" could not be made to come real in her mind. She thought of how she had earned her living for years, in offices, budgeting for everything she spent. "I suppose we could be described as rich?" she asked wonderingly at last, trying to relate this fact to the life she lived, to the country around them, to their future.

"I suppose we could," agreed Tom, snorting with amused laughter. He liked it when Julia made it possible for him to think of her as helpless. "Most of the credit goes to Kenneth," he added. "All the work he did during the war is reaping dividends now."

Julia looked at him; then sardonically at Kenneth, who was shifting uncomfortably in his chair. Tom persisted with good-natured sarcasm, getting his own back for Kenneth's gibes over the war: "This is getting quite a show-place; I got a letter from the Government asking me if they could bring a collection of distinguished visitors from Home to see it, next week. You'll have to act as hostess. They're coming to see Kenneth's war effort." He laughed. "It's also been very profitable."

Kenneth shut his mouth hard; and kept his temper. "We are discussing my future wife," he said coldly.

"So we are," said Julia.

"Well, let's finish with the thing. I shall give the girl a thumping, expensive honeymoon in the most glossy and awful hotels in the sub-continent," continued Kenneth grimly. "She'll love it."

"Why shouldn't she?" asked Julia. "I should have loved it too, at her age."

"I didn't say she shouldn't."

"And then?" asked Julia again. She was wanting to hear what sort of plans Kenneth had for another farm. He looked at her blankly. "And then what?"

"Where will you go?"

"Go?"

It came to her that he did not intend to leave the farm. This was such a shock she could not speak. She collected herself at last, and said slowly: "Kenneth, surely you don't intend to live here?"

"Why not?" he asked quickly, very much on the defensive.

The atmosphere had tightened so that Julia saw, in looking from one man to the other, that this was the real crisis of the business, something she had not expected, but which they had both been waiting, consciously or unconsciously, for her to approach.

"Good God," she said slowly, in rising anger. "Good God." She looked at Tom, who at once averted his eyes. She saw that Tom was longing uneasily for her to make it possible for Kenneth to stay.

She understood at last that, if it had occurred to either of them that another woman could not live here, it was a knowledge neither of them were prepared to face. She looked at these two men and hated them, for the way they took their women into their lives, without changing a thought or a habit to meet them.

She got up, and walked away from them slowly, standing with her back to them, gazing out of the window at the heavily-starred winter's night. She said: "Kenneth, you are marrying this girl because you intend to have a family. You don't care tuppence for her, really."

"I've got to be very fond of her," protested Kenneth.

"At bottom, you don't care tuppence."

He did not reply. "You are going to bring her here to me. She'll feel with her instinct if not with her head that she's being made use of. And you bring her here to me." It seemed to her that she had made her sense of outrage clear enough. She turned to face them.

"The prospect of bringing her 'to you' doesn't seem to me as shocking as apparently it does to you," said Kenneth drily.

"Can't you see?" she said desperately. "She couldn't compete . . ."

"You flatter yourself," said Kenneth briskly.

"Oh, I don't mean that. I mean we've been together for so long. There's nothing we don't know about each other. Have I got to say it . . ."

"No," said Kenneth quietly. "Much better not."

Through all this Tom, that large, fair, comfortable man, leaned back in his chair, looking from his wife to his half-brother with the air of one suddenly transported to a foreign country.

He said stubbornly: "I don't see why you shouldn't adjust yourself, Julia. After all, both Kenneth and I have had to adjust ourselves to . . ."

"Quite," said Kenneth quickly, "quite."

She turned on Kenneth furiously. "Why do you always cut the conversation short? Why shouldn't we talk about it? It's what's real, isn't it, for all of us?"

"No point talking about it," said Kenneth, with a sullen look.

"No," she said coldly. "No point." She turned away from them, fighting back tears. "At bottom neither of you really cared tuppence. That's what it is." At the moment this seemed to her true.

"What do you mean by 'really caring'?" asked Kenneth.

Julia turned slowly from the window, jerking the light summer curtains across the stars. "I mean, we don't care. We just don't care."

"I don't know what you are talking about," said Tom, sounding bewildered and angry. "Haven't you been happy with me? Is that what you are saying, Julia?"

At this both Kenneth and Julia began laughing with an irresistible and painful laughter.

"Of course I've been happy with you," she said flatly, at last.

"Well then?" asked Tom.

"I don't know why I was happy then and why I'm unhappy now?"

"Let's say you're jealous," said Kenneth briskly.

"But I don't think I am."

"Of course you are."

"Very well then, I am. That's not the point, though. What are we going to do to the girl?" she asked suddenly, her feeling finding expression.

"I shall make her a good husband," said Kenneth. The three of them looked at each other, with raised brows, with humorous, tightened lips.

"Very well then," amended Kenneth. "But she'll have plenty of nice children. She'll have you for company, Julia, a nice intelligent woman. And she'll have plenty of money and pretty clothes and all that sort of nonsense, if she wants them."

There was a silence so long it seemed that nothing could break it.

Julia said slowly and painfully: "I think it is terrible we shouldn't be able to explain what we feel or what we are."

"I wish you'd stop trying to," said Kenneth. "I find it unpleasant. And quite useless."

Tom said: "As for me, I would be most grateful if you'd try to explain what you are feeling, Julia. I haven't an idea."

Julia stood up with her back to the fire and began gropingly: "Look at the way we are. I mean, what do we add up to? What are we doing here, in the first place?"

"Doing where?" asked Tom kindly.

"Here, in Africa, in this district, on this land."

"Ohhh," groaned Tom humorously.

"Oh *Lord*, Julia," protested Kenneth impatiently.

"I feel as if we shouldn't be here."

"Where should we be, then?"

"We've as much right as anybody else."

"I suppose so." Julia dismissed it. It was not her point, after all, it seemed. She said slowly: "I suppose there are comparatively very few people in the world as secure and as rich as we are."

"It takes a couple of bad seasons or a change in the international set-up," said Kenneth. "We could get poor as easily as we've got rich. If you want to call it easy. We've worked hard enough, Tom and I."

"So do many other people. In the meantime we've all the money we want. Why do we never talk about money, never think about it? It's what we are."

"Speak for yourself, Julia," said Tom. "Kenneth and I spend all our days thinking and talking about nothing else. How else do you suppose we've got rich?"

"How to make it. Not what it all adds up to."

The two men did not reply; they looked at each other with resignation. Kenneth lit a cigarette, Tom a pipe.

"I've been getting a feeling of money the last few days. Perhaps not so much money as . . ." She stopped. "I can't say what I feel. It's no use. What do our lives add up to? That's what I want to know."

"Why do you expect us to tell you?" asked Kenneth curiously at last.

This was a new note. Julia looked at him, puzzled. "I don't know," she said at last. Then, very drily: "I suppose I should be prepared to take the consequences for marrying the pair of you." The men laughed uneasily though with relief that the worst seemed to be over. "If I left this place tomorrow," she said sadly, "you simply wouldn't miss me."

"Ah, you love Kenneth," groaned Tom suddenly. The groan was so sudden, coming just as the flippant note had been struck, and successfully, that Julia could not bear it. She continued quietly, lightly, to wipe away the naked pain of Tom's voice: "No, I don't. I wish you wouldn't talk about love."

"That's what all this is about," said Kenneth. "Love."

Julia looked at him scornfully. She said: "What sort of people are we? Let's use bare facts, just for once."

"Must you?" breathed Kenneth.

"Yes, I must. The fact is that I have been a sort of high-class concubine for the two of you . . ." She stopped at once. Even the beginning of the tirade sounded absurd in her own ears.

"I hope that statement has cleared your mind for you," said Kenneth ironically.

"No, it hasn't. I didn't expect it would." But now Julia was fighting hard against that no-man's-land of feeling in which she had been living for so long, that under-sea territory where one thing confuses with another, where it is so easy to drift at ease, according to the pull of the tides.

"I should have had children," she said at last, quietly. "That's where we went wrong, Tom. It was children we needed."

"Ah," said Kenneth from his chair, suddenly deeply sincere, "now you are talking sense."

"Well," said Tom, "there's nothing to stop us."

"I'm too old."

"Other women of forty have children."

"I'm too—tired. It seems to me, to have children, one needs . . ." She stopped.

"What does one need?" asked Tom.

Julia's eyes met Kenneth's; they exchanged deep, ironic, patient understanding.

"Thank God you didn't marry me," he said suddenly. "You were quite right. Tom's the man for you. In a marriage it's necessary for one side to be strong enough to create the illusion."

"What illusion?" asked Tom petulantly.

"Necessity," said Kenneth simply.

"Is that the office this girl is going to perform for you?" asked Tom.

"Precisely. She loves me, God help her. She really does, you know . . ." Kenneth looked at them in a manner of inviting them to share his surprise at this fact. "And she wants children. She knows why she wants them. She'll make me know it too, bless her. Most of the time," he could not prevent himself adding.

Now it seemed impossible to go on. They remained silent, each face expressing tired and bewildered unhappiness. Julia stood against the mantelpiece, feeling the warmth of the fire running over her body, but not reaching the chill within.

Kenneth recovered first. He got up and said: "Bed, bed for all of us. This doesn't help. We mustn't talk. We must get on, dealing with the next thing." He said good night, and went to the door. There he turned, looked clear and full at Julia with his black, alert, shrewd eyes, and remarked: "You must be nice to that girl, Julia."

"You know very well I can be 'nice' to her, but I won't be 'nice' for her. You are deliberately submitting her to it. You won't even move two miles away on to the next farm. You won't even take that much trouble to make her happy. Remember that."

Kenneth flushed, said hastily: "Well, I didn't say I wouldn't go to the other farm," and went out. Julia knew that it would take a lot of unhappiness for the four of them before he would consent to move himself. He thought of this house as his home; and he could not bear to leave Tom, even now.

"Come here," said Tom gently, when Kenneth had left the room. She went to him, and slipped down beside him into his chair. "Do you find me stupid?" he asked.

"Not stupid."

"What then?"

She held him close. "Put your arms round me."

He held her; but she did not feel supported: the arms were as light as wind about her, and as unsure.

In the middle of the night she rose from her bed, slipped on her gown and went along the winding passages to Kenneth's bedroom, which was at the other end of the house.

It was filled with the brightness of moonlight. Kenneth was sitting up against his pillows; he was awake; she could see the light glinting on his eyes.

She sat herself down on the foot of his bed.

"Well, Julia? It's no good coming to me, you know."

She did not reply. The confusing dimness of the moon, which hung immediately outside the window, troubled her. She held a match to the candle, and watched a warm yellow glow fill the room, so that the moon retreated and became a small hard bright coin high among the stars.

She saw on the dressing-table a new framed photograph.

"If one acquires a wife," she said sarcastically, "one of course acquires a photo to put on one's dressing-table." She went over and picked it up and returned to the bed with it. Kenneth watched her, alertly.

Slowly Julia's face spread into a compassionate smile.

"What's the matter?" asked Kenneth quickly.

She was not twenty-three, Julia could see that. She was well over thirty. It was a pretty enough face, very English, with flat broad planes and small features. Fair neatly-waved hair fell away regularly from the forehead.

There was anxiety in those too-serious eyes; the mouth smiled carefully in a prepared sweetness for the photographer; the cheeks were thin. Turning the photograph to the light Julia could see how the neck was creased and furrowed. No, she was by no means a girl. She glanced at Kenneth; and was filled slowly by a sweet irrational tenderness for him, a delicious irresponsible gaiety.

"Why," she said, "you're in love, after all, Kenneth."

"Whoever said I wasn't?" he grinned at her, lying watchfully back in his bed and puffing at his cigarette.

She grinned back affectionately, still lifted on a wave of delight; then she turned, and felt it ebb as she looked down at the photograph, mentally greeting this other tired woman, coming to the great rich farm, like the poor girl in the fairy story.

"What are you amused at?" asked Kenneth cautiously.

"I was thinking of you as a refuge," she explained drily.

"I'm quite prepared to be."

"You'd never be a refuge for anyone."

"Not for you. But you forget she's younger." He laughed: "She'll be less critical."

She smiled, without replying, looking at the **pictured** face. It was such a humorless, earnest, sincere face, the eyes so serious, so searching.

Julia sighed. "I'm terribly tired," she said to Kenneth, turning back to him.

"I know you are. So am I. That's why I'm marrying."

Julia had a clear mental picture of this Englishwoman, who was soon coming to the farm. For a moment she allowed herself to picture her in various situations, arriving with nervous tact, hiding her longing for a home of her own, hoping not to find Julia an enemy. She would find not strife, or hostility, or scenes—none of the situations which she might be prepared to face. She would find three people who knew each other so well that for the most part they found it hardly necessary to speak. She would find indifference to everything she really was, a prepared, deliberate kindness. She would be like a latecomer to a party, entering a room where everyone is already cemented by hours of warmth and intimacy. She would be helpless against Kenneth's need for her to be something she could not be: a young woman, with the spiritual vitality to heal him.

Looking at the pretty girl in the frame which she held between her palms, the girl under whose surface prettiness Julia could see the anxious, haunted woman, the knowledge came to her of what word it was she sought: it was as though those carefully smiling lips formed themselves into that word. "Do you know what we are?" she asked Kenneth.

"Not a notion," he replied jauntily.

Julia accepted the word evil from that humorless, homeless girl. Twice in her life it had confronted her; this time she took it gratefully. After all, none other had been offered.

"I know what evil is" she said to Kenneth.

"How nice for you," he returned impatiently. Then he added: "I suppose, like most women who have lived their own lives, whatever that might mean, you are now beginning to develop an exaggerated conscience. If so, we shall both find you very tedious."

"Is that what I'm doing?" she asked, considering it. "I don't think so."

He looked at her soberly. "Go to bed, my dear. Do stop fussing. Are you prepared to do anything about it? You aren't, are you? Then stop making us all miserable over impossibilities. We have a pleasant enough life, taking it for what it is. It's not much fun being the fag-end of something, but even that has its compensations."

Julia listened, smiling, to her own voice speaking. "You put it admirably," she said, as she went out of the room.

Jean Stafford

A Country Love Story

Born in California and raised in Colorado, Jean Stafford wrote many years later, "I could not wait to quit my tamed-down native grounds. As soon as I could, I hotfooted it across the Rocky Mountains." From 1940 to 1948 she was married to the poet Robert Lowell, and during that time she wrote her first two novels, Boston Adventure *(1944) and* The Mountain Lion *(1947). Highly regarded by fellow writers for her "coldly brilliant prose style," Ms. Stafford has published several collections of short stories, among them* Children Are Bored on Sunday *(1953) and her* Collected Stories, *for which she was awarded the 1970 Pulitzer Prize for fiction.*

An antique sleigh stood in the yard, snow after snow banked up against its eroded runners. Here and there upon the bleached and splintery seat were wisps of horsehair and scraps of the black leather that had once upholstered it. It bore, with all its jovial curves, an air not so much of desuetude as of slowed-down dash, as if weary horses, unable to go another step, had at last stopped here. The sleigh had come with the house. The former owner, a gifted businesswoman from Castine who bought old houses and sold them again with all their pitfalls still intact, had said when she was showing them the place, "A picturesque detail, I think," and, waving it away, had turned to the well, which, with enthusiasm and at considerable length, she said had never gone dry. Actually, May and Daniel had found the detail more distracting than picturesque, so nearly kin was it to outdoor arts and crafts, and when the woman, as they departed in her car, gestured toward it again and said, "Paint that up a bit with something cheery and it will really add no end to your yard," simultaneous shudders coursed them. They had planned to remove the sleigh before they did anything else.

But partly because there were more important things to be done, and partly because they did not know where to put it (a sleigh could not, in the usual sense of the words, be thrown away), and partly because it seemed defiantly a part of the yard, as entitled to be there permanently as the trees, they did nothing about it. Throughout the summer, they saw birds briefly pause on its rakish front and saw the fresh rains wash its runners; in the autumn they watched the golden leaves fill the seat and nestle dryly down; and now, with the snow, they watched this new accumulation.

The sleigh was visible from the windows of the big, bright kitchen where they ate all their meals and, sometimes too bemused with country solitude to talk, they gazed out at it, forgetting their food in speculating on its history. It could have been driven cavalierly by the scion of some sea captain's family, or it could have been used soberly to haul the household's Unitarians to church or to take the womenfolk around the countryside on errands of good will. They did not speak of what its office might have been, and the fact of their silence was often nettlesome to May, for she felt they were silent too much of the time; a little morosely, she thought, If something as absurd and as provocative as this at which we look together—and which is, even though we didn't want it, our own property—cannot bring us to talk, what can? But she did not disturb Daniel in his private musings; she held her tongue, and out of the corner of her eye she watched him watch the winter cloak the sleigh, and, as if she were computing a difficult sum in her head, she tried to puzzle out what it was that had stilled tongues that earlier, before Daniel's illness, had found the days too short to communicate all they were eager to say.

It had been Daniel's doctor's idea, not theirs, that had brought them to the solemn hinterland to stay after all the summer gentry had departed in their beach wagons. The Northern sun, the pristine air, the rural walks and soundless nights, said Dr. Tellenbach, perhaps pining for his native Switzerland, would do more for the "Professor's" convalescent lung than all the doctors and clinics in the world. Privately he had added to May that after so long a season in the sanitarium (Daniel had been there a year), where everything was tuned to a low pitch, it would be difficult and it might be shattering for "the boy" (not now the "Professor," although Daniel, nearly fifty, was his wife's senior by twenty years and Dr. Tellenbach's by ten) to go back at once to the excitements and the intrigues of the university, to what, with finicking humor, the Doctor called "the omnium-gatherum of the school master's life." The rigors of a country winter would be as nothing, he insisted, when compared to the strain of feuds and cocktail parties. All professors wanted to write books, didn't they? Surely Daniel, a historian with all the material in the world at his fingertips, must have something up his sleeve that could be the *raison d'être* for this year away? May said she supposed he had, she was not sure. She could hear the reluctance in her voice as she escaped the Doctor's eyes and gazed through his windows at the mountains behind the sanitarium. In the dragging months Daniel had been gone, she had taken solace in imagining the time when they *would* return to just that pandemonium the Doctor so deplored, and because it had been pandemonium on the smallest and most discreet scale, she smiled through her disappointment at the little man's Swiss innocence and explained that they had always lived quietly, seldom dining out or entertaining more than twice a week.

"Twice a week?" He was appalled.

"But I'm afraid," she had protested, "that he would find a second year of inactivity intolerable. He does intend to write a book, but he means to write it in England, and we can't go to England now."

"England!" Dr. Tellenbach threw up his hands. "Good *air* is my recommendation for your husband. Good air and little talk."

She said, "It's talk he needs, I should think, after all this time of communing only with himself except when I came to visit."

He had looked at her with exaggerated patience, and then, courtly but authoritative, he said, "I hope you will not think I importune when I tell you that I am very well acquainted with your husband, and, as his physician, I order this retreat. *He* quite agrees."

Stung to see that there was a greater degree of understanding between Daniel and Dr. Tellenbach than between Daniel and herself, May had objected further, citing an occasion when her husband had put his head in his hands and mourned, "I hear talk of nothing but sputum cups and X-rays. Aren't people interested in the state of the world any more?"

But Dr. Tellenbach had been adamant, and at the end, when she had risen to go, he said, "You are bound to find him changed a little. A long illness removes a thoughtful man from his fellow-beings. It is like living with an exacting mistress who is not content with half a man's attention but must claim it all." She had thought his figure of speech absurd and disdained to ask him what he meant.

Actually, when the time came for them to move into the new house and she found no alterations in her husband but found, on the other hand, much pleasure in their country life, she began to forgive Dr. Tellenbach. In the beginning, it was like a second honeymoon, for they had moved to a part of the North where they had never been and they explored it together, sharing its charming sights and sounds. Moreover, they had never owned a house before but had always lived in city apartments, and though the house they bought was old and derelict, its lines and doors and windowlights were beautiful, and they were obsessed with it. All through the summer, they reiterated, "To think that we own all of this! That it actually belongs to us!" And they wandered from room to room marveling at their windows, from none of which was it possible to see an ugly sight. They looked to the south upon a river, to the north upon a lake; to the west of them were pine woods where the wind forever sighed, voicing a vain entreaty; and to the east a rich man's long meadow that ran down a hill to his old, magisterial house. It was true, even in those bewitched days, that there were times on the lake, when May was gathering water lilies as Daniel slowly rowed, that she had seen on his face a look of abstraction and she had known that he was worlds away, in his memories, perhaps, of his illness and the sanitarium (of which he would never speak) or in the thought of the book he was going to write as soon, he said, as the winter set in and there was nothing to do but work. Momentarily the look frightened her and she remembered the Doctor's words, but then, immediately herself again in the security of married love, she caught at another water lily and pulled at its long stem. Companionably, they gardened, taking special pride in the nicotiana that sent its nighttime fragrance into their bedroom. Together, and with fascination, they consulted carpenters, plasterers, and chimney sweeps. In the blue evenings they read at ease, hearing no sound but that of the night birds—the loons on the lake and the owls in the tops of trees. When the days began to cool and shorten, a cricket came to bless their house, nightly singing behind the kitchen stove. They got two fat and idle tabby cats, who lay insensibly beside the fireplace and only stirred themselves to purr perfunctorily.

Because they had not moved in until July and by that time the workmen of the region were already engaged, most of the major repairs of the house were to be postponed until the spring, and in October, when May and Daniel had done all they could by themselves and Daniel had begun his own work, May suddenly found herself without occupation. Whole days might pass when she did nothing more than cook three meals and walk a little in the autumn mist and pet the cats and wait for Daniel to come down from his upstairs study to talk to her. She began to think with longing of the crowded days in Boston before Daniel was sick, and even in the year past, when he had been away and she had gone to concerts and recitals and had done good deeds for crippled children and had endlessly shopped for presents to lighten the tedium of her husband's unwilling exile. And, longing, she was remorseful, as if by desiring another she betrayed this life, and, remorseful, she hid away in sleep. Sometimes she slept for hours in the daytime, imitating the cats, and when at last she got up, she had to push away the dense sleep as if it were a door.

One day at lunch, she asked Daniel to take a long walk with her that afternoon to a farm where the owner smoked his own sausages.

"You never go outdoors," she said, "and Dr. Tellenbach said you must. Besides, it's a lovely day."

"I can't," he said. "I'd like to, but I can't. I'm busy. You go alone."

Overtaken by a gust of loneliness, she cried, "Oh, Daniel, I have nothing to *do!*"

A moment's silence fell, and then he said, "I'm sorry to put you through this, my dear, but you must surely admit that it's not my fault I got sick."

In her shame, her rapid, overdone apologies, her insistence that nothing mattered in the whole world except his health and peace of mind, she made everything worse, and at last he said shortly to her, "Stop being a child, May. Let's just leave each other alone."

This outbreak, the very first in their marriage of five years, was the beginning of a series. Hardly a day passed that they did not bicker over something; they might dispute a question of fact, argue a matter of taste, catch each other out in an inaccuracy, and every quarrel ended with Daniel's saying to her, "Why don't you leave me alone?" Once he said, "I've been sick and now I'm busy and I'm no longer young enough to shift the focus of my mind each time it suits your whim." Afterward, there were always apologies, and then Daniel went back to his study and did not open the door of it again until the next meal. Finally, it seemed to her that love, the very center of their being, was choked off, overgrown, invisible. And silent with hostility, or voluble with trivial reproach, they tried to dig it out impulsively and could not—could only maul it in its unkempt grave. Daniel, in his withdrawal from her and from the house, was preoccupied with his research, of which he never spoke except to say that it would bore her, and most of the time, so it appeared to May, he did not worry over what was happening to them. She felt the cold, old house somehow enveloping her as if it were their common enemy, maliciously bent on bringing them to disaster. Sunken in faithlessness, they stared, at mealtimes, atrophied within the present hour, at the irrelevant and whimsical sleigh that stood abandoned in the mammoth winter.

May found herself thinking, If we redeemed it and painted it, our house would have something in common with Henry Ford's Wayside Inn. And I might make this very observation to him and he might greet it with disdain and we might once again communicate. Perhaps we could talk of Williamsburg and how we disapproved of it. Her mind went toiling on. Williamsburg was part of our honeymoon trip; somewhere our feet were entangled in suckers as we stood kissing under a willow tree. Soon she found that she did not care for this line of thought, nor did she care what his response to it might be. In her imagined conversations with Daniel, she never spoke of the sleigh. To the thin, ill scholar whose scholarship and illness had usurped her place, she had gradually taken a weighty but unviolent dislike.

The discovery of this came, not surprising her, on Christmas Day. The knowledge sank like a plummet, and at the same time she was thinking about the sleigh, connecting it with the smell of the barn on damp days, and she thought perhaps it had been drawn by the very animals who had been stabled there and had pervaded the timbers with their odor. There must have been much life within this house once—but long ago. The earth immediately behind the barn was said by everyone to be extremely rich because of the horses, although there had been none there for over fifty years. Thinking of this soil, which earlier she had eagerly sifted through her fingers, May now realized that she had no wish for the spring to come, no wish to plant a garden, and, branching out at random, she found she had no wish to see the sea again, or children, or favorite pictures, or even her own face on a happy day. For a minute or two, she was almost enraptured in this state of no desire, but then, purged swiftly of her cynicism, she knew it to be false, knew that actually she did have a desire—the desire for a desire. And now she felt that she was stationary in a whirlpool, and at the very moment she conceived the notion a bit of wind brought to the seat of the sleigh the final leaf from the elm tree that stood beside it. It crossed her mind that she might consider the wood of the sleigh in its juxtaposition to the living tree and to the horses, who, although they were long since dead, reminded her of their passionate, sweating, running life every time she went to the barn for firewood.

They sat this morning in the kitchen full of sun, and, speaking not to him but to the sleigh, to icicles, to the dark, motionless pine woods, she said, "I wonder if on a day like this they used to take the pastor home after lunch." Daniel gazed abstractedly at the bright-silver drifts beside the well and said nothing. Presently a wagon went past hauled by two oxen with bells on their yoke. This was the hour they always passed, taking to an unknown destination an aged man in a fur hat and an aged woman in a shawl. May and Daniel listened.

Suddenly, with impromptu anger, Daniel said, "What did you just say?"

"Nothing," she said. And then, after a pause, "It would be lovely at Jamaica Pond today."

He wheeled on her and pounded the table with his fist. "I did not ask for this!" The color rose feverishly to his thin cheeks and his breath was agitated. "You are trying to make me sick again. It was wonderful, wasn't it, for you while I was gone?"

"Oh, no, no! Oh, no, Daniel, it was hell!"

"Then, by the same token, this must be heaven." He smiled, the professor catching out a student in a fallacy.

"Heaven." She said the word bitterly.

"Then why do you stay here?" he cried.

It was a cheap impasse, desolate, true, unfair. She did not answer him.

After a while he said, "I almost believe there's something you haven't told me."

She began to cry at once, blubbering across the table at him. "You have said that before. What am I to say? What have I done?"

He looked at her, impervious to her tears, without mercy and yet without contempt. "I don't know. But you've done something."

It was as if she were looking through someone else's scrambled closets and bureau drawers for an object that had not been named to her, but nowhere could she find her gross offense.

Domestically she asked him if he would have more coffee and he peremptorily refused and demanded, "Will you tell me why it is you must badger me? Is it a compulsion? Can't you control it? Are you going mad?"

From that day onward, May felt a certain stirring of life within her solitude, and now and again, looking up from a book to see if the damper on the stove was right, to listen to a rat renovating its house-within-a-house, to watch the belled oxen pass, she nursed her wound, hugged it, repeated his awful words exactly as he had said them, reproduced the way his wasted lips had looked and his bright, farsighted eyes. She could not read for long at any time, nor could she sew. She cared little now for planning changes in her house; she had meant to sand the painted floors to uncover the wood of the wide boards and she had imagined how the long, paneled windows of the drawing room would look when yellow velvet curtains hung there in the spring. Now, schooled by silence and indifference, she was immune to disrepair and to he damage done by the wind and snow, and she looked, as Daniel did, without dislike upon the old and nasty wallpaper and upon the shabby kitchen floor. One day, she knew that the sleigh would stay where it was so long as they stayed there. From every thought, she returned to her deep, bleeding injury. He had asked her if she were going mad.

She repaid him in the dark afternoons while he was closeted away in his study, hardly making a sound save when he added wood to his fire or paced a little, deep in thought. She sat at the kitchen table looking at the sleigh, and she gave Daniel insult for his injury by imagining a lover. She did not imagine his face, but she imagined his clothing, which would be costly and in the best of taste, and his manner, which would be urbane and anticipatory of her least whim, and his clever speech, and his adept courtship that would begin the moment he looked at the sleigh and said, "I must get rid of that for you at once." She might be a widow, she might be divorced, she might be committing adultery. Certainly there was no need to specify in an affair so securely legal. There was no need, that is, up to a point, and then the point came when she took in the fact that she not only believed in this lover but loved him and depended wholly on his companionship. She complained to him of Daniel and he consoled her; she told him stories of her girlhood, when she had gaily gone to parties, squired by boys her own age; she dazzled him sometimes with the wise comments she made on the books she read. It came to be true that if she so much as looked at the sleigh, she was weakened, failing with starvation.

Often, about her daily tasks of cooking food and washing dishes and tending the fires and shopping in the general store of the village, she thought she should watch her step, that it was this sort of thing that *did* make one go mad; for a while, then, she went back to Daniel's question, sharpening its razor edge.

But she could not corral her alien thoughts and she trembled as she bought split peas, fearful that the old men loafing by the stove could see the incubus of her sins beside her. She could not avert such thoughts when they rushed upon her sometimes at tea with one of the old religious ladies of the neighborhood, so that, in the middle of a conversation about a deaconess in Bath, she retired from them, seeking her lover, who came, faceless, with his arms outstretched, even as she sat up straight in a Boston rocker, even as she accepted another cup of tea. She lingered over the cake plates and the simple talk, postponing her return to her own house and to Daniel, whom she continually betrayed.

It was not long after she recognized her love that she began to wake up even before the dawn and to be all day quick to everything, observant of all the signs of age and eccentricity in her husband, and she compared him in every particular—to his humiliation, in her eyes—with the man whom now it seemed to her she had always loved at fever pitch.

Once when Daniel, in a rare mood, kissed her, she drew back involuntarily and he said gently, "I wish I knew what you had done, poor dear." He looked, as if for written words, in her face.

"You said you knew," she said, terrified.

"I do."

"Then why do you wish you knew?" Her baffled voice was high and frantic. "You don't talk sense!"

"I do," he said sedately. "I talk sense always. It is you who are oblique." Her eyes stole like a sneak to the sleigh. "But I wish I knew your motive," he said impartially.

For a minute, she felt that they were two maniacs answering each other questions that had not been asked, never touching the matter at hand because they did not know what the matter was. But in the next moment, when he turned back to her spontaneously and clasped her head between his hands and said, like a tolerant father, "I forgive you, darling, because you don't know how you persecute me. No one knows except the sufferer what this sickness is," she knew again, helplessly, that they were not harmonious even in their aberrations.

These days of winter came and went, and on each of them, after breakfast and as the oxen passed, he accused her of her concealed misdeed. She could no longer truthfully deny that she was guilty, for she was in love, and she heard the subterfuge in her own voice and felt the guilty fever in her veins. Daniel knew it, too, and watched her. When she was alone, she felt her lover's presence protecting her—when she walked past the stiff spiraea, with icy cobwebs hung between its twigs, down to the lake, where the black, unmeasured water was hidden beneath a lid of ice; when she walked, instead, to the salt river to see the tar-paper shacks where the men caught smelt through the ice; when she walked in the dead dusk up the hill from the store, catching her breath the moment she saw the sleigh. But sometimes this splendid being mocked her when, freezing with fear of the consequences of her sin, she ran up the stairs to Daniel's room and burrowed her head in his shoulder and cried, "Come downstairs! I'm lonely, please come down!" But he would never come, and at last, bitterly, calmed by his calmly inquisitive regard, she went back alone and stood at the kitchen window, coyly half hidden behind the curtains.

For months she lived with her daily dishonor, rattled, ashamed, stubbornly clinging to her secret. But she grew more and more afraid when, oftener and oftener, Daniel said, "Why do you lie to me? What does this mood of yours mean?" and she could no longer sleep. In the raw nights, she lay straight beside him as he slept, and she stared at the ceiling, as bright as the snow it reflected, and tried not to think of the sleigh out there under the elm tree but could think only of it and of the man, her lover, who was connected with it somehow. She said to herself, as she listened to his breathing, "If I confessed to Daniel, he would understand that I was lonely and he would comfort me, saying, 'I am here, May. I shall never let you be lonely again.' " At these times, she was so separated from the world, so far removed from his touch and his voice, so solitary, that she would have sued a stranger for companionship. Daniel slept deeply, having no guilt to make him toss. He slept, indeed, so well that he never even heard the ditcher on snowy nights rising with a groan over the hill, flinging the snow from the road and warning of its approach by lights that first flashed red, then blue. As it passed their house, the hurled snow swashed like flames. All night she heard the squirrels adding up their nuts in the walls and heard the spirit of the house creaking and softly clicking upon the stairs and in the attics.

In early spring, when the whippoorwills begged in the cattails and the marsh reeds, and the northern lights patinated the lake and the tidal river, and the stars were large, and the huge vine of the Dutchman's-pipe had started to leaf out, May went to bed late. Each night she sat on the back steps waiting, hearing the snuffling of a dog as it hightailed it for home, the single cry of a loon. Night after night, she waited for the advent of her rebirth while upstairs Daniel, who had spoken tolerantly of her vigils, slept, keeping his knowledge of her to himself. "A symptom," he had said, scowling in concentration, as he remarked upon her new habit. "Let it run its course. Perhaps when this is over, you will know the reason why you torture me with these obsessions and will stop. You know, you may really have a slight disorder of the mind. It would be nothing to be ashamed of; you could go to a sanitarium."

One night, looking out the window, she clearly saw her lover sitting in the sleigh. His hand was over his eyes and his chin was covered by a red silk scarf. He wore no hat and his hair was fair. He was tall and his long legs stretched indolently along the floorboard. He was younger than she had imagined him to be and he seemed rather frail, for there was a delicate pallor on his high, intelligent forehead and there was an invalid's languor in his whole attitude. He wore a white blazer and gray flannels and there was a yellow rosebud in his lapel. Young as he was, he did not, even so, seem to belong to her generation; rather, he seemed to be the reincarnation of someone's uncle as he had been fifty years before. May did not move until he vanished, and then, even though she knew now that she was truly bedeviled, the only emotion she had was bashfulness, mingled with doubt; she was not sure, that is, that he loved her.

That night, she slept a while. She lay near to Daniel, who was smiling in the moonlight. She could tell that the sleep she would have tonight would be as heavy as a coma, and she was aware of the moment she was overtaken.

She was in a canoe in a meadow of water lilies and her lover was tranquilly taking the shell off a hard-boiled egg. "How intimate," he said, "to eat an egg with you." She was nervous lest the canoe tip over, but at the same time she was charmed by his wit and by the way he lightly touched her shoulder with the varnished paddle.

"May? May? I love you, May."

"Oh!" enchanted, she heard her voice replying. "Oh, I love you, too!"

"The winter is over, May. You must forgive the hallucinations of a sick man."

She woke to see Daniel's fair, pale head bending toward her. "He is old! He is ill!" she thought, but through her tears, to deceive him one last time, she cried, "Oh, thank God, Daniel!"

He was feeling cold and wakeful and he asked her to make him a cup of tea; before she left the room, he kissed her hands and arms and said, "If I am ever sick again, don't leave me, May."

Downstairs, in the kitchen, cold with shadows and with the obtrusion of dawn, she was belabored by a chill. "What time is it?" she said aloud, although she did not care. She remembered, not for any reason, a day when she and Daniel had stood in the yard last October wondering whether they should cover the chimneys that would not be used and he decided that they should not, but he had said, "I hope no birds get trapped." She had replied, "I thought they all left at about this time for the South," and he had answered, with an unintelligible reproach in his voice, "The starlings stay." And she remembered, again for no reason, a day when, in pride and excitement, she had burst into the house crying, "I saw an ermine. It was terribly poised and let me watch it quite a while." He had said categorically, "There are no ermines here."

She had not protested; she had sighed as she sighed now and turned to the window. The sleigh was livid in this light and no one was in it; nor had anyone been in it for many years. But at that moment the blacksmith's cat came guardedly across the dewy field and climbed into it, as if by careful plan, and curled up on the seat. May prodded the clinkers in the stove and started to the barn for kindling. But she thought of the cold and the damp and the smell of the horses, and she did not go but stood there, holding the poker and leaning upon it as if it were an umbrella. There was no place warm to go. "What time is it?" she whimpered, heartbroken, and moved the poker, stroking the lion foot of the fireless stove.

She knew now that no change would come, and that she would never see her lover again. Confounded utterly, like an orphan in solitary confinement, she went outdoors and got into the sleigh. The blacksmith's imperturbable cat stretched and rearranged his position, and May sat beside him with her hands locked tightly in her lap, rapidly wondering over and over again how she would live the rest of her life.

Paule Marshall

Brooklyn

Although she was born and raised in Brooklyn, Paule Marshall is a second-generation American of Barbadian descent. Since graduating with honors from Brooklyn College in 1953, she has worked as a librarian and as a feature writer for Our World. *The recipient of a number of grants, among them a Guggenheim fellowship and a Rosenthal Award from the National Institute of Arts and Letters, Paule Marshall has published two novels,* Brown Girl, Brownstones *(1959) and* The Chosen Place, The Timeless People *(1970), and a collection of four long stories,* Soul Clap Hands and Sing *(1961). Ms. Marshall presently lives in New York City.*

A summer wind, soaring just before it died, blew the dusk and the first scattered lights of downtown Brooklyn against the shut windows of the classroom, but Professor Max Berman—B.A., 1919, M.A., 1921, New York; Docteur de l'Université, 1930, Paris—alone in the room, did not bother to open the windows to the cooling wind. The heat and airlessness of the room, the perspiration inching its way like an ant around his starched collar were discomforts he enjoyed; they obscured his larger discomfort: the anxiety which chafed his heart and tugged his left eyelid so that he seemed to be winking, roguishly, behind his glasses.

To steady his eye and ease his heart, to fill the time until his students arrived and his first class in years began, he reached for his cigarettes. As always he delayed lighting the cigarette so that his need for it would be greater and, thus, the relief and pleasure it would bring fuller. For some time he fondled it, his fingers shaping soft, voluptuous gestures, his warped old man's hands looking strangely abandoned on the bare desk and limp as if the bones had been crushed, and so white—except for the tobacco burn on the index and third fingers—it seemed his blood no longer traveled that far.

He lit the cigarette finally and as the smoke swelled his lungs, his eyelid stilled and his lined face lifted, the plume of white hair wafting above his narrow brow; his body—short, blunt, the shoulders slightly bent as if in deference to his sixty-three-years—settled back in his chair. Delicately Max Berman crossed his legs and, looking down, examined his shoes for dust. (The shoes were of a very soft, fawn-colored leather and somewhat foppishly pointed at the toe. They had been custom made in France and were his one last indulgence. He wore them in memory of his first wife, a French Jewess from Alsace-Lorraine whom he had met in Paris while lingering over his doctorate and married to avoid returning home. She had been gay, mindless and very excitable—but at night, she had also been capable of a profound stillness as she lay in bed waiting for him to turn to her, and this had always awed and delighted him. She had been a gift—and her death in a car accident had been a judgment on him for never having loved her, for never, indeed, having even allowed her to matter.) Fastidiously Max Berman unbuttoned his jacket and straightened his vest, which had a stain two decades old on the pocket. Through the smoke his veined eyes contemplated other, more pleasurable scenes. With his neatly shod foot swinging and his cigarette at a rakish tilt, he might have been an old *boulevardier* taking the sun and an absinthe before the afternoon's assignation.

A young face, the forehead shiny with earnestness, hung at the half-opened door. "Is this French Lit, fifty-four? Camus and Sartre?"

Max Berman winced at the rawness of the voice and the flat "a" in Sartre and said formally, "This is Modern French Literature, number fifty-four, yes, but there is some question as to whether we will take up Messieurs Camus and Sartre this session. They might prove hot work for a summer-evening course. We will probably do Gide and Mauriac, who are considerably more temperate. But come in nonetheless. . . ."

He was the gallant, half rising to bow her to a seat. He knew that she would select the one in the front row directly opposite his desk. At the bell her pen would quiver above her blank notebook, ready to commit his first word—indeed, the clearing of his throat—to paper, and her thin buttocks would begin sidling toward the edge of her chair.

His eyelid twitched with solicitude. He wished that he could have drawn the lids over her fitful eyes and pressed a cool hand to her forehead. She reminded him of what he had been several lifetimes ago: a boy with a pale, plump face and harried eyes, running from the occasional taunts at his yamilke along the shrill streets of Brownsville in Brooklyn, impeded by the heavy satchel of books which he always carried as proof of his scholarship. He had been proud of his brilliance at school and the Yeshiva, but at the same time he had been secretly troubled by it and resentful, for he could never believe that he had come by it naturally or that it belonged to him alone. Rather, it was like a heavy medal his father had hung around his neck—the chain bruising his flesh—and constantly exhorted him to wear proudly and use well.

The girl gave him an eager and ingratiating smile and he looked away. During his thirty years of teaching, a face similar to hers had crowded his vision whenever he had looked up from a desk. Perhaps it was fitting, he thought, and lighted another cigarette from the first, that she should be present as he tried again at life, unaware that behind his rimless glasses and within his ancient suit, he had been gutted.

He thought of those who had taken the last of his substance—and smiled tolerantly. "The boys of summer," he called them, his inquisitors, who had flailed him with a single question: "Are you now or have you ever been a member of the Communist party?" Max Berman had never taken their question seriously—perhaps because he had never taken his membership in the party seriously—and he had refused to answer. What had disturbed him, though, even when the investigation was over, was the feeling that he had really been under investigation for some other offense which did matter and of which he was guilty; that behind their accusations and charges had lurked another which had not been political but personal. For had he been disloyal to the government? His denial was a short, hawking laugh. Simply, he had never ceased being religious. When his father's God had become useless and even a little embarrassing, he had sought others: his work for a time, then the party. But he had been middle-aged when he joined and his faith, which had been so full as a boy, had grown thin. He had come, by then, to distrust all pieties, so that when the purges in Russia during the thirties confirmed his distrust, he had withdrawn into a modest cynicism.

But he had been made to answer for that error. Ten years later his inquisitors had flushed him out from the small community college in upstate New York where he had taught his classes from the same neat pack of notes each semester and had bandied his name at the hearings until he had been dismissed from his job.

He remembered looking back at the pyres of burning autumn leaves on the campus his last day and feeling that another lifetime had ended—for he had always thought of his life as divided into many small lives, each with its own beginning and end. Like a hired mute, he had been present at each dying and kept the wake and wept professionally as the bier was lowered into the ground.

Because of this feeling, he told himself that his final death would be anticlimactic.

After his dismissal he had continued living in the small house he had built near the college, alone except for an occasional visit from a colleague, idle but for some tutoring in French, content with the income he received from the property his parents had left him in Brooklyn—until the visits and tutoring had tapered off and a silence had begun to choke the house, like weeds springing up around a deserted place. He had begun to wonder then if he were still alive. He would wake at night from the recurrent dream of the hearings, where he was being accused of unstated crime, to listen for his heart, his hand fumbling among the bedclothes to press the place. During the day he would pass repeatedly in front of the mirror with the pretext that he might have forgotten to shave that morning or that something had blown into his eye. Above all, he had begun to think of his inquisitors with affection and to long for the sound of their voices. They, at least, had assured him of being alive.

As if seeking them out, he had returned to Brooklyn and to the house in Brownsville where he had lived as a boy and had boldly applied for a teaching post without mentioning the investigation. He had finally been offered the class which would begin in five minutes. It wasn't much: a six-week course in the summer evening session of a college without a rating, where classes were held in a converted factory building, a college whose campus took in the bargain department stores, the five-and-dime emporiums and neon-spangled movie houses of downtown Brooklyn.

Through the smoke from his cigarette, Max Berman's eyes—a waning blue that never seemed to focus on any one thing—drifted over the students who had gathered meanwhile. Imbuing them was his own disinterest, he believed that even before the class began, most of them were longing for its end and already anticipating the soft drinks at the soda fountain downstairs and the synthetic dramas at the nearby movie.

They made him sad. He would have liked to lead them like a Pied Piper back to the safety of their childhoods—all of them: the loud girl with the formidable calves of an athlete who reminded him, uncomfortably, of his second wife (a party member who was always shouting political heresy from some picket line and who had promptly divorced him upon discovering his irreverence); the two sallow-faced young men leaning out the window as if searching for the wind that had died; the slender young woman with crimped black hair who sat very still and apart from the others, her face turned toward the night sky as if to a friend.

Her loneliness interested him. He sensed its depth and his eye paused. He saw then that she was a Negro, a very pale mulatto with skin the color of clear, polished amber and a thin, mild face. She was somewhat older than the others in the room—a schoolteacher from the South, probably, who came north each summer to take courses toward a graduate degree. He felt a fleeting discomfort and irritation: discomfort at the thought that although he had been sinned against as a Jew he still shared in the sin against her and suffered from the same vague guilt, irritation that she recalled his own humiliations: the large ones, such as the fact that despite his brilliance he had been unable to get into medical school as a young man because of the quota on Jews (not that he had wanted to be a doctor; that had been his father's wish) and had changed his studies from medicine to French; the small ones which had worn him thin: an eye widening imperceptibly as he gave his name, the savage glance which sought the Jewishness in his nose, his chin, in the set of his shoulders, the jokes snuffed into silence at his appearance. . . .

Tired suddenly, his eyelid pulsing, he turned and stared out the window at the gaudy constellation of neon lights. He longed for a drink, a quiet place and then sleep. And to bear him gently into sleep, to stay the terror which bound his heart then reminding him of those oleographs of Christ with thorns binding his exposed heart—fat drops of blood from one so bloodless—to usher him into sleep, some pleasantly erotic image: a nude in a boudoir scattered with her frilled garments and warmed by her frivolous laugh, with the sun like a voyeur at the half-closed shutters. But this time instead of the usual Rubens nude with thighs like twin portals and a belly like a huge alabaster bowl into which he poured himself, he chose Gauguin's Aita Parari, his languorous form in the straight-back chair, her dark, sloping breasts, her eyes like the sun under shadow.

With the image still on his inner eye, he turned to the Negro girl and appraised her through a blind of cigarette smoke. She was still gazing out at the night sky and something about her fixed stare, her hands stiffly arranged in her lap, the nerve fluttering within the curve of her throat, betrayed a vein of tension within the rock of her calm. It was as if she had fled long ago to a remote region within herself, taking with her all that was most valuable and most vulnerable about herself.

She stirred finally, her slight breasts lifting beneath her flowered summer dress as she breathed deeply—and Max Berman thought again of Gauguin's girl with the dark, sloping breasts. What would this girl with the amber-colored skin be like on a couch in a sunlit room, nude in a straight-back chair? And as the question echoed along each nerve and stilled his breathing, it seemed suddenly that life, which had scorned him for so long, held out her hand again—but still a little beyond his reach. Only the girl, he sensed, could bring him close enough to touch it. She alone was the bridge. So that even while he repeated to himself that he was being presumptuous (for she would surely refuse him) and ridiculous (for even if she did not, what could he do—his performance would be a mere scramble and twitch), he vowed at the same time to have her. The challenge eased the tightness around his heart suddenly; it soothed the damaged muscle of his eye and as the bell rang he rose and said briskly, "Ladies and gentlemen, may I have your attention, please. My name is Max Berman. The course is Modern French Literature, number fifty-four. May I suggest that you check your program cards to see whether you are in the right place at the right time."

Her essay on Gide's *The Immoralist* lay on his desk and the note from the administration informing him, first, that his past political activities had been brought to their attention and then dismissing him at the end of the session weighed the inside pocket of his jacket. The two, her paper and the note, were linked in his mind. Her paper reminded him that the vow he had taken was still an empty one, for the term was half over and he had never once spoken to her (as if she understood his intention she was always late and disappeared as soon as the closing bell rang, leaving him trapped in a clamorous circle of students around his desk), while the note which wrecked his small attempt to start anew suddenly made that vow more urgent. It gave him the edge of desperation he needed to act finally. So that as soon as the bell rang, he returned all the papers but hers, announced that all questions would have to wait until their next meeting and, waving off the students from his desk, called above their protests, "Miss Williams, if you have a moment, I'd like to speak with you briefly about your paper."

She approached his desk like a child who has been cautioned not to talk to strangers, her fingers touching the backs of the chair as if for support, her gaze following the departing students as though she longed to accompany them.

Her slight apprehensiveness pleased him. It suggested a submissiveness which gave him, as he rose uncertainly, a feeling of certainty and command. Her hesitancy was somehow in keeping with the color of her skin. She seemed to bring not only herself but the host of black women whose bodies had been despoiled to make her. He would not only possess her but them also, he thought (not really thought, for he scarcely allowed these thoughts to form before he snuffed them out). Through their collective suffering, which she contained, his own personal suffering would be eased; he would be pardoned for whatever sin it was he had committed against life.

"I hope you weren't unduly alarmed when I didn't return your paper along with the others," he said, and had to look up as she reached the desk. She was taller close up and her eyes, which he had thought were black, were a strong, flecked brown with very small pupils which seemed to shrink now from the sight of him. "But I found it so interesting I wanted to give it to you privately."

"I didn't know what to think," she said, and her voice—he heard it for the first time for she never recited or answered in class—was low, cautious, Southern.

"It was, to say the least, refreshing. It not only showed some original and mature thinking on your part, but it also proved that you've been listening in class—and after twenty-five years and more of teaching it's encouraging to find that some students do listen. If you have a little time I'd like to tell you, more specifically, what I liked about it. . . ."

Talking easily, reassuring her with his professional tone and a deft gesture with his cigarette, he led her from the room as the next class filed in, his hand cupped at her elbow but not touching it, his manner urbane, courtly, kind. They paused on the landing at the end of the long corridor with the stairs piled in steel tiers above and plunging below them. An intimate silence swept up the stairwell in a warm gust and Max Berman said, "I'm curious. Why did you choose *The Immoralist?*"

She started suspiciously, afraid, it seemed, that her answer might expose and endanger the self she guarded so closely within.

"Well," she said finally, her glance reaching down the stairs to the door marked EXIT at the bottom, "when you said we could use anything by Gide I decided on *The Immoralist,* since it was the first book I read in the original French when I was in undergraduate school. I didn't understand it then because my French was so weak, I guess, but I always thought about it afterward for some odd reason. I was shocked by what I did understand, of course, but something else about it appealed to me, so when you made the assignment I thought I'd try reading it again. I understood it a little better this time. At least I think so. . . ."

"Your paper proves you did."

She smiled absently, intent on some other thought. Then she said cautiously, but with unexpected force, "You see, to me, the book seems to say that the only way you begin to know what you are and how much you are capable of is by daring to try something which tests you. . . ."

"Something bold," he said.

"Yes."

"Even sinful."

She paused, questioning this, and then said reluctantly, "Yes, perhaps even sinful."

"The salutary effects of sin, you might say." He gave the little bow.

But she had not heard this; her mind had already leaped ahead. "The only trouble, at least with the character in Gide's book, is that what he finds out about himself is so terrible. He is so unhappy. . . ."

"But at least he knows, poor sinner." And his playful tone went unnoticed.

"Yes," she said with the same startling forcefulness. "And another thing, in finding out what he is, he destroys his wife. It was as if she had to die in order for him to live and know himself. Perhaps in order for a person to live and know himself somebody else must die. Maybe there's always a balancing out. . . . In a way"—and he had to lean close now to hear her—"I believe this."

Max Berman edged back as he glimpsed something move within her abstracted gaze. It was like a strong and restless seed that had taken root in the darkness there and was straining now toward the light. He had not expected so subtle and complex a force beneath her mild exterior and he found it disturbing and dangerous, but fascinating.

"Well, it's a most interesting interpretation," he said. "I don't know if M. Gide would have agreed, but then he's not around to give his opinion. Tell me, where did you do your undergraduate work?"

"At Howard University."

"And you majored in French?"

"Yes."

"Why, if I may ask?" he said gently.

"Well, my mother was from New Orleans and could still speak a little Creole and I got interested in learning how to speak French through her, I guess. I teach it now at a junior high school in Richmond. Only the beginner courses because I don't have my master's. You know, *je vais, tu vas, il va* and *Frère Jacques*. It's not very inspiring."

"You should do something about that then, my dear Miss Williams. Perhaps it's time for you, like our friend in Gide, to try something new and bold."

"I know," she said, and her pale hand sketched a vague, despairing gesture. "I thought maybe if I got my master's . . . that's why I decided to come north this summer and start taking some courses. . . ."

Max Berman quickly lighted a cigarette to still the flurry inside him, for the moment he had been awaiting had come. He flicked her paper, which he still held. "Well, you've got the makings of a master's thesis right here. If you like I will suggest some ways for you to expand it sometime. A few pointers from an old pro might help."

He had to turn from her astonished and grateful smile—it was like a child's. He said carefully, "The only problem will be to find a place where we can talk quietly. Regrettably, I don't rate an office. . . ."

"Perhaps we could use one of the empty classrooms," she said.

"That would be much too dismal a setting for a pleasant discussion."

He watched the disappointment wilt her smile and when he spoke he made certain that the same disappointment weighed his voice. "Another difficulty is that the term's half over, which gives us little or no time. But let's not give up. Perhaps we can arrange to meet and talk over a weekend. The only hitch there is that I spend weekends at my place in the country. Of course you're perfectly welcome to come up there. It's only about seventy miles from New York, in the heart of what's very appropriately called the Borsch Circuit, even though, thank God, my place is a good distance away from the borsch. That is, it's very quiet and there's never anybody around except with my permission."

She did not move, yet she seemed to start; she made no sound, yet he thought he heard a bewildered cry. And then she did a strange thing, standing there with the breath sucked into the hollow of her throat and her smile, that had opened to him with such trust, dying—her eyes, her hands faltering up begged him to declare himself.

"There's a lake near the house," he said, "so that when you get tired of talking—or better, listening to me talk—you can take a swim, if you like. I would very much enjoy that sight." And as the nerve tugged at his eyelid, he seemed to wink behind his rimless glasses.

Her sudden, blind step back was like a man groping his way through a strange room in the dark, and instinctively Max Berman reached out to break her fall. Her arms, bare to the shoulder because of the heat (he knew the feel of her skin without even touching it—it would be like rich, fine-textured cloth which would sooth and hide him in its amber warmth), struck out once to drive him off and then fell limp at her side, and her eyes became vivid and convulsive in her numbed face. She strained toward the stairs and the exit door at the bottom, but she could not move. Nor could she speak. She did not even cry. Her eyes remained dry and dull with disbelief. Only her shoulders trembled as though she was silently weeping inside.

It was as though she had never learned the forms and expressions of anger. The outrage of a lifetime, of her history, was trapped inside her. And she stared at Max Berman with this mute, paralyzing rage. Not really at him but to his side, as if she caught sight of others behind him. And remembering how he had imagined a column of dark women trailing her to his desk, he sensed that she glimpsed a legion of old men with sere flesh and lonely eyes flanking him: "old lechers with a love on every wind . . ."

"I'm sorry, Miss Williams," he said, and would have welcomed her insults, for he would have been able, at least, to distill from them some passion and a kind of intimacy. It would have been, in a way, like touching her. "It was only that you are a very attractive young woman and although I'm no longer young"—and he gave the tragic little laugh which sought to dismiss that fact—"I can still appreciate and even desire an attractive woman. But I was wrong. . . ." His self-disgust, overwhelming him finally, choked off his voice. "And so very crude. Forgive me. I can offer no excuse for my behavior other than my approaching senility."

He could not even manage the little marionette bow this time. Quickly he shoved the paper on Gide into her lifeless hand, but it fell, the pages separating, and as he hurried past her downstairs and out the door, he heard the pages scattering like dead leaves on the steps.

She remained away until the night of the final examination, which was also the last meeting of the class. By that time Max Berman, believing that she would not return, had almost succeeded in forgetting her. He was no longer even certain of how she looked, for her face had been absorbed into the single, blurred, featureless face of all the women who had ever refused him. So that she startled him as much as a stranger would have when he entered the room that night and found her alone amid a maze of empty chairs, her face turned toward the window as on the first night and her hands serene in her lap. She turned at his footstep and it was as if she had also forgotten all that had passed between them. She waited until he said, "I'm glad you decided to take the examination. I'm sure you won't have any difficulty with it"; then she gave him a nod that was somehow reminiscent of his little bow and turned again to the window.

He was relieved yet puzzled by her composure. It was as if during the three-week absence she had waged and won a decisive contest with herself and was ready now to act. He was wary suddenly and all during the examination he tried to discover what lay behind her strange calm, studying her bent head amid the shifting heads of the other students, her slim hand guiding the pen across the page, her legs—the long bone visible, it seemed, beneath the flesh. Desire flared and quickly died.

"Excuse me, Professor Berman, will you take up Camus and Sartre next semester, maybe?" The girl who sat in front of his desk was standing over him with her earnest smile and finished examination folder.

"That might prove somewhat difficult, since I won't be here."

"No more?"

"No."

"I mean, not even next summer?"

"I doubt it."

"Gee, I'm sorry. I mean, I enjoyed the course and everything."

He bowed his thanks and held his head down until she left. Her compliment, so piteous somehow, brought on the despair he had forced to the dim rear of his mind. He could no longer flee the thought of the exile awaiting him when the class tonight ended. He could either remain in the house in Brooklyn, where the memory of his father's face above the radiance of the Sabbath candles haunted him from the shadows, reminding him of the certainty he had lost and never found again, where the mirrors in his father's room were still shrouded with sheets, as on the day he lay dying and moaning into his beard that his only son was a bad Jew; or he could return to the house in the country, to the silence shrill with loneliness.

The cigarette he was smoking burned his fingers, rousing him, and he saw over the pile of examination folders on his desk that the room was empty except for the Negro girl. She had finished—her pen lay aslant the closed folder on her desk—but she had remained in her seat and she was smiling across the room at him—a set, artificial smile that was both cold and threatening. It utterly denuded him and he was wildly angry suddenly that she had seen him give way to despair; he wanted to remind her (he could not stay the thought; it attacked him like an assailant from a dark turn in his mind) that she was only black after all. . . . His head dropped and he almost wept with shame.

The girl stiffened as if she had seen the thought and then the tiny muscles around her mouth quickly arranged the bland smile. She came up to his desk, placed her folder on top of the others and said pleasantly, her eyes like dark, shattered glass that spared Max Berman his reflection, "I've changed my mind. I think I'd like to spend a day at your place in the country if your invitation still holds."

He thought of refusing her, for her voice held neither promise nor passion, but he could not. Her presence, even if it was only for a day, would make his return easier. And there was still the possibility of passion despite her cold manner and the deliberate smile. He thought of how long it had been since he had had someone, of how badly he needed the sleep which followed love and of awakening certain, for the first time in years, of his existence.

"Of course the invitation still holds. I'm driving up tonight."

"I won't be able to come until Sunday," she said firmly. "Is there a train then?"

"Yes, in the morning," he said, and gave her the schedule.

"You'll meet me at the station?"

"Of course. You can't miss my car. It's a very shabby but venerable Chevy."

She smiled stiffly and left, her heels awakening the silence of the empty corridor, the sound reaching back to tap like a warning finger on Max Berman's temple.

The pale sunlight slanting through the windshield lay like a cat on his knees, and the motor of his old Chevy, turning softly under him could have been the humming of its heart. A little distance from the car a log-cabin station house—the logs blackened by the seasons—stood alone against the hills, and the hills, in turn, lifted softly, still green although the summer was ending, into the vague autumn sky.

The morning mist and pale sun, the green that was still somehow new, made it seem that the season was stirring into life even as it died, and this contradiction pained Max Berman at the same time that it pleased him. For it was his own contradiction after all: his desires which remained those of a young man even as he was dying.

He had been parked for some time in the deserted station, yet his hands were still tensed on the steering wheel and his foot hovered near the accelerator. As soon as he had arrived in the station he had wanted to leave. But like the girl that night on the landing, he was too stiff with tension to move. He could only wait, his eyelid twitching with foreboding, regret, curiosity and hope.

Finally and with no warning the train charged through the fiery green, setting off a tremor underground. Max Berman imagined the girl seated at a window in the train, her hands arranged quietly in her lap and her gaze scanning the hills that were so familiar to him, and yet he could not believe that she was really there. Perhaps her plan had been to disappoint him. She might be in New York or on her way back to Richmond now, laughing at the trick she had played on him. He was convinced of this suddenly, so that even when he saw her walking toward him through the blown steam from under the train, he told himself that she was a mirage created by the steam. Only when she sat beside him in the car, bringing with her, it seemed, an essence she had distilled from the morning air and rubbed into her skin, was he certain of her reality.

"I brought my bathing suit but it's much too cold to swim," she said and gave him the deliberate smile.

He did not see it; he only heard her voice, its warm Southern lilt in the chill, its intimacy in the closed car—and an excitement swept him, cold first and then hot, as if the sun had burst in his blood.

"It's the morning air," he said. "By noon it should be like summer again."

"Is that a promise?"

"Yes."

By noon the cold morning mist had lifted above the hills and below, in the lake valley, the sunlight was a sheer gold net spread out on the grass as if to dry, draped on the trees and flung, glinting, over the lake. Max Berman felt it brush his shoulders gently as he sat by the lake waiting for the girl, who had gone up to the house to change into her swimsuit.

He had spent the morning showing her the fields and small wood near his house. During the long walk he had been careful to keep a little apart from her. He would extend a hand as they climbed a rise or when she stepped uncertainly over a rock, but he would not really touch her. He was afraid that at his touch, no matter how slight and casual, her scream would spiral into the morning calm, or worse, his touch would unleash the threatening thing he sensed behind her even smile.

He had talked of her paper and she had listened politely and occasionally even asked a question or made a comment. But all the while detached, distant, drawn within herself as she had been that first night in the classroom. And then halfway down a slope she had paused and, pointing to the canvas tops of her white sneakers, which had become wet and dark from the dew secreted in the grass, she had laughed. The sound, coming so abruptly in the midst of her tense quiet, joined her, it seemed, to the wood and wide fields, to the hills; she shared their simplicity and held within her the same strong current of life. Max Berman had felt privileged suddenly, and humble. He had stopped questioning her smile. He had told himself then that it would not matter even if she stopped and picking up a rock bludgeoned him from behind.

"There's a lake near my home, but it's not like this," the girl said, coming up behind him. "Yours is so dark and serious-looking."

He nodded and followed her gaze out to the lake, where the ripples were long, smooth welts raised by the wind, and across to the other bank, where a group of birches stepped delicately down to the lake and bending over touched the water with their branches as if testing it before they plunged.

The girl came and stood beside him now—and she was like a pale-gold naiad, the spirit of the lake, her eyes reflecting its somber autumnal tone and her body as supple as the birches. She walked slowly into the water, unaware, it seemed, of the sudden passion in his gaze, or perhaps uncaring; and as she walked she held out her arms in what seemed a gesture of invocation (and Max Berman remembered his father with the fringed shawl draped on his outstretched arms as he invoked their God each Sabbath with the same gesture); her head was bent as if she listened for a voice beneath the water's murmurous surface. When the ground gave way she still seemed to be walking and listening, her arms outstretched. The water reached her waist, her small breasts, her shoulders. She lifted her head once, breathed deeply and disappeared.

She stayed down for a long time and when her white cap finally broke the water some distance out, Max Berman felt strangely stranded and deprived. He understood suddenly the profound cleavage between them and the absurdity of his hope. The water between them became the years which separated them. Her white cap was the sign of her purity, while the silt darkening the lake was the flotsam of his failures. Above all, their color—her arms a pale, flashing gold in the sunlit water and his bled white and flaccid with the veins like angry blue penciling—marked the final barrier.

He was sad as they climbed toward the house late that afternoon and troubled. A crow cawed derisively in the bracken, heralding the dusk which would not only end their strange day but would also, he felt, unveil her smile, so that he would learn the reason for her coming. And because he was sad, he said wryly, "I think I should tell you that you've been spending the day with something of an outcast."

"Oh," she said and waited.

He told her of the dismissal, punctuating his words with the little hoarse, deprecating laugh and waving aside the pain with his cigarette. She listened, polite but neutral, and because she remained unmoved, he wanted to confess all the more. So that during dinner and afterward when they sat outside on the porch, he told her of the investigation.

"It was very funny once you saw it from the proper perspective, which I did, of course," he said. "I mean here they were accusing me of crimes I couldn't remember committing and asking me for the names of people with whom I had never associated. It was pure farce. But I made a mistake. I should have done something dramatic or something just as farcical. Bared my breast in the public market place or written a tome on my apostasy, naming names. It would have been a far different story then. Instead of my present ignominy. I would have been offered a chairmanship at Yale. . . . No? Well, Brandeis then. I would have been draped in honorary degrees. . . ."

"Well, why didn't you confess?" she said impatiently.

"I've often asked myself the same interesting question, but I haven't come up with a satisfactory answer yet. I suspect, though, that I said nothing because none of it really mattered that much."

"What did matter?" she asked sharply.

He sat back, waiting for the witty answer, but none came, because just then the frame upon which his organs were strung seemed to snap and he felt his heart, his lungs, his vital parts fall in a heap within him. Her question had dealt the severing blow, for it was the same question he understood suddenly that the vague forms in his dream asked repeatedly. It had been the plaintive undercurrent to his father's dying moan, the real accusation behind the charges of his inquisitors at the hearing.

For what had mattered? He gazed through his sudden shock at the night squatting on the porch steps, at the hills asleep like gentle beasts in the darkness, at the black screen of the sky where the events of his life passed in a mute, accusing review—and he saw nothing there to which he had given himself or in which he had truly believed since the belief and dedication of his boyhood.

"Did you hear my question?" she asked, and he was glad that he sat within the shadows clinging to the porch screen and could not be seen.

"Yes, I did," he said faintly, and his eyelid twitched. "But I'm afraid it's another one of those I can't answer satisfactorily." And then he struggled for the old flippancy. "You make an excellent examiner, you know. Far better than my inquisitors."

"What will you do now?" Her voice and cold smile did not spare him.

He shrugged and the motion, a slow, eloquent lifting of the shoulders, brought with it suddenly the weight and memory of his boyhood. It was the familiar gesture of the women hawkers in Belmont Market, of the men standing outside the temple on Saturday mornings, each of them reflecting his image of God in their forbidding black coats and with the black, tumbling beards in which he had always imagined he could hide as in a forest. All this had mattered, he called loudly to himself, and said aloud to the girl, "Let me see if I can answer this one at least. What *will* I do?" He paused and swung his leg so that his foot in the fastidious French shoe caught the light from the house. "Grow flowers and write my memoirs. How's that? That would be the proper way for a gentleman and scholar to retire. Or hire one of those hefty housekeepers who will bully me and when I die in my sleep draw the sheet over my face and call my lawyer. That's somewhat European, but how's that?"

When she said nothing for a long time, he added soberly, "But that's not a fair question for me any more. I leave all such considerations to the young. To you, for that matter. What will you do, my dear Miss Williams?"

It was as if she had been expecting the question and had been readying her answer all the time that he had been talking. She leaned forward eagerly and with her face and part of her body fully in the light, she said, "I will do something. I don't know what yet, but something."

Max Berman started back a little. The answer was so unlike her vague, resigned "I know" on the landing that night when he had admonished her to try something new.

He edged back into the darkness and she leaned further into the light, her eyes overwhelming her face and her mouth set in a thin, determined line. "I will do something," she said, bearing down on each word, "because for the first time in my life I feel almost brave."

He glimpsed this new bravery behind her hard gaze and sensed something vital and purposeful, precious, which she had found and guarded like a prize within her center. He wanted it. He would have liked to snatch it and run like a thief. He no longer desired her but it, and starting forward with a sudden envious cry, he caught her arm and drew her close, seeking it.

But he could not get to it. Although she did not pull away her arm, although she made no protest as his face wavered close to hers, he did not really touch her. She held herself and her prize out of his desperate reach and her smile was a knife she pressed to his throat. He saw himself for what he was in her clear, cold gaze: an old man with skin the color and texture of dough that had been kneaded by the years into tragic folds, with faded eyes adrift behind a pair of rimless glasses and the roughened flesh at his throat like a bird's wattles. And as the disgust which he read in her eyes swept him, his hand dropped from her arm. He started to murmur, "Forgive me . . ." when suddenly she caught hold of his wrist, pulling him close again, and he felt the strength which had borne her swiftly through the water earlier hold him now as she said quietly and without passion, "And do you know why, Dr. Berman, I feel almost brave today? Because ever since I can remember my parents were always telling me, "Stay away from white folks. Just leave them alone. You mind your business and they'll mind theirs. Don't go near them.' And they made sure I didn't. My father, who was the principal of a colored grade school in Richmond, used to drive me to and from school every day. When I needed something from downtown my mother would take me and if the white saleslady asked me anything she would answer. . . .

"And my parents were also always telling me, "Stay away from niggers,' and that meant anybody darker than we were." She held out her arm in the light and Max Berman saw the skin almost as white as his but for the subtle amber shading. Staring at the arm she said tragically, "I was so confused I never really went near anybody. Even when I went away to college I kept to myself. I didn't marry the man I wanted to because he was dark and I knew my parents would disapprove. . . ." She paused, her wistful gaze searching the darkness for the face of the man she had refused, it seemed, and not finding it she went on sadly, "So after graduation I returned home and started teaching and I was just as confused and frightened and ashamed as always. When my parents died I went on the same way. And I would have gone on like that the rest of my life if it hadn't been for you, Dr. Berman"—and the sarcasm leaped behind her cold smile. "In a way you did me a favor. You let me know how you—and most of the people like you—see me."

"My dear Miss Williams, I assure you I was not attracted to you because you were colored. . . ." And he broke off, remembering just how acutely aware of her color he had been.

"I'm not interested in your reasons!" she said brutally. "What matters is what it meant to me. I thought about this these last three weeks and about my parents—how wrong they had been, how frightened, and the terrible thing they had done to me . . . And I wasn't confused any longer." Her head lifted, tremulous with her new assurance. "I can do something now! I can begin," she said with her head poised. "Look how I came all the way up here to tell you this to your face. Because how could you harm me? You're so old you're like a cup I could break in my hand." And her hand tightened on his wrist, wrenching the last of his frail life from him, it seemed. Through the quick pain he remembered her saying on the landing that night: "Maybe in order for a person to live someone else must die" and her quiet "I believe this" then. Now her sudden laugh, an infinitely cruel sound in the warm night, confirmed her belief.

Suddenly she was the one who seemed old, indeed ageless. Her touch became mortal and Max Berman saw the darkness that would end his life gathered in her eyes. But even as he sprang back, jerking his arm away, a part of him rushed forward to embrace that darkness, and his cry, wounding the night, held both ecstasy and terror.

"That's all I came for," she said rising. " You can drive me to the station now."

They drove to the station in silence. Then, just as the girl started from the car, she turned with an ironic, pitiless smile and said, "You know, it's been a nice day, all things considered. It really turned summer again as you said it would. And even though your lake isn't anything like the one near my home, it's almost as nice."

Max Berman bowed to her for the last time, accepting with that gesture his responsibility for her rage, which went deeper than his, and for her anger, which would spur her finally to live. And not only for her, but for all those at last whom he had wronged through his indifference: his father lying in the room of shrouded mirrors, the wives he had never loved, his work which he had never believed in enough and, lastly (even though he knew it was too late and he would not be spared), himself.

Too weary to move, he watched the girl cross to the train which would bear her south, her head lifted as though she carried life as lightly there as if it were a hat made of tulle. When the train departed his numbed eyes followed it until its rear light was like a single firefly in the immense night or the last flickering of his life. Then he drove back through the darkness.

D.H. Lawrence

Odour of Chrysanthemums

All through the 1920's, D. H. Lawrence and his wife Frieda moved incessantly, seeking a community where he could feel a vital connection with natural life. After brief periods in Ceylon, Australia, the United States, and Mexico, they returned finally to a village outside Florence, Italy, and there he wrote his last novel, Lady Chatterley's Lover *(1928). Two years later, in the south of France, D. H. Lawrence died of tuberculosis at the age of 44. Always a prodigious worker, Lawrence wrote nearly fifty books in his lifetime, achieving recognition not only as a novelist and short story writer, but also as a poet, essayist, and literary critic.*

1

The small locomotive engine, Number 4, came clanking, stumbling down from Selston with seven full wagons. It appeared round the corner with loud threats of speed, but the colt that it startled from among the gorse, which still flickered indistinctly in the raw afternoon, out-distanced it at a canter. A woman, walking up the railway line to Underwood, drew back into the hedge, held her basket aside, and watched the footplate of the engine advancing. The trucks thumped heavily past, one by one, with slow inevitable movement, as she stood insignificantly trapped between the jolting black wagons and the hedge; then they curved away towards the coppice where the withered oak leaves dropped noiselessly, while the birds, pulling at the scarlet hips beside the track, made off into the dusk that had already crept into the spinney. In the open, the smoke from the engine sank and cleaved to the rough grass. The fields were dreary and forsaken, and in the marshy strip that led to the whimsey, a reedy pit-pond, the fowls had already abandoned their run among the alders, to roost in the tarred fowl-house. The pit-bank loomed up beyond the pond, flames like red sores licking its ashy sides, in the afternoon's stagnant light. Just beyond rose the tapering chimneys and the clumsy black headstocks of Brinsley Colliery. The two wheels were spinning fast up against the sky, and the winding engine rapped out its little spasms. The miners were being turned up.

The engine whistled as it came into the wide bay of railway lines beside the colliery, where rows of trucks stood in harbor.

Miners, single, trailing and in groups, passed like shadows diverging home. At the edge of the ribbed level of sidings squat a low cottage, three steps down from the cinder track. A large bony vine clutched at the house, as if to claw down the tiled roof. Round the bricked yard grew a few wintry primroses. Beyond, the long garden sloped down to a bush-covered brook course. There were some twiggy apple trees, winter-crack trees, and ragged cabbages. Beside the path hung dishevelled pink chrysanthemums, like pink cloths hung on bushes. A woman came stooping out of the felt-covered fowl-house, half-way down the garden. She closed and padlocked the door, then drew herself erect, having brushed some bits from her white apron.

She was a tall woman of imperious mien, handsome, with definite black eyebrows. Her smooth black hair was parted exactly. For a few moments she stood steadily watching the miners as they passed along the railway: then she turned towards the brook course. Her face was calm and set, her mouth was closed with disillusionment. After a moment she called:

"John!" There was no answer. She waited, and then said distinctly:

"Where are you?"

"Here!" replied a child's sulky voice from among the bushes. The woman looked piercingly through the dusk.

"Are you at that brook?" she asked sternly.

For answer the child showed himself before the raspberry-canes that rose like whips. He was a small, sturdy boy of five. He stood quite still, defiantly.

"Oh!" said the mother, conciliated. "I thought you were down at that wet brook—and you remember what I told you——"

The boy did not move or answer.

"Come, come on in," she said more gently, "it's getting dark. There s your grandfather's engine coming down the line!"

The lad advanced slowly, with resentful, taciturn movement. He was dressed in trousers and waistcoat of cloth that was too thick and hard for the size of the garments. They were evidently cut down from a man's clothes.

As they went slowly towards the house he tore at the ragged wisps of chrysanthemums and dropped the petals in handfuls among the path.

"Don't do that—it does look nasty," said his mother. He refrained, and she, suddenly pitiful, broke off a twig with three or four wan flowers and held them against her face. When mother and son reached the yard her hand hesitated, and instead of laying the flower aside, she pushed it in her apron-band. The mother and son stood at the foot of the three steps looking across the bay of lines at the passing home of the miners. The trundle of the small train was imminent. Suddenly the engine loomed past the house and came to a stop opposite the gate.

The engine-driver, a short man with round grey beard, leaned out of the cab high above the woman.

"Have you got a cup of tea?" he said in a cheery, hearty fashion.

It was her father. She went in, saying she would mash. Directly, she returned.

"I didn't come to see you on Sunday," began the little grey-bearded man.

"I didn't expect you," said his daughter.

The engine-driver winced; then, reassuming his cheery, airy manner, he said:

"Oh, have you heard then? Well, and what do you think——?"

"I think it is soon enough," she replied.

At her brief censure the little man made an impatient gesture, and said coaxingly, yet with dangerous coldness:

"Well, what's a man to do? It's no sort of life for a man of my years, to sit at my own hearth like a stranger. And if I'm going to marry again it may as well be soon as late—what does it matter to anybody?"

The woman did not reply, but turned and went into the house. The man in the engine-cab stood assertive, till she returned with a cup of tea and a piece of bread and butter on a plate. She went up the steps and stood near the footplate of the hissing engine.

"You needn't 'a' brought me bread an' butter," said her father. "But a cup of tea"—he sipped appreciatively—"it's very nice." He sipped for a moment or two, then: "I hear as Walter's got another bout on," he said.

"When hasn't he?" said the woman bitterly.

"I heerd tell of him in the 'Lord Nelson' braggin' as he was going to spend that b——afore he went: half a sovereign that was."

"When?" asked the woman.

"A' Sat'day night—I know that's true."

"Very likely," she laughed bitterly. "He gives me twenty-three shillings."

"Aye, it's a nice thing, when a man can do nothing with his money but make a beast of himself!" said the grey-whiskered man. The woman turned her head away. Her father swallowed the last of his tea and handed her the cup.

"Aye," he sighed, wiping his mouth. "It's a settler, it is——"

He put his hand on the lever. The little engine strained and groaned, and the train rumbled towards the crossing. The woman again looked across the metals. Darkness was settling over the spaces of the railway and trucks: the miners, in grey sombre groups, were still passing home. The winding engine pulsed hurriedly, with brief pauses. Elizabeth Bates looked at the dreary flow of men, then she went indoors. Her husband did not come.

The kitchen was small and full of firelight; red coals piled glowing up the chimney mouth. All the life of the room seemed in the white, warm hearth and the steel fender reflecting the red fire. The cloth was laid for tea; cups glinted in the shadows. At the back, where the lowest stairs protruded into the room, the boy sat struggling with a knife and a piece of white wood. He was almost hidden in the shadow. It was half-past four. They had but to await the father's coming to begin tea. As the mother watched her son's sullen little struggle with the wood, she saw herself in his silence and pertinacity; she saw the father in her child's indifference to all but himself. She seemed to be occupied by her husband. He had probably gone past his home, slung past his own door, to drink before he came in, while his dinner spoiled and wasted in waiting. She glanced at the clock, then took the potatoes to strain them in the yard. The garden and fields beyond the brook were closed in uncertain darkness. When she rose with the saucepan, leaving the drain steaming into the night behind her, she saw the yellow lamps were lit along the high road that went up the hill away beyond the space of the railway lines and the field.

Then again she watched the men trooping home, fewer now and fewer.

Indoors the fire was sinking and the room was dark red. The woman put her saucepan on the hob, and set a batter-pudding near the mouth of the oven. Then she stood unmoving. Directly, gratefully, came quick young steps to the door. Someone hung on the latch a moment, then a little girl entered and began pulling off her outdoor things, dragging a mass of curls, just ripening from gold to brown, over her eyes with her hat.

Her mother chid her for coming late from school, and said she would have to keep her at home the dark winter days.

"Why, mother, it's hardly a bit dark yet. The lamp's not lighted, and my father's not home."

"No, he isn't. But it's a quarter to five! Did you see anything of him?"

The child became serious. She looked at her mother with large, wistful blue eyes.

"No, mother, I've never seen him. Why? Has he come up an' gone past, to Old Brinsley? He hasn't, mother, 'cos I never saw him."

"He'd watch that," said the mother bitterly, "he'd take care as you didn't see him. But you may depend upon it, he's seated in the 'Prince o' Wales.' He wouldn't be this late."

The girl looked at her mother piteously.

"Let's have our teas, mother, should we?" said she.

The mother called John to table. She opened the door once more and looked out across the darkness of the lines. All was deserted: she could not hear the winding-engines.

"Perhaps," she said to herself, "he's stopped to get some ripping done."

They sat down to tea. John, at the end of the table near the door, was almost lost in the darkness. Their faces were hidden from each other. The girl crouched against the fender slowly moving a thick piece of bread before the fire. The lad, his face a dusky mark on the shadow, sat watching her who was transfigured in the red glow.

"I do think it's beautiful to look in the fire," said the child.

"Do you?" said her mother. "Why?"

"It's so red, and full of little caves—and it feels so nice, and you can fair smell it."

"It'll want mending directly," replied her mother, "and then if your father comes he'll carry on and say there never is a fire when a man comes home sweating from the pit. A public-house is always warm enough."

There was silence till the boy said complainingly: "Make haste, our Annie."

"Well, I am doing! I can't make the fire do it no faster, can I?"

"She keeps wafflin' it about so's to make 'er slow," grumbled the boy.

"Don't have such an evil imagination, child," replied the mother.

Soon the room was busy in the darkness with the crisp sound of crunching. The mother ate very little. She drank her tea determinedly, and sat thinking. When she rose her anger was evident in the stern unbending of her head. She looked at the pudding in the fender, and broke out:

"It is a scandalous thing as a man can't even come home to his dinner! If it's crozzled up to a cinder I don't see why I should care. Past his very door he goes to get to a public-house, and here I sit with his dinner waiting for him——"

She went out. As she dropped piece after piece of coal on the red fire, the shadows fell on the walls, till the room was almost in total darkness.

"I canna see," grumbled the invisible John. In spite of herself, the mother laughed.

"You know the way to your mouth," she said. She set the dust-pan outside the door. When she came again like a shadow on the hearth, the lad repeated, complaining sulkily:

"I canna see."

"Good gracious!" cried the mother irritably, "you're as bad as your father if it's a bit dusk!"

Nevertheless, she took a paper spill from a sheaf on the mantelpiece and proceeded to light the lamp that hung from the ceiling in the middle of the room. As she reached up, her figure displayed itself just rounding with maternity.

"Oh, mother——!" exclaimed the girl.

"What?" said the woman, suspended in the act of putting the lamp-glass over the flame. The copper reflector shone handsomely on her, as she stood with uplifted arm, turning to face her daughter.

"You've got a flower in your apron!" said the child, in a little rapture at this unusual event.

"Goodness me!" exclaimed the woman, relieved. "One would think the house was afire." She replaced the glass and waited a moment before turning up the wick. A pale shadow was seen floating vaguely on the floor.

"Let me smell!" said the child, still rapturously, coming forward and putting her face to her mother's waist.

"Go along, silly!" said the mother, turning up the lamp. The light revealed their suspense so that the woman felt it almost unbearable. Annie was still bending at her waist. Irritably, the mother took the flowers out from her apron-band.

"Oh, mother—don't take them out!" Annie cried, catching her hand and trying to replace the sprig.

"Such nonsense!" said the mother, turning away. The child put the pale chrysanthemums to her lips, murmuring:

"Don't they smell beautiful!"

Her mother gave a short laugh.

"No," she said, "not to me. It was chrysanthemums when I married him, and chrysanthemums when you were born, and the first time they ever brought him home drunk, he'd got brown chrysanthemums in his button-hole."

She looked at the children. Their eyes and their parted lips were wondering. The mother sat rocking in silence for some time. Then she looked at the clock.

"Twenty minutes to six!" In a tone of fine bitter carelessness she continued: "Eh, he'll not come now till they bring him. There he'll stick! But he needn't come rolling in here in his pit-dirt, for *I* won't wash him. He can lie on the floor——Eh, what a fool I've been, what a fool! And this is what I came here for, to this dirty hole, rats and all, for him to slink past his very door. Twice last week—he's begun now——"

She silenced herself, and rose to clear the table.

While for an hour or more the children played, subduedly intent, fertile of imagination, united in fear of the mother's wrath, and in dread of their father's home-coming, Mrs. Bates sat in her rocking-chair making a "singlet" of thick cream-colored flannel, which gave a dull wounded sound as she tore off the grey edge. She worked at her sewing with energy, listening to the children, and her anger wearied itself, lay down to rest, opening its eyes from time to time and steadily watching, its ears raised to listen. Sometimes even her anger quailed and shrank, and the mother suspended her sewing, tracing the footsteps that thudded along the sleepers outside; she would lift her head sharply to bid the children 'hush,' but she recovered herself in time, and the footsteps went past the gate, and the children were not flung out of their play-world.

But at last Annie sighed, and gave in. She glanced at her wagon of slippers, and loathed the game. She turned plaintively to her mother.

"Mother!"—but she was inarticulate.

John crept out like a frog from under the sofa. His mother glanced up.

"Yes," she said, "just look at those shirt-sleeves!"

The boy held them out to survey them, saying nothing. Then somebody called in a hoarse voice away down the line, and suspense bristled in the room, till two people had gone by outside, talking.

"It is time for bed," said the mother.

"My father hasn't come," wailed Annie plaintively. But her mother was primed with courage.

"Never mind. They'll bring him when he does come—like a log." She meant there would be no scene. "And he may sleep on the floor till he wakes himself. I know he'll not go to work tomorrow after this!"

The children had their hands and faces wiped with a flannel. They were very quiet. When they had put on their nightdresses, they said their prayers, the boy mumbling. The mother looked down at them, at the brown silken bush of intertwining curls in the nape of the girl's neck, at the little black head of the lad, and her heart burst with anger at their father, who caused all three such distress. The children hid their faces in her skirts for comfort.

When Mrs. Bates came down, the room was strangely empty, with a tension of expectancy. She took up her sewing and stitched for some time without raising her head. Meantime her anger was tinged with fear.

2

The clock struck eight and she rose suddenly, dropping her sewing on her chair. She went to the stair-foot door, opened it, listening. Then she went out, locking the door behind her.

Something scuffled in the yard, and she started, though she knew it was only the rats with which the place was over-run. The night was very dark. In the great bay of railway lines, bulked with trucks, there was no trace of light, only away back she could see a few yellow lamps at the pit-top, and the red smear of the burning pit-bank on the night. She hurried along the edge of the track, then, crossing the converging lines, came to the stile by the white gates, whence she emerged on the road. Then the fear which had led her shrank. People were walking up to New Brinsley; she saw the lights in the houses; twenty yards farther on were the broad windows of the "Prince of Wales," very warm and bright, and the loud voices of men could be heard distinctly. What a fool she had been to imagine that anything had happened to him! He was merely drinking over there at the "Prince of Wales." She faltered. She had never yet been to fetch him, and she never would go. So she continued her walk towards the long straggling line of houses, standing back on the highway. She entered a passage between the dwellings.

"Mr. Rigley?—Yes! Did you want him? No, he's not in at this minute."

The raw-boned woman leaned forward from her dark scullery and peered at the other, upon whom fell a dim light through the blind of the kitchen window.

"Is it Mrs. Bates?" she asked in a tone tinged with respect.

"Yes. I wondered if your Master was at home. Mine hasn't come yet."

" 'Asn't 'e! Oh, Jack's been 'ome an' 'ad 'is dinner an' gone out. 'E's just gone for 'alf an hour afore bed-time. Did you call at the 'Prince of Wales'?"

"No——"

"No, you didn't like——! It's not very nice." The other woman was indulgent. There was an awkward pause. "Jack never said nothink about—about your Master," she said.

"No!—I expect he's stuck in there!"

Elizabeth Bates said this bitterly, and with recklessness. She knew that the woman across the yard was standing at her door listening, but she did not care. As she turned:

"Stop a minute! I'll just go an' ask Jack if 'e knows anything," said Mrs. Rigley.

"Oh no—I wouldn't like to put——!"

"Yes, I will, if you'll just step inside an' see as the' childer doesn't come downstairs and set theirselves afire."

Elizabeth Bates, murmuring a remonstrance, stepped inside. The other woman apologized for the state of the room.

The kitchen needed apology. There were little frocks and trousers and childish undergarments on the squab and on the floor, and a litter of playthings everywhere. On the black American cloth of the table were pieces of bread and cake, crusts, slops, and a teapot with cold tea.

"Eh, ours is just as bad," said Elizabeth Bates, looking at the woman, not at the house. Mrs. Rigley put a shawl over her head and hurried out, saying:

"I shanna be a minute."

The other sat, noting with faint disapproval the general untidiness of the room. Then she fell to counting the shoes of various sizes scattered over the floor. There were twelve. She sighed and said to herself: "No wonder!"—glancing at the litter. There came the scratching of two pairs of feet on the yard, and the Rigleys entered. Elizabeth Bates rose. Rigley was a big man, with very large bones. His head looked particularly bony. Across his temple was a blue scar, caused by a wound got in the pit, a wound in which the coal-dust remained blue like tattooing.

" 'Asna 'e come whoam yit?" asked the man, without any form of greeting, but with deference and sympathy. "I couldna say wheer he is—'e's non ower theer!"—he jerked his head to signify the 'Prince of Wales.'

" 'E's 'appen gone up to th' 'Yew,' " said Mrs. Rigley.

There was another pause. Rigley had evidently something to get off his mind:

"Ah left 'im finishin' a stint," he began. "Loose-all 'ad bin gone about ten minutes when we com'n away, an' I shouted: 'Are ter comin', Walt?' an' 'e said: 'Go on, Ah shanna be but a'ef a minnit,' so we com'n ter th' bottom, me an' Bowers, thinkin' as 'e wor just behint, an' 'ud come up i' th' next bantle——''

He stood perplexed, as if answering a charge of deserting his mate. Elizabeth Bates, now again certain of disaster, hastened to reassure him:

"I expect 'e's gone up to th' 'Yew Tree,' as you say. It's not the first time. I've fretted myself into a fever before now. He'll come home when they carry him."

"Ay, isn't it too bad!" deplored the other woman.

"I'll just step up to Dick's an' see if 'e *is* theer," offered the man, afraid of appearing alarmed, afraid of taking liberties.

"Oh, I wouldn't think of bothering you that far," said Elizabeth Bates, with emphasis, but he knew she was glad of his offer.

As they stumbled up the entry, Elizabeth Bates heard Rigley's wife run across the yard and open her neighbor's door. At this, suddenly all the blood in her body seemed to switch away from her heart.

"Mind!" warned Rigley. "Ah've said many a time as Ah'd fill up them ruts in this entry, sumb'dy 'll be breakin' their legs yit."

She recovered herself and walked quickly along with the miner.

"I don't like leaving the children in bed, and nobody in the house," she said.

"No, you dunna!" he replied courteously. They were soon at the gate of the cottage.

"Well, I shanna be many minnits. Dunna you be frettin' now, 'e'll be all right," said the butty.

"Thank you very much, Mr. Rigley," she replied.

"You're welcome!" he stammered, moving away. "I shanna be many minnits."

The house was quiet. Elizabeth Bates took off her hat and shawl, and rolled back the rug. When she had finished, she sat down. It was a few minutes past nine. She was startled by the rapid chuff of the winding-engine at the pit, and the sharp whirr of brakes on the rope as it descended. Again she felt the painful sweep of her blood, and she put her hand to her side, saying aloud: "Good gracious!—it's only the nine o'clock deputy going down," rebuking herself.

She sat still, listening. Half an hour of this, and she was wearied out.

"What am I working myself up like this for?" she said pitiably to herself, "I s'll only be doing myself some damage."

She took out her sewing again.

At a quarter to ten there were footsteps. One person! She watched for the door to open. It was an elderly woman, in a black bonnet and a black woolen shawl—his mother. She was about sixty years old, pale, with blue eyes, and her face all wrinkled and lamentable. She shut the door and turned to her daughter-in-law peevishly.

"Eh, Lizzie, whatever shall we do, whatever shall we do!" she cried.

Elizabeth drew back a little, sharply.

"What is it, mother?" she said.

The elder woman seated herself on the sofa.

"I don't know, child, I can't tell you!"—she shook her head slowly. Elizabeth sat watching her, anxious and vexed.

"I don't know," replied the grandmother, sighing very deeply. "There's no end to my troubles, there isn't. The things I've gone through, I'm sure it's enough——!" She wept without wiping her eyes, the tears running.

"But, mother," interrupted Elizabeth, "what do you mean? What is it?"

The grandmother slowly wiped her eyes. The fountains of her tears were stopped by Elizabeth's directness. She wiped her eyes slowly.

"Poor child! Eh, you poor thing!" she moaned. "I don't know what we're going to do, I don't—and you as you are—it's a thing, it is indeed!"

Elizabeth waited.

"Is he dead?" she asked, and at the words her heart swung violently, though she felt a slight flush of shame at the ultimate extravagance of the question. Her words sufficiently frightened the old lady, almost brought her to herself.

"Don't say so, Elizabeth! We'll hope it's not as bad as that; no, may the Lord spare us that, Elizabeth! Jack Rigley came just as I was sittin' down to a glass afore going to bed, an' 'e said: "Appen you'll go an' sit wi' 'er till we can get him home.' I hadn't time to ask him a word afore he was gone. An' I put my bonnet on an' come straight down, Lizzie. I thought to myself: 'Eh, that poor blessed child, if anybody should come an' tell me of a sudden, there's no knowin' what'll 'appen to 'er.' You mustn't let it upset you, Lizzie—or you know what to expect. How long is it, six months—or is it five, Lizzie? Ay!"—the old woman shook her head—" time slips on, it slips on! Ay!"

Elizabeth's thoughts were busy elsewhere. If he was killed—would she be able to manage on the little pension and what she could earn?—she counted up rapidly. If he was hurt—they wouldn't take him to the hospital—how tiresome he would be to nurse!—but perhaps she'd be able to get him away from the drink and his hateful ways. She would—while he was ill. The tears offered to come to her eyes at the picture. But what sentimental luxury was this she was beginning? She turned to consider the children. At any rate she was absolutely necessary for them. They were her business.

"Ay!" repeated the old woman, "it seems but a week or two since he brought me his first wages. Ay—he was a good lad, Elizabeth, he was, in his way. I don't know why he got to be such a trouble, I don't. He was a happy lad at home, only full of spirits. But there's no mistake he's been a handful of trouble, he has! I hope the Lord'll spare him to mend his ways. I hope so, I hope so. You've had a sight o' trouble with him, Elizabeth, you have indeed. But he was a jolly enough lad wi' me, he was, I can assure you. I don't know how it is . . ."

The old woman continued to muse aloud, a monotonous irritating sound, while Elizabeth thought concentratedly, startled once, when she heard the winding-engine chuff quickly, and the brakes skirr with a shriek. Then she heard the engine more slowly, and the brakes made no sound. The old woman did not notice. Elizabeth waited in suspense. The mother-in-law talked, with lapses into silence.

"But he wasn't your son, Lizzie, an' it makes a difference. Whatever he was, I remember him when he was little, an' I learned to understand him and to make allowances. You've got to make allowances for them——"

It was half-past ten, and the old woman was saying: "But it's trouble from beginning to end; you're never too old for trouble, never too old for that——" when the gate banged back, and there were heavy feet on the steps.

"I'll go, Lizzie, let me go," cried the old woman, rising. But Elizabeth was at the door. It was a man in pit-clothes.

"They're bringin' 'im, Missis," he said. Elizabeth's heart halted a moment. Then it surged on again, almost suffocating her.

"Is he—is it bad?" she asked.

The man turned away, looking at the darkness:

"The doctor says 'e'd been dead for hours. 'E saw 'im i' th' lamp-cabin."

The old woman, who stood just behind Elizabeth, dropped into a chair, and folded her hands, crying: "Oh, my boy, my boy!"

"Hush!" said Elizabeth, with a sharp twitch of a frown. "Be still, mother, don't waken th' children: I wouldn't have them down for anything!"

The old woman moaned softly, rocking herself. The man was drawing away. Elizabeth took a step forward.

"How was it?" she asked.

"Well, I couldn't say for sure," the man replied, very ill at ease. " 'E wor finishin' a stint an' th' butties 'ad gone, an' a lot o' stuff come down atop 'n 'im."

"And crushed him?" cried the widow, with a shudder.

"No," said the man, "it fell at th' back of 'im. 'E wor under th' face, an' it niver touched 'im. It shut 'im in. It seems 'e wor smothered."

Elizabeth shrank back. She heard the old woman behind her cry:

"What?—what did 'e say it was?"

The man replied more loudly: " 'E wor smothered!"

Then the old woman wailed aloud, and this relieved Elizabeth.

"Oh, mother," she said, putting her hand on the old woman, "don't waken th' children, don't waken th' children."

She wept a little, unknowing, while the old mother rocked herself and moaned. Elizabeth remembered that they were bringing him home, and she must be ready. "They'll lay him in the parlor," she said to herself, standing a moment pale and perplexed.

Then she lighted a candle and went into the tiny room. The air was cold and damp, but she could not make a fire, there was no fireplace. She set down the candle and looked round. The candlelight glittered on the lustre-glasses, on the two vases that held some of the pink chrysanthemums, and on the dark mahogany. There was a cold, deathly smell of chrysanthemums in the room. Elizabeth stood looking at the flowers. She turned away, and calculated whether there would be room to lay him on the floor, between the couch and the chiffonier. She pushed the chairs aside. There would be room to lay him down and to step round him. Then she fetched the old red tablecloth, and another old cloth, spreading them down to save her bit of carpet. She shivered on leaving the parlor; so, from the dresser drawer she took a clean shirt and put it at the fire to air. All the time her mother-in-law was rocking herself in the chair and moaning.

"You'll have to move from there, mother," said Elizabeth. "They'll be bringing him in. Come in the rocker."

The old mother rose mechanically, and seated herself by the fire, continuing to lament. Elizabeth went into the pantry for another candle, and there, in the little penthouse under the naked tiles, she heard them coming. She stood still in the pantry doorway, listening. She heard them pass the end of the house, and come awkwardly down the three steps, a jumble of shuffling footsteps and muttering voices. The old woman was silent. The men were in the yard.

Then Elizabeth heard Matthews, the manager of the pit, say: "You go in first, Jim. Mind!"

The door came open, and the two women saw a collier backing into the room, holding one end of a stretcher, on which they could see the nailed pit-boots of the dead man. The two carriers halted, the man at the head stooping to the lintel of the door.

"Wheer will you have him?" asked the manager, a short, white-bearded man.

Elizabeth roused herself and came from the pantry carrying the unlighted candle.

"In the parlor," she said.

"In there, Jim!" pointed the manager, and the carriers backed round into the tiny room. The coat with which they had covered the body fell off as they awkwardly turned through the two doorways, and the women saw their man, naked to the waist, lying stripped for work. The old woman began to moan in a low voice of horror.

"Lay th' stretcher at th' side," snapped the manager, "an' put 'im on th' cloths. Mind now, mind! Look you now——!"

One of the men had knocked off a vase of chrysanthemums. He stared awkwardly, then they set down the stretcher. Elizabeth did not look at her husband. As soon as she could get in the room, she went and picked up the broken vase and the flowers.

"Wait a minute!" she said.

The three men waited in silence while she mopped up the water with a duster.

"Eh, what a job, what a job, to be sure!" the manager was saying, rubbing his brow with trouble and perplexity. "Never knew such a thing in my life, never! He'd no busines to ha' been left. I never knew such a thing in my life! Fell over him clean as a whistle, an' shut him in. Not four foot of space, there wasn't—yet it scarce bruised him."

He looked down at the dead man, lying prone, half naked, all grimed with coal-dust.

" ' 'Sphyxiated', the doctor said. It *is* the most terrible job I've ever known. Seems as if it was done o' purpose. Clean over him, an' shut 'im in, like a mouse-trap"—he made a sharp, descending gesture with his hand.

The colliers standing by jerked aside their heads in hopeless comment.

The horror of the thing bristled upon them all.

Then they heard the girl's voice upstairs calling shrilly: "Mother, mother—who is it? Mother, who is it?"

Elizabeth hurried to the foot of the stairs and opened the door:

"Go to sleep!" she commanded sharply. "What are you shouting about? Go to sleep at once—there's nothing——"

Then she began to mount the stairs. They could hear her on the boards, and on the plaster floor of the little bedroom. They could hear her distinctly:

"What's the matter now?—what's the matter with you, silly thing?"—her voice was much agitated, with an unreal gentleness.

"I thought it was some men come," said the plaintive voice of the child. "Has he come?"

"Yes, they've brought him. There's nothing to make a fuss about. Go to sleep now, like a good child."

They could hear her voice in the bedroom, they waited whilst she covered the children under the bedclothes.

"Is he drunk?" asked the girl, timidly, faintly.

"No! No—he's not! He—he's asleep."

"Is he asleep downstairs?"

"Yes—and don't make a noise."

There was silence for a moment, then the men heard the frightened child again:

"What's that noise?"

"It's nothing, I tell you, what are you bothering for?"

The noise was the grandmother moaning. She was oblivious of everything, sitting on her chair rocking and moaning. The manager put his hand on her arm and bade her "Sh—sh!!"

The old woman opened her eyes and looked at him. She was shocked by this interruption, and seemed to wonder.

"What time is it?" the plaintive thin voice of the child, sinking back unhappily into sleep, asked this last question.

"Ten o'clock," answered the mother more softly. Then she must have bent down and kissed the children.

Matthews beckoned to the men to come away. They put on their caps and took up the stretcher. Stepping over the body, they tiptoed out of the house. None of them spoke till they were far from the wakeful children.

When Elizabeth came down she found her mother alone on the parlor floor, leaning over the dead man, the tears dropping on him.

"We must lay him out," the wife said. She put on the kettle, then knelt at the feet, and began to unfasten the knotted leather laces. The room was clammy and dim with only one candle, so that she had to bend her face almost to the floor. At last she got off the heavy boots and put them away.

"You must help me now," she whispered to the old woman. Together they stripped the man.

When they arose, saw him lying in the naïve dignity of death, the woman stood arrested in fear and respect. For a few moments they remained still, looking down, the old mother whimpering. Elizabeth felt countermanded. She saw him, how utterly inviolable he lay in himself. She had nothing to do with him. She could not accept it. Stooping, she laid her hand on him, in claim. He was still warm, for the mine was hot where he had died. His mother had his face between her hands, and was murmuring incoherently. The old tears fell in succession as drops from wet leaves; the mother was not weeping, merely her tears flowed. Elizabeth embraced the body of her husband, with cheek and lips. She seemed to be listening, inquiring, trying to get some connection. But she could not. She was driven away. He was impregnable.

She rose, went into the kitchen, where she poured warm water into a bowl, brought soap and flannel and a soft towel.

"I must wash him," she said.

Then the old mother rose stiffly, and watched Elizabeth as she carefully washed his face, carefully brushing the big blond moustache from his mouth with the flannel. She was afraid with a bottomless fear, so she ministered to him. The old woman, jealous, said:

"Let me wipe him!"—and she kneeled on the other side drying slowly as Elizabeth washed, her big black bonnet sometimes brushing the dark head of her daughter-in-law. They worked thus in silence for a long time. They never forgot it was death, and the touch of the man's dead body gave them strange emotions, different in each of the women; a great dread possessed them both, the mother felt the lie was given to her womb, she was denied; the wife felt the utter isolation of the human soul, the child within her was a weight apart from her.

At last it was finished. He was a man of handsome body, and his face showed no traces of drink. He was blond, full-fleshed, with fine limbs. But he was dead.

"Bless him," whispered his mother, looking always at his face, and speaking out of sheer terror. "Dear lad—bless him!" She spoke in a faint, sibilant ecstasy of fear and mother love.

Elizabeth sank down again to the floor, and put her face against his neck, and trembled and shuddered. But she had to draw away again. He was dead, and her living flesh had no place against his. A great dread and weariness held her: she was so unavailing. Her life was gone like this.

"White as milk he is, clear as a twelve-month baby, bless him, the darling!" the old mother murmured to herself. "Not a mark on him, clear and clean and white, beautiful as ever a child was made," she murmured with pride. Elizabeth kept her face hidden.

"He went peaceful, Lizzie—peaceful as sleep. Isn't he beautiful, the lamb? Ay—he must ha' made his peace, Lizzie. 'Appen he made it all right, Lizzie, shut in there. He'd have time. He wouldn't look like this if he hadn't made his peace. The lamb, the dear lamb. Eh, but he had a hearty laugh. I loved to hear it. He had the heartiest laugh, Lizzie, as a lad——"

Elizabeth looked up. The man's mouth was fallen back, slightly open under the cover of the moustache. The eyes, half shut, did not show glazed in the obscurity. Life with its smoky burning gone from him, had left him apart and utterly alien to her. And she knew what a stranger he was to her. In her womb was ice of fear, because of this separate stranger with whom she had been living as one flesh. Was this what it all meant—utter, intact separateness, obscured by heat of living? In dread she turned her face away. The fact was too deadly. There had been nothing between them, and yet they had come together, exchanging their nakedness repeatedly. Each time he had taken her, they had been two isolated beings, far apart as now. He was no more responsible than she. The child was like ice in her womb. For as she looked at the dead man, her mind cold and detached, said clearly: "Who am I? What have I been doing? I have been fighting a husband who did not exist. *He* existed all the time. What wrong have I done? What was that I have been living with? There lies the reality, this man." And her soul died in her for fear: she knew she had never seen him, he had never seen her, they had met in the dark and had fought in the dark, not knowing whom they met nor whom they fought. And now she saw, and turned silent in seeing. For she had been wrong. She had said he was something he was not; she had felt familiar with him. Whereas he was apart all the while, living as she never lived, feeling as she never felt.

In fear and shame she looked at his naked body, that she had known falsely. And he was the father of her children. Her soul was torn from her body and stood apart. She looked at his naked body and was ashamed, as if she had denied it. After all, it was itself. It seemed awful to her. She looked at his face, and she turned her own face to the wall. For his look was other than hers, his way was not her way. She had denied him what he was—she saw it now. She had refused him as himself. And this had been her life, and his life. She was grateful to death, which restored the truth. And she knew she was not dead.

And all the while her heart was bursting with grief and pity for him. What had he suffered? What stretch of horror for this helpless man! She was rigid with agony. She had not been able to help him. He had been cruelly injured, this naked man, this other being, and she could make no reparation. There were the children—but the children belonged to life. This dead man had nothing to do with them. He and she were only channels through which life had flowed to issue in the children. She was a mother—but how awful she knew it now to have been a wife. And he, dead now, how awful he must have felt it to be a husband. She felt that in the next world he would be a stranger to her. If they met there, in the beyond, they would only be ashamed of what had been before. The children had come, for some mysterious reason, out of both of them. But the children did not unite them. Now he was dead, she knew how eternally he was apart from her, how eternally he had nothing more to do with her. She saw this episode of her life closed. They had denied each other in life. Now he had withdrawn. An anguish came over her. It was finished then: it had become hopeless between them long before he died. Yet he had been her husband. But how little!

"Have you got his shirt, 'Lizabeth?"

Elizabeth turned without answering, though she strove to weep and behave as her mother-in-law expected. But she could not, she was silenced. She went into the kitchen and returned with the garment.

"It is aired," she said, grasping the cotton shirt here and there to try. She was almost ashamed to handle him; what right had she or anyone to lay hands on him; but her touch was humble on his body. It was hard work to clothe him. He was so heavy and inert. A terrible dread gripped her all the while: that he could be so heavy and utterly inert, unresponsive, apart. The horror of the distance between them was almost too much for her—it was so infinite a gap she must look across.

At last it was finished. They covered him with a sheet and left him lying, with his face bound. And she fastened the door of the little parlor, lest the children should see what was lying there. Then, with peace sunk heavy on her heart, she went about making tidy the kitchen. She knew she submitted to life, which was her immediate master. But from death, her ultimate master, she winced with fear and shame.

2 3 4 5 6 7 8 9 10 11 12 13 14 15   88 87 86 85 84 83 82 81 80 79 78 77 76 75